Praise for *A Strange and Stubborn Endurance*

"Many a reader longing for a sense of homecoming in the realm of romantic fantasy will find it in *A Strange and Stubborn Endurance.*"

—Jacqueline Carey, *New York Times* bestselling author of the Kushiel's Legacy series

"Meadows has constructed a world to get lost in, and this is a book to savor."

—Everina Maxwell, author of *Winter's Orbit*

"Meadows has written something beautiful, and if you need a book to light a fire in your heart, let it be this one. . . . A queer romance for the ages."

—*Tor.com*

"I flew through this book and enjoyed every page of the journey. . . . I loved that this was a gripping political fantasy, but I loved even more that it was wrapped around a stubbornly kindhearted romance."

—Freya Marske, author of *A Marvellous Light*

"A satisfying balance of romance and action, with political intrigue that is both elaborate and plausible, and rich, fascinating world-building."

—Malka Older, award-winning author

"Blending intrigue and queer romance, *A Strange and Stubborn Endurance* stitches together two cultures and reembroiders gender conventions. Meadows combines the personal and political through an elegant voice, and finds time for tender moments of healing."

—E. J. Beaton, author of *The Councillor*

"A heartfelt, meticulously observed romance, a page-turning mystery, and a world that feels real enough to live in."

—H. G. Parry

Also by Foz Meadows

The Manifold Worlds Series

An Accident of Stars
A Tyranny of Queens

The Rare Series

Solace and Grief
The Key to Starveldt

A Strange and Stubborn Endurance

FOZ MEADOWS

Tor Publishing Group
New York

This is a work of fiction. All of the characters, organizations, and events portrayed in this novel are either products of the author's imagination or are used fictitiously.

A STRANGE AND STUBBORN ENDURANCE

Map by Jennifer Hanover

A Tor Book
Published by Tom Doherty Associates / Tor Publishing Group
120 Broadway
New York, NY 10271

www.tor-forge.com

The Library of Congress has cataloged the hardcover edition as follows:

Names: Meadows, Foz, author.
Title: A strange and stubborn endurance / Foz Meadows.
Description: First edition. | New York : Tor, 2022. |
"A Tom Doherty Associates book."
Identifiers: LCCN 2022008297 (print) | LCCN 2022008298 (ebook) |
ISBN 9781250829139 (hardcover) | ISBN 9781250829146 (ebook)
Subjects: LCGFT: Fantasy fiction. | Romance fiction. | Novels.
Classification: LCC PR9639.4.M43 S77 2022 (print) |
LCC PR9639.4.M43 (ebook) | DDC 823/.92—dc23
LC record available at https://lccn.loc.gov/2022008297
LC ebook record available at https://lccn.loc.gov/2022008298

ISBN 978-1-250-82929-0 (trade paperback)

First Tor Paperback Edition: 2023

Printed in the United States of America

0 9 8 7 6 5 4

For Liz and Sarah, Chris and B,
who braved the Yelling Bowl.

Author's Note

A Strange and Stubborn Endurance contains on-page depictions of rape, suicidal ideation, and self-harm. While the narrative arc is one of healing, readers should nonetheless be aware of this content in order to engage with it on their own terms.

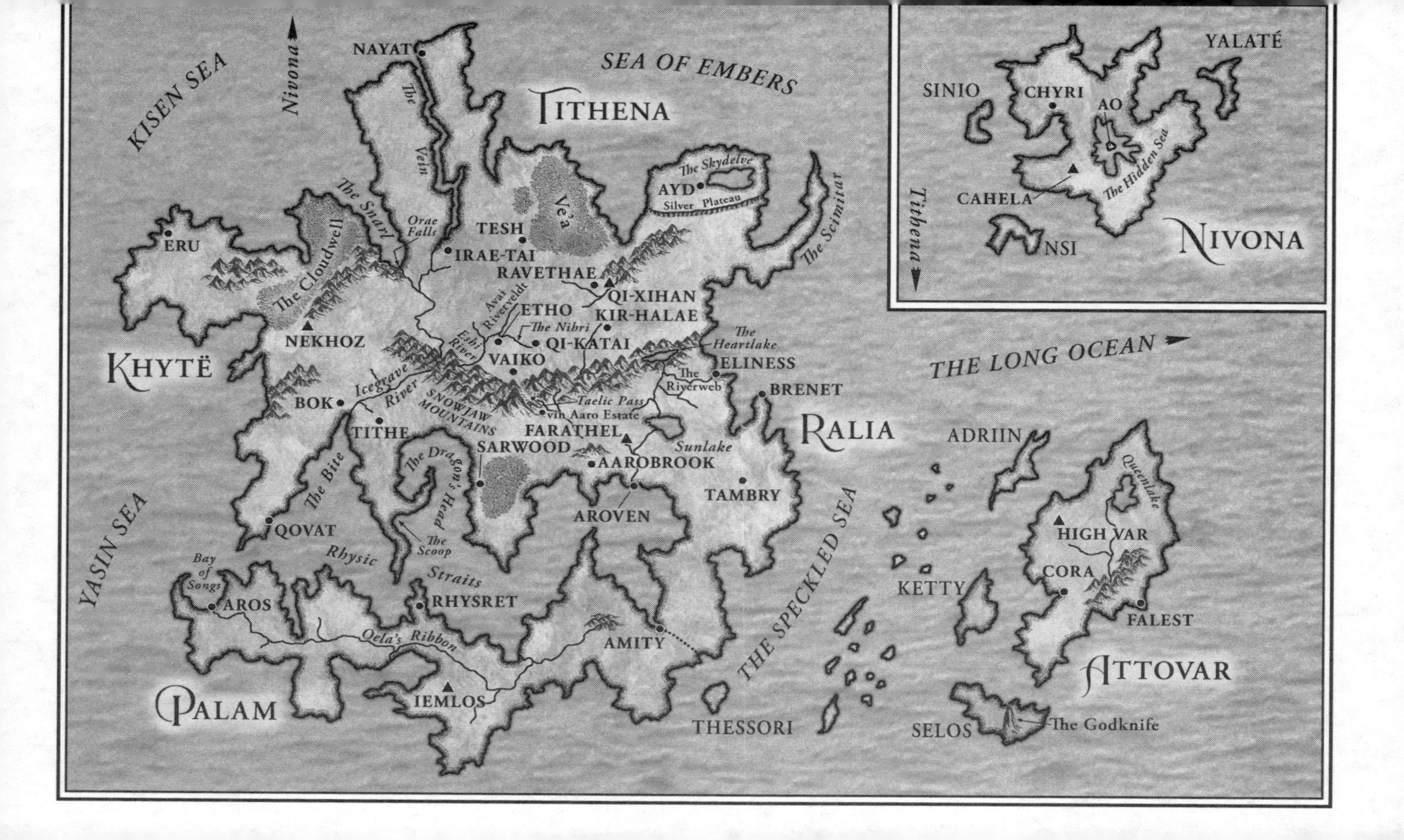

KISEN SEA
Nivona
NAYAT
SEA OF EMBERS
TITHENA
The Vein
The Snarl
Orae Falls
ERU
The Cloudwell
TESH
Ve'a
AYD
The Skydelve
Silver Plateau
The Scimitar
IRAE-TAI
RAVETHAE
QI-XIHAN
Avai Riverveldt
ETHO
KIR-HALAE
The Nibri
NEKHOZ
Esbi River
QI-KATAI
The Heartlake
KHYTË
VAIKO
ELINESS
The Riverweb
BRENET
Icegrave River
BOK
SNOWJAW MOUNTAINS
Taelic Pass
vin Aaro Estate
TITHE
FARATHEL
RALIA
SARWOOD
Sunlake
The Dragon's Head
AAROBROOK
TAMBRY
The Bite
AROVEN
QOVAT
The Scoop
YASIN SEA
Bay of Songs
Rhysic Straits
AROS
RHYSRET
Oela's Ribbon
AMITY
THE SPECKLED SEA
PALAM
IEMLOS
THESSORI
THE LONG OCEAN
ADRIIN
KETTY
Queenlake
HIGH VAR
CORA
FALEST
ATTOVAR
SELOS
The Godknife
SINIO
CHYRI
AO
YALATÉ
Tithena
CAHELA
The Hidden Sea
NSI
NIVONA

Part One

VELASIN

1

We'd scarcely entered Father's new lands when I realised how little I cared that I'd never inherit them. It was a genteel epiphany, as such things go: though surprised, I neither reined Quip to a jarring halt nor made any pronouncements to Markel, who was paid to endure my rambling. Instead, I wondered whether I should pride myself on my apparent humility—a somewhat ironic paradox, to be sure—or worry at my total lack of ambition. Certainly, had my next-eldest brother lived to share in the same restrictions, he would have been angry enough for the both of us; but then, Revic had always been quick-tempered. My missing him didn't change the fact that his death had removed an ugly complication from our father's advancement, though acknowledging it left a bad taste in my mouth. Where Revic had always coveted Nathian's status as heir, I'd never expected more than my third son's modest sinecure, and though I was hardly indifferent to the prospect of greater wealth, I deemed myself allergic to the increased responsibilities it so frequently engendered.

No, I decided, inhaling a lungful of crisp, clean air. *Little Jarien can have it all, and welcome.* My infant half-brother, Father's son by his new wife and, through her, heir to all I surveyed, was a fraternal blank slate. Whatever relationship we might one day have was untainted by the childhood I'd shared with Revic and Nathian, and though that unpleasant template might yet reassert itself, I was disinclined to borrow such a worry so preemptively.

That being settled within me, I found myself admiring the new vin Aaro lands—which is to say, the old vin Mica lands—as a traveller might, without thought to their upkeep or earnings. We'd passed a small township earlier on, and since ignored the diversions of smaller, only occasionally signposted roads that presumably led to the various other farms and hamlets now under Father's purview. Before vin Mica's folly, trade had flourished along this route, goods moving to and from neighbouring Tithena and Khytë through a single pass in the otherwise forbidding Snowjaw Mountains. Though tenants and traders here had likely suffered for their previous lord's mismanagement, the physical beauty of the land, at least, remained untouched. The road on which we travelled wound prettily through late-fruiting orchards and gentle hills, the bright grass dotted with flowers. The autumn sky was powder blue, shading to lilac around the gleaming caps of the distant peaks, which shone white this late in the year. Pleasant birdsong coloured the air like music.

Though Markel was seldom impressed by views lacking in mortal architecture, on this occasion, he deigned to be impressed by nature's handiwork, peering curiously about us. As we crested a gentle rise, he nudged his sorrel mare, Grace, a little closer to Quip and snapped his fingers twice, signalling his intention to speak.

From any other servant, it would have been impertinence—and indeed, was often mistaken for such by those who didn't know that Markel was mute. We'd worked out an etiquette long ago, and though his snapping still struck certain officious types as presumptuous, it worked for us.

"Yes?" I asked, turning to watch his signs.

Reins looped over the saddle horn, Markel signed, "It's very different to Aarobrook."

I snorted. "Much as fine lace is different to canvas, yes." And then, in signs—for use of the skill kept it fresh for me—"We should see the main house, soon."

Markel grinned and nodded, resuming his hold on the reins. Despite (or perhaps because of) my tendency to use him as a captive audience, he was sharp enough to hear what I left unsaid: that for all my eagerness to leave the capital—and moons, but I'd been eager!—I still didn't know why Father had summoned me here in the first place, and was therefore blind to what we might expect. His letter had said only that he wished to see me at my earliest convenience, to discuss "some family matters, best addressed in person." The ambiguity of it gnawed at me, and what little peace I'd felt on so calmly accepting my half-brother's future accession to titles and properties I might have otherwise coveted vanished in an instant.

Had Father learned of my indiscretions? Both recently and otherwise, I'd committed so many that I didn't bother to narrow down what stories might have reached him, or from which sources. My life in Farathel had become little more than a string of offences against propriety; that I regretted only a few of them, and for more complex reasons than simple contrition, didn't make me any less keen to avoid their consequences, nor did it blunt my desire to escape, however briefly, the circumstances of their creation. It was equally possible, however, that the summons entailed only news of pleasant things—an increase in my sinecure; the expected birth of a new niece or nephew, or—moons!—another half-sibling; some propitious detail about the estate—and a certain self-interest wouldn't let me forget it.

Unable to sway me one way or the other, hope and fear formed a bipartisan knot of anxiety in my gullet, which felt a little like being seasick and a lot like being drunk, and by the time we reached the estate proper and rode into the main courtyard, my back was as lathered with sweat as Quip's flanks were not.

Whatever else could be said of the late Lord Ennan vin Mica—and there was a lot to be said, his lateness being unlamented by virtually everyone who hadn't joined him in it—he'd certainly loved his horses. The grandeur of the stables reflected this fact, and if the estate's grooms were at all perturbed by the still-recent change in their livery, it didn't show in their enthusiasm. I'd scarcely dismounted before a wiry, capable-looking man appeared to take Quip's reins from me, while a short youth did the same with Markel's

Grace. They had the stamp of father and son, or possibly uncle and nephew; their eyes were the same watchful grey, while their noses shared a distinctive crook. Their skin was lighter than Markel's tawny brown or my own dark olive—a deep tan that came partly from outdoor living, but whose golden undertones suggested more than a drop of Tithenai blood. Looking so unlike my own sire, I always marvelled at such likenesses in others, though as she'd been the handsomer parent, did I say it myself, I never grudged a whit of my mother's heritage.

"I'm Lord Velasin vin Aaro," I said—redundantly, it seemed, for they must have known me, lack of paternal resemblance or not. "And this is Markel, my valet." I hesitated, casting him my usual questioning glance. Markel considered, then gave a minute shake of his head to indicate that no, on this occasion, he didn't want me to give these strange servants the *my valet is mute* speech. He carried a slate and a clever chalk pen to aid in making himself understood by strangers who proved inimical to either silence or pantomime, but didn't always wish to be preannounced as an oddity (as he'd once put it). Turning back to the grooms, I said, "Is my father in residence?"

"Aye, my lord," said the elder, head jerking towards the house. "The butler will see you right." He eyed the meagre bags strapped behind our saddles, one brow rising in surprise. "Should I have your things brought up, my lord?"

"Yes, with my thanks," I replied, and headed straight on, Markel following close behind. I was three paces from the main door when it swung open, revealing a harried-looking butler, two very large dogs and the noblewoman who was—in law, if not in raising—my stepmother, Lady Sine vin Aaro, formerly Sine vin Mica. She was freckled and clever-looking, a scant three years my senior, her reddish-gold hair escaping from a series of upcoiled braids. Little Jarien wasn't in evidence, but if the spit-stains on the shoulder of her gown were anything to go by, he wasn't too far distant. I'd met her once before, though briefly, on the day of her wedding; she'd been polite but understandably flustered, and I'd been too distracted to try and observe her more closely.

Now, though, she favoured me with a smile I was inclined to think genuine, holding out her hands for me to take and kiss, which I did. By the standards of women of our class, she'd come late to marriage and motherhood both, but inasmuch as I was placed to judge, they both looked well on her.

"You made good time," she said, laughing as the dogs nosed between us. I dropped her hands in favour of scratching their ears, my panic settling somewhat at the contact. "We weren't expecting you until supper, though even then, my lord seemed to doubt you'd arrive before tomorrow."

"I have a history of tarrying," I said. "But the weather is fine, and I"—*needed to get away*—"was moved by filial piety."

"That will doubtless please my lord to hear," said Lady Sine, and for a moment, her gaze was shrewd as Markel's. "Though he might wonder at the occasion."

My reply was forestalled by the sudden appearance of the man himself, trailed by a nursemaid carrying baby Jarien. Remarriage certainly suited Father; I hadn't seen him so hale in years. His paunch was gone, new muscle firming his arms and shoulders, eyes bright, skin clear. Even before the awful wrangling of what was now called the Dissension, the decade or so in which a loose cadre of antagonistic nobles had stoked political strife within Ralia, and which had finally ended, somewhat anticlimactically, with the exposure of Lord Ennan vin Mica's plans for rebellion and the arrest, imprisonment and/or execution of his various co-conspirators, my mother's death had wearied him on a level I'd been too young to fully comprehend, for all that I witnessed it daily. But not even civil peace had eased him as Lady Sine did; or perhaps that was Jarien's doing, if not the two in combination. Either way, his positive transformation threw into sharp relief my own, inverse trajectory, and in that moment, had he asked for the truth, I would have confessed to everything—even, perhaps, beyond my culpability.

But he did not ask; just clapped my shoulder, fingers squeezing briefly against the bone, and bade me welcome.

"Your timing is better than you know," he said. And then, eyes crinkling: "It's good to see you, Vel." He didn't acknowledge Markel, but that was as expected.

With his typical quiet skill, he herded our whole panoply back inside: wife, servants, dogs and youngest sons, the front door shutting neatly behind us.

Given this friendly greeting, it was hard to imagine I was in any serious disgrace, and yet my traitor brain refused to abandon the possibility wholesale. As such, I endured the subsequent hours of niceties in an agony of tension. Not that I betrayed this fact beyond a slackening of my usual chatter, but as I was more often the party addressed than addressing, that was hardly incongruous. I was shown the estate, Lady Sine enlightening me as to various features and points of historical interest, all learned during her childhood there, while noting certain recent improvements, such as the addition of magelights and, in the courtyard, an artifex sculpture set within a fountain.

This latter surprised me greatly: while Father had as much respect for magecraft as any Ralian nobleman, he'd never had much interest in artistry or aesthetics, and while the magic underpinning the sculpture was truly impressive—a series of embedded cantrips which caused the carving of a great water serpent to glow, roar and even move when certain control words were spoken—it was hardly utilitarian. I ventured as much to Lady Sine, fishing to see whether she'd had to fight him over its acquisition, but she only laughed.

"Varus is quite fond of it, actually," she said. "He thinks of it as an investment piece." She hesitated, then said, "There's plans to reopen the Taelic Pass to trade with Tithena, and hopefully that will bring Khytoi trade, too. They've always been famed for their artifex as well as furs, and if all goes well, he's hoping it'll make a good impression on their merchants. And, well." She laughed. "He likes that Jarien likes it."

Her smile softened at the mention of her son, and the conversation turned swiftly to talk of his development. Both then and later, I offered up as much admiration of Jarien as one with no real knowledge of infants can for a six-month-old; I praised the quality of the rooms I was given and the food I was offered, both of which were exceptional; and only then, at the tail end of supper, did Father finally invite me into his study.

Though the room was wildly different to its predecessor at Aarobrook—which was Nathian's now, though I struggled to picture it—enough of the order and furnishings were the same that, instantly, some inward sense transported me back in time. As children, Nathian, Revic and I were only ever admitted to the vin Aaro study at times of great praise or censure, and so it had held a kind of grave magic for us all, like a cave of wonders. It was where I'd been caned for breaking a tenant's window while flinging rocks at a hornet's nest, and where I'd been awarded my choice of Father's prize books for having mercy-killed a beloved hound instead of delegating the task to a servant.

I remembered the cane, and the book, and the dog, and for the second time that day, I battled the urge to confess.

"Sit down, Vel," said Father, motioning to one of a pair of armchairs. I obeyed, careful to fold my hands in my lap, lest I grip the leather and give myself away through whitened knuckles—a redundant effort, as the next words out of his mouth were, "Relax, boy! I can see you're tense, though the Lord Sun alone knows why. Or, well," he amended, scrubbing a rueful hand through his beard, "perhaps that's unfair of me. After all, I can hardly blame you for wondering where you stand. If Revic—"

He broke off, and we shared a certain fond, pained expression at all that the absence entailed. "I know," I said softly, and left it at that.

"Well," said Father, after a moment. "Well, then." He set his hands on his knees and met my gaze. "Let me speak plainly. Though His Majesty granted me vin Mica's holdings on the condition that their inheritance falls, not to my eldest sons, but to Jarien, and to any other children with which Sine might yet bless me—" He coloured, just a little, in presumed remembrance of the efforts made in getting them, and I stared very hard at the opposite wall, the better to suppress an embarrassed laugh. "—still, my elevation might yet benefit you."

"My sinecure, you mean?" I asked, hardly daring to hope.

"In a manner of speaking, yes. I mean for you to marry."

At this, my lungs and brain forgot how breathing worked, denying me that function for seconds that passed like minutes. My poleaxed expression must have been the expected response, however, for Father waited out my breathlessness with no apparent chagrin.

"How?" I finally managed. "And to whom? My sinecure cannot be increased so greatly as all that, surely!"

"It isn't," came the blunt response. "I don't propose that you could or should support a wife, Vel—in fact, I mean the opposite."

"You want a wife to support *me*?"

"And why not?"

I stared at him. "In principle," I said, pulse galloping in counterpoint to my careful speech, "I have no objection." A bald-faced lie; I had every objection, though none I dared to voice. "But in all practicality, Father—and I say this with no false modesty—what good Ralian heiress would have me? They are not such abundant creatures as to have no better prospects than a sinecured third son, no matter your elevation." Not that the vin Aaros had risen in rank, per se, but as any good Ralian knows, there are lords and there are *lords,* and since being awarded vin Mica's holdings in the still-recent aftermath of the Dissension, Father was now much closer to the latter than the former.

"*Ah,*" said Father—pleased, as though I'd hit upon the crux of it. "A *Ralian* heiress, no; I would not force you to swim such waters against your inclination. But a Tithenai girl, Vel—there, *there* you have value."

"A Tithenai girl," I echoed faintly. I could no more swallow the concept than water could swallow oil. "You—that is, you mean—I—"

"Velasin," said Father, not unkindly. "*Think*. These lands abut the Taelic Pass; there's no closer route to Tithena west of the capital. More Khytoi trade passes through Tithena than Ralia; and Nivonai trade, too! That fool vin Mica let those trading routes fall to ruin and the pass itself to banditry—even engaged in border raids himself against the Wild Knife, if the rougher tales are to be believed, though if not, he certainly sanctioned them—but now he's dead, Shade keep him, and His Majesty is keen to make reparations. The reigning lord of Qi-Katai, Tieren Halithar Aeduria, has an unmarried daughter of twenty-two, and has said in missives that he's willing to make an alliance. You'll go to *her*, Vel, and Qi-Katai is a city of trade—of libraries, even, and theatre, and craft; and I know you speak the language, thanks to those court-friends of yours. And even if you didn't, many there speak Ralian; you won't lack for civilisation, nor for anything else, and should you wish to visit home, the distance is not so great."

His tone was enamoured, wheedling, but I chilled all over at the implications. *You'll go,* he'd said, and *you won't lack*—not *you could,* or *you wouldn't*. There might have been a mason present to carve the words in stone, for all the give I sensed in them, and it took every scrap of self-possession I had to say, with barely a quaver, "So this—this is finalised, then? You've arranged it?"

"Yes," said Father, and though he was discomforted in the admission, at least he did me the courtesy of not looking away. "You've always been a good son, Vel—a good third son, supportive of your brothers and uncovetous of their dues. I watched you with Jarien earlier, and unless I miss my guess, you bear him no ill-will, though many in your position would. I know you haven't sought marriage"—and here he reached out, squeezing my chair's arm as if in proxy for my withheld hand—"but I wouldn't propose it now, even though it please my king, if I thought it was not also a reward to you; a fitting, good thing for a loyal son."

I wanted to scream, but could not. I wanted to weep, but dared not. I looked at him, and all at once, the dreadful ironies of my flight from Farathel—of why I'd left, and in what hopes—rose up to choke me, gales of awful laughter locked behind my teeth. My smile was a rictus. I bowed my head, and let another memory of childhood obeisance carry me through.

What do you say, Velasin, when Father gives you something?

"Thank you, sir," I croaked out.

My hoarseness he took for a sign of joy; my shock, he took for awe. Still gripping my chair, he spoke in excited tones of the Tithenai envoy due to arrive sometime tomorrow, bearing the marriage contracts; of any arrangements I might want to make, to have my Farathel possessions carefully shipped to Qi-Katai, and whether I'd take Markel with me; of the Tiera Laecia Siva Aeduria, who was to be my wife, and her many apparent virtues. I listened in a half-dead daze, and so missed the knock on the study door that broke my father's speech. Instead, I saw only the butler, bowing at the threshold; heard only his cruel, absurd pronouncement:

"I'm sorry to interrupt, my lords, but there's a visitor inquiring after Lord Velasin."

"A visitor?" asked Father, brow wrinkling in puzzlement. "Not the Tithenai envoy already, surely!"

"No, my lord. Our guest is Ralian—a Lord Killic vin Lato."

The bottom dropped out of the world.

"I know of the house, but not him," said Father, oblivious to the wreck of me. "A friend of yours, Vel?"

That's one way of putting it. "Yes, Father," I said, though how I kept my voice steady, I'll never know. "I—I was not expecting him. He must have sought me out." *Please, please send him away.* But I couldn't ask for it; not without raising questions, and I felt too stupid to lie.

"He's very welcome, then," said Father. To the butler, he added, "He can have the oak room, Perrin, but send him through to the games hall while it's made up—Lord Velasin can meet him there. And do offer him a tray, would you? Late as it is, he's likely starved."

"Yes, my lord," said Perrin, and left.

"Well!" said Father, bright and final. "We can discuss the particulars more tomorrow, but as your friend has come all this way, I shan't keep you from him—unless," he said, with a certain slow awareness of my discomfort, "you'd rather I make your excuses? Sun knows, I'd understand if you'd rather take some time to yourself—"

"No," I said. The word felt tacky and strange in my mouth, like a half-cooked mushroom. Killic was persistent; as unpalatable as I found the prospect, it was best to deal with him now. "I'll see him."

"Good lad," said Father, and as we both came to our feet, he clapped my shoulder again, more gently than before. "I'm proud of you, Vel. Of all of us."

You wouldn't be, I thought, *if you knew.*

"Thank you," I said, and watched him turn left down the corridor, towards his wife and the son too young to have yet disappointed him.

Which left me—false, dutiful creature that I was—to greet Lord Killic vin Lato: the man who, until a mere fortnight past, had been my lover in Farathel.

2

Being both a coward and a pragmatist, I didn't go straight to the games hall, but headed instead to my own rooms, knocking a gentle pattern on the door to Markel's chamber. As with his finger-snapping, this particular rhythm had a meaning unique to us: *Attend me quickly—I need your discretion.*

Within moments, Markel opened the door, stepping neatly aside to let me through. As his master, I was technically within my rights to enter unheralded, but as he could hardly cry out in the event that I was interrupting a private moment—and as I preferred to offer courtesy as a habit, the better to ensure its meaningful reciprocation—I found it more expedient than rudeness.

As Markel shut the door, I faced him and spoke in our shared, silent language, which ran no risk of being overheard.

"Killic is here," I signed. "I can guess what he wants, and I don't intend to give it to him."

Markel's eyebrows shot up. Being my valet, he knew more about my personal life than I sometimes cared to remember, but he was loyal to me, and I trusted him implicitly. Gestures halting, he asked, "Do you want me to deal with him?"

"Not quite," I replied. "Just—" I hesitated, hands stalled helplessly in midsign. "—just keep him from my bed, and me from his. You know I can't be trusted."

"He didn't deserve you," Markel signed fiercely.

It wasn't a new sentiment from him; nonetheless, it touched me, and in a fumbling flurry of signs, I said, "Father has betrothed me to a Tithenai girl. An envoy comes with the contracts tomorrow; I don't know how soon afterwards I'm expected to leave, but she lives in Qi-Katai." I spelled out the city name letter by letter, watching Markel's eyes go wide. "I have no desire to lose your service, but if you didn't wish to come, I would understand; I'd see you happily placed—"

Markel made a rasping noise and shook his head, the rare vocalisation enough to stop me cold. In quick, sharp gestures, he signed, "We are friends. You saved me. Of course I will come to Qi-Katai. Besides," he added, gaze softening slightly, "who else would keep you from yourself?"

"Too true," I replied, and briefly clasped his hands in mine: a renewal of faith on both our parts. "Should I do anything foolish with Killic, you have my permission—no, my instruction—to douse me in cold water."

Markel laughed his silent laugh. "I'd sooner douse Killic."

"A tempting alternative. Should the need arise in either case, I trust you to use your judgement."

He nodded sagely, perching on the edge of his narrow bed. At twenty-one, Markel was three years my junior, and yet he managed his romantic attachments with the ease of a much older man. Once upon a time, I'd begged him for the secret of it: all my life, I'd been taught that women were fickle and hard to woo, but in my experience, men were a far more terrifying prospect. Was one sex truly so much simpler than the other, I'd asked, or was I just doing something wrong?

"I don't know what men want," he'd replied. "But many women, I'm told, are quite impressed by a silent man who listens and writes, and is skilled with his hands." And then he'd grinned, and wiggled his fingertips at me.

Recalling that particular conversation, I felt my heart clench anew at how badly wrong things had gone with Killic. It was hard enough, in Ralia, for men of my inclination—and women, too, though I'd known far fewer of them—to form relationships in the first place, such that it hurt all the more when they ended. Though our existence was not criminalised under crown law, as it was in Attovar, the Doctrine of the Firmament still held considerable power, casting our failure to embody "the order and symmetry of nature" as a degenerate perversion, and what the Doctrine taught, most people believed. Social sanctions could be every bit as effective as legal ones—more so, at times, as they could be justified by anything while being bound by nothing—and among the nobility, social standing was everything. Except among our circle of like-minded friends and acquaintances, Killic's and my involvement had been, of necessity, secret, but now I wondered bitterly if things would've been any different, had living openly been an option. If any part of Killic's betrayal had been sculpted by the pressures of circumstance—no. I severed that line of thought at once. Indulging it would lead me nowhere good.

My misery must have shown in my face, for Markel clicked once: a sound to precede the giving of a personal opinion. I gave him my full attention, and this time, his signing was tentative.

"Killic cannot follow you to Qi-Katai, and you cannot return with him to Farathel. That much is done. If you wanted to—to say farewell, in whatever way, this is your last chance. I do not like the man, but I would not begrudge you that."

My throat tightened. Markel looked at me steadily, compassion in his bright brown eyes. In such moments—and there had been many between us—the lines between our stations had a tendency to blur, if not evaporate completely. Markel was handsome, his shaved head showing the fine lines of his face to best advantage, but if there'd ever been a time when I desired him, it was long past. He was my friend, the closest one I had, and though he didn't hide his opinion of Killic, he still understood my own, more complex feelings towards him.

"I will think on it," I replied—and there, too, was another advantage of signing: that it remained accessible when my spoken voice shrivelled and died. "Thank you, Markel."

He shrugged and smiled, the expression wryly fond.

After a moment, I said aloud, "If you could compose an inventory of our possessions at Farathel, sorted by what ought to come, what we'd like to have and what can be abandoned, I would be grateful."

"And if I leave something out?" he signed.

I snorted. "Then we probably neither need nor want it."

"Impeccable logic, truly."

"Quite right," I said, then hesitated, thoughts snagging on a particular locked and warded chest in my possession, or more accurately its contents, both of which I took care to maintain discreetly. Coughed. "Though, ah. There's a small chest in my room, made of rosewood, you might not have seen—"

Markel shot me a withering look. "I'm very aware of your rosewood chest."

"Ah," I said, an embarrassed flush creeping up my chest. "Well then. Very good." And with that, I summoned my courage, or what little of it remained, and went to see Killic.

He was, as promised, in the games hall, looking as polished and composed as no man who'd ridden hard and fast from Farathel—and he surely must have done so, to have arrived so hot on our heels—had a right to be. Though it shamed me, I watched him for several moments before he noticed my presence, unable to quite shake Markel's suggestion of a farewell. I could accuse Killic of many things, but ugliness—the physical kind, at least—wasn't one of them. His wheat-coloured hair was tied back in a tail, accentuating the strong line of his jaw. He was pale by Ralian standards, but still with that distinctive, olivine warmth to his skin that the Palamites and some Attovari lacked, set off by a pair of dark brown eyes. He was broad-shouldered, dressed in earthy colours accentuated by hints of gold thread: an understated fashion choice by his usual standards, but one that suited him. He was picking delicately through the contents of the tray Perrin had brought him, pausing intermittently to wipe his fingers on a linen square.

My betraying boot squeaked on the hall floor, and he looked up, finally seeing me.

Both of us froze.

My heart began to pound, and all at once, the events of the day—of the past fortnight—seemed unutterably absurd. It made no more sense that I was betrothed to some unknown Tithenai girl than that Killic, my lover of almost a year, would ever betray me so cruelly. I stood there like a lump as Killic rose, closing the gap between us. He stopped within arm's reach of me, hand raised to touch my sleeve; but at the last second, he seemed to think better of it, exhaling sharply as the hand fell to his side.

"All the way from Farathel," he said, lowly, "I wondered what I might say to you—what explanation I could possibly give—to make you reconsider. And now I'm here, and I have no words for you, Aaro: no word but *please.*"

It was like being slapped. My own hands clenched in outrage. "You thought to *explain*?" I asked, voice deadly soft. "Not to apologise or beg, but to *explain*?" My nails dug into my palms. "There are no words to sway me, Killic. Not even *please,* though you use it rarely enough."

He flinched, to my satisfaction. "Aaro, darling—"

I hissed him to silence, grabbing his arm. "Not in here!"

Having no notion of the habits of Father's servants and the risk of eavesdropping, I all but dragged him out of the hall, retracing the path of Lady Sine's earlier tour to the gardens. Killic came easily enough, though he huffed under his breath as though it were all a ridiculous precaution; as though we were not in my father's house, on my father's sufferance, attempting to say in public things which ought only be said in private.

All three moons were bright and clear, the garden lit with their dappled rose-gold light. I finally dropped Killic's arm beside a tree, in sight of the stables but—I hoped—shielded from the house, and resolved to stand my ground.

"Darling," Killic said again, more softly than before, "I'm sorry. I'm so sorry, truly."

I shook my head, hating the part of me that wanted to believe him. "You went to bed with Avery," I said, as much to remind myself as to make him acknowledge it. "Not once, Killic, but dozens of times—hundreds, for all I know!—and he wasn't even the only one—"

"Aaro—"

"—just the one I *caught* you with, and now you come here, you come to explain—" I laughed, a sharp bark that cut the night air. "—and even if you did, it doesn't matter anymore, because I'm *betrothed,* of all the ridiculous things, to a Tithenai girl in Qi-Katai, and even if I still wanted you, Killic—even if I were minded to forgive and forget, which I'm certainly not—I'm not returning to Farathel, and we're done, *I'm* done—" I was near to shouting, my throat hot and tight. "—and there's nothing you can say to undo any of it."

I was shaking, miserable; I wanted him to go. Yet when he cupped my jaw and drew me in, I could no more have pushed him away than grown antlers. He kissed me deeply, pressing me back against the tree, and I knew it was neither apology nor farewell, nor even comfort, but only Killic's need to say he owned me still; that I craved him enough to let him do as he wanted. I gripped his shirt, but didn't kiss back: just hung there, suspended in something like grief, until his mouth lifted from mine.

"I slept with others, yes," he said, voice rough with an honesty I'd seldom heard. "But it was you I laughed with, you I trusted, you I always returned to. You've a hold on me, Aaro—I didn't know how much of one until you left, until there was this absence where you've always been. Your Tithenai girl can marry another; come home with me." He moved in close again, trailing kisses along my jaw, my neck, murmuring promises between each one. "I'll never stray again. I'll make a place for you, something paid. Be part of my household. Just mine. Please."

I tipped my head back, overwhelmed, and stared at the glowing moons. Once, such an offer would've meant everything to me, and been favoured by Father into the bargain, however ironically; now, even without our fallout and my apparent engagement, my family stood higher than his, making the proposition borderline scandalous. Oblivious, Killic kissed my throat, hands sliding down to grip my waist, and almost—almost—I acquiesced, thinking it a bittersweet farewell. But then he murmured, "There you go, darling," as though my lack of a no was the same as a yes, and I tensed beneath him, shoving at his chest.

"No, Killic." And then, when he didn't stop, "*No,* I said!"

Killic made a frustrated noise and resisted my efforts to free myself, pinning my hips to the tree. "You don't know what you want," he said, and tried to kiss me again. I jerked my head aside, but he only laughed, biting at the soft skin beneath my jaw. He stepped back a little, and for half a breath I thought that was it, relaxing my guard and my hold on him both; but when I moved, he used it against me, pulling and grabbing and spinning until he'd turned me completely around, my stomach and cheek against the bark, his chest against my back.

"You don't know what you want," he echoed, kissing the nape of my neck. I tried to turn, but I'd never been a fighter, and Killic, despite his love of formal duels, was also an accomplished brawler.

"No," I said again, struggling against him, "no, no, stop—"

"Shhh." He grabbed my right wrist and twisted it, pinning the arm behind me. The punishing angle meant I could do nothing with my left hand but hang on to the tree, swatting feebly as he went for my belt. I'd already been afraid, but that was the moment I truly began to panic. With awful, visceral clarity, I realised I couldn't cry for help without betraying myself to whoever answered: Killic, it seemed, was beyond such concerns, but discovered or not, I would have to live with whatever consequences he forced me to. I'd never had any great gift for magic, but in that moment it felt impossible that none of the simple charms or tricks I'd mastered could avail me here; it was just that my head was a roaring void, and none of what little I'd learned would come to me. *Fire,* I thought wildly, *I could call fire, set him alight—*

But fire spreads fast in a garden. Even had the charm come to me, I didn't dare.

My tears spilled over, hard and fast. Struggle turned my breathing ragged, pain in my shoulder and elbow as Killic held me firm. Above the roar of my pulse, I heard him murmuring in my ear—*quiet, darling; let me show you, let me have you, Aaro, Aaro*—and then he got his hand on me, and my traitor body was not so frightened as to not respond. Killic laughed at that, warm and pleased, and I choked out a sob whose meaning he either ignored or wilfully misconstrued. I tried to prise his hand away, but only succeeded in strengthening his grip; he ground his own arousal against me, insistent and unrelenting, and in that moment, I despaired of myself as I never had before. I couldn't flee, it seemed: not from Farathel, not from my duty and certainly not from Killic.

And so I went limp against the tree, and let him do as he wanted.

There is a kind of drunkenness—one that some men seek, though I seldom do—where time feels wounded, gaping holes self-suturing into ragged continuity, until minutes pass as seconds, hours as minutes. I'd taken little wine at dinner, but under his hands, I endured the same effects as if I'd emptied bottles. Time jumped and shoved at me, until I felt only fragments of each moment. Killic brought me off—or brought my body off, at least; I was scarcely present—with his usual efficiency, taking his own enjoyment against my buttocks and between my pressed thighs, hands bruisingly hard to hold me where he wanted even once he dropped my arm, and then I went strangely blank. It couldn't have been for more than a moment, but when I came back to myself, I was on my knees, my trousers around my thighs. My fingers clenched in the night-cool dirt, and I bowed my head, not wanting to look at any of him, though more than his face was bare. Killic gripped my jaw, his fingers digging in—hard, as he was still hard—but though it hurt, I refused to open my mouth for his greedy use.

"Have it that way, then," he snarled, and forced me to take him in hand instead, his grip pinning mine in place. I didn't look at him, but stared at the ground, so numb I heard nothing beyond his grunts until a sudden blaze of light illuminated us both.

"Well!" said a dry, unfamiliar voice. "That's certainly unexpected."

The shock of being caught brought me back to myself as nothing else could have. Killic dropped his hold on me; I jerked to my feet and stumbled backwards, struggling to reconfine such parts as he'd left loose. *Shame* is not a strong enough word for what I felt; I was paralysed, so sick at heart I almost lost my stomach. I kept my eyes on the ground, not wanting to see who'd discovered us; and yet a part of me already knew, though silenced by shock and fear.

And then I heard my father's voice—he came from the house, boots crunching on the gravel path—and started to shake anew.

"Envoy, greetings! We weren't expecting you until tomorrow."

"Clearly," said that same wry voice, as someone else laughed in the background.

"What do you—" Father started to ask, and then—I cannot describe it otherwise—I felt the moment he saw me; the moment he *knew*. For all that I'd managed to cover myself, the tableau we made was unmistakeable.

No silence of my life had ever felt more deafening.

"I think, Lord vin Aaro," the envoy said, "that we ought to speak in private, don't you?"

"Yes," growled Father, and when I dared to look at him, the glance he spared me was venomous. "We ought." He looked at Killic with a mix of disgust and fury. "*You,* sir, will either leave this estate at once, or not at all. Do we understand each other?"

Killic's head bobbed in frightened agreement, his disregard for consequence wholly forgotten. He didn't even look at me; just clutched himself and fled to the stables.

Father watched him go, then turned back to the envoy, stiff with humiliation. "This way," he said, and led the Tithenai inside. Perhaps it was a trick of the light, but I felt the envoy spared me a sympathetic glance before following him; Father, however, paid me even less notice than Killic had, and I shrank on myself, more chastened than if he'd yelled.

The house doors shut, and the night fell to silence. Abandoned, debauched and utterly disgraced, I slid to the ground and sobbed.

3

I don't know how long I sat there; only that I was shivering by the time Markel found me. I flinched from his hands when he tried to help me up, and instantly hated myself for it. He crouched down, trying to catch my eye, but I couldn't look at him. I hated myself for that, too, and shivered all the harder, hunching sideways against the tree. I scarcely felt human, like a whipped cur cowering from thunder, and when Markel snapped his fingers three times—his signal for urgency—it was reflex alone that saw me lift my head.

"You need to come inside," signed Markel. "Please, Velasin. Let me help you."

I stared at him, bereft. Unable to find my voice, I signed with shaking hands, "Is Killic gone?"

"He fled nearly an hour ago, and good riddance!"

I had a dim recollection of noise near the stables, but nothing more; even so, a little tension bled from me. Markel must have noticed, for he tried again to help me rise, this time by reaching for my hand. I cried out, floundering backwards, scrambling to my feet almost as an afterthought. He looked at me in shock, his own palms bared to show he meant no harm, and I nearly doubled over with renewed weeping, unable to explain to him that my hands were soiled, that I couldn't bear to dirty him.

"I'm sorry," I whispered. "I'm sorry, Markel."

I let him usher me inside, though having divined my aversion to touch, he kept his distance, herding me when I faltered like a shepherd with an errant sheep. In this way he brought me to my rooms, where a steaming bath was laid out behind a paper screen, a servant's stool at the foot of the tub and all my bathing implements on a folding table beside it. Markel looked from me to the bath and back again, one eyebrow raised in silent inquiry.

"I'll get in," I said. "I'll—I'll undress myself."

Markel nodded, evidently satisfied with this, but he still looked troubled. I turned away and began to fumble at my clothes, hands shaking all the while. I felt like a crab without its shell, soft and vulnerable when I finally entered the tub. The water was hot, almost scalding: I wanted to scrub myself clean, obliterate every sign that Killic ever touched me, but though I'd bathed with Markel present for nearly a decade and never felt him an imposition, I suddenly wanted privacy.

"I would be obliged," I said, voice curiously flat, "if you could find me some brandy. Doubtless, Father—" I faltered, swallowing around my shame. "—doubtless he won't want to give me anything, after what he saw, but I think—if you could try—"

Markel bowed low and slipped from the room like a shadow.

For several moments I simply sat, drained in a way I could scarcely articulate. Distantly, I noted that my hips and wrist were bruised from Killic's hands, but if Markel had noticed, he wouldn't have thought it odd; I'd carried similar marks before, from encounters whose roughness came from passion, not—

I shied away from naming what had happened, embracing instead a different angle of misery. In my mind, there was no question that I'd ruined my life irreparably: the envoy would dissolve the betrothal; Father would be shamed before King Markus and the Tithenai both; my disgrace would be made public; I'd lose my sinecure—maybe even be formally disinherited, stripped of the vin Aaro name—and after what Killic had said and done, I couldn't go back to Farathel. Markel was all I had in the world, but if I could no longer afford to keep him, he didn't deserve to be yoked to me through a loyalty I'd so manifestly failed to deserve.

On the table beside the bath lay soap, a washcloth, a mirror, nail scissors, a hot towel and a cold one, a shaving brush, shaving soap and a cutthroat razor. It would take Markel at least ten minutes to find the brandy, by my estimate: the estate was large, and unlike me, he hadn't had the benefit of Lady Sine's tour. I felt so strange, so alien and cold, that it scarcely seemed a conscious decision to pick up the razor, studying the blade. I could bleed out in ten minutes, if I cut myself deeply enough; the warm bath would aid in that. Absently, I wondered whether wrists or throat would be the better choice: I wasn't sure I had the stomach for more than one cut, but if I missed the jugular, I'd have to try again.

Despite the heat of the bath, I began to shake. I pressed the sharp of the blade to my wrist, but didn't bear down, though I willed myself to do so. I couldn't understand my own hesitation: what did I have to live for? I thought of Markel, who'd been so considerate as to draw the bath before bringing me inside; who'd set everything in its proper place; and who, if I succeeded, would be the one to find me.

Tears stood in my eyes. I wanted to be selfish, but I was too afraid of the pain, too conscious of Markel's return. I steeled myself to press harder, and a thin red line appeared on my skin, stinging sharply in the damp air. This small success shocked me into stopping; I stared stupidly at the blood, and was still staring minutes later, when Markel returned. I didn't see him enter, nor did I hear the door. All I recall is the urgent repeating triple-snap of his fingers, clicking and clicking until I finally looked at him. He was kneeling beside me, eyes wild with fear, and all at once, I realised that if I had truly hurt myself, he wouldn't have been able to call for help; would instead have had to leave me and run for it, scrambling to write the terrible truth on his slate, for none in my father's household knew his signs.

It was this thought that broke me. Though not a perfect analogue to the helpless fear of crying out I'd felt at Killic's hands, it was close enough that I couldn't bear to inflict it on him; felt newly monstrous, in fact, for ever having considered it.

"Take it," I croaked, "moons, please, take it from me—"

Markel snatched the razor, flinging it away. I stared at him, breathing hard, then grabbed the soap and started scrubbing my palms, arms, stomach, genitals; everywhere I could reach, sobbing at I knew not what. The soap stung in my bleeding wrist, which made some mad part of me fixate on it, hands working hard and fast along the cut.

Markel clicked his fingers again, just once. I looked up from my scrubbing. Keeping his eyes on me, Markel reached out and, very slowly, took the soap away, too. This time, I didn't shy from his touch, but shuddered with something like relief. I felt drained beyond endurance, bleak and weak and lost.

"I've ruined us," I rasped. "I've ruined everything."

Markel shook his head.

I wanted to tell him to leave my service before my reputation could work against him, but I hadn't the strength for an argument. Instead, when Markel gripped my arm, I let him help me out of the bath, towelling myself dry with a bare minimum of effort. I'd scarcely managed to tug on a nightshirt before collapsing onto the bed, and even then, it was Markel who pulled the covers over me. I shut my eyes, listening to him pad about the room, extinguishing the lights. I felt safer in the dark. Hidden. Anonymous, even. Which felt appropriate, all things considered; soon enough, I'd be nothing in truth.

I fell asleep to the sound of Markel's breathing.

If I dreamed at all that night, I have no memory of it. Come morning, it was Markel's hand on my shoulder that woke me, worried eyes scanning my face. Small wonder: I ached all over, as if with fever, and couldn't have looked much better.

"Yes?" I said, voice rough. "What's happened?"

Markel hesitated, then signed, "Your father wants to see you."

I tensed, some childish part of me convinced that hiding beneath the covers would see the problem evaporate. Abruptly, Markel looked furious, but not at me. He thumped to his knees, his hands on a level with my eyes, and began to sign, swift and passionate.

"I will not lose you. Not to Killic, not to your father, and not to yourself. Not like this. You still have options, and even though they be risky, I will stand with you, whatever you choose. Just get up! There are no more razors here, and whatever you fear has happened, I do not think things are simple. The Tithenai envoy is still here. Your father's mood is baffled, not angry. Something has happened overnight, and I need you to get up, I need you to fight for yourself as you once fought for me. Please, Velasin." His eyes entreated me along with his words. "Please get up."

And somehow, for his sake, I managed it.

I dressed myself, still reticent to be touched in so intimate a fashion by anyone else, even Markel. He accepted my unease without comment, handing me my clothes instead. I stubbornly did not think of Killic; of what he'd done to me. In the daylight, I knew exactly what word described his actions, but couldn't yet bear to confront it. Whatever distinctions I might draw between consensual liaisons and—and the other thing, I didn't believe for a second that Father would; not where two men were concerned.

The cut on my wrist had scabbed cleanly and was hidden beneath my sleeve; so long as I didn't look at it, I could forget its presence. But though my jaw was unshaven, when I glanced in the mirror, the faint bruising left there by Killic's grip stood out to me like a brand. I felt it with every effort at speech, with every gulp and swallow. It wasn't so distinctive as to invite comment—unlike the marks on my hips, these bruises were faint and small, their cause not obvious unless you knew what to look for—but it was more than enough to keep me unsettled.

I dressed for travel.

The walk to Father's study felt longer than it ever had in anticipation of any childhood punishment. The door was closed, forcing me to knock like a penitent, empty stomach churning.

"Enter," Father called.

I obeyed.

The first shock, on opening the door, was finding him standing behind his desk in the company of an older woman who could only be the envoy. The second shock, on looking more closely, was the realisation that she was not a *she* at all, but one of Tithena's third-gender souls, called kemi, whose existence—or rather, the acknowledgement of whose existence—so intrigued and scandalised the Ralian court. The Doctrine of the Firmament was nearly as scathing about those who professed an identity beyond male or female, or who knew themselves to be other than what their born bodies suggested, as it was about men like me; as such, I couldn't help but feel a spark of kinship for the envoy. Adjusting my assumptions and internal language both, I reassessed thim, striving to correct my misapprehensions. Though thir face seemed feminine to me, both beardless and unstubbled, thir chest was completely flat, a fact emphasised by thir slim-fitted Tithenai robes. Even so, it was the robes that were the real clue: I knew little enough of Tithenai culture, but kemi were intriguing to Ralians like myself, and thus I recognised the significance of the green braid design on thir collar.

If Father was aware of this distinction, however, he chose to ignore it.

"This is Envoy Keletha," he said, voice flat and tense. "You owe her an apology."

Slowly, I turned to face thim. Keletha was, I guessed, around sixty years of age, silver-haired and bronze-skinned, with sharp eyes the colour of flint. Thir expression was calm and steady, but thir poise was that of a powerful force contained, like a great cat watching potential prey. With nothing to lose, I took a breath and gambled.

In Tithenai, using modifiers appropriate to a kem, I said, "My sincerest apologies, envoy. I am—" My voice cracked, betraying me. "—I am more ashamed than you know."

A slow, considering smile crossed Keletha's face. "I was surprised, I admit," thei said, the self-reference affirming my choice of grammar. "I am more surprised now, however. And more impressed." Thei inclined thir head. "Your apology is unnecessary, Tiern Velasin. Nonetheless, I accept it." Turning to Father, thei added, in flawless, unaccented Ralian, "Your son has excellent manners. I commend your raising of him."

Father flushed, unable to deny the praise without slighting the one who gave it. "Thank you," he said, curtly. And then, to my utter shock, he seemed to crumple, knuckles braced on his sturdy desk as his head hung down, despairing. "Gods forgive me my trespasses," he murmured. "That I even consider this blasphemy—" He broke off, head jerking up again, eyes widening at the envoy. "Forgive me. I am beyond my element."

"I take no offence," said Keletha, though the twitch of thir lips said otherwise. "May I be the one to speak?"

Father nodded, waving a weary hand at the selfsame chairs we'd sat in only yesterday, while he, in turn, collapsed into the seat behind the desk. Caught off guard, I followed Keletha's lead in sitting, hunting for clues in thir face, but finding none.

When we were seated, Keletha said, "Forgive me a personal question, my lord, but do your tastes encompass women, too?"

My shock at such a bald inquiry was nothing compared to Father's. He made a gut-punched noise, as though the very notion wounded him. It would have been easy to lie, and for the sake of my tattered Ralian honour, I ought to have done so. But the words would not come; I raised my hands to sign, which would have been easier, but checked myself at the last, and said aloud, though faintly, "No, envoy. Just men."

Father swore and gripped his desk. The wood creaked audibly. The envoy didn't look at him, but kept thir eyes on me. "My thanks for your honesty," thei said. "Can I assume, then, that contrary to your sire's assurances, you did not consent to taking a wife?"

The question left me fixed between the hammer and the anvil. I was sluggish with shock, but couldn't shake the suspicion that the envoy was, in some strange and unexpected sense, on my side. And yet I couldn't bring myself to wholly damn my father either, least of all when I had no sense of the possible implications of doing so.

"I am a dutiful son," I said at last, "and duty is consent enough for such purposes. And besides," I added, unable to quite keep the bitterness from my tone, "he didn't know."

"Damn right I didn't," Father muttered.

I flinched, and the envoy frowned.

"Well, then," Keletha said. "In that case, Lord Velasin, might you be amenable to an alternate arrangement?"

I stared at thim. "Such as?"

"It seems," said Father, grinding the words like grist, "that the Tiera Laecia has a—a *brother.*"

"But what—" I began, then stopped, heart seizing as it hit me.

I knew, of course, that marriage in Tithena had more valid permutations than the Ralian sort; indeed, I could hardly have been ignorant of it. Even before the current fad had popularised that nation's language among Farathel's elite, the Tithenai word for a husband's husband had long been used as court-cant for men like me, with some other, more intimate implications thrown in for the bargain. The first time I'd heard that whispered word, *litai,* was seared into my memory; I'd lied to myself before then, but in that moment, I'd felt branded by the term, as undeniably bound to it as if some storybook sorcerer had evoked my true name.

Not that magic worked that way in practice, a distant, slightly hysterical part of me thought. Real magic was like an invisible muscle everyone was born with, but which only a few could use without proper training, just as only some people could wiggle their ears or curl their tongues as children. And with or without that native spark, you still had to work at it, and work hard, mastering charms before you could so much as attempt the more complex marriages of power, intent and focus required for cantrips or spells, just as any man who aspires to lift boulders must first begin with stones.

I felt like I'd been thrown a boulder now.

"You want me to marry a man?" I said, faintly.

"The Tiern Caethari Xai Aeduria, yes," said Keletha. "He's Laecia's elder by six years. The two of you would suit each other well, I think."

I didn't know what to say to that, and so said nothing. Killic's bruises pulsed on my jaw.

"It seems a neat solution, all things considered," Keletha went on, turning back to Father. "The terms of the betrothal remain the same, your king and my tieren are still given proof of mutual goodwill, and your son"—thir gaze flicked briefly to me—"is offered a match more suited to his tastes."

"I will be shamed," said Father, stiffly. "To have a child of mine so claimed—to have the claiming *known*—"

"Careful, my lord," said Keletha, sharply. "That reticence runs perilous close to insult. Or do you imagine no greater repercussions to such a refusal?"

Father, like me, sought refuge in silence. After a moment, the envoy said, in easier tones, "Besides, there's ample historical precedent for such a match. Not many in recent years, I grant you, but as mending those newer hostilities is why we proposed this alliance in the first instance, that hardly seems a reasonable objection."

"True," Father grudged. "The point is well-taken."

Keletha looked at me. "Do you object, Lord Velasin?"

I almost laughed; the notion that I had any say in a matter so clearly decided was absurd, and even had I wished to dissent, my father's gaze drilled into me, commanding I salvage the mess I had made of his plans.

"No, envoy," I said, softly. "I do not object."

Keletha smiled. "It's settled, then. A son for a son." Thei came to thir feet, approaching Father's desk. "Is tomorrow too soon to depart? I wish neither to slight your excellent hospitality nor overly impose on it, but in either case, it seems a shame to waste good travelling weather."

"Tomorrow is fine," said Father. He rose and offered thim a tense, tight bow. "My thanks, envoy. I appreciate your . . . flexibility."

Keletha inclined thir head, spared me a parting glance and left, presumably to make whatever arrangements thei now deemed necessary. Not that I was in much of a state to consider what these might be; my head was spinning, unable to fully grasp the turn events had taken. I felt adrift, like flotsam at the mercy of inescapable tides.

"Get up," said Father suddenly, voice harshened by the envoy's absence. I leapt to my feet, trembling beneath his stare. He was breathing hard, but when he next spoke, his voice was soft and deadly. "I will say this once, and once alone. The fact that this wreck of a situation is deemed salvageable by Tithenai perversity does not make it so by any civilised measure. You have disgraced yourself, and me, with a completeness I never thought possible. You will retain your name and sinecure only because to strip you of them would attract more comment—and provoke more insult—than I have any desire to navigate, and because I believe your exile will be punishment enough."

"Exile?"

"You cannot come home again," said Father. "Not to Aarobrook, and certainly not here. So long as I live, you will remain absent." He bared his teeth in an ugly smile. "This bed is of your making, Velasin; you will damn well lie in it. Now get out."

I fled.

4

I had no destination in mind, but let my feet carry me where they would, until I fetched up on a rooftop terrace overlooking the gardens. I could scarcely breathe; I felt as though my lungs were shrinking, each breath shallower than the last, until the resultant dizziness forced me to my knees. The posture recalled what Killic had done, which only made things worse: I leaned my forehead against the stone and tried to breathe deep, but my body refused to cooperate. My throat burned, and for a hysterical moment, I wondered if it were possible to die of such self-induced panic.

A slim hand landed on my shoulder, rubbing forth and back in a soothing rhythm.

"Easy now," Lady Sine murmured. "Take a breath, Vel, and hold it. Good. That's good. And out again. There you go. Easy."

She kept up her patter and contact both until the fit had passed. When I was able to look up, I found her kneeling beside me, heedless equally of dirt and propriety. Her kindness left me lost for words, both on its own account and in contrast to her husband's lack of same.

"I don't understand," I said, blankly. "Do you not despise me?"

"It would make me hypocrite indeed, were that the case," she said. Her smile was a complex thing, both soft and sad. "Whatever our differences, I cannot rightly shame you for a fear I've known myself."

"Oh," I said, dumbly. *Oh.* "It is just—" I gulped, struggling for words, hands spread in supplication. "—with a wife, I couldn't have—I wouldn't have touched her, I would have had space—there would have been expectations, yes, but not—she would not—" I raised an unconscious hand, brushing Killic's bruises. "—but this, now—in *this* arrangement, things might—he might *take*—and I cannot endure it again, I *cannot*—"

The lady's hand flew to her mouth in shock, and only then did I realise what I'd said. My eyes went wide, head shaking in a silent plea for retraction, but she would have none of it.

"You were forced last night?"

I nodded miserably.

"Had he done it before?"

I shook my head.

"But you—the two of you, I mean—before this, you were—" She faltered, clearly uncertain of the terminology, then gamely ventured, "—lovers?"

Another nod.

She exhaled sharply. "*Fiend,*" she hissed, and with such vehemence that I trembled, assuming her compassion had run its course. Seeing my reaction, however, she cursed—an unladylike invective—and said angrily, "Not *you,* Vel, gods! I meant *him.*"

She tried to take my hand, but as with Markel, I flinched from it, tucking both hands safely between my knees. Her sharp gaze raked my jawline, noting the bruises there, and by the way her expression changed, she understood their significance.

"I didn't fight," I said, softly. "Or not well enough, at least."

"That is to his discredit, not yours."

"Few in this house would agree with you, my lady. Certainly, my father does not." I swallowed, unable to meet her gaze. "Whatever lurid tales you've heard, what was—the act that was interrupted did not—it did not seem, would not have seemed—and even had it done, they would draw no distinctions—"

I found I couldn't continue, but in truth, there was no need. Lady Sine set a hand on my knee and squeezed, and for a minute or so, we sat in silence, sharing a strange camaraderie.

"I am the last of my house," she said, by and by. She stared straight ahead, as though the gardens were visible through the stonework. "Those of my kin who did not die in my uncle's attempt at rebellion were executed or exiled for their part in it." I winced, ashamed of the ease with which I'd put the circumstances of Lady Sine's marriage to my father—or rather, her perspective on them—to the back of my mind. What had she felt for Lord Ennan vin Mica, I suddenly wondered? Did she mourn his death, or resent what he'd brought her to? "I was tried and held to have been innocent of participation," she went on, "but guilty of concealing it. With such a verdict rendered, marriage"—she waved a cynical hand—"seemed a better fate by far than dying. But I was still afraid."

I shut my eyes, not sure I could ask the question if I looked at her, then opened them again, because she deserved the courtesy of it. "And did my father justify that fear?"

"He did not," she said, after a beat. "He was very patient. And kind, too, in his own way. I did not wish to defer the inevitable, though had I asked him to wait, he would have done so. He has never pressed me, nor held my uncle's sins to my account, and though I did not look for such, I am grown fond of him. Very fond. And happy, as you may see." She hesitated, then said, "Perhaps you, too, will be so fortunate."

"Perhaps," I echoed, though I held no hope of it; not after what Killic had done. His predations had left me with an intense sense of my own vulnerability: I'd risked rough treatment before, and been threatened with same, but enduring it was something altogether different, and doubly so at the hands of a man I'd trusted. In that suffocating aftermath, what terrified me most of all was not the knowledge that I might be overpowered again, but that I would once more be too cowardly to fight.

Though not, perhaps, a part of me thought, *too cowardly to die.*

"I have no right to ask it," I said, "but may I have a boon of you, Lady Sine?"

"So long as it be not impossible, yes."

I took a deep breath, staring at my hands. "Markel is very dear to me, and exceedingly clever. Should the need arise, will you find him a worthy place?"

Her head jerked up, eyes wide with alarm. "Is that truly a possibility?"

I looked within myself, and then at her. My voice, when I finally spoke, was steel. "I will not be forced, my lady. Not again. If such is what I can expect in Qi-Katai—if that is what I find—then yes, it will come to that. You may count on it."

"I would offer you sanctuary," she said, a note of desperation in her voice. "Velasin, if it was in my power, I would offer you sanctuary, but your father—I cannot intercede with him on this, I cannot risk—"

"I do not ask it of you. Only care for Markel, if you can. That's all I want."

She shut her eyes. "You have my word."

"Thank you," I said, and squeezed her knuckles.

After that, there wasn't much more to be said. Lady Sine stayed with me for another few minutes before excusing herself to see to Jarien; she kissed my cheek, and I knew it for a farewell. I sat awhile on the roof alone, then finally went to find Markel, explaining to him—in signs again, for I had no wish to be overheard—that I was now bound for a husband instead of a wife, and that we were leaving tomorrow. Markel responded by producing his list of our Farathel possessions, along with some thoughts on their dispersal. Approving it all, I bade him give it to Lady Sine, who seemed more likely to see my wishes enacted than Father did, and tried not to terrify myself with the prospect of anyone breaking into my rosewood chest.

And then I stared at the wall for some minutes, unmoored by the realisation that, having left our Farathel home in a rush, I would never return there again.

Despite the expense, I'd chosen to live in the capital because the hustle and bustle, the abundance of bright young noblemen coming and going and getting themselves up to mischief in the interim, provided the perfect cover for hiding in plain sight, for men like me. Other large Ralian cities afforded similar opportunities, but none so ripe with intrigue as Farathel, and what else were indolent third sons good for, but engaging in publicly spirited nonsense and privately tawdry affairs? It had been a life circumscribed in all things by the need for discretion and the limits of my sinecure—it had certainly not been perfect—and yet the knowledge that I'd lost it so completely, so quickly, was like having a hand cut off.

How was I to occupy myself in Qi-Katai? I was as ill-suited to an uneventful existence as I was to solitude. Without a social circle to keep track of, gossip to pursue, novelties to investigate or excursions to plan, my brain would pace itself into a mania inside of a week, and that was in a city where I knew the rules. How would I live, if my husband kept me as constrained as some Ralian noblemen kept their wives? How was I meant to cope with any of this?

Though devoid of appetite, I forced myself to eat a little bread and fruit, and then went back to bed, taking what comfort I could in pillows and eiderdown. Depending on the weather and our general luck, it would take us two or three weeks to reach Qi-Katai. I wondered if I should hope for delays, but like Lady Sine, I found that I would rather not postpone the inevitable, whatever it might be.

When it came time for supper, I didn't go down to eat with the household and envoy, but remained in my room, where Markel brought me a tray. We ate together in a silence less companionable than it might have been, had I not been so on edge. In addition to the food, Markel brought me word from Keletha's people that thei intended for us to leave at dawn: as such, once our meal was done, he dutifully laid out our clothes for the morrow, then took our scanty luggage down to the stables. I swallowed, hoping the grooms would give him no trouble. Even had he not been mute, the servant of a man in disgrace was inherently more vulnerable than one whose master flourished, and if Father's servants wished to take their disgust at me out on Markel, there was little I could do to stop it. I waited for his return in an agony of anticipation, tormenting myself with images of him beaten and bloodied, unable to cry out, but when he returned, it was in good time, with no sign of disarray on his person.

My rest that night was fitful: a combination of nerves and overtiredness from my earlier lethargies. I didn't dream of Killic, but of nameless hands holding me down, twisting and grabbing, and woke in a sweat to find Markel standing over me in the grey light.

"Did I cry out?" I asked him, hoping I had not.

He shook his head and signed, "Dawn. I was coming to wake you."

I made my ablutions swiftly, opting again to dress myself unaided. Markel made no comment at this, but performed his own chores, and soon enough, the pair of us were outside at the stables, milling in a subdued confusion of grooms and Tithenai riders.

This latter contingent numbered twelve, not including Keletha; it was the first time I'd paid them any attention, and was surprised to find that five of them were women. I thought of Lady Sine, and found the prospect strangely cheering. I was yet too raw to hope that Tithena meant anything good for me, but as Keletha had thus far shown me a greater acceptance than Father had, the possibility existed that our travelling companions might prove similarly tolerant. For all I was fluent in Tithenai, Keletha was only the third native speaker I'd ever had occasion to test it on. I understood the language, knew that it contained both terms and concepts that Ralians found peculiar, but that was a far cry from understanding how Tithenai culture functioned. For all I knew, my impending marriage, though legally binding, would be just as great a source of gossip and ridicule in Tithena as Ralia.

Swinging up into Quip's saddle, I heard some witty groom snigger, "Mount up, my lord."

Several others chuckled at the joke, and though Keletha frowned censure at those of our party who joined in, the head groom did nothing at all.

A pang went through me then, a preemptive wave of homesickness for everything I'd lost. I wasn't surprised that Father hadn't risen to see us off, and yet it still pained me to think that I was so easily discarded. Lady Sine's absence was a mixed blessing: after her kindness to me, I would have liked to see her again, if only from a distance, but such a glimpse would have hurt in a different way. It was Perrin the butler alone who watched our departure, and with what seemed to me an expression of thinly veiled relief.

Only two days earlier, I'd ridden into the vin Aaro lands and calmly accepted my lack of any claim on them. Now I rode out for the first, last time, and tried to accept that Father had abandoned his claim on me.

As the Tithenai moved into an apparently practiced formation, I found myself riding at Markel's side, placed between the pack mules and the vanguard. There were spare mounts, too—a trio of rouncies strung along behind one of the outriders—and for the first time, I began to appreciate the sheer physical distance we'd have to travel. I had always been an accomplished rider, but my skills had never been tested in any more strenuous context than the steeplechase races held between nobles in Farathel—which were hardly safe, to be sure, yet not exactly comparable to weeks in the Snowjaw Mountains. My experience of cross-country riding was limited to a handful of hunts at the estates of friends, controlled rides through well-groomed fields and woodlands. But even after the fall of House vin Mica and His Majesty's efforts to clear our side of the Taelic Pass of bandits, the way to Qi-Katai was far from safe. I found myself conjuring visions of bad weather, rockfalls, unexpected snow, broken limbs—all the perils that might keep us from our destination.

Three weeks past, I might have been afraid. But in the pale dawn light, with grief behind and grief ahead, I found I relished the danger. Either it would kill me, and potentially spare me the trouble of making my second attempt to achieve the same ends, or else it would strengthen me; and moons, but I needed strength! For despite my despair and my words to Lady Sine—despite that I was steeling myself to the prospect—I didn't want to die. Revic had been the fighter in my family, and he was dead of too much drink and too little sense; but perhaps that meant his mantle had, in some sense, passed to me. I would fight with wits, I decided, and such courage as I could muster in the circumstances. I had little faith in succeeding, but if I made no attempt at all, then I might as well fling myself from the first high place we came to.

Two thoughts came to me then, and both related to Markel. Glancing at him, I drummed my fingers pointedly on my saddle horn, tapping out my *attend-discreetly* knock. Markel's head jerked up at the sound, gaze narrowing as he looked at me. Being sure to keep my gestures small, I signed to him, "How strong is your knowledge of Tithenai?"

Markel considered the question. "Not as strong as it was," he replied. "But strong enough. And under these conditions, it ought to come back quickly."

I nodded, pleased. When I'd first undertaken to learn the language, I'd practiced with Markel: teaching him the written form had solidified my own understanding considerably, and once I began to speak it aloud, he'd been my first audience, head shaking or fingers snapping to indicate an error as he scribbled corrections on cards. His knowledge soon yielded surprising boons: the court's faddish adoption of Tithenai as an elite language of secrets and romance led most nobles to assume a servant would never speak it. Markel was already underestimated by such people due to his muteness; they spoke carelessly around him as it was, but were soon proven utterly indiscreet when lapsing into Tithenai. I'm not ashamed to say we made a game of it, and for a time, my reputation in Farathel as a man who knew everything worth knowing was strong enough to precede me in many quarters.

But after taking up with Killic, I'd let my involvement in such intrigues slacken: I'd hardly been celibate prior to that, but brief encounters were different to an ongoing affair. Not wanting to leave either of us vulnerable to exposure by needlessly provoking conflict,

I'd taken a step back—except, of course, when Killic had bade me do otherwise, and always to his advantage.

I shoved the memories aside, lest sickness and fury sway me. *Focus,* I thought sternly, and returned my attention to Markel. Taking a steadying breath, I signed to him, "Good. I want to play the listening game. Don't let them know you know, and report back to me."

Markel smiled a sharp, gleeful smile. "I was hoping you'd say that."

His enthusiasm sparked my own. I might have been out of my depth in some respects, but spying, listening, playing court politics? That, I could do, and whatever the cultural differences between Qi-Katai and Farathel, some human similarities surely went deeper than language.

Which brought me to my second, more immediate concern. "Even so, they need to know you're mute. Not just to avoid causing offence, if someone speaks to you; riding out here is dangerous. If you get into trouble or spot some coming, you need to be able to call for help in a way they'll understand."

Markel looked at me, a strange expression on his face. After a moment, he signed, "I'll whip-whistle. One note if I see trouble, two if I need help. Will that do?"

I nodded. "Perfect. I'll let the envoy know."

That being settled, I nudged Quip's flanks and rode up the column in search of Keletha, noting as I passed that every Tithenai rider was armed. I found the envoy in conversation with a glowering, muscular man on a dish-faced gelding, and waited politely to one side. The man broke off when he noticed me, while Keletha turned in the saddle and smiled, head tilted inquiringly. In Ralian, thei asked, "Are you well, my lord?"

As tempting as it was to reply in the same language, my Tithenai was rusty, and from the little I'd heard so far, I suspected my accent was terrible. Determined to improve before we reached Qi-Katai, I declined the easier option and said, in Tithenai, "As well as can be expected. If I'm not interrupting, may I have a moment, envoy?"

Beside us, the big man grunted in surprise. Keletha laughed, thir crow's-feet crinkling pleasedly. "Of course," thei said—in Tithenai, this time. And then, in belated introduction, "This is my second, Tar Raeki Maas. Raeki, this is Tiern Velasin vin Aaro."

Tar was a Tithenai title, indicating a rank that meant something like lieutenant-captain. As such, I accorded Raeki a respectful nod. As for my being called *tiern,* the title was not quite equivalent to Ralian lordhood, but whether it constituted a step up or a step down for me—or a step sideways, even—was yet to be seen.

Raeki looked me over, seemingly unimpressed with what he saw. At last, he said, "I can't decide if you sound more like a farmer or an Attovari."

"I sound like a Ralian courtier, which is worse than either. Both options are complimentary in comparison."

Raeki snorted. "I can well believe it."

Keletha shot him a look of mild irritation. "I believe the tiern had something to say?"

"Yes," I said, suppressing a smile at Raeki's chastened expression. "My, uh, my—" I fumbled for what to call Markel; there was no direct equivalent to *valet* in Tithenai, while the closest term I could think of had sexual implications in Farathel's court slang, and I wasn't sure if this was a Ralian adaptation or part of the Tithenai meaning. Calling him my servant in the generic felt inadequate; he was more than that, and I needed the envoy to know it, if he was to be shown respect. Eventually, I said, "—my friend, Markel, is mute. He cannot shout, but if he sees trouble, he'll whistle once; if he's in trouble himself, he'll do it twice. I'd ask that you inform your riders of this."

"He'll whistle?" Raeki asked, dubiously. "Can mutes do that?"

"Markel!" I yelled in Ralian, turning in the saddle. "Show the man you can whistle!"

Markel complied, with ear-splitting effect. Several Tithenai shouted in alarm, while one of the pack mules put its ears back and brayed. Markel grinned and waved. I raised a brow at Raeki.

"Is that sufficient, tar?"

"It'll do," he said, and promptly wheeled his horse around, presumably to inform his fellows.

Throughout all this, Keletha had remained conspicuously silent. Now, however, thei fixed me with a curious look.

"I had understood that Markel was your servant"—thei used the Ralian word—"not your friend. Am I mistaken in this?"

"He can't be both?" I countered.

"Perhaps my knowledge of Ralian customs is faulty, but I'd have thought it very unusual, yes."

"According to Ralian customs, everything about me is unusual," I said bitterly. "Why should my relationship with Markel be any different?"

Keletha looked startled. "Is he your lover, then, too?"

I choked. "Of course not! What do you take me for?" I gripped the reins, as though I could control my anger as easily as I did Quip's head. "Do you think I'd have been anywhere near Killic if I had another waiting for me?"

"I don't know, tiern," said Keletha, calmly. "Would you?"

"No!"

"I'm glad to hear it, for Tiern Caethari's sake."

I looked away, a sour knot in my stomach. The envoy, however, wasn't done with me.

"I am being rude, I know," thei said, in that same, steady voice. "But rude to a purpose. I'm bringing you to marry one to whom I owe my loyalty; as such, I'd be remiss to ask no questions. Do you desire your servant, Tiern Velasin?"

I gritted my teeth. "No, envoy."

"And what of Lord Killic? Should I expect him to follow us now, as I'm told he followed you from Farathel?"

The prospect stopped me cold. Would he try to find me again?

As furious as Father was, I couldn't imagine he'd make any effort to keep Killic's secret, and especially not when revealing him was the obvious way to draw attention away from House vin Aaro. I might be the disgraced lord sent to marry a Tithenai man, but Killic would be known for having chased me to my family's lands and, by his actions, risked the whole betrothal in the first place. Though our relationship had been known to some in our Farathel circle, the scandal of it would doubtless cause the majority to cut him, and all things considered, I couldn't imagine the reaction of his own family would be any more forgiving than Father's. If Killic truly felt he had nothing else left—if any of what he'd said to me had been sincere—he might well try to reclaim me.

My bruised jaw throbbed; I couldn't speak. The world had grown too small, too tight. I didn't answer Keletha, but kicked Quip forwards, urging him to a gallop. He snorted approval and met the challenge, eager to stretch his legs. Behind me I heard someone shout, but I had no fear of being so swiftly caught. The Tithenai mounts were strong and stolid, rouncies bred for mountain crossings and packwork, but Quip was a courser, deep-chested and fast. Over open ground like this, I scarcely needed the advantage of a head start in order to break away, and the column wasn't made for speed. The passing air stung my eyes to tears. I swallowed a sob and urged Quip faster, the prospect of being pursued by Killic more than I could bear.

And what if he did appear—what then? I couldn't decide which option was worse: that Killic would think I'd consented to his touch, or that he'd think his violation of me, like his infidelity, was something I either could or should forgive. *But what if it is?* some inner voice whispered. *You didn't fight, not really. You climaxed. And Killic, at least, is a man you know. Who's to say that Tiern Caethari Aeduria isn't a monster?*

I could flee, I thought wildly. *Whatever I do now, Father has still disowned me. Do I really care so much for his reputation that I'd rather risk more and greater abuse for the sake of those who despise me?*

Wretchedly, it seemed, I did. Or at least, I couldn't think of where else to go, should I choose to completely abandon all sense of honour. I had saleable skills, but no experience in selling them, and no one to vouch for my expertise save Markel. I felt a sudden, furious rush of sympathy for every Ralian woman who'd ever been the subject of marital bartering; I was ashamed of my prior indifference to the phenomenon, and wondered, with a certain, sick fascination, if being raised in expectation of such a fate made enduring it any easier. Remembering Lady Sine's testimony, I doubted it.

The gorge rose in my throat. All at once, Quip's furious pace was too much for me: I reined him back through canter and trot, peeled off from the road and dismounted just in time to vomit. I'd eaten little enough that could be thrown up, but it was still unpleasant. Bile stung my lips and nostrils, and even after I rinsed my mouth with water from my saddle's canteen, the bitter aftertaste lingered.

Shakily, I put my arms around Quip's neck and buried my face in his mane. He whickered, lipping the back of my shirt, offering a form of equine comfort. I hated that I could be so easily shaken; that all my resolve to fight, to test myself against the mountains, could be overthrown by the simple mention of Killic's name. I tried to tell myself that Killic wasn't the problem, that I was only angry at his selfishness in betraying me, his carelessness in seeing us caught—he'd scarcely hurt me, after all, the bruises minor in comparison to the harm he might've inflicted had he breached me—but it wouldn't take. I shook my head, trembling and furious, empty stomach churning. I'd told him to stop, and he'd kept me pinned—

The memory of it proved too much. I staggered away from Quip and gagged, though I'd nothing else to bring up but bile. I made a pathetic noise, hugging myself with one arm as I drained my canteen dry. I wiped my mouth on my sleeve, and where it rode up, I saw my cut wrist: a thin, scabbed line that represented everything I feared.

A sudden whistle pierced my reverie. I lifted my head, aware of the nearby thud of hooves, and sure enough, there was Markel, turning Grace away from the Tithenai column in determined pursuit of me. I laughed, because it was that or weep, and tugged my errant sleeve down again, covering the cut.

"I'm fine," I said, as soon as he was in earshot.

Markel shot me a look that was equal parts disgusted at the lie and worried for it, swinging down from the saddle. He strode over to me and took in the scene—the horsehairs on my cheek and shirt, the mess I'd made in the grass—and gripped my arm, tight and brief.

"You are not well," he signed, too agitated to click first, as he usually would. "There is something badly amiss with you, Velasin."

I made a choking noise. "Is it really so shocking?" I signed back. "What am I to make of any of this? I've been betrayed and bartered away to I know not whom, and I cannot—I am afraid—" I froze in midsign, alarmed by my own admission, then forced myself to continue, echoing it apurpose. "I am afraid. Moons help me, but I'm so afraid, and I'm trying not to be for both our sakes, but there it is."

"What did the envoy say, that made you fear?"

I clenched my hands, not wanting to admit to it, but knowing I must. "Thei suggested Killic might return."

Markel hissed. "Should he make that mistake, I will deal with him. Sharply."

"Sharply?"

"Sharply. He will not be missed."

Markel looked at me steadily as he said it, his signs as clear and unwavering as his gaze. I knew he meant it; and more, that he was skilled enough to enact the threat, should it come to that. At his request, I'd ensured he had a bodyguard's training, and beyond his gifts with blade and fist, he'd proved a peerless archer, though he seldom had occasion to carry a bow.

His bow, like the rest of our life, was back in Farathel, and possibly never to be seen again, depending on the trustworthiness of whoever ended up in charge of our possessions. I swallowed a new wave of grief and made myself look at him.

"I cannot ask such a thing of you."

"Nor would you," Markel signed. "And that is why I offer."

Distantly, I worried at what my life had come to, that I found the promise of murder touching. I smiled at the irony of it, which Markel—correctly—took for my assent. I clapped him on the shoulder, he rolled his eyes, and we both remounted, steering our horses back to the Tithenai column.

"Ralians," Raeki muttered, and got us all moving again.

By accident more than design, I found myself riding once more beside Keletha, while Markel took up his previous place behind me. The envoy looked me over, brow pinched in worry.

"I apologise, Tiern Velasin. That was . . . provocative of me. Needlessly so."

I sighed, too tired to willingly make an enemy of thim. "And my flight was needlessly dramatic. I accept your apology, envoy. I am not myself."

Keletha sighed angrily. "And why should you be? I mean no disrespect to your nation otherwise, but most Ralians are singularly stupid on the topic of sex. I can scarce believe your father treated you as he did, nor that he made his contempt so plain to me. Fifteen days on mountain roads, and I had rather ride them over again than subject myself to his hospitality."

Thir declaration took me aback. "That's why we left so soon? He offended you that much?"

"Offence to my own person, I can endure well enough," said Keletha. "Being an envoy, I've certainly had enough practice, both in Tithena and elsewhere. But direct, unprovoked offence to my people? That, I will not tolerate." Thei gestured behind us, indicating two of the female riders. "Kita and Mirae are five years married, and that *butler*"—thei spat the Ralian word—"refused to let them share a bed, in keeping with his master's sense of propriety."

I felt obscurely shamed. "My apologies, envoy."

"It is not your place to apologise, but his to have done better. And of course," thei added, offhand, "his insult to you was also an insult to me."

"I'm sorry?"

"The betrothal agreement never specified your marriage to Tiera Laecia; only that you would marry the chosen scion of Clan Aeduria as affirmed by me for the purposes of alliance. Though your father seems to have missed the importance of it, those contracts gave you status as an Aeduria the moment I arrived." Thei shot me a puzzled look. "Did you not realise that, when you read them?"

"They were never given to me to read," I said. "I'd barely been told about it before you arrived, and afterwards, Father was hardly inclined to explain the fine print."

Keletha looked horrified. "Ayla forgive me," thei whispered. "You didn't *know*?"

I blinked, confused. "But you must have known that, surely. When we met with Father, you said you understood that I hadn't consented to the betrothal."

"That's not what I said at all!" Keletha exclaimed. "Lord Varus said you were eager to marry the tiera, and when I arrived and found otherwise, I asked if you'd given your consent—to which you replied that duty was consent enough, and that your father was unaware of your preference for men. Which led me to believe that either you'd feigned enthusiasm to him, which he had then reported, or you had dutifully agreed to marry against your inclination, which he had interpreted as enthusiasm. What I did *not* think is that you'd been given no forewarning at all, nor been consulted in the slightest!" Thir tone was genuinely distressed. "For the love of every saint, why didn't you object when I asked?"

"You think I had a *choice*?" I gaped at thim, incredulous. "Had I refused, I would've been disinherited! The second you left the room, Father told me the only reason I was allowed to keep my name and my, my—" I flailed for the Tithenai word for *sinecure,* and came up short. "—my income, is because you might take offence if they were stripped from me! I am *exiled,* envoy!" I was yelling, I realised distantly, but unable to stop myself. "Whether I marry your tiern or not, I can never go home, and you have the gall to ask why I didn't *object*?"

Keletha's face went ashy with shock. A small part of me was vindicated by thir distress, but mostly I was exhausted by the whole business. When I spoke again, my voice was hoarse, and I realised I was perilously near to weeping.

"I'm sorry that my unwillingness distresses you, envoy. I wish I could be otherwise. In so many ways, I wish I could be other than I am. But I am only myself, beyond alteration. Refusing my duty earns me nothing and strips me of everything, and so I consent to it, even when it pains me. And for now—for you, and me, and your Tiern Caethari Aeduria—that must be enough. You cannot ask any more of me." I tried to smile, and failed. "I have nothing else to give."

And before thei could respond to that, I bowed my head and wheeled Quip around, Markel following silently as I took up my previous place behind the mules.

5

That first night, after hours of riding steadily uphill, we camped in the shadow of the Snowjaw Mountains. Though the autumn weather had been pleasant when we set out, it had grown steadily colder the higher we climbed, and would doubtless only grow more so once we entered the Taelic Pass. The clothes I'd brought with me were ill-suited to the drop in temperature, but Markel's foresight had at least seen me dressed in layers, which was better than nothing. It ought to have been miserable, but I was too tired to care about the thinness of the bedroll Raeki gave me, or to offer complaint at the night wind chilling my neck. After my spat with Keletha, I'd spent the day in silence, ignoring every effort made to draw me into conversation. It was churlish, but at that point, I'd felt entitled to a little pique. Markel, who understood me better than anyone, made no attempts to sign with me, though he did pass me food at intervals, glaring pointedly until I ate. We slept back-to-back, the better to guard against the cold, but though I woke twice from nightmares about Killic, sweating and shaking, Markel never stirred, and when dawn came, I didn't speak of it.

The days that followed were gruelling in every sense, but thankfully devoid of peril; almost anticlimactically so. The Taelic Pass was a narrow defile, barely wide enough in parts for two wagons to pass abreast, cast in almost perpetual shadow by the dizzying loom of the peaks. Sheer cliffs towered on either side, broken only occasionally by boulders, scree and, even more rarely, the skinny lines of goat-tracks, though the animals themselves kept a wary distance, presumably having learned caution from the long predations of bandits and hungry farmers. Light snow fell from time to time, melting icily where it kissed my skin, and I shivered to think how much worse the crossing would be in a month or so, with the onset of winter.

I took to avoiding Keletha; indeed, I avoided everyone other than Markel, inasmuch as doing so was possible, submitting myself to only as much conversation as felt necessary to improve my Tithenai accent while keeping from being a nuisance. As Markel told it—as planned, he'd been listening in on the Tithenai conversations—there were two competing theories in play to explain my odd behaviour, neither of which was surprising. Indeed, they mirrored Keletha's first suspicions: either I was still in love with Killic and heartsick at his abandonment, or else I pined for Markel himself. Depending on the speaker, Markel's nonreciprocation was attributed to his being too simple to have any sexual desires at all, to his being interested only in women, or else to the fact that he was pining for me in turn, the both of us too Ralian to act on our obvious feelings. We both laughed quietly at that last theory, though I noted which riders thought Markel simple—the muleteer Daeri and the tracker Shathan—and ignored them more fully than I did the others.

If Markel learned anything else of Tiern Caethari, he kept it to himself, for which I was duly grateful; Kita had boasted in passing that my betrothed was a skilled warrior, and I'd felt myself go ashen with the memory of Killic's violence. The closer we came to Qi-Katai, the more dread I felt. My nightmares, too, became more intense, and despite the cold, I took to sleeping farther from Markel, wanting to neither wake nor worry him with my thrashing. Back in Farathel, I had a silk eye-mask charmed to aid in sleep—its capabilities didn't extend to altering the shape of dreams, but I knew from experience that it could, at the least, decrease the likelihood of bad ones. I longed for it with a hopeless, angry frustration: I was far more sentimentally attached to various other possessions, but in my exhausted state, it was the mask on which I fixated, making it a surrogate for everything else I more keenly feared to lose (or to have exposed, in the case of my rosewood chest).

After a few days, however, my anger turned inwards: had I been a more assiduous student of magic, I might've made myself a makeshift mask, to say nothing of easing the discomfort of our trip through the mountains in any number of other small ways; that I had failed to do so was proof of my poor character. Never mind my conspicuous lack of that vital, native spark for magecraft, rendering such studies as I had undertaken three times as laborious and twice as risky as was so for a natural talent; never mind, too, that the smatter of charms I did know was still more than many without that skill could boast. I was too angry to be rational and too miserable to be kind to myself, and so, on the nights when I struggled to sleep, which was most of them, I ran my thoughts through the basic mantras taught to novice scholars of magecraft, a self-punishment that was simultaneously an attempt to bore myself to sleep:

> Magic is intention channelled by will and executed by power. Charms are a simple use of intention; cantrips are a variable manipulation of intention; spells are complex products of intention. All magic derives from ambient power, including the strength of the caster. The caster is both a source of power and a conduit for it; the stronger the caster, the greater their ability to imbue or draw from sources beyond themselves, including latent sources. An ambient source is elemental, active and continuous; a latent source is inert and finite. Anything the caster wishes to manipulate, he must first understand in detail—

Unsurprisingly, this didn't help in the least.

Night after night, the sleeplessness continued to take its toll on me. Markel was clearly worried, as was Keletha, but their concern only made me feel worse. Though it was easier to push aside their scrutiny while we were still in the mountains, once we crossed into

Tithena and began our descent, I knew that, once we'd spent a night indoors, my excuses would no longer hold water.

As we picked our way down the path between the mountains' flanks, the tiny town of Vaiko was clearly visible in the distance, though *town* felt like an overly generous moniker for such a small settlement. A patchwork of ruins in varying stages of disrepair spread out around the inhabited remainder like the threat of time made manifest, sagging wood and tumbled stone hemmed in by the dilapidated remains of fences. Unsown fields, now barely recognisable as such, had been reclaimed by weeds and wildflowers; if not for a skinny herd of sharp-eyed, collared goats and a pair of disinterested cows grazing in an unkempt but sturdily fenced-in pasture, I would've thought the place abandoned.

Our destination was the simply named Mountain Inn. As the largest remaining structure in Vaiko, it ought to have taken pride of place in the failing township; instead, it was situated off to one side like an afterthought, or perhaps a sentinel, a lone beacon of welcome against the oncoming night. Whatever other complaints could be levied against our lodgings, however—the rooms themselves were small, unglamorous and in much need of repair, while the food on offer was both sparse and simple—the quality of the beds was not among them. Prior to turning in, I'd hoped the luxury of a real mattress might prove sufficient to see me rested, but to no avail. My fears refused to leave me be, resulting in yet another tense, restless night, and when I finally staggered down late to breakfast the next morning—I'd already sent Markel ahead, still opting to dress unaided—even Raeki, who cared for me little enough, looked openly concerned.

"Ruya's grace, tiern!" he exclaimed. "Did you sleep at all, or just sit up moping all night?" Raeki, it transpired—like Keletha, Kita and Mirae—subscribed to the yearning-for-Killic theory of my behaviour, though as he didn't know I knew, I could hardly tell him otherwise.

"No," I rasped, voice rough with lack of sleep. "I was whittling trees from firewood." It was a Tithenai expression I'd heard the tracker Siqa use, meant to imply the idle passing of time to no good purpose, and I rather liked it.

"You do seem tired, tiern," said Keletha, looking at me with worried eyes. For the first time since our spat, I felt a pang at having ignored thim so totally. "We're only a few days out from Qi-Katai and making good time. If you wanted to rest before arrival, to find your ease—"

"There is no ease in this," I said, "and if rest were so simply obtained, I'd not be short of it."

Keletha looked almost wounded. "If there's anything I can do to help—"

"There isn't."

Beside me, Markel clicked his fingers once. I glanced at him, and he signed, "You're scaring them, and me. If you won't let anyone help, at least be aware that we're trying."

The rebuke stung. "Your trying is the problem," I signed back, my gestures choppy and harsh. "I've told you again and again that there's nothing to be done, yet everyone persists in offering, as though if I only tried hard enough, this would somehow be easier—as though I don't know what I want—"

I broke off, pulse thundering. *You don't know what you want,* Killic had said, and in that moment, he might have been speaking the words in my ear, the memory was so vivid. Despite having barely sat down, I shoved away from the table and stood again, stalking out to the stables. I hadn't wept since that first day of travel, the close quarters having offered few opportunities for such private grief, but as I started saddling Quip, I came perilously close. I felt as though I were riding to my own execution, and though I'd tried hard not to dwell on the vow I'd made to Lady Sine, the closer we came to Qi-Katai, the harder it was to think of anything else.

"Tiern?"

I squeezed my eyes shut, tense in every muscle. Of everyone who might have come after me, why did it have to be Raeki? Silently,

I counted to three, finished checking Quip's bridle and turned to face him.

"Yes, tar? You have something you'd like to say to me?"

"I do, as a matter of fact." He crossed his arms and stepped forwards, glowering. "You're a spoiled, ungrateful brat, you know that, tiern? Ruya's grace, I understand this wasn't your first choice, but you might at least make an effort! Tiern Caethari's a good man, one of the best I've ever known, and Keletha is hardly lacking in honour. Your lover isn't coming back, tiern, and I tell you now, you're heading for something better—"

Something in me snapped. I didn't think; just dropped Quip's reins and barrelled forwards, punching Raeki hard in the face.

"He's not my *lover*!" I spat, shoving him away. "I know exactly what you think of me—what *all* of you think of me—and none of you has the right of it. Do you understand me, Raeki?" My voice cracked. "Do you?"

Raeki didn't answer. Slowly, he raised a hand to his nose, dabbing at the tiny trickle of blood my inexperienced violence had produced. He rubbed his fingertips together, expression unreadable as he looked from them to me. Too late, I recalled that Raeki was as muscle-bound and competent as I was not, and when he took another step forwards, I flinched.

Naked surprise flashed across his face. "You truly think I'd strike a tiern?"

"Why not?" I said. "I hit you first." And my hand was throbbing as a result, for all I knew enough form not to tuck my thumb.

He hissed an incredulous breath. "Ralians! It's a wonder your country even functions."

"I don't care what you think of me, tar." My smile was ghastly as I took Quip's reins. "One way or another, you'll be free of me soon."

I started leading Quip forwards, and was almost out the stable door before Raeki called after me, "Tiern? Where are you going?"

"Qi-Katai," I said, not bothering to stop.

He chased after me, watching in utter bafflement as I mounted up. "We're still eating breakfast!"

"So eat. The road is straight, and I've nowhere else to go. You'll catch me easily enough."

Just then, Markel came hurrying out of the inn, a frustrated look on his face that turned into comic outrage when he saw me mounted. Keletha was hard on his heels, along with half the riders; the other half, presumably, were still eating.

Markel snapped his fingers three times, but didn't wait for my response; just moved in front of me and held Quip's head, glaring fiercely.

All at once, I realised the absurdity of it. I hung my head and started to laugh, though the sound was sawed and rough.

"I'm sorry," I said. Moons! I felt as though I'd done nothing but apologise since leaving Farathel. It made me laugh harder, Quip shifting irritably from foot to foot. "I'll wait. I'll wait right here. Go back and finish your food."

Keletha gave a diplomatic shrug. "There's little enough to finish. As you say, tiern, as close as we are, we might as well make good t—"

An arrow sprouted from the envoy's shoulder, punching through with a soft, wet *thunk*. Quip tossed his head and shied in shock, which is all that saved me from the second shaft; it whipped past my head with a noise like a hornet, embedding itself in the inn's wall. I stared at it, uncomprehending.

Then everything happened at once.

Keletha staggered, swearing as thei gripped the arrow. I yelled at Markel to get inside, but he ignored me, moving to support Keletha as Raeki roared furious orders. Heart pounding, I wheeled Quip in a tight circle, putting my back to the inn, and caught a flash of sunlight from a small rise a hundred yards to the west. Another arrow sang past me, hitting Siqa square in the chest; he grunted and dropped, a stunned look on his face, and suddenly ten or more armed men were coming over the rise, swords drawn and screaming.

"To arms! To arms!" Raeki bellowed, swearing as yet another arrow whipped by, but though the riders rushed to obey him, half of them were still running out from breakfast and most were unarmed: even Raeki himself had only a belt-knife, his sword nowhere in sight.

Time seemed to slow, the scene taking on a strange, fey cast. I formed my view of things as if from a great distance, ascribing no emotional significance to the pitchfork leaning on the stable wall, the realisation that there was only one archer, my status as the sole rider ahorse. It was so surreal, I scarcely thought at all. And yet I acted: kicking Quip forwards; snatching the pitchfork; shouting as I rode at our assailants. I'd carried spears on boar-hunts before, and though their balance and weight were vastly different from that of a farm implement, at least I knew how to steer with my knees. The pitchfork was light by comparison, and rather than wield it as a lance—even in my disconnected state, I knew I couldn't brace against such an impact as it would likely make—I swung out and down with it like a greatsword: a double-handed blow aimed squarely at the foremost runner.

Clearly, he wasn't expecting such a counterattack: he froze in shock, his sword too short to compensate for the longer range of the pitchfork, and my stroke connected savagely with his collarbone. The judder and crunch nearly rocked me from the saddle. Pain shot through my arms and shoulders, but I kept my seat and my grip on the pitchfork both, not stopping to look at the damage I'd wrought. A man on my left took a swing at Quip, but flinched in the delivery and missed; whoever our assailants were, they were hardly professionals. Behind me, I heard crashing and screams as the two groups closed with each other, which left me almost at the rise, the archer my only target.

My adversary seemed to realise this in the same instant I did: he'd been shooting from behind a boulder, but a single stone was scant protection from a charging horse, for all that he had an arrow nocked. He paled and fired, and as I came within strides of him, pain blossomed in my thigh, a burning ache where his arrow sank into the muscle. Dropping the bow, the archer tried to flee, but couldn't outrun Quip. As though by someone else's will, my arm rose and fell, driving the tines of the pitchfork hard into his unarmoured back. The impact jolted less than before, as I didn't attempt to keep hold of the haft; even so, my shoulder wrenched, and I slumped over the saddle horn, sweating and gasping in belated fear. My thigh was wet with spreading blood, the pain increasing with every second. The arrow had struck me oddly, which was a mixed blessing: it hadn't penetrated as deeply as a clean shot would have done, but the queer angle lent it no steadiness; every slight movement or press of air was like a cruel hand jiggling the shaft.

Whatever manic energy had carried me across the field abandoned me like mist at dawn. I felt sick with cold and pain, panting as I reined Quip to a walk. He snorted, flanks twitching as if in outrage at the presumption of our attackers, and turned back towards the inn with scarcely a touch. I just had time to notice that the fight was done before my vision greyed out, leaving me slumped over Quip's mane. The next thing I knew, Markel was at my stirrup, fingers clicking frantically in a bid to get my attention. Raeki was beside him, and Kita, and Mirae, all of whom were staring at me with expressions I couldn't fathom. Markel, however, looked tense and frightened: a smear of blood daubed his cheek, and my stomach clenched at the thought of him being injured.

"Are you all right?" I asked, in Ralian. "I told you to get inside, but you never listen, you—"

"Not his blood," said Raeki, getting in ahead of Markel's signs. "It's Keletha's, from pulling the arrow."

"Oh. That's good. That's good, Markel." I swayed in the saddle, not sure if I was more in danger of passing out or throwing up. Switching to Tithenai, I asked, "Is Quip all right? One of those villains swung at him—"

"He's fine," said Raeki, eyeing the arrow in my thigh. "You, though, tiern—that needs to come out, and carefully."

I managed a shaky laugh. "No argument there."

At that, I didn't so much dismount as topple, sliding gently sideways until Markel and Mirae caught me jointly, arms around my shoulders. As they half dragged, half carried me forwards, Raeki gave an unsolicited report as to what had happened. The archer, it emerged, had claimed our only fatality: as well as shooting Keletha, Siqa and me, he'd also put a shaft through Shathan's eye, killing him instantly. Otherwise, our attackers had been a poorly armed, inexpert rabble: the first man I'd struck with the pitchfork had been leading them, and with him down, three others had surrendered instantly, leaving Raeki and his people to make short work of the remainder.

"Good," I mumbled, dizzy with pain. "Well done, tar."

"Lay him on the table," Raeki said, and my helpers complied, levering me down onto a surface still littered with breakfast crumbs. My head clunked against the wood, though I scarcely felt it over the pain in my leg. I hissed as the limb straightened, and suddenly Raeki was looming over me, his expression grave.

"I can't push the arrow through, tiern," he said. "It's not in deep enough for that."

"Pull it out, then," I gasped.

"It's going to hurt—"

"It hurts now!"

"I mean," he growled, "that we'll need to hold you down. Do I have your consent for that?"

I gulped, suddenly terrified for a whole new reason. Rationally, I knew, the context bore no resemblance to Killic's restraint of me, yet reason seemed not to apply in such moments. It was like being haunted: I had no control over what apparently innocent thing would suddenly turn spectre, making me fear his hands, his voice, as though it were happening again; as though, in some ugly sense, it was happening still.

Desperately, I looked from Raeki to Markel, Markel to Raeki. "I'll be still," I pleaded. "You needn't hold me."

Almost, Raeki smiled. "I don't doubt your bravery, tiern, but it's less a question of will than reflex. Whatever you mean to do, you'll move, and be hurt the worse for it."

I made a noise that was neither laugh nor sob. My head fell back again, hands clenched to stop their trembling. I tried to find some comfort in the fact that being so afraid at least distracted me somewhat from the pain in my leg, but didn't quite succeed.

"Do it fast, then."

"Yes, tiern." He hesitated, glancing at Markel. "You want him to take your shoulders?"

I nodded, and for propriety's sake, I signed the question.

"Of course," Markel replied, and quickly moved to do just that. His grip on me was gentle, but I still felt claustrophobic at the sight of him, and when Raeki braced a heavier hand on my injured thigh, just above the shaft, while Mirae held my other leg, I truly began to panic. My breathing quickened sharply; I turned my head away, trying to focus on the blank wall, but not being able to see who held me was somehow worse.

And then Raeki gripped the arrow-shaft, his other hand clamped on my thigh, and *pulled*.

Pain was a bright explosion. I roared and bucked, fighting the restraint, only to be held down again, and through the sick, sharp ache in my leg, I felt tears sting my eyes. I made an ugly choking noise as the arrow came free, my vision swimming as I started to bleed more heavily. Abandoning the uninjured leg, Mirae compressed the wound while Raeki examined the arrowhead and made a satisfied noise. Carefully, he peeled a tiny strip of fabric from the metal tip, waving the bloody thing at me.

"Got it all!" he exclaimed. "You're lucky I'm so good at this, tiern—you don't want to leave cloth in a wound."

I swallowed in lieu of nodding, tipping my head back to meet Markel's gaze.

"Let go now, please," I rasped in Ralian. He lifted his hands instantly, and though Mirae still clutched my leg, I breathed a little easier.

And then, for a mercy, I passed out.

When I came to again, it was to find my leg dressed and bandaged, Markel keeping watch beside me. He smiled, the expression one of pure relief, and signed, "Are you back with us?"

"I think so," I replied, blinking dazedly. "How long was I out?"

"Not long. Mirae"—his sign for her was a corkscrew gesture, mimicking her tight black curls—"says it should heal well. She sewed you up. I watched her; she's got a good eye, and all her tools were cleaned with boiling water and alcohol. She used magic, too; a soldier's charm to keep out new infections. You'll be able to put weight on the leg, but don't do anything too strenuous, or you'll pull the stitches."

"I'll try," I said aloud, though the thought left me feeling strangely hollow. Before I could fathom why, however, Keletha appeared. Thir face was pinched and a little pale, thir injured arm snugged in a makeshift sling, but otherwise, the envoy seemed no worse for wear. Thei smiled at me, and though thei didn't ask Markel to give us privacy, he did so of his own accord, bowing slightly to Keletha before flashing me a quick, discreet sign: *going to listen.* I nodded and watched him depart, leg throbbing in time with his footsteps.

"Do we know who attacked us?" I asked, as much to distract myself from the pain as because I wanted the answer.

Keletha pulled up Markel's seat, forestalling me with a wave of thir hand. "First things first: drink this." Thei reached into thir coat and passed me a small metal flask, the contents of which were clearly alcoholic, some sort of spirit mixed with what I guessed, from the smell, was essence of poppy. "Marvellous stuff. It'll help."

"My thanks," I said, and accepted gratefully, taking a long swallow before handing it back. Keletha gave an approving nod, returned the flask to the inner pocket of thir riding coat, and rested thir free hand in thir lap.

"Good. Now, to answer your question, according to the three who surrendered, they're displaced farmers. Desperate men, as a rule; they saw us ride in last night and thought to try their luck this morning." Thei gave a lopsided shrug. "It happens, sadly. It's why we ride armed."

I frowned at thim. "Displaced farmers?"

The envoy sighed. "When your father's predecessor, Ennan vin Mica, first inherited his family holdings, one of his first acts was to strip the border patrols that kept bandits from his stretch of the Snowjaw Mountains. At the same time, he raised both the levies on his tenants and the taxes on traded goods from Tithena, Khytë and Nivona, and in that first harsh winter, many people suffered. Of course, this was all some twenty years ago, and the Taelic Pass was still a regular trade route, for all that vin Mica scorned foreign coin. When his own people began to prey on traders, trying to recover some of what he took from them, he turned a blind eye, so long as it was other folk they were robbing. And after enough years—as the trade up here became riskier and riskier, and the eastern routes more populous—everything on the Tithenai side that relied on it suffered, too. The Khytoi clans took their furs and leathers, artifex and craftwork straight to Qi-Katai, bypassing Vaiko completely; most Nivonai stopped coming so far south at all. And without that secondary trade to enrich the markets here, Tithenai traders had less and less business to do.

"The land here is arable, but there are more and bigger farmholds closer to Qi-Katai, and with three days' ride to the city and back, there's not much profit to be made if you're only selling vegetables. But livestock is almost as attractive to bandits as trade caravans, and when that became a risky prospect, there was a knock-on effect. Crop farmers sold to their neighbours, traders and everyone else who supported the caravans; but when the caravans dried up, so too did the businesses associated with their passage. So as the livestock farmers left, the crop farmers had fewer and fewer ways to make a living, which meant their neighbours had less food, which meant there was less for everyone to trade, and the whole thing fell apart. And with Qi-Katai so close—though not close enough for anything else—it was easier far for the merchants to simply relocate instead of digging in."

The run-down state of Vaiko suddenly made a lot more sense. "In other words," I mumbled, "Ralian greed put an arrow in my thigh."

"Quite," said Keletha, wryly. "Albeit via an indirect route. We were caught off guard, which Raeki is furious about, because we swept this area on the way to your father's estates and thought it long safe. Apparently, we were wrong."

"Lucky us." I took a deep breath, forcing myself to ask the question, though part of me was already sure of the answer. "Only the three who surrendered lived?"

Keletha hesitated. "Yes, tiern."

I shut my eyes, stomach churning sickly. "So the two I—the ones I rode down, I mean, they didn't—they're both—"

"You killed them, yes."

"Oh." I opened my eyes again, staring at the rafters. "That's new. I haven't—I hadn't—ah, killed. Before. And now I have, apparently. Twice."

"Yes."

"With a—" I couldn't think of the Tithenai word, and so substituted the Ralian. "*—pitchfork.*"

"It was bravely done, regardless of your choice of implement."

I snorted, lethargy stealing through me as the poppy began to work. "*Bravery,*" I said, voice dripping with disgust. "You flatter me, envoy."

Keletha cocked thir head. "You think your actions foolish?"

"I think—" I said, and stopped, the truth too ugly to speak. "I think," I said instead, "that charging archers with *pitchforks* is seldom intelligent." Grimacing, I eased myself upright, swinging my legs carefully over the edge of the table. "No offence to Mirae," I said, "but I've had more comfortable sickbeds."

"Should you be up?" thei asked, alarmed.

I raised an eyebrow at thim. "Should you?"

"Hah."

"Look," I said, after a moment. "Just tell me what's happening, and I'll act accordingly. But if I have to stay lying down indefinitely, it's not going to be on a table."

Keletha sighed again, free palm running over grey braids. "Siqa is badly hurt. We can't risk moving him, and even if we could, there's the prisoners to think of, and—and Shathan's body to bring home for burial." Thei bit thir lip, considering. "With the innkeep's cooperation, I'd like to leave a token guard here until we can send help from Qi-Katai—that way, Mirae can tend to Siqa, and the bandits can stay in the cellar. Kita can take the fastest horse and ride ahead, report our situation—it's a risk, but she'll make better time alone—while the rest of us go on as planned. But if you'd prefer to rest—"

"I already told you, envoy: rest isn't easily come by. If it's all the same to you, I'd rather keep moving."

Keletha looked at me for a long moment. I don't know what thei saw in my face, but finally, thei nodded.

"Moving it is. I'll let Raeki know, though I'd take it as a kindness to Mirae's handiwork if you'd wait here."

"Of course," I said, and as thei vacated Markel's chair, I levered myself into it, the spasming of my sore leg pleasantly muted by the poppy. Almost, Keletha looked set to speak again, but seemed to think better of it, heading off to reorganise our departure without another word.

Finally alone, I closed my eyes, a gnawing emptiness in the pit of my stomach. I wasn't a fighter, and yet I hadn't hesitated to ride into—well, not *battle,* which seemed too grand a word for it, but *danger,* certainly. Keletha had called it bravery, and even Raeki had looked impressed, which made me want to laugh at the irony.

I didn't know whether I'd acted as I had because I wanted to live, or because I hoped to die; only that, either way, I hadn't succeeded.

Forty minutes later, our diminished, wounded party left for Qi-Katai. I felt a strange, disconnected sense of loss, although I couldn't quite tell from what. I'd killed two men, my former home was as far behind me as it had ever been, and I'd no way of knowing if our Farathel possessions would ever make it to Qi-Katai, let alone whether I'd still be there to receive them if they did. I had what little I carried with me; I had Quip; and I had Markel, for as long as he consented to put up with me. I tried to imagine fleeing back to Farathel with so little to my name and had to choke down an inappropriate burst of laughter. The capital was as barred to me as it was to Killic, now that we'd been exposed—arguably more so, as my going there would mean fleeing a marriage endorsed and required by the crown. All I could do was go forwards, into whatever small scrap of future remained for me.

I didn't look back.

Part Two

CAETHARI

6

It was nearly a fortnight since Keletha's courier-bird had arrived at Qi-Katai proclaiming that the vin Aaro betrothal was settled, not on Laecia's behalf, as everyone had expected, but *Caethari's.* Cae still hadn't come to grips with it. Technically, of course, his marriage had always been a possible outcome: when Tithenai families had multiple unwed children of marriageable age and established consent, a betrothal offer was rarely made specific to an individual, but extended to the immediate clan, the better to ensure the strongest possible match. Knowing the Ralian hatred for men like him, Cae had assumed, not unreasonably, that the honour of marrying Velasin vin Aaro would be all Laecia's—as, indeed, had Laecia herself. As best he could tell, his sister had looked on the match as something of an intellectual challenge, and was rather put out at being denied her experiments in it; Cae, however, was furious, and at no one more so than himself.

Saints, he'd even been asked his opinion on whether they ought to modify the betrothal contracts in deference to Ralian sensibilities, and he'd argued against it! Not, of course, because he'd wanted to stay in contention for the match: he'd simply hated the idea of denying his own rightful status—his worthiness as a person—just because some asshole Ralian disliked what he did with his cock. And now look where his cursed principles had gotten him: hiding from not only Laecia, who was determined to have him enact her wildly impractical plans for *civilising Velasin,* as she called it, but from their elder sister, Riya, who wanted to give him *marital advice.*

Years ago, Cae had fought—and, miraculously, killed—a rabid

bear. It had been a defining moment of his youth, the most terrifying thing he'd ever faced. Even now, his ribs still bore the parallel marks of claw-scars from the encounter, and for ages afterwards, he'd secretly slept with a talisman charmed to guard against nightmares. It hadn't always worked, of course—the charm was focussed on keeping his body calm, not sorting the contents of his mind—but he'd nonetheless taken comfort from its presence.

Given the choice between facing down another bear and listening to Riya pass judgement on his sexual habits, he felt certain he'd take the bear. *At the very least,* Cae thought sourly, *I'd flip a coin.*

Ducking out the servants' door to the lower hall of the Aida, he headed swiftly for the Court of Swords, hoping to work off some of his nervous energy via a sparring session with whoever was available, or else by running his hardest combat patterns. He'd been doing a lot of both since learning of his betrothal: as keen as his sisters were to interrogate him, even they understood that interrupting his active pursuits was never a wise course of action, and especially not if their real goal was to let him incriminate himself. Using his body kept him centered: he never felt so decisive as when he was moving, as though the whole world slowed and gave him time to pick the best course of action. But if he stood still—if he let himself be trapped in conversations designed to trick him into speaking ahead of his thoughts—there was no telling what he might say.

Which was the other thing Cae was angry about, or at least deeply frustrated by: no matter who he asked or where he searched, he couldn't seem to learn anything about Velasin vin Aaro beyond his former residence in Farathel, the Ralian capital; his age—twenty-four to Cae's twenty-eight—and the fact that, despite his family's recent elevation, he wasn't eligible to inherit their lands. Keletha's note had been cramped and brief, stating only that thei planned to make a swift return journey, and that thei thought Velasin a "good match" for Cae, whatever that meant. He'd swallowed his pride enough to ask if Laecia had learned anything of the man—she'd sent out queries through her personal network of trader, mage and traveller friends for any hint of gossip—but either she genuinely knew nothing of interest, or she'd mastered the art of lying to him barefaced, which was too terrifying a prospect to countenance.

Either way, the fact remained that, until Keletha returned, he simply didn't have enough information to know how he ought to feel. It was the worst sort of chicken and egg problem: he needed to first meet Velasin in order to know how to act when he first met Velasin, and after nearly a fortnight's wait, the contradiction of it had driven him to frustration.

He was almost to the armory when a sudden shout made him look up. Across the flagged expanse of stone, a rider on a lathered horse came cantering through the upper gates, dismounting almost before they'd pulled the animal to a halt. It was an unusual enough sight that Cae instantly headed over. To reach the Aida, the rider had already passed the many guarded gates of Qi-Katai; that they'd still ridden hard to the summit could only mean their business was with someone in the Aida itself.

Coming close, he recognised the rider a half-second after noticing that they weren't wearing courier's colours.

"Kita!" he exclaimed, hastening the last few steps to clasp the warrior's arm. "Saints, what's happened to Keletha? Are you well? What news?"

Wearily, Kita scrubbed a wrist across her forehead, which only succeeded in smearing about the sweat and dirt that coated her. "We made good time through the Taelic Pass, but were attacked at Vaiko, at the Mountain Inn," she said. "Bandits—just a small party, we'd swept the area on the way to Ralia, but they caught us early, disorganised, and they had an archer." She took a deep breath, swaying slightly on her feet. "We lost Shathan. He was the only fatality, but there were several wounded, one badly—Siqa took an arrow to the chest, and the envoy had to leave him behind with Mirae and the prisoners."

Cae swore. "And the rest? What happened?"

"Envoy Keletha was shot in the shoulder," said Kita, looking both chastened and angry. "And your—and Tiern Velasin also took an arrow. He was hit in the thigh." A strange look crossed her face. "He rode the archer down with a pitchfork—took out the leader with it, too, though I would've sworn he'd rather flee than help us. I don't think he'd even seen combat before; certainly, he isn't fond of it. When I first mentioned you were a fighter, tiern, he nearly had a fit." She shook her head in bewilderment. "I told the postern guard to send a retrieval squad for those who stayed on at Vaiko with the prisoners, but everyone else is scarcely a day behind me."

Cae's pulse leapt. Forcing a calm he didn't feel, he asked, "Have you any other reports to make?"

"No, tiern," said Kita, casting longing eyes in the direction of the barracks. "Though the envoy bid me answer any, ah, personal questions you might have."

"You've ridden hard and well," said Cae, valiantly suppressing his desperate curiosity. "It would be a poor reward to make you answer before you've rested. Go, see to your horse's needs and your own, then find me in my apartments at your convenience."

Kita's weary expression bloomed with gratitude. "My thanks, tiern. I won't keep you waiting long." Yet even, so she hesitated. "Have you any other instruction for me?"

"Yes," said Cae. "Say nothing at all of Velasin to either my sisters or their people until you've spoken to me."

"Of course, tiern." With a parting bow, Kita turned and led her lathered horse away to a well-earned rest.

Cae watched her go, fighting the impulse to call her back. The saints, it seemed, had a perverse sense of humour, but what else could be expected from a pageant of mortals elevated to a nebulous immortality by divine whim? Velasin himself, of course, was unlikely to believe in the saints, which only made it all the more ironic—what was it Ralians believed in again? The doctrine of something-or-other to do with the heavens; he never could remember the Ralian word for it, being far more hung up on how faith in the sun and the moons could sensibly translate to a hatred of men who fucked men or women who fucked women, or anyone who was kemi or metem; but then, that was Ralians for you, forever twisting themselves in knots over false propriety.

Probably that was something he ought to ask Kita about, actually: Was Velasin a believer? What would that even look like, for a man of his inclinations? The question skittered along Cae's spine like an errant insect, making him wince uncomfortably. His own beliefs were rather more habit than faith, and something he tended not to poke at too closely, the present moment excepted: the gods were the moons, and the moons were real enough, so why not the stories that went with them? Everything else was better left to more thoughtful minds than his.

Fingers clenching, Cae strode away, retracing his route to the Aida proper and trusting in speed to keep him safe from sisterly intervention. Happily, he made it to his apartments without being accosted, and spent the next forty minutes agitatedly pacing the length of his receiving room, flipping his second-favourite knife in increasingly intricate patterns. This particular habit was one of the many reasons why he'd given up keeping personal servants: it tended to make them nervous, and nervous servants were, in Cae's experience, prone to clumsiness. These days, he preferred to have his apartments maintained by the Aida's general staff, and what the arrangement lacked in personal nuance it more than made up for in privacy.

Except, of course, that he'd soon be sharing his space with Velasin vin Aaro, whose habits were wretchedly unknown. Cae gritted his teeth, the knife-blade flashing back and forth. It was years since he'd given his general consent to the prospect of marriage, and while he didn't want to remain unattached forever, this wasn't exactly how he'd thought it would happen. Saints, he'd spent the better part of a decade riding against Ralian bandits and noblemen both, thanks to Ennan vin Mica's idiocy, and now he was meant to *marry* one? What was Keletha *thinking*?

In a burst of frustration, Cae turned and flung the knife at a target-board he'd hung on the wall for exactly that purpose. It sank in deep with a satisfying *thunk,* and he'd scarcely pulled it out again when, at long last, someone knocked on the door.

It was Kita, newly scrubbed and freshly attired in the uniform of the Aida's own guard, the pins on her tunic denoting both her rank and her place under Raeki's command. She gave a short, formal bow, her right palm resting over her heart.

"Dai Kita Valichae, reporting as instructed," she said. Her hair was still wet, the short spikes leaking damp trails down to her collar. Cae stepped aside, waving her to the visitor's chair on one side of the room's main table and taking his own seat opposite. Unusually for her, Kita looked nervous, which Cae, with a sinking heart, took to mean she had nothing favourable to report of Velasin—or at the very least, nothing simple. Resolving to learn first, judge later, Cae flattened his palms on the desk and said, "I trust, Dai Kita, that I may rely on your discretion?"

Instantly, she sat a little straighter. "Of course, tiern."

"Good. In exchange, you have my permission to speak freely. I, ah—" He hesitated, trying to find the right words. "As you might imagine, this match is not what I'd expected. Any information that might help me prepare for it would be greatly appreciated."

Kita flushed, then blurted, "We think he's in love with someone else. Tiern Velasin, I mean—the night we reached vin Aaro's estate, he was caught in the act with another man—" She paused, visibly fumbling for the Ralian word. "—Lord Killic vin something, and that's, I mean—it's why the betrothal was made to you instead of Tiera Laecia, because Tiern Velasin has no interest in women, and after what the envoy saw, it wasn't like his father could pretend otherwise, though I'm told he tried to argue it didn't matter. Saints, he was *furious* over it—he threw Lord Killic out in the dark, said he'd kill him if he stayed, and Tiern Velasin—"

She broke off suddenly, as though ashamed of herself, and Cae, who was feeling increasingly uneasy, had to prompt her to continue. "What of him?"

"He gave no consent to marry," she said, swallowing. "Even given his preferences, the envoy thought—she assumed, we all did—that he'd at least been asked beforehand if he wanted to wed, but apparently not, and his father threatened to disinherit him if he didn't agree to it."

Cae felt faintly sick. "Do you know what became of his lover?"

"Fled," said Kita, equally scornful. And then, more sadly, "The tiern pines for him, I think. He's certainly not happy. Can't say I blame him for that, under the circumstances. Even so—" She paused, frowning, then said at last, "—I still feel that there's more to it all than we know. He talks to us, sometimes—his Tithenai is very good, though his accent needs work—but we never seem to learn much about him; I'm not sure if he's warmed to any of us, for all that he's polite."

Cae winced. *Ruya's grace, is any of this salvageable?* "You also said he attacked the bandits with . . . a pitchfork, was it? And was wounded?"

"Shot in the thigh," Kita confirmed, "though Mirae saw him right. The bandits attacked during breakfast; Tiern Velasin was the only one of us mounted. He—"

"Why was that?" Cae interrupted.

"I'm sorry?"

"Why was Velasin mounted, if the rest of you were still eating?"

"Oh." She flushed again, looking troubled. "He was . . . I don't know, tiern. He hadn't slept well on the road, but even after a night indoors, he still looked half-dead. The envoy offered to delay the journey, give him more time to rest, but he said no, that it wouldn't help. I think he argued with his servant, too, though it's hard to tell when they speak in signs, but—"

"Signs?"

"His servant is mute," said Kita quickly. "Markel, he's called. They're close to each other, though I don't know the story behind it, and they speak in signs, like this." She made a series of shapes with her hands, then snorted. "Some of the others think Markel's the one he's really in love with, not Lord Killic, but I don't think so. Whatever the tiern's problem is, I don't think being shy about who he wants has anything to do with it. But either way, it looked like he argued with Markel, and then he stormed out."

"And that somehow led to Velasin, what—riding off alone?"

"More or less," said Kita. "Tar Raeki went to talk to him and found the tiern in the stables. I don't know what they said to each other, but the tiern brought his horse out all the same, saying he wanted to get to Qi-Katai, and that's when the bandits struck. Not that they seemed to have the first clue what they were doing, but the tiern still accounted for two of them—and the most skilled two, it seems. Tar Raeki didn't know what to think about that."

Cae blinked, utterly bewildered. "Am I understanding this correctly?" He raised a hand, counting the contradictions off on his fingers. "Velasin is Ralian, but indiscreet enough to get caught with his lover in his father's gardens. He doesn't want to marry me, but he's still in a hurry to get here. He's not a fighter, but he killed two bandits armed with a saints-forsaken *pitchfork,* of all the ridiculous things, and even though he spends all his time talking to a mute servant, none of you know what he's saying, because it's in *signs.*" He made an exasperated noise and ran a hand down his face. "Can you tell me anything about the man that makes *any* degree of sense, or is he a walking mystery?"

Kita bit her lip, her expression somewhere between embarrassed and amused. "He . . . likes horses?"

"Horses," Cae said flatly.

"Well, he knows his way around them, and he takes excellent care of his courser. Doesn't delegate his maintenance, for all he's got Markel there. And he learns fast, too. The first day out, his Tithenai accent was *terrible*—there's a fashion for it in Farathel, apparently—but he sounds much better now. Like someone from Irae-Tai, perhaps, instead of an Attovari merchant."

"Small mercies," Cae muttered. He rubbed his temples; the

conversation was starting to give him a headache. Remembering his earlier line of thought, he asked, "Is he devout?"

Kita blinked at him, startled. "No," she said, after a moment. "No, I don't think so. If he is, he keeps it quiet. Then again, I'm not sure I'd know what faith looks like on a Ralian, so take that as you will." She shrugged apologetically.

Cae sighed. "Anything else?"

"He's brave, I think," said Kita, thoughtfully. "Dutiful, certainly, in a Ralian way. He treats his servant kindly, which always tends to speak well of a person, and though he's argued with the envoy, he's never been rude—and he understands thim being a kem, too, which is unexpected. Or at least, I've never heard him use the wrong forms or make the sort of jokes some foreigners do, even when he's angry. He sulks a bit, and his moods are odd, but he's never complained, like some noblemen would, at the lack of creature comforts."

It was thin enough praise, but Cae took heart from it nonetheless. He inhaled deeply, steadying himself, and debated briefly whether or not to ask his final question.

Curiosity, however morbid, won out over restraint. "And is he—to look upon, I mean, is he, ah—"

Kita rescued him from his embarrassment, smiling only slightly. "He's well-favoured," she said. "For a man. And a Ralian too, I suppose."

Cae nodded, refusing the temptation of asking for more details. "Thank you, Dai Kita." With as much dignity as he could muster, he stood. "That was . . . very enlightening."

"Of course, tiern," said Kita, bowing.

The second she was gone from the room, Cae leaned his head on the door and groaned. *Enlightening* was one word for Kita's testimony; *baffling* was another. No matter how he examined the facts, he couldn't get any clear sense of Velasin's motives. Was he resigned to the prospect of marriage, or in mourning for his lover? Had he been caught out by accident, or on purpose? Possibly the same convention didn't apply in Ralia, but in Tithena, it wasn't uncommon for any parties in previously undisclosed relationships to arrange to be seen together if an open betrothal was issued. Had Velasin sought to break the match with Laecia, unaware that Cae would then be offered as a substitute? Or was it just bad timing? Or something else altogether? Did he accept his preference for men, or was he leashed by guilt?

Almost, he regretted asking for Kita's report, because the most important question of all—*Can I possibly make this work?*—wasn't one she could answer. Sighing, Cae shoved away from the door and resumed his earlier pacing, the knife appearing in his hands as if of its own volition. *Contingencies,* he thought. *That's the key to it.* In battle, if the information you received about the enemy's position was unreliable, you made different strategies to account for all the most likely permutations. Not that he was in any rush to think of Velasin as an enemy, but Cae had always been better at tactics than diplomacy, and as the ultimate goal in this instance was a tolerable marriage, it seemed sensible to play to his strengths.

Flipping the knife up, over and back again, he began to map out his plans for Velasin vin Aaro.

7

"You're blushing," Laecia remarked. "Don't you agree that he's blushing, Riya?"

"I don't know," Riya said, pretending to study Cae. "If anything, I think he's a little pale."

"Saints, give me strength," Cae muttered, staring out over the parapet. The worst of it was, he *hadn't* been blushing until Laecia suggested it, but now that she had, he could feel the heat rising along his throat. He scowled, pushing his shoulders back, and wished a silencing ailment on his sisters.

"I think I see them," Riya said—too casually, given her own vested interest in Keletha's arrival. Through long years of practice, Cae declined to rise to the bait.

"Really?" he said instead. "I don't."

"Spoilsport," Riya muttered. "I liked you better before the bear."

His lips quirked at the old complaint. "Alas that I killed it."

"Alas indeed."

"Alas that it didn't kill *you* instead," grumbled Laecia, who'd always been irked by the in-joke. "Then *I* might be getting a husband today, and Riya would tell me all her filthy married jokes instead of saving them to spring on you at inappropriate moments. Which is a waste, by the way," she added, glaring at Riya. "You're just worried I'll tell them to him first."

"Are you saying you wouldn't, sister dearest?"

"I'm saying *I'd* tell them better."

"Such a shame, then, that your repertoire is so lacking!"

"It would lack less," Laecia said, "if I were ever in a position to *learn from experience.*"

"I'm not listening," Cae said loudly, in the forlorn hope that this might somehow make it true.

"If you want to have sex, have sex!" said Riya, ignoring him. "It's not as if you lack for options."

"I happen to have standards."

"Which is why you wanted to marry the Ralian, sight unseen?"

"No, I *expected* to marry the Ralian. There's a difference, Ri."

"Well, you're not marrying him *now,* are you?" Riya said, exasperated. "So go have sex!"

Cae put a hand to his eyes. He would've prayed for them to stop, but once they did, they'd inevitably circle back to—

"I can't right now," said Laecia, primly. "I'm waiting to meet our new brother-in-law. Oh! Is that them, do you think?" And she pointed down to the winding streets below.

Cae was on the brink of walking away when Riya said, excitedly, "It is! I'd know Keletha's piebald anywhere," and all at once his sisters were crowding close again, taking turns to try and determine which of the riders was Velasin vin Aaro.

Despite the ridiculousness of it—he'd meet the man soon enough, once Keletha's party reached the Aida—Cae couldn't resist the urge to join in, even though he couldn't tell much more at his present distance than the colour of Velasin's horse.

"That must be him," said Laecia, indicating a dark-haired, olive-skinned figure on a neat bay courser. "Which makes *him*"—her finger drew a line in the air, indicating a shaven-headed man on a sorrel mare—"the servant, Markel."

Riya turned to Cae, the picture of innocence feigned, and asked, "Do you feel threatened, brother?"

"I do not," said Cae. He'd known, of course, that Kita would wind up answering his sisters' questions as well as his own, which had evidently led to their hearing about the Killic vs. Markel debate; that did not, however, mean he had to like it. *Sides* had been taken, saints help him: the second Riya had declared that Markel sounded the more likely prospect, Laecia had opted for the alternative, and unless Cae's husband-to-be did something radical to dispel either rumour, he predicted he'd be hearing about Velasin's Secret Love for the foreseeable future. *And not just from Riya and Laecia,* he thought grimly. For all he tried to avoid it, Qi-Katai was as much a hotbed of gossip as any major city, and in Cae's experience, it was even money as to who was worse: soldiers, merchants, servants or his own cursed family.

As Riya and Laecia resumed their bickering about Velasin's unknown lover, Cae leaned his elbows on the wall and watched the party ride closer. For all that they'd been a small group even before the attack at Vaiko, they'd accrued a number of extra guards on their ride through the lower city, and as word had spread about Velasin's identity—the betrothal having hitherto been kept secret—crowds had begun to gather, curious onlookers lining the streets to gawk at the Ralian noble.

It happened just after they passed through the Amber Gate, which marked the last stretch before the Aida proper. The narrowness of the gate forced the riders to temporarily pass in single file before the street widened again—an architectural decision that was immensely helpful in the event of siege, but inconvenient otherwise—and as Cae watched helplessly from on high, a bystander suddenly broke from the crowd and rushed at Velasin's horse. Cae didn't have to see the blade to know the man was armed—and nor, evidently, did Velasin's servant, whose own mount shot forwards just in time to intercept the attacker.

Distant cries floated on the air. Riya's hand flew to her mouth in shock, while Laecia made a startled noise, gripping the stone. Cae's stomach clenched: the guards moved in, restraining the man, but the servant—Markel—was clearly injured, swaying in the saddle. Heedless of the continuing risk, Tiern Velasin dismounted, staggering beneath the servant's weight as Markel toppled sideways. Then Velasin, too, collapsed, and Cae's heart leapt into his throat before he remembered the tiern's injured leg, which must have given way beneath him.

Wrenching back from the parapet, Cae began to run, his guard detail following close behind. He hadn't paced his shortcuts through the Aida's upper levels in years, not since he'd still been a soldier in training, but his memory of them went deep, and before long, he'd left his guards behind, a single man being able to vault and leap and dodge in ways that a squad could not.

Breaking out into the courtyard, he cast around for a horse and, for a mercy, found one being led somewhere by a young groom. The poor girl squeaked in fright as Cae snatched the reins from her, yelling about an emergency, but didn't protest. The horse, a grey palfrey, gave a disapproving snort at this sudden change in plans, but responded quickly nonetheless. The stirrups were far too short, so Cae went without rather than taking the time to adjust them, looping the irons over the saddlehorn as he kicked the mare to a canter.

Halfway to the Amber Gate, he reined aside as a trio of riders came bolting up in the opposite direction: two uniformed guards—one from Jade Market, the other from the Amber Gate—and Tar Raeki Maas, the latter holding an injured Markel before him, one arm wrapped around his chest to keep the servant upright. He just had time to catch Raeki's angry gaze before they all went thundering past to the Aida, and then he was alone again.

Not for long, however: just as Cae steered the palfrey back into the road, a fourth rider came barrelling around the corner, and only the quick reflexes of both their mounts prevented a collision. Cae's palfrey shied, dancing sideways with her ears laid back as the other rider tried to continue straight past.

"Which way?" he shouted, waving a frantic hand at the nearby crossroads. "Which way did the riders go?" He was dishevelled and sweating, black hair coming loose from its tie to frame a fine-boned face, a week's growth of stubble accentuating the pleasing lines of his lips and jaw. His flushed skin was a warm, appealing olive shade, but there were dark circles beneath his hooded eyes, and despite the day's heat, he was visibly shaking.

Velasin vin Aaro.

After Kita's report, Cae had worked out several potential ways to approach his betrothed, but none of them had included Velasin being in distraught pursuit of his injured servant. Cae swallowed, momentarily struggling with the question of whether to identify himself before answering. Thankfully, the habit of command kicked in, priorities realigning in response to the situation. Wheeling his borrowed palfrey up alongside Velasin's bay, he nodded back the way he'd come and said, "Follow me, tiern!"

"Thank you!" Velasin gasped, and then they were riding together, horses snorting as they cantered up the slope.

Passing back through the upper gates and into the courtyard, Cae almost laughed to find that the groom was just where he'd left her, staring about with an anxiousness that melted away the second they drew to a halt.

"My thanks for the loan," he said, thrusting the reins at her. "Returned with interest."

She gaped at him. "You want me to take both horses, tiern?"

"If you'd be so kind, Ren—?"

"Vaia, tiern. Ren Vaia Skai."

"—Ren Vaia. This is the new Tiern Velasin vin Aaro, and *this*—" He looped the bay's reins over its head as Velasin dismounted. "—is his faithful steed. He's just arrived from Ralia, so treat him kindly, you understand?"

The girl nodded rapidly, eyes wide. "Yes, tiern!" she said, and hurried to comply, clicking her tongue as she chivvied both beasts along.

Which, thanks to the unusual emptiness of the courtyard, left Cae alone with Velasin. The injured tiern took a step forwards, paled and almost fell over, remaining upright seemingly through sheer stubbornness. Only then did Cae realise the extent of the problem: Velasin's left thigh was wet with blood, the dark stain spreading across his breeches. Most likely, he'd pulled his stitches open. Hissing in dismay, Cae moved to help him.

"Here," he said, extending an arm, "you can lean on me—"

"No!"

Cae jerked back, startled. Velasin just stared at him, wide-eyed and tense as a wire.

After a moment, Cae nodded at his leg. "You can't walk on that unsupported, tiern. I don't mean to importune you, but under the circumstances—"

"You keep calling me tiern," said Velasin, cutting him off. "You know my full name, even." He eyed Cae with visible unease. "Who are you?"

Inwardly, Cae sighed; outwardly, he straightened. "Tiern Caethari Aeduria," he said, softly. "Or Cae, if you like."

"Of course," said Velasin, shutting his eyes. "Of course you are." He laughed, the sound cracked and humourless. In Ralian, he said, "The moons are mocking me."

In the same language, Cae replied, "I didn't know your moons had a sense of humour."

"It depends on who you ask," said Velasin, switching back to Tithenai. As Kita had said, his accent was lilting—pleasantly so, as though he were from a prosperous clan in Irae-Tai; a university family, perhaps.

"I saw what happened," Cae said, into the silence. "From the parapets of the Aida. I was coming to help."

Velasin's face crumpled. "That blow was meant for me. If Markel dies—"

"I pray he won't."

"My thanks," he whispered. And then, as though he feared the answer, "Can you take me to him? I know there are other things to discuss, but Markel's mute—he won't be able to speak if I'm not there, and Tar Raeki might not think to tell the healers."

"Of course," said Cae. "But you'll have to trust me at least enough to lean on, tiern. That leg won't hold your weight."

Velasin looked away, considering. Cae frowned: whatever his objection to public touching, the tiern clearly needed help, and it was an effort to keep from saying as much. After a moment, however, Velasin nodded. Cae approached him carefully, wondering if he was hiding an additional injury—cracked ribs, perhaps, or a shallow cut, something that a supportive arm could easily make worse. Some people were secretive about their hurts that way, whether soldiers or civilians, and while Cae wasn't one of them, he understood the impulse. As such, he tried to be gentle, fingertips grazing Velasin's side in search of any tender spots, and it was only when Velasin inhaled sharply, tensing again, that Cae realised such a lingering touch conveyed some very different implications.

"Sorry," he muttered, flushing at the error, and promptly snugged his arm around Velasin's ribs. "There. You can lean on me, now."

Velasin shuddered and complied, letting Cae take his weight as they started forwards. He was limping badly, breath hissing with each step, and Cae couldn't decide which he was more: frustrated with Velasin's stubbornness, or impressed by his tenacity.

Working on the not unreasonable assumption that Raeki had taken Markel straight to the infirmary, Cae headed there, silently grateful for the fact that they didn't have to tackle any stairs. In fact, it was becoming increasingly clear that, regardless of the state of his servant, Velasin himself needed medical attention: he was breathing hard and, pressed as close as they were, Cae could feel his heart pounding.

"Is it much farther?" Velasin gritted out.

"Don't tell me you can't keep up," said Cae, shifting to get a better grip on him.

"Why should I struggle? You're practically carrying me."

"What, so you think *I* can't manage?"

"You said it, not me."

"Funny," Cae huffed, mouth twitching despite himself. "Such a singular wit you Ralians possess."

"You Tithenai set a low bar."

"Hah!"

"See?" said Velasin, panting a little. "You laugh, but it isn't funny."

"What can I say? I'm starved for good entertainment."

"Sorry to disappoint you, then, but I'm terrible company."

"I won't argue that point. We've only just met, and you're already bleeding on me."

"In my defence, you sent my horse away."

"I don't know how you do things in Ralia," Cae said, taking the final corner, "but here, it's generally frowned upon to ride indoors."

Velasin chuckled weakly. "And you call us backwards?"

"Yes, but to your faces. We're polite like that."

"This marriage is off to a terrible start," said Velasin—and just like that, the humour between them vanished. Cae swallowed hard and brought them to a halt, nodding awkwardly at the infirmary door.

"Through here," he said, and didn't look at Velasin as he steered them both inside.

Cae paused at the threshold, taking in the scene. Markel was laid out on a nearby bed, his shirt pulled up to reveal a deep wound in the vulnerable flesh below his ribs. The two guards stood back from him, engaged in a hissing argument about whose fault it all was, while Raeki hovered and swore under his breath, watching as the healer, Ru Zairin Ciras, issued sharp instructions to thir underlings.

Recognising Cae, the arguing guards snapped to attention, but before either Raeki or Ru Zairin could speak, Velasin stumbled between them, shoving his way to the bedside.

"Markel? Are you awake? Markel!"

The servant's eyes rolled open, focussing hazily on Velasin, and with a sudden burst of effort, he raised his hands and began to sign. The gestures were alien to Cae, but Velasin clearly understood them, for he began to translate, speaking aloud in Tithenai as his gaze remained fixed on Markel.

"The man who attacked him said they acted in the name of the Wild Knife, who will not suffer Ralians to live in Qi-Katai."

"He *what*?" choked Cae, aghast. "But it's not—that doesn't make any sense!"

Velasin turned and glared at him. "Why not? The Wild Knife rode against vin Mica for years—he'd have every reason to hate my being here! Are you honestly going to pretend otherwise?"

"I'm going to *pretend* nothing," Cae snapped back, "because *I'm him*!"

For a pointed moment, everyone went still.

"Oh," said Velasin, swaying slightly. He gripped the edge of Markel's bed, trying to steady himself, and all at once, Cae realised how pale he was. "Do you want me dead, then?"

"I don't," said Cae, already moving towards him. "Tiern, your leg—"

"Damn," said Velasin softly, and fainted.

8

It was just as well, Cae thought grimly, that there'd been no ceremony planned to mark Velasin's arrival, or else a great many people would have been inconvenienced beyond himself. As it was, instead of showing his betrothed around the Aida, as had been his preferred strategy for the afternoon, he found himself traipsing across it for far less pleasant reasons. Though the Jade Market guard had suggested, with some degree of affront, that Markel's "supposed testimony" about his assailant didn't count for anything, as they had "only the Ralian tiern's word" that he'd said anything at all, Cae was not so foolish. However clumsy the attempt, not only had someone tried to kill Velasin, but they'd had the gall to do it in Cae's name—and, by extension, the name of Clan Aeduria.

And that was unacceptable—not just personally, though it stung Cae's pride, but politically, too. In all his panic over Velasin the person, he'd barely digested the implications of Velasin the diplomatic tie to Ralia. What would it mean, if Cae's clan—the ruling family of Qi-Katai—were thought to have so violently baulked at a marriage endorsed, however distantly, by the monarchs of two nations? The bigger ripples would be slower to come, but Cae shuddered to think of them forming nonetheless.

After an anxious ten minutes in the infirmary, where Ru Zairin had assured him that Markel would live and that Velasin was merely suffering the combined effects of blood loss, stress and exhaustion, for which the only real cure was rest, Cae finally judged himself able to leave. Of necessity, he took Raeki with him and headed straight for Keletha's apartments. Halfway there, however, they were intercepted by a red-faced servant who'd clearly been trying to hunt them down: the tiern and tar, she panted out, were to meet Tieren Halithar in the Green Study as quickly as possible.

Arriving at this new destination—which was, conveniently, on the opposite side of the Aida—Cae and Raeki found not only the tieren in attendance, but Keletha, Riya and Laecia. Sketching his father a hasty bow, Cae hurried in and took a seat, Raeki scrambling to do likewise. The Green Study was a small but finely appointed and imposing room: the tieren's location of choice for private meetings. He sat at the head of the oblong table, scarred hands flat on the polished wood, and said, in wintry tones, "Now that we're all assembled, I'd be very much obliged if *someone*"—he stared pointedly at Cae—"would enlighten me as to what in Zo's name has been going on."

As though he were giving a parade report to a commanding officer—which, in a sense, he was—Cae took a deep breath, spared a brief, acknowledging glance for each member of his audience, and told his version of events, beginning with what he'd seen atop the Aida and ending with Velasin's collapse in the infirmary. When he was finished, Tieren Halithar motioned for the next person—Riya, in this case—to speak. In that fashion, they went around the table, with Keletha and Raeki both beginning their accounts, not with their arrival at Qi-Katai, but the attack at Vaiko. Though Kita had covered most of those details in her first report to him, an odd jolt ran through Cae on hearing Raeki's and Keletha's versions: he'd met Velasin now, and even without the betrothal, he would've been hard-pressed not to feel invested in his actions.

Of the events in Qi-Katai, there was precious little new information to be had. The Amber Gate guards had arrested Markel's assailant, but beyond Keletha's confirmation of Markel's own account—namely, that the man had claimed to be acting on behalf of the Wild Knife—there was nothing to explain his motives, nor would there be until the guards had completed their own interrogation.

"He came out of nowhere!" Raeki fumed, when Keletha finished speaking. "Ruya's grace, but that's a poor excuse. We should have anticipated more resistance, taken more steps to ensure his safety—"

"*Should have done* unsinks no boats," said the tieren. His voice was calmer than it had been at the outset, which Cae took as a positive sign. "In any case, Tar Raeki, it was I who thought that discretion would better serve our interests than spectacle in this matter; even had you disagreed, you would have been overridden."

"All the same, tieren," said Raeki, waving a frustrated hand, "after Vaiko, I ought to have been prepared—not that I think the two are connected," he added quickly, as Riya's brows shot up. "That would be absurd. Bandits are a fact of life, and anyone organised enough to have orchestrated two attacks in two different places would have surely picked sturdier cat's-paws than some terrified yokels and a single raving malcontent."

"Ordinarily, I'd agree with you," Cae said, frowning. "But you must admit, the coincidence is striking." He glanced at Keletha. "With your permission, envoy, once the retrieval squad returns with your prisoners, I'd like to question them myself."

Keletha spread thir hands. "Of course, tiern. I had no plans for them beyond the obvious."

"I'll make sure they're brought to the Amber Gate garrison," Raeki said. "Might as well keep them all under one roof, if only for convenience's sake."

"And what if someone tries again?" Cae asked.

Laecia made a face at him. "You truly think that's likely?"

"I think I'd rather prepare for an attack that doesn't come than be complacently vulnerable to one that does. Even if the man today was acting alone—even if his claim to support me is the work of delusion—his actions force us to consider that there's more and stronger anti-Ralian sentiment in Qi-Katai than we realised. Now that the betrothal is known, we ought to be prepared to encounter pushback. We don't want anyone thinking that the Aedurias are so faithless as to sabotage an agreed-upon alliance with attempted murder."

"Let alone make such a piss-poor job of it," Laecia muttered.

A meaningful silence settled over the gathering. Though it was Tieren Halithar who'd initially proposed the marriage alliance with Ralia, he'd proceeded only after his liege, the Asa Ivadi Ruqai, had approved the idea in writing. If anything befell Velasin, it wasn't just Farathel they had to worry about, but Qi-Xihan, too.

His father shot him an assessing look. "You have a plan, Caethari?"

"Not much of one," Cae admitted. He drew a breath, acutely aware of his sisters, and forced himself to disregard their judgement. "Just . . . being my betrothed offers Velasin a certain degree of protection, but as my spouse, he'll be safer still."

"Inasmuch as there's a better range of punishments available for anyone who harms him, you mean," said Laecia, sounding sceptical.

Riya, however, took Cae's side. "If it acts as a deterrent, why not? It's not as though there's much else to be done."

Keletha coughed, politely attracting Cae's attention. Thei looked strangely guilty, fingers laced on the tabletop. "You know that Tiern Velasin hasn't read the betrothal contracts? That his consent, while technically given, is a product of his sense of duty, and not his informed will?"

"I do," said Cae, stomach twisting at the reminder.

"Then you should consider that he likely has no notion of the difference between Ralian weddings and our own. I had intended to explain it all to him during the journey, assuming he had any questions, but—" Thei shrugged, frustrated. "—he didn't want to speak to me, and clearly had little enthusiasm for the topic even had I insisted."

Laecia pricked up her ears. "Meaning what, in a practical sense?" she asked eagerly, and Cae was hard-pressed not to roll his eyes. *Civilising Velasin, indeed!*

"In Ralia, the legal union and the public celebration of its success are the same event," said Keletha. "Meaning, I doubt it would ever occur to Tiern Velasin that a noble marriage might be effected swiftly, or in private."

"They do it all at once? Even the arranged marriages?"

"Just so."

"But that's absurd! What can strangers possibly have to say about each other during the speeches?"

"Their families speak for them, I believe."

Laecia looked scandalised. "That's all the more reason *not* to marry him now!" she exclaimed. "If someone is determined to act, your marriage vows won't stop them. The poor man's likely frightened enough already, and now you're going to, what—skip the grace period and make things completely uncivilised by our standards as well as his?"

Cae flushed guiltily. "With our father's blessing, yes," he said, looking again to Tieren Halithar. "Though only if Velasin agrees."

The tieren considered, then gave a slow, thoughtful nod. "That sounds a sensible precaution," he said. "I'll send for the justiciar, should Velasin consent."

Cae let out a breath of relief. "Thank you, Father."

"What a beautiful day for a wedding," Riya drawled, mouth quirked with amusement. Laecia only scowled.

"As for the rest of it," the tieren said, ignoring his daughters, "I expect to be kept updated. Tar Raeki, you have my authority to investigate this matter however you see fit; if anti-Ralian sentiment is organising within the city, I want it found and dealt with."

Raeki bowed in his chair.

"Riya, Laecia—I'd appreciate your thoughts on the matter, too. Keep your ears open, and if you should hear anything of interest from your respective quarters, pass it on to me, or to Tar Raeki—or to your brother, should it concern either himself or Velasin directly. Now." He slapped his palm on the table. "If the rest of you will excuse us, I have other matters to discuss with Keletha."

Accepting the dismissal, Cae rose and left. For once, his sisters refrained from comment, heading off to Laecia's apartments without stopping to importune him with their opinions—though Riya, being Riya, still cast him a sly look. In stolid contrast, Raeki offered a brusque farewell, then promptly hurried off in the opposite direction, eager to begin his investigations. Keletha, of course, remained behind, continuing in conference with the tieren.

Which left Cae alone, wondering how in Ruya's grace he was going to explain the situation to Velasin.

He mulled his options en route to the infirmary, though in truth, the decision didn't take long. Even if he'd had a knack for subtlety, there wasn't time for it, and Velasin struck him as someone who'd been lied to enough already. Taking Keletha's advice to heart, Cae resolved to speak as plainly as possible, to answer any questions Velasin might have, and to accept it with good grace should the tiern reject his proposal, though he hoped it didn't come to that. In Cae's observation, mistrust was poison to marriages, even dispassionate ones, and for all he'd hoped that his eventual political marriage might also be something of a love match, in his practical heart, he'd assumed at the least that his partner would be someone he could rely on; who would come to rely on him in turn.

Keeping this in mind, Cae nodded to himself and entered the infirmary. Except for Markel and Velasin, the beds were empty, and despite the earlier presence of multiple junior healers, Ru Zairin Ciras seemed to be working alone, thir attention focussed on the myriad contents of the room's medicine table. Though thei looked up and acknowledged Cae with a respectful glance, thei didn't rise, continuing thir measurement of substances which were doubtless of great medical significance, had Cae been able to identify them. Taking this apparent disinterest as a sign that both patients were in no immediate danger, Cae approached Velasin's bed, noting as he passed that Markel was fast asleep.

Velasin, however, was only drowsing, and at the sound of Cae's footsteps, his head lifted from the pillow. Moving slowly, so as not to startle him, Cae pulled up a chair and sat at a respectful distance from Velasin's bedside, waiting quietly as the tiern blinked himself back into wakefulness. He looked a little better than before, though still plainly exhausted: the whites of his eyes were bloodshot, the circles beneath them dark, the hooded lids drooping. He lay atop the blankets, freshly washed, shaved and dressed in borrowed Tithenai clothes, his own evidently having been taken for cleaning. The looser fit suited him, Cae thought, then promptly wondered at his own opinion.

"Hello," said Velasin blearily. "What day is it?"

"Saintsday, the twentieth of Kidae," Cae replied. And then, when Velasin still looked confused, "The year is 1409."

"Yes, thank you, I'm not quite that addled," Velasin said waspishly. With a little effort, he levered himself upright, so that his back was resting against the headboard. He blinked, belatedly registering Cae, and something shuttered in his expression. "Do you have need of me, tiern?"

Something about the question irked Cae, though he couldn't have said what. "Isn't it possible that I'm just here to check on you?"

"I don't know. Is it?"

Just in time, Cae recalled that actually, he wasn't there for politeness's sake alone, and bit back his native retort. Instead, he sighed. "It's not, as it happens, though I'd ask you to believe that I'm still concerned for your well-being."

"I'll consider the prospect," Velasin muttered. "What is it you want, tiern?"

"I want you to marry me."

"That hardly seems a new development, or else I wouldn't be here."

"Today."

"Ah."

"It's not—it's not what you might think," Cae said, hating his own sudden awkwardness. "In Tithenai custom, the legal marriage is always a brief act, and usually private. There's often a smaller marriage-gathering a little after the ceremony, to introduce the new spouse to local friends and family, but we don't usually hold a full celebration between both clans until a month or so afterwards, to show that the marriage is working. But I'm told the Ralian way is different?"

"You could say that," said Velasin. He seemed a shade paler than before, his fingers twitching against the sheets. "I'll confess, I'd thought I might have more time. To, ah. To acclimate, I suppose." He tried to smile, but it was forced, and just a little fearful. Inwardly, Cae winced.

"May I speak plainly, tiern?"

"I'd be very grateful if you did."

"I'm concerned for your safety," Cae said, bluntly. "The attack today, the fact that it was apparently carried out in my name, the prospect that there might be others who threaten you—it unsettles me. As my, my husband—" He stumbled a little over the word, surprised by how intimate it sounded. "—you would be more secure, legally speaking, than as my betrothed, and though it's a smallish sort of shield, I'd hoped it might prove a deterrent. Ordinarily, we'd wait a week or so before formalising the union, a sort of . . . a sort of courtship, I suppose, in which we'd get to know each other, called a grace period. And if you'd truly prefer it that way, I won't object; I want to respect your wishes. But under the circumstances, I thought it might be better—"

"Yes," said Velasin. "I see." He looked . . . *resigned* wasn't quite the word for it, though it came close. Withdrawn, somehow, yet also a little fey. He glanced across the room at Markel, and just for a moment, his expression became complicated, sad. "Your surgeon gave him a sedative," he said, softly. "To help speed the healing. I'm told he'll likely sleep until after sunrise." He turned back to Cae, his features smoothing into practiced blankness. "Does this brief, private marriage of yours require much walking? I can manage a little distance, I think, but I'm under strict orders not to pull a second set of stitches."

"We can have the justiciar and the official witnesses come to my apartments," Cae said, then promptly corrected himself. "To *our* apartments, I mean. Damn." *I'll have to get used to that.*

Velasin opened his mouth, but didn't speak. Instead, he glanced away, swallowed—and then, without any further discussion, swung his legs over the bed and stood. "Lead on, then," he said, with only the barest shake in his voice. "Let's see these fabled apartments."

Cae hesitated, studying him. "You can lean on me again, if you want."

"I'll manage alone."

"I'd prefer you didn't," Ru Zairin interjected, without looking up. "Pride supports many things, tiern, but seldom injured legs."

Velasin looked like he wanted to argue, but lacked the strength for it. "As you wish," he said instead, and stayed where he was as Cae, who'd learned an early respect for healers, moved to prop him up. Though requiring less help than before, Velasin still leaned heavily on him, and Cae marvelled anew at the sheer contrary stubbornness of the man. *You'd almost think he likes being hurt,* he thought to himself, then promptly dismissed the notion as uncharitable, and therefore unhelpful.

As they reached the infirmary's threshold, the tiern stopped and turned, forcing Cae to do likewise. Jaw working soundlessly, Velasin looked again at the sleeping Markel, but when he spoke, his words were directed at Ru Zairin.

"When he wakes," he said, steadily, "tell him . . . gods, I don't know. Just tell him I'm sorry, will you?"

"Of course," said Ru Zairin, blinking. The healer was clearly bemused by the request, but Cae thought he understood: the way Ralians conceived of marriage, and as close as the two of them were, both master and servant would doubtless have expected Markel to play some significant part in things, which opportunity was now denied him. Almost, Cae was tempted to say that he'd still get his chance, the public celebration having ample scope for such gestures, but given Velasin's tiredness, he thought the details of that event could wait.

Instead, he remained silent, waiting until Velasin moved to lead him out into the Aida.

9

Despite the tieren's promise to inform the justiciar of Cae's intentions, his continued conference with Keletha meant that events had outpaced him. Though Cae sent a runner while still en route to his—*their,* damn it, *their*—apartments, the justiciar, it seemed, was set to take his time in arriving. Velasin, for his part, was drained from the walk, and after Cae delivered a brief summation of where everything was, the tiern asked simply if he might lie down again.

Which question rendered Cae belatedly, acutely aware of their potential sleeping arrangements. Though his apartments weren't small, both the service chamber and the guest suite had long since been repurposed as, respectively, a library and a storeroom—which meant, of course, that the only bed available was his own. He'd anticipated their making changes to the space together during their courtship period, as was common, and so hadn't considered the more immediate logistics of rooming together. Cae's attempt at explaining this was almost painfully awkward, while Velasin's reaction to hearing it could best be described as *tense.*

"I can have the spare room made up for you tomorrow," Cae added hastily, because at this point, the last thing either of them needed was the additional awkwardness of sleeping together—of *co-sleeping,* saints!—while still virtual strangers. "But you can lie down here for now, and I'll just, ah, give you some privacy—"

As Velasin lay down in their—no, no, in *his,* saints help him, *his*—bed, Cae beat a hasty retreat to the receiving room, pacing as he flipped his knife, and before too long, he'd made several new dents in his throwing board. He was angry at himself, hindsight having informed him of a dozen different, better ways he could've handled the situation, the most obvious being for one or other of them to sleep in a different apartment. But navigating unplanned personal conversations with sense and dignity had never been one of Cae's strong suits; hence the efforts his sisters routinely made to trick him into them. In such moments, he had a disconcerting tendency to betray himself, and though it would have been the work of a moment to knock on the bedroom door, apologise and offer to spend the night elsewhere, a tiny, selfish part of him didn't want to.

Because for all Velasin's odd manners, alternately bristling and flinching—for all that he was road-weary, tired and injured—Cae would have been lying if he'd claimed to not find him attractive. It wasn't just his looks, though he certainly had those: it was his dry sense of humour, the obvious compassion he had for Markel, the flashes of fire and courage that underscored his actions. From the little he'd seen, Velasin was exactly the sort of person to whom Cae was naturally drawn, and though the feeling didn't seem to be mutual, he couldn't help hoping that a little forced proximity might give them some common ground, however awkward the context.

Though Velasin hadn't originally wanted to marry, the circumstances were such that he—that *they*—could hardly do otherwise, least of all without consequence. Velasin, surely, was even more aware of that fact than Cae himself, and yet his personal reservations seemingly remained strong enough that he hadn't taken the logical step of trying to work *with* Cae, to make the most of the arrangement, preferring to stumble along like a horse resentfully harnessed.

Frustrating, Cae decided, didn't begin to cover it.

By the time the justiciar finally arrived, trailing the customary witnesses for Ayla, Zo and Ruya, Cae's pacing had just about worn a groove in the floor. He was halfway to the bedroom to collect Velasin when the tiern appeared of his own volition, blinking owlishly as he clung to the doorframe. His dark, wavy hair was loose to his shoulders, long threads sticking messily to his pillow-creased cheek, and for the first time since he'd arrived in Qi-Katai, his eyes were clear. His irises weren't brown, Cae realised belatedly, but hazel, flecked with golds and greys, hooded in a way that looked both languid and intelligent now that he was no longer on the brink of exhaustion, and something about the observation made his throat dry up.

"I'm awake," said Velasin, sounding thoroughly grumpy about it—though for once, his tone seemed more the product of having been woken from sleep, and less because he objected wholesale to the situation in which he found himself. The distinction, Cae told himself, was absolutely not an endearing one.

Almost, he could've sworn he heard Riya laughing.

For how long the justiciar had taken to arrange it, the union itself took scarcely any time at all. Tradition required that the two of them stand, which Velasin managed with gritted teeth, refusing to lean on Cae again because, as he put it, "I can damn well rest my hand on a book without you holding the other one."

"The word *stubborn* does you a disservice," Cae muttered, but didn't press the issue.

With that, the justiciar set his copy of the Laws on the table between them—it was an enormous old thing, the leather cover stained and pitted from years of use—and began to speak the litany of union. Cae recognised it from Riya's ceremony, when the vows she'd taken first before state and gods were renewed again in the sight of family, and felt abruptly light-headed. *Saints, give me strength. We're really doing this.*

"As marriage is made for mortals, let it be governed by mortals," the justiciar said, his voice a pleasant tenor, "yet also witnessed by the divine, as all that is mortal is witnessed. In keeping with the laws of Tithena and Qi-Katai, and in honour of the contracts made by kin and clan, I invoke the witness of Ayla, the Mother of Saints; of Zo, the Father of Change; and of Ruya, the Child of Luck, in this, the mortal union of Tiern Caethari Xai Aeduria, scion of Clan Aeduria and the city of Qi-Katai, to Tiern Velasin Averin vin Aaro, scion of House vin Aaro and the kingdom of Ralia." He inclined his head towards the book. "Please, set your hands on the Laws."

Both Cae and Velasin complied, their littlest fingers brushing. The minute contact stirred the hairs on Cae's arm.

"Tiern Caethari. Do you swear to uphold this union with Velasin Averin vin Aaro, the product of mortal law and divine witness, in the spirit of peace and prosperity?"

"I do," said Cae, not daring to look at Velasin.

"Tiern Velasin. Do you swear to uphold this union with Caethari Xai Aeduria, the product of mortal law and divine witness, in the spirit of peace and prosperity?"

Velasin's voice was a rasp. "I do."

Nodding, the justiciar laid his palm across both of theirs, pressing briefly down.

"The law has so witnessed," he intoned, and stepped aside as, one by one, the divine witnesses echoed the gesture.

"Ayla, the Mother of Saints, has so witnessed."

"Zo, the Father of Change, has so witnessed."

"Ruya, the Child of Luck, has so witnessed."

"As it is witnessed, so let it be," the justiciar said. "Now join hands, and meet each other."

Heart pounding, Cae took Velasin's palms in his—he held them gently, feeling how the other man wanted to pull away—and dropped a light kiss on the knuckles of each hand. Velasin inhaled sharply; he clearly hadn't expected the gesture, but after a moment, he shakily inverted his grip and did the same for Cae, a bare brush of lips on skin before letting go.

"You are husbands," the justiciar said, and smiled at the pair of them. "May you live happily together."

All that remained was to add their names to the city's Marital Register—a different, slimmer tome produced by the witness for Zo. Cae signed his own name, then watched as Velasin did likewise. He had elegant handwriting, especially when set alongside Cae's own, spikier style. By tradition, as Cae's marital status was a matter of public interest in Qi-Katai—and particularly in this instance, as the whole purpose of rushing the marriage was to offer Velasin greater legal protection—the justiciar would post a public notice confirming the marriage to the boards outside the justiciary, where other such unions, births and deaths were recorded. From there, the gossip-runners who earned their coin by spreading such news through the city would do the rest; though likely as not, the rumours would've begun to spread the second the justiciar and witnesses were sighted en route to the Aida.

And just like that, it was done; they were married. The justiciar bowed to both of them, but didn't overstay his welcome, leading the witnesses back out of Cae's—no, *their*—apartments with commendable efficiency.

The instant the door shut behind them, Velasin sagged, falling heavily into the nearest seat, which happened to be an armchair. He looked dazed, staring up at Cae with a sort of blank acceptance that was almost comical. "So," he said. "What now? Is there feasting? Music? Revelry? You'll have to forgive me, tiern, if I'm not quite up to dancing."

The use of his title hit Cae like a slap, though he was at a loss to understand why. That they'd joined hands and said the words didn't make either one of them less an alien to the other, and yet some foolish part of him had evidently thought just that. Refusing to be baited—if this marriage started badly, it would not be on his account—he took a deep breath and said, "No dancing. But I could call for some food, if you like."

The ghost of a smile flitted over Velasin's face. "Feasting it is, then."

It was only when his stomach rumbled quiet agreement that Cae realised how late it was. It seemed impossible that so much had happened in the space of a single day, and yet it also felt like no time at all since he'd stood atop the Aida with his sisters, waiting to catch his first glimpse of the man who was now his husband.

Cae rang the bell, composing a mental list of suitable foods. Nothing too complicated, he thought, but the sort of things he might request when fresh off the road: dishes that were warm and filling, but which didn't sit too heavily on the stomach. And wine, perhaps, had they any to match his choices.

Into the silence, Velasin asked, softly, "Do I keep my name?"

It was a painfully naked question, and when Cae turned, he found that Velasin had drawn up his knees beneath his chin, a forearm bracketing his shins, so that he was curled in the armchair like a cat in a flower-box.

"If you wish to, yes," said Cae. "Though legally, you belong to Clan Aeduria." He hesitated, then said, "Should you prefer to remain a vin Aaro, I would not be offended—"

"I don't," said Velasin, gulping a little. "Prefer. I do not . . . I am not who I was." He forced a laugh, hugging his legs. "As my father has cast me off, I see little reason to honour him by pretending otherwise. In this, I can be an Aeduria."

Mouth unaccountably dry, Cae said, "We are lucky to have you, I think."

Velasin's head jerked up at that, cheeks colouring slightly. "The man who stabbed Markel didn't seem to think so."

Cae had no answer to that, but was saved from attempting one by the arrival of a servant, to whom he gave instructions regarding dinner. The servant bowed and hurried off again, indulging in only a single curious glance at the new tiern.

"I don't recognise half of what you just ordered," Velasin said, "but I must say, it sounds delicious."

Lips quirked, Cae settled himself into a chair that was neither so close to Velasin's as to encroach on his space nor so distant as to make conversation difficult and said, "May I ask you something?"

"That rather depends on what it is," replied Velasin, a flash of his earlier wariness returning.

Cae elected to ignore this. "You speak excellent Tithenai, yet know nothing about us as people. I merely wondered what possessed the Ralian court to pick our language to elevate, of all possible options, instead of, say, Attovarin or Khyto."

Velasin laughed, the first such genuine sound that Cae had heard from him. "The obscurity was the point. There are few Tithenai in Farathel these days, though plenty of older Tithenai texts are still held in high esteem, and private languages, I'm told, are good for speaking secrets. It also sounds quite lovely, to a Ralian ear—good for poetry, for those so inclined. And of course," he added, gesturing between them with a wry flick of his wrist, "you have all these wonderful, salacious, sensational words for improper things, like *husbands of husbands*. It's like learning to swear all over again. Though I'll admit, it's left me a little confused as to whether certain words are lewd in the original context, or merely judged as such by prurient Ralian standards."

"For example?" Cae asked, intrigued.

"Well, for one thing," said Velasin, "you don't have a word for valet"—he used the Ralian term—"but I wasn't sure what I might really be saying, if I called Markel my body-servant. In Farathel, the term has . . . particular implications."

"And here, too," said Cae, wincing in apology. "It's . . . the position is sometimes given innocently, but more often than not, it's an appointment of pretext—a way for a wealthier person, a noble or merchant or the like, to keep a lover of lower status close to them. Marriage across classes does happen, of course, but where the purpose of union is alliance, there will always be those who—well. I doubt you need a lesson in those elements of human nature."

"Indeed, I don't," murmured Velasin. He shivered slightly, curling his arm more tightly about his legs.

It was a fragile moment, one that threatened to shatter beneath the slightest stress. Not wanting to risk their tentative rapport, Cae took the hint and changed the subject, asking instead about Velasin's siblings. Happily, that seemed to prove a safer topic, and one that enabled Cae to share some anecdotes about his own sisters.

"Laecia lives here still," he said, when Velasin asked, "though Riya is only visiting. Her wife owns a spectacular house in Kir-Halae, and their current desire is to fill it with children. Riya being Riya, of course, she's determined to negotiate known paternity instead of contracting with one of Zo's sons, and though I don't think Kivali has a preference either way, she's happy enough to indulge her."

"I—what?" said Velasin, looking thoroughly confused. "I'm sorry, tiern; I think I was listening with my Ralian ear. She's negotiating *what*?"

"Known paternity," said Cae. "As neither of them can sire a child on the other, they're negotiating for, ah, outside help. Or Riya is, rather; though I believe it's Kivali who wishes to bear first."

Velasin gave a choking laugh. "That sound you hear is the distant, outraged shrieking of Ralian moral conservatives. Do, please, help me drown it out with details!"

Bemused, Cae said, "There's really not much to tell. Known paternity is hard to negotiate mainly because it constitutes an alliance without marriage: the child is tied to three clans, which can make for some tricky legal caveats, especially if there are half-siblings involved, or are likely to be in the future. Which is why contracting with Zo's sons is more usual: they're temple-sworn dedicates, and any child they sire is considered a gift from the god. Of course, for obvious practical reasons, the priests still keep records of mortal blood relations, but otherwise, it's a simple enough process."

Velasin sat quietly, digesting the implications. When he next looked at Cae, his expression was tentative, all teasing gone. "And is there, a . . . a reverse process, too?"

"Ayla's daughters," Cae said, throat suddenly dry. "There is magic that assists the process, just as with Zo's sons—that is, there is no need for, ah, traditional physical relations in either instance, though things can still be done that way if desired." He coughed, neck heating as he looked away. "But in either case, yes, there are options, adoption being the most obvious alternative."

"Even between two men?"

"Even then."

Velasin's voice, when he spoke again, was very soft. "I had not considered that."

Cae swallowed, not knowing what to say. Whether through luck or mischance, however, he was saved the effort of replying by the arrival of dinner. He was a little embarrassed by how much food he'd apparently requested, though it hadn't seemed so much at the time. Flushing slightly, he dismissed the servant and began to set out the tray's contents himself, talking as he did so.

"I wasn't sure what you might like," he said, "so I asked for—well, a bit of everything, I suppose. There's egg soup with noodles, goat vahta—it's a sort of, well, a sort of meat and sauce dish, with chickpeas and kilia seeds, if you know what those are. And this is field rice, for all the different things mixed in, and some steamed fish, and I think, ah—rabbit shanks with leeks? And some wine, if you want wine. I'm sorry," he said, feeling at once an utter fool. "I'm not used to doing this."

"It smells wonderful," Velasin said, and crept up out of the armchair, easing himself to the table like a hungry stray. He ate tentatively to begin with, as though more in doubt of his hunger than the quality of the food, but after the first few bites, he became ravenous, trying a little of everything with such eagerness that he burned himself on the fish. Cae laughed at that, and found he was hungry enough in turn that, despite his initial worries, they managed to get through almost everything.

It was a pleasant meal, and for the first time since the justiciar's departure, Cae let himself imagine that this might actually work: that Velasin might be willing to pull in harness with him after all. Though he quieted again when Cae finally summoned a servant to take the remains of the meal away, he didn't seem as tense as he had earlier, and once they'd both made their ablutions, the only remaining hurdle was the sleeping arrangements.

In what Cae told himself was a tactical decision, he let Velasin enter the bedroom first, waiting a minute or so before following.

Much to his relief—or possibly his disappointment—he found that Velasin had doused the lights, and after taking a moment for his eyes to adjust, he peeled off his clothes and donned the thin hip-wrap he usually wore to bed, its linen soft and worn.

Pulse loud in his ears, he eased himself beneath the covers. From what he could make out, Velasin was still mostly clothed, though whether that was a personal affectation or a Ralian habit, Cae didn't know. Beside him, he felt the tiern—felt his *husband* tense, curling sharply away to the other side of the mattress. As signals went, it was unequivocal, and though, to his considerable surprise, Cae realised he would have been amenable to a more—well, to *more,* whatever it might entail—having so precariously won whatever trust they shared, he had no intention of raising the issue.

"Good night," he said instead, softly.

Velasin didn't reply, though he clearly wasn't asleep. Suppressing a sigh, Cae closed his own eyes and, despite the awkwardness of it, fell asleep as deeply and quickly as only a soldier can.

He woke some hours later, disoriented, groggy and alone. Cae blinked in the darkness, wondering what had woken him, if not Velasin's departure—the blankets opposite were rucked and cold, clearly vacant for some time—until he heard the sound of muffled crying.

At that, Cae came bolt awake. Standing silently, he crept to the door and eased it worriedly open.

He froze.

Velasin sat at the table in the receiving room, illuminated by a single, stunted candle. His cheeks were wet with tears, and in his right hand was Cae's second-favourite knife, the one he so often found himself flipping from hand to hand.

The tip of it was pushed to Velasin's throat.

10

"I can't do it," Velasin said. His knuckles clenched around the knife, the silvery blade made molten in the candlelight. He looked at Cae, eyes wet and pleading. "I can't do it, I can't, I'm sorry."

"Can't do what?" said Cae. He was calm and still, the way he sometimes felt in the eye of a battle, but though he didn't move, his guts were churning.

"Can't find the vein, for one thing." Velasin's smile was ghoulish with grief. "Can't wait, for another."

"You can't *wait*? For what?"

A tremor ran through Velasin's hand, the movement visible only in the way the knife-light flickered. "I can't wait," he rasped, staring straight at Cae. "I can't—can't lie in there, tonight or tomorrow or the night after that, and wait for you to force me."

Cae's stomach roiled in horror. "I wouldn't—Velasin, I swear, I couldn't—I would never—why would you even think—?"

"We're married," Velasin said. He sounded utterly broken. "I came to you. My father sent me as he would a bride, and I know, I never thought before what they must feel, all those women betrothed by their families, but I can't—I *can't*—"

"Oh, saints," Cae whispered. The epiphany was appalling. "You came here thinking I'd, what—rape you? *That's* how Ralians marry?"

"Yes. No. I don't know." And then, absurdly, as though he weren't the one holding a knife to his own throat, "Please don't hurt me."

"I won't." Slowly, so slowly, Cae began to inch towards him. "I won't hurt you, Velasin, I promise. I'll swear by anything you like."

Velasin shuddered, enough that a tiny prick of blood bloomed on his throat. Cae froze again, and was trying to think what else to say when Velasin said, so quietly that it was almost inaudible, "Killic promised, too."

"What do you—" Cae started to say; and then it clicked, and his voice refused to work. He stared at Velasin, replaying anew every flinch and fearful glance, reconsidering his aversion to touch in this ugly new light. *Oh, saints.* "Killic abused you?"

"Killic forced me," Velasin said, voice cracking on the admission, and all at once, he was speaking in a choppy mix of Ralian and Tithenai, the words coming thick and fast. "We were together in Farathel, but I saw—I saw he strayed, he betrayed me, and so I left him, I broke it off, and then I went home when Father wrote, but Killic followed and tried, he tried to win me back, and I said no, I told him *no,* but he grabbed my arm and *twisted,* and I just—I couldn't call out or they'd hear me, they'd *see,* and he kept—he touched—and I couldn't, I couldn't—I *couldn't*—but the envoy saw, and thei thought—thei thought I *wanted*—and Father was so furious, he wouldn't—there's no difference to him, he just wanted me gone, and I didn't—moons, I couldn't even tell *Markel,* I just—I should've fought, I thought I must have wanted it—I wanted to die, I tried to die but I couldn't do it, just like now, I couldn't, I can't, I *can't,* oh, gods—"

He dropped the knife, and Cae moved in a flash, snatching up the blade and flinging it away. Velasin stared at him, breathing hard, and Cae didn't think: just dropped to his knees and said, in halting Ralian, "On my life—on my house, on the name Aeduria—I swear by my saints and your moons together, I would sooner die than force you, or allow you to be forced. I *swear* it, Velasin."

Velasin made a wounded noise, and for an awful moment, Cae was afraid he was going to run. Instead, he shoved his chair away and slid to his knees in turn, gasping as he leaned his forehead on Cae's collarbone. Cae raised his eyes in mute relief, hands hovering over his husband's sides.

"Can I hold you? Do you want that, or—?"

"Please," Velasin whispered, and as Cae pulled him close, he clung to him and sobbed, his shoulders shaking violently. Cae soothed him as he might a grieving soldier, by breathing in deep and out again, the rhythm steadying both of them. Later, he could be angry, but right now, he was calm, calm, calm, and little by little, Velasin came back to himself, until his sobs were nothing but breath, and the only tears left were cold.

All at once, a terrible thought occurred to Cae. There were many things Killic might have done to Velasin, but there was one particular type of violation that would have lent a whole new level of agony to almost a fortnight spent on horseback in the immediate aftermath. It hardly mattered that his husband had already visited the infirmary; not even Ru Zairin would think to check for such an injury unless prompted to do so. "Velasin," he said urgently, voice twisting around the words, "when he hurt you—are you still hurt? Do you need healing?"

Velasin shook his head. "No," he said, softly. "He didn't . . . he spared me that, at least. He used my thighs. He tried—tried to have my mouth, too, but I wouldn't, so he grabbed my hand—"

He broke off, shuddering. Cae shut his eyes and held him as tightly as he dared, relieved beyond measure when Velasin hugged back. Steadily, the pressure of contact soothed them both, until they began to relax their grips on one another.

When Velasin shifted against him, Cae let the fingers of one hand ghost across the back of his head, tangling briefly in soft black hair before letting go altogether. Velasin swayed and knelt upright, breathing deeply as Cae pulled his own hands into his lap.

"Do you think we can start again?" Velasin asked in Tithenai. His voice was rough, but his face was light in a way it hadn't been before, and the change squeezed something deep in Cae's chest.

"I think we might," he said, voice raw. "After all, we are married."

"True," said Velasin. He took a shaky breath and said, "I'm

not . . . I don't think I can be a very good husband. But a friend, perhaps? Can we be that?"

"We can," said Cae, swallowing. "Friends, then?"

"Friends," said Velasin, and gripped the edge of the table, pulling himself to his feet.

This time, he didn't protest Cae's help in limping back to bed, though he still flinched at having his arm held, even briefly.

"Sorry," he mumbled, crawling under the covers. With the bedroom door open and the candle beyond it still burning, there was just enough light to illuminate his flush, and in that moment, he looked very young. "I don't mean to pull away, I just—"

"It's all right. You don't have to explain." Cae moved to his own side of the bed, uncertain of whether to get in or not. "Unless you want to, of course."

"Perhaps," said Velasin. "Are you going to lie down?"

"That depends on you, I think."

"Oh." He seemed to consider this, then blinked. "I . . . yes. You can—we can do that. Unless you'd rather—?"

"No, no," Cae said hastily, and slid back in before he could lose his nerve.

The bed was big enough that they weren't touching; nonetheless, there was an unequivocal intimacy to it, especially when Cae rolled on his side, so that they were facing each other.

Quietly, Velasin said, "Being held, or if my hands are grabbed—some part of me panics, since. Not every time, but often enough. Knowing I ought to be safe doesn't help. I just react."

"It happens, sometimes. When people—when you've suffered a particular thing, or witnessed something terrible, I think there's a part of the brain or heart, wherever the instinct lies, to fight or flee, that overrides mortal reason." He thought of the rabid bear he'd killed in youth, the way he'd jumped at shadows for months afterwards, but didn't speak of it, not wanting to risk insult by comparing Velasin's reactions to those of a child. "It should grow less, with time."

Should, Cae knew, was far from a guarantee. But though the more difficult implications had clearly occurred to both of them, they remained unvoiced.

Under Cae's watchful gaze, Velasin slowly fell asleep. It always amazed him, the way even the most agitated, battle-bloody veteran could drift off once the fighting stopped, and yet it happened with the regularity of sunrise. The spirit might protest, but the body still needed respite from its adventures, and after such an ordeal as Velasin had had—a series of abominable betrayals beginning in Farathel and continuing in Qi-Katai—Cae no longer wondered at his exhaustion, but marvelled that he'd endured so much despite it.

Velasin's face was softer in repose, though no less appealing to look at. Rather than play the voyeur, Cae rolled away and stared at the opposite wall, a sea of thoughts churning within him. Though he closed his eyes, sleep wouldn't come, and after shifting position for the fourth time in as many minutes, he realised abruptly that he was furious.

He glanced at Velasin, assessing. He seemed deeply asleep, but what if he woke and found Cae gone? What if he tried to hurt himself again? The sight of him weeping, a knife to his throat, had burned itself into Cae's memory, and the prospect of failing to prevent a reoccurrence of that event—or worse, being somehow the cause of it—made him shudder. But he also needed to trust Velasin, and if this was truly to be a starting point between them, then he couldn't begin the friendship by assuming it false. On his own account, too, he desperately needed to move; to expel the violent anger chewing, tumour-like, through his body.

Exhaling in a long, slow breath, Cae rose from bed and padded out into the receiving room. Having first found and hidden the knife, he pulled on a worn silk robe, grabbed a scrap of parchment, and penned a quick explanatory note to Velasin, saying that he'd gone for a walk to ease his thoughts, but would return before dawn. Ducking back into the bedroom, he set the note on his pillow, reassured himself that Velasin was definitely sound asleep, and headed out into the Aida, knotting the robe across his stomach.

As always, moving invigorated him. His anger surged with every step, clarifying into something clean and sharp, and by the time he reached Keletha's apartments, he felt as dangerous as he ever did on the brink of battle.

He knocked three times and waited. Like Cae, Keletha kept no personal servants, though in thir case, it was more because thei spent so much time travelling. Sure enough, it was Keletha who answered the door, alert despite the late—or possibly, now, early—hour. Thir brows rose in surprise.

"Tiern? Has something happened?"

"Of a sort," he said, tersely. "May I come in?"

By way of answer, Keletha stepped aside. Thir receiving room was smaller than his own, or else the proliferation of heavily laden shelves conspired to make it seem that way. Maps and charts were everywhere, and as he shut the door, Keletha waved at the space with an air of vague apology.

"It gets away from me," thei said. "I swear, when it comes to unchecked proliferation, books are worse than spring hares." And then thei frowned—though not, Cae thought, at him—and shook thir head. "Forgive me. My thoughts tend to wander at night. You're here for a reason, tiern. How may I serve you?"

"With honesty," Cae said. It would have been polite to sit. He didn't. "As an envoy, you're entitled to keep your secrets; required to, even. But in your capacity as a friend to me—as a scion of Clan Aeduria—I ask you for the truth."

He looked Keletha in the eye, took a breath—and promptly released it, realising belatedly that what he most wanted to ask (*Did you know it was rape, what Killic did to Velasin?*) would be an abominable breach of his husband's trust. He shook his head, angry with himself all over again for even considering such a betrayal, let alone thinking to ask such a pointless question of Keletha. Of course thei hadn't known; the idea that the envoy could've witnessed such abuse without outrage, let alone left Velasin to suffer through its aftermath in silence, was absurd.

Instead, Cae gritted his teeth and asked, "Do you know how marriage works in Ralia?"

"Yes?" said Keletha, clearly confused. "You know I do, tiern."

"Then answer me this," he said. "Why, in all your preparations, did you fail to consider that a man forced into obedience without consent—a Ralian man, with a Ralian concept of wedding nights—might come here in the terrified expectation of being raped?"

Keletha's mouth formed a horrified O of shock.

Cae's nails cut into his palms, voice low and furious. "You failed him, envoy. You failed him *badly.* He came here ready to die in preference to being forced, do you understand that? If I hadn't—" He looked away, overwhelmed by the terrible *almost* of Velasin's actions. To have woken too late—to have never known the *why* of it—the prospect chilled his heart. When he could speak again, he said, more softly, "I don't tell you this in blame alone, but to ensure that the error is never repeated. If King Markus is sincere in his desire to reaffirm friendship with Tithena—if my own marriage is seen to work—then we may well see more Ralian betrothals, and I wouldn't wish Velasin's fear of them on anyone."

At that, the rage went out of him, replaced by a sort of empty shock, as though his own belated terror had only just caught him up. He reached for the nearest chair and sat down heavily, watching in silence as Keletha withdrew a dusty decanter and two clean glasses from a nearby cabinet. Carefully, thei poured out two measures of what proved to be Ralian brandy, sweet and sharp as summer. Keletha claimed a second chair, and the pair of them sat in silence.

Cae drank gratefully, surprised by the strength of his agitation. Or perhaps it wasn't surprising at all, under the circumstances. He didn't know what to think, beyond sheer relief that he'd talked Velasin down.

Opposite him, Keletha toyed with thir glass, fingers tapping patterns on the rim before suddenly stilling. "Oh, *saints,*" thei breathed. "I truly am a fool."

"What is it?"

"The day we rode out, Tiern Velasin's jaw was bruised. I thought it an older injury, for the marks were faint, but the shape, the size and dispersal—they were likely fingerprints." Thei stared at Cae, their expression horrified. "All the way here, I thought his fear was incongruous, but what if Killic forced him? We saw so little, and they parted so swiftly . . . Saints, it makes sense of everything." Thei set the glass down with an angry thump. "What was I *thinking*?"

Almost, Cae was tempted to answer, but by the look on the envoy's face, thir internal self-flagellation was more effective than anything he could say. Instead, an altogether more useful thought occurred to him, and the more he considered it, the more correct it felt.

"Envoy," he said, slowly, "if what you saw was truly assault . . . you were there."

Keletha flinched. "Forgive me, tiern. I should have known; I should have stopped him—"

"No, that's not—I mean, of course, yes, if you'd realised, but that isn't—" He caught thir gaze and held it. "—Keletha, you were *there.*"

The envoy's eyes widened in comprehension. "The betrothal contracts. As soon as I entered vin Aaro's lands, Tiern Velasin had status as an Aeduria."

"Which means that *Killic,*" Cae said, spitting the name, "can be prosecuted fully under Tithenai law, assuming he ever comes here. And assuming, of course," he added, unwilling to confirm the accuracy of Keletha's guess, "that your theory is correct."

Keletha frowned. "The Ralian crown might extradite him, should you ask it, but that could prove a double-edged sword."

"Because it would be public, you mean?"

"That, and they'd be more likely to damn Killic simply because he prefers men in the first place than from any concern that he'd forced one."

Cae swore. "Those suppurating, stiff-necked—"

"Quite," said Keletha, dryly. "But in either case, tiern, I'd consult with your husband before taking any action on his behalf. He might equally resent the effort as thank you for it. And of course, I could be wrong." More softly, thei murmured, "Saints, I hope I'm wrong."

Knowing thei weren't, Cae drained the last of his brandy to hide his wince. "I should go to him," he said. "He was asleep when I left, but I dislike the thought of him waking alone." At Keletha's raised eyebrow, he added, "We have agreed to be friends, it seems. It's more than I'd hoped for this morning."

The admission left him feeling curiously vulnerable, though if thei noticed, Keletha gave no sign. Instead, thei saw him to the door, promising an envoy's discretion in all things pertaining to Velasin and Killic. Angry or not, Cae would never have spoken at all if he hadn't felt assured of Keletha's silence; nonetheless, he was grateful to have it confirmed.

With that, he left the envoy's apartments, padding quietly back to his own. The Aida was silent around him, slumbering in a predawn gloom. Passing the infirmary, he poked his head in to check on Markel, staying just long enough to confirm that the servant was breathing comfortably. Satisfied, he left again.

Outside his own rooms, however, he experienced a lurch of anxiety. What if Velasin had woken in his absence? But though the candle-stub still guttered on the table, Cae entered to find that his husband remained safely abed, sprawled in deep slumber beneath the covers.

Sighing with relief, Cae removed his robe and climbed in beside him. Velasin murmured sleepily at the minor disturbance, but otherwise didn't stir, and within moments, Cae, too, was asleep. His dreams were the usual faint nonsense, nothing disturbing, and as such, he slept well.

When he woke again, it was to Velasin shaking him, an urgent hand gripping his shoulder.

"What is it?" he asked, knuckling the sand from his eyes. And then, recalling the night's events, "Are you all right?"

"I'm fine, but it's not—something's happened." Velasin knelt by the bedside, a worried look on his face. "Tiern, it's your father. He was attacked last night."

Cae went cold all over. "*What?*"

"He's alive," Velasin said quickly, as Cae leapt out of bed, "and not too badly hurt, Kita said, but that's not the problem—or not the whole problem, anyway."

Cae stared at him, incredulous. "My father's attacked, and that's not the whole problem?"

"No," said Velasin, rising to his feet. He bit his lip, face pale. "The problem is that the one who did it claimed to be acting in your name. They said it was a message, tiern. The will of the Wild Knife."

Part Three

VELASIN

11

Though I hadn't yet met my father-in-law, I felt certain that gratitude was an inappropriate response to learning that he'd been attacked in his sleep. Nonetheless, I *was* grateful—not for the attack itself, as I bore Tieren Halithar no ill-will, but because I desperately needed to believe that Markel hadn't been stabbed on my account alone; and as the tieren was evidently being targeted by the same people who'd come after me, then whatever motivated them was, if still political, not uniquely personal. It was a selfish reaction to have, and I felt badly for it, especially given Caethari's distress; and yet the miracle was that I felt anything at all. For the second time in as many weeks, I'd tried and failed to die by my own hand, but where my first survival had left me numb with the terror of worse fates, the second felt like a kind of absolution.

Despite my actions the night before—or despite his, rather—I wasn't yet sure if I trusted Caethari; only that a part of me, at least, was prepared to try. Perhaps that made me a fool, and perhaps it made me an optimist, but however much I feared to live, I was more afraid to die. Friendship, in my Ralian conception of things, seemed a strange (though not undesirable) expression of husbandry, especially in my case, but lacking any alternative, I was willing to see where it took me.

As metaphorical as that particular destination might have been, Tieren Halithar's chambers were a decidedly literal one, and far more readily accessed. Not unsurprisingly, Caethari was in a hurry to do just that. Though he'd relaxed somewhat once reassured that his father's injuries were minor, he nonetheless began to dress with alacrity, heedless in his speed—or possibly more through habit—of any physical modesty. As he strode past me, snagging fresh clothes from a cedar chest, I found my gaze drawn to the hipwrap in which he slept, the thin, pale linen clinging to his golden skin in ways that left blessed-cursed little to the imagination. The night before, I'd been too distraught to care that he'd been virtually naked: now, though, it left me flushing. To my Ralian sensibilities, the hipwrap was essentially a skirt—albeit an impossibly immodest one—and therefore the sort of thing I'd never expected to see on a man. I was hardly a sexual innocent, and yet the contrast of his warrior's musculature with that flimsy, feminine-seeming fabric rendered me more dry-mouthed than if he'd been buck naked.

Which comparison, moments later, was put to the test when he disrobed entirely, setting aside the hipwrap as he donned a pair of nara: blended hemp trousers worn in Tithena with little reference to station or, it seemed, gender, such differences rather being reflected in the subtleties of style and fabric. Quietly flustered, I looked away until he'd finished dressing.

"Velasin? Are you well?"

I cast desperately around for some reasonable response—and, to my great relief, found one instantly. "Yes," I said. "It's just—I have no clean clothes." And I held out my arms, the better to demonstrate the creased, unpresentable state of the borrowed things in which I'd slept.

Caethari's expression went from startled to irritated to wry in less time than it took me to blink. "Damn!" he muttered. "I didn't even think to see where your saddlebags ended up."

"They wouldn't help much," I pointed out. "All I have is filthy, and it's little enough in the first place."

When I'd originally left Farathel—a departure that both seemed and was a lifetime ago—I'd packed barely any clothes: I'd been in a hurry to leave, eager to sacrifice my wardrobe for convenience, and was still stung enough over Killic's betrayal in any case that I'd seen little point in trying to dress fashionably. After trekking through the mountains to Qi-Katai, and with two pairs of breeches now ruined by bloodstains, I was left without even the basic comfort of familiar clothing.

"Damn," Caethari said again, and all at once, I was acutely aware of the fact that, having first kept the man from sleep with my dramatics, I was now keeping him from his father's side for far more frivolous reasons. I wanted to cringe from myself; my despair, it seemed, was not so easily shucked, but was rather intent on adapting. Though I thought it ridiculous, part of me wanted to sink into the floor.

"You should go," I offered, with a calm I didn't feel. "My wardrobe can wait, and you hardly need me there."

Caethari looked at me strangely. "Or you could just borrow my clothes. We're close enough in size."

I opened my mouth. Closed it again. "Or we could do that," I said, and stood there like a sunstruck mule as Caethari returned to the cedar chest and plucked out a pair of pale green nara, a cream loop-necked undershirt, and a sort of fitted tunic-vest, called a lin, to go over it all. I accepted the clothes, not sure if he expected me to change while he watched, or if the possibility that I might find this awkward hadn't yet occurred to him.

Seemingly, it was the latter: after a beat of silence, he made a small *oh!* of understanding and turned his back, which gesture, if not affording me total privacy, was nonetheless polite. With my freshly stitched and magicked leg still tender, I moved gingerly, fumbling with the unfamiliar ties of the Tithenai clothing.

"Can you manage?" Caethari asked. His head moved slightly, then stilled, as though he'd checked a native impulse to turn.

"Slowly, but yes," I grunted. "I'm sorry to inconvenience you—"

"You're not an inconvenience, Velasin. You're my husband."

"Many Ralian women claim that the one is synonymous with the other."

Caethari snorted. "That's because many Ralian women are married to Ralian men."

"As are you, tiern." I bit back a wince, weight resting on my bad leg as I pulled on the clean nara. Though the fit was a little loose, it was manageable.

"Isn't that a contradiction in terms?" Caethari asked.

"Isn't what a contradiction?"

"I would've thought this marriage was an utterly un-Ralian institution. Ralian men do not marry men of any persuasion; therefore, either you're not married to me, or you're not a Ralian man."

I don't know what possessed me to say it, except that the remark was there, and I was preoccupied enough with the undershirt not to think through the implications. "Maybe so, but as we're not married at all by Ralian standards, the question is moot."

"We're not?"

I faltered, only belatedly realising the trap I'd laid for myself. Striving to keep my tone offhand, I said, "In Ralia, a marriage isn't considered valid until it's been consummated. And as we, ah—well. Well."

"Oh," said Caethari, and even with his face hidden, I could practically *hear* him blushing. He drew an awkward breath, then said, "Still, that seems a secondary problem. If Ralian men can only marry women, then consummation should hardly make a difference."

"Point taken," I said quickly. "So which is it, then?"

"Which what?"

"Either we're not married, or I'm not a Ralian man. You can look, now," I added, self-consciously straightening the lin.

"I would've thought that was your—" Caethari turned, faltering slightly. "—decision." He looked me over, then murmured, "Though you certainly don't look like a Ralian man."

"Maybe I'm not one, then."

Caethari exhaled slowly. I didn't know him well enough to read his expression, though it seemed a curious mix of blankness and complexity. I studied him, trying to get a sense of the man. His eyes were a dark, rich brown, and deeply expressive, though what they were saying just then I had no idea; only that their softness stood in contrast to the sharper lines of nose, cheek, jaw. Yesterday, he'd been scrupulously clean-shaven; this morning, however, faint stubble was starting to show against his luminous bronze skin. He had an attractively martial build—powerful arms, broad shoulders, thick thighs and, though I'd been attempting not to notice it, an especially well-formed arse—but unlike any Ralian soldier I'd ever known, his hair was long, straight and ink-black, bound in a braid that fell over one shoulder.

For an absurd moment, I was tempted to reach out and tug on it, just to see how he'd react.

"Boots," I said instead, "just let me find my boots—"

I pulled them on quickly, ignoring the sting to my leg, and headed out into what Caethari had called the receiving room, relieved to find that, while I was still limping, it was neither unduly painful nor impossible to walk unassisted. Having no prior experience with magical healing on such a scale, I'd assumed whatever cantrips Ru Zairin had spoken over my wound in addition to thir stitching would be little better than Mirae's charm against infection. Evidently, I'd been mistaken.

"Wait!" said Caethari, as I reached the door. I halted, and he came up beside me, handsome brow slightly furrowed. "Your leg. Will you be all right?"

"I'll let you know if I'm not."

He nodded, but in a way that said that wasn't really what he'd been asking. "I don't know what's happening here," he said, looking intently at the door. "Why someone tried to kill you—why they're trying to kill my father. I've never been good at politics, and I've little patience for dealing with them. But I do mean to see you safe."

You already have. Even thinking the words made my stomach churn; there was no possibility of speaking them. I flexed my hand on the door, spent precious seconds trying to find something I *could* say, and finally settled on, "You might not be good at politics, but I am." Which was to say, I had a knack for navigating the cliques and factions, scandals and intrigues that constituted life among Farathel's young nobility—which, given its frequent overlap with the doings of court and the orders of the crown, was more or less the same thing. "We are married. And friends, or trying to be. And I—" It was my turn to falter, looking at him. "—I have a vested interest in this. If I can help, I will."

"I'll keep that in mind," Caethari said. "My thanks." He reached for the door handle, but paused, flashing me a curious look. "You said it was Dai Kita who brought the news?"

"It was."

"But she didn't stay, to give her report in person?"

"She offered to," I admitted. "But I—well. I wasn't sure of the etiquette, of whether I should let her in while you slept. These are your chambers. In Ralia, it wouldn't be done."

"Because she's a soldier, or because she's female?"

"Both, really." I hesitated, suddenly unsure of myself. "Did I do the wrong thing?"

"No, not at all. As my spouse, you have a say over who can enter our apartments, and when. It just didn't occur to me that you might not know that." He flashed me a rueful look. "Apparently, I'm not very good at being married."

The comment startled a laugh from me. "Don't worry, tiern. I'm hardly one to judge."

We shared a brief smile at our mutual incompetence. Caethari opened the door for me, and together, we headed out into the Aida.

12

To say that Tieren Halithar was annoyed by the attack on his life would be something of an understatement. He was *livid,* and to such an extent that, unlike and despite his visitors, he was yet to concern himself with dressing. Beneath a lavish silk robe, he wore nothing but a long blue hipwrap, and if not for the fact that I'd already seen Caethari wearing almost the same thing, I would have been scandalised. Yet even more undressed than not, it was impossible to see him as anything other than imposing—imposing and, though it flustered me to admit it, rather handsome, which was not something I'd ever expected to think of any in-law, hypothetical or otherwise. For all that he was in his middle fifties, he was still impressively fit, the whipcord musculature of his arms and torso evident beneath the robe. His grey hair, like Caethari's, was worn in a long braid, though where his son's reached barely past his shoulder-blades, the tieren's hung to his waist. It swished as he moved, like the tail of an angry cat.

"In *my chamber*!" he was saying—for Caethari's benefit, and possibly my own. "If I'd had my sword to hand, I would have gutted them!"

"We don't doubt it," Tiera Riya muttered, in the tones of one who'd already heard the same declaration several times and was starting to tire of it. The tieren ignored her, unselfconsciously running the fingers of his left hand along the length of bandage wrapping his right forearm. The wound, as Kita had said, was a deep, defensive slash, sustained when the tieren had blocked his assailant's knife strike. Otherwise, he seemed largely unharmed—a point which Caethari, on entering, had been quick to ascertain.

"But they fled?" he asked, frowning at his father.

"As soon as they missed their mark." The tieren scowled. "And no, before you ask, I didn't get a good look at them—they were all in black, hair covered. Nothing visible except their eyes, and it was dark enough that I only noticed the whites. Wretched cowardly, to try and stick me in my sleep!"

"What woke you?" Caethari asked.

"Damned if I know," said Tieren Halithar. "Instinct, if I want to flatter myself, but more likely overconfidence; getting in the way they did, they must've been incautious in the final approach."

"And what way was that?" Caethari gestured to the chamber door, which was as sturdy a thing as any man could want between himself and a potential assailant. "Not through the door, surely."

"Through the window," the tieren said grimly. "And seemingly without rope, despite how high up we are. I would've assumed some climbing trick, but once I came after them, they jumped off the sill and out like the drop was nothing. Startled me almost as much as the cut, if I'm honest—thought they'd gone straight to suicide. But when I looked down, they were already on their feet and running, and by the time anyone reached the ground outside, they were long gone." He glanced at the head of his personal guard, a stone-faced woman called (or so Caethari had whispered) Tar Katvi Tiru, who looked quietly furious at having had her perimeter so thoroughly breached. "You suspect they used magic, tar?"

"It's the most logical explanation," Tar Katvi grudged. "I'm no expert, but I've sent one of my people to Ruya's Order to ask about the possibilities." She shook her head. "An old commander used to tell a story about an adventurer friend who knew a cantrip to let him climb sheer rock, but I always figured it for a tall tale. Seems like I might've been wrong. Still doesn't explain how they got down so fast, though."

Tiera Laecia shot her father a look too laden for me to interpret.

"How strange, that your assailant was able to wring such usefulness out of magic."

"Indeed," Tiera Riya echoed, as dryly as her sister.

"Magic," the tieren snorted. Looking at me, he said, "I've never had much patience for it. Most of the time, it's years of study to learn a shortcut for something better done mundanely, but every so often, it sneaks up on you." He thumbed at his bandage again, then dropped his hand, glancing pointedly at Caethari. "Together with their invocation of your name, it makes whoever did this either exceedingly smart, or exceedingly stupid."

Caethari's voice was pained. "They truly claimed to be acting on my behalf?"

"'The Wild Knife sends his regards.' That's what they said, right as they jumped from the window. Couldn't even tell you anything useful about their voice; it was half-muffled in the first place, no distinctive accent, middle pitch. It could've been anyone." He glanced at Raeki, who stood stiffly to one side. "Your prisoner has divulged nothing of use, I take it?"

"No, tieren," said Raeki. He sounded furious about it. "He won't even tell us his name, which is making things considerably harder. If I had some idea of his background, where he's from, then maybe I'd know the right questions to ask, but so far, he'll only repeat the same thing he told Tiern Velasin's servant: that the Wild Knife and his followers won't suffer Ralians to live in Qi-Katai."

I felt the shift in attention like a physical current. In addition to Raeki, Tar Katvi and Tiera Riya, the room's other occupants were Keletha and Tiera Laecia, all of whom were staring at me. The tieren's gaze was heaviest of all. Looking at me, but addressing Caethari, he said, "I take it you married him, then?"

"He consented to have me, yes," Caethari replied. And then, with a breath that implied a degree of formality absent when we'd first entered, "I present my husband, Tiern Velasin Aeduria."

"Tiern," said both tars at once, and sketched me identical bows. Keletha's gaze was curiously intent, while Laecia looked me over with a quick, assessing scrutiny that made me feel like a horse her rival had bought ahead of her; which is to say, as though she were trying to establish what defects she might have inadvertently spared herself, the better to feel comforted. "Congratulations," she said mildly.

Riya shot me an amused look. "Welcome to the family."

"Welcome," the tieren echoed, a certain gruff fondness in his voice, which I assumed had more to do with his love for Caethari than any native approval of me. "I don't suppose you can shed any light on all this?"

I'd opened my mouth to deny that I could when something occurred to me. "Possibly not," I said, voice slow as I thought it through, "but—forgive me, tieren—am I right in thinking that the betrothal with my family was a secret?"

"Inasmuch as Qi-Katai has secrets, yes," said Tieren Halithar. "Certainly, the correspondence between your father and myself was largely private, though of course, those present here and certain other officials were informed of it when I wrote to Asa Ivadi for permission to proceed, including the Ralian ambassador in Qi-Xihan. Doubtless, rumour flared with Dai Kita's return, but otherwise, there was very little known." He frowned, as though only just seeing why this mattered.

"It's just," I said, with a sideways glance at Caethari, "originally, I wasn't meant to marry your son. Originally, I was meant for Tiera Laecia. And from what I understand, whoever might have known about the betrothal itself, *very* few beyond your family knew about Keletha's missive." I'd caught that particular piece of gossip while in the infirmary, as more than one of Ru Zairin's aides had been taken aback by the news that I was marrying Caethari. "Which begs the question: Was the decision to attack me in the Wild Knife's name made by someone who knew I was coming to *marry* the Wild Knife, or by someone who thought I was marrying his *sister*?"

Very quietly, Raeki swore, while Tieren Halithar looked equal parts angry and thoughtful. "Now, that *is* an interesting question," he murmured. "The alternatives change the implications considerably."

"How so?" countered Tiera Laecia. "If the stated goal is Ralians out of Qi-Katai, then striking at Velasin was hardly contingent on who he was here to marry."

"If the stated goal were truly as simple as all that, yes," Tiera Riya retorted. "And if our dear brother-in-law had been the only one attacked, then I might even agree with you. But attacking father—killing him, even—would hardly have removed Velasin. This isn't just about dislike of Ralia as personified by an individual, but about such politics as underlie his presence. That being so, and as they were determined to bring Cae into it in either case, then yes: who they thought he was marrying *does* matter."

Tiera Laecia glared at her sister. "Perhaps you're giving whoever did this too much credit. Perhaps they merely aimed to make a statement, regardless of any subtler implications."

"Possibly," said the tieren, breaking in ahead of his elder daughter, "but strategically, it makes more sense to assume an intelligent adversary than a foolish one. If the point—even secondarily—was to make you question whether your brother had killed your betrothed, then there's a clear intent to sow dissent in Clan Aeduria. But if Caethari was seen to have killed his *own* betrothed, then that message is of greater consequence to Ralia and House vin Aaro than to us. Do you see? Relations with Ralia suffer both ways, but in only one scenario is Aeduria actively divided against itself."

Tiera Laecia flushed at the rebuke, though I frowned at the tieren's conclusion. "Forgive me," I said, "but I feel I'm missing something. If Caethari is seen to want me dead in either instance, then why are his hypothetical actions only rendered divisive if taken against Tiera Laecia's betrothed, instead of his own? Would your matchmaking not be slighted either way, tieren? Unless—" I looked between Caethari and Tiera Laecia, Tiera Laecia and the tieren, took in the sudden discomfort exhibited by all three, and nodded my understanding. "Ah, I see. Because none of you *but* Tiera Laecia would believe him capable of it. Or at least, she might not think him capable of sabotaging himself, but would certainly fear him capable of sabotaging *her*."

A scowl appeared on the tiera's face, which, together with her deepening flush, told me I'd hit my mark.

Into the sudden conversational vacuum, Tiera Riya said, "Very well-observed, Tiern Velasin. You're a clever man. That being so, what *I* want to know is why you still consented to marry my brother—a man you'd never met, and had no reason to trust—after hearing him clearly implicated in the attack on you. I listened to Dai Kita's report of your journey here, and Keletha's, and Tar Raeki's. By all accounts, you were hardly eager; mostly, in fact, you seemed terrified. Yet here you stand, by my brother's side—in my brother's clothes, unless I'm mistaken—a married man, in seemingly no doubt at all as to Cae's innocence."

"Riya—" Caethari growled, but she forestalled him with a raised hand.

"I'm not trying to impugn your husband's judgement," she said, gaze still on me. "Only to follow his logic. I prefer to know where I stand with people—and where they stand in relation to me."

If the scrutiny to which I'd been subjected earlier had felt intense, it was nothing to how it seemed now. My heart began to pound; I stared at Tiera Riya, focussing on the details of her appearance—her bright eyes, a honey shade lighter than that of her father and brother; the intricate, upcoiled braids of her hair, meticulous even at this early hour; the elegant cut of her blue silk robe; the plain gold twists of jewellery adorning her at wrist, ear, throat—and tried to think of what answer to give, that was honest enough to be both helpful and believed. I couldn't possibly voice the full truth, which was that, as Caethari had kept me from suicide only last night, it didn't make sense for him to want me dead. All he would've needed to do was show me where to cut.

What I finally said, when I could bring myself to answer, was, "I didn't know, before coming here, that my betrothed was the fabled

Wild Knife, and by the time Markel—by the time my servant told me what his attacker had said, your brother had already aided me." I didn't trust myself to look at Caethari, but in that moment, I wanted to. "He was kind to me; I hadn't expected kindness. And after I collapsed in front of him—or after I woke again, rather—I thought, it would have been an easy thing, for the tiern to hurt me while I slept, had that been his intention. And if he'd truly wanted me dead before the marriage took place, why offer to marry me sooner? I am—" I sucked in air, squaring myself against the impenetrability of Tiera Riya's gaze. "—I am not so trusting a person, tiera, as you might imagine. But I am alive now, despite the many opportunities your brother was yesterday afforded to render me otherwise. That being so, why shouldn't I work from the assumption of his innocence?"

"Why not indeed?" Keletha echoed. "Respectfully, tiera, I feel that we're getting off topic. The issue isn't Velasin's trust, but the motives of those who attacked him."

"Just so," said the tieren, shooting Keletha an approving look. And then, abruptly weary, "Patient saints, I should've seen this coming."

"Seen what coming?" asked Riya.

"City factions, forming around the three of you." The tieren waved a hand to indicate his offspring. "Thinking to act in your names or in what they suppose to be your best interests, the better to curry favour with whichever of you they desire to see inherit the tierency. There was a little flutter of it when you and Kivali married—" He glanced at Riya, who looked first startled, then thoughtful. "—but I ought to have anticipated that a Ralian match would bring more and greater interest." He snorted. "In fact, I did consider it; but there was no sign of anything so serious brewing already."

"To that end," said Keletha, "I propose Tar Raeki attempt a new line of inquiry with his prisoner—reticent or not, his reaction to the question might tell us something useful—while Tar Katvi continues her investigation into how your assailant gained entry to the

Aida in the first place, leaving the rest of us to get on with our mornings. Unless anyone here thinks that news of an attack on the tieren will somehow be made less conspicuous by a break in our normal routines?"

Despite his sternness, Tieren Halithar looked vaguely amused. "As the envoy speaks, so shall it be. Go on, all of you; we've stood about talking long enough, and I've other business aplenty to attend to."

At this, both tieras looked equally outraged. "But father—" they began, then stopped in mutual horror at their synchronicity. Beside me, Caethari suppressed a snort, though poorly enough that his sisters noticed. Turning their glares away from each other and onto him, they swept from the room like a pair of wind-whips, leaving us mere mortals storm-tossed in their wakes. More sedately, Caethari offered a parting bow to his father—which I, still unsure of the etiquette, copied—and then we, too, departed.

"Come on," Caethari murmured, leading us down the hall. "Let's go and check on Markel."

I followed him readily, taking note of the various twists and turns of the mazelike Aida. Given its elevated perch at the centre of Qi-Katai, I wasn't sure if it was more properly a palace, a fort or a citadel; to my eye, it contained elements of all three. It was exactly the sort of massive, twisting, complicated space my childhood self would've yearned to explore, and I suddenly felt an ache for that boy, both sad and fond, that we'd ended up here in the least likely way imaginable.

Oblivious to my thoughts or possibly just lost in his own, Caethari picked this moment to say, "You should know, with Laecia—it's not that she hates me, or that she's unintelligent, or anything like that. But she competes with me, and what she can't bear is that it's a one-sided competition. Riya plays her games, but I never do—or not on purpose, anyway—and it frustrates her fiercely, though I've never really understood why. It's like—" He scratched at his unshaven jaw, square nails raking against the stubble. "—saints, I don't know—"

"She worries you think you're too good to engage with her," I said. "Tiera Riya might win the bulk of their exchanges, but she still sees Tiera Laecia as worthy of playing in the first place."

Caethari shot me a startled look. "Ruya's grace! You got all that from a single meeting?"

"More or less," I said, wryly. "But don't think me too great a savant. My brothers are much the same. Or were, rather," I amended, feeling the usual pang. "Revic always hated being the second son. He wanted what Nathian had—to be heir, to be respected—and always, *always,* he wanted to impress Father. So he'd try to compete with Nathian in everything, but most of the time, Nathian wouldn't rise to it. Of course, in his case, it was because he knew Revic really was better at most things and didn't want to look weak by losing—which Revic also knew, or at least suspected, and *that* just made him angrier." I smiled a little despite myself, though the feelings the memories stirred were bittersweet. "Denied the opportunity of taunting Nathian, he'd try to beat me instead."

"And did he succeed?"

"That depends on your definition of beating. Let's just say, I learned early on that appearing to lose by a narrow margin earned me more peace than winning by a large one, and acted accordingly."

"Hah! No wonder you're so practiced, then."

"Family is the best preparation for politics, tiern. Ask anyone."

"It seems I've married a cynic."

"Not cynical," I said, as we reached the infirmary. "Just realistic." And before Caethari could respond, I opened the doors and headed in.

Ru Zairin looked up as I entered, clearly relieved to see me. Like Mirae, thei had the kinky hair and dark brown skin that most commonly betokened Nivonai heritage; unlike Mirae, thir petal-shaped eyes suggested they also claimed some Khytoi blood. Though I'd run across both Nivonai and Khytoi in Ralia, they'd rarely been migrants or the descendants of same; transplants to Ralia were far more often Attovari or Palamites, all but the palest of whom were less easily distinguished as such at a casual glance. In Tithena, by contrast, there'd been sufficient friendly intermingling with Nivona and Khytë for long enough that, in a major city like Qi-Katai, there was far more diversity than I'd ever seen before. It was oddly wonderful, and though I'd come from a different place altogether, it made me feel just a little less alien.

"Ah, tiern!" the ru exclaimed. "Excellent timing—your servant is awake, but as I speak neither Ralian nor his signing-speech, I've been at a loss as to how to communicate with him."

Sure enough, I found Markel sitting up in bed, a pinched, worried look on his face that burst into sheer relief as I approached. A surge of emotion ran through me then: shame, that I'd ever countenanced my abandonment of him; relief, that he was awake and recovering; guilt, that I hadn't come sooner. I forced it all down as I sat beside him, clasping his hands and squeezing tight. He gripped me back, then released me in favour of signing, a rapid flow of words as he glimpsed Caethari.

"They said you were married yesterday. Is it true? Are you all right? Did he hurt you?"

I shut my eyes, overwhelmed by his concern, and shook my head. When I opened them again, I signed, "We're married, it's true. But he hasn't hurt me, and I don't believe he will."

"But he's the Wild Knife!" Markel's signs were emphatic. "The man who stabbed me worked for him!"

"No, he didn't. It was a lie."

"How can you know that? How can you trust in anything he says?"

"Because," I began, then hesitated. I didn't want to admit the truth, but of all people, Markel deserved to hear it. Taking a shaky breath, I signed, "Because I tried to die last night. I was afraid and weak, the way I was in Ralia, but he stopped me, just as you did. Why do that, if he wanted me dead?"

Markel made a scraped noise of distress. "You tried to die?"

I swallowed, startled to find myself on the brink of tears. "I'm sorry," I said—aloud, in Ralian, knowing Caethari could hear me. "I won't do it again. I was afraid."

"Your fear makes me afraid," signed Markel.

I had no answer to that; could only hang my head. But after a moment, Markel snapped his fingers, and I looked up again.

"Would you ask the healer how I am? Thei looked at me when I woke, but didn't say anything."

Nodding, I turned to Ru Zairin and asked in Tithenai, "How is he?"

"Very well, under the circumstances," Ru Zairin said. "The blade went beneath his ribs, but missed the major organs. A flesh wound, though an inconvenient one. I'd recommend he stay in bed for the next couple of days at least—I'll be giving him regular poppy for the pain, of course, but he won't have to sleep through it all, and I know some cantrips that will help to speed his recovery."

Though Markel, of course, had heard all this, I went through the show of repeating it in Ralian. He nodded comprehension, looking equal parts tired, annoyed and resigned, and I realised, with a fresh surge of guilt, that I wouldn't be able to stay with him: even without the threat of attack, I was newly married, new to the Aida, and needed to learn my place here for both our sakes.

From over a decade's companionship, I knew that, though Markel was largely at peace with his muteness, still he found it frustrating, as anyone would, to be shut out of conversation. In Farathel, at least, like me, he'd had a small circle of friends who understood and made room for him, but my marriage had stolen his life as surely as it had severed me from mine. For all that he'd made light of it on the journey here, insisting that his friendships could be maintained by correspondence, I saw now how fully he'd been set back—put among those to whom his muteness was not only new, but who, thanks to me, assumed him ignorant of Tithenai, too.

Caethari came to stand at the bedside, hesitant as he glanced from me to Markel. And then, in Ralian—and to Markel, not me—he said, "We have some Ralian books, in the Tierena's Library. A few novels, even. I could have the librarian bring them to you, if you wanted."

We both froze, completely taken aback. After a moment, Markel regained enough composure to nod, eyes wide as he signed at me, "Did you ask him to make that offer?"

"I didn't!" I signed back.

Markel digested this information. He looked at Caethari for a long moment, studying him, looking for any trace of mockery or insincerity in his words. But there was none to be found, and when he realised this, Markel nodded again, put his right palm flat to his heart, and bowed to the tiern, inasmuch as his injury allowed him to. It was a small, awkward gesture, but deeply felt, and Caethari must have sensed that, for he didn't laugh at it. "I'll have one of the librarians bring you a selection, then."

Switching back to Tithenai, he turned to me and said, "I imagine . . . that is, I assume you'd like Markel to stay in our apartments? I'm not trying to preempt you," he said hastily, at the likely stunned expression on my face, "but if I'm to have the second room made up for you today, it would make sense to have the servants' chamber reassembled at the same time, too. Just in case."

"Just in case," I echoed, faintly. "Yes, I would—please. I would like that."

Caethari nodded, looking unaccountably self-conscious. "And, ah . . . the signing, that you do? The hand-language? I, well. I understand if it's a private thing between the two of you, but as we're to share space, I would—if you could teach me a few signs, at least, for ease of use, I would appreciate it."

"I—yes. Of course, I—"

Markel snapped his fingers twice, and I broke off to look at him.

"Tell him I speak Tithenai," he signed, a fierce light in his eyes. "Tell him I'll teach him myself, if he wishes. And anyone else who asks."

A lump rose in my throat. I nodded to Markel, took a moment to compose myself, then said to Caethari, "May we speak privately?"

"Of course," he replied, a worried crease between his brows. With a parting nod and a murmured *excuse us, please* to both Ru Zairin and Markel, he led me back out to the hall, ushering me through to a small, unoccupied room adjacent to the infirmary. Though the lingering scent of dried flowers said it had once been used for herbal storage, it was now furnished with two small sleeping cots, a wooden desk stacked with basic amenities for writing and personal hygiene, and several shelves of medical texts. As such, I took it for a space held in common use by Ru Zairin's assistants during busy shifts, though as suggested by the fine layer of dust, it wasn't much required at present.

"We won't be overheard in here," Caethari said, pulling the door shut. Light came in from a high, square window set in the opposite wall, though I didn't know what it looked out on. He made as if to step close to me, but stopped himself, fingers flexing at the aborted motion. Worriedly, he asked, "Have I offended you?"

"Gods, no!" I shook my head. "I just—I wanted to tell you, quietly, that Markel understands Tithenai. Though I'd take it as a kindness if you kept that to yourself, for now. It's just, people tend to speak freely around him, and after the attack on your father, it could be quite useful."

Caethari looked momentarily startled; then he laughed. "Remind me never to underestimate either of you. But, ah. Thank you for telling me."

Belatedly, I realised my own tension. "You're not angry?"

"Do I seem angry?"

"No, but you—" I gulped, fighting a sudden urge to fidget. "Many would be, in your place." And though I tried to suppress it, I found myself remembering Killic's anger on learning that Markel could understand him perfectly—anger he'd been quick to couch in terms of his own embarrassment at having so often ignored him, but anger nonetheless. I didn't speak his name, but something in my expression must have betrayed me. Caethari looked minutely furious, but his voice was soft as he asked, "Killic?"

I didn't answer; which was, in its own way, answer enough. He hissed a breath, looking away from me. After a moment, he said, in that same, soft voice, "I could have him arrested, you know. If you wanted."

I jerked my head up, staring at him. "What?"

"He'd have to be in Tithena, of course," Caethari said. "But technically, you were already bound to Aeduria when he assaulted you, by right of betrothal and Keletha's witness. That makes him subject to our laws. I just. I thought you should know. It's an option."

All the breath went out of me. If the room's sole chair had been readily accessible, I would've sat down; as it was, I swayed a little, resting my hand on the wall. Very badly, I wanted to cry—and moons, but I hated the impulse; I felt as though I'd scarcely stopped weeping in weeks. I wasn't moved by fear or grief or pain, nor even relief, but had rather been scraped so thin by their recent excesses that tears, it seemed, had now become my first response to any strong emotion.

"I'll consider it," I croaked.

Caethari looked pained. "I'm sorry. I shouldn't have brought it up like that. Did you, ah." He inclined his head at the door. "Did you want to go back in with Markel? You can do that, I'll just—I'll see about the rooms, the library—" And he started to move past me, back towards the door.

Without thinking, I grabbed his arm, halting him. "Caethari?"

He inhaled sharply, staring at my hand; I pulled it back, and found my gaze locked with his.

"I—thank you," I said, feeling myself flush. "For the books, for Markel. For—for speaking to him directly, instead of through me. Most nobles—most people, even—they don't bother to do that. They assume he's dim-witted, or they don't see the point, because he can't speak back. We'd both be glad to teach you his signs. They're . . . they're useful to know."

"I imagine so."

All at once, the room felt too close. "We should go back in," I said, mouth dry.

"You go ahead," said Caethari, sounding equally rough. "If you're—if you don't mind, I have duties to see to, and other things, but I wouldn't keep you from him—"

"I won't stay all day, I know I need to learn the place—"

"You can find me at any time, the servants will know where I am—"

"I don't want to get in your way—"

"You're not in the way, Velasin, saints!—"

We both broke off, which is how I realised that, despite my protestations, I'd been drifting closer to him. I jerked away, shocked, and before I could further distress or incriminate myself, I fled back to the infirmary and the safety of Markel's bedside.

13

I wasn't surprised when Caethari didn't follow me, though despite his kindness—or perhaps because of it—I was also slightly relieved. He flustered me badly; I didn't know what to make of it. That Markel trusted him—that he'd *given* Markel a reason to trust—was utterly unprecedented: in all the years he'd been with me, not a single nobleman had ever asked to learn his signs nor spoken to him directly, as an equal, without first being prompted to do so. That Caethari had done both on his own initiative said more about his character than any other consideration he'd yet offered, and as such, it came as no shock when Markel signed, "He seems like a good man."

"I think so," I replied; and yet I also worried at how easily the appellation came. Last night, I'd chosen to believe in Caethari's goodness instead of dying, such that now, in daylight, I badly wanted that trust to be justified by more than my own raw need. The idea that I might be mistaken in him was intolerable, but I'd been betrayed too badly—and too recently—to ignore the possibility. Markel's acceptance of him shook me, because I trusted Markel's assessment of him more than my own; and yet I couldn't escape the fact that Markel's trust was based, in part, on my own reassurances.

Was Caethari truly a good man? Or had my own low standards rather served to elevate a simple kindness to the status of an extraordinary one? That he hadn't raped me—had rather, in fact, expressed horror at the concept—was surely the lowest possible standard to which any partner might reasonably be held. Likewise, the fact that he hadn't let me die didn't mean he was someone I could happily live with; only that I was alive to make the distinction. His treatment of Markel counted for something, as did his willingness to let me have my own space in his apartments, but ultimately, I barely knew the man.

And yet, I was married to him. I couldn't go back to Ralia or my family, and even if the option had been available to me, I was beginning to realise that I no longer wanted to. Caethari was my husband, and if ours was to be a functional, friendly relationship, then to some extent, I *had* to trust him, or else remain perpetually fearful of the alternative. But I was still trapped; that I'd gone willingly into the cage—that I found it more hospitable than expected, even—didn't change my inability to leave it. And without that freedom, I couldn't ultimately *choose* to trust anything about my situation, because the choice itself was an illusion.

Abruptly, I regretted telling Caethari that Markel could speak Tithenai. It had been an unquestionable advantage, and now it was lost forever. Yet for Markel's sake, I couldn't regret agreeing to teach him signs: regardless of my trust, Caethari was one more person for Markel to talk to who was willing to talk to him, and as such, the loss of my privacy was no loss at all, when weighed against Markel's gain.

All this passed through my head in the time it took Markel to shift position, wincing as he resettled himself on the mattress. He was lying down again, but his head was propped up with an extra pillow, and it was only then, when I looked around to see where thei had got to, that I noticed the absence of Ru Zairin. Following my gaze, Markel snapped his fingers and said, "Thei went to get breakfast. For both of us, I think." He hesitated, then asked, "The man who stabbed me—if the Wild Knife didn't send him, who did?"

I answered in signs, explaining the new attack on Tieren Halithar,

Raeki's investigation into the culprit and everything else of note that had been said in his absence. When I was done, Markel thought for a moment, then signed, "It feels like we're back in Farathel."

My mouth twisted wryly. "There is that sense of familiarity, yes. Though people in Farathel weren't often trying to kill us."

Markel's ironic expression mirrored my own. "Not often, no."

Behind me, the door creaked open to readmit the absent Ru Zairin, thir wiry arms laden with a large tray of breakfast things.

"Ah!" thei exclaimed, on seeing me. "Tiern, hello—I wasn't expecting you back, or I'd have brought more food. Though please help yourself, by all means."

The tray's contents did smell tempting—at a glance, they included several hot, savoury bread rolls, two cups of spiced milk and a selection of unfamiliar sliced fruits—but as I had no wish to deprive either Markel or the healer of their repast, I shook my head and stood.

"My thanks, but I should be going," I said in Tithenai. "For starters, I intend to find out what's become of our horses and saddlebags; I'd hate to think of any of them being lost or mistreated."

"Very good, then." Ru Zairin set the tray on thir desk. From the little I'd seen of thim, Ru Zairin struck me as being a precise, efficient sort of person. I gauged the healer to be in thir middle forties: thir close-cropped curls were peppered with silver, while laughter lines marked thir mouth.

"If you're hungry," thei said, "I'd recommend stopping by the lower kitchens and introducing yourself to the cook. Ren Valiu is always keen to feed newcomers; knowing her, I expect she's already set something aside for you, just on the off-chance."

"Thank you," I said, oddly touched by the remark. And then, to Markel, in Ralian, "You'll be all right alone?"

Markel grinned. "I'll be fine," he signed. "Go learn your way around."

With a parting bow, I did just that, departing the infirmary in search of the stables. Having taken the route only once before, and from the opposite direction, it took me some time to retrace my steps. Though I passed several guards and servants, I didn't ask for help, wanting to try and get my own sense of the Aida, and as none of them challenged my right to be there, I assumed that word of my appearance, presence and marital status was already circulating. The realisation was disconcerting in its familiarity: I'd been known in Farathel, too, and the more Qi-Katai and its politics reminded me of the court, the more I felt, if not at home, then certainly in my element.

Which was not, of course, the same as feeling—or being, even—safe.

When I finally reached the courtyard into which I'd initially ridden with Caethari, I took a moment to orient myself. The open space faced west, and so was cast in the Aida's shadow, though gold limned the tops of the gated stone walls that faced down onto the city. The flagged stones were smooth and symmetrical, the space stretching out in either direction like a wonky rectangle: to my right, it eventually narrowed into a slim path cutting between the Aida and the outside wall, while to my left was a cluster of buildings, the stables chief among them. Even at a distance, I could smell the faint, betraying waft of leather polish and fresh hay, manure and horse-sweat. I headed there at once, hopeful that Quip and Grace had been well-tended.

The stables, like everything in the Aida, soon proved larger and more complex on the inside than the outer façade made clear. They occupied three distinct levels: a storage loft above, a main stable on the ground floor, and then a secondary, underground level accessible via a sloping ramp in the floor, the open space above it fenced off with a wooden rail. I stared down at it, not having encountered such an arrangement before, and so was caught slightly off guard when a middle-aged groom approached.

"Can I help you, tiern?" he asked.

"Hopefully, yes," I said, and explained about wanting to look in on our horses. "I don't know where Grace went," I said, remembering how Raeki had ridden in holding Markel, "but there was a groom, a young woman, who took charge of Quip, along with a grey palfrey."

A flash of panic crossed the groom's face, though he quickly smoothed it away. "Was the groom so high"—he raised a hand, indicating a height approximately level to my breastbone—"with a freckled nose? Wearing red and grey livery?" As distinct, I assumed, from his own red and black.

"I don't recall what her nose was wearing," I said, unable to help myself, "but otherwise, yes. That sounds about right." Not that I'd paid her much notice, having been far more concerned with Markel, but I remembered her height, or her lack of it.

"Ren Vaia Skai," said the groom, with a tense expression. "She's not part of the Aida's general staff; she's in personal service to Yasa Kithadi Taedu. The grey palfrey is the yasa's own mount." He lowered his voice, as though fearful of being overheard. "I heard she was wroth with Vaia, for letting the tiern take her horse. I doubt either one of them will be very pleased to see you."

Now, that *was* interesting. I was still coming to grips with Tithenai honorifics, which were just distinct enough from their Ralian equivalents to feel somewhat alien, but yasa was a rank even higher than tieren, being closer to a duchess than anything else. If this Yasa Kithadi was resident in Qi-Katai, it spoke to something complicated that Tieren Halithar was the one in charge of the city. Had we been in Ralia, in the absence of other evidence, I'd likely have attributed the discrepancy to the yasa's gender, but this was Tithena, where women clearly occupied any number of roles denied them in my home country. And besides, the groom was scared, which he wouldn't be if Yasa Kithadi were truly some defanged snowcat.

"I take it the yasa and the tieren don't get along, then?" I asked.

"You could say that," the groom hedged. "It's more that—well.

Not wanting to speak ill of Yasa Kithadi"—meaning, he wanted to speak ill of her very much indeed, but feared the consequences of doing so—"it's just that she's . . . *particular* about her horses. Very particular. And it's easy enough for *her* to say no to a tiern, should the need arise, but Ren Vaia could hardly have done it—not that Tiern Caethari's an unreasonable man," he added hastily, eyes widening at the potential slight to my husband, "but it's, well—it's his rank, you know, and Vaia's very young—"

"I understand," I said. "I'm not looking to get the girl in trouble. I just want to know where my horses are."

The groom licked his lips, clearly pained. "I think the yasa took them, tiern. To her own stables, at the Little Aida."

"The Little Aida?"

"It's, well, it's the yasa's residence now, though it used to be Tierena Inavi's, before she left, which is part of why Tieren Halithar mislikes her being there, if you'll excuse the gossip. It's connected to the Aida proper by that covered walkway behind the Triple Gardens—have you seen them yet, tiern?" I shook my head, unwilling to disturb the flow of information, and the groom went on, "Well, they're hard to miss, if that's where you're headed; not that you couldn't just head through the horseway, mind, but the yasa tends to look upon that as a liberty if it's not for stable business."

I blinked. "The horseway?"

He waved a hand at the ramp leading down to the lower level. "It's a sort of road, tiern. It cuts beneath the Aida—or between the lower cellars, at any rate—so's we can move riders and horses about discreetly if there's a siege, or day to day, so's we don't have to take the long way 'round the walls. I think it had some fancier name to begin with, but we all just call it the horseway."

"Right," I said, and promptly latched on to an even more pressing mystery. Used as I was to Ralian women being summarily excluded from the business of their husbands, and understanding that many married nobles kept separate quarters, it hadn't struck me as odd that Caethari's mother had been absent in the aftermath of the attack on Tieren Halithar. Now, though, it seemed I was missing something important. "Forgive me, but did you say that Tierena Inavi *left*?"

"Yes, tiern?" The question seemed to puzzle him. I took this to mean my startlement was more Ralian than I'd realised, and so tried again.

"This would be the tiern and tieras' mother?"

"Yes, tiern."

"And she's, what—" I tried to conjure some suitably plausible reason as to why a powerful matron might vacate her home and family. "—on a pilgrimage?" Such excursions were popular among Ralian noblewomen. Shrines and temples dedicated to the moon goddesses Riva, Asha and Coria were common destinations for those who wished good marriages for their daughters; those seeking aid for or intercession with their own husbands prayed to the Lord Sun; and any prayers for sons and brothers went to the First Star, heir to the Lord Sun's heavenly kingdom. (Where and how Ralian women worshipped on their own account had always been somewhat opaque to me; Sky was the mother of the Lord Sun's children, but as it was her scandalous love of the Lord Sun's brother, Earth, which had produced both humankind and the natural world, the Doctrine of the Firmament endorsed no temples to her; and if any existed regardless, I didn't know of them.)

But then, I recalled belatedly, the whole question was moot in any case, as Tithena didn't follow the Doctrine of the Firmament. The moons were different gods for them—I'd been married under their auspices only yesterday—but whether that faith included pilgrimages, I had no idea.

Seemingly not, if the baffled look the groom gave me was any indication. "No, tiern," he said, eyebrows creeping up of their own accord. "She just moved on, when she and the tieren divorced."

My mouth hung open for several seconds before I thought to close it. "I see," I said, though I didn't see at all; wanted nothing so much as to pepper the man with questions. But I didn't, because even had the poor groom been an appropriate target for my curiosity, his increasingly twitchy body-language betrayed his anxiousness to return to the duties from which I'd kept him, though as I was still an unknown quantity, he was doubtless too wary to say so.

I had no purse on me, nor any Tithenai currency; nonetheless, I felt it polite to offer him something. "May I ask your name?" I said, and inwardly cursed when the question made him tense.

"Ren Taiko Arith," he said, nervously.

I offered him a slight bow. "My thanks, Ren Taiko. I have no coin to hand, but if you stop by the lower kitchens this evening and tell Ren—" I struggled to recall the cook's name. "—ah, Ren Valiu that I sent you, I'll be sure she saves you a bottle of whatever you like best."

Taiko's eyes bugged. "My sincerest thanks, tiern, but a whole bottle—it's too much, surely!"

"Then consider it gratitude in advance for taking good care of my horses, once I've returned them to you. And of course," I added, as an afterthought, "I'll be certain not to tell Yasa Kithadi who sent me in her direction."

This time, Taiko's relief was palpable. He bowed low and deep, and I felt the satisfaction of having made an ally. "My thanks, tiern," he said, and at my nod of acknowledgement, he promptly returned to work.

I cast a final, longing glance at the entrance to the horseway—I'd certainly have to make time to explore it—and headed back out to the courtyard. Based on the fact that Ru Zairin's bread rolls had still been steaming when they reached the infirmary, I judged that the lower kitchens must be quite close by, and so returned in that direction, nosing about the unfamiliar halls until I found the common mess, which led directly into Ren Valiu's domain.

The cook, when I found her, proved to be a sensible, curvaceous woman somewhere in her late thirties; her head was shaved to fine dark stubble—"The better to keep my hair from the food!" she said cheerfully, noticing my double take—and her right arm was tattooed from wrist to shoulder, a single, continuous portrait of water and water-creatures intermittently stamped with spindly black glyphs.

"May I ask—?" I began, but as with my interest in her lack of hair, she'd clearly preempted the question.

"Spent ten years as a merchant fleet cook," she said, proudly. "These"—she tapped the glyphs—"are trade symbols for different ports; got one for each I visited. See this?" She indicated a mark like a divining rod with a bar beneath the fork. "That's the mark for Aroven, in Ralia. Never did make it as far upriver as Farathel, but—" She sighed, smiled. "—you can't have everything!"

"I've visited Aroven several times," I said. "The docks and markets there were always wonderful."

Ren Valiu laughed. "That they are, tiern! But here, now—you look half-starved! What with all the uproar last night, nobody's had time for a proper breakfast, but I've set aside plenty of jidha, just in case. Come, help yourself!"

As she steered me towards a tray of the same savoury rolls Ru Zairin had been carrying—they were still hot, despite the hour, as she'd kept them aside in a warming oven—I decided I liked the cook immensely. The jidha proved delicious, filled with a mix of (Ren Valiu said) red bean paste, anise and rabbit gravy, and though I didn't know exactly what was meant by this last ingredient, I couldn't deny that the overall effect was wonderful. Seeing my appreciation, Valiu swiftly presented me with a cup of spiced milk—called khai, I learned—to wash it down, which beverage proved equally to my liking. If not for the matter of the missing horses, I might well have lingered in the kitchens for some time; as it was, however, I regretfully declined the offer of a third jidha, and passed on the promise I'd made to Ren Taiko.

"I hope that won't inconvenience you," I said, "but as Yasa Kithadi apparently has my saddlebags"—which contained, among other things, the promissory documentation that enabled me to access my sinecure from any of several banks—"there wasn't much else I could give him."

Valiu shot me a respectful look. "Not at all, tiern," she said. "It was an offer well-made."

Warmed by her approval as much as the khai, I asked for, and was given, a set of easy directions to the Triple Gardens and the Little Aida. There was already a certain native mischief to Ren Valiu's round face, but it shone more readily when she said, "The yasa is an interesting person. She'll either love or loathe you, but it won't always be obvious which is which."

"That sounds ominous," I said dryly.

Ren Valiu only laughed.

Thus fortified, I followed her instructions, exiting the common mess via a different door than the one through which I'd entered. A quick walk through a switchbacking hall—or as quick as I could manage, with my stitched-up leg still throbbing—soon brought me outside again, revealing a central garden surrounded by the Aida on three sides. Following a cobbled path around the northwest border, I passed the section of greenery designated the Triple Gardens—so-called, Ren Valiu said, because its three sections grew herbs, fruit and flowers, respectively—and fetched up at the same covered walkway that Ren Taiko had mentioned. The Little Aida was at the end of it: a lonely, hexagonal structure that seemed at once too stocky to be a tower and too tall to be anything else. The stables lay at the eastern edge, separated from the Little Aida by a neat, square courtyard with a central fountain and bordered on the other side by an open stretch of lawn. The grass was rich and green, but for all it was clearly well-tended, it was also haphazardly dotted with small pink wildflowers, the kind Ralians called kideyes and which Tithenai called sika, though I'd always known them as weeds by any name.

So why were they growing here?

It was a minor thing to wonder about, perhaps, but if years of dealing secrets in Farathel had taught me anything, it was never to underestimate the significance of small incongruities.

As I approached the main door of the Little Aida, a liveried servant in black boots, grey nara, white undershirt and red lin came hurrying out to meet me. She was short, curvy and quite beautiful, her wide, dark eyes emphasised by a pair of lacquered black spectacles, though I put her age at little older than twenty. Her black hair was sun-streaked brown in places, the pronounced, springy ringlets suggestive of a midpoint between Mirae's tightly kinked curls and my own loose waves. Her skin was a gleaming warm brown, darker than the more common Tithenai shades of gold and bronze, though not necessarily Nivonai, and when she smiled, her teeth were white and perfect.

"Tiern Velasin!" she said. Her voice was warm, deeper than I'd expected. "Welcome! We didn't expect that word would reach you quite so soon."

"I'm sorry?" I said. "Word of what? I came in search of my horses."

"Oh!" She looked genuinely surprised. "Our runner didn't find you, then?"

"Your runner?" I asked, bemused.

She ducked her head prettily; indeed, she was such a natural beauty, I began to suspect she could hardly have done otherwise. She radiated a sort of clever joy, and though it made me inclined to like her, it also put me on my guard, if only because she wasn't what I'd expected. *Like the flowers,* I thought, and dutifully filed away the comparison.

"My apologies, tiern," she said. "I've come at this all backwards. I'm Ru Telitha Kairi, sworn in service to Yasa Kithadi Taedu." She offered me a small, polite bow.

I blinked, struggling to rework my notion of her status. Not a servant, then, but a scholar, for all that she wore her patron's colours. Then something Ren Taiko had said clicked with an earlier comment of Caethari's, and I lit up with sudden understanding.

"You're in charge of the Tierena's Library," I said. I'd meant it as a question, but it somehow came out a statement, and Ru Telitha's smile became a grin, as though I'd performed a sleight-of-hand trick at the dinner table.

"I am," she said, "though the yasa considers it *her* library, and was rather upset at Tiern Caethari's decision to offer your body-servant *her* books without prior consultation."

Possibly it was a slip, and possibly it was a direct insult; or more likely, I realised, it was Yasa Kithadi's insult in Ru Telitha's mouth, though whether it was meant maliciously or in mere speculation by either of them was unclear.

"Markel isn't my body-servant," I said, politely. "He's ostensibly my valet"—I used the Ralian word, and noted her clear comprehension of it—"but before that, he's my friend."

It wasn't an admission I'd often made in Ralia, given the scarcity of people who'd have either sanctioned or believed it. Nonetheless, it was true, and had only grown more obviously so since we'd crossed into Tithena, where such distinctions were seemingly enforced in different ways, in accordance with different logic.

"Oh!" said Ru Telitha again, but where her first such exclamation had been unfeigned, this time, the artifice of it was clear. And more, I judged, was *meant* to be so: the insult had been a test—of my comprehension; of my temperament; of the truth of the rumour; it hardly mattered which—and by her acknowledgement, Ru Telitha let me know, not necessarily that I'd passed (which verdict, I suspected, was the ultimate prerogative of her mistress), but that I hadn't failed.

For a moment, the clean air over Qi-Katai tasted distinctly of Farathel's heat. I almost laughed.

"Please pardon any offence," said Ru Telitha, brown eyes bright.

"None taken," I replied. "After all, it's hardly a new error." I let that hang a moment, then said, "May I assume, then, that as you were evidently expecting me, Yasa Kithadi has requested that I present myself?"

Ru Telitha nodded. "If you follow me, I'll take you to see her now, and you can discuss the question of Ralian books."

I considered pressing the issue of the horses, but decided it would do me little good at present. Instead, I touched two fingertips to my forehead—a Ralian bow to a scholar, which she also seemed to recognise—and gestured for her to lead me onwards.

"It would be my pleasure."

14

Often as children, before Nathian finally declared himself to be too old for it, my brothers and I played seek-me through the Aarobrook estate. We all took turns as seeker, and in keeping with my established code of self-preservation, I usually let Revic and Nathian find me with relative ease while being sure to delay my finding of Revic especially. If they noticed this consideration in me, however, my siblings had none for each other: it maddened Nathian how consistently Revic eluded him, while Revic managed to be both a bad winner *and* a bad loser, gloating in triumph and petty in defeat.

Thus it was that, during one such game in early winter, when they'd spent the whole afternoon bickering over who was best at it, I finally lost my patience and determined to prove them both wrong. With Revic as seeker, I took myself off to a hiding place I knew he'd never found before, settled in, and waited. Unbeknownst to me, however, Revic found Nathian almost instantly, and the resulting fistfight saw them both corralled and punished by Father, who was too angry at their misconduct to ask why they'd been fighting in the first place. As such, my own absence went unnoticed for hours. I don't know how long I remained in hiding; only that I stayed put long after I'd realised that the game was over. The winter cold sank into me, chilling my core, and yet I refused to move, convinced in some obscure, childish way that, if I went inside, I'd be conceding to my brothers forever.

By the time I was finally discovered—my brothers didn't know my hiding place, but my favourite groom did—I was blue with cold, completely hypothermic. When I woke from the subsequent delirium, it was to find my father sitting anxiously at my bedside, face creased with a worry he seldom let me see. At his insistence, I coughed out the whole story, though I could barely speak. The effort was such that I passed out again almost instantly, but in the space between dreams and waking, I heard Father whisper, "Yours is a strange and stubborn endurance, Velasin." And then, more softly still, such that I might almost have imagined it: "Just like your mother's."

A strange and stubborn endurance. The words might have been a prophecy, for they never quite ceased to be relevant: not in my childhood, and certainly not to my adult self. I'd recalled them often over the years, and as Ru Telitha led me into Yasa Kithadi's receiving room, where my leg twinged hard enough that I nearly stumbled, I heard them again as if spoken.

"Are you quite all right?" asked Yasa Kithadi, eagle-eyed. She was a slim, tall, sharp-featured woman somewhere in her sixties. She wore the bulk of her long silver hair in the same sort of single braid as Caethari and the tieren, with smaller, more complicated braids around the crown of her head—though what that might have betokened, I didn't know—while her weathered bronze skin spoke to many years spent outdoors. There was something instantly familiar about her, though I couldn't place it; and in any case, I was distracted.

"I'm well, yasa," I said, but sat down fast and gracelessly when she waved me towards a chair. I flexed my leg a little, wincing at the pull in the stitches. It was hardly a sizeable wound, but the arrow had sunk deep in the muscle, and since Tar Raeki had pulled it out, I'd not exactly lain idle. I'd asked Ru Zairin about the possibility of using magic alone to close the wound in place of stitches, but thei'd looked at me with a scholar's indulgent weariness for a layman's questions and said that, in this instance, stitches would be preferable. Rather than explain any of this to Yasa Kithadi, I gave the thigh a demonstrative pat. "Just a little sore."

Her sharp gaze narrowed, and from the corner of my eye I saw

Ru Telitha pull up a chair and sit, listening intently. "Ah, yes. The bandits. You were attacked at Vaiko, I believe?"

"We were. A dawn ambush."

"I hear you killed two men."

"I did," I said. My voice stayed calm, but my pulse jumped. "With a pitchfork."

"A pitchfork!" Her fine brows arched. "How very *innovative.*"

"That's one word for it, certainly."

"I also hear," the yasa said, choosing to ignore this remark, "that prisoners were taken?"

"Three prisoners, yes."

"And that a retrieval squad was sent for them, oh, three days ago?"

"I believe so."

"And that Tiern Caethari wonders if their attack is connected at all to the one on your servant?"

"I—what?"

Yasa Kithadi smiled. "You didn't know?" she asked. "He thinks that both attacks—or all three attacks now, presumably—might have a common factor. Not that it's an especially strong suspicion," she added, as offhandedly calm as if she hadn't just twisted a knife in me, "but it's strong enough that he's ordered the Vaiko prisoners be brought to the same guardhouse as your man from the Amber Gate."

"He hasn't mentioned it." *But he could have.*

Yasa Kithadi waved a hand. "Doubtless he thinks it a premature conjecture."

"Doubtless," I echoed, hollowly.

It was a weightless moment, like being submerged in deep water. I looked at Yasa Kithadi—at the twist of her mouth, neither soft nor satisfied; at her slate-pale, unreadable eyes—and as if such epiphanies were a reflex of self-preservation, I suddenly understood why she looked so familiar.

"Now," she began, "about your servant—"

"You're Envoy Keletha's sister," I blurted.

Yasa Kithadi paused on an inhale, head tilted as if to confirm that she'd heard me correctly. Now that I'd noticed it, her resemblance to Keletha was so striking, I wondered that I hadn't spotted it instantly.

"Yes," she said, slow and regal. "Keletha is my kinthé." The Tithenai word for a kem sibling. "And my elder, too, though only by half an hour."

"You're twins?"

My surprise was oddly delightful to her; she laughed, pure and pealing. "Do you not have twins in Ralia, Tiern Velasin?"

"We do, yasa, though I've met very few"—I opted to gamble on flattery—"and none so fascinating."

She snorted, amused. "Were that not so manifestly true, young man, I'd take you for a sycophant."

My mind raced, steadily piecing a theory together. I was conscious of Yasa Kithadi watching me—and Ru Telitha, too, though with greater speculation and less intensity than her mistress—and realised we'd reached the brink of yet another test. Meeting the yasa's gaze, I said, "It seems a curious thing to me, that envoys have no titles and discard their family names."

"It marks them as equals to everyone," said Yasa Kithadi, "the better to negotiate equally."

I bit my lip; I was missing something. In Tithena, it seemed, primogeniture was much more a guideline than a requirement, and certainly not circumscribed by gender. If Keletha had willingly renounced thir noble status—if thir title had passed to Yasa Kithadi—then why was Tieren Halithar still the ruler of Qi-Katai?

Unless, of course, the city had never belonged to the yasa at all. *But if her territory lies elsewhere, then why is she resident here? It can't just be proximity to Keletha, and anyway, Ren Taiko said the Little Aida belonged to the tierena first.*

But the tierena left . . .

I stared at Yasa Kithadi, watching her watch me. There was something decidedly feline about the whole business, as though we were poised on the brink of a conflict that might just as easily dissolve as culminate. Frustrated, I resisted the urge to fidget. In Farathel, the answer would've been obvious, because I understood how Farathel worked. But in Tithena—

The problem hit me like a slap.

"Forgive my dullness, yasa," I said. "I seem to be very Ralian today."

She laughed at that, another genuine sound. "You can hardly help it, tiern. Though I'm curious to hear why you think it relevant."

"Because it makes me miss the obvious; or at least, what's obvious in Tithena."

"Such as?"

"Such as the fact that titles, descent and marriage don't always work the way I expect them to." I took a breath and gambled again. "Divorce is rare in Ralia, and the process becomes exponentially more complicated the higher the ranks involved. Before I heard it mentioned, it would no more have occurred to me to think the tieren divorced than to assume his mother-in-law would remain in a place his wife had willingly left."

Almost imperceptibly, Yasa Kithadi stiffened. "And yet, it seems, you've thought exactly that."

"Am I right, yasa?" She didn't reply, but her expression told me everything. "You're Tierena Inavi's mother." And therefore Caethari's (and Riya's, and Laecia's) grandmother. Which also made Keletha their grandkiun, assuming I had the terminology right, but in the moment, I was far more interested in where Yasa Kithadi's power actually lay.

"Inavi is my only child," the yasa said, voice steady. "When she married Halithar, her children became heirs to my domain as well as his, though as she never held the title of yasa herself, my grandchildren cannot claim it by birth alone; only by named inheritance or, if none is named, by majority approval of the Conclave." Which meant, though she didn't say so, that there could only be one such inheritor. "And as she joined Clan Aeduria instead of bringing

Halithar into Clan Taedu, she was never called yasera once she married; only tierena. But when she *divorced*"—her jaw clamped on the word, eyes flashing with old anger—"the contracts stipulated that she rescind her born title, so that it couldn't be transferred to any other spouse or children she might subsequently acquire, but would remain in trust for her Aedurian heirs. Halithar, of course, was *gracious* enough to let her continue to call herself tierena, and she was *gracious* enough to accept."

Yasa Kithadi's voice dripped with sarcasm, but for Tierena Inavi as much as Tieren Halithar, and I found myself wondering exactly what had caused Caethari's parents to separate, that the yasa was the only person I'd met so far who seemed angry about it.

A tic worked in her jaw. "Inavi has since remarried—some middling man of middling rank, supposedly kind and comely enough—I've never met him and never wish to—but has borne no further children, which is doubtless a sort of mercy." She snorted. "She may yet do so, of course—she's not quite old enough for it to have passed beyond possibility—in which case, I'll have a new headache to contend with."

I waited to hear more, but when she remained silent, I realised she was expecting me to draw my own conclusions.

"The tiern and tieras," I said. "They're not just Tieren Halithar's heirs. They're yours."

"For all the good it does me," Yasa Kithadi muttered, though less bitterly than expected. "I *asked* Inavi to name an official heir before the divorce, when she still had the authority, but she wouldn't do it; she said her children were still too young for her to make a proper decision. And I said, if they're really so young, then don't leave them! But off she went, and now I'm stuck with the damned responsibility."

Carefully, I asked, "Is it really such an onerous chore?"

The yasa shot me a pitying look. "Are you really so stupid, tiern?"

"I might be wiser," I shot back, stung, "had I more information to work with. I've scarcely been here a day, and yet you expect me to understand how everything works, what all this means to you. And I'm trying, yasa," I said, belatedly lowering my tone, "but as I said, it's not always obvious."

For a long, tense moment, the yasa said nothing. I'd almost forgotten Ru Telitha entirely, she was so silent. Then Yasa Kithadi blinked and sighed, as though I were a wilful child consistently failing a simple lesson.

"You are, I suspect, being Ralian again," she said. In her mouth, the word *Ralian* felt like a synonym for *stubborn,* or possibly *backwards.* I might have objected to that, if the judgement had been less accurate. "What do you think my being a yasa entails? What do you think we *do*?"

Sensing another test, I said, "What do I think other yasas do? Or what do I think *you* do? Because, Ralian or not, it seems to me there's a difference."

Yasa Kithadi's smile was hard and, very faintly, approving. "Clever boy," she said. "My primary holdings are in Ravethae, though I also own property in Qi-Xihan." The capital city, of which I knew virtually nothing beyond its name. "I administer from here as best I can, though my people are capable enough. And if I declared an heir tomorrow, I could go straight home. But not with a clean conscience." She sat back in her chair, hands folded, and raised a challenging eyebrow. "Now why is that, do you think?"

I glanced at Ru Telitha, her face carefully schooled to blankness, and for the first time, it occurred to me to wonder at her inclusion in our conference. I didn't fully understand what being ru meant in Tithena: it was a scholar's rank, not a noble one—though it could be held by nobles—and entailed a certain amount of respect, particularly within their field of study. But even though we'd strayed from the ostensible topic of books and libraries without ever really touching on it, Yasa Kithadi had neither asked Ru Telitha to leave nor indicated discomfort with her presence.

Firmly setting that mystery aside for later, I returned to the question she'd posed me. Why wouldn't Kithadi name an heir? What did I know about her? Only that she seemed as angry at her daughter as she did at Tieren Halithar—

Oh.

"You won't name your heir because the tieren hasn't named his. You're both—" I stared at her, sickly fascinated. "Moons, it's a stalemate, isn't it? You're each of you waiting for the other one to die, so the one who lives can choose without contest, or without—wait." I held up a hand, head spinning with the implications. "*Can* the one person inherit both titles, theoretically speaking?"

"Theoretically, yes," said Yasa Kithadi. "But it doesn't happen often, and both the Conclave and Her Majesty Asa Ivadi tend to dislike it when it does, because it makes things . . . complicated, shall we say. Especially in an instance such as this, where the two clans involved aren't just titled, but the hereditary heirs to potentially conflicting responsibilities." At my inquiring look, she elaborated, "Clan Aeduria has governed Qi-Katai for several generations by royal fiat, while Clan Taedu has a confirmed, inheritable seat on the Conclave, which has authority over certain aspects of governance, both nationally and within the capital."

"Complicated indeed," I said. "And you don't want that?"

"Neither of us wants that," the yasa said, sharply. "Not for preference, anyway. But that doesn't mean we won't do it rather than lose our candidate."

"But if one of you dies without a named heir, the legal default is primogeniture, correct?"

"Assuming nobody mounts a challenge, yes."

"So you can't be fighting over the right to name Tiera Riya, or there'd be no point: even if you outlived the tieren, he'd still get his way in death, because she's the eldest, and vice versa. Which makes her, what—your fallback option?"

"That's one way of looking at it," said the yasa. "The other is that we both think she's competent, a good choice in either instance. We both want her to inherit something, and we don't mind who from."

"But she's not your first choice," I said, slowly, "because you each have a favourite." I swallowed. "The *same* favourite?"

"Now *that,*" the yasa declared, "is the real question, isn't it? Neither of us can hide how we feel about Riya, but as for Caethari and Laecia—well. I know who I favour, and I think I know who Halithar favours, but neither of us is sure. Which makes things rather difficult, you see? Because if we truly favour the same person, then our stalemate is entirely sensible: our two first choices are each assured an inheritance, and whoever lives longest decides the distribution."

I inhaled sharply. "But if one of you wants Caethari, and the other one wants Laecia—"

"—then in saying so, we'd be effectively disinheriting Riya, and neither of us wants to do *that,* either."

"Moons, what a mess." I rubbed my temples, trying to wrap my head around the various permutations. "You won't name an heir and risk Riya losing everything, but you won't name Riya and risk your favourite losing everything, either."

"Quite," said the yasa. "And thus, I'm stuck."

"With the greatest possible respect, yasa, you're betting that a healthy man more than ten years your junior is going to die first. That seems like a fairly skewed gamble."

The yasa snorted. "Halithar acts as if he's still a buck of Caethari's age, which is hardly conducive to his longevity, and as Ru Zairin could tell you, women who survive their childbearing years tend to outlive men, especially if we're not married to one. Which, being widowed, I'm not," she added, with a certain dark smugness.

My brain, which was struggling to process this wealth of new information, made a sudden belated connection. "And last night, someone tried to kill the tieren in his son's name—ostensibly because of me, clearly because of wider political problems, but also—very conceivably—because of your dispute over choosing an heir?"

"Very conceivably," she agreed, her tone abruptly weary. "Ayla's blessed arse, but I'm sick of this nonsense!"

I let out a strangled laugh. "And here I thought you asked me in here to talk about books."

"Oh, *books.*" The yasa waved an irritable hand. "Saints, boy, this was never about *books,* I just needed a pretext! Telitha can take your man as many books as he wants, once I'm done with you."

"And is that why you took my horses, too?"

"Do I look like a horse-thief?" she countered. "Of course it was! But the books were, I thought, a much better excuse, for all that they're not what brought you here."

My stomach gave an uneasy lurch. "And may I ask *why* you wanted to see me, yasa? Or why, at least, you felt the need to disguise your reason for seeing me?"

"Because," she said, and though her gaze was intense, her voice was almost gentle. "You've been dropped into the middle of this without any notion of what it means, and as Caethari has a tendency to try and pretend the whole matter away—and as you're now a material piece on the board, so to speak—I thought you deserved an explanation."

Suddenly, my earlier conversation with Caethari made a great deal more sense. If Laecia was aware that the two of them were in direct competition for an unassured inheritance—if she understood that only Riya was guaranteed anything—then it was small wonder that she might think him capable of sabotage. After all, she was third and youngest of her siblings, a position with which I was intimately familiar, and yet possessed of a temperament closer to Revic's than my own. Caethari was her Nathian, the elder brother whose disinterested refusal to engage only made her more determined to prove herself; which left me to be like Riya, or Riya to be like me, the pair of us sufficiently secure in our respective intellects and futures to engage the other two without fear of failure.

It was a neat analogy, and therefore a treacherous one. I was in no danger of overly associating Nathian with Caethari—the obvious differences aside, I hardly wanted my husband to remind me of my brother—but likening Laecia to Revic and Riya to myself was the sort of thing that could easily get me in trouble. I didn't know either woman, but if I lapsed into thinking I understood them *fundamentally,* I put myself at risk of presumption, ignorance, false security. And regardless of whether the attack on me—or was that *attacks*?—had truly resulted from anti-Ralian sentiment or wider politicking, I couldn't afford to think sloppily.

"My thanks, yasa," I said to her, bowing from the waist. "This has all been very enlightening."

"I should hope so," she said, dryly. "And now, Tiern Velasin, if you don't mind, I'll leave Ru Telitha to show you to your horses—assuming, of course, that you trust her to choose some books unsupervised?" I nodded, and she clapped her hands in dismissal. "Excellent! Off with the pair of you, then."

Carefully, I rose from the chair. My leg felt much better for the rest, and within a few steps, I was almost walking normally.

At the door, however, I stopped and turned. "May I ask a final question, yasa?"

Yasa Kithadi looked up. "You may."

"The groom who loaned your palfrey out, Ren Vaia Skai—did you truly punish her?"

Her gaze narrowed. "I did."

"For letting the tiern take your horse, or to make my coming here seem more plausible?"

"Neither," she said, abruptly cold. "I punished her because Silk is *mine,* not some courier's rouncy, and yet Vaia saw fit to ride her without permission. Not that I owe *you* an explanation."

"My apologies, yasa," I said, bowing again, but Yasa Kithadi had already turned away in disgust.

Unable to quite decide if knowing the truth was worth the loss of the yasa's goodwill, I followed Ru Telitha back through the Little Aida, which was somewhat easier to navigate than its counterpart, and out to the stables. Sure enough, I found that both Quip and Grace had been well-tended, their tack polished and oiled, and our saddlebags, as best as I could tell, left unmolested. Not that they'd contained much of value, but it was a relief to find my promissory documents intact, as money was one of the many things I was yet to discuss with Caethari, and I disliked the thought of being rendered wholly dependent on him.

At my request and Ru Telitha's instruction, two liveried grooms were promptly dispatched through the horseway to deliver both mounts and tack into the care of Ren Taiko, which left me to deal with the saddlebags. Rather than entrust them to a servant, I slung one over each shoulder, grunting in slight amusement at my resemblance to a pack mule, and turned to face Ru Telitha.

"Markel will read almost anything," I said, in answer to the unasked question, "but he's very fond of adventure tales and myths, if you have any."

Ru Telitha smiled. "I think we just might," she said. She moved to take her leave, but hesitated, just as I'd done with Yasa Kithadi. "Forgive my curiosity, tiern, but the signs you speak with Markel—did you invent them yourself, or are they an existing language?"

Combining the note of genuine interest in her voice with both her title and knowledge of Ralian, I made a leap. "I take it you're a scholar of languages, ru?"

"And customs, yes. I studied in Irae-Tai, at the university. I did hope to learn in Farathel, too, but I understand that female scholars aren't much prized in Ralia."

"They're not, I'm sorry to say."

Her eyes crinkled. "Ironic, given my interests."

"Ironic indeed. And to answer your question, no, I didn't invent our signs. We, ah—" I hesitated, wondering how much I had the time or inclination to divulge, and finally settled on, "—we taught each other. First from a book, which was difficult, and then with the help of a fishmonger, which was . . . instructive." And a highly redacted version of things, besides.

Telitha looked at me as though she couldn't quite decide if I was joking. "A *fishmonger*?"

I sighed. "It's a long story. But the book we initially used was called *The Fivefold Tongue,* by Adoryc Lillain—he was an Attovari monk turned explorer, I think, but he wrote in Ralian."

"I know his work!" Ru Telitha said, excited. "I've read his treatises on the development of trade-languages in the Rhysic Straits, but I didn't know he'd written a book on signs! Do you still have it, by any chance?"

"I think I might, actually. Or at least, I did. But I don't know if it's among the things being sent to me here, or if—" I swallowed, a sudden lump in my throat. "—if it will survive the journey." Or even begin one in the first place. Though Markel had entrusted our list of possessions to Lady Sine, I could easily imagine Father intervening to ensure that they never reached us at all, preferring to sell or dispose of anything I'd touched.

Unbidden, I pictured Father breaking into my rosewood chest in pursuit of valuables and being confronted instead with various tools and materials meant to aid in a litai's pleasure. The image was so horrifying that it almost looped around into being comic. Almost. I felt myself freeze at the prospect, some deep well of shame I hadn't known was in me boiling up like sediment stirred from a lakebed.

I'd been silent too long, I realised abruptly, and with a wrench of will, I turned my attention back to Telitha and said, with forced cheer, "But if it does turn up, you're welcome to borrow it—though I warn you, it's hardly a perfect guide to what Markel and I speak. Adoryc tried his best, but it doesn't really, ah . . . it's hard to describe in text."

"I can imagine!" Telitha flashed another dazzling smile, then stepped back and bowed. "It's been a pleasure to meet you, Tiern Velasin. I look forward to seeing what Ren Markel thinks of my books." And with that, she turned and left the stables, leaving me to resettle the saddlebags on my shoulders.

Simultaneously relieved of old burdens and laden with new ones, both literal and figurative, I headed back to the Aida. This time, to sate my curiosity, I went through the horseway. The downward slope of the entrance ramp was tough on my leg, while the uneven weight of the saddlebags further complicated matters, but I judged the inconvenience worth it for the novelty. As promised, the horseway was a straight, paved tunnel that cut a straight line beneath the Aida, being both wide and tall enough for three armoured riders to pass abreast, and in that sense, it was fascinating. Even so, it wasn't long before my thoughts turned inwards again, spiralling back to the problem of Caethari.

Much to my churning irritation, I realised I needed to have a proper conversation with my husband, and soon. As things stood, I didn't even have a key to our apartments—though in fairness, I hadn't yet seen them locked—and while we'd talked a lot about my instability, our respective families and Markel's good health, we'd scarcely exchanged a single word of practical use to our cohabiting future. Annoyingly, I was forced to acknowledge that this was far more my fault than his—Caethari, after all, had been willing to talk from the outset, and had only refrained from doing so in deference to my grief. I wanted to be angry at him for failing to mention his theory about the Vaiko bandits being linked to Markel's stabbing, but there, too, rationality prevented it: between my trying to die and the attack on Tieren Halithar, I could scarcely claim he'd had ample opportunity. And after everything Yasa Kithadi had done to conceal her interest in me, it wouldn't have been fair to accuse him of failing to warn me on that count, either.

Maybe I can be angry at him for not giving me any legitimate reasons for anger, I thought, not without a certain bitter irony. It wasn't even a subtle problem: if I'd truly been able to blame Caethari for something, it would've helped to counterbalance my trusting him, thereby lending the latter emotion a greater air of objective legitimacy. Instead, the fact that he'd done nothing obviously wrong had the paradoxical effect of making me worry that he really had, and I was just too foolish to see it.

I indulged in these thoughts until I finally exited the horseway, trudging up into the stables by the same ramp I'd seen earlier. Though the saddlebags were truly starting to weigh on me, I stopped to check that both horses were being cared for, and was happy to find Ren Taiko in the process of currying Quip. We didn't speak, but I offered him an approving nod, patting Quip's nose as he whuffled softly into my palm, before heading off again.

By the time I'd navigated my way back to Caethari's apartments, I was exhausted. Once in the receiving room, however, I found a trio of servants hard at work restoring the servants' chamber and the guest suite—or my room, as it now was—to a habitable state, which mostly seemed to involve moving furniture to and fro, and arguing about where everything ought to be stored.

If there had only been one servant in the apartments, I might have been too wary to relax. Instead, the fact that there were three of them—and that two of the three were women—proved strangely reassuring. Murmuring something about resting my leg, I went through into Caethari's room, dumped the saddlebags on his clothes chest and collapsed onto the bed, where I fell instantly and very deeply asleep.

I woke again to the sound of frantic knocking. Bleary and disoriented, I sat up and called out "Yes? Who is it?" before I'd even fully opened my eyes.

"It's Dai Kita, tiern."

"Kita?" I struggled to my feet, relieved that I'd been too tired to undress, and opened the door to her. "What is it?"

Her expression was somewhere between furious and frightened. "Tiern, I'm so sorry, we don't know who, but there's been—we're looking for whoever did it, but you should, you should come—I don't know what to say—"

"Show me," I said, my stomach leaden with dread. Kita had been less flustered when telling me of the attack on Tieren Halithar; whatever had happened now must be truly awful. She led me through the Aida at pace, and when we emerged into the courtyard—I'd slept into the late afternoon, the setting sun bathing the stone in orange-gold light—I saw there was a crowd in front of the stables. I could hear crying inside, and the panicked snorting of horses, and the closer we came to the source of both sounds, the sicker I felt.

With Kita beside me, I entered the stables. Beyond the ramp to the horseway, Ren Taiko knelt by a spreading pool of blood. He was sobbing into his hands, and I knew then what I was going to see, yet couldn't seem to stop myself from looking.

"I'm sorry, tiern," Ren Taiko choked out, the words a watery hiccup. "I failed you, I failed him, I'm so, so sorry—"

The blood was Quip's, his sweet head tacky with it. His throat had been slit, his body left to lie on the floor of his open stall. The sight numbed something in me, or maybe I'd been numb already, but it was several long seconds before I could raise my gaze high enough to see what had been scrawled—in Quip's blood, of course; what else would such a person use?—on the wooden wall behind him, the written Tithenai dark against the wood:

FIRST THE HORSE. THEN THE RIDER.
—THE WILD KNIFE

15

I went to my knees, unable to do otherwise. I felt like I was unravelling, the skein of myself spooling out and out, until there was nothing left. Of its own volition, my hand settled on Quip's nose, stroking the velvety skin, a horrible echo of the last, unknowing pat I'd given him. I was crying, I knew that, but silently, as though my tears were completely divorced from the rest of me. Distantly, I was aware of Ren Taiko's wailing apologies, of Kita leading him away, of other figures coming to look at my dead, beloved horse, but none of it truly registered.

"Tiern, please." It was Kita again; she must have come back, though I didn't know when. "Please come away."

"He didn't deserve this," I said. I was cold all over, utterly immobile. "He was a good horse."

"Yes, he was. But tiern, you should get up—"

"It's all right, Kita." Caethari's voice, low and warm. "You help with the grooms. I'll stay with him."

"Of course, tiern." The relief in her tone was evident. I heard vanishing footsteps, and then she was gone again.

Caethari crouched down beside me, just outside the spread of blood—which had, I realised belatedly, ruined yet another item of clothing. He stayed there for a moment, statue-still in the edge of my vision. "Velasin?" he asked, softly.

Perhaps it was just that he'd already seen me in a far worse state and could therefore be under no illusions as to my lack of stoicism, but something in his tone broke me. I looked at him, unable to keep my voice from cracking.

"I raised him from a foal. Seven years, he was mine, he brought me safe through the mountains, and now—"

"I'm so sorry," he said, and put a hand on my shoulder. A gentle touch, not a presumption, offering only what I consented to accept. Even so, I didn't mean to lean into him, but my body seemed to have other ideas, the desire for comfort as reflex as my tears. Boneless, I buried my face in Caethari's neck and clung to him, thinking dimly, *What else are husbands for, if not this?*

He shifted to his knees and sighed, his right hand lightly cupping the back of my head, the left a bare, warm pressure against my ribs.

"I don't have anything left," I said in Ralian, the words small and muffled against his shoulder. "What else can they take from me?"

It was a rhetorical question, but though Caethari didn't answer, my own paranoia had no such compunctions. *Markel,* it whispered. *They could still kill Markel. Or maim you, or rape you, or send you back to Killic, or Father—*

I must have whimpered, for Caethari made a soothing noise, thumb stroking against my scalp. "We should get up," he murmured. "Can you rise?"

I wasn't sure that I could, but I nodded anyway. He helped me stand, then hesitated, as though he didn't know whether to keep ahold of me or let go. Craving contact even at my pride's expense, I clung on, pressing close. Accepting this, Caethari looped an arm around my waist and walked me out of the stables, back through the courtyard and into the Aida, not stopping until we reached his apartments, where he promptly steered me into a chair. I sat gratefully, faint and sick.

"Can I get you anything?"

"No," I said—in Tithenai, this time—and then amended my answer. "Maybe some water?"

He quickly obliged me, filling a glass from a convenient pitcher. I gulped it down, and as I wiped my face on my sleeve—or his sleeve, rather; I was still wearing his clothes—I realised I'd stopped crying.

"Thank you," I said, setting the glass on the table. I took a deep breath, probing my own emotions. "I . . . I think I'm all right, now." Or as all right as I could be, under the circumstances. I didn't wish to belittle Quip, but no matter how much I'd loved my horse, his loss couldn't grieve me more than Markel's wounding had; nor my own, for that matter. Or maybe I was just too tired to feel the full scope of what I'd lost, Quip's death a spectre yet waiting to haunt me.

That last thought had the feel of truth. I was fatigued in every sense: I had no outrage left to tap, and so lay fallow for future grief, my heart an unsown field.

Caethari made a relieved noise, hands moving distractedly over the furniture as he paced the receiving room.

"Zo's balls, but I don't understand this!" he said. "There's no consistency to it, no logic. If this is some anti-Ralian coalition at work, then I must say, they've got some fairly strange priorities."

I considered this statement and was surprised to find I agreed with it. "You're right," I said, blinking up at him. "The attack on me, that was public, open, committed by someone zealous enough that they didn't care if they were caught and competent enough that they almost succeeded. The attack on the tieren, though—that was covert, tentative. He was much harder to access, which suggests the assailant should've been more skilled, but they missed their stroke and fled instantly, didn't bother to stay and fight. *They* cared about being caught, I think. And Quip—"

I bit my lip, using numbness as an excuse to consider the matter. Caethari waited me out, until I finally said, "Quip makes the least sense of all. Killing a horse, that's a scare tactic and a, a—" I fumbled for the Tithenai word, then settled on the Ralian. "—a de-escalation. A step down," I added, at his look of incomprehension.

"A step down?" he asked. "What do you mean? A step down from what?"

"I mean that they've gone from attacking the tieren in his own chambers to killing a foreigner's horse. Doesn't that seem odd to you? Lesser crimes usually precede greater ones, not the other way around."

His eyes lit with understanding. "You mean de-escalation," he said, and I nodded to acknowledge the Tithenai term. "That's . . . a very good point, actually." He raised a curious eyebrow. "It's also not something I'd expect someone who's neither soldier, guard nor magistrate to think of."

"Farathel is an interesting place," I said, dryly. Caethari laughed, but as he didn't press the question, I judged the comment had had the desired effect. (Though from the look he shot me, I suspected he knew that, too.)

"Your grandmother," I said, changing the topic, "thinks this all has something to do with inheritance politics."

"You've met my grandmother?" he said, startled.

"She arranged an introduction earlier today," I said, wryness creeping into my tone of its own accord. "She thought I might appreciate knowing about her battle of wills with your father as to who'll inherit what."

Caethari grimaced. "Saints, I hope she's wrong. Bad enough to live with that wasp-nest hanging over my head; the last thing I want is other people poking it with sticks."

"She also said you thought that the bandit attack might be related to all this, too."

I said it carefully, gauging his reaction, but there was nothing in the way he frowned and raked his hair that suggested he'd intended to keep it a secret. "I don't think it's *likely*," he admitted, "but it's certainly possible. I don't want to rule anything out until I know for sure."

"What I don't understand," I said, refusing to feel relieved, "is why whoever this is—this group, or the person behind them—keeps bringing you into it. I mean, if this were just about me, my presence in Qi-Katai, then I can see a certain logic in claiming to act on your behalf. But attacking the tieren? Killing my horse? Why would the Wild Knife sanction either action? And more, how can they possibly think that *we'd* believe it?"

"And here I thought you were smarter than that," said a wry voice from the doorway.

Both of us jumped, staring in shock as Tiera Riya let herself into the room. She was dressed in riding clothes, her expressive mouth curved in exasperation. Plainly, she'd overheard some of our conversation, but how much, I didn't know. I made a mental note to ask Caethari if, in fact, there was such a thing as a locked door in the Aida.

"You have a theory, sister?" Caethari asked, recovering quickly.

"I don't have a *theory,*" the tiera scoffed, leaning against the sideboard. "I have an *observation.* And what I *observe,* little brother, is that the pair of you are missing the obvious."

"Which is?"

"That Velasin shouldn't trust you."

I stilled, not sure if her words were a threat or warning; Caethari, though, looked furious.

"You really think I'd hurt him?" he growled. "You honestly believe—"

"Oh, for the love of Zo's sainted ballsack!" she snapped. "I don't mean that you're *dangerous,* Cae—I mean that he shouldn't *know* that, let alone trust it!"

"He—what?"

The tiera made a frustrated noise. "Try and be rational for a moment, would you? Velasin arrived yesterday. He doesn't know you—he doesn't even know this *country*—but he knows the Wild Knife fought against Ralians, and after what happened to Markel—after what happened to Father, even—he's got several compelling reasons to be wary of you. By all rights, finding his horse dead with your name on the wall ought to have sent him running in the opposite direction; at the very least, he should be wondering if you're involved, if he's safe, if he can trust any of us. But *instead*"—and here she glared at me—"you let my brother comfort you—let everyone *see* him comfort you—and haven't once asked for any reassurances. It's not *normal,* and it's certainly not the reaction that whoever did this wanted."

"Oh," said Caethari, which neatly summed up my reaction, too. I flushed in embarrassment, then flushed all the harder when I accidentally caught Caethari's eye and found *him* blushing, too. We looked away from each other, absurdly chastened (and possibly, part of me considered, something more than that).

Tiera Riya waved a hand between us. "You see? The pair of you don't make any damn sense. I can *almost* stretch to blaming it on mutual attraction"—my cheeks flamed at that—"but neither of you is, I think, *quite* so stupid or naive as to let that override everything else. And right now, there's a lot being overridden. So." She crossed her arms and glared, for all the world like a schoolteacher disciplining miscreants. "Either you tell me right now why you really trust each other, or I undertake to ferret it out myself. And believe me," she said, with another pointed look in my direction, "you *don't* want that."

For a long moment, nobody said anything. Caethari braced his palms on the table, fingers flexing against the grain, and said, low and even, "Riya, please. It's none of your business what we d—"

"I tried to kill myself."

Caethari's head jerked up. He stared at me; the tiera looked utterly taken aback. I swallowed, shrugging as though the admission cost me nothing, and fixed my gaze on the wall.

"I was . . . very frightened," I said, a note of black laughter colouring the understatement. "I thought, when your brother married me, that I'd be forced—that *he* would force me. And I'd already been attacked twice, as you say. It seemed . . . better, easier, to just get it over with." I took a breath, and made myself look at Tiera Riya. "He found me holding myself at knifepoint, like this." I put two fingertips to my jugular, over the tiny nick the blade had made, and kept them there, tilting my chin. "He didn't have to talk me down. He could've simply pressed, just so"—I pushed my fingers in—"or goaded me to die. Nobody would have blamed him for it. And if you'd asked Markel—if you'd thought to ask Markel, that is, with pen and paper—he would've told you I'd tried before, when Keletha first came to us."

I smiled at her. The expression felt ghastly on my face, and when she blanched, I let my fingers drop. "Of course I'm afraid, tiera. I'm just more scared of myself than of your brother."

Right from the first, the Tiera Riya had struck me as a woman who was seldom confounded by others. Nonetheless, she was clearly on the back foot now, and part of me felt a perverse sense of pride in having provoked the reaction.

"Now, assuming I've answered your question," I said, in the silence of her shock, "would you mind giving us some privacy? I think I'd quite like to get maudlin drunk, if it's all the same to you." And I rose from the chair, heading towards my newly furnished chamber.

"You corresponded," the tiera said, suddenly.

I paused, but didn't turn. "I'm sorry?"

"As part of the betrothal negotiations. I'll put it about that the two of you corresponded, built up a rapport. You cared for each other before you met, and that's why you trust that the Wild Knife wouldn't hurt you." More sardonically, she added, "That, of course, and Caethari's actions against vin Mica helped your father's ascension, albeit indirectly. I'll say you bonded over it."

I huffed a small laugh. "You're really very good at this, tiera. No wonder your grandmother likes you."

I heard her inhale, shocked and deep. "As are you, tiern. Clearly." A beat later, she added: "And please, no titles between us. Just Riya is fine."

"Riya, then," I said, inclining my head.

"Do I get a say in any of this?" Caethari asked, more curious than despairing.

"No," said Riya, just as I asked, "Why? Do you want one?"

This time, it was the tiern's turn to laugh. "Not especially," he said. "Sweet saints, but I hate politics!"

"You should've been born a hermit," Riya deadpanned. And then, more softly, "Your confidence is my confidence. You have my discretion in this."

"Thank you," I said, and waited in place until I heard her leave, the door clicking shut on her footsteps.

Behind me, Caethari said, "You didn't have to do that."

"Perhaps not. But it's done."

"I—" He hesitated long enough that I turned again, watching him with a calm I didn't quite feel. There was, I realised, blood on his nara, though less than the quantity soaking my own. "I went to Keletha last night, while you slept. I told thim . . . well. I told thim what you'd feared our marriage would mean—what you were willing to do to escape it—and thei realised the truth about what Killic did to you, though I didn't confirm it. I'm sorry for breaching your confidence, but I was . . . upset, more so than I'd realised at first. And I didn't want the mistake repeated in the future, should there be other alliances made with Ralia."

"Mistake?"

"Or misunderstanding, rather. That a Tithenai marriage isn't—that it doesn't—that it carries no Ralian expectations."

"Oh," I said, digesting this. I considered being angry about it, but found I couldn't muster up the energy. "That's . . . good to know, then."

Caethari nodded, relaxing a little. "I've assigned a guard to Markel, as a precaution. He was very upset about your horse; I had to coax him to stay put. I don't expect he's in danger, but just in case—"

"Thank you," I said in a rush. The thought of such a measure being necessary—or worse, insufficient—threatened to put my heart in my throat, and I didn't want it there. "I appreciate it, truly."

He nodded again, and I realised this was awkward for him; that he didn't quite know how to treat me. I snorted softly. That was one thing we had in common: I hardly knew how to treat myself, either.

"Do you really want to get drunk?" Caethari asked, after a moment.

I considered the prospect, sighed and shook my head. "I wish I wanted to get drunk. It would be simpler, somehow. But no, I don't think I do."

"What do you want, then?"

I opened my mouth to answer, but stalled unaccountably. Swallowed. Paused, my neck still flushed from Riya's comments, and wondered why some reckless, treacherous part of me was tempted to answer, *You, I think.*

Depending on how I looked at it, the impulse was ridiculous for all the same reasons it wasn't, but in the end, what stopped me was the fact that it *was* an impulse. Assuming he even wanted me that way, Caethari deserved better than to be a bad decision, and so I ignored the part of me that longed to curl up and be held (and possibly more than held) without any care for the consequences, and said, "Well, for starters, I'd like for both of us to not be covered in horse blood. Maybe a decent wash, some clean clothes. Dinner. And then, if it's not too much trouble, we could have an adult conversation about my finances and yours, and the keys to these rooms, and any other relevant family politics your grandmother neglected to explain."

"That sounds . . . very sensible," Caethari said. "Though also draining. Might I request the inclusion of wine in this adult conversation?"

"You may," I said magnanimously.

Caethari grinned, rang for a servant and made it so.

Though I'd managed a cursory wash in the infirmary the day before, the bath I had then, in the bathing chamber of our apartments, felt like the best kind of luxury, not least because the Aida boasted indoor plumbing. Left alone while my husband summoned a tailor, I scrubbed myself until my skin smarted, the water so brackish beneath the lather that I could scarce understand how anyone in Qi-Katai had tolerated my proximity before then. I tried my best to keep my stitches dry, my bad leg raised along the edge of the tub, but with little success, for all that I forwent shaving for the sake of keeping my balance. I anticipated a scolding from Ru Zairin in my near future, but in the moment, I didn't care, and only the knowledge that Caethari needed the room himself kept me from languishing.

When I finally emerged, wrapped in a borrowed silk robe—I'd been offered a hipwrap, too, but felt too self-conscious to don it just yet, feeling paradoxically less naked in my smallclothes—it was to find the tailor had arrived. Though Caethari's eyes widened a little at the sight of me, he didn't comment on my comparative state of undress, but coughed, ducked his head and introduced me to Ren Lithas Vael, stating that everything I ordered was to go on his account and to be delivered speedily. Then he went to make his own ablutions, leaving me alone with the tailor.

I felt nervous at the prospect of being measured, but Ren Lithas was a consummate professional. Though there were times when I flinched or stiffened as he laid his tape on me, he never remarked upon it, waiting until I'd relaxed again before proceeding. All the while, he maintained a genial patter about styles and cuts and Tithenai fashions, which had far more permutations than just the lin and nara I'd assumed to be the default, and though I followed next to none of it, I found his voice soothing, nodding vague agreement at various junctures. Ren Lithas didn't comment on my ignorance, either, but maintained the same, small smile throughout, and when he finally pronounced himself satisfied with my measurements, he straightened, bowed, reiterated his commitment to bringing me a full set of new things as quickly as possible, and left.

Only then, with Caethari still bathing, did I finally inspect my new room. My expectations weren't great, but neither were my needs: so long as I had a place to sleep alone, I was prepared to make do.

Instead, I found myself gawking, slightly overawed at how much effort had gone into outfitting the space, not only due to the speed with which the transformation from storage room had been effected, but because of the obvious care taken to make it comfortable.

The bed was spacious enough to have slept three people, the wooden frame carved with leaping hares and crouching snowcats. The mattress was soft, the ticking stuffed with feathers and covered in soft linen, the sheets themselves sumptuous cotton dyed a rich, welcoming blue. The pillows were thick, while the quilted coverlet was silk on one side, cotton on the other, all coloured to match the sheets. I had a full glass mirror, framed in bronze, set beside a gorgeous camphor clothes chest, the polished wood carved with vines and spirals, flowers and feathers. A knotted silk tapestry covered one wall, depicting a forest scene. I had a nightstand, a cushioned reading chair, a basin and ewer for simple washing and a small cabinet, one drawer of which contained candles and brushes and other mundane, useful things. My boots, which I'd removed to bathe, had been swiftly polished and set beside the chest, and there was even an empty set of shelves for such books and personal effects as hadn't yet arrived, or which I might presumably accrue. There was a window, too; shuttered now, but when opened, it looked out on the Aida's gardens, and though the floor was smooth, cool stone, a thick rug covered most of it.

A lump rose in my throat at the consideration, and it was some moments before I noticed that a clean pair of nara, presumably another donation from Caethari, had been laid out for me alongside the lin and undershirt I'd been wearing earlier. After a brief hesitation, I pulled on the nara and undershirt, but left the lin; it was evening, after all, and I was accustomed to dressing less formally in my own rooms at such an hour.

When I reemerged, I found that Caethari had done likewise; and more, that both our dinner and the promised wine had arrived.

"I didn't order so much food this time," Caethari said, smiling a little. "Still, you seem to have won Ren Valiu's favour."

"How so?" I asked, taking a seat at the table in the receiving room.

"These," he said, indicating a shallow blue bowl. It was full of apparently edible balls, about as big around as the circle between my pinched thumb and index finger, covered with a crackly golden-brown glaze. I blinked, not recognising the dish, though given how new I was to Tithenai cuisine, that was hardly surprising.

"What are they?"

"They're called little suns," Caethari said. "Caramelised dough balls made with honey, chives, ginger and a sort of sweet spice, I can't remember the name of it, but Ren Valiu is famous for hers. She doesn't make them for just anyone. You, ah. You must've made a good impression."

"How do you know they're not for you?" I asked, helping myself to a serving of poached fish.

Caethari snorted. "Believe me, if I'd done anything Ren Valiu thought worth celebrating, I'd know about it."

I rolled my eyes at that, and began to eat my fish. It was delicious, the white flesh melting in my mouth, the buttery sauce perfectly offset by the peppery taste and crisp texture of the surrounding greens. Either Ren Valiu was a truly exceptional cook, I decided, or Tithenai food was inherently spectacular. It was an innocuous thought, but it warmed me, and after the day I'd had, I resolved to enjoy whatever comfort I could find. I refused to think of poor, loyal Quip lying dead in his stable. I hadn't thought to ask what would be done with his body, and though I had a niggling sense the lapse would haunt me later, in the moment, I swallowed around my grief and let it pass.

"I'm sorry for my grandmother," Caethari murmured, apropos of nothing. He didn't look up from his own meal, determinedly chasing a slippery slice of fish with the edge of his kip, the thin, two-tined utensil the Tithenai seemed to use for everything that wasn't soup. "I should've known she'd find a way to ambush you."

"It's no bother," I said, surprised to find I meant it. "She was . . .

well. I won't go so far as to say *pleasant,* but—refreshing, maybe? Interesting, at the very least."

"She certainly is that." He lifted the wine bottle inquiringly; I nudged my glass towards him, watching as he poured. The wine was pale gold and lightly chilled, a perfect complement to the fish.

"So," I said, when the subsequent silence threatened to grow awkward. "What do I do now?"

Caethari blinked at me. "In what sense?"

"In the ongoing sense. As your—as your husband," I said, hating that I blushed; that I looked aside without even meaning to. *Litai.* A husband's husband. Such a small word, to mean so much! "I have a modest sinecure, my own Ralian funds, but no sense of how to use them here."

"How would you like to use them?"

I made a frustrated noise. "That's not—I mean to say, in Ralia, if I were married—if I'd been in a position to be married there, rather—I'd have holdings of some sort, a house or estate, and my wife would be its castellan. Any inheritance she claimed would go towards the upkeep of our household, and she would—" My face heated further. "—that is, if we were blessed with children, their raising would fall to her. Likely, too, she would have domestic hobbies, a social circle and her own occupations, and I would encourage her in that, as Nathian does his wife, but I am—I am, by my own sense of things—by virtue of having come to your house, to your lands, as a Ralian bride would come—I cannot avoid the assumption, however flawed, that I am *your* wife, in the occupational sense, and that such duties as I consider wifely are now *my* duties.

"But this, here—" I waved a hand at the walls of the Aida, snatching a gulp from my wine in passing. "—this is not a house, or an estate. It's a castle, or near enough to one: its functioning, so far as I can tell, has nothing to do with me. You have no heir for me to raise, nor can we amuse ourselves with the getting of one." The words twisted in my mouth, more bitter than I'd intended. "And as my being here at all is a seed of conflict, finding a social circle seems . . . difficult, at present. So I ask you, tiern: What am I to do for you? How do I function here? What is expected of me? Or what is expected of you, that a spouse might aid in?"

Caethari's mouth hung open a little. We stared at each other, the air between us wreathed with steam from Ren Valiu's fish, and then my husband shook himself: a genteel shiver, as if he was recalling his thoughts from some scattering distance.

"I have some small holdings," he said at last, "about a week's ride from here, at Avai, in the farmlands of the riverveldt. I hold them in my own right, irrespective of other inheritance politics, though I seldom go there. I am . . . I have always held myself to be a soldier first, a landholder second. And my properties were a gift from my mother—one of her last to me, before she left, which complicates my feelings towards them." He bit his lip, uncertain. "My grandmother—Yasa Kithadi—did she tell you about Tierena Inavi?"

"A little," I admitted. "She seemed angry at her, and at your father, though it wasn't clear why." I hesitated, then said, as neutrally as I could, "I was surprised to learn of their divorce. It's a rare thing in Ralia. I can't say I understand it."

"Nor do I, in truth. Or not fully, anyway." Caethari sighed, toying with his kip. "I was fourteen when she left. Their parting seemed amicable enough, but if it were truly so, then I can't understand the reason for their separation. Divorce, here—it's accessible, but seldom used when no fault is levied between partners, as the conventions of consent are meant to weed out any base incompatibilities at the outset."

I tried to keep my expression blank at that, but by the way Caethari flushed, I must have failed. My heart began to pound, but before I could steel myself to ask the vital how of it—to divine how I might escape him, should I ever feel pressed, without betraying my reasons for asking—Caethari said, in a pained, struggling burst, "If you do leave me, Velasin, I would ask—I have no right to ask,

I know, but I would—if you did—I would take it as a kindness, if you would levy no faults against me. I know you didn't choose this, that your consent has been abominably violated, and if you wished to go, I would be monstrous to blame you, or to stop you, whatever the consequences. But if you levy fault, it's a mark—it's a stain on me, that might well stop me wedding again, and I have tried—I am trying—I don't want—"

"Caethari," I said softly, and he fell as sharply silent as if I'd slapped him. His dark eyes were wide, and my throat felt tight as I said, "I've come this far for duty, and I have nowhere else to go. I will try to stay, to, to—to make whatever life is here to be made, if I can. But if I can't, and you are good enough to let me go in peace, then no: I will not fault you. I will promise you that much."

"My thanks," he said, voice hoarse. And then, with a weak attempt at laughter, "Ruya's grace, how did we get to this? I didn't even answer your question."

I took the change in topic gratefully. "You said you had country holdings?"

"Yes, and if you truly want to administer them—or just to visit them, even—I can arrange it for you. But I am, as I said, a soldier: I reside in Qi-Katai, not only because I prefer the city, but because it keeps me near my revetha, should we be called up to fight again."

"Your revetha," I said, testing the Tithenai word. "That's—that's like your garrison, or unit?" I used the Ralian terms, not sure if either was the correct equivalent.

"More or less," Caethari said. "We don't really have a standing army in the Ralian sense, but each city has a revetha—a core of trained soldiers paid a stipend to maintain that training and induct new trainees, who have the authority to call up local levies or conscript new troops for specific causes, should the need arise. The stipend keeps us bound to the military, but leaves us free to pursue other work and duties if we're not in service. Our rahan—our commander, you'd say, or near enough—has the authority to deploy us on her own recognizance, in defence of Qi-Katai and its territory; as does the tieren, should he need to supplement the city's own guard. Otherwise, we serve only at the order of Qi-Xihan, by order of Asa Ivadi or majority approval of the Conclave."

"You're led by a woman?" I blurted, unable to keep the surprise from my tone, though this was hardly the most salient point of Caethari's explanation. Even knowing that women served as soldiers here, I still hadn't quite considered that they'd hold such a rank.

Caethari looked amused. "I am. Rahan Nairi Siurin. Why?" He quirked an eyebrow, considering. "Does that offend your Ralian sensibilities?"

"Not quite," I hedged. He continued looking at me until I sighed and said, "It would have done, once. Growing up, I didn't exactly have a frame of reference for female warriors. I didn't think less of women, exactly; I just assumed they were capable of less, or less capable at certain things, though I suppose that's much the same thing when you get right down to it. Until one day, I watched a fishmonger's wife first lay out four grown men in a bar-brawl, then quick-talk them into paying her damages, and—well. It was hard to maintain my old views after that, not least because it made me wonder why it took excelling at something masculine for me to be impressed by female competence. If women were meant to be valued for their feminine skills, then why were the skills themselves devalued? I'd like to say that was when I stopped making assumptions about what certain people are capable of, but it's a hard habit to break. I've seen what Kita and Mirae can do—what women in Farathel can do, regardless of whether they're ever appreciated for doing it—but I'm not used to seeing it mean something real, something tangible like rank, or unchallenged respect."

"Well, by the usual Ralian standards, you're not doing too badly." Caethari raised his glass in mock respect, and I did likewise, lips quirking in an almost-smile. "Nairi's a friend, and a good leader. I'd like you to meet her, actually. Which brings me back to the point, *again.*" He sipped his wine, then set it down. "It's customary, in the first week after a marriage, for the couple to host a gathering, the better to introduce an incoming partner to—how did you put it? To their potential social circle within the city. Which, under the circumstances, is going to be rather more political an affair than not, I'm afraid."

"Clearly," I said.

Caethari made a face. "Quite. And that's on my list of tasks for tomorrow, once I've consulted with Tar Raeki and my father—and my sisters, Zo help me—about how best to arrange it, assuming you have no objections."

"None at all."

"Thank you. But in answer to your original question, unless you want to manage my riverveldt holdings, your duties here are whatever you want them to be. I mean that sincerely," he said, in response to my incredulous snort. A faint blush coloured his cheeks. "If you ever—if we ever wanted a child, you would have as much of their raising as I did, or as you wanted, but otherwise—what did you do in Farathel?"

The question caught me enough off guard that I answered honestly. "Little of worth, and much that was questionable." I gulped at his inquiring look, and clarified: "I gambled, tiern, with secrets as well as coin. I played at intrigues, raced horses, took lovers, made enemies and indulged in every foolishness for which younger sons are famous. And I studied, when I remembered enough of myself to bother, though that was less and less, after Killic." Shame roiled through me, hot and sour. I looked away. Mine felt a small life, when phrased in such terms.

"What did you study, Velasin?"

The question was gentle, coaxing. I hunched my shoulders against it, and said to the floor, "Languages, sometimes. It's how I learned to sign, and to speak Tithenai. Magic, occasionally, though I have no great knack for it. Otherwise, histories. Stories. Songs. Whatever caught my fancy."

"Then study here, if it pleases you," Caethari said. And then, haltingly, "As we are friends, it would please me to see you happy."

"I will do my best to oblige you, then," I said, cheeks hot. "As a friend."

We both fell silent, staring at our food. The fish had gone cold, and as tasty as it was, I found I had no more appetite. I tried to summon a pertinent question—something about his mother, perhaps, or his soldier's life—but couldn't find the words. Instead, I drained my wine, the liquor cool-hot in my throat, and privately beseeched the moons for strength.

Someone rapped smartly on the main door. I jumped, startled, while Caethari jerked upright to answer it, clearly as glad of the interruption as I was.

"Who—" he began, then stopped, surprised. "Raeki?"

"Forgive me, tierns." Raeki stood in the doorway, offering us each a jerky bow. To Caethari, he said, "It's the prisoner, the one who stabbed Ren Markel. I told him what we discussed this morning—that you, not Tiera Laecia, had married Tiern Velasin—and he went pale as rice. He wants to speak to you in person. I've tried to get him to talk to me instead, but he won't budge. Says he'll confess to the Wild Knife alone, or not at all. So I came to tell you myself, to see how you want to proceed."

My heart clenched in my chest. Caethari's expression hardened. "I'll speak to him," he said, stonily. "Now."

"Me, too."

The words were out before I could stop them. Both men turned to stare at me: Raeki was clearly startled, but Caethari looked more considering. I straightened my back, determined. "It was me he meant to hurt, but Markel he stabbed. Whatever grudge he bears me, or thinks he bears, I want to hear it for myself."

For a moment, I thought Caethari was going to refuse me; certainly, Raeki was shooting him looks to that effect. Instead, the tiern nodded, his expression grave. "Then you shall," he said. "The sooner this mess is resolved, the better for all of us."

Raeki looked pained. "Tiern, with all due respect—"

"Have Alik saddled for me," Caethari said, cutting him off.

"And for Velasin—" He hesitated, glancing at me. "Will you take Markel's horse, or would you prefer another?"

I couldn't have said why, but riding Grace would've somehow been a greater betrayal of poor, dead Quip than accepting an unknown mount.

"Another," I said. "If it please you."

Caethari nodded. "Then Velasin can ride Luya," he said, returning his attention to Raeki. "See it done, and we'll meet you in the courtyard."

"Tiern," said Raeki, and bowed again, shooting me an unfathomable look before striding off.

"Thank you," I said. "I—thank you."

"There's nothing to thank me for," Caethari said. He cast a last, lingering look at the untouched bowl of little suns and suppressed a regretful sigh. "Come, then. Let's dress and go. The night is warm enough; you shouldn't need a coat if you wear your lin."

"Yes, mother," I said, unable to help myself.

The teasing remark startled a burst of laughter from Caethari. It crinkled his eyes, and something in me lurched. Good humour looked well on him. *He deserves better,* I thought, *than to be married in misery.*

"Be quick," he said, and headed into his room.

I watched him go, then retired to mine, shrugging into my borrowed lin. Already, I was second-guessing my decision to accompany him, if only because riding some other mount so soon after Quip's death felt obscurely disrespectful. I tugged my boots on, forcing my doubts aside. Markel had taken a knife for me; the least I could do was try to find out why, dead horse or no dead horse.

I left the room and shut the door, and tried to pretend I hadn't flinched from the mirror.

Part Four

CAETHARI

16

The upper city of Qi-Katai was eerie at night, the blocky dark of buildings swathed against the deeper blacks of sky and distance. Lamps at street level cast more shadows than pools of light, the stones glowing fishbelly-orange and star-white in their brief halos, then receding into charcoal. Though Cae longed to race to the guardhouse, he forced himself to keep Alik at a fast walk, alert for the few pedestrians abroad at such an hour. The middle and lower cities were more lively, taverns and pleasure-shops, theatres and nightmarkets all plying their various, interconnected trades, but above the Amber Gate, where respectable citizens dwelled and the merchants shut their doors at sundown, the loudest sound was of their passage, clopping hooves and jingling tack and murmured conversation.

Two of three moons rode low in the sky, the Eye a bare gold sickle chasing the fuller, rose-hued bloom of the Hand, while the striped Heart was nowhere to be seen. They made him think of Velasin, and as Cae glanced at his husband, he felt a surge of new fury at the fate of his horse. The Aida's stables should have been *safe,* and Cae didn't know which prospect disturbed him more: that despite all the extra guards on watch since his father's attack, an assailant had snuck in anyway; or that someone already trusted within the Aida was responsible for the butchery.

Aware of Cae's scrutiny, Velasin looked up. His long fingers clenched on Luya's reins, a minute flinch in response to being watched. The reflex made Cae feel sick in a different way. He swallowed the feeling, and said, in a leap that felt more logical than it sounded when spoken aloud, "You pray to the moons?"

Velasin's mouth curved. "I certainly swear by them. Whether that counts as praying depends on your definition, though if it helps, I never expect an answer."

"You don't believe in your gods?" He wasn't sure why it mattered; he was hardly devout himself.

"A contradictory statement," Velasin observed. "You'd give me ownership of those I disavow."

"So you are apostate?"

"Better to say I'm cynical."

"In my experience, cynics believe in the gods; just not in their kindness."

"A realist, then." Velasin tipped his chin to the sky; the gesture coincided with their passing a streetlamp, and its brief light licked up his throat like a burning tongue. "I see the moons, tiern; I see the sun, the sky, the stars. I've never seen the gods."

"Nor have I," Cae admitted. "Though I'll confess, I sometimes feel better for knowing they're there."

Velasin cast a glance at the sky. "Which is which?" he asked. "I mean, which moon is which god?" He laughed. "It feels somewhat rude, not knowing."

Glad of his husband's good humour, Cae took a hand from the reins and pointed. "Ruya's Eye," golden-hued, smallest of the three, "Ayla's Hand," middle-sized and rosy, "and Zo's Heart, though he's hidden now." He gestured to a low, empty space in the sky, as if apologising for the absence of the largest, distinctively banded moon. "Mostly, we just say the Eye, the Hand, the Heart." He paused, then said, "I've never known their names in Ralian."

Replying in that language, Velasin said, "We call them the Lord Sun's Daughters—Riva, Asha, Coria." He named them in the same order Cae had, pointing as he went. "Lesser goddesses, the Doctrine of the Firmament says, who offer luck and favour to mortals who catch their notice. Sometimes, in the older tales, they even take human form and marry kings and heroes, though they always return to the sky once their heirs are born." He hesitated, and when he switched back to Tithenai, his gaze seemed far away. "My mother always prayed to the moons; their stories were her favourites. Father always grumbled about that—said she should've prayed to the First Star, in honour of her sons—but she never did. She was stubborn about it, like me. Strange and stubborn." A complex expression flitted across his face, fey and lovely. "So even when she died, I never quite lost the habit."

"How did she—?"

"A miscarriage. The child had barely quickened, but she took an infection from losing him all the same."

Reflexively, Cae made Ayla's warding sign against the misfortunes of childbirth, tapping two fingers to navel, then lips. "Saints ease her grief, and yours."

"It was a long time ago," Velasin said, but though he shrugged, there was old pain in the words. "I can't imagine what she'd make of my being here. Sometimes—" He broke off, expression twisting into an almost-smile. "Sometimes I think she always knew what I was, and loved me anyway. But mostly I think I only have such thoughts because she isn't here to gainsay them."

"Tierns," said Raeki, cutting in before Cae could reply, "we're here."

And so they were, Cae realised belatedly: they'd passed beneath the Amber Gate without him even noticing, and there was the guardhouse, demarcated as such by the quartet of yellow lanterns around the main door, while a smaller pair, set farther back from the front, lit the way to the stables.

As they dismounted, a skinny groom came rushing out to take their reins, throat bobbing deferentially at the three of them. Cae looked the lad over sharply, a pang of paranoia making him pay more attention than usual, but didn't stop him from leading the horses away, Luya snorting softly behind Alik and Raeki's black gelding, Sarus.

"He's been stewing all day," said Raeki, as they entered the guardhouse. Though they'd scarcely spoken since leaving the Aida, the tar had a habit of treating lengthy breaks between conversations as mere pauses. "I told him about your marriage this morning; he clammed up for a couple of hours, then asked for you the first time. I said he could speak to me, and he refused. Went through it all three more times before I came to you." He hesitated, as though only belatedly considering that Cae might have preferred an earlier interrogation, and said, "Figured a longer wait would make him more eager to talk, tiern—and, well. I didn't want to borrow you from your husband if I could avoid it."

"Sure you didn't," Velasin muttered, enough wry rancour in his tone that Raeki flushed.

Cae smothered a laugh. "You did well," he said, flicking Velasin an amused look, which his husband returned with a roll of his eyes. Their humour vanished, however, as Raeki led them through to the cells, the guards on duty hastening out of their way. Their reaction gave Cae pause: guards had a different discipline from soldiers, but while he appreciated their deference to Raeki, he disliked their lack of cohesion. Even with the tar in charge, he'd expected their superior to be underfoot, either protesting the need for their investigation or trying to involve himself in it. Instead, the Amber Gate guards were conspicuous in their silence, and when he noticed Cae noticing, Raeki clicked his tongue in disgust.

"Varu Shan Dalu went home," he said, in answer to Cae's unasked question. "He seems to think my being here is the same as him being on leave. I can't decide if he's lazy, incompetent or just desperate to establish that any investigative errors are mine alone, but from what I've heard, it seems to be part of a longstanding pattern of behaviour when higher-ups are around."

Cae frowned. "Better to borrow milk than trouble—"

"—but neglect sours all," said Raeki, completing the proverb. "I'll have Kita look into it, tiern. I doubt it's related to anything, but I'd sooner be sure than not."

"Good," said Cae, though it came out vaguer than he'd intended; Velasin was mouthing *better milk than trouble* to himself, brow furrowed perplexedly at the phrase, and Cae was distracted by a sudden urge to smooth the lines from his forehead. The impulse caught him off guard; he shook his head in private negation, fingers flexing abortively.

Focus, he told himself, and looked away.

Passing the cells, whose few occupants were either asleep or pretending to be, they reached an interview room whose locked door was flanked by a pair of guards. They straightened at the sight of Raeki, one standing back as the other hurried to let them in.

"He's been quiet since you left, tar," said the one with the key, her voice a deferential murmur. Raeki huffed his lack of shock, gaze flicking briefly to Velasin. Clearly, he still disliked his being there, but was too politic to say so. Cae pretended not to notice the subtler hint, and stepped through the door with Velasin and Raeki at his heels.

The room was small and square, the prisoner bound to one of two chairs set on either side of a wooden desk. The room was illuminated by a roof-hung lantern, while a tiny barred window set high on the opposite wall admitted nothing but a slice of dark sky and the pungent smell of horse.

The prisoner lifted his head, eyes widening as the three men entered. Instantly, Cae was struck by the fact that, whatever else could be said of the man, he was clearly no professional assassin. He was middle-aged, thin-limbed but paunchy, his square hands soft and uncallused where they fidgeted on the table. His clothes were plain, but not quite nondescript, though Cae suspected they'd been meant to appear so: his undyed linen undershirt was plain enough, but the dark brown lin worn over it bore clear signs of having been altered, loose threads poking along the hems where some adornment or other—embroidery, most like—had been ripped away. A glance beneath the table showed boots too well-maintained and newly soled to have belonged to a poor man, and when coupled with the faint piping on his otherwise dull nara, all Cae saw was a merchant of middling prosperity attempting, rather badly, to seem other than he was.

This suspicion was confirmed the instant the prisoner opened his mouth: his accent was pure Qi-Katai mercantile, polished diction twisted by the telltale curlicue vowels invariably affected by anyone who spent enough time either speaking Khyto with fur-traders or listening to their heavily accented Tithenai.

"My tiern," the man said, sounding desperate already, "please, you must understand, I never intended—"

"Don't lie to me," Cae snapped. "You clearly *intended* a great deal. What I want to know is why, and on whose orders, as they clearly weren't mine. You can start by telling me your name."

The man gulped. His jaw was grey-stubbled and unshaven, his hair cropped just above his collar.

"I'm called Baru, tiern, but please—"

"Baru who?"

"Ren Baru K—"

A thin, black bolt punched into his neck, its entry turning his clan-name into a garbled rasp. Baru's eyes went impossibly wider, shock and pain flaring in his face, blood bubbling on his lips.

"The window!" Raeki bellowed. "Tiern, get down! It came through the wind—"

The insect-zing of a second bolt cut him off, embedding itself in Baru's throat directly beside the first. Unable to raise his bound wrists to the wound, the prisoner could only loll as blood spurted from his neck, soaking bolts, flesh, cloth and table.

"Find the shooter!" Cae shouted. "Go, now!"

Raeki cursed and tore off, all but dragging the door guards behind him. Cae darted around the table, sliding his hand through the slick of blood on Baru's neck, trying to stop the bleeding, but though he pressed and swore, it was too late. Between them, the bolts had torn the man's jugular open, and as he pressed futilely around the wound, Cae felt the last red gush of his pulse before the beat faltered and died.

"Saints," he whispered, half furious, half perversely awed at the accuracy of the shots. He glanced at the window, trying to figure it: the gaps between the bars were less than three fingerwidths, and though the bolts had gone so deep as to suggest close range, they'd still been shot at an angle by someone whose night-eyes were compromised by the necessity of firing into a lit room. Even factoring in the potential greater accuracy of a crossbow, it was impressive—and given how close together the bolts had come, the weapon itself was likely expensive.

Dazed by the suddenness of it all, Cae stepped back from the body, staring in disgust at his bloodied hands. He turned, looking for something to wipe them on—and only then, as their gazes locked, did he remember Velasin.

"Don't—stay there," Velasin said, his voice a shaky rasp. He took a step back, towards the door. "Just wait."

Cae took a reflexive half-step towards him, then held firm, throat tight with inexplicable anxiety as his husband vanished from sight. His pulse felt loud in his ears. Through the window, he could hear Tar Raeki's pursuit of the shooter, angry footsteps and hissed instructions, yet somehow, he already knew they'd make no capture. Whoever had killed Ren Baru knew what they were doing: if they'd been able to get in position on the guardhouse without being detected—they'd most likely shot from atop the stables, he thought distantly—then they'd likely planned an escape route, too. *Or else they're a guard themselves,* he thought, hating the necessity of such cynicism. Varu Shan Dalu's convenient absence itched at him. Something was badly amiss in all this, and he hated not being able to fathom it.

His hands dripped red on the stone floor, slow and sticky.

He looked up at the sound of returning footsteps. Velasin stood in the doorway, clutching a clay jug and a washrag. He was pale but determined, straight-backed in his refusal to look at the body.

Instead, he stared straight at Cae as he approached him, stopping just within arm's reach.

"Hands," he said, softly. "Hold them out."

Cae obeyed, watching in something akin to shock as Velasin poured the water over his palms, then set the jug down on the table. Carefully, he dipped the cloth in what remained of the contents, grasped Cae gently at wrist and knuckle, and started wiping the blood away. Inasmuch as he'd ever considered the matter, Cae had thought his hands too callused to have retained much heightened sensitivity, but the slow, wet drag of the cloth between his fingers and along his wrists dispelled the notion utterly. Velasin didn't speak; the only sounds were Cae's own breathing, loud in the dead man's silence, and the gentle drip of water.

"You don't have to do this," he managed, shivering at the secondhand touch.

"I know," Velasin said; then, "*Shhh,*" stifling Cae's incipient protest, gaze flicking briefly up before refocussing on his hands.

It shouldn't have felt intimate. It shouldn't have been anything but perfunctory, a courtesy. Ruya's grace, it should at least have been *brief,* but Velasin took his time, and Caethari let him.

Seconds after Velasin finally stepped away, Tar Raeki returned, flushed and furious.

"We're searching the streets," he panted, "but the glimpse I caught, they went over the rooftops—over and down the walls, like a fucking spider—saints, but I hate assassins!"

"That makes two of us," Cae said. He rubbed his face, abruptly tired. "I haven't the wits for this, Raeki. Did they know he was going to talk, or would they have killed him anyway? Is there a spy in the guardhouse, or was the killer just paying attention?"

Raeki's jaw worked soundlessly. "Tiern—"

"He tried to kill me," Velasin said. His voice was curiously flat. He stared at the body, only the finest tremor in his arms belying the impassivity of his features. "He stabbed Markel. And now he's dead, and it doesn't balance anything; there's no justice in this.

Only more blood for some poor sod to clean up, and more questions left unanswered."

"And yet, we'll ask them anyway," Cae murmured. "How else to find the truth?"

"If I could answer that," said Velasin, "I'd be a rich man indeed."

"Fuck," Raeki said, his expression bleak.

They had a long night ahead.

17

By the time they finally returned to the Aida, it was deep night, the sky skittish with stars. Cae felt as though he'd aged a good decade: with Ren Baru's murderer lamentably uncaught, he and Raeki had interviewed each member of the guardhouse, trying to determine the extent of their culpability. Unsurprisingly, they'd learned little of use, except that the Amber Gate guards were routinely lax in protecting their own building from the outside: no one had seen the assassin arrive, and none besides Raeki had seen them flee. As several guards admitted to having freely discussed both Ren Baru's capture and his subsequent decision to talk—details which, while not strictly secrets, ought nonetheless to have been treated with greater discretion—Cae was reluctantly forced to conclude that incompetence was a more likely culprit for the leak than malice. Even if there was a guard, or guards, who'd actively betrayed the imminence of Ren Baru's confession, with so much readily accessible gossip serving the same function—and with so many nervous at the tiern's presence—there was no telling who it was.

Even so, Cae had made note of several guards who'd seemed warier, less honest than the rest, and quietly instructed Raeki to interview them more thoroughly tomorrow. It was just one item on an ever-increasing list of chores: he'd held off on having the body of Velasin's horse cremated, uncertain if there were any Ralian rituals his husband might want to enact instead, but the decision couldn't wait much longer. There was their marriage-gathering to organise, which meant consulting with his sisters and grandmother about the guest list, and of course, the prisoners from Vaiko and the rest of Keletha's riders would likely arrive tomorrow, which meant yet more questions, more interrogations. Added to that, it was traditional for soldiers to personally inform their superior officers after a marriage—not that Nairi was a stickler for that sort of thing, but he certainly owed her the courtesy of it, and anyway, she was one person Velasin ought to meet before being thrown to the wolves . . .

He glanced at Velasin, the two of them walking exhaustedly along the hall. Before he'd started interviewing the guards, Cae had offered his husband the opportunity to return to the Aida without him, but he'd refused, preferring to ask the Amber Gate guards about the city, its customs, Tithena in general. Cae had been so preoccupied with his own affairs, he hadn't given these conversations much thought, but as he unlocked their apartment door, it occurred to him that Velasin was both subtle and clever, never mind his exceedingly personal interest in the matter. Despite his casual approach, he'd likely been investigating, too.

"Why do I get the feeling that you learned more tonight than I did?" Cae asked, shutting the door behind them.

"Because you're a clever man," said Velasin. "And because people say more when they think you're not really listening." He shrugged off his lin, throwing it ahead of him into his chamber, one hand rubbing distractedly at his sore leg. "We should compare notes over breakfast, but right now, I need sleep."

"Likewise," said Cae, hovering on the threshold of his chamber and the receiving room. Their abandoned meal was still on the table; he could have called a servant to tidy up, but felt too weary to bother. He hesitated, uncertain what to say, and finally settled on a simple, "Good night, Velasin."

His husband flashed him a tired smile. "Good night, tiern."

And then he vanished into his room, so that Cae had no choice but to do likewise. He shut his door, dazedly changed into a clean hipwrap and climbed into bed, fully expecting to pass straight out. But though he ached with tiredness, sleep wouldn't come. His thoughts were too busy, churning through the assaults on Clan Aeduria—threats made in his own name. Bare days ago, he'd been angry at the thought of marrying a foreign stranger; now he lay awake worrying for Velasin's safety. Bad enough that some nameless coterie wanted him dead—did he really have to exhibit all the self-preservation instincts of a duckling, too? The man seemed wholly incapable of acknowledging his own limits, let alone sticking to them: though wounded, lonely and terrified, he'd thrown himself straight into Qi-Katai's politics, grappling with both Kithadi and Riya—no mean feat at the best of times—while dismissing his own injuries.

He's going to get himself killed, Cae thought, and instantly regretted it, seeing again the trembling knife in Velasin's hand, the pleading look on his face. What sort of man walked into death like that? How much compassion did it take, to wash your would-be killer's blood from the hands of a man you feared to touch? Cae rolled onto his stomach, eyes screwed shut in a futile attempt at sleep. It wasn't just the marriage vows, though they were certainly part of it: he felt bound to his husband in some deeper sense, responsible for protecting him—from assassins, from himself. Staying angry would've been easier, but he found he couldn't be angry with Velasin; only at circumstance.

And what circumstances were these, exactly? Assuming their fledgling marriage didn't end in divorce—a prospect that made Cae uneasy for any number of reasons—would it ever feel truly comfortable? He'd engaged in dalliances with men, women and kemi before, some more involved than others and one serious in particular, but those were all years in the past. Protecting the farmsteads of Vaiko, patrolling the Taelic Pass for bandits, clashing with the late Ennan vin Mica's men, he'd earned a reputation as the Wild Knife—would that he could go back in time and throttle whoever popularised that wretched nickname!—and since then, he'd learned to be leery of bedmates approaching him for novelty's sake. In public, Nairi had rolled her eyes at his unfathomable reticence to, as she put it, *sleep with people more interested in your achievements than your status* ("They're usually interested in both," was Cae's muttered rejoinder), but in private, where they could afford to ignore the tension between their respective ranks, her reaction was more wryly sympathetic.

"You know," she'd said, the last time he'd turned down such an offer, a good seven months back, "if I didn't know any better, I'd think you were saving yourself."

"I am," he'd replied, somewhat testily. "*From them.*"

"*From,* yeah, that's good, that makes sense. *Saving from* is sensible." Her warm gaze was both teasing and sincere. "But are you sure there's not a bit of *saving for* there, too?"

"Nairi, I swear by Ruya, Zo and Ayla together, if you're going to bring up Liran—"

"You said it, not me!"

"Look me in the eye and tell me you weren't thinking of him."

"I don't have to look you in the eye," said Nairi, throwing a nutshell at him. "I'm your commanding officer."

"And?"

"And I was thinking of him, yes, but so were you! Ruya's grace, Cae, it's been how many years?"

"Not enough to shut you up, apparently."

Nairi made an exasperated noise. "Look me in the eye and tell me you're completely over him."

"I don't have to look you in the eye," said Cae, aggressively shelling a nut. "I'm your liege."

"You're an idiot, is what you are," said Nairi—and then, with her usual battlefield mercy, she changed the subject.

Now, as Cae recalled the conversation, he realised he truly hadn't thought of Liran since then, except in passing. It was a strange epiphany, enough so that his first instinct was to doubt it. He probed the edges of his memory, testing the extent of his emotional indifference, and was surprised and pleased to find that it held up to private scrutiny. Doubtless, were Liran himself to suddenly materialise, Cae's reaction would be rather more complex, but even so, there was a weird relief to knowing that time and distance really had worked their curative magic, for all that they'd taken a roundabout route to doing so. The relief was short-lived, however, as he realised that Riya would likely insist on inviting Liran to their marriage-gathering, and with tradition being what it was—

Cae groaned, face smushed into the pillow. "I am a terrible husband," he mumbled, kicking himself all over again. His contrition was such that he almost wanted to knock on Velasin's door and confess immediately, but was forced to concede that both of them were far too tired for such a conversation; trying now would only do more harm than good. Like so much else, it would have to wait until morning.

It was a long time before sleep came, and when it did, it settled only lightly. He spent the night tossing and turning, just conscious enough to wonder if he was dreaming without being able to formulate a cogent answer.

When he finally woke the next day, his eyes were gritty, his muscles sore. He made a resentful noise, stretching under the sheets. Nairi would say he was getting soft. In the field, on patrol, he was accustomed to sleeping in rough conditions, rising far earlier than he did in the Aida, but just at that moment, Cae didn't care. Even so, and as tempted as he was to go back to sleep, he forced himself to his feet, spine cracking, his braid sleep-loosened but still intact. Yawning, he padded out into the receiving room and stopped, arrested by the unexpected sight of Velasin.

His husband was sitting with his legs tucked up in a comfortable chair, a half-eaten little sun in one hand, a steaming cup of khai in the other, staring sleepily into the middle distance. He was dressed in the same borrowed robe he'd donned last night, the green silk worn soft with age and use. Unlike last night, however, he clearly had nothing on beneath it—no nara, no hipwrap, not even his smallclothes—and though the robe was belted closed, his sideways posture tugged the fabric askew. In truth, it had fallen half off his right shoulder, leaving him bare from collarbone to navel, a lean expanse of lightly defined musculature and dark olive skin, one small, brown nipple fully visible, the other barely concealed. His hair was tousled and unbound, soft against his slender throat.

"Good morning," Cae said, dry-mouthed, unable to manage anything else.

Velasin startled, his khai sloshing in his cup, hazel eyes widening as he lurched into a flurry of embarrassed motion.

"Ah, hello!" he exclaimed, attempting to simultaneously set his khai down and pull his robe closed without getting up, eventually succeeding in both tasks, but not before Cae had learned that Velasin was capable of a dusky flush that extended from cheek to chest. "I, ah—I don't usually wake so early, but a servant came to take away our dinner things, they brought the khai—"

"Are you apologising? It sounds like you're apologising, but I can't for the life of me think why, or about what."

Velasin opened his mouth. Closed it again, tucking the robe a little more securely around his hips—Cae manfully didn't stare—and finally said, "You looked surprised to see me. I wasn't sure if I'd disturbed your routine, or if I ought to have woken you."

Surprised, Cae thought distantly. *Yes. Let's go with that.* Out loud, he said, "I'll admit to a little confusion, but only on account of a bad night's rest."

Velasin grimaced in sympathy. "That makes two of us. I—I dreamed of Quip, and after that, I never quite settled again."

Early as it was, it took Cae a moment to recall that Quip was the name of Velasin's butchered horse, and when he did, he sat down heavily in the nearest available chair. "It shouldn't have happened," he said, rubbing at his face. "Saints, I'm amazed you haven't run screaming."

"I considered it," Velasin said, "but I'm not sure my leg would hold."

Cae laughed weakly, reaching for the pot of khai and the empty cup beside it. As he poured, he was conscious of Velasin watching him. Pulse ticking, he blew the steam from the milk and sipped. It was just the right blend of spicy and sweet, doing wonders to settle his inexplicable jumpiness.

"How are the little suns?" he asked, nodding at the bowl.

Velasin's lips quirked. "Delicious, as promised. Is Tithenai food universally exceptional, or am I just being spoiled?"

"A little of both, I expect."

Velasin nodded, head bowed over his khai. Absently, he reached up and looped a lock of hair behind his ear. "I've brought you so much trouble," he said, lightly. "Hardly a fair trade, when you keep feeding me delicacies."

"Is Ralian cuisine really so terrible?" said Cae, who was feeling unusually ill-equipped to handle such a benign conversation.

"It's not *terrible,*" said Velasin. "It's just not *this.*" And to demonstrate, he popped the little sun he'd been holding in his mouth, devouring it with evident relish.

As Velasin swallowed and licked his lips, Cae wondered which particular god or saint he'd so displeased, to be subjected to this level of torment first thing in the morning. He was already doing his level best to accept his cohabitation with a beautiful man he was on no account to flirt with, let alone touch; he didn't need such a vivid reminder of all the reasons why he might want to.

"Speaking of less pleasant things," he forced himself to say, "there's some matters we ought to discuss sooner rather than later."

Velasin sighed. "I rather thought there might be."

"Would you, ah—that is, if you'd prefer to dress first, I was thinking I'd wash—"

"Of course!" The flush returned, though less of it was visible than before. Velasin flowed to his feet, one hand securing the front of his robe as he headed towards his room. "Please, we should both be comfortable—"

"I won't be long, it's just—"

"These are your apartments, tiern, you hardly need hurry on my account."

"*Our* apartments, and I don't want to keep you waiting."

"Believe it or not, I am capable of patience."

"I never claimed otherwise! I—" Cae fell abruptly silent, smiling stupidly at Velasin, who was smiling at him. No, not just smiling—*grinning,* the bright expression transforming his features from beautiful to extraordinary. The breath caught in Cae's chest, though he somehow retained the power of speech. "We are rather hopeless at all this, aren't we?"

"Just a bit," said Velasin, and with a huff of laughter, he vanished into his room.

Cae turned in such a daze that he very nearly smacked his forehead into the bathroom door.

"Right," he muttered, "right, right—"

His ablutions were perfunctory: as much to wake himself up as for any other reason, he opted for a quick, cold shower, after which he towelled himself dry and set about rebraiding his damp hair, fingers moving swiftly through the familiar patterns. He stopped short of walking naked through the receiving room, though it was a near thing—he was accustomed to doing so, and only recalled at the last second that Velasin might object—and hurried to dress in his own room, forcefully shoving any and every inappropriate thought to the back of his mind.

Velasin, too, made quick work of his morning routine, emerging scarcely a minute after Cae. Of necessity, he was still wearing borrowed clothes, the same outfit he'd worn last night. Why the sight of him thus attired should prove enticing in an entirely different way to his former near-nakedness, Cae didn't know; only that it did, and that he needed to get a firm grip on his imagination. *And on certain other parts.* As ever, that particular inner voice was a mix of Riya and Nairi, but for once, Cae didn't resent its intrusion. His room was yet his own, and what he did to himself with the door closed, or thought about while doing it, was only Velasin's business if he wanted it to be. Which he didn't, and wouldn't, which was why that door was going to stay closed in the first place. So.

So.

"Are you all right?" asked Velasin, seating himself at the table. He'd pulled his hair back into a tail, but messily enough that a few fine strands still framed his face.

"Fine," lied Cae, and took his own seat opposite.

It was going to be a very long day.

"So," he said, picking what he hoped was the least of many fraught topics as a starting point. "I know it's not the most pleasant thing to discuss, but your horse . . . is there any Ralian custom you wish to observe in terms of, ah. Burial?"

Velasin jerked in his seat. "What?"

"Your horse," Cae said again. "I wasn't sure if there was something in particular you wanted to do, some ritual or prayer—"

"You wouldn't," said Velasin, then stopped. Licked his lips, which motion Cae tracked involuntarily. Started again, voice softer than before. "That is, you wouldn't think it strange of me?"

"Why should I?" said Cae. "When Tithenai mounts fall in battle, we honour them in death. Under the circumstances, this seems little different."

Velasin's throat worked silently for a moment. "In Ralia, we wouldn't . . . most of my station would think it odd to pay a dead animal such respect. Improper, even." Somewhat choked, he added, "I assumed he'd already been taken away for butchering."

"He hasn't," said Cae. And then, because he found himself oddly perturbed by the notion, "Do Ralians keep no pets, then?"

"No, we do. And if they're infirm or mortally injured, a great value is placed on giving them the kindness of a quick death. But anything beyond that, any mourning or sentiment in their absence, is generally considered excessive. I . . ." He hesitated, the fingers of one hand fidgeting with his sleeve. "What rites *do* you perform, for a fallen horse?"

"Little enough," said Cae. "We cremate them, but keep a braided lock of their mane or tail as a keepsake. Most soldiers have theirs lacquered, for waterproofing."

Velasin swallowed. "I would like that," he said, softly.

"I'll see it done, then." He sipped his khai and pointedly did not stare as Velasin scrubbed a wrist across his eyes. "There's also the matter of our marriage-gathering."

"Ah, yes." Velasin blinked, his expression of grief morphing into polite attention with an ease that would've been impressive, had it not been so jarring. "I recall you speaking of two such events?"

"A smaller and a larger one, yes. The former is meant to introduce whichever partner has moved to live with the other—you, in this case—to their new friends and neighbours; the latter is a bigger affair, meant to show that the marriage is stable, and won't be held for some months yet." *Assuming you don't leave me before that point,* he thought, but did not say. "The smaller, though; that ought to be held soon."

"What qualifies as soon?"

"Within the week."

"Ah," said Velasin. A strange expression flashed across his face. "Forgive me, but . . . will that allow enough time for your mother to get here?"

"My *mother*?" said Cae, unable to keep the surprise from his voice.

Velasin winced. "I'm sorry, that was Ralian of me. I'd just assumed—"

"No, no, it's fine, I understand." He swallowed, trying to school himself against the sudden, unexpected twisting in his chest. "It's not—that is, in other cases—even where parents are divorced, it's common for both to attend a child's marriage-gathering. But this is only the smaller, and like I said, it's more to introduce you to people here than to the whole extended family—that's why

Kivali's not rushing to be here, either, for all she loves a good party. But the larger one . . . my mother most likely will come, then. But that's months away yet. For now, you can think of this as a warm-up." He smiled, relieved to return to more certain conversational waters. "Obviously, you won't be expected to help with the organisation—"

"Obviously," Velasin deadpanned, with just a spark of humour.

"—but there's, ah. There's a tradition you should be aware of?" He winced, hating to hear it come out as a question. "I can ask that we ignore it, of course, but as it's likely to be brought up, you should at least know what's being asked about—"

"What tradition?"

Cae flushed. "Kissing," he said. "Or three kisses, rather. Three kisses each. From—well, the third is meant to be between the couple, but the other two can be claimed by guests, so it's really five in total."

"Kissing," said Velasin, flatly.

"It's meant to symbolise a farewell to—well, to single life, or to past relationships, whichever applies in the context." He gestured helplessly. "It can be platonic, too, it just . . . usually isn't, because the third kiss, the one between spouses, is meant to show what's being chosen instead of what came before, and the expectation is that you stay close with your friends and family. People look forward to it, not least because—well. If you're still on good enough terms with a former lover to invite them, it's expected that they get to kiss your new spouse."

"Your *spouse*?" asked Velasin, surprised. "Not you?"

Cae stared at the ceiling. "It does happen," he allowed, "but it's considered a bit gauche, frankly."

Several seconds ticked by in silence. "And do you, as it happens, have a former lover with whom you are on good terms?"

"I do."

"Ah."

"Quite."

There was a pause, at which point Cae felt obliged to grace Velasin with some eye contact. He was met, in return, with a look of startling intensity, and yet the surrounding expression gave him no clue as to its meaning. "So," said Velasin slowly, "just to be clear, at this small marriage-gathering, both you and I are to be publicly kissed in a non-platonic fashion by two as-yet-unknown persons, though in all likelihood, your former lover will opt—and, indeed, be expected—to kiss me, after which we will both make a show of kissing each other. Do I have it right?"

"You do," said Cae, "but as I said, we don't have to participa—"

Velasin burst out laughing.

"I think I love Tithena," he said, grinning from ear to ear. "You have such novel ideas!"

"So you . . . don't object?"

"My dear Caethari," Velasin drawled, "I may be out of my depth and at potential risk of assassination, but never let it be said that I don't know how to have *fun.* Not, of course, that you've actually seen me *have* fun yet"—a note of apology bled into the words, paired with a softly self-deprecating smile—"but rest assured, making a spectacle of myself by kissing strange men at parties is one of my foremost skill sets."

Despite himself, Cae laughed. "I'll believe it when I see it."

Velasin threw a little sun at his face; Cae caught it, his reflexes easily equal to the task, and popped it smugly into his mouth. Velasin pouted. "What else is on today's agenda, then?" he asked, pointedly eating a little sun of his own.

Cae sighed. "Aside from informing Nairi about our marriage, most everything else involves sorting out this Wild Knife mess. Mirae and the others ought to arrive today, along with the prisoners we took at Vaiko—I'd originally thought to house them in the Amber Gate guardhouse, keep everyone under one roof, but after what we saw last night, I think I'd rather put them elsewhere."

"Understandably so," murmured Velasin.

Belatedly, Cae recalled that his husband had asked his own questions of the Amber Gate guards. "What was your impression of them?" he asked, curious. "The guards, that is, not the bandits."

Velasin stretched his arms above his head, the motion drawing attention to the narrow taper of his waist beneath his borrowed lin. "They were sloppy. Inattentive. Used to disorder. Granted, I'm new to Qi-Katai and Tithena both, but something there felt very wrong."

"I'm inclined to agree with you," Cae said. He paused, letting his disparate thoughts cohere into something useful. "The assassin, last night," he finally said. "Those shots they made between the bars. Did that seem uncanny to you?"

"Uncanny as in freakishly difficult, or uncanny as in magically assisted?"

"The latter."

"Huh." Velasin propped his chin on a fist. "It's not a bad thought, especially given how your father's chambers were breached. There are charms and cantrips for accuracy, for clear sight, for target-honing—that's not to say our target isn't simply an expert marksman, but it's not beyond the realm of possibility, either."

"I confess, I know precious little about magic," Cae admitted. "My father has no time for it, outside of medical contexts."

"You've never tried your hand at it?" asked Velasin, surprised.

"Not since I was a child. Which isn't to say I think that magic is childish," Cae added hastily, "just that—well. My interests tended to lie elsewhere, and in truth, it's a good thing they did."

"Why so?"

"Because mages here are trained by Ruya's Order, and once you swear an oath of temple-service, you're disqualified from holding certain public offices and titles, including the tierency. It's a matter of allegiance: the temples serve the gods first, while the rest of us serve the crown. Trying to do both at once is contradictory. You can be self-taught, of course, or hire private tutors, but past a certain level of skill it's . . . frowned upon, let's say, to take the gods' gift without offering them your service, and there's plenty of cautionary tales about nobles being corrupted by a desire to wield both divine and earthly power. Laecia always had the most aptitude, but there's a reason she's never pursued it." He blinked. "Is it not the same in Ralia?"

"Somewhat the opposite, actually; mages are almost exclusively noblemen. The odd individual might give up his rank to serve a religious order—that much is the same, and for the same reasons—but it's got nothing to do with magic. It's considered a gentleman's skill, you see. Who else could be trusted with it?" Velasin snorted and leaned back in his chair, chewing meditatively on a little sun. "My favourite tutor used to say that magic is energy steered by will informed by knowledge. Without all three, you'll either accomplish nothing or set fire to your own eyebrows, and even with all three, you still need a construct or an anchor to define your intentions, or else you'll set fire to someone else's eyebrows."

"Do you know any spells, then?"

"Spells? Moons, no." Velasin laughed. "*Spells* are complicated, messy things—far too many components for a layperson like me. I attempted a cantrip once and just about got away with it, but that was after weeks of practice; I didn't quite subject myself to the full horrors of magical overextension, but it was a very near thing, and nothing I'd want to experience again in a hurry. I do know a few charms, though. Just simple things, nothing fancy."

Cae leaned forwards, eager despite himself. "Show me."

"What, now?"

"Why not?"

Velasin raised an eyebrow. "I would've thought you'd object to me starting a fire in your apartments."

"Our apartments," Cae corrected automatically. Then, blinking, "You can make fire?"

"I can start one, certainly. Like tapping sparks from a flint, but without the flint." He gestured with an elegant, long-fingered hand.

"Fire needs fuel and air to burn, so it can't come from nowhere, but a spark is more like lightning, a little zap to start things off. *That,* I can make. But, as I said, I assume you'd prefer me not to do so at the breakfast table."

"Another time, then," said Cae, fascinated. "What other charms do you know?"

"I can purify water, or take the salt from it." He wrinkled his nose. "There's a word for that in Ralian, but I don't know it in Tithenai."

"Desalinize?"

"Yes, that sounds right. But surely you've seen that used plenty of times; I'd be shocked if none of your soldiers know it."

"I have, and they do," Cae agreed, lips twitching in a smile. "My father counts it as a medical usage of magic, albeit from the preventative side of things, and therefore sensible."

Velasin snorted. "Very sensible." He paused, as though assessing whether Cae was still interested in the topic of charms. Having established this was so, he went on, "Otherwise, I can untie knots—I'll admit I learned that one for the sake of bootlaces in winter, I can never unpick the damn things in the cold—and detangle hair, which is largely the same, except that I mostly use it for Quip's mane. Used, I mean," he said, eyes dimming at the reminder that his horse was dead. "He never liked being snagged by the comb."

"Velasin—"

"Will you come with me, to see Markel? I want to check in on him before we head out for the day."

"We?"

"Yes, we. On the investigative front, at least—I won't infringe on your meeting with Nairi or the party organisation, but I refuse to sit around like a lump while someone out there is trying to kill me, and possibly your father, while blaming it all on you." He'd been sitting forwards as he spoke, but all at once, his posture slumped again. "Unless you'd rather me keep away, of course."

"Not at all!" Cae said quickly. "I'd welcome your company." It was, after all, only practical: the closer Velasin was to him, the easier he'd be to protect, and they still had a great deal of getting-to-know-each-other to do.

Velasin smiled at him, and Cae ignored a sudden, wildly inappropriate urge to lean across the table and kiss the corner of his mouth.

Practical, he told himself firmly. *That's all.*

18

With the day's agenda set, Cae accompanied Velasin down to the infirmary—letting Velasin lead, to help improve his knowledge of the Aida—to check on Markel. As they walked, he recalled his desire to learn Markel's signs, and decided this was as good a time as any to make a start on that.

"How do I say hello to Markel?" he asked.

Velasin startled, looking at him as if he'd grown antlers. "What?" And then, a confused beat later, "In Ralian?"

"What?" Cae blinked at him, bemused. "I meant in signs."

"Oh!" Velasin's confusion melted into delight. "I mean, for hello, we just wave, the same as anyone else. But if you wanted to say his name—" He held up his hands and made a swift, two-part sign, then paused and made the same sign again, only slower.

Carefully, Cae raised his own hands and copied, stopping as he did so. Velasin followed suit, and Cae turned to face him, as conscious of how he positioned his hands as he'd ever been with his weapons tutors.

"Nearly," said Velasin. "Here, like this—" and he reached out, taking Cae's hands in his own, showing him how to move his fingers just so. It was a purposeful touch, perfunctory, and yet Cae's skin felt hot when Velasin pulled away. Tongue thick in his mouth, he copied the sign as shown, and was rewarded with a beaming smile of approval.

"Well done!"

"How do you come up with signs for names, anyway?" he asked

as they started to walk again. "Is there an alphabet, or do they just exist?"

"There is an alphabet, yes, and you can use it to spell out words and names, but once you know a person, you make a sign that means *them,* like—like a nickname, of sorts, made up of other signs. Markel's sign means Sharp Luck. He chose it himself, when we first started learning together, because—well. He felt it summed up a lot of his life, at that point."

As intrigued as he was, Cae thought this sounded like the start of a longer story for a different time, and so angled his curiosity in another direction. "What does your sign name mean, then?"

Velasin let out a startled laugh, a slight blush warming his cheeks. "Mine is much less interesting, I'm afraid." He demonstrated a different, two-part sign that only required the use of one hand. "It just means Third Son."

"And is that what Markel calls you? Or is there an honorific in there, a *my lord* or suchlike?"

"No honorifics. He calls me my name, as I call him his." He ducked his head, looking oddly flustered. "We've never told anyone that before. It would've been considered . . . odd, in Ralia."

There was a lot Cae wanted to say to that, but none of it felt appropriate. Instead, he waited a beat, then asked, "How do I say good morning?"

In relatively short order, he'd learned how to say *good morning, how are you, sorry, please* and *thank you* with passable confidence, and had also been told what various finger-snaps meant between the two of them. As practiced as he was at learning combat patterns, he'd never learned anything quite like this, and inwardly resolved to improve on that front.

When they entered the infirmary, Cae was surprised to find that Markel, far from being alone, had more company than just Ru Zairin and thir apprentices: Ru Telitha was also present, sitting at his bedside with a small pile of books on her lap and a now-empty breakfast tray on a nearby table. He experienced a brief frisson of worry at this—as lovely as Ru Telitha was, she was also unquestionably Yasa Kithadi's agent, and he mistrusted his grandmother's meddling on principle—but firmly told himself to get over it. *Not the point, Caethari,* he thought, and came to hover at the foot of the bed as Velasin hurried to the side unoccupied by Ru Telitha.

Speaking Ralian—which jolted Cae for a moment, until he recalled that Markel's knowledge of Tithenai was still a secret—Velasin said, "How are you feeling? Is there anything I can get you?"

Markel smiled, replying with a flurry of signs. Whatever he said relaxed Velasin considerably; Cae hadn't realised his husband was strung so tight until he saw the tension vanish, and mentally scolded himself for being inattentive.

"He should be back on his feet tomorrow," said Ru Zairin, choosing this moment to wander over. Thei stood a little to Cae's right, looking between Velasin and Markel. "He'll still need to take it easy, of course, but I'll perform another healing cantrip once he's had time to digest his breakfast, and if that goes well, then I'll sew him up."

Dutifully (if unnecessarily) Velasin relayed this to Markel in Ralian, who nodded gravely. Satisfied that all was understood, Ru Zairin then turned to Velasin and said, one eyebrow pointedly raised, "As for you, tiern, how are your stitches holding?"

Velasin had the grace to look a little chastened. "Admirably," he said. "Do you, ah—do you wish to see them?"

Ru Zairin let the question hang for a moment, then shook thir head. "So long as there's no bleeding or inflammation, you should be fine—but if you see any signs of either, come to me immediately, you understand?"

"Yes, ru."

"Good." Ru Zairin swept them all with thir gaze, nodded politely and then headed back to thir workbench.

Seizing the moment, Cae caught Markel's eye and clumsily signed, "Good morning, Markel. How are you?"

A slow, broad smile spread across Markel's face. He signed a slow response, glancing at Velasin as he did so. Translating, his husband said, "He says he's feeling much better, and thanks you for asking."

"I'm glad to hear it," Cae replied. He nodded a belated acknowledgement to Ru Telitha, who'd been watching this all with an expression of polite interest, and said, "Good morning, ru. I hope my grandmother was not unduly inconvenienced by my volunteering the Tierena's Library for Markel's use?"

Ru Telitha smiled prettily. "Yasa Kithadi is always pleased to assist her family."

Cae swallowed an extremely uncharitable remark. "Please convey my thanks to her, then."

"Of course."

While they'd been talking aloud, Markel and Velasin had begun signing to one another, a quick back-and-forth that Cae found fascinating. He had no idea what they were saying to one another; Markel looked concerned at first, but his expression evened out at whatever Velasin said in reply, and by the end, both men looked, if not quite happy, then certainly in accord with one another.

"Ru Telitha," said Velasin—aloud, and in Tithenai, "I entrust Markel to your company. Please pass on my thanks to your mistress, for the loan of her books."

"It is no trouble, tiern," said Ru Telitha.

Velasin nodded, then looked to Cae. "Next order of business?"

"Next order of business," Cae affirmed, and with a parting goodbye to all present, including Ru Zairin, they headed back out to the Aida.

This time, it was Cae who took the lead: they needed to find Raeki, assuming the tar was available to be found, and Velasin had not yet been to the Aida's barracks.

"I told Markel about what happened last night," said Velasin, as they turned a corner. "And that we're investigating. He wants me to be careful, which isn't anything new."

"I can't say I blame him."

Velasin shot him a quelling look, which Cae ignored. "Regardless, I also gave him the bare bones of your relationship to Yasa Kithadi and the inheritance tangle. He knows that Ru Telitha works for her, and unless he opts to tell her himself—which he might, in due course; we'll see how things play out—Ru Telitha doesn't know that he speaks Tithenai, so in the event that she lets anything useful slip, he'll pass it on to us."

Cae grimaced. "My thanks. I hate how blasted complicated everything is. I'm no good at politics."

"Politics is just people, only bigger."

"I'm not very good at people, either."

"I find that extremely hard to believe."

"Well," Cae allowed, "perhaps I'm good at some people."

"You've certainly won Markel over. I—if you like, I could teach you the hand-sign alphabet later?" He offered this last hesitantly, as though still unsure of Cae's interest.

"Please," said Cae, trying to inject as much sincerity into the word as possible. "If we can, I'd like to make time to learn a little every day."

Velasin nodded, looking quietly pleased. "We can do that," he said, and then blinked, as though a thought had just occurred to him. "Speaking of languages, when and how did you ever learn Ralian? It didn't occur to me to ask, before."

"Ah," said Cae. "Well, it's reasonably common as a trade-language, here—the Attovari and Palamites tend to speak it more often than they do Tithenai, so we were all taught the basics as children—but in my case, it was a matter of practicality." He hesitated, hoping that Velasin would take the inference. When he didn't, Cae sighed and said, "I spent the better part of a decade fighting Ralians in the Taelic Pass. It's hard to interrogate captives if you don't speak their language."

Velasin winced. "Oh."

"It's not—" Cae blurted, feeling a sudden need to explain himself, to dispel any lingering fears his husband might have on that account, "—it's not that I've ever born Ralians any ill-will." He flinched at the lie, then amended, "Or, well, no. That's not true. Early on, when I was younger and vin Mica's actions first started to affect us, I was furious; I took it as a damning indictment of your whole nation, and the first few times I rode out against Ralian bandits, I felt myself a proper defender of Tithena." He shook his head, grimacing at the folly of his younger self. "Then I opened my eyes and saw I was raising my sword against, not selfish killers, but desperate men driven by fear and poverty. Some were rough and greedy, yes, but no more so than you'd find among people anywhere, and once our own folk started to turn criminal under the same conditions . . . well. It was hard to hold the idea that we were inherently special, they inherently flawed. The waste of life and livelihood, that's what stung, and yet I couldn't do anything to fix the root of it. All I could do was fight." He shrugged and looked away, obscurely embarrassed by the admission.

"I'd heard," said Velasin haltingly, "that you rode against vin Mica himself a time or two."

"It's likely," Cae admitted. "More than once, our patrol camps or the traders we escorted suffered raids by well-armed men, better trained and more coordinated than was usual, and we never did catch their leader. It could well have been him. But they never announced themselves as such, and they didn't wear his colours."

"They wouldn't have," said Velasin, softly.

An awkward silence followed. As it hung between them, they emerged from the Aida's hallways into the Court of Swords, where a group of soldiers was already engaged in training exercises. The sight of them left Cae with a prickling, guilty self-consciousness about the fact that he'd had no time for training of his own since before Velasin's arrival. Nairi had a sixth sense for such things, and would doubtless rib him mercilessly for it when he finally reported in.

Shoving these unhelpful thoughts aside, Cae cast around for a familiar face and was relieved to find one in the form of Kita, who was supervising as two younger recruits went through a series of block-and-parry drills.

"Dai Kita!" he hailed her.

She turned, lips twitching as Cae and Velasin approached. "Good morning, tierns," she said, touching her right hand to her left breast and bowing slightly. "How can I be of assistance?"

"We're looking for Tar Raeki," said Cae. "Do you know where he might be found?"

"I do, at that. He passed by here not long ago, on his way to speak with Tar Katvi."

"Excellent! My thanks, Dai Kita. As you were."

"Tiern," she said again, repeating her half-bow, and with a quick flash of smile to Velasin, she turned back to her recruits.

"Tar Katvi has an office near the mess hall," Cae said, as they started walking again. "This is good; we can speak to them both at once without having to trek down to Amber Gate again."

"I still can't see the pattern in all this," said Velasin. "What was the point in attacking your father? If you can even call it an attack."

Cae glanced at him sharply. "What does that mean?"

"I don't know. Sorry." Velasin shot him an apologetic look. "It's just, the more I think about it, the odder it seems. Whatever magic was used to break into the tieren's rooms, it's hardly common stuff. Whoever this is went to a lot of trouble to learn it—or even more trouble to have their tools spelled for them, if they aren't a practicing mage—and then they go and waste it all by waking the target and missing their strike? Did they truly have no plan for moving silently; no plan for if your father fought back? And yet they made absolutely sure to say that the Wild Knife sent them, even when it would've made more sense to flee in silence."

Cae digested this analysis, and was disturbed to find no clear-cut flaws. "You think it was a stunt," he said, slowly. "A misdirection."

"Perhaps," said Velasin, not meeting his gaze. "I only wonder, what if the real goal wasn't to harm the tieren, but to sow dissent in your family? Or at the very least, to make us aware that whatever anti-Ralian faction is using your name has more power than we realised. A warning-shot, to let us know their capabilities."

Both prospects were unsettling. "Whatever they mean, they claim to do it in my name," said Cae, unable to keep the growl from his voice. "Do they truly think I've sanctioned them? Is there someone out there pretending to be my liaison to their group, or do they just assume I'll support their actions? Ren Baru seemed to think so, but he was clearly expendable. If they lied to him about my involvement while still using my name, that suggests they're using me as a false figurehead. But to what end?"

Velasin made a frustrated noise. "Ren Baru's attack on Markel—he didn't live long enough to confirm that he thought I was wed to your sister, not you, but the way he reacted when Raeki told him suggests so. But everything that's happened since then . . . they *know* we're married now. So why haven't they changed tactics?" He came to an abrupt standstill, so that Cae kept going for an extra step and then had to turn and face him. "But if they had changed . . . how would we tell? It's not like we've got their original checklist to compare it against." He looked at Cae, a strange light in his eyes. "We need to find the negative space."

Cae blinked at him, uncomprehending. "The what?"

Velasin started moving again, obliging Cae to do likewise. "Maybe the term doesn't translate; it's what Ralian artists call the space around an image. If I drew a portrait of you—just a portrait, no background—then all the blank paper would be the negative space. But sometimes, artists use the negative space to make a sort of trick picture, a second picture that reverses the lines of the first . . . oh, I'm not explaining this properly!" He clicked his teeth, walking faster. "What I mean is, we need to look at what these people *have* done, since I married you, to find the shape of what they *haven't;* to try and see how their plans have changed. Weren't we just saying yesterday—was it only yesterday? Moons!—that killing Quip was a de-escalation; that it didn't make sense?"

"You made that leap first, I believe," said Cae.

Velasin waved an irritable hand, as if his own intelligence were of little consequence. "Either way, the point is that this might explain it. We've been trying to see the shape of a plan, but what if we ought to be looking for a plan bent out of shape?"

"I think you might be right," said Cae, punctuating the comment with a gentle grab to Velasin's elbow as he went to steer the wrong way down a junction.

Velasin startled at the contact. "What?"

Cae's lips twitched, the only outward sign of the sudden surge of fondness he was struggling to conceal. "Velasin. Do you know the way to Tar Katvi's office?"

"No?"

"Because I do."

"Ah." Velasin flushed, an embarrassed smile flickering on his lips. "Yes. Quite. Lead on, tiern."

Cae did so, and within minutes they'd arrived at Tar Katvi's door. A quick knock was answered by Raeki, whose glower at being interrupted smoothed out into relief when he saw who the visitors were.

"Tierns," he said, bowing them through. "Please, come in."

Tar Katvi was seated behind her desk, an expression of weary annoyance etched on her features. She stood as they entered, but sat with relief when Cae waved her back down.

"How goes the investigation?" he asked, taking one of the visitors' chairs as Velasin took the other.

"Slowly," said Raeki, leaning against Tar Katvi's desk. "I met with the tieren's intelligencer, and while he's keeping an ear to the ground about anti-Ralian sentiment, before this, he wasn't aware of any groups who affiliated themselves with or overly esteemed the Wild Knife." He made a frustrated noise. "If only we'd gotten anything from Ren Baru before that bastard shot him—"

"I'd lay money he was a merchant," said Cae. "There was a touch of Khyto in his vowels, too—not a native speaker, but I'd wager he dealt with Khytoi traders enough to have picked it up. It's not much of a starting place, but together with his name, it's better than nothing." Khytë was a mountainous nation north and west of Tithena, known mostly in Qi-Katai for their trade in furs, pelts, leather and artifex, though that was far from their only commerce. Cae's education as a potential heir to the tierency had covered their basic customs, systems of governance, imports and exports, but to his shame, he'd forgotten most of it through lack of use. Riya and Laecia had always been better at scholarly pursuits.

Raeki looked first stunned, then focussed. "It certainly is that," he said, exchanging a meaningful look with Tar Katvi. "I'll send someone trustworthy to investigate as soon as we're done here."

Cae mentally cursed himself for not having shared that particular observation with the tar last night. But then, they'd both been so busy that it hadn't seemed pressing, and on top of everything else—

"Speaking of which," he said, "I take it you'll be speaking with those Amber Gate guards today?"

"Yes, tiern; and their commander, Varu Shan Dalu. Something there stinks, and I don't like it one bit."

"Good," said Cae. "On which note, when Mirae and the others return with the Vaiko prisoners, I'd rather keep them in the Aida." He glanced at Tar Katvi. "Unless that would prove troublesome for you, tar?"

Tar Katvi shook her head. "Not at all, tiern." She glanced at Raeki, took a breath and added, "I've just been writing up a report for the tieren about the magic used to break into his chambers. According to Ruya's Order, there are a variety of different magics that could've been used to scale the wall, but only a very few, very complex spells or cantrips that could've allowed such a swift, safe descent. The Order does keep records of mages with the ability to perform at such a high level, but only of those who are temple-certified; anyone less . . . officially taught will be harder to find." She straightened. "Still, I have the names, and they might yet lead us somewhere. If our culprit ever studied in the temples and was talented enough to be memorable, a former colleague might recall them." She laughed dryly. "Or maybe we'll get lucky, and the first temple-certified mage we speak to will confess."

"Thank you, Tar Katvi," said Cae. He rubbed his forehead, hating how little they had to go on. "And what about Velasin's horse? Do we have any leads on who might've done that, at least?"

Raeki winced. "Not as yet, tiern. Last night, I had my people talk to all the grooms who were working yesterday and a few who weren't, and I went through their statements first thing this morning. From all the goings in and out, we can pinpoint when it must've happened, but there are no witnesses."

"Nobody?" said Velasin, angry and disbelieving. "How do you kill a horse in a busy stable and not be seen?"

Raeki shot him an apologetic look, which Cae knew was genuine; however the tar felt about Velasin personally, he held a special loathing for the mistreatment of animals. "Right before it happened, there was a commotion out in the yards. Tiera Riya's seneschal rides a stallion, and just as he returned from the city, a groom was leading a mare in heat over to the Little Aida. The mare's lead-rope snapped, the stallion threw his rider, and every groom in the place was trying to grab either one or the other, never mind trying to keep the seneschal safe. The whole furore lasted less than ten minutes, but that was enough, and the sound of it would've covered any noise from the stables besides."

Velasin frowned. "That seems . . . unduly convenient, for whoever killed Quip. Whose mare was it, and why was she headed for the Little Aida?"

"Yasa Kithadi keeps no stallions as a rule," Cae explained. "As such, she often allows her stable to be used as boarding for mares in heat who aren't to be put to stud."

Raeki nodded. "The mare belongs to one of the Aida's guards—Dai Tarsa Xon. Nothing untoward in her being moved when she was; it's not like our assailant has the ability to make a mare's heat start on command. The tiera's seneschal returning when he did, though . . . someone could've arranged for the two to intersect." He glanced at Cae. "With your permission, tiern, I'll speak to Tiera Riya's man myself. He told the guard who questioned him yesterday that he was running errands for his mistress, but perhaps there's something more to it."

Cae nodded. "Please do. If Riya makes a fuss at all, just send her my way and I'll explain. And—" He hesitated, glancing at Velasin. "—if you pass that way, I'd appreciate you asking the stables to cremate my husband's horse, and to save a braid of hair for him."

"Of course, tiern," said Raeki, bowing. "Is there anything else?"

Cae shared another look with his husband, who nodded approval. "Yes, as it happens," he said, and proceeded to lay out the chain of logic they'd worked through together on the way over; or which, more accurately, Velasin had worked through while Cae listened. Both tars looked thoughtful—Tar Katvi especially so, at the idea that the strike on Tieren Halithar was never meant to be fatal—and remained silent for several seconds when Cae was done.

"Well," said Raeki. "That certainly does bear thinking about. If Ren Baru was lied to, mind, it could be that what's happening now would've happened regardless of who Tiern Velasin married, but that business with the horse . . . without wanting to discount the threat to my tieren's safety, it's the horse that troubles me most."

"Why?" asked Tar Katvi, getting in a breath ahead of Cae himself.

"Because it's personal," Raeki said. "And worse, if that damn scramble in the yards yesterday was truly an accident—if nobody pulled the seneschal's strings or placed that mare just so—then killing the horse was a crime of opportunity. And if that's the case—"

"—then our villain lives in the Aida," Cae finished. "Or at least has access to it."

The prospect left a mix of worried and sickened expressions on all their faces. "I'll speak to all the guards," said Tar Katvi, after a moment. Her voice was dark, her expression darker. "Tighten security everywhere, not just around the tieren's and tierns' quarters. If we're harbouring a rat in our ranks, I want to know about it."

"Your lips to Zo's ears," murmured Raeki. Then, to Cae, "If that's all, tiern, I've a day's work to get to. Might I be excused?"

"Certainly," said Cae, whose own docket was far from empty. He glanced at Velasin. "Where to next?"

"Actually," said Velasin slowly, "if Tar Raeki doesn't object, I thought I might . . . that is, I could walk with him to the stables. Oversee Quip's burning." He ducked his head, glancing uncertainly at Cae. "Assuming that's permitted, of course?"

"Of course," Cae said, softly.

"Not that I'm trying to run out on you," Velasin added quickly, "but as we discussed, you've tasks to do that don't require my presence. You can collect me again, afterwards. I'll be—well, I assume you'd know where a horse-cremation would take place better than I do, but if I'm not there, then I'll either be with Markel or in your apartments."

"Our apartments," Cae said. "And yes, that makes sense."

Velasin smiled—a little sadly, but understandably so, given what he was about to do—stood, and proceeded to follow Raeki out of Tar Katvi's office. Cae lingered just long enough that they wouldn't have to walk awkwardly down the same hallway after they'd already farewelled each other, then rose in turn, thanked Tar Katvi for her time and headed off to take care of his own emotionally laborious tasks: arranging the marriage-gathering, and telling Nairi about it.

19

To Cae's enormous relief, once he ran Keletha to ground in thir apartments, it turned out that the bulk of the marriage-gathering arrangements had already been made. When he expressed his surprise and delight at this discovery, Keletha rolled thir eyes and smacked him over the head with a rolled-up scroll, and none too gently, either.

"Tiern Caethari," thei said, thir voice as dry as Attovari wine. "Please do me the courtesy of assuming that I know how to do my job! I had little else to occupy my evenings on the road home from Ralia than to draft lists of things to be done once your marriage took place, and establishing a guest list was among the easiest." Thei cast around on the overburdened table and unearthed a clipboard with several attached pages, thumping it against his chest. "There. Sit down and read that, and tell me if there's anyone I've omitted, or included who you'd rather not be there."

"Yes, grandkiun," he said meekly, offering up the rare familial title as a sign of contrition. Technically, neither of them was meant to acknowledge the relationship—envoys gave up their kin-names and kin-ties both—but private conversations between close relatives were understood to be an exception.

"Wretch," muttered Keletha, not without a certain degree of fondness.

Keletha's guest list was, of course, perfect: in addition to such selective members of Qi-Katai's aristocratic, political and mercantile circles as were expected to be invited, the members of his revetha with whom he was closest were all there, as was Liran. Also attached to the clipboard were suggestions for food, which Cae was happy to leave to thir discretion—and, by proxy, to the discretion of his sisters, who had evidently already spoken to Keletha about the matter.

"When do you think we should hold it?" Cae asked. The guest list wasn't huge—around a hundred people, including family, which counted as small by the standards of the Tithenai nobility—but it was still a large enough event that the Aida's staff would need time to prepare, while the guests were owed the courtesy of at least a day in which to prepare themselves. For bigger, more elaborate parties, it was standard to send an invite no less than seven days before the event itself, but marriage-gatherings were different: once the justiciar's notice was posted, as theirs had been, anyone likely to be invited would know to expect one soon. All the real panoply would be reserved for the festivities held in a month or so, when the marriage was shown to be working; this was just an appetizer.

"Three days from now," said Keletha, after a moment's consideration. "That's Ruyasday, twenty-fifth Kidae. Unless the tieren has any objections, I'll have the invites written up and sent out by this afternoon." Thei hesitated, expression turning troubled. "After our last conversation about Tiern Velasin, I can't help but ask—have you told him about the, ah, party tradition?"

"I have, yes," said Cae. "I was worried, too, but he laughed and said it sounds fun."

Keletha looked visibly relieved. "Well, that's something." Thei fixed Cae with an assessing look. "All this Wild Knife trouble notwithstanding, how are the two of you getting along?"

"Just fine," said Cae.

"Just fine?"

"Absolutely fine." And then, because Keletha was still looking at him in a way that was unpleasantly reminiscent of Yasa Kithadi, "We've agreed to be friends."

"Well, that's certainly better than nothing."

"Yes, it is."

Keletha raised an eyebrow, looking very much like thei wanted to ask for more details. Rather than provide them, Cae stood up, apologised and cited his—extremely legitimate!—business elsewhere as a reason why he couldn't linger. Keletha clearly wasn't fooled, but allowed him to escape regardless, and Cae took the out with relief.

As he walked, he had an idle, hopeful thought about maybe running into Velasin at the stables, and promptly quashed it as unlikely. Poor Quip would be cremated in one of the powerful furnaces that burned beneath the Aida, providing heat not only for the laundries and hot water pipes that ran throughout the structure, but also the communal baths used by guards and servants alike. Recalling the awful sight of Velasin kneeling in his horse's blood, Cae clenched his jaw. Raeki was right: the killing of Quip was personal, brutal, menacing in a way that somehow went beyond everything else. For all the culprit had taken the time to scribe a bloody threat on the wall, the politics hardly seemed the point. But who in Qi-Katai could hate Velasin the man, as opposed to Velasin the unknown Ralian? He'd hardly been here long enough.

Had the crime taken place in Ralia, however . . . as little as Cae knew of his husband's life before this, there was one name that leapt instantly to mind. *Killic.* Lord Killic vin Lato, may he rot where he lay, was certainly capable of such cruelty. As he reached the stables, Cae entertained a short, vicious fantasy of Killic being caught skulking about the Aida, remanded in ungentle custody and then subjected to Tithena's sharpest justice, preferably at his own hands. It was impossible, of course—Keletha and Raeki had been neither shadowed nor leapfrogged on the Taelic Pass, to say nothing of what had happened at Vaiko—but just for a moment, he let himself indulge the fantasy.

"Tiern!" exclaimed a groom, shaking Cae from his thoughts. "Do you require assistance?"

"I'd like Alik saddled, please," he said. The groom bowed acknowledgement and hurried off to comply, leaving Cae to his own devices.

Surrounded by the scent of sweat, hay and horse, Cae walked slowly forwards, looking for the place where Quip had fallen. Sure enough, there was a dark, red-brown stain on the stone before an unhappily empty stall. The terrible words on the wall had been cleaned from the wood, but blood was harder to remove from porous stone, and Cae suspected it would be a while until this particular stall was used again. Grooms had their own superstitions, and what could be more ill-omened than the site of a murdered horse?

In short order, Alik was brought to him, tack gleaming and immaculate. Alik nosed at his shoulder, and Cae scratched indulgently at his ears. "Thank you," he said to the groom.

He'd expected the man to bow and leave, but instead, he hesitated. "Tiern," he said, voice trembling. "I don't mean to importune you, but—Tiern Velasin. How is he?"

Belatedly, Cae recognised the groom: Ren Taiko, who'd found Quip's body. "He's seeing his horse cremated," he said, gently. "Other than that, he's as well as he can be."

"I failed him," Ren Taiko whispered. "Tiern, I'm so sorry."

"It wasn't your fault," said Cae. "Truly, ren."

Ren Taiko lifted his head, a terrible light in his eyes. "I won't fail again, tiern. I swear by Ayla, Zo and Ruya, until this murdering fiend is caught, these stables won't be left unattended!"

Cae didn't quite know what to say to that, but was thankfully spared the necessity of a reply, as Ren Taiko promptly ducked his head, bowed and hurried off. Cae watched him vanish into the tack room, let out a sigh and swung himself onto Alik's back. There was no more excuse for stalling: now that Keletha was sending out invites to the marriage-gathering, it would be unforgiveable to let Nairi receive hers before Cae had so much as spoken to her in person.

It was a pleasant, sunny morning, the late-autumn air crisp and clean as he rode out of the Aida. He walked Alik at first, letting the gelding stretch his legs, then raised him to a trot as he passed the Amber Gate, sparing a sour glance for the guardhouse as it went by in his periphery. Doubtless he'd be back there again at some point: whatever came of Raeki's investigations, it was clear the place needed a thorough shake-up.

Qi-Katai's revetha was located in the middle city, slightly above the smithy district and abutting the Iron Market, where the armaments made below were sold. Despite the early-morning bustle thronging the streets, Cae made good time, and was soon pulling up at the open gates to the compound.

The two men on guard duty recognised him instantly. "Congratulations, tiern!" called one, while the other grinned and whip-whistled.

"Your jealousy is noted!" Cae replied, making a semi-obscene hand gesture at the whistler, who laughed in reply.

Beyond were the training yards, which were busier than the Aida's as a matter of course. Cae dismounted in short order, tied Alik to a hitching-post on a long enough rein that he could drink from the trough, and wove his way through the familiar, comforting bustle. As rahan, Nairi rated personal quarters on the second floor of the barracks; her office, however, was in the administrative block, and so he headed there first, exchanging hellos in passing with people he recognised.

He found Nairi ensconced behind her desk, her frown framed by the two teetering stacks of paperwork that were undoubtedly its cause. He took a moment to watch her from the open doorway, then rapped smartly on the frame. She lifted her head and glared at him, though more for the noise than the interruption. Her blue-black skin looked almost iridescent in the sunlight, while her head was freshly shaven enough to gleam beneath its stubble.

"There you are," she said, as though he were a favourite mug misplaced in the kitchen. "I was wondering when you'd show up."

"Here I am," he said, helping himself to the visitors' chair. "Reporting in to tell you, officially, in your capacity as my rahan, that I am newly married."

"You don't say," Nairi drawled. She stared at him for a good three seconds, just long enough for Cae to wonder whether she really was offended he'd taken so long to tell her, before bursting into laughter. "Gods, your *face*!" she cackled, slapping the desk. "What, did you honestly think I'd chew you out for not getting down here sooner?"

"The thought had crossed my mind."

Nairi shot him a withering look, though she was still smiling. "Seriously, though. Congratulations! Or, well," she amended, a hint of curiosity creeping into her tone, "hopefully congratulations?"

"The former," he said, and was touched by her clear relief. "Which isn't to say it's not complicated, but—we're friends. That's enough, for now."

"The Wild Knife, married to a Ralian," she mused. "Who would've predicted it? Not me, certainly."

Cae felt an obscure pang. Nairi had known him long enough to have seen his early anger at Ralia's incursions into the Taelic Pass firsthand, and though they both knew he'd grown since then, hearing it referenced suddenly felt shameful. "Nai, you know it's not like that," he said.

Nairi's eyebrows rose. "I know," she said. And then, a heartbeat later, "Does it truly not feel strange?"

"Perhaps," Cae admitted, "but not for that reason. It's just . . . complicated."

"Ralians usually are," drawled Nairi. "Saints know, they tie themselves up in knots enough over nothing. I'm just surprised they agreed to let one of their men become your husband."

"Like I said, it's complicated."

"Hm." All at once, her gaze sharpened. "I do hear, though, that there was some trouble when he arrived? Something about an assailant going after his servant?"

"Trouble indeed, and not just when he arrived," said Cae. Knowing he could trust her discretion, he gave Nairi a quick rundown of everything that had happened, beginning with the attack at Vaiko and ending with the murder of Ren Baru, omitting only Velasin's personal traumas. Her expression went from troubled to grim, finally settling on worried.

"Saints, Cae, you don't do anything by halves, do you?" she said, when he finished his recitation.

Chagrined, he replied, "Apparently not."

Nairi sighed. "I'd offer to help, but I suspect if there was anything useful for me to do, you'd have asked it of me already."

"Correct."

"Still. If nothing else, I can keep my eyes sharp at your marriage-gathering—I assume I rate an invite? Teasing!" she added, when he straightened in indignation. "Prickly today, aren't you?"

"Just a bit," he allowed, slouching again.

"Cae," said Nairi, and all at once, her tone was unbearably gentle. "Is Liran coming, too?"

"He is," said Cae, "but truly, Nairi, he's not—that's no longer an issue. It hasn't been for a while now."

She levelled him with an assessing look, then blinked, apparently determining that he meant it. "Huh," she said. And then, because she, like his sisters, was far too observant for his personal comfort, "So. This Tiern Velasin—what's he like?"

Cae manfully resisted the urge to squirm away from the question, but couldn't quite suppress a sigh. "Impossibly stubborn. Witty. Kind. So clever he cuts himself with it. Brave." *And utterly beautiful.*

Nairi's face softened; she knew him far too well. "Oh, Cae."

"Don't," he said, running a hand down his face. "Please, Nai. It's not—there are complications. Nothing I can speak of, and nothing to his discredit, but . . . complications, nonetheless."

"When are there not?" she said, a touch sadly. She looked like she wanted to say more, but whatever look Cae shot her mercifully did the trick. "At any rate, I'll see for myself soon, won't I?"

"You will," he said. "Keletha's aiming to get the invites out this afternoon, but barring further incidents"—he made the sign against tempting fate, tapping his left shoulder, forehead and right shoulder—"the marriage-gathering should be in three days."

"I'll clear my extremely busy schedule," Nairi said dryly.

With the serious business out of the way, they indulged in some casual conversation, which mostly consisted of Nairi catching him up on the soldier-gossip he'd missed the past few days. The long-running saga of Cae's squadmates Xani and Seluya, who'd been on-again, off-again since approximately the dawn of time, had once more veered back into on-again territory, with the result that half the revetha was in on a betting pool as to how long it would last this time. They were just unpicking the odds when a nervous young dai poked his head in and said, "Sorry to interrupt, rahan, but the quartermaster has an issue that requires your oversight."

Nairi sighed. "Tell thim I'll be right there."

The dai saluted and hurried off. Cae stood along with Nairi, the two of them clasping hands as she came around the desk.

"We'll catch up again soon," she said. And then, with just a touch of smirk, "Go be with your *husband.*"

Cae's neck flushed hot. "I will," he said, loudly. "He's very good company!"

"I'm sure he is," said Nairi, waggling her eyebrows.

Cae turned away, heading to where he'd left Alik. "Fine, goodbye, I hate you!"

"Hate you too!" she called cheerfully after him.

The ride back up to the Aida was less pleasant than the ride down had been. The temperature had risen with the sun, and the city's pale stone seemed to magnify the unseasonal heat, while any fresh breeze was broken up by the buildings. Cae was sweating by the time he passed the Amber Gate, and the instant Alik was safe in the stables, he went in search of a wash and some fresh clothes.

Without much thinking about it, he headed straight to the communal bathhouse, something he often did after training in the

Court of Swords or a vigorous ride. Stripping perfunctorily in the outer chamber, he had one of the attendants take his dirty things to be laundered and then strode naked into the rinse-room, sighing with relief as he stood beneath the flow of cold water. The temperature change was a refreshing shock: just what he needed. Ordinarily, he would've progressed to the second chamber, where the heated baths and showers were, but today, he decided against it; he'd only wanted to cool down, get the sweat off, and it wasn't like he'd worked his muscles hard enough to need the heat. He'd even managed to keep the bulk of his hair dry, too, thus sparing himself the trouble of having to rebraid it.

Mood vastly improved, Cae snagged a fresh towel from the linen cubby, wrapped it firmly around his hips, redonned his boots, which were the only garment now left to him, and, heedless of propriety, walked out into the Aida, grinning cheerfully at every guard, servant and passerby who gawked at his semi-naked state. Probably someone would chastise him later, but just at that moment, he couldn't find it within himself to care.

By the time he made it back to his (no, their, *their*) apartments, he was practically dry. Feeling pleased with himself, he removed his boots at the door, stepped inside, and startled at the sight of Velasin, the likelihood of whose presence he'd somehow managed to forget. Velasin likewise froze in turn, so that they were stuck gawking at each other.

"Oh," said Cae, stupidly.

Velasin was wearing Tithenai clothes—not Cae's borrowed garb, but new things tailored to his form. Evidently, Ren Lithas had been as good as his word about the speed of their creation, and the results were making it hard for Cae to function. Velasin was wearing Aeduria colours: forest-green nara, a pure white undershirt whose billowing sleeves cinched tight at the wrists and a gold-and-cream lin striped with green, the fit of which perfectly emphasised both the breadth of his chest and his tapered waist. His hair was still pulled back, but for the first time Cae noticed that his ears were pierced, for all that they were currently devoid of ornamentation. *I should buy him something,* he thought distantly. *Something gold.*

And here, by comparison, stood Cae, clad only in a borrowed towel.

"You seem to have had an adventure, tiern," said Velasin faintly, breaking the silence. That beautiful dusky blush was staining his cheeks, and Cae hated and loved that he now knew how far down it went.

"Ah. Yes. Sorry," said Cae, grinning ruefully. "This is, ah—I just got back from the revetha and it's hot out, so I wanted a wash. I went to the communal baths and usually when I do that I've got spare clothes waiting for me ahead of time, but I didn't today, so I just . . . walked back up here."

"You walked."

"Yes."

"In your towel."

"Right."

"Right," said Velasin. "Right, that's—certainly. Yes. But, ah—I was actually referring to those." He gestured towards Cae's ribs.

The scars from the bear attack had been there for so long that, even when staring down at his own naked torso, it took Cae several confused seconds to realise what his husband was referring to. When he finally understood, however, he looked up and laughed.

"Oh, these!" He patted the long, raised lines. "It was a rabid bear, years ago."

"A rabid *bear*?" Velasin looked genuinely horrified. "Sweet moons bless, you're lucky it didn't tear you in half!"

"At the time, we were more worried it might've given me the water-sickness. Transmission is usually through bites, not scratches, but what I got was hardly a lovetap. I was lucky on both counts." He hesitated, not wanting to sound a braggart while also wanting, just a little, to brag, and added, "I did kill it, though. As sick as it was, the poor thing was much weaker than it should've been. I'd speared it through, but it kept on moving, impaling itself. That's how it got me—one last swipe as it came in range, with half a spear through its back."

"How old were you?"

"Fifteen."

Velasin made a shocked noise. "I'm not sure I could be that brave now, let alone at fifteen."

Cae snorted. "Being fifteen is four parts bravery to six parts foolishness. Deciding to hunt down a rabid bear was definitely the latter."

Velasin grinned at that—and then, abruptly, appeared to recall that Cae was still half-naked, and that this was a source of embarrassment to him. Coughing, he turned to face the wall, waving a hand towards Cae's bedroom. "You should get dressed, tiern. Don't let me keep you waiting."

20

I'll be out in a moment," Cae said, suddenly paranoid that Velasin would take his absence as an excuse to leave. He didn't shut his door all the way, but left it ajar, shedding his towel as he grabbed new clothes from the chest and dressed with unprecedented speed. He hurried out while still donning his lin, and was unduly relieved to find that Velasin, who'd shown no sign of being about to rush off, was exactly where he'd left him.

"Sorry about that," said Cae, straightening his undershirt.

Velasin turned, a faint smile twitching his lips. "There's nothing to forgive, tiern."

"Caethari," said Cae, suddenly. "Can you, I mean—if we are to be friends, I'd ask that you use my name."

"Caethari, then," said Velasin, after an awkward beat. He looked away, his flush returning. "My apologies. I don't mean to keep putting you at arm's length, but I'm not . . . good, at this."

"Neither am I."

"You know what I mean."

Cae blinked. "I'm not sure I do."

Velasin gestured tightly. "I mean that you're not—you're not damaged."

"Neither are you."

"There's really no need to coddle me."

"I'm not!" said Cae, uncertain how the conversation had gotten away from him. "Velasin, you might be adrift, you might be hurt and healing, but you're not *damaged.*"

"I feel damaged," he said, softly.

Cae inhaled, staring at the floor as he struggled to find his words. Finally, he said, "I can't tell you how to feel about yourself, but I can say I don't share the sentiment. That's not how I think of you. That's never how I've thought of you."

"That's . . . oddly reassuring." Velasin lifted his head, and just like that, the tiny smile was back. "I'm sorry, ti—Caethari. I have a terrible knack for maudlin self-indulgence, and I'm rather used to Markel being around to snap me out of it."

"He'll be out of the infirmary tomorrow, Ru Zairin said. Then he'll be up here with us." Cae gestured to the newly restored servants' chamber, which despite the name was scarcely any smaller than Velasin's own room. "Is there anything missing from his quarters that you'd want me to add, or anything present you think should be removed?"

Velasin shook his head. "It looks extremely comfortable," he said. "I shouldn't think Markel would want to change anything, but I'll let you know if he does." He hesitated. "You truly don't mind him being here with us? I can't help but feel that we're crowding you out of your own apartments."

"*Our* apartments, Velasin, and you're hardly crowding me."

"I'm sorry. I suspect I'm being Ralian again." He sighed. "It's just that I'm . . . unaccustomed, let's say, to the idea that a relationship between two men isn't something to be ashamed of."

Cae's neck grew hot. "But we're not—I mean, we're married, certainly, but we aren't—"

"That's not what I mean," said Velasin quickly. "I mean . . . even if we weren't married, because this is Tithena, I wouldn't have to be careful of how much time I spend with you, to stop other people from gossipping about what we are to each other. I don't have to keep offering to leave to spare you the trouble of telling me to go, because you're not worried we might be found out. I know you keep calling these *our* apartments, not yours, but if two men live together in Ralia, admitting it so casually—it's the kind of slip that could cost you everything. I can't acclimate to it overnight."

Cae's stomach twisted. He'd never given much thought to how it must be for Ralian men who shared his inclinations, and inasmuch as he'd thought about Velasin's romantic history prior to learning about Killic, he'd more or less assumed that, on some level, Velasin would simply be happy to live in a country where things were easier for him. Now, though, he felt a surge of dread to realise that, for his husband, their marriage had begun from a place of bitter irony: in gaining the freedom to live openly with a man, Velasin had lost all freedom to choose his own partner, rendering it pointless.

The knowledge raked him, sharp as bear-claws. "I didn't know," he said, which felt woefully inadequate but was all he had to offer. "I didn't think—"

"Please," said Velasin, voice taking on a desperate edge, "don't pity me more than you already do. I'm not sure I could take it."

"This isn't pity!" Cae snapped. And then, taking a deep breath, "This isn't pity," he said again, more calmly. "I just . . . I hate that there's no way to make this easier. I hate that I can't be better for you."

"That *you* can't be better?" Velasin stared at him, throat working as he swallowed. "Ti—Caethari, there's no better for you to be. All I've done since arriving is attract trouble, and still you've been kinder, more accommodating and better humoured about it than I have any right to expect. Whatever deficiencies exist in this marriage are all on my part."

"That's ridiculous."

"That's factual," Velasin countered, crossing his arms. "Name me one thing you've done so far that could possibly merit reproach."

Softly, Cae said, "I forced you to share a bed with me."

Velasin froze. "That isn't—that wasn't your fault, that was *me*—"

"It doesn't matter. I knew we were strangers to one another. If I'd stopped to think for even a moment, I would've had the staff set you up with your own chambers that first night, not assumed I could rush you into my space."

"I'm glad you rushed," said Velasin. His words startled them both; Cae stared at him, unable to look away from those languid, gold-grey eyes.

"But—"

"If I'd been alone that first night, I'd have been no less terrified; I'd just have had more space to work myself into a fit. Or to have done something foolish." His fingers twitched abortively, like he wanted to reach out but didn't quite dare. Instead, he stepped closer. "I never thanked you. For talking me down."

Cae's mouth went dry. "Don't thank me for being decent."

"Decency is one thing; compassion is another. I haven't—" He glanced away, jaw working. "I keep prickling at you. Bristling over nothing. You deserve better from a spouse than whatever it is I bring, but you still—" He turned back, expression shaky, and before Cae could so much as brace himself, Velasin leaned up and kissed the corner of his mouth. His lips were soft, and Cae shivered at the contact, tingling all over as Velasin pulled back. He wanted to reach for him, pull him in for a real kiss; could only stare at Velasin's mouth, lips parted on a shaky exhale.

"Thank you," Velasin said quietly.

"Any time," Cae managed. "Velasin, I—"

There was a loud knock on the door.

Cae tensed, stifling a curse. He glanced desperately at Velasin, trying to convey his willingness to ignore whoever it was until they went away, but was promptly foiled in this desire by the sound of a cheerful, all-too-familiar voice.

"Caethari! Don't ignore me, I know you're in there—half the Aida saw you walk back up in only a *towel*!" called Laecia.

Cae groaned. Velasin rolled his eyes, not unkindly, and waved at the door in a *best get it over with* fashion.

Smoothing out his lin, Cae spared a final glance for his husband, whose cheeks were still beautifully flushed, and opened the door to his wretchedly interrupting little sister.

"Ah, so you do know what clothes are!" said Laecia, beaming. She pushed past Cae without waiting for a response. "That's a relief; I thought you might've been having some sort of episode. Oh, hello, Velasin!"

"Tiera Laecia," said Velasin, politely inclining his head.

Laecia laughed. "Why so formal? You almost married me and now you're my brother-in-law; that makes you more entitled to use my name than most." She whirled on the spot, smiling impishly at them. She was dressed all in blue—pale blue undershirt, sky-blue lin, and ocean-blue nara in a new, fashionably loose style that resembled a Ralian lady's split riding skirt—and her glossy black hair was braided in a crown around her head. "Cae's half-naked jaunt notwithstanding, I'm here to ask the pair of you to have lunch with me. Now, in my apartments."

Cae looked uncertainly at Velasin. He felt off-balance; his mouth still burned with the imprint of Velasin's lips. His husband, still flushed, gave a minute shrug, which Cae interpreted to mean, *She's your sister. What am I to do about it?*

Carefully, he said, "We've a busy slate today, Laecia. With everything that's happening—"

"With everything that's happening," she countered, her firm tone eerily like Riya's, "you still need to eat. And today, right now, you're eating with me." She stepped in closer, grinning at him. "I simply won't take no for an answer."

"Then we graciously accept," said Velasin, coming to Cae's rescue. "Please, lead on."

Laecia dimpled approvingly at him and headed off, the two of them following in her wake. As they reached the corridor, Cae was frustrated to see that Velasin had smoothed his face into a pleasant mask, all trace of earlier sentiment gone. *You kissed me,* Cae thought at him, *you kissed me and I don't know why. What did you mean by it? Was I meant to kiss you back? I wanted to kiss you back, but what would've happened if I did?*

"You're unusually quiet," said Laecia, turning to raise a brow at him. "Did your walk of shame strip you of eloquence, or does husbandry require more brainpower than you're accustomed to sparing?"

"Questions like these," said Cae, rallying to the familiar bicker-banter, "are exactly why Riya won't tell you her married jokes."

"I think it's because she doesn't actually have any and won't admit it."

"Kivali wouldn't put up with a humourless wife."

"Kivali puts up with *Riya*."

"I stand by my statement."

"So do I." And then, before Cae could reply to this, "Velasin, tell me—are you burdened with any elder sisters?"

"Sisters, no," said Velasin, "but I'm the youngest of three brothers."

Laecia turned, eyes lighting up. "The youngest of three! I knew I liked you for a reason. Tell me, are they both insufferable?"

"Revic was . . . difficult, while he lived," said Velasin, offering an awkward smile. "But Nathian has always been very much as he is now, even when we were children."

"That sounds familiar," Laecia muttered, and said nothing else until they reached her apartments, which were one level down from Cae's and at the opposite end of the wing.

With a guilty lurch, Cae realised it had been quite some time since he'd last visited with Laecia like this. She'd redecorated her receiving room, too: a plush wool rug in shades of white, blue and black now covered the floor, matching the gauzy white and blue hangings on the walls. Even the dining table was new, gleaming wood stained a dark honey shade and large enough to comfortably seat six matching chairs, the backs carved to depict leaping river-dolphins.

It was also, at present, laden with a small feast. Cae hadn't thought he was hungry, but he was no sooner seated than his mouth began to water. Laecia flashed him a smug look: she'd taken a chair at the head of the table, with Cae to her right and Velasin to her left.

"Eat!" she said, and promptly began to serve herself. As Velasin followed suit, Cae had no excuse not to do likewise, and so set aside his misgivings to pile his plate with sweet smoked rabbit with spiced honey sauce, savoury greens, field rice and pork dumplings.

Laecia had also provided wine, pouring herself a modest glass, but Cae—like Velasin, he noted—abstained from this so early in the day, sticking to the pitcher of water flavoured with lemon, mint and ginger.

For a brief while, the only sounds were those of a good meal, interspersed with Velasin's surprised, pleased murmuring as he expanded his knowledge of Tithenai food.

"You should try these, too," said Cae, depositing a dumpling on Velasin's plate.

"Mmm," said Velasin, nodding gratefully. He swallowed his mouthful of rabbit, speared the dumpling with his kip, popped it in his mouth and then said, far more emphatically, "*Mmmm!*"

Laecia looked between them, smirking. "That's adorable," she drawled. "And here I was worried, Velasin, that you'd be off-put by all the unfamiliar cuisine!"

Velasin swallowed again. "Impossible," he said. "If only someone had told me about Tithenai food, I'd have emigrated years ago."

"Is Ralian cooking truly that bad?"

"Not bad, exactly." Velasin hesitated, his attention caught by the last dumpling in the shared bowl. Manners were clearly preventing him from taking it, so Cae did the logical thing and gave it to him, earning himself a truly brilliant flash of smile. Velasin speared it and said, "It's more that it's very heavy, very rich. In small servings, it can be truly divine, but eaten every day, I find, it gets a bit sickly." He ate the dumpling with relish.

"And how have you been, Laecia?" asked Cae, as much because he wanted to know as to give his husband some quality time with his food. He was belatedly conscious of the fact that they hadn't really sat down and talked about his marrying instead of her, and it made him feel awkward, not least because he didn't know if Laecia's ambitions still ran towards *civilising Velasin,* as she'd called it.

"Oh, you know," said Laecia airily, gesturing with her kip. "I'd been planning my own marriage-gathering before—well, everything, and it seemed a shame to waste the work, so I've been coordinating with Keletha to incorporate my thoughts into yours. I hope you don't mind, only—"

"No, not at all," said Cae. "I . . . thank you." Uncertain if he'd be stepping into a trap by saying so out loud, he ventured, "You've been very gracious about all this."

Laecia snorted. "*Gracious.* What a stupid way of putting it! I'm glad you two are getting along, but respectfully, what would I want with a husband who won't bed me? It defeats the whole purpose!"

Cae winced, achingly aware that Velasin had stilled. He wanted to reach for him, just a touch to let him know he didn't agree without having to share any of their private business aloud with his sister, but Velasin's hands were out of range.

"Perhaps we have different ideas of marriage, tiera," said Velasin, tone deceptively mild, "but especially in a diplomatic marriage, I wouldn't think bedplay to be the *whole* purpose."

"Well, perhaps not," allowed Laecia, seemingly oblivious to the new undercurrent of tension. "But it's not insignificant, either. You can hardly call a diplomatic union successful if both parties are courting lovers from the outset while ignoring each other." She paused, raising a delicate eyebrow. "Unless, of course, such a lover was preexisting?"

Far too late, Cae recalled Laecia and Riya's debate over whether Velasin was more likely in love with Killic or Markel, and which side each had taken.

"I have no lover," Velasin said stiffly. "Whatever else you think of me, know that I would not so dishonour your brother."

Laecia *tsk*ed. "You're being Ralian, Velasin. A lover is no dishonour; it's only when you favour them to the exclusion of your spouse that the trouble starts. So if you *did* have one—"

"*Laecia,*" Cae snapped, sharply enough that she jumped in her seat. Through gritted teeth, he said, "Whatever game you think this is, it isn't one to me. Stop harrying my husband."

Laecia's gaze flicked between them, quick and assessing, before she inclined her head at Velasin. "My apologies," she murmured. "That was rude of me."

"Think nothing of it," said Velasin.

"She should absolutely think something of it," Cae countered, injecting as much older-sibling emphasis into the words as possible.

Laecia didn't quite slouch in her seat as she'd done when they were children, but something in the set of her shoulders suggested that she wanted to. "Well, then," she said, "a change of conversation! Caethari, what should we talk about?"

Literally anything else, Cae thought but did not say. "I'm open to suggestions."

"Horses," Velasin said, after a semi-awkward beat. "I . . . after what became of Quip, I suppose I'll be needing a new mount. Ti—Laecia, do you have any recommendations?"

Cae didn't actually sigh with relief, but it was a near thing. Laecia brightened instantly, launching straight into a rundown of the pros and cons of visiting Qi-Katai's horsemarkets versus buying directly from a particular stable. Cae was even able to join in, and for a blissful ten minutes or so, the three of them were able to speak comfortably with each other.

The tension was just starting to leave Cae's shoulders when, as had happened in his own apartments, the moment was broken by a knock on the door. Groaning, he muttered, "What *now*?"

"Nothing good, I'd imagine," said Velasin lightly, tucking a wavy thread of hair behind his ear.

Ignoring the pair of them, Laecia rose to answer the door, and was visibly startled to find a grim-faced Riya on the other side of it.

"Ri!" she exclaimed. "What in Zo's name—"

"Sorry to interrupt," she said, not sounding sorry at all as she pushed past Laecia (in exactly the same manner, Cae couldn't help noticing, that Laecia had pushed past him), "but Dai Mirae and her prisoners just arrived in the Aida."

Cae's heart gave an ugly lurch. They'd been expecting Mirae, so her return alone couldn't be the cause of Riya's upset—and she was upset, for all that she exhibited it as a thrumming, angry tension.

Velasin seemed to sense this, too; he came instantly to his feet. "What's happened? What's wrong?"

"It seems," said Riya, mouth a tight line as Cae stood in turn, "that they've picked up an extra person en route to Qi-Katai. He's . . . not exactly a prisoner, but Dai Mirae wasn't quite comfortable styling him a guest, either. Right now, she's minding him in the Court of Swords, but she wants you to come and tell her where to put him."

"Who is it?" Cae asked, but even as he voiced the question, some terrible instinct already knew the answer.

"Lord Killic vin Lato," said Riya.

Part Five

VELASIN

21

Killic.

I froze where I stood, heart thumping against my ribs. It didn't make sense; it shouldn't have been possible, but my thoughts were too scattered to understand why.

"Lord Killic!" exclaimed Laecia, in a jarringly thrilled tone of voice. She shot me a look that was equal parts sly and curious, and together with her earlier insinuations, I belatedly recalled the Killic vs. Markel debate among Keletha's riders and realised which side she'd taken.

A tingling numbness swept through me, putting me at a queer remove from my own flesh. I didn't faint or black out, but I somehow lost my awareness of the room and the people in it for just long enough that, when Caethari appeared at my elbow, I didn't know how he'd gotten there. I flinched, moving away before he could touch me, speak to me, do anything that might crack me open in front of his sisters, and found myself bowing to Riya.

"Thank you for informing us," I said, my tone as even as I could manage. "Would you please tell Mirae we'll be down shortly, once I've . . . conferred with Tiern Caethari? In private," I added, to ensure that Laecia couldn't invite herself into our confidence.

Riya frowned—I was, after all, imposing on her, treating my husband's elder sister like a message-runner—but after a moment, she nodded and said, "Of course."

I felt light-headed as I watched her leave. When Caethari next moved to stand beside me, I didn't react except to say, without turning to look at his remaining sister, "Tiera, thank you for the meal. Our apologies for having to cut things short."

Possibly Laecia replied to that, or possibly not; my awareness swam as I left the room, walking blindly down the still-unfamiliar hall as my breathing grew louder and faster, faster and louder.

"Velasin," Caethari said, voice tense with worry. "Velasin, you need to c—"

"Moons help me, if you tell me to calm down, I will *bite* you!" I snarled in Ralian. I came to a stop, chest heaving, shaking, and ripped my gaze to the floor to avoid Caethari's expression.

"You need to calm your breathing," he said softly, keeping to Tithenai. "Stay angry, stay upset, feel however you need to feel right now, but you'll hurt your lungs if you can't breathe evenly."

"Shut up," I croaked, ungrateful and furious. I sucked in air, too fast and too shallow, throat abominably tight. "Shut up, I can't—I can't do this here, someone will *see* me—"

"There's a guest apartment two doors down. We can talk in there."

I nodded, still unable to look at him but pathetically grateful for the featherlight touch of his hand on my shoulder, steering me in the right direction. I shut my eyes, trusting his guidance, and didn't open them again until he drew me to a halt. We were in a neat, unfamiliar room, not dissimilar in layout to Laecia's but on a smaller scale, the furnishings far less lavish. I cared only that there was a vacant chair, into which I collapsed with trembling legs, still struggling—stupidly, wretchedly—to breathe, spots dancing in the edges of my vision.

Though the floor was bare stone, Caethari knelt beside me, placing a warm hand on my arm.

"Breathe in," he murmured, and somehow I complied, holding the breath until he gave a gentle squeeze and said, "Breathe out."

I hated that it worked; hated that I needed it at all, and yet it did, and *I* did, and despite the shame I let him soothe me, following his soft instructions until my vision cleared and my chest stopped aching.

"Why is he here?" I finally managed, instead of something far more appropriate like *thank you* or *I'm sorry.* I raised my head and looked at Caethari, wanting answers he couldn't possibly provide. And then, reverting to Tithenai, "*How* is he here? I don't understand. I don't understand at all."

"Nor do I," said Caethari, "but we can find out."

Rational. Be rational, Velasin. What happens next? "A lot will depend," I forced myself to say, "on how he reacts when he sees me."

Caethari's hand twitched against my arm. "You don't have to see him."

"Yes. I do." I forced myself to meet his gaze; to ignore the softness in it. "For one thing, I know him better than you, and for another, his reaction will tell us a great deal." I laughed bitterly. "I'm holding out no hope that he'll recognise what he did to me for what it was, but whether he's angry, or thinks to win me back, or whether someone sent him here, someone from Ralia"—the possibility occurred to me only as I spoke it—"or he's come by his own volition, we need to know."

"Do we, though?"

I stared at him. "What?"

"Does it matter why he's here, or under what auspices? He hurt you, Velasin." Caethari's dark eyes flashed. "Remember what I told you, about the betrothal contracts? You had status as an Aeduria the moment Keletha laid eyes on you. Under Tithenai law, he's a criminal. We can hold him as such."

The concept was startling. For all that I recalled the conversation, it hadn't felt real; more like a story told to soothe a frightened child. I sat with the implications a moment, then realised I was thinking of it in terms of Ralian justice—I had no real concept of how such a crime would be dealt with in Tithena.

"If . . . if we did arrest him," I asked, testing the concept, "would it be public? He's Ralian, and a nobleman. There would be diplomatic consequences, surely."

"The Ralian ambassador would have to be told," Caethari said, "but it wouldn't necessarily be public. There's . . . I wouldn't call it overlap, exactly, but a friction between the judicate and the tierency when it comes to cases involving the nobility. Any noble accused or accuser has the right to have their case heard before the tieren, but in addition to rendering a verdict, the tieren can decide to turn the case over to the judicate instead, which is mostly what my father prefers to do. But when it comes to our family . . . technically, we have a right to what's called tieren's privilege, to deal with certain domestic crimes in-house, in accordance with our own wishes, and we could do that here." He hesitated, then added, "If tieren's privilege is invoked, it's strongly preferred that we notify the judicate of both crime and punishment, so there's an external record of what happened, but it's not technically *required.* But Velasin, none of that is an obstacle. It doesn't have to matter."

"But it does matter. It matters to me," I said. And then, because he was still looking at me with that gentle determination, I choked out, "Caethari. If we arrest him, people will know what he did to me. Not many, perhaps, but enough. There'd be a record of it."

Caethari froze.

"I don't want that," I whispered. "Please, I can't—I can't deal with that on top of everything else."

"No one would think less of you—"

"*I think less of me!*" I shouted, coming to my feet. My eyes were hot, my throat clenched against grief with all the efficacy of a fist around water. Caethari stood, expression pained, but neither spoke nor moved as the words poured out of me, jagged and bloody. "I should've fought him. Should've done more than just stand there and take it. He took his hands off me more than once, I could've—but I *came,* Caethari, do you know how disgusting that feels, that any part of me enjoyed it? Because it's not like he tried to fuck me raw, not like he punched his way inside and took what he wanted—*that* would've been worse, *that* would've left me with deeper hurts than bruises. Shouldn't I be grateful for that, for his *courtesy*? How can it even affect me at all, when I let it happen; when *what*

I let happen was nothing compared with what it might've been?" I scrubbed a hand across my eyes, furious at the tears I felt there. "Why couldn't he just stay *away*?"

"Velasin," said Caethari, and just that, just the sound of my name spoken with so much feeling, undid me as nothing else could. I wanted to turn away, but when he angled his body in a tacit offer of comfort I froze, unable to either retreat or accept. I shook my head mutely, angry and embarrassed and a dozen other things, and all Caethari did was still his hands and smile crookedly, as if to say he understood. Some hungry, animal part of me wanted to throw myself forwards, to press my cheek to his shoulder, face tucked into his throat, but I didn't trust myself with it. Bad enough I'd already kissed him, overcome by anxiety and gratitude and the fact that he kept on *existing* near me, kind and witty and beautiful. Teasing him with the promise of something I didn't dare offer would be unspeakably cruel to both of us, and so I just stood there, trembling with misery.

"I'm sorry." I exhaled the words, not sure for which of us I meant them more.

Caethari made a rough noise and shook his head. His fingers twitched abortively. "There's nothing to be sorry for."

I didn't believe him, but it was a nice thought. I forced myself to step past him but, in my shocky state, passed too close. Our shoulders brushed, and my arm lit up as if burned.

"What do you want to do?" he asked, after several seconds of silence.

"I don't know. I don't think I can handle what would happen if we brought him before the judicate, not on top of everything else, but invoking tieren's privilege still wouldn't keep things quiet, if we had to rope the ambassador in. But if we just let him go, I'd know he was out there, and that—I don't want that, either."

Caethari considered this. "What if," he said, slowly, "we only threaten him with arrest?"

I turned to stare at him. "What?"

"Threaten him," Caethari repeated. "Give him the choice: either stay here and be arrested for rape, or leave and never come back. He's hardly going to call your bluff and say, *Yes, please, arrest me.* No rapist wants to be branded as such."

The words set off a ripple of realisation through me, association to concept to thought until I had a beautiful, perfect idea. As simple as it would've been to chase Killic out of Qi-Katai, I wanted there to be consequences for his actions beyond my terror; wanted to ensure that he couldn't do to anyone else what he'd done to me. I explained my plan to Caethari, and his gaze went sharp with approval—and with relief, though whether at the prospect of holding Killic accountable or of there being something he could do for me, I wasn't sure. Possibly it was both, though in the moment, that felt too overwhelming to contemplate.

"Yes," he said, when I was finished. "Yes, we can do that."

We discussed the practicalities, which happily turned out to be practical. The thought of seeing Killic in person still made my stomach churn, but I had a plan now, and Caethari's support. The task would grow no easier for being delayed.

"All right," I said, just a thread of shake in my voice. "I'm ready now."

Steadying myself, I let Caethari precede me out of the room, then moved alongside him as we began the walk to the Court of Swords. As we passed a pair of servants, Caethari flagged them down and, after ascertaining that neither was on urgent business for anyone else in the Aida, gave them our instructions.

"Tierns," they said in unison, and hurried off to comply.

The nearer we came to the Court of Swords, the more anxious I felt. Still, if there was one thing life in Farathel had prepared me for, it was concealing my true feelings while dealing with Ralian nobles, and so I swallowed and steeled myself to the task.

The sun beamed down on the courtyard, glaringly bright against the pale stone; bright enough that it took a few blinks for my eyes to fully adjust.

"Is that him?" Caethari murmured, indicating with a tip of his chin.

I followed his gaze, and for two confused seconds didn't quite recognise the bedraggled figure standing alongside Mirae. But then he moved, and even in profile there was no mistaking that fine-jawed face, no matter the state of the rest of him.

"Yes," I whispered.

Caethari put a hand to my shoulder and gave a quick, supportive squeeze before letting go, falling a step behind me. Knowing he was there to watch my back was almost as good as having Markel with me—and moons, I'd have to tell Markel everything after this, I owed him that much—but when it came to my feeling safe, there was no higher compliment.

Killic hadn't yet spotted us: his head was tilted upwards, brown eyes wide as he stared at the bulk of the Aida. He looked . . . *wretched* wasn't quite the word—his posture was still firm, his clothes were his own—but given his usual standards of deportment even under difficult conditions, he was more dishevelled than I'd ever seen him. He was still wearing the exact same clothes he'd worn at my father's estate, though the gold embroidery was missing from his shirt, which was visibly torn in places, and the whole ensemble was marred by dirt, sweat and other stains. His hair was tied back, but messily so, and when he finally turned towards us, I saw there was a bruise on his left cheek.

At the sight of me, he did a double take, presumably as unprepared for my current appearance as I'd been for his. And then he smiled—a genuine smile of pleasure—and nausea rattled through me as I realised exactly how awful this was going to be.

"Tierns!" said Mirae, bowing to myself and Caethari. "Apologies for disturbing you, but I wasn't quite sure what to do with this one."

"You did the right thing," said Caethari. "We'll take it from here. You're dismissed."

"Thank you," said Mirae, sighing with relief. She flashed me a quick, encouraging smile and then hurried off to the barracks, doubtless eager both to wash and reunite with Kita.

That left Killic, who'd remained silent throughout the exchange. He looked me up and down in a way that made me want to peel my skin off, taking in my Tithenai clothes, the closed expression I'd set on my face, before finally speaking in Ralian.

"Aaro, darling. I know you must be cross with me, but please—can we talk?"

Caethari inhaled sharply at this. Killic startled, as if noticing him for the first time, and then added, with a pointed glance at me, "In private, perhaps."

"Killic," I said, replying in the same language, "allow me to introduce my husband, Tiern Caethari Xai Aeduria."

Killic paled. "*Husband?*" he croaked. "Aaro, don't joke, that isn't funny—"

"I'm not joking," I said. His confusion caught me by surprise; Mirae and the other guards all knew I'd been destined for Caethari, so why hadn't anyone told him? The answer came to me almost as soon as I'd thought the question: unlike me, Killic had no great facility with languages, and though he'd attained a selective, fumbling knowledge of Tithenai to keep up with Farathel's intrigues, he lacked the fluency to communicate with a native speaker, and especially one who knew only a smatter of Ralian.

"But," said Killic, staring at me with something very like despair, "that's not—you told me you were set to wed a Tithenai girl, not a *man*."

Any response I might've made touched too closely on things I didn't want to say in public. "Come inside," I said, tone clipped to hide how angry I was. "We can talk there. *All* of us," I added, when Killic cast a frustrated glance at Caethari.

Without speaking, Caethari took the lead, fingers brushing my arm in passing. We'd already decided where to house Killic for the duration of his (hopefully brief) stay, but as I still lacked a functional working knowledge of the Aida's halls, it fell to Caethari to take us there.

Mercifully, Killic remained silent as he walked beside me, staring around at the Aida with uncharacteristic meekness. His behaviour unnerved me: I was half convinced it was all some sort of calculated act to win my sympathy, but that didn't stop me from feeling like a fool for having dreaded him so. I didn't yet know the details of how he'd come to be here, but if the bruise on his cheek and his filthy clothes were anything to go by, his travels hadn't gone smoothly, and I wasn't above feeling a flash of petty vindication at the thought.

Our destination was an isolated guest room on the ground floor of the Aida, set closer to the barracks than anything else. According to Caethari, it was ordinarily reserved for his rahan, Nairi, when she came to stay, though it was also offered up to relatives of the Aida's guards whenever they visited. One of the servants we'd spoken to earlier was already waiting at the door; he bowed to Caethari, handed over three small metal objects and then left.

The two-room interior was sparsely but comfortably furnished: a small, private washroom lay behind a curtained divider on the left, while the single main room boasted a bed, a storage trunk and four chairs around a wooden table, on which had been laid a jug of water, three clay mugs and a plate bearing fresh bread rolls and a pat of fragrant goat's cheese. There was even a tiny butter-knife to help spread the one on the other, though round-edged as it was, not even a desperate man would think to use it as any sort of weapon.

"Sit," I said, unable to muster up a *please* to go with it, and only once Killic had chosen his seat on one side of the table did I take my own opposite. Caethari, however, stayed standing behind me: a comforting, silent presence.

Rallying somewhat now that we were indoors, Killic slouched in his seat, cast a sour look at Caethari and said, "Has he words at all, your *husband,* or does he just loom?"

"He speaks when there's someone worth speaking to," I said, finally letting some of my anger bleed into my voice. "Killic, what in the hells are you *doing* here?"

"I came for *you*!" he snapped. And then, a little desperately, "By the First Star, Aaro, was that not obvious? What else would I want in a place like this?"

"I don't know," I said, coolly. "Perhaps you just wanted a change of scene." I folded my arms, as much to hide the trembling of my hands as for any other reason. "Tell me how you ended up with Mirae."

"Who? Oh, *her*." He wrinkled his nose; Killic had always had little patience for women, which I'd largely attributed to his being pressured to marry one, but his dismissive tone made my jaw clench. Oblivious to my reaction, he schooled his face into what I thought of as his coaxing expression, a look of almost-contrition-but-really-defensiveness reserved for when he meant to explain, politely, why he was absolutely justified in his actions.

"Well," he said, "after all that . . . unpleasantness in the garden, I was forced to leave at some speed—you can't blame me for abandoning you, Aaro, your father was quite firm about it—so I backtracked a few miles to a little public house; still technically within the vin Aaro demesne, I believe, but frankly I was too upset to go farther. I barely slept a wink, but when I woke, I had the most brilliant idea—why not set out ahead of you, and be there to meet you in Qi-Katai?"

He pronounced it the Ralian way, *Qui-Katay*, and as this was the least objectionable of the many things wrong with what he'd just said, I fixated on it as a point of sanity.

Killic paused, as if waiting for me to comment. When I didn't, he continued anyway. "So I bought some supplies from the public house—not the best fare, in hindsight, but I didn't want to lose any time—and set out immediately for the Taelic Pass. Of course I had to be careful to skirt the estate, but I made good time regardless." He blinked. "When did you depart?"

"A day after you," I gritted out. No wonder Raeki hadn't noticed us being followed: Killic had been ahead the whole time.

"That soon!" he exclaimed. Then, chagrined, "Well, I can't say I blame you for rushing; your father must've been in a terrible state—I daresay my own will be just as bad, once the gossip reaches him. But that's a problem for another day." He flapped a dismissive hand. "At any rate, a man alone travels faster than a caravan, so I thought I'd make it through the pass to Tithena with time to spare. As it turned out, however, I'd been a bit overambitious." He smiled a smile that was meant to charm, disarm; to downplay the utter impulsive foolishness of what he'd done into something to be laughed about over drinks. I'd found it endearing once; now, it only grated.

Killic paused again, clearly expecting me to show some softness towards him. When I didn't, he frowned as though I was being unreasonable. "Come now, Aaro—I know you're cross, but you have to at least give me credit for trying. I came all this way to be with you!"

I went rigid, my pulse beating hard in my throat. I locked my teeth and forced myself not to react, not to say anything that would either encourage him or derail the conversation from its present direction. I'd confront him about it all soon enough, but for my own peace of mind, I needed to know what had happened, or the worries and what-ifs would keep me up more than the nightmares already did.

"And then?" I asked. I kept my voice level, but only barely; I had a distant sense that my current composure would level an exacting cost later, but it was too late to back out.

"And then," said Killic, who was starting to sound put out, "I had several hungry days, and my horse threw a shoe, but I still almost made it through the pass—and would've done, if not for those wretched bandits."

"Bandits," I said, flatly. I heard Caethari shift behind me, but didn't dare turn to look at him.

Killic gave a disgusted snort. "They were a poxy rabble; if I'd been properly armed and not half-starved, I'd have seen them off in a trice. But as it was, they captured me—not without resistance, for all the good it did"—he touched the bruise on his cheek—"and took me back to their squalid little camp in the foothills. Happily, they spoke Ralian—one was even fluent; I think he must've started life as one of old vin Mica's tenant farmers, before everything went sideways—but unhappily, they didn't believe me when I said I was travelling alone, with nothing more valuable to offer than my horse and purse. They still took both, of course," he added darkly, "but they were convinced I was scouting ahead for some bigger party.

"When your lot came down the pass behind me, they more or less figured they were right, and set out to ambush you. Of course, they took my horse and left me tied up; I had a hell of a time getting my hands free on a handy rock, and once I'd finally staggered down to see what happened and found that little inn-place you'd been staying at, it was all over bar the shouting: you'd gone on ahead, and none of those guards you left behind spoke Ralian, which left me in a bit of a bind—it's not like the bandits were keen on translating for us, and in any case, the one who was fluent in Ralian was dead. Still, I was able to convey the fact that I was a friend of yours and wanted to see you, and they agreed to bring me along. So here I am, and really, Aaro, I think I've been quite patient about all this—haven't you a single kind word to spare me, after all I did to get here?"

"A kind word," I said. It came out a growl, so unlike my usual voice that Killic looked taken aback. "Even if all you'd done was betray me with Avery and then follow me home uninvited, you wouldn't be welcome here, but that *damn well* isn't all you've done, and you know it!" I was shouting, shaking; I came to my feet without meaning to. "That *unpleasantness in the garden,* as you call it—that was *rape,* Killic! You twisted my fucking arm and *forced* me; you had the arrogance to get caught in the act, and now you follow me here as if I should *want* you?"

Killic's eyes went wide. "Rape? Aaro, darling, don't be dramatic—it was rough play, yes, we were caught up in the moment, but that's nothing we haven't done before—"

"I told you no, and you didn't stop!"

"Of course I didn't, when you were so clearly enjoying yourself!" He smirked. "Or have you forgotten that part? *I'm* the one who was interrupted before he could get any pleasure."

Rage washed through me in waves of heat and cold. "I will never forget a second of what you did to me," I hissed. "Whatever excuses you care to make, we both know the truth of it."

Killic's smirk broadened. "But does he?" he asked, softly.

Shaken as I was, it took me a moment to recall Caethari's presence. I looked from Killic to Caethari and back again, unable to fathom his inference—and then it clicked, and I felt sick to think that I'd ever cared for Killic.

He didn't think Caethari understood Ralian. He'd only heard him speak Tithenai to Mirae and the servant, and because he'd stayed so quiet since, he'd interpreted that silence as ignorance, just as he'd once done with Markel. He'd gone to such pains, on learning of Markel's intelligence, to apologise; to assure us that he'd meant no offence; to frame the whole thing as a misunderstanding, his anger as the product of surprise instead of venom—and me, selfish, lonely, foolish coward that I was, had let myself be charmed into forgiveness. He'd never slighted Markel afterwards, or I wouldn't have stayed, but I'd made the mistake of thinking his contrition sincere, and not just a means of placating me back into his bed.

But now Killic had made the exact same error all over again, completely unaware of the parallel: he'd learned nothing, and now was trying to compel me with the threat to reveal our former relationship to Caethari.

Mistaking my silence for fear, Killic leaned forwards. "Why don't you sit down, hm? Let's talk about this rationally."

Leashing my anger, my shock and disgust, I glanced at Caethari. His face was impassive, but I was startled to find I knew him well enough to discern the effort he was putting into keeping it that way. Hoping he could read my intentions, I silently begged him to stay quiet just a little longer; to let Killic fully incriminate himself. The whole thing hurt like poison, but some part of me needed this: needed Caethari to witness Killic at his worst, so that I could stop torturing myself with the terrible fear that somehow, I'd exaggerated it all.

So I sat, heart thrumming against my ribs, and spat out, "Talk, then."

Killic sighed. "The thing is, Aaro, I'd have happily been your secret if you'd wedded a woman, but I've too great an instinct for self-preservation to square up against someone in my own weight class." He smiled sharkishly. "So, as you're clearly not inclined to run away with me—and as my future prospects in Ralia will doubtless look rather grim, once word gets out about us—I'd like you to set me up with, let's call it a generous loan, courtesy of your new husband's coffers."

I dug my fingernails into my palms. "And in return?"

"And in return," Killic purred, "I won't tell him that we're lovers."

"We aren't lovers, Killic; not anymore. You raped me."

"Whatever I did, you wanted it." His smile turned predatory, all semblance of courtesy gone. "You'd want it again, if your man there gave us some privacy."

"I beg to differ," Caethari said, coldly and in Ralian. He set a hand on my shoulder. "You will get nothing but what you deserve, Lord Killic vin Lato."

22

All the blood drained from Killic's face, his bruise standing out as starkly as if he'd just been slapped. He stared between us, furious at having been tricked, then turned to me with a look of pure venom.

"You're a sweet little fuck, Aaro, but the novelty wears off. Your *husband* will find that out soon enough. I—"

Caethari moved so fast, I didn't even register it. One moment he was beside me, and the next he had his hand on the back of Killic's neck, gripping hard as he smashed his cheek into the table. Killic made a choking noise; he tried to wriggle out of the chair, but Caethari held it firmly in place, his eyes black with fury.

"I'd ask you to apologise," he growled, "but we both know you wouldn't mean it, and even if you did, words wouldn't be enough. You disgust me." He gave Killic's neck a final, pushing squeeze and then stepped back, leaving Killic to gasp and splutter against the table.

"Barbarians," he choked out, "you're all barbarians—"

Someone knocked on the door.

Caethari caught my eye, a silent question as to whether I wished to proceed. I nodded, my body thrumming with more feelings than I could possibly identify, and only then did he move to answer it.

A bemused Ru Zairin entered, carrying a small medical bag in one hand.

"Perfect timing, ru," said Caethari, switching back to Tithenai.

Ru Zairin frowned, taking in the tableau. "It's my pleasure, tiern, though your message was rather mysterious." Thei glanced at Killic. "I take it this is the patient?"

"He's about to be," Caethari said, grimly.

Ru Zairin's expression hardened. "Tiern Caethari," thei said, voice sharper than I'd yet heard it. "If you are planning on torturing this man, I'm not only ashamed of you, but insulted that you'd think I'd be a party to it."

"Torture? No. I'm enacting justice." Caethari's hands twitched by his sides. "This man, ru, is a confessed rapist. I've just heard the proof of it from his own mouth, in addition to which he has tried to blackmail my husband. He is also, however, a Ralian nobleman, and so rather than subject us all to the inevitable diplomatic circus that would result from attempting to bring him before the judicate, Tiern Velasin has suggested a rather more Ralian solution, invoked under tieren's privilege."

"Has he now," said Ru Zairin, casting me a look that was far too knowing by half. I swallowed hard, forcing myself to endure thir scrutiny: Caethari hadn't outright said that I was Killic's victim, but under the circumstances, there was little else to explain both my visibly shaken state and Caethari's fury. "And in what way does this solution of yours involve medical treatment, tiern?"

"Branding," I said, my voice sounding shocky and hollow to my own ears; I couldn't imagine how much worse it was to the others. *You're a sweet little fuck, Aaro, but the novelty wears off.* "In Ralia, rapists are branded on the backs of their hands. Anyone there who sees it will know what it means, as will most sailors who've ever passed through Ralian waters." I swallowed. "I wouldn't advocate for it here if I wasn't—it's just that I can't . . . there must be consequences."

If Ru Zairin hadn't understood before that I was the subject of Killic's violence, thei certainly did now. Thir expression grave, thei murmured, "I see."

"We don't ask you to perform the branding," Caethari said. "I know that would go against your oaths. But though he may deserve the pain"—and here he flashed an ugly look at Killic, who was trying and demonstrably failing to follow the conversation, a pinched, confused look on his face—"Tiern Velasin asks that you numb him beforehand and tend the burn afterwards."

Ru Zairin hesitated, then nodded. "It is . . . irregular. But criminal though he may be, I will see that his hurt his minimal. And," thei added, flashing Caethari a meaningful look, "I fully expect to be given a more detailed explanation in due course."

Caethari inclined his head. "Of course, ru. You have my thanks."

With that agreed upon, Caethari reached into his pocket and withdrew two of the items he'd been given by the servant: a matched pair of plain metal bracelets. Moving slowly, he returned to Killic's side of the table—Killic watched him suspiciously all the while—until he was close enough to strike. Killic's reflexes were good, but Caethari's were better: he grabbed Killic's forearms, grappled them flat to the table and slipped a bracelet over each of his wrists.

"*Anchor,*" said Caethari, still holding Killic in place. A frisson of magic rippled through the room, and Killic yelped as two things happened simultaneously: the bracelets tightened, fitting as snugly around his wrists as if they'd been molded there, while also becoming fixed in place, so that even when Killic stood, trying wildly to tug himself free, he couldn't lift his arms from the table.

"You bastard!" he snarled, bent at an awkward angle by virtue of his pinned arms. Dirty hair fell into his eyes. "What is this?"

"You would call them anchor-cuffs," said Caethari mildly. "I've found them useful in the past, for restraining Ralian captives. They're keyed to my voice, so don't bother trying to figure out the release word." Killic, who'd been in the process of doing just this, swore violently. "And this—" Caethari reached once more into his pocket, withdrawing a slim metal rod with a flat, wedge-shaped tip that looked like the head of a screwdriver. "—is a soldering pen."

Killic's eyes went wide; he glanced at me, stricken. "Aaro, please tell me this isn't what I think it is."

"It's exactly what you think it is," I said quietly, "and a good deal kinder than you deserve." I motioned to Ru Zairin, who opened thir medical case and withdrew a small vial and syringe. Killic began to thrash in place at the sight of this, but was unable to do more than lift his elbows a hair or so off the table, leaving him bent forwards. "It's a sedative," I told him, voice flat in a way that had nothing to do with calm. "We don't mean to torture you."

Killic let out a hysterical laugh. "Is that so?"

"I would sit, if I were you," said Caethari, nudging his chair back in easy range. "You don't want the doctor's hand to slip."

Killic swore violently but had the sense to comply. He was trembling now, real fear in his eyes as he looked at me, desperate in a way he hadn't been even moments earlier. "Aaro," he pleaded, "I'm sorry, I'm so sorry, please don't do this, I was wrong, I recant—I shouldn't have done it, I'll never do it again—I was just caught up, I was mad with how much I missed you, *please*—"

He broke off, whining in his throat as Ru Zairin, who spoke no Ralian and thus had been ignoring this desperate monologue, took advantage of Killic's preoccupation to locate the big vein in the crook of his elbow. He tapped it a few times, frowned, and readied the syringe.

"Hold still," said Caethari, and Killic complied, wincing as the needle went in. Ru Zairin administered the sedative with practiced ease, a small swab ready to daub away the bead of blood that welled at the exit point.

"Please," Killic panted, staring at me. "Please, Aaro, if you ever loved me—"

"I did, is the thing," I said, softly. "And you betrayed that love in every way that mattered."

Killic moaned, eyes drooping, and slowly lowered his head to the table. As though spellbound, the three of us watched in silence as Killic passed into unconsciousness, shoulders slumping as his breathing went deep and even.

"That should keep him under for a good half-hour or so," said Ru Zairin, helping thimself to an empty chair. "You'll excuse me if I avert my gaze for this next part; I understand the necessity, but I'd rather not watch it all the same."

"Of course," said Caethari. He pressed a button on the soldering pen, which was powered by what I understood to be a comparatively simple (yet extremely useful) cantrip—unlike the anchor-cuffs, which were a fascinating and no doubt expensive bit of spellwork I'd not seen before—and within moments, the tip began to glow red-hot. Caethari studied it, then turned his gaze on me, his dark eyes gentle. "Velasin, you don't need to watch this, either."

"Yes, I do."

"He isn't owed your witness."

"I know," I said. "But you are."

Caethari startled. "What?"

"You're doing this for me," I said, unable to look away from him, though I felt as though I'd catch fire from the force of his attention. "For my sake, you're ignoring your customary justice and burning a Ralian mark on a Ralian's hand. You would not do it otherwise. The least I can do is watch."

Slowly, Caethari nodded. "As you wish."

The brand, as I'd described it to him earlier, was a simple thing: a circle barred by two horizontal lines and one vertical. No artistic skill was required to render it beyond the most basic grasp of penmanship and a stomach strong enough to endure the scent of burning flesh.

As Ru Zairin helped thimself to one of the rolls with goat's cheese—every surgeon I'd ever met was accustomed to eating despite their surrounds, and Ru Zairin had been drawn away from thir lunch—Caethari pulled up a chair alongside the unconscious Killic and began, with painstaking carefulness, to draw the brand on the back of his dominant hand.

Traditionally, the brand would be like a cattle-brand: a single piece of iron heated over a fire and pressed directly to bare skin. But soldering pens were not uncommonly used for the job, either, partly because they allowed for the brand to be modified—since their advent, alternate marks were sometimes given to the rapists of married women or underage girls, to say nothing of introducing different brands for different crimes altogether—but mostly because a great many Ralian judges, in my experience of the breed, were sadists. A traditional brand got the punishment over and done with too quickly, but a soldering pen allowed the pain—and, theoretically, the lesson the pain was meant to impart—to go on far longer.

Killic was spared that pain by virtue of Ru Zairin's sedative, but his flesh burned all the same. It smelled like crisping pork, and the comparison alone was enough to make me gag. As if thei could read my thoughts, Ru Zairin gestured with thir half-eaten roll.

"Taste and smell are quite linked," thei remarked. "Often, I find, it's easiest to use one to block out the other."

I nodded grimly. The advice was sensible, but I was far too nauseated to take it, and though my stomach churned, I couldn't look away from the terrible work of the soldering pen as it carved the brand into Killic's skin.

The whole process didn't take long, and yet it felt as though an eternity had passed by the time Caethari turned off the pen and put it back in his pocket.

I stood on wobbly legs and made myself look at the finished product, which was as neat a condemnation of its bearer as any I'd ever had the misfortune to see up close.

"Thank you," I rasped, and realised abruptly that I was going to be sick. I staggered over to the curtained washroom and threw up into the latrine. *So much for Laecia's lunch,* a part of me thought hysterically. I lifted my head, panting like a sunstruck dog, and tried to get ahold of myself. Nobody came in after me, for which I was pathetically grateful, and when I finally returned to the main room, Ru Zairin was murmuring a cantrip over Killic's freshly bandaged hand, the anchor-cuffs already removed from his wrists.

"I'd advise letting him rest up for a day before he heads out again, so that I can make sure the burn isn't festering," thei said, "but under the circumstances, I'll understand if that isn't possible."

"He can have a day," I said, the taste of bile still fresh in my mouth. I walked to the table, poured myself a cup of water, swilled my mouth clean and swallowed until the cup was empty. "I'd prefer him under lock and guard, but he can have one day."

"Very good," said Ru Zairin. "In the interim, Tiern Velasin, I suspect you could do with some rest yourself."

I smiled horribly. "You're not wrong."

With enviable ease, Caethari bent at the knees and scooped Killic into his arms, carrying him over to the bed and laying him unceremoniously on top of the covers. I felt an absurd pang of anger at the sight, too deep and complicated to unwrap in the moment, and willed it away as Caethari came to stand beside me.

He looked me over, handsome brow furrowed. His inky hair was still pulled back in the same perfect braid he'd worn all morning, barely a hair disturbed despite his trip to the revetha and his subsequent change of clothes. It made me want to dishevel him; to unbind his braid and sink my fingers into the dark, silky mass. The strength of the longing took me aback, guilt souring in my throat. Bad enough I'd kissed him in a moment of weakness; I didn't have the luxury of further complicating the fragile accord between us.

"Are you all right?" he asked, then instantly grimaced, shaking his head at himself. "I'm sorry, that was a stupid question. Do you want company?"

I managed something that was almost laughter. "I hardly know what I want," I said. "I think—Ru Zairin is right, I do need rest, but before that . . . I need to speak to Markel. Alone."

"Of course," said Caethari. He hesitated. "I'll have a guard placed on the door, then speak to Mirae and the others, to see that Killic's presence is kept as confidential as it can be at this point."

I nodded, squashing down the misery that accompanied the thought of people knowing anything about my history with Killic. I'd flinched from invoking Tithenai justice due to the certainty of spectacle, but it was impossible to suppress all knowledge of his being here, especially given the existing, albeit wildly inaccurate, gossip among the guards regarding my feelings for him. Ru Zairin, too, knew more than thei had mere minutes ago, and while a part of me shuddered at the reveal, I still preferred to have the ugly truth spoken aloud, in private, to the prospect of it being written down and seen by strangers, all outside my control.

Either way, the brand on Killic's hand was bandaged for now, and while a former sailor like Ren Valiu might know what it meant, the chances were that few others in the Aida would. If I was lucky, all that would circulate was a whisper that the new tiern's ex-lover had come for him and been turned down in favour of Tiern Caethari.

If I was lucky.

"Ru Zairin, if you have no objections, I'll accompany you to the infirmary," I said. "Ti—Caethari, I'll . . . come find you when I'm done."

"Or you could rest," he said, not ungently.

"Or that."

He smiled at me, the expression soft and complex, and though I smiled back, I quickly turned away before I could embarrass myself about it, letting Ru Zairin precede me out of the room.

I trailed a step behind thim all the way back to the infirmary. We didn't speak, though the good ru looked vaguely troubled whenever thei turned to check that I was following. When we entered, I was privately relieved to find Ru Telitha absent, though she'd left behind a pile of books, a clipped sheaf of paper depicting notes about Markel's signs, and a pencil, suggesting that she meant to return. I was likewise surprised that, despite the return of Mirae's party, which had included the injured Siqa, Markel was still the only patient in the infirmary. It belatedly occurred to me that, although Keletha had also taken an arrow, I hadn't once seen thim come in there, either. I asked Ru Zairin about this, and thei rolled their eyes.

"Envoy Keletha is almost as stubborn as you," thei said. "I'm accustomed to running thim to ground over medical matters for which thei refuse to seek treatment. As for Siqa, he's in need of recuperative rest, but prefers to do so in his own quarters. Don't mind me, by the by," thei added, returning the medical supplies thei'd used on Killic to their usual places. "I'm off to get a proper lunch." And with a final, meaningful glance in my direction, thei departed the infirmary, the door shutting softly behind them.

Markel smiled at me, setting aside the book he'd been reading. He straightened his back against the cushions, wincing only a little as the movement jostled his healing wound, and all at once the full impact of the morning's events hit me like a hammer. I made my way to the chair Ru Telitha had left vacant and sat down heavily, but before Markel could sign the question I saw in his eyes, I clasped his hand between mine and pressed my forehead against it, shaking as I struggled to breathe.

"I'm sorry," I rasped. "Markel, I'm so sorry. You took a blade for me, and I haven't been honest with you." I lifted my head, hating the worry I saw in his face. "I need to tell you the truth about Killic."

And so I did—in signs, as much because I didn't trust my voice as to prevent being overheard. I told him the truth of what had happened in the garden; why I'd twice raised a blade to myself. He was so distressed that he made a rare vocalisation, a rough, hurt noise as he grabbed my hands and squeezed them, offering comfort as I wept; and then, when I could sign again, I told him the rest of what he'd missed that day, starting with Laecia's lunch and ending with Killic's brand, omitting only the barely-a-kiss I'd so foolishly given Caethari.

When I finally finished, Markel held my hands in a brief, tight grip, then signed, "You owe me no apologies. I'm furious that he hurt you, and your branding him is kinder by far than I would've been, were the choice mine to make. But you didn't have to tell me, or apologise for not telling me sooner."

"Yes, I did," I signed back. I bit my lip, recalling that we no longer lived in Ralia—that, in all probability, we would never live there again—and decided to be brave. "You have acted as my servant because, for as long as we've known each other, there was no other acceptable way for us to associate. You are my dearest friend, Markel, and have been for years. That you were willing to serve me, to stay with me, to endure the slights of Farathel—that's something I can never repay. I would have been lost without you, a dozen, a hundred times over. But here, I think—I hope—that you might have more opportunities. You are clever, hard-working, quick to learn, and Tithena is a nation that rewards those qualities more than Ralia does. I would—" I faltered, throat closing with the selfishness of what I was about to ask. "—I would beg you to stay with me a little longer at least, until I am acclimated here, but after that, whatever you wish to do, whether it is here or elsewhere, you will have my support."

Markel stared at me for two full seconds; then he grabbed my arms and hauled me up for a hug. The embrace was no less heartfelt for being slightly awkward—I was too conscious of his injury to be sure where to rest my weight—and it cracked something open in me, or possibly mended what was already cracked, or maybe both of those things at once.

Markel pressed a kiss to my forehead and let me go, his expression one of fond exasperation.

"You really are ridiculous," he signed. "Of course I'm not going anywhere! I don't need you to tell me what I can or can't do in Tithena—and yes, there could well be more opportunities for me here than there were in Ralia. Ru Telitha"—he spelled out her name using the sign alphabet I was yet to teach Caethari, then introduced a new sign for her that translated literally to Bright Scholar—"has been telling me all about the universities; how anyone who passes the tests can attend. And in time, I might be interested, especially if, as she suggests, there might be a way to make signing more common."

He smiled crookedly, reaching over to give my cheek a quick double pat, like a maiden aunt indulging an errant nephew over sherry. "But you are my friend, Velasin. I owe you at least as much as you feel you owe me—more, I would argue, but that is a debate for another time. And as your friend, I know that you have a terrible habit of pushing away the people closest to you whenever you feel you're being a burden on them." He fixed me with a stare that was as firm as it was kind, so that any denial I might've made died on my fingertips. "Telling me about Killic is not a burden. Your feelings are not a burden. *You* are not a burden, and whatever happens in the future, I am not about to rush off and leave you just because things here are complicated." He snorted. "After all, when have our lives not been complicated one way or another?"

I hardly knew what to say to that, and it must've shown on my face, because Markel's next act was to take mercy on me and change the subject. "Caethari appears to be treating you well."

"He is," I replied, so relieved not to be talking about my innermost fears that even my marriage felt like a safer topic of conversation. "All the way here, I was so afraid, and yet he's been impossibly kind. We have agreed to be friends, and once this Wild Knife mess is sorted out, I think we might even succeed at it."

Markel touched my hand, featherlight. "I'm sorry about Quip. I know how much he meant to you."

"He was a good horse," I said aloud, the words inadequate to the pang of grief that accompanied them, and so I reached into my pocket and handed him the braid of horsehair, as yet unlacquered, that I'd been given as a keepsake. Markel examined it gently, thumb stroking the braid, and returned it to me.

"Have you eaten?" I asked him, needing a reprieve from emotional matters.

Markel grinned at me. "Ru Telitha went to fetch us some lunch not long before you arrived. I expect she'll be back soon."

I raised an eyebrow; I was very familiar with that particular grin. "Oh, will she? And I suppose you'd like some privacy when that happens?"

"I wouldn't object to it."

I laughed, as relieved to be capable of the sound as I was happy that one of us, at least, was able to flirt sensibly. "Should I take this to mean that you're feeling better?"

"Very!"

"In that case, I'll leave you be," I said, and rose to my feet.

"Take care of yourself," signed Markel. "I know you're out of practice, but please try."

I flapped a hand in not-quite-acknowledgement and left the infirmary, feeling somewhat lighter than I had on entry, if no less exhausted. Sleep would perhaps have been sensible, but just at that moment I lacked the wit to go and rest, as three separate people had now suggested I do, half out of fear that being alone with my own thoughts would cause my pending bill of distress to come due, and half out of sheer contrariness. Instead, I headed out into the main courtyard, testing the strength of my healing leg. It ached in a background sort of way, but wasn't actively bothering me, which I took for a positive sign. I didn't want to be still or unoccupied, but I didn't quite trust myself to seek out Caethari either, and on that basis I decided to go for a walk.

Picking a direction more or less at random, I set off at a pace neither brisk nor slow and pretended I had a greater purpose than aimless wandering. I made it as far as the Triple Gardens before my stomach began to gurgle unpleasantly, a none-too-gentle reminder that my lunch had ultimately ended up outside my body.

"Yes, yes," I grumbled, the disapproving trio of Markel, Caethari and Ru Zairin looming large in my imagination. "I know."

I backtracked to the kitchens and the domain of Ren Valiu. She was clearly in her element, yelling orders to undercooks and scullions while beating an aromatic mixture in a large wooden bowl with startling enthusiasm. Yet when she saw me, she smiled and beckoned me over, producing a plate of fresh jidha from somewhere nearby and pressing it into my hands, unasked.

"Thank you," I said, stunned.

Ren Valiu *tsk*ed. "I feed people, and you need feeding. No thanks required."

I hesitated. "Did Ren Taiko ever come to claim that bottle I promised him?"

"No, tiern." Her expression turned grave. "I offered, but he wouldn't accept. Said you'd gifted it on the condition that he look after your horse, and as he'd failed in that, he couldn't take it."

My stomach twisted unpleasantly. "If you see him again, please give it to him," I said. "On my insistence. He didn't fail. What happened to Quip . . . that wasn't something grooms are meant to guard against."

"I'll do that, tiern."

"My thanks for the food," I said, and hurried back outside before either her kindness or her approval could inspire yet another complex feeling I'd have to deal with.

I ate as I walked, the jidha just cooled enough not to burn my mouth, and was almost back to the Court of Swords when someone hailed me.

"Velasin!" called Caethari. I turned towards the sound of his voice and saw him jogging over, Raeki following at his heels. I swallowed a mouthful of jidha and cast about unsuccessfully for somewhere to put the plate as my husband reached me. "Velasin, Raeki's guards just got back from asking around about Ren Baru, and they think they've found him. Or found out his identity, rather."

"Ren Baru Kasha," said Raeki, coming to stand beside Caethari. His expression was grim. "A local merchant known for selling Khytoi furs, among other things. None of his associates have seen him for days, but apparently he was well-known for his hero worship of the Wild Knife."

"We know where he lived," said Caethari. "The guards haven't been inside yet—they reported back first—but we're going to head there now. Do you want to come?"

I thrust the plate at Raeki, who did an outraged double take while accepting it with a scowl. "Let's go."

23

Ren Baru Kasha's house was a narrow two-storey building at the lower edge of the upper city. It was three streets away from his shopfront in the cloth district, where furs, fabrics and other fine materials were sold, and where the best tailors in Qi-Katai made their living—including, Caethari informed me, Ren Lithas Vael. From the outside, there was little to distinguish the building from those on either side of it, no sign of disturbance or violence. We reined our horses and dismounted, leaving them in the care of one of the two guards Raeki had insisted accompany us. Taking the lead with the other guard, a wiry, sharp-faced woman named Dai Sirat Lo, Raeki walked up to the door and knocked. There was no answer, but we'd been expecting that: by all accounts, Ren Baru lived alone. Raeki waited an extra few seconds for good measure, then nodded to Dai Sirat.

"Go ahead."

Reaching into her pocket, Dai Sirat withdrew a set of lockpicks and had the door open in a startlingly short amount of time. I whistled, impressed with the skill, and she flashed me a crooked grin as we entered the house.

A narrow set of stairs opposite the door went straight up to the next level, while the small foyer opened into a living area. Though the windows were open, the buildings on either side were tall enough that little light came in through them, but Ren Baru had evidently been prosperous enough to afford magelights: glass balls that shone with captured daylight, but which could be dimmed or extinguished with a touch. Caethari sighed, casting these an envious look.

"I've a fondness for magelights," he admitted, raising a finger to switch on the nearest globe, "but my father thinks them a frivolous expense. And in his defence, most rooms in the Aida are sufficiently bright during the day not to need them, while the candles we purchase keep us in good accord with the Chandlers' Guild. Regardless, I have always found them beautiful. Even here." He smiled sadly.

This was the second time the tieren's apparent dislike of magic had cropped up in conversation, and I made a mental note to inquire about it later. Though finicky and eccentric in its applications, I'd never before met a nobleman who scorned magecraft as my new father-in-law evidently did, and I wanted to know why.

"Ren Baru kept two employees, as far as we know," said Raeki, still moving ahead of us. "A housekeeper and a shop assistant. Both showed up for work in the days since he was arrested, and both made reports about their employer's apparent absence to the Sable Street guardhouse, but nobody from Amber Gate reached out to them." He made a disgusted noise. "If you've an unknown criminal in custody, it ought to be standard procedure to contact other guardhouses for their missing persons' reports—I've said so for years, but does anyone listen?"

Caethari and Dai Sirat exchanged a look at this, which told me the complaint was a long-standing one. Nor did Raeki appear to expect an answer; instead, he huffed and glared at the settee, as though to hold it personally responsible for the failings of Qi-Katai's law enforcement.

Behind the living area was a well-stocked kitchen, the apparent domain of Ren Baru's housekeeper, and, off to one side, a small cupboard. When neither room revealed anything of interest, Raeki instructed Dai Sirat to make a thorough search of the living area while the three of us went to check upstairs.

The wooden steps creaked under our feet, and when we reached the landing, the floorboards were just as noisy. To our left, a linen cupboard set in the wall divided a bathroom and a study, while Ren Baru's bedroom was straight ahead.

"Study first," said Caethari.

The walls were covered with ledger-filled shelves; Caethari gravitated towards them, plucking a random volume and scanning the contents, while I turned my attention to the heavy oak desk placed to take advantage of the room's one window. It was surprisingly neat, with stacks of paper on one side and an expensive quill and inkpot set on the other. The blotter was new, speckled with only a few stains of dark ink, but I was more interested in the desk's two drawers, one on either side.

"Found anything?" asked Raeki. He was holding the door open, watching us work.

"Sales ledgers," said Caethari, reshelving his book. "We should have them looked through, to see if he was in debt, who his main associates were."

Raeki nodded. "I'll check the bathroom," he said.

As the tar stepped away, the heavy door swung shut of its own accord, fitting silently into the frame. I opened the first drawer and found the usual clutter I'd expect in a desk drawer: sealing wax, a penknife, spare quills, a small pot of red ink and a sheaf of letters bound with a ribbon, which I absently passed to Caethari. The second drawer was heavier than the first; it stuck fast, as ifthe wood had warped at some point. Still, I managed to wrangle it open, revealing a bundle of cheap paper pamphlets of the kind invariably sold in cities, detailing everything from major trade news and military successes to salacious gossip and rumours.

"Scandal sheets," I said, thumbing through them. None of the dates were consecutive, but they were all a few years old at least to judge by the yellowing paper, and my brows rose as I realised what linked them. "All chronicling the exploits of the Wild Knife."

Caethari winced, taking them from me. "I always hated these stories," he muttered. "And the name itself, for that matter. *Wild Knife.*" His lip curled.

"It's not a self-styled title, then?" I asked, daring to tease him.

"One time," he muttered, looking delightfully embarrassed, "*one time* I brought an escaping bandit down with a throwing knife, and I've never since heard the end of it."

"In fairness," I said, "you do keep a knife and a throwing board in your apartments."

"*Our* apartments," Caethari huffed.

I smiled despite myself.

Closing the sticky drawer was as difficult as opening it had been. I jiggled it in place, and was startled when something heavy and metallic, which must previously have been kept to the back by the stack of pamphlets, rolled to the front with a *clunk.* I picked it up, staring dumbly at my find.

It was a crossbow bolt, identical to the ones that had punched through Ren Baru's jugular.

Caethari inhaled sharply. "Is that—?"

"It is." I held it up for my husband's benefit. "A bolt."

Caethari swore. "Raeki needs to see this."

At that, I heard a sound from the hall. Thinking Raeki done with the bathroom, I rose and headed to the door, pulling it open—

A blade slashed towards me, missing my throat by a hairsbreadth. My assailant was clad all in black, their whole face hidden except for their eyes, and I had just enough time to register that they perfectly matched Tieren Halithar's description of the intruder who'd broken into his rooms before the knife flashed again and I dodged with a yell, stumbling backwards.

"*Raeki!*" I yelled.

My attacker froze—as did I, which was a grave mistake, as it afforded them a crucial space in which to shove me roughly at Caethari before bolting for the bedroom. As my husband and I collided, Raeki dashed past with his sword drawn, the study door already swinging shut again.

"Stop!" roared Raeki, but whoever it was ignored him. Tearing through the hall, Caethari and I reached the bedroom door just in time to see my assailant launch themselves from the windowsill to the wall of the building adjacent, a jump of some nine feet.

There ought to have been no handholds, but as the three of us rushed to the window, we saw the intruder slap their gloves and boots to the naked brick and somehow, impossibly, cling on like a gecko. They climbed with startling speed until they reached the rooftop, where they pulled themselves over the edge and began to run.

Shouting frustration, Raeki turned and bolted downstairs, yelling for Dai Sirat to give chase. Caethari and I stayed rooted to the spot, watching as the black-clad stranger reached the end of one roof and then leapt to another, the pattern repeating until they vanished from sight. Caethari was rigid; he'd dropped the letters and scandal sheets, the fingers of both hands digging into the windowsill.

"That's them," he said, voice tense. "That's the person who struck my father."

"We'll catch them," I said, trying to project a certainty I didn't feel.

Caethari turned to me. "Are you all right?"

"I'm fine."

"They didn't cut you?"

"No." I exhaled slowly, shaky in the aftershock. "No, they missed." A dark twist of humour entered my voice. "Again."

When Caethari didn't respond to that, I crouched by his feet and carefully gathered up the dropped papers; the letters were still contained by the ribbon, but the scandal sheets were lighter, unbound, and some were moving in the breeze, blowing under the bed and across the floor.

"Fuck," said Caethari, belatedly noticing the mess he'd made. He crouched down so fast that we almost banged heads, then jerked his hand away when we both reached for the same pamphlet. He laughed at that, sheepish enough that any sting I'd felt was soothed, and helped to gather up the scattered paper.

"Whoever it was, they must've been in here the whole time," Caethari murmured, looking around the space. "Why didn't they run when we were still downstairs?"

"Maybe they hoped we'd leave without finding them," I said, then paused, considering. "Attacking me was a gamble; I doubt they knew we were coming. But then they missed—they seem to be making a habit of that—and when I called Raeki, they realised they were in danger of getting boxed in and caught, so they fled."

"Which begs the question," Caethari murmured, running a hand over the carving on Ren Baru's wardrobe, "did they act because we found the bolt, or because we were about to head to the bedroom?"

I'd put the bolt in my pocket while tidying the dropped papers, but withdrew it again, weighing it in my palm. I had little knowledge of crossbows—my firsthand experience of archery was restricted to Markel's marksmanship and hunting parties—and I didn't know whether it was heavier than it ought to be, or if I was just ignorant.

"Does this bolt seem odd to you?" I asked, handing it to Caethari.

He frowned as he took it, examining the metal. "Not exactly. It's a distinctive make, but so were the ones we pulled from Ren Baru."

"What do you mean, distinctive?"

"It's a heavier type of bolt, meant to punch through armour. But the weight means they're harder to aim accurately over distance and they won't shoot as far, which means they're usually used more in close combat." His frown deepened. "Which makes it even stranger, that they were used to kill Ren Baru. That shot would've been hard enough to make without using heavy bolts."

I sighed. "Unless there's magic involved, something to increase the range or the accuracy of the bow itself."

Caethari nodded, glancing back at the window. "From what we just saw, I'd wager our target is wearing spelled gloves and boots. Why not a spelled crossbow, too?"

By mutual agreement, we headed back down the creaking stairs and out to where the second of Raeki's guards, Dai Moras Mara, was still holding the horses, a tense expression on his face. He looked up eagerly at our approach, asking, "What happened, tierns? Tar

Raeki sent Sirat off at a run, then scrambled away himself to look for witnesses."

Caethari filled him in on the details of the intruder, though he omitted any mention of the papers and the bolt we'd found. Dai Moras looked wistfully towards the alley where his fellows had vanished, for all the world like a hound denied scraps at table. I glanced at Caethari, unsure of what it was or wasn't my place to suggest, and was relieved when he said to Dai Moras, "You should stay here and keep guard for them. Tell Tar Raeki that Velasin and I are returning to the Aida."

"Yes, tiern," said Dai Moras, and handed over our horses without another word.

We mounted up and began to ride. I was on Luya again, and though he was a perfectly serviceable horse, I missed the fluid bond I'd had with Quip; the years of training that meant I could steer with my knees or guide him with only the lightest rein and know how he'd respond.

"Spelled bow, spelled clothes, a dead merchant," Caethari murmured, more to himself than to me. He stared into space for several moments, then shook himself and said, "That list of mages Tar Katvi had, from Ruya's Order. What if we're looking in the wrong place entirely?"

I caught his meaning instantly. "You think we should be looking for artifex sellers, not mages?"

"I think we should investigate both."

I considered the little I knew about artifex sales in Tithena, whose primary point of difference to the same trade in Ralia, as I understood it, was the lack of religious oversight. Though any gentleman of good standing might learn magic in Ralia, the creation of artifex for anything other than personal use was strictly controlled and monitored by the temples. Without a temple licence, no mage was permitted to sell or otherwise distribute their creations, while imported artifex underwent heavy scrutiny to ensure that nothing immoral, heretical or otherwise antithetical to Ralian values was circulated among the populace. I'd always thought it a lot of scaremongering nonsense—after all, the temples thought my attraction to men was immoral, which showed what use their strictures were—but it did mean that tracking down the origins of a particular artifex was comparatively easy. But in Tithenai, I suspected, this would be a much more difficult endeavour.

"Where should we start, then?" I asked, by way of easing into the topic.

Caethari made a frustrated noise. "I don't know. The Aida doesn't have many dealings with artifex sellers, and there must be hundreds in Qi-Katai, never mind the merchants bringing things in from elsewhere. It might narrow things down, knowing that these are high-quality items, but even so—" He broke off, a look of vague embarrassment dawning on his face. "Oh."

"Oh what?"

"I think I know who we need to see," Caethari said, "but it's . . . awkward. Slightly. That is, it might be awkward for you, and certainly for me to show up unannounced, but he'll be fine, it's just—"

"Caethari," I said, amused, and his mouth snapped shut like the maw of a carnivorous plant. "Who is it?"

"Ru Liran Faez," he said. "My, ah, former lover. The one who's coming to the marriage-gathering."

I sat with that a moment, studying Caethari's expression. He looked every bit as nervous as he had when he'd explained the kissing tradition, a light flush warming his cheeks and throat. Flushed was a distractingly good look on him, and so it took me longer than usual to recognise the source of his apprehension.

"Oh!" I said. "You're worried I might be jealous."

"The thought had crossed my mind."

"Are you still in love with him?"

Caethari startled. "No."

"Still sleeping with him?"

"Of course not!"

"Then why should I be jealous?" I laughed. "Really, tiern; I know we're married, but we've also only just met. I've no right to that sort of jealousy, and in any case, we've agreed to be friends; and what sort of friend would I be, to begrudge you intimacy?" I swallowed a little at that, my own words cutting too close to Laecia's unknowing remarks at lunch. *What would I want with a husband who won't bed me? It defeats the whole purpose!* I shoved the thought aside and added, as much for my own sake as for Caethari's, "In any case, as I'm apparently destined to kiss him—or be kissed by him, sorry—three days from now, I can hardly object to meeting him beforehand."

Caethari blinked at me. "My apologies, Velasin, but I'd rather thought you'd be more Ralian about it. Especially given—well." He ducked his head, flashing a worried glance at me, and this time I knew instantly what he was referring to: the fact that, prior to his worse offences, Killic had been unfaithful to me.

I stared at my hands where they gripped Luya's reins, trying to work through the sudden snarl of emotion that had lodged itself under my breastbone.

"Forgive me," Caethari said, softly. "I shouldn't have brought it up."

"No," I said. "If we are to be friends, we ought to be honest about such things." I was silent for a long moment, letting my ears fill with the background noise of Qi-Katai, the steady clip-clop of hooves on the sloping street. "Killic's betrayal," I said at last, "his first betrayal, I mean—that cut me deep, because we'd agreed to be exclusive, and I thought it meant something. Not many like us are truly monogamous in Ralia—or at least, not in Farathel; not at court. It's too dangerous to appear too heavily fixated on one person, you see, so the general feeling is, if you have to be seen to share your favours anyway, then why not enjoy the sharing?"

I shrugged, though the sting of it was not so easily shaken off, and forced myself to continue. "But Killic . . . Killic swore himself to me, and I was fool enough to believe him. Moons, if he'd told me he wanted to bed someone else, I probably would've said yes, because I thought—I thought I had his heart." I swallowed. "If he'd asked, it would've been part of the trust between us, and we could've negotiated it in good faith. But he didn't, and it wasn't." My throat rasped on the words, and I hated—suddenly, acutely—that I could still be this angry about Killic's infidelity, when what he'd done afterwards had been so much worse. I pressed my knuckles hard against the pommel so that I didn't jerk poor Luya's reins and said, striving for evenness, "I can't be jealous of Ru Liran. Even if you were still involved, you've made no promises to me that loving him would break."

"And is marriage not a promise?" Caethari asked, gently.

My mouth twisted of its own accord. "A promise of a different sort," I said, not trusting myself to look anywhere other than Luya's mane. "A contract, not a vow. But one I nonetheless take seriously," I added, both because it was true and because I didn't want Caethari to think I disdained our marriage entirely.

"I hate that you were forced to this," Caethari said suddenly. I glanced at him, unsettled by the genuine distress in his tone. "I feel as if I've stolen you, like some ogre in a story."

"A handsome ogre, if so," I said, trying to lighten things. "And even if you have stolen me, it was not from anything to which I either could or would return, had I the option." I realised it was true as I said it; Caethari shot me a startled look, which forced me to explain. "Had my preferences never been revealed, I would've wed your sister in dutiful misery, and without wanting to slight her in the least, I don't think her tolerance for my inadequacies would remotely compare to what yours has been."

"Velasin—"

"And had the alliance never been offered," I said, running roughshod over whatever implausibly kind thing Caethari had been about to say, "I would still be in Farathel, lonely and hurt and trying to sift through my acquaintances to see who might take my side over Killic's. When my father summoned me home, I still hadn't told our mutual friends that we'd parted." I smiled, the expression as small as my past horizons. "Stolen me? As well to say a caged bird can be stolen by the sky."

His leg brushed mine as our horses drew close, and then he leaned over and gripped my arm, squeezing hard enough that I met his gaze. "Stop belittling yourself," Caethari said. His hand released me, but his eyes did not; they pierced me, sharp as obsidian and just as beautiful. "You are not inadequate."

"Please," I said, and it came out shaky. The conversation had already brought me perilously close to the edge of everything I'd been blocking out of my mind all day; too much kindness and I'd be lost. "Please, not here. You can fight me about myself tomorrow all you wish, but please—not now."

I didn't expect him to listen, which was perhaps unfair; but then, very little about the last few hours had been anything else. Something complex flickered in Caethari's expression, and then—to my profound relief—he nodded and pulled away.

"So," he said, after a good minute had ticked by and I'd had time to master myself. "Would you object to seeing Liran now? Provided he's home, of course," he added. "He might not be, but it's on our way to check; his residence is near the Jade Market."

"By all means, lead on," I said, and let my curiosity about Ru Liran Faez distract me from myself.

24

Caethari led us expertly through the interweaving streets of the upper city at a brisk trot, until we reached a broad residential avenue just two turns back of the vaunted Jade Market. Here, the tall houses were more considerately spaced than in Ren Baru's former neighbourhood, with hitching posts for visiting horses set at intervals along the length of the street.

"Are all these individual homes?" I asked, trying to better attune my perspective. In Farathel, buildings of this size would be considered too small for the richer nobility, yet still too grand for most anybody else to afford, unless they were split into multiple occupancies.

"Only a very few," said Caethari. "Most are fashionable apartments—very popular with the young nobility and upwardly mobile merchant scions who like to be seen to mingle with artists and artisans without actually having to support them." He said this with a note of wry amusement, as though quoting a witty assessment made by someone else.

I took an intuitive leap and asked, "Is that what Ru Liran says?"

Caethari did a double take, then graced me with a broad, soft smile that crinkled the edges of his eyes. "Saints, you're sharp," he said, reining his horse to a standstill. "Yes, as it happens. And here we are!"

We dismounted together, leaving the horses hitched to one of the many convenient posts. "So which is Ru Liran?" I asked.

"Which is he what?"

"Young nobility, upwardly mobile merchant scion, artist or artisan?"

Caethari laughed. "A little of all four, on a good day. He's the middle son of a noble house, like me—his proper title is Ciet Liran, but he hates to use it; says he'd rather be known for his scholarship than his birth."

Ciet was a rank a step below tiern. "A man of good sense, then," I said.

"Extremely. As to the rest—" Caethari waved a hand as we ascended the steps leading up to a generous, three-level building made from pale gold stone. "—he dabbles."

We stopped before a large white door set with a bold bronze knocker styled in the shape of a snowcat's head. Caethari knocked, and within moments the door opened to reveal a uniformed kem standing in a small foyer.

"Tierns Caethari and Velasin to see Ru Liran, if he's at home to visitors," said Caethari.

The kem flashed a quick smile and nodded, waving us in. "Ru Liran is in," thei said. "Please, go ahead."

Murmuring thanks, Caethari led me out of the foyer and over to the staircase. "The ground floor is the main kitchen and laundry for both apartments, along with the servants' quarters," he said as we climbed, noting my interest in the layout. "Each tenant's personal servants have access, as do the tenants themselves." And then, as we passed the first landing, "Liran is on the top floor."

Unlike the stairs in Ren Baru's apartment, the two flights up to Ru Liran's door were both silent and carpeted, ensuring the wealthy tenants wouldn't be bothered by the sounds of neighbours and servants going about their business. We reached a second landing and stopped before another door, where Caethari once again knocked.

"Just a moment!" someone called from the other side. There was a scuffing sound, and then the door swung open to reveal, not a servant, but Ru Liran himself. He was wearing nothing but a hip-wrap and a pale gold robe, which seemed to glow against the deep, warm brown of his skin. His long, black locs were pulled back from his face with a twist of gold wire, showing off the elegant line of his throat, and there was a paintbrush tucked behind one heavily earringed ear. His face lit up at the sight of Caethari, and only an interested quirk of his fine, dark brows betrayed any surprise at seeing me there, too.

"Cae!" he exclaimed, delighted. "If I'd known you were coming, I would've dressed." He glanced at me, and I could see the moment when he realised who I must be. "And this is your husband, yes? Tiern Velasin?"

"A pleasure to meet you, Ru Liran," I said, flustered by more than his hipwrap.

"Just Liran, please," he said, and stepped aside to wave us in. "Come, sit down! What brings you to my corner of Qi-Katai?"

Inside, the main room of the apartment was light, airy and beautifully decorated, an eclectic mix of colour and comfort that nonetheless spoke to a singular aesthetic. An easel stood before a nearby window, though as the canvas it supported faced away from the room, I could only guess at the subject of Liran's art.

"If you've got the time, we were hoping to pick your brains about something," Caethari said, sitting down on a plush green settee. I hesitated, then sat beside him, acutely aware of the press of his leg against mine.

Fastening his robe more closely, Liran sat down in an armchair opposite and leaned forwards, clearly interested. "I'm listening."

Caethari shot him a meaningful look. "It's about a confidential matter. I'd never accuse you of being indiscreet, but—"

"Oh, you *liar,*" said Liran, mouth curved with humour. "We both know you have, and we both know I deserved it. But on this occasion, yes, I solemnly pledge to mind your privacy—and that of your husband, of course, to whom you *will* properly introduce me at some point, yes?"

"Of course," said Caethari, abashed.

"Good, then." Liran crossed his hands at the wrists and flicked his fingers. "Now. Tell me what secret business requires my intellect."

And Caethari did so, sparing no detail: everything from the attack at Vaiko to the disappearance of the unknown intruder through Ren Baru's bedroom window. He spoke like a soldier giving a report, laying out the chain of events with calm, even precision. Liran listened closely, and though he didn't interrupt at any point, his expressive features showed the full range of his feelings. I found myself watching him throughout, partly because I already knew what had happened and therefore had no reason to pay close attention, but mostly because he was one of the most exquisitely handsome men I'd ever seen. He was luminous.

"And so we've come to you," Caethari finished. "If our target is buying or stealing artifex instead of creating them, then I thought you might know where to look for that sort of high-end, specialist magecraft."

"That is . . . quite a lot to take in," said Liran, leaning back in his chair. He looked at me, his gaze sympathetic. "It seems Qi-Katai has met you with a fairly poor reception."

I shrugged, lips quirking at the understatement. "I don't take it personally."

"You'd be more than entitled to."

"Perhaps. I just don't see that it would help."

"True," said Liran, grinning. It was a very beautiful grin, and while I'd been completely sincere in telling Caethari that I wasn't and wouldn't be jealous of Liran, I was certainly feeling intimidated. This was the man to whom I would be invariably compared, if not by Caethari himself, then certainly by others. I was not so harshly self-deprecating as to think myself ugly or untalented, but even at my best, I wasn't half so warm and charming as Liran appeared to be, to say nothing of being neither an artist nor an expert on artifex sellers.

"Hm," said Liran, who'd been staring thoughtfully into space. "The kind of spelled gear you're describing is a little outside my usual wheelhouse, but it does have some intriguing implications. That spell to jump safely from a height, for instance—I wonder how it worked? Did it regulate descent, or redistribute the force of the landing impact, or something else altogether?" He tapped a finger against his lips. "It would've had to take mass into account, surely—but hm, no, that suggests a tailored spell, and we're looking for generic components, or generic enough to be purchased. Tailored to mass within set parameters? That could be risky, but—ah! An air cushion! Now *that* seems promising." He beamed at us. "Not to downplay your difficulties, Cae, but this is a marvellous puzzle!"

"I'm so glad we could entertain you," Caethari said dryly.

"As well you should be," Liran replied. "These other artifex—the crossbow, the gloves and boots—those aren't as uncommon as you might think. They're specialist equipment, certainly, but not necessarily bespoke, although they might well be proprietary." He toyed with one of his locs, brow furrowed as he thought. "In fact," he said, slowly, "taken together with the jumping spell, what it most makes me think of is hunting."

"Hunting?" I said, surprised.

"Hunting, yes. But oh! No, not the sort you're likely familiar with," Liran said, seeing my expression. "Not Ralian chase-through-the-manicured-woodland hunting; I mean the kind the takes place in high mountains." He shot a sharp glance at Caethari. "Khytoi hunters might use this kind of gear to chase down snow-cats and silk chamois, for instance. I understand many prefer crossbows for such work, as the bolts are both less damaging to the hides and easier to transport, while that jumping spell makes much more sense as a safeguard against falling from heights than as a unique creation."

"Khytoi again," said Caethari, frowning. "It could be a coincidence, but . . ."

"Quite," Liran said, stretching languorously against his chair. "Of course, I don't imagine this is some sort of Khytoi *plot*, but at the very least, I'd suspect your target is familiar enough with Khytoi merchants to know where to acquire their gear—which they do sell in Qi-Katai, as far as I know, but not openly, and not to many people." He grinned cheekily. "Give me another day or two, and I ought to be able to scrounge up a list of names to investigate."

I stared at Liran, thoroughly impressed. "If this is what it looks like when you're working outside your wheelhouse, I'm almost afraid to see what you'd consider a specialist topic!"

All at once, Liran's expression turned, not exactly cool, but undeniably reserved. "Cae," he said carefully, "may I ask, did you enlighten your husband as to *why* I have an interest in magic?"

Caethari blinked at him, nonplussed. "No. Why, should I have done?" And then, a moment later, both sheepish and worried, "Oh."

Liran rubbed his face. "Saints preserve me. This is awkward, isn't it?"

"What's awkward?" I asked, glancing confusedly between them. I'd clearly misstepped, but I didn't know how, and that made me anxious.

Caethari grimaced. "I'm sorry. I didn't think."

"Thinking never has been your strong suit," Liran agreed. I would've taken offence at this on Caethari's behalf, but it was clearly an old line between them, as Liran's tone was wry and Caethari unbothered. Liran sighed, then said to me, "Tiern Velasin—"

"Just Velasin," I said, feeling a sudden urge to offer him the same intimacy he'd offered me.

Liran's lips twitched. "Velasin," he amended, "I don't normally go around making a song and dance about my personhood, especially not to new acquaintances, but as I'll be at your marriage-gathering—I received the invite an hour ago, by the way; I'm looking forward to attending," he added to Caethari, who ducked his head in acknowledgement, "—and as you are, not to put too fine a point on it, Ralian, I'd rather tell you myself than have some wag decide to spring it on you for the sake of seeing how you react."

By this point, I was thoroughly baffled. "Tell me what?"

"That my interest in magic stems from my having originally been thought a girl," said Liran bluntly. "I knew myself to be otherwise quite early on, and there's nothing shameful about it here, but I understand that in Ralia, things are . . . different."

The pause that followed was sufficiently pregnant to be considered past due. I absorbed the admission, understanding why Liran had opted to make it even as I hated having put him in such a position, and said, "That is certainly true. But I am not, ah—in this respect, I am not very Ralian."

Liran raised an assessing eyebrow. "Oh?"

I flushed, struggling to think how best to express myself. The body-altering magics to which Liran referred were tittered about in Farathel in much the same salacious way that other Tithenai concepts were, but while Ralian lacked equivalent terms for kemi or a husband's husband, it boasted a distressing number of vicious epithets for people like Liran.

Finally, I said, "I will not excuse my home nation. We are abominable about many things. But as I know from experience, despising a thing doesn't stop it from existing." I swallowed, meeting Liran's gaze. "I have known men and women like you before, though they haven't always had access to body-magic. Ralia does not treat them kindly, and yet they have invariably been kind to me. One woman—" I stopped, not knowing if such details were necessary or even wanted, but Liran motioned for me to continue, and so I obliged him. "One woman I know is a healer. Before I met her, I don't think I'd ever heard of being metem"—I used the Tithenai term, relieved not to have to lean on the least-offensive Ralian slur I could think of—"but whatever ignorance I had, she was patient with me. More than that, though, she saved my best friend's life. Markel's life," I added, for Caethari's benefit.

Beside me, my husband made a sound of surprise. Up until then, it hadn't felt incongruous that he didn't know how Markel and I had met—it was a story I'd seldom had occasion to tell; or rather, for which I'd traditionally lacked a trustworthy audience—but all at once, that felt wrong.

Liran's brow furrowed. "Markel—this is the servant Cae mentioned? The one who was stabbed in your place?"

"That's him," I said, "though he's more my friend than anything else. He always has been, really, though explaining that in Ralia is . . . difficult."

"Happily, we're not in Ralia," said Liran. "I'd love to hear the full story."

There was nothing barbed in the statement; only genuine curiosity. I glanced at Caethari and, on seeing that he, too, looked interested, decided, *Why not?*

"I met Markel when I was not quite fourteen," I said. "My father had brought my brothers and I to Farathel on business—he'd only wanted to bring Nathian at first, to teach him his duties as heir, but Revic kicked up such a fuss about being left behind that in the end, he brought all of us. But that evening, he had an engagement that none of us was invited to, and so we were left in the apartment and told, very firmly, that we weren't to go out unaccompanied."

Caethari snorted. "That seems an ambitious expectation of three young noblemen."

"And so it proved to be," I said, wryly. "Nathian wanted to go out, of course—he was eighteen, practically a grown man—but he'd also been left in charge, and he took that seriously, if only because it gave him permission to boss Revic and me around. Revic was sixteen then, and he wanted to sneak out to the brothels—Nathian was scandalised, of course, which only made Revic more determined to embarrass him, saying lewder and lewder things until they were nearly at each other's throats. Which is when I, foolish younger son, decided to intervene." I winced at the memory. "I told them both to calm down, and that made Revic so angry, he said the only reason I didn't want to come to the brothels was because there wouldn't be any boys for me to fuck. Later, I realised that he didn't actually *know* my inclinations—he only suspected, or else was just trying to get a reaction—but even so, it's not the sort of accusation one makes lightly in Ralia.

"I froze up; I was terrified. But Nathian was furious at him—absolutely outraged that he'd say something so obscene about his little brother." I gave a bitter laugh, the irony still sharp a decade later. "They really did come to blows then, and I got caught in the middle of it. A more undignified scrap you've never seen, all of us flailing and kicking and punching! We made such a noise that the cook came in, and Revic jumped up and ran out of the house, yelling that he could do what he liked and neither of us could stop him. I begged Nathian to go after him, but he refused; just went up to bed to nurse his black eye in private."

"You were worried about Revic, after what he said?" asked Liran, clearly surprised.

I laughed. "The worry was purely selfish, I assure you. Nathian might've been in charge, but if Father came home and Revic was gone, I knew he would've held us both responsible. So I decided to find him myself. Which . . . well. I was, as I said, not quite fourteen, alone and on foot in the capital city, which I'd never explored before. Revic had a head start on me, and I thought I was so *clever*, knowing that there'd likely be brothels by the river docks. You could see the river from our apartment, so I thought it would be an easy walk." I paused, chagrined at my younger self. "It wasn't. By the time I realised my error, I'd covered enough distance that I didn't want to go back empty-handed, but I didn't have a purse on me to pay for a cab, either. So I just kept going."

"Stubborn," Caethari murmured, with something suspiciously like fond exasperation.

"Stubborn," I agreed, "and also, in this instance, extremely foolish. It was dark by the time I fetched up in one of the seedier red-light districts, and it hadn't occurred to me that knocking on a brothel door and asking if my brother was there was not, in fact, a good strategy."

Liran let out a scandalised burst of laughter. "Tell me you didn't actually do that!"

"I did," I admitted. "The doorman at the first establishment I went to just laughed at me; the second took a swing at my head, and the third said I was too young for custom, but that if I wanted work, the Blue Feather over on Kestrel Street was always looking for pretty boys. After that, I figured I needed a different approach." I rolled my eyes. "That being so, my next genius move was to start stalking the alleys *behind* the brothels, looking for a private way in."

Caethari groan-laughed into his hands. "Saints, Velasin!"

"Yes, yes." I shot him a flustered look. "Even so, I was lucky. Nobody bothered me, and to my annoyance, the only back doors I found were all either locked or guarded—all but one." My throat tightened abruptly; even a decade later, the memory was sharp and clear as crystal. "I'd crouched down when I saw the door open, thinking it might be left ajar, that I could sneak my way inside. Instead, a man came out—a big man, one of the bruisers who kept the clientele in line—and threw someone into the alley. It was a boy, just a small boy, younger than me, and the sound he made when he hit the cobbles . . . I had nightmares about that sound for years afterwards. Like wet meat being dropped on the kitchen floor." I shuddered, running a hand over my face.

"I didn't find out the details until later, but it was Markel. He was an orphan; he worked at the brothel as an all-purpose servant, fetch and carry, barely paid. He'd been saving his coins under a floorboard, but the bruiser found them and figured he deserved a nice bonus. Markel stole them back, but the bruiser found out, told everyone he was a thief, and Markel couldn't defend himself—he's mute, you see," I said, for Liran's benefit, "and nobody was minded to fetch him a pen or wait for him to draw signs in the dust to explain himself. So the bruiser beat him bloody and left him for dead, all with his employer's permission. And so I found him there, and I couldn't . . . I couldn't just *leave* him. So I picked him up—he was skin and bone; we owned dogs that weighed more—and I went to try and find help."

Silence fell between us. I stared at the floor, belatedly conscious of the weight of Caethari and Liran's attention, and when I continued, my voice was rougher than before. "You can imagine, two boys in the dark, one crying for a doctor, the other near dead. I was a nobleman's son; I was used to people heeding me. The idea that I could call for aid and not find it—the idea that an injured child could be thrown away like garbage—it was a side of the world I'd never seen before. Adults cursed at me when I went to them for help, or turned away, or threw things. I was so distraught, I hadn't had the sense to run back the way I'd come, towards the wealthier districts—but then, if I had done, I'd probably have landed in a different sort of trouble altogether. So instead, I went farther into the poor quarter, yelling and knocking on doors for help. And finally, someone answered.

"Her name was Aline. She made it her job to help those who needed it most; the poor folk, the people with nowhere else to go. She took us in, used magic to keep Markel living and mundane medicine to soothe his other hurts. I probably should have entrusted him to her care and gone home, but he hadn't woken up, and I knew that if I left him there, I wouldn't be able to come back. So I stayed. I passed out on the floor beside him and woke up in a panic the next day, which is when I realised that Aline, ah . . . did not resemble any lady I'd met before." I grinned, embarrassed by my old ignorance but happy to think of Aline herself. "She was frank with me about metem and patient with my questions, and I realised that her life, the suspicion and fear with which she lived, was a cousin to my own experience. So I told her that I liked men, and she was so kind about it—she was the first soul I ever told, and she gave me advice that made my ears burn at the time, but oh, I was grateful for it later!"

All of us laughed at that, a shared camaraderie. Liran's bright smile was back, and I ducked my head, embarrassed by how much it affected me. "Markel woke up a short while later; I was frightened at first, thinking the beating had damaged his voice, but Aline found him something to write with—he'd been taught his letters, but little else; he'd puzzled out spelling on his own—and he told us the mutism wasn't new, though he didn't know if he'd been born that way or if it was due to some accident in his infancy. We talked like that, back and forth, with Aline watching over us, and it felt . . . it felt like being a person. Not a nobleman, not somebody's son or brother, just a person. He was eleven, and he didn't know who I was, and I liked him. Not, not romantically," I added, glancing at Caethari, "but. I liked him, and he liked me, too, and I knew he didn't have anywhere else to go.

"So I just . . . took him home with me." I chuckled. "I spent the whole walk back trying to come up with reasons why Father ought to give him a job, why it was the right thing to do—I thought I'd be in trouble, you see, for running away and staying out all night, and I didn't want the trouble to stick to Markel. But when we got back, Father was so relieved to find me alive and whole, he didn't ask any questions; I just blurted out the first lie that came to mind—that I'd gone to find Revic, and Markel had been hurt protecting me from ruffians—and he accepted it. So when I asked if Markel could train to be my valet, he agreed to that, too. And he's been with me ever since.

"It was three years before we had a chance to go back and look for Aline. It was hard work tracking her down—even once we found the right district, the locals were protective of her; they didn't want some noble getting her in trouble—but we managed in the end. I gave her all the coin I had on me, and I thanked her, very profusely, for the bedroom advice." I grinned. "We've always kept in touch since then; I funded her healing early on, but she has a good head for investments, and she's supported herself quite nicely on those earnings for a while now."

I fell silent, rubbing self-consciously at the back of my neck. There was a brief quiet, during which my stomach churned with anxiety at the thought that I'd blundered again somehow, and then Liran broke it with a huff of gentle laughter.

"You're a very surprising person, Velasin Aeduria. Has anyone told you that?"

My cheeks burned; Liran was the first person other than Caethari to name me *Aeduria* instead of *vin Aaro,* and it affected me in ways I hadn't anticipated. "Mostly, I just get called stubborn," I said. "I'll take *surprising* as a compliment."

"As well you should; it was meant as one," he replied, and I flushed all over again. Moons, why did he have to be so good-looking? Even Caethari's handsomeness didn't fluster me this much, though that had more to do with the inherent mortification of knowing he'd seen me at my worst than any level-headedness on my part. Some terrible gremlin impulse connected one thought to the other, and just for a moment, I imagined how Caethari and Liran must've looked together.

The mental image was so overwhelming that I choked on nothing, resulting in startled looks from the pair of them.

"Don't mind me!" I wheezed, red-faced and ridiculous. "I'm fine, that was just—nothing. Absolutely nothing."

"Would you like some tea?" asked Liran, concerned. "Elit is out at the moment"—I assumed Elit was his servant—"but I'm certain I can brew a pot without setting fire to anything."

I shook my head, swallowed and managed to get myself under control. "My thanks for the offer, but there's no need, truly."

"You're certain you're well?" asked Caethari. I nodded firmly, and was relieved beyond words when he relaxed and said, "In that case, Liran, I'm afraid we ought to head back to the Aida. We told Tar Raeki we were headed there, and given all that's happened, I wouldn't put it past him to send out a search party if we delay too long."

Liran laughed. "We can't have that now, can we? Do send the good tar my regards."

We stood, and though I cast a wistful glance towards Liran's easel, I didn't manage to sneak a glimpse at his painting.

"I'll let you know as soon as I find anything," Liran promised at the door. "Would you prefer I send a messenger or come in person?"

"In person, if you can," said Caethari, his tone apologetic. "I hate to suspect that any of the Aida's staff would intercept a message, but after what happened to Velasin's horse—"

Liran grimaced in understanding, then changed expressions with lightning speed and smiled at me. "It's been a pleasure to meet you, Velasin." A spark of mischief touched his gaze. "I was already looking forward to the marriage-gathering, but now I'm even more excited to attend." And before I could brace for it, he leaned in and gave me a kiss on the cheek.

I stood there, stunned, as he did the same to Caethari, and then he was gone, retreating back into his apartment as if it were nothing.

"Well," said Caethari, after a moment. He flashed me a look that was meant to be wry, though it didn't escape my notice that, like mine, his face was warmer than usual. "That was Liran."

"It certainly was," I said, and led the way back down the stairwell.

25

We returned to the Aida without further incident, arriving at the stables to find an anxious, scowling Raeki pacing before their entrance.

"Where have you been?" he barked at Caethari. "I thought something had happened to you!"

"We stopped to visit a friend, that's all," Caethari replied, swinging down from his mount and handing the reins to a hovering groom. As I did likewise, Raeki's hackles visibly relaxed.

"Well, good," he muttered. "We didn't catch the runner, if you were wondering—Dai Sirat did her best, but they were off over the rooftops too fast. She lost them within a block."

"Even so, the excursion wasn't a total loss," said Caethari. He reached into his pocket, withdrawing the bolt we'd found, and handed it to Raeki. "Confirm that this is a match to the ones that killed Ren Baru, would you? And have someone go through his ledgers; it's a thin chance, but we need all the help we can get at this point."

"Consider it done, tiern." Raeki hesitated. "Did you wish to examine the pamphlets and letters yourself, or would you prefer I have them looked at, too?"

Caethari glanced expectantly at me, and an embarrassing moment passed before I realised he wanted my opinion. I coughed to cover my surprise and said, "Why not look them over first, then see if they need the tar's attention?"

My husband grinned. "What Velasin said."

"Very good, tiern."

As Raeki departed, we made it all of three steps towards the Aida before a young servant came running up, skidding to a halt before us.

"Tiern Caethari!" she said earnestly. "Tieren Halithar requests that you and your husband, and your husband's servant, join him tonight for dinner. Please be in the Garden Hall at sunset."

"Ah," said Caethari, who'd no more been expecting it, from the look on his face, than I had. "That would be, ah—yes, of course. Of course we'll be there. Thank you."

"Yes, tiern," said the servant, and promptly dashed off again.

"Should I be worried?" I asked, only half joking, as we started to walk again.

"No, not at all!" Caethari ran a hand through his hair and sighed. "I shouldn't be surprised that he wants to meet you properly—and Markel, too—but today has been, ah . . ."

"Exhausting?"

"Yes. That." He flashed me a tired smile. "Riya and Laecia will most likely be there, too; I love them both, but on this occasion, I'd much rather hole up in our apartments with a bottle of wine. Two bottles, even."

"Now there's a lovely thought." I paused. "Do we need to tell Markel, or will he know already?"

By way of answer, Caethari swore and changed direction, heading towards the infirmary.

We found Markel once more attended by Ru Telitha, the two engaged in an intimate yet animated conversation that was, from the look of things, half signed and half written.

"Hello, Markel," I said, sparing a smile for his companion. "Tieren Halithar has invited us to dinner tonight. Do you feel up to it?"

Markel nodded. "I've been feeling a little cooped up," he signed, "though Telitha has been excellent company. Dinner would be lovely."

Ru Telitha's mouth hung open as she glanced between us. "You speak Tithenai?" she exclaimed.

Markel froze as I bit back a curse: distracted as I was, I'd forgotten to switch to Ralian.

"He does," I said, wincing a little at the hurt look that flashed across Ru Telitha's face. "But please, ru, don't bear a grudge against him for not telling you. I asked him to keep it a secret."

Ru Telitha looked slightly mollified at this, though there was a trace of pout to her expression when she turned to Markel and said, "And here you've been letting me translate for you all day!"

Markel grinned. "I'm sorry. If it helps, you did an excellent job, and it's comforting to know that you never tried to trick me with a wrong translation."

"Hmm," said Ru Telitha. She cast me a speculative glance, and I knew that Yasa Kithadi would be told of Markel's polylingualism within the hour. It might've concerned me more, had I not already reached the very limit of my capacity to care about petty court intrigues. "Well, then. I suppose that means you do have a straight face, after all." This last to Markel, and evidently in reference to some earlier conversation of theirs; his grin broadened, prompting Ru Telitha to give an exaggerated sniff and adjust her glasses.

"I'll have some clean things sent for you, if that's acceptable," Caethari said, with a questioning glance at me.

Markel pulled a face. "Better still, convince Ru Zairin to let me have a proper wash."

I laughed, translating this chagrined request for the others. "I'll do my best," said Ru Telitha. "When do you need him ready?"

"Sunset, in the Garden Hall."

"I'll be there," signed Markel.

With that established, Caethari and I resumed the walk to our apartments, moving in swift, silent sync to avoid further interruption.

Mercifully, we made the journey undisturbed, letting out mutual sighs of relief as the door shut behind us.

"I claim the first bath!" I said. "You've already had a second wash; your need is not as great."

"Arguable, but I'll allow it," Caethari said, lips twitching in amusement. "Besides which, I might as well see if there's anything in these letters. I'm not sure we'll be quite that lucky, but you never know."

"I'll beseech the moons on your behalf," I said, and ensconced myself in the bathroom.

Steam filled the air as I ran the hot water, and for the first time in hours, I let myself relax. Undressing, I left my new clothes folded on the hamper and busied myself with other ablutions as the tub steadily filled. There was a small glass jar of bath salts on a corner shelf, and I indulged myself by sprinkling some in the water. A pleasant aroma spread through the air, jasmine cut with something sharper and more mineral. Sighing with relief, I turned off the taps and sank into the bath, eyes closing as I rested my head on the gleaming ceramic tile.

My thoughts swirled. I didn't want to process the morning's events, not the meal with Laecia and certainly not anything to do with Killic, and so I fixed instead on Liran and Caethari. It was easy to imagine them as a couple: their friendship was full of teasing familiarity, shared jokes and mutual respect, to say nothing of how beautiful they looked together. It was hard to understand why they weren't still involved, in fact—but then, I realised, I had no framework for relationships ending gracefully. I thought again of Caethari's parents, whose divorce would've been unfathomable in Ralia, and wondered if I'd ever hear the full story of it; or if I'd ever know what had parted Caethari and Liran, for that matter. Would it come up at the marriage-gathering? Was it the kind of thing I'd be permitted to ask about, or was I simply expected to let it be?

My arousal came on so slowly, I almost didn't notice it, until suddenly the idle sweep of my fingers across my thighs was idle no longer. I made a small, shocked noise and stilled in place, acutely conscious of the fact that, ever since that night in the garden, I hadn't once seen to my own release. Inasmuch as I'd been consciously aware of this, I'd put it down to circumstance—the close, public quarters of outdoor travel were hardly conducive to such things—but even once I'd been given my own room, I hadn't bothered. Or had, perhaps, been scared to try, given recent experiences.

Killic had taken enough from me. I refused to let him have this, too.

I shut my eyes, skin burning for reasons that had nothing to do with the heated bath, and shuddered as I took myself in hand. Pleasure sang through me, dizzying in its sudden urgency. I tipped my head back as my breathing quickened, images of Caethari and Liran blurring through my mind. I thought of Caethari as I'd seen him that morning—naked except for a borrowed towel and damp from the showers, all firm, thick muscle and gentle eyes—and imagined what might've happened next, had I any skill at seduction, the nerve to attempt it with him and the contents of my rosewood chest to hand.

In a different setting, I might've been embarrassed by how strong and sudden my climax came on; instead, I was overwhelmed, barely managing to stifle a cry by biting down hard on my lip. My vision swam, pulse thrumming in my ears. I lay as if stunned, staring up at the ceiling as if I'd never seen one before, and almost laughed from the sheer relief of knowing such pleasure was mine, still, to summon; that I'd not, as I'd half begun to fear, been cut off from it forever. That worry felt almost foolish now, as I languished in my own, skin-tingling aftermath, but it was a foolishness I much preferred to the alternative.

When I finally bestirred myself sufficiently to reach for the soap, I felt lighter than I had in days. A fragment of music came to me, a Ralian folk tune that Nathian would never confess to being fond of, and I began to hum it under my breath as I washed. I ran fresh water to rinse my hair, emptied the tub, and toweled myself dry, refusing to let the impending prospect of dinner with my in-laws dim my mood.

Emerging from the bathroom, I found my husband frowning at Ren Baru's letters, flipping repeatedly from one page to another as though trying to puzzle out a code.

"Any joy?" I asked him.

Caethari looked up and visibly startled at the sight of me, eyes going wide. My cheeks heated, but after his performance that morning, I refused to feel embarrassed for wearing only a towel in the privacy of my own quarters, and silently dared him to comment on it with a pointed raise of my eyebrow. I might've lacked his enviable physique, but I was far from hideous.

"Ah," said Caethari, after a moment. "Ah—not as such, no. I'm just . . . confused." He gestured to the letters. "As far as I can tell, they're neither written by nor addressed to Ren Baru; the only signature is an initial, and nobody in them is named. They're love letters, of a sort, though rather bleak in flavour: a young woman, unhappily betrothed, writing to beg her lover to return home and kill her fiancé."

"Bleak indeed," I agreed. "Does the lover oblige her murderousness, or is the tale left hanging?"

"A little of both, it seems." Caethari set the letters on the table. "Reading between the lines—I don't have the lover's letters, but whatever he said is referenced in her replies—the lover was prevented from returning, though he vowed to kill her husband if she were wed when he came back, and the lady was left in fear of what would happen to her."

"An unpleasant tale," I said, suppressing a tiny shiver of sympathy for the woman in question.

"Unpleasant, yes," said Caethari, frowning still, "but also very odd."

"Odd how?"

Caethari paused. "It's hard to say," he said, sounding frustrated. "It's not one thing, but lots of little details altogether. Why were her family forcing her to marry in the first place? Why was her lover kept secret? Why doesn't she state her intention to divorce, if she's so opposed to the union?"

"Perhaps she's Ralian," I joked, a little darkly. "None of your Tithenai courtesies would apply in that instance."

Caethari stared at me. "Velasin, you're *brilliant*!"

I flushed more at the praise than I had at his staring. "Don't be absurd. The letters are written in Tithenai, aren't they? What would a Ralian lady be doing writing in Tithenai?"

"You speak Tithenai," he pointed out. "And it makes perfect sense, if her lover is Tithenai and her fiancé not."

"That doesn't explain what her letters were doing in Ren Baru's drawer."

"One mystery at a time," Caethari said. He rose from his chair and headed for the bathroom, passing close enough that his undershirt brushed my shoulder.

I shivered a little, rooted in place, and it wasn't until I heard the door click that I recalled my rather pressing need to dress. And yet, the moment I was safe in the privacy of my room, I didn't move to find clothes at all; just flopped face-first onto my unmade bed and pillowed my head on my elbow. I didn't mean to fall asleep, but the next thing I knew, Caethari was knocking on the door and calling, in faintly worried tones, "Velasin? Are you all right in there?"

"I'm fine," I croaked back, rolling onto my side. I blinked muzzily, aware that the room was darker than it had been, the fading sunlight leaving silver dusk in its wake. "What time is it?"

"Nearly sunset."

"Oh!" I sat up, limbs stiff and chill from resting in one position without the benefit of a blanket, and hurriedly started to dress. It was a small mercy that I'd slept facedown, or else I'd have creased my hair into some ridiculous shape and looked a fool at dinner. As it was, its usual wave was slightly more pronounced on one side than the other, which I solved by tying it back with a ribbon.

Silently blessing Ren Lithas, I pulled on another set of new clothes, checked my appearance in the mirror, and hurried out to Caethari, who rose from his seat at the table as I emerged.

"Sorry," I said, smoothing a self-conscious hand over my hair. "I fell asleep."

"I don't blame you," he said. He looked me over—not salaciously, but to confirm I was well—then gave a small nod. "Are you ready to go?"

I smiled. "As I'll ever be."

I hadn't yet been to the Garden Hall, so Caethari led the way as we left the apartments, taking new twists and turns through the Aida. After a few minutes, he coughed and said, "Technically, this is me presenting you to my family. So they may be, ah . . . inquisitive, as to how you're settling in."

I snorted. "Frankly, so long as none of them tries to stab me or Markel, I'll consider it a success."

Caethari laughed at that, and as we turned the next corner, we arrived before a pair of elaborately carved double-doors, one of which was open.

"After you," he said.

With a small twinge of nervous foreboding, I stepped through.

The Garden Hall, it transpired, was so named because its long side walls were lined with lush, living plants. Elaborate raised planters of stone and wood were filled with rich earth where fruits and flowers grew, while the ceiling overhead alternated stone and glass in a checkered pattern, ensuring that the vegetation didn't lack for light. A long wooden table dominated the centre of the room, while the rear wall housed another pair of double-doors, both of which were thrown open to reveal a semicircular stone balcony—we were on the third floor of the Aida, I belatedly recalled.

The effect was so beautiful that it took me a moment to notice that the room was lit, not by candles, but magelights, the first I'd seen in the Aida, flower-shaped enclosures of coloured glass set atop metal stands shaped like twining vines. I glanced at Caethari, lips parted on a question about this apparent exception to his father's rule, and found there was a sad smile on his face.

"This room was my mother's doing," he said, softly. "It used to be called the Stone Hall, but she never liked it then—said it was too cold. So she chose and tended the plants herself, had the glass installed in the ceiling, and she insisted on the magelights, so that nothing could burn by accident."

"One of her better decisions, frankly," said a familiar voice.

We turned, Caethari sketching a fluid bow to Yasa Kithadi. "Hello, grandmother."

"Yes, yes." She waved him up with an irritable flick of her fingers, then turned her attention to me, gaze raking over my Tithenai clothes. "You've cleaned up passably well, I see."

"It's all the tailor's doing, I assure you."

"I can well believe it," she replied, glancing around the room. "Tch. I see Halithar has left his guests to arrive first. Typical!"

"We're family, not guests," said Caethari, not unreasonably.

To my great surprise, Yasa Kithadi laughed at that, a sudden cackle that cracked through the room like the sound of breaking pottery. "Hah! It's true, it's true." She patted him affably on the shoulder and headed to the table, selecting a chair apparently at random and sitting down.

I cast Caethari a confused look. "Isn't there a seating order?"

"What?"

"A seating order," I repeated. "You know, set places for us to sit at."

"Not for a private dinner, no."

I sighed. "I'm being Ralian again, aren't I?"

Caethari flicked me a grin, and something about it caused all the remembered heat from my time in the bath to come rushing back at once. "Perhaps just a little," he said. "But that's hardly a defect."

As we moved to take seats of our own—both opposite Yasa Kithadi, which I enjoyed; Ralian seating arrangements insisted on spouses sitting across the table from one another—there was a cheerful clamour at the door as both tieras entered, engaged in playful argument. Immediately after them came Markel, who smiled and headed towards me. I watched him move, noting that he was nowhere near his usual speed, his stride hitching slightly as he favoured his side, and yet relief bloomed in my chest to see him up and about at all.

As Markel sat to my left, Caethari leaned forwards and signed hello to him. Markel signed back, and the ease between them settled an anxiety I hadn't known I'd been feeling.

The tieras, meanwhile, were yet to sit, Laecia having diverted them both to examine one of the magelights.

"You see?" she said, raising a hand to gesture at it. "Fine artifex work is no less a skill than any other type of craftsmanship!"

Riya shook her head. "A glassmaker made the glass, not a mage. The mage spelled it, yes, and I agree that such work is craftsmanship, but the creation of artifex is a collaboration, not a singular skill."

"And yet, the glassmaker wouldn't have made the glass if not for the mage's instruction," Laecia countered. "If a tailor makes use of fabric crafted by a weaver, we don't call the final suit of clothes a collaboration; we thank the tailor."

"That's a different case altogether!" Riya protested. "The cloth is the weaver's final product, and might be used for anything or by anyone who purchases it. But when the glassmaker made this piece"—she extended a hand, not quite touching the flower-shaped globe—"they were commissioned to do so for a set purpose. That makes it a collaboration."

"Even so, the tailor cannot work without the weaver. What makes it so different, really?" And then, before Riya could reply, "You underestimate the importance of magic, just like everyone else in this family."

"I do not!" Riya retorted. "In fact, I—"

Yasa Kithadi coughed pointedly, raising a brow at her granddaughters. "And what am I, part of the decorations?"

Instantly, the tieras left off their debate and came to pay dutiful greetings to their grandmother, with Laecia leaning in to give her a kiss on the cheek. Despite having solicited this attention, Yasa Kithadi waved them both off with as much apparent unconcern as she had Caethari, though she looked quietly pleased when they sat down on either side of her.

"Everyone's here, then? Excellent!" came a voice from the door. We all turned our heads, and there was Tieren Halithar, arriving at last with Keletha. The dining table had far more spaces than there were people, and with the six of us already clustered in the middle, my Ralian instincts braced for an evening of awkwardly shouted conversation, should the tieren and envoy choose to sit at the top and tail, respectively. But instead of this, and far more sensibly, Keletha sat down at Riya's left, with the tieren on Caethari's right. No ceremony, as my husband had said: just a family dinner, which made me feel all the happier at Markel's inclusion.

At no discernible signal—except, perhaps, the tieren's entry—servers began to file in, laying plates and utensils before us all.

"Well, Riya," said Tieren Halithar, "how goes your quest to negotiate a sire for my future grandchild?"

Riya pulled a face. "Men are terrible," she declared. "Thank the saints I'm not burdened with finding them attractive!"

"You should've asked Kivali to do the negotiating, in that case," Caethari teased.

"We flipped a coin for it," Riya said wryly. "I lost."

Yasa Kithadi snorted at that, and whatever small lingering awkwardness there was vanished as the family eased into the rhythms of conversation, bantering and making fun. Even the eldest joined in, with Keletha chaffing thir sister for her insistence on receiving a physical invite to our marriage-gathering, "when you already live here, and know perfectly well you're invited!"

"Observing the proprieties is still important," the yasa replied, shooting her twin an amused glance. "And in any case, your handwriting needs the practice. The last report I had from you looked like a bird had walked in ink."

"My handwriting is perfectly legible," Keletha shot back. "Your eyesight, on the other hand—"

"My eyes are just fine!"

"And Ru Zairin agrees with that, do thei?"

"Oh, you hypocrite!" Yasa Kithadi said, leaning forwards and pointing a finger at Keletha. "Telling me to seek out the ru for my eyes, when you'll barely consent to let thim look at your arrow-wound!"

"My shoulder is healing perfectly," said Keletha, with great dignity. "I don't need to be poked at."

"Hah!"

The argument broke off as the servers returned, setting a mouth-watering array of dishes between us. I faltered a little, uncertain of the protocol, until Caethari murmured that everything was to be shared.

"Oh!" I said, so enthused by the prospect that I didn't know where to start.

"Here," said Caethari. He set about serving me a little of each dish, explaining what it was as he did so. I flushed at his kind attention, insisting that he serve himself, too—and when he ignored me, I took matters into my own hands, grabbing a serving spoon to start putting food on his plate. I caught Markel smirking at me as I did so and paused in midmotion.

"What?" I asked him, noting that he'd already helped himself to the leeks and rabbit.

"Nothing," he signed, eyes gleaming with mischief. "You're just very sweet together, that's all."

I made an affronted noise. "I have not ever been, nor will I ever be, *sweet,*" I told him in Ralian, ignoring his snort as I slid a steaming piece of fish onto Caethari's plate. My husband chose to reward my kindness with betrayal, translating our byplay for the rest of the table.

"Oh, I don't know," said Laecia, grinning. "You seem very sweet to me."

My neck warmed; I didn't know what to say to that, largely because I wasn't yet familiar enough with Laecia to know how to tease her.

"Velasin is exactly as sweet as he needs to be," Caethari said lightly. "Pass the greens, would you?"

"Anything for my dearest brother," said Laecia, rolling her eyes.

The conversation quieted as we began to eat, which was a relief: I was still enraptured with Tithenai food and had no desire to concentrate on very much else while sampling the dishes Caethari had picked for me. None of the flavours seemed to clash, the different spices and sauces complementary without being tame, and I tuned out the people around me as I indulged myself, savouring each bite.

As such, it was an even more jarring shock than it might otherwise have been when, out of nowhere, Tieren Halithar said, "By the by, Caethari, is there a reason why there's a Ralian nobleman locked up in the Aida?"

Caethari stilled, his kip raised halfway to his mouth. "There is," he allowed.

The tieren raised a thick silver eyebrow. "A good reason, is it? So good that you didn't see the need to consult with me about it?"

Caethari winced a little at that. "My apologies, Father. It all happened very quickly. But," he added, before the tieren could speak again, "I also thought that, for diplomatic reasons, it was better for you to have plausible deniability about his, ah . . . circumstances."

"Did you now," said Tieren Halithar. He levelled a fearsome stare at his son; a stare from which I might have quailed, had I been in Caethari's position. But my husband just stared measuredly back, and after a moment the tieren huffed and slapped a hand on the table. "Well! What's done is done, and I trust you to have done it for good reason. Should his visitation be prolonged, however—"

"It won't be," Caethari said quickly. "He'll be on his way again tomorrow."

"Good," said the tieren, and with that, he went straight back to his dinner.

And that was it. I stayed frozen in place, heart racing, waiting for someone else to ask about Killic, to demand an explanation, but nothing happened. When I looked up again, only Laecia seemed perturbed, frowning at her father as though she'd had something to say or ask, but didn't want to venture it when he'd so clearly set the matter aside.

Markel nudged me gently, getting my attention. Hands low, he asked, "Are you all right?"

I took a moment to consider my feelings, and was surprised when they coalesced into calm. "Yes," I signed back. "Oddly, I think I am."

"Good," he replied, and popped a dumpling in his mouth.

The rest of the meal was anticlimactic by comparison. The teasing, friendly conversations started up again once the main course was finished, filling the lull before the sweet with the banter of family members who, for all their differences, genuinely appeared to like one another. It wasn't what I'd been expecting, and I wondered if that said more about my life than anything that had happened since Father summoned me back from Farathel, or if the two were more linked than I cared to acknowledge.

The sweet, when it was served, was delicious—a chilled sorbet that melted in the mouth, pairing beautifully with the pale, sweet wine the servers brought out with it.

By the end of the meal, everyone had been laughed both with and at—including Markel, who'd joked with Caethari and me—resulting in a warmly convivial mood that defied my every experience of such dinners. Using me as a translator, Markel excused himself first, bowing thanks to Tieren Halithar for his inclusion, but pleading a need to rest.

"Of course," said the tieren, acknowledging Markel with a deep nod. "I'm only sorry your first experience in Qi-Katai was one of injury."

I feigned a translation to Ralian, though Yasa Kithadi shot me a look that said Ru Telitha had already informed her of Markel's linguistic proficiencies. It made me wonder if she'd also spoken to Tieren Halithar, who'd invited him in the first place; but then I recalled their strange, silent tug-of-war over their respective successors, and decided against it. More likely, it hadn't occurred to the tieren that Markel wouldn't understand the conversation; unless, of course, he'd been counting on it as grounds for speaking so freely. It was a cynical thought, and one that jarred with the pleasant evening we'd just had. I didn't want to think ill of my father-in-law, but I was too accustomed to Markel being discounted by others to neglect the prospect entirely. Still, that he'd bothered to invite him at all was a positive sign, and I decided to treat myself to a tiny bit of optimism.

By the time Caethari made our excuses, Laecia and Keletha had switched seats, the better to engage in spirited, separate arguments with their respective siblings. I bowed to the tieren on my way past, acknowledging his look of amusement at the overlapping debates, and sighed a happy, satiated sigh.

"That was . . . nice," Caethari said, as we walked back to our apartments. "We haven't had a dinner together like that in forever, and when we last did, it was much more aggressive." He grinned at me. "Perhaps you're a soothing influence on my family."

I burst out laughing at that. "I've been called a lot of different things, but a *soothing influence* isn't one of them."

"Oh?" His smile turned cheeky. "And I suppose that means you aren't sweet, either?"

"Absolutely not," I said, and walked faster to hide my sudden blush.

It hadn't escaped me that I was starting to feel decidedly non-platonic about my husband, but having agreed to be friends with him, I couldn't bear the thought of making things difficult between us. I wasn't sure I could trust myself: did I want him because he was there and kind, or because he was Caethari? I didn't want to believe that I was so starved for affection that even the simplest niceties could make me starry-eyed in such a short span of time, but Caethari was so much *more* than what I was used to—more open, considerate, playful; more *present,* simply by virtue of our relationship being public and legitimate here—that even the smallest gestures felt magnified.

Returning to our apartments, Caethari sighed with relief as he slipped off his boots by the doorway. He glanced at me, his expression suddenly shy. "I'm not tired enough for sleep yet, I don't think," he said.

"Me neither," I said, heart pounding.

Caethari nodded. "Do you know how to play kesh?"

"I do." In fact, I was rather good at it; as was Markel.

"Fancy a game, then? I've a board somewhere."

"By all means," I said. "I might put my lin away, though, if you've no objections."

"Of course not," said Caethari, and ducked his head as I went through to my bedroom.

It wasn't until I'd pulled the lin over my head that I caught sight of the paper, and then only from the corner of my eye. I turned, frowning, and draped the lin over the edge of the bed as I went to investigate. The paper wasn't anything I recognised; just a folded scrap, unremarkable except for the fact that it was in the middle of my unmade bed, and definitely hadn't been there when I'd left for dinner.

I picked it up, wondering if it had perhaps blown in from somewhere, but when I unfolded it, the message I found scrawled there made my stomach clench.

I'm so sorry.

Part Six

CAETHARI

26

Cae slept little and restlessly that night, stirring at every tiny creak or half-imagined noise that drifted in through door and window. He'd roused Raeki and half the Aida after Velasin found the note on his bed, but none of the servants or guards he questioned had seen anyone near their apartments. He'd wanted to keep going, to have every single member of the Aida's staff brought before him until he found some answers—and he might well have done so, if not for Keletha firmly insisting that he delegate the task to thim. He grimaced at the memory over a cup of khai, a little wry and a lot stressed. Keletha's actual injunction had been to *stop spooking your husband and let me deal with this before you pace a hole in the floor,* and it probably said something about Cae's recent priorities that the need to reassure Velasin trumped his constant desire for action.

Velasin had been understandably shaken at the time, but now, over breakfast, he just looked tired.

Clearly, neither of them had managed a good night's rest.

"Markel moves in today," said Velasin. He was holding his khai to his lips, though Cae was yet to see him drink any. "I'll feel better for having him near me."

"Me, too," Cae admitted. Velasin shot him a look, and Cae amended, "I mean that I'll feel better for having him near you, too."

"Oh," said Velasin, flushing into his khai. "That's . . . good to know."

For neither the first nor last time, Cae remembered the brush of Velasin's mouth against the edge of his own and shivered. He didn't think he was imagining it, that his husband was warming to him, but no matter how much some eager, desirous part of himself wanted to draw Velasin close and kiss him properly, the consequences if he misstepped were too horrible to contemplate. How much longer would it take to regain Velasin's trust, if Cae rushed him now?

And anyway, the desirous voice whispered, *you'll still get to claim a kiss at the marriage-gathering.*

Cae shoved the thought aside out of panicked self-preservation. If he spent the next two days dwelling on Velasin's mouth, he'd never get anything done, and there were—unfortunately, infuriatingly—more pressing matters to deal with.

He was about to suggest they speak to Raeki first when someone knocked urgently on the apartment door. Instantly, they both tensed; Cae looked at his husband and, after a brief, silent conversation, rose to see who it was.

He'd been expecting Raeki, or perhaps Keletha, and was therefore surprised to find Ru Telitha before him, her curls pulled severely back from her face. He stepped aside to let her in as much out of shock as politeness, and the second the door closed again, she spoke.

"Yasa Kithadi needs you both to come to the Little Aida, right now."

"Now?" said Cae, in the same breath that Velasin asked, "What's happened?"

"It's best you see for yourselves," said Ru Telitha. Her tone was anxious, her expression tense. "Please. The yasa wouldn't ask if it wasn't urgent."

Cae exchanged another look with Velasin. They were both already dressed for the day, lacking only their boots, and Velasin was on his feet in an instant.

"Lead the way," he said.

Ru Telitha didn't speak as she hurried them through the Aida's hallways, taking them out to the Triple Gardens via the shortest route. Nobody passed them as they traversed the covered walkway, but when they reached the courtyard that separated the Little Aida from the stables, it was towards the latter building that Ru Telitha turned.

"In here," she said, holding the swing-door open to admit them. "The stall at the far end."

The first thing Cae noticed was the restlessness of the horses, stamping and shifting as they whinnied to each other. The second was a scent that had no place in a stable, but which had been everywhere when Quip was killed.

"Oh, gods," Velasin whispered, shivering as they passed the open mouth of the horseway. "Not another one."

"Not in the way you're thinking," came Yasa Kithadi's voice. She emerged from the open door of the stall, her face set in hard lines. Her appearance was shocking: hair unpinned, still clad in her nightclothes under a barely tied dressing gown, her soft indoor slippers covered with straw and muck.

Not just muck, Cae realised. Blood.

"In there," the yasa murmured. "Don't go in, just—look."

Cae looked, and almost wished he hadn't. Beside him, Velasin swore.

Lying dead on the floor of the stall, beneath the hooves of the same grey palfrey Cae had borrowed to ride to Velasin's rescue—a horse now half-saddled, tack hanging askew as she pressed herself to the wall, ears pinned back—was a young groom. She was almost unrecognisable: her head had been staved in by multiple hard blows, but the red and grey of her livery, coupled with her slight form, summoned her name regardless.

"Ren Vaia Skai," he whispered. He looked at his grandmother, bleak and shocked. "What happened here?"

"Murder," said Yasa Kithadi, eyes flashing. "Though we're *meant* to think it an accident."

"How could—" Cae started, but stopped when Velasin squeezed his arm.

"Look at the rear hooves," he murmured. Cae did so, inhaling sharply to see they were tacky with gore. "She was kicked to death." Velasin glanced at Yasa Kithadi, and added, "Or so we're meant to believe?"

"Had I no other reason to find this suspicious," the yasa said, "the choice of horse would give me pause." She glanced at the still-spooked palfrey, who was clearly unhappy to have a body in her stall. "I've had Silk since she was a filly, and she's never so much as bitten a groom, let alone kicked them. And Silk *knew* Vaia." Her voice trembled, slim fingers clenching by her sides. "Either Silk was compelled somehow—hurt or spelled or goaded into action—or else some human hand did the deed, and smeared false proof on her hooves. Either way, this was no accident."

Cae was still processing this when Velasin said, "But you have another reason for suspicion?"

"Yes," said the yasa. She hesitated, then called to Ru Telitha, who'd moved closer as they spoke, "Please have Silk put in a separate stall, and keep guard over—over the body." She swallowed hard, and the brief glance she spared for the remains of Ren Vaia was full of pain. "Sweet little fool," she whispered. "Why didn't you come to me?"

But Ren Vaia was beyond answering.

Silently, Yasa Kithadi led them into the Little Aida, through the main atrium and up the stairs, towards her private quarters. Cae exchanged an uneasy glance with Velasin, but neither spoke as the yasa brought them into her personal parlour and gestured for them to wait as she ducked into her bedroom.

"Here," she said, returning. "I found this on my pillow when I woke."

Cae took the folded piece of paper, from which a lower edge

had been torn, and held it open for both of them to see. The brief note read:

> *Please forgive me. I have always tried to be worthy of your service. I thought I was being loyal to the Aedurias but I was deceived. I have nowhere else in the world to go, but I must go somewhere. I fear I am no longer safe.*
>
> *Vaia*

"She wrote my note," said Velasin, shocked. Reaching into his pocket, he withdrew the scrap he'd found on his bed and held it up to the torn corner of Vaia's farewell. It was a perfect match, as was the scrawled handwriting. He swallowed, looking at Yasa Kithadi. "Did . . . does this mean she killed Quip?"

"I don't know." Yasa Kithadi plucked at her dressing gown, then sat down heavily in a plush armchair, looking as vulnerable as Cae had ever seen her. "Clearly, she did *something,* but that hardly narrows it down. I have a hard time imagining her climbing through Halithar's window dressed all in black, or killing that merchant who stabbed your friend"—her eyes flicked to Velasin with this—"but she was certainly involved."

"Whoever deceived her, she doesn't name them," Cae said, staring at the note.

His grandmother made a noise that was equal parts disgust and frustration. "Vaia knew I would've acted had she done so, but evidently didn't trust that I'd be able to keep her safe from retaliation. So she demurred, and then they killed her anyway, on the floor of my stable." Yasa Kithadi thumped an angry fist on the armrest. "Fucking gods, I hate this!"

"Yasa," said Velasin, "are we the first you've told of this?"

"Of course," she said, lifting her chin. "I ran to the stables as soon as I found my note—I guessed she might try to take Silk again, the foolish girl!—but when I saw . . . the body," and here she faltered, gulping over the ugly truth, "I had Telitha fetch you at once. The whole Aida knew you'd found a note of your own last night; it wasn't a stretch to think they had the same origin."

Velasin nodded, then turned to Cae. "What does Ru Zairin know of pathology?"

"Thei know enough," said the yasa, answering for him. "If you're thinking thei can give us a rough time of death, I'm inclined to agree with you. But." A certain familiar steeliness returned to her expression; Yasa Kithadi rose from her chair and came to stand before them. "I'd wager my whole inheritance that whoever did this is still in the Aida. We need to let them think themselves successful; let them think we look on Vaia's death as an accident. It's too late to keep your note a secret, but only Telitha knows of mine, and I'd like to keep it that way."

"Agreed," Cae said promptly. Velasin nodded, too, and Yasa Kithadi relaxed, just a fraction.

"If that's the plan," said Velasin, "then we need an explanation as to why you summoned us over here first thing in the morning, if not to see the body. Whoever this is, we've got to assume they're paying attention to what happens next."

"Sharp lad," said the yasa, a rare note of approval shading her tone. "What do you suggest?"

Velasin glanced at Cae, soliciting any suggestions, but this sort of deception had never been Cae's forte. He shook his head, thoughts running in a different direction. How had the killer incited Silk to kill Ren Vaia? Assuming that was the case, of course—the theory that they'd staved in her head and staged the scene afterwards was equally as likely. Ru Zairin would perhaps be able to tell the difference, but if it was, to thir eyes, a clear-cut case of murder, then they'd need to bring thim in on the secret.

"Markel," Velasin said at last. "He's moving into our apartments today, and after seeing him at dinner last night and discussing him with Ru Telitha, you wanted to gift him something. When Ru Telitha brought us back past the stables, the horses were unsettled, so we went to investigate." He paused, frowning. "Though that doesn't quite track if anyone saw you go to the stables earlier, or if we were seen coming into the Little Aida together just now; but then, anyone who saw all that would know we were lying regardless."

"I'll chance it if you will," said Yasa Kithadi. "I don't think we've been watched thus far—aside from anything else, there's not a lot of nearby cover to watch from, if you're trying to be secretive—and I suspect whoever this is won't have risked loitering."

"More likely, they'll be waiting for the news of Vaia's death to spread," said Cae.

His grandmother nodded in sharp agreement, then pursed her lips at Velasin. "A gift, is it?"

Velasin quirked a smile. "Should you consent to give one."

"Hmph." She waved a hand. "We can say we forgot about it in the uproar, but I'm sure Telitha can pick out a book for him. She's quite enjoyed ferrying half the library to and fro."

With that agreed, they returned to the stable, where a grey-faced Ru Telitha was still keeping guard over Vaia's remains. Velasin beelined to her side, hand tentatively outstretched as if he wanted to offer comfort but wasn't sure how well it would be received—a problem Ru Telitha solved by letting out a choked sob and falling against him. Though clearly startled, Velasin put his arms around her, sending Cae a troubled glance over the top of her head.

"I'll fetch Raeki and Ru Zairin," Cae said. "You three stay here."

"Of course," said his grandmother, and with that Cae began to run. He was fit and healthy, but the exertion stood as a neat reminder that he'd had no time to practice his combat patterns or spar with Nairi since before Velasin's arrival. He resolved to return to his routines as soon as he was able, though when that might be exactly, he had no idea.

He found Raeki, who had *not* been neglecting his combat patterns, training in the Court of Swords, and gasped out the news that they'd found a body. A smatter of nearby guards, grooms and servants all tutted and gasped, while Raeki swore and hurried out of the training ring.

"Zo's sainted ballsack, this is all we need!" he growled. "Will you—"

"Ru Zairin is next on my list," Cae said.

Raeki made a gruff noise of approval, yelled at the bystanders to stop gawking and be about their business and hastened off towards the Little Aida. This left Cae, chased by whispers, to make his way to the infirmary, where he found Ru Zairin puttering over thir desk.

"Hello, tiern," thei said, blinking in surprise at Cae's entrance. "If you've come for Markel, I'm afraid I've already discharged him—he should be on his way to your apartments just now, as a matter of fact. I'm surprised you didn't pass him in the halls."

Cae shook his head. "I came from the Little Aida," he said, not having to feign a whit of his distress or urgency. "There's been a death, ru. We need you to look at the body."

Ru Zairin paled, then straightened. "Of course," thei said, gathering up thir medical kit with the ease of long practice. "Take me there. What happened?"

As they walked, Cae gave thim the details, including the fabricated tale about why he and Velasin had been there in the first place. Ru Zairin listened grimly until their arrival at the stables, at which point Cae fell silent.

Both his grandmother and Ru Telitha were still present, the latter tucked up against the former's side like a baby chick under its mother's wing, while Velasin stood by the stall door with Raeki.

"It's all yours, ru," said Raeki.

Nodding, Ru Zairin entered the stall, grimacing slightly at the smell. As Cae and the others watched, thei withdrew a selection of implements from thir bag and set about examining the body. Cae was used to death—he'd killed before, though seldom in cold blood; he preferred the heat of a skirmish—but this aspect of aftermath was new to him. When soldiers and bandits died fighting, there was no need for post-mortem advice: if you yourself weren't the cause of death, you generally knew who was. Trying to fathom weapon from wound was an art which Cae—perhaps mercifully—had never had to practice.

"She's been dead since the darkest part of the night," said Ru Zairin, now examining the ruined skull. "You say there was a horse in here?"

"My palfrey, Silk," said Yasa Kithadi, voice tight.

Ru Zairin nodded absently, hands hovering over the pulped and broken flesh. "A shod horse kicking hard enough, long enough could certainly do this type of damage." Thei straightened. "I'd need to do a closer examination to be sure, but there's straw and horse-hair embedded in the fractures, and nothing to suggest it was done with a stave or a hammer. Nothing that I can see, at least."

"You can't be more precise?" asked the yasa.

Ru Zairin sighed. "Some of my colleagues at the Medical College in Irae-Tai are working on a cantrip to show an echo of whatever weapon caused a given injury, but thus far, there's too many potential variables to yoke the intention verbally. In the absence of such a tool, I am forced to rely on experience alone."

"Of course," said Yasa Kithadi, inclining her head. She, too, was starting to look pale, leaning as much on Ru Telitha as being leaned against.

"Can we move her now?" asked Raeki, voice gruff. "Poor slip of a thing, to be left in the filth like that."

"If you'd be so kind, you could carry her to the mortuary for me," Ru Zairin said, softly.

Velasin blinked in surprise. "The Aida has a mortuary?"

"Just a small one," Cae said. "It's under the cold rooms."

"I'll need to shrive her first," said Raeki, ignoring the byplay. "Do we have a winding sheet?"

"We should have something inside," said Yasa Kithadi stiffly. "Excuse us, please, and I'll—I'll have Telitha bring it out to you."

The two women turned and departed together, Yasa Kithadi

visibly shuddering. Cae felt a pang of sympathy at the sight: his grandmother could be unflinching at times, sharp and hard and overbearing, but she still had a tender side, and for all the calm she'd shown thus far, he could tell she was badly rattled. *And Ren Vaia was sworn directly to her service, too. Of course she takes it personally.*

The awkward, heavy silence that followed was broken by Velasin. "Tar Raeki," he said, "as it seems there's been no foul play, would you object to my passing the news to Ren Taiko, to tell the other grooms? I believe he had a kindly relationship with Ren Vaia, and would want to hear of it firsthand, not by rumour."

Cae fought to keep his face expressionless at that. He'd expected to bring Raeki in on their suspicions of murder—although, he realised a beat later, Velasin could hardly say so just then, not with Ru Zairin still present.

"Of course, tiern." Raeki hesitated, glancing between them, then said, "That Ralian we've kept overnight. Is it still your wish to have him escorted out of Qi-Katai at the earliest convenience?"

"Oh, very much so," said Velasin.

"I'll see it done after the mortuary, then."

Another silence ensued, this one broken by the returning footsteps of Ru Telitha, who came bearing a plain cambric sheet. She flashed Cae a look that was too full of feeling to easily interpret beyond the obvious shock and grief, then beat a quiet retreat back to the Little Aida.

"Here we go," said Raeki, taking the sheet into the stall. "Gently now, that's it."

As tar and ru began the process of shriving Ren Vaia, Velasin turned and made for the horseway, leaving Cae to follow. The cooler air underground was also cleaner, lacking the lingering scent of death that permeated the stables above, and he breathed in deep for what felt like the first time in hours.

"I spoke to Ren Taiko yesterday," he murmured to Velasin. "He said he was watching the stables, wanting to keep them safe."

"Fuck," said Velasin.

Emerging into the Aida's main stables brought them into the midst of chaos, the sounds of which had reached them well before they mounted the ramp. Cae had been thinking they'd have to track Ren Taiko down, but he'd reckoned without the lightning speed of gossip and the fact that several grooms had been listening when he came to fetch Raeki. They'd barely crossed the horseway's threshold when Ren Taiko hurried up to them, his expression distraught.

"My tierns, is it true? Is Vaia dead?"

"It is," said Velasin, softly. "I'm so sorry, ren."

Ren Taiko made an anguished noise and shook his head. "Oh, poor girl, poor girl! Poor foolish girl! What happened to her?"

Cae exchanged a quick glance with his husband, then said, "It looks as though she attempted to take the yasa's palfrey for a nighttime ride, and was kicked in the head." No need to go into the details of how badly kicked, or to what effect; saints knew, a single blow was often all it took.

Something about the thought prickled at him, suggesting a need for further investigation. He tucked it carefully away and refocussed on Ren Taiko, who was doing his best not to sob into his hands.

"Poor Vaia!" he moaned. "Tierns, I beg you, please don't judge her too harshly. She was always so good with the horses, good with her duties, but these last few days, there's been something wrong. Ever since she borrowed Silk, and she'd never done a thing like that before, not once, but since that day—the day you arrived, tiern, not that it's got anything to do with you"—he bobbed his head nervously in Velasin's direction—"but ever since then, she's been acting off." He wrung his hands. "I should've done more to talk to her, after that awful business with your horse, tiern; it was clear she blamed herself, but I was too shaken up my own self."

"Why did she blame herself?" Cae asked.

"For causing the fuss beforehand," said Ren Taiko. "I told her, it wasn't her fault for moving the mare when she did—there was a mare in heat, tierns, you must've heard, a stallion broke loose to mount her and the stables emptied to deal with it. Vaia was only doing her job, she couldn't have known some, some *monster* would take advantage to slip in and kill a defenceless beast!" He ran a trembling hand down his face. "But now she's dead, too, poor thing!"

27

Velasin jerked but didn't speak. Cae murmured further condolences to Ren Taiko, who accepted them with a shuddering nod and a promise to tell Vaia's friends what had happened. He turned away, leaving the tierns alone, and Velasin stared after him, his hooded eyes lit with an odd intensity.

"Markel," he said abruptly. "We need to find Markel and tell him what's happened."

Cae had no argument with that. "He'd already left the infirmary when I went to get Ru Zairin," he said. "He's probably already in our apartments."

Velasin made a frustrated noise and started walking. "So much for giving him a proper welcome. He finally gets out of bed, and where are we? Investigating a suspicious death."

"I'm sure he'll understand," said Cae, and distracted Velasin from his annoyance by asking him to demonstrate some more hand-signs.

They reached the apartments without further incident, which felt like a tiny miracle. "Markel?" Velasin called, hurrying into the main room. "Markel, are you here? Oh, thank goodness." This last as Markel emerged from what was to be his new bedroom, looking demonstrably relieved to see the pair of them.

Cae signed him a greeting, still feeling a little fumble-fingered but encouraged by Markel's answering smile, then said aloud, "Sorry we weren't here to greet you. Something's happened."

Instantly, Markel's expression turned grave. "Tell me," he signed, and Cae allowed himself a moment of pride at his comprehension before Velasin replied with a flurry of gestures, too fast and fluid for Cae to follow. He looked between them, trying to get a sense of the conversational rhythm, and was concentrating hard enough that he actually startled when Velasin said, out loud, "Moons, I'm sorry! That was rude of me."

"Not at all!" said Cae. "It's not as if you're discussing anything I don't already know."

"Even so," said Velasin. "Markel and I often sign together, but that's no excuse for excluding you."

"Even so," Cae echoed, "there's no offence taken. Truly, Velasin."

Velasin drew breath as if to argue, but seemed to think better of it. Instead, he nodded and sat down at the table, prompting Cae and Markel to do likewise, and recommenced his narrative out loud—in Ralian this time, to Cae's amusement.

When the telling was done, Markel looked worried. He signed a question to Velasin, who nodded and said, "Yes. Killic is still leaving."

"Good," signed Markel fiercely.

All at once, the stray thought Cae had been struggling to conceptualise since the conversation with Ren Taiko flowered into coherence. "Overkill," he blurted.

"What?"

"Ren Vaia's head being kicked in like that. It was overkill. That amount of damage, to break the bone . . . I can imagine a horse trampling someone, but standing still and striking the same spot, over and over?" His mouth twisted into a grim line. "Whoever did this was *angry.*"

Velasin paled. "Oh, moons," he whispered. "It's my fault. The note, the note she left me—the whole Aida heard about it, including whoever Ren Vaia was running from. They knew they'd been betrayed and went after her. If I'd only kept quiet—"

"Don't," said Cae, catching Velasin's hand and gently squeezing his fingers. "Don't blame yourself. Blame whoever did this."

Velasin made a choked noise that was almost laughter. "I'm trying," he said, "but it's hard not to feel responsible."

"What happened to Ren Vaia is no more your fault than mine, that whoever this is keeps acting in the name of the Wild Knife," Cae said firmly. "Velasin—"

"The Wild Knife." Velasin sat bolt upright, eyes wide. "Cae, whoever did this *didn't blame the Wild Knife.*"

Cae stilled, heart pounding stupidly. *You called me Cae,* he wanted to say, *you used my name, please, do it again,* but this wasn't the time, and he forced himself to focus with a brutal wrench of will.

"You're right," he said, slowly. "Which . . . why? The two things are clearly connected, so why drop the pretence now? Because it wasn't working?"

"Possibly," said Velasin, "but we still don't know what they've been trying to achieve, or for what reason." He held up a hand, ticking incidents off on his fingers. "First they have Ren Baru try to stab me, but he gets Markel instead. Then they break into the tieren's rooms and cut his arm, but get away thanks to what we think is a Khytoi hunter's artifex gear. They kill my horse—possibly after using Ren Vaia to create a distraction, emptying the stables—and murder Ren Baru in custody with a spelled crossbow, but when we visit Ren Baru's house, we find an identical bolt in his drawer, and the same person who cut Tieren Halithar makes a rushed attempt at killing me before fleeing out the window. And then, last night, Ren Vaia tries to escape, and is murdered in turn—but instead of claiming her death for the Wild Knife, they try to make it look like an accident." He shook his head, baffled. "None of it makes any clear sense, but there must be a logic to it!"

Markel clicked his fingers and, when he had Velasin's attention, began to sign.

"He wants me to translate," Velasin said. "Markel says, if the bolt was in Ren Baru's house, it didn't get there by accident. What if the crossbow was his? But if so, why didn't he use it to try and kill me—us—instead of a knife, that day at the Amber Gate? It would've been easier, and he would've been much more able to escape. But if the crossbow was his, or at least in his house, then whoever killed him knew it was there. Didn't you say they only struck after you found the spare bolt in his desk? Crossbow quarrels are sold in sets. Maybe they didn't notice one bolt was missing at first, especially if they were in a hurry, but afterwards they panicked and went back for it, except that you got there first."

Cae nodded, frowning in thought. "And if the killer had access to the crossbow, why not fetch it earlier to use on my father?"

"Unless," said Velasin, now speaking for himself, "like we already speculated, they never meant to kill the tieren at all."

Cae stood without meaning to, pacing back and forth. His throwing knife had been left on a nearby bureau; he picked it up, tossing it from hand to hand as he worked through the implications. "Ren Baru had the crossbow, but he used a knife instead. Why a knife? And why keep a bolt in his office drawer?" He flipped his blade again, back and forth, resisting the urge to fling it into the target. "He was a merchant. He dealt with the Khytoi, but he wasn't a hunter. So why did he buy the crossbow if he wasn't going to use it?"

"Because he didn't buy it at all," said Velasin suddenly. Cae stopped pacing and looked at him, arrested by the brightness of his eyes. "The bow, the climbing artifex, the jumping spell—say Liran *was* right, and it's all Khytoi hunting gear. Doesn't it make more sense to think they were all acquired together? And we already know Ren Baru was a patsy—he really thought he was acting on the Wild Knife's orders, or at least to your benefit, but the second Raeki told him I was marrying you, not Laecia, he panicked. So."

Velasin drummed his fingers on the table, impatient with his own intelligence, tongue peeking out of his mouth as he thought. "So, let's say our mastermind wants Ren Baru to kill me—never mind why, when they're clearly capable of murder themselves—but for whatever reason, they want a fall guy, or at least some plausible distance between them and the crime. You saw those pamphlets in Ren Baru's drawer, heard Raeki's report: the fact that he idolized the Wild Knife was no secret to those around him. Knowing this, our killer convinces him that you need me dead, and gives him the spelled crossbow. It has to be spelled, of course it does—Ren Baru was no hunter, he didn't have any experience with that sort of weapon. And maybe that's why he went with the knife, in the end: he didn't feel confident shooting. But I think he chose a knife, specifically, to impress you. A knife to show the Wild Knife he was worthy."

"Saints," said Cae, rubbing a hand over his face. "That's just stupid enough to be plausible."

"Say I'm right," said Velasin. "Say he sat at his desk while he mulled it over, the bolt in one hand and his blade in the other, weighing up the choice. He puts the bolt back—as a souvenir, maybe—and goes to kill me. But he screws it up. Markel takes the blade instead—" He paused, shooting a look of fond, exasperated worry at his friend, who rolled his eyes and shrugged in response. "—and Ren Baru gets arrested. Clearly he was under orders not to say anything in the event that he did get caught, and the killer must've trusted him to hold to that at least a bit, or else I don't see why they would've waited the extra day to kill him. But then—huh." He stopped, staring into the middle distance, then murmured to himself, "So why *did* they wait?"

Markel clicked again, which brought Velasin out of his daze to act as translator for some emphatic signing. "Markel says, the real question is, what changed between the time Ren Baru was arrested and his murder, besides the attack on the tieren? Assuming they ever had some bigger plan for Ren Baru, like setting him up for a later fall, that must've changed when he was caught. If they'd tried to break him out of the guardhouse, even if they'd failed, it would've looked like he was part of a wider conspiracy, but instead, they killed him outright. So what changed? What did he know that they couldn't risk him telling us, and why did they only decide he was expendable after the attack on Tieren Halithar?"

Cae had always thought Markel clever, but his incisiveness still took him aback. He rubbed his chin, which was scratchy with stubble, and kept on flipping his knife. "What happened that day?" he said, as much to himself as to Velasin and Markel. "There's no use speculating about unknowns, so assume it was something we witnessed. Whoever this is, they're either based in the Aida or have access to it. We met with my father, and Tar Katvi sent someone to Ruya's Order to ask about magic—could that have been it?"

"I met your grandmother that day, too," said Velasin. "Could it have anything to do with her inheritance?"

Cae winced. "Saints, I hope not." He forced himself to consider the prospect, then shook his head. "No. It doesn't make any sense—if someone wanted to tip the scales or speed things up, they would've killed my father outright, not just threatened him, and in all this, nobody has come after me, Riya or Laecia."

"True," said Velasin, grimly. "They came after Quip instead. And right after that, we went down to the Amber Gate guardhouse, because—"

"Because Ren Baru wanted to talk," Cae said, significance thrumming through him. "Because of what you said about marrying me instead of Laecia; that it changed his motives. *That* was what made him talk, so it's not unreasonable to assume that's what made the difference."

Markel clicked. Translating once more, Velasin said, "So who was at the meeting?"

Cae froze in place. "No," he said, swallowing hard. "I know why you're asking, Markel, but—no. Aside from Raeki and Tar Katvi, it was family only: Keletha, my sisters, my father. If I start doubting any of them without solid evidence . . ." He tailed off, unable to finish the sentence.

"Besides which," said Velasin, coming to his rescue, "the meeting didn't stay secret. Tar Katvi sent a messenger to Ruya's Order, and Raeki went to the Amber Gate guardhouse. The whole Aida knew about the attack, and I'd wager the gossip afterwards flew thick and fast."

Markel nodded agreement, but his expression was mulish. He

propped his chin on a fist and stared pensively at Cae; or rather, at the knife he was still absently flipping from hand to hand. Cae floundered a little under the scrutiny, but not so badly as to lose his rhythm, and after a moment he recollected his train of thought.

"So, the killer learns that Ren Baru wants to speak to me in person, and knows they have to act. They drop him with the crossbow—we don't know when they fetched it back from Ren Baru's house, but they'd clearly reclaimed it by then—but afterwards, they realised they were missing a potentially incriminating bolt and went back to look for it."

"You missed out Quip," said Velasin. "They killed my horse first. Which." He frowned, dark brows knit together. "Quip's death was always odd," he said, softly. "But now it feels even more so. Why stop to kill my horse if you were rushing to kill Ren Baru? We know Ren Vaia can't have done it, even if she was involved—she was leading the mare in heat; she didn't have time—but if his killing was orchestrated and not just a crime of opportunity . . ."

"Then what?" asked Cae, though he had a dreadful feeling he knew the answer.

Velasin sighed heavily. "Then we're most likely dealing with two killers, not one. Or with a second accomplice in the Aida, at the very least; it's *possible* our friend in black made time to kill Quip before collecting their crossbow and racing down to the guardhouse, all somehow without being seen, but—"

"But it's not likely," Cae finished. He stopped flipping his knife, sighted the target on his wall and, taking aim, said, "FUCK!"

The knife thudded home with a dull *whump.* Cae watched it quiver in place, then let out a tense exhale and amended, somewhat sheepishly, "Sorry."

"Don't be," said Velasin, blinking at him with what Cae fervently hoped was amusement rather than fear. "But in the future, I'd appreciate a warning before you do that." Markel, who was grinning, signed something in response, and Velasin translated with a chuckle, "Excellent shot, though."

"You should see me do it from horseback," Cae muttered, reclaiming his seat at the table.

Velasin offered him a lopsided grin. "And here I recall you telling me that the Tithenai don't ride indoors."

"We save it for special occasions."

"Really? Does that mean I can expect to see you mounted at our marriage-gathering?"

"You can see me however you like," said Cae, the naked words tripping out of their own accord.

A beat passed, in which Cae's skin heated in sympathy with Velasin's instant flush. He swallowed, knowing he needed to fix the moment, recover the conversation, but had no idea what to say. "Ah, that is—"

"I'm sorry," said Velasin.

Cae stared at him. "What are you sorry for? I'm the one who said it."

"Yes, but I'm—I made it awkward, I—"

"If you did, then so did I."

"That isn't—"

Markel clicked twice, which startled them both into silence. He was grinning hugely, looking between them like all his festival days had come at once, and when his gaze settled on Velasin, he signed something that only made his husband's flush darken. Velasin signed furiously back at him, and suddenly they were engaged in the quietest yet most intense argument Cae had ever witnessed. It was the only time he'd been happy not to be fluent in their signs, though that didn't stop him from burning with curiosity as to what, exactly, was being said.

After nearly a minute of this, Velasin made what even Cae knew to be a universally rude gesture, to which Markel poked out his tongue and sat back with his arms crossed, looking smug and not the least bit cowed.

Velasin coughed. "Right. So. As we were saying, before we were sidetracked—"

"Murderers," said Cae, thrilled with the change in subject. "Or a murderer and an accomplice. One or the other."

"Quite. And we still don't know why they killed Quip, not really."

"I think we do, actually," said Cae, the realisation as sudden as it was compelling. "Like Ren Vaia's killing, whoever this is, you made them angry. It was *you* who suggested that Raeki tell Ren Baru you'd married me instead, and as that was apparently the right line of questioning—"

"Killing Quip was a punishment," said Velasin. He looked abruptly exhausted. "It was personal, just like we thought. I made them angry, so they killed my horse and tried to make me scared of you." He smiled a watery smile. "At least they failed in one of those things."

All at once, Cae wanted to kiss him. He'd wanted to kiss him before now, multiple times, but in that moment, the strength of his longing all but knocked the breath from his lungs. It made him ache, to see the edges of Velasin's grief and not be able to smooth them away. He wanted to lean in, cup his cheek and stroke a thumb across the bone; wanted to tuck a loop of that soft, dark hair behind his ear and kiss him, over and over, until those beautiful gold-grey eyes were hooded with laughter, not sadness.

But he couldn't. He couldn't, because he'd promised Velasin safety and friendship, and kissing him played no part in that unless Velasin wanted it to.

Murderers, he reminded himself. *A traitor in the Aida, and a killer of whose origins and motives we know nothing.*

"I hate this," Cae said aloud. He stood up again, restless energy twitching through his limbs. "I hate just sitting here, waiting for the next damn thing to happen."

"What do you propose instead, then?" Velasin said, somewhat tartly. "Walking out into the city and shouting for an honourable duel on the off-chance they take you up on it?"

Markel clicked at this, but didn't say anything; just shot his friend a withering look. Velasin coughed in response and muttered, "Sorry. That wasn't fair of me. I hate it, too."

"I know," said Cae. He rolled his shoulders, feeling the need for activity, and made a decision. "Ah, saints' breath! I'm all caught up in my head, and that's no good for either of us. I'm going to go swing a sword around until I'm more myself. Not indoors," he added, at Velasin's look of alarm, "I mean I'll do some training, out in the Court of Swords. Run some combat patterns, maybe, or find a sparring partner."

"Oh," said Velasin. And then, a beat later, "Would you object to an audience?"

"Not in the least," said Cae, suppressing a tiny thrill.

28

Cae told himself, quite firmly, that he wasn't showing off. He'd often run combat patterns wearing nothing but his nara and a thin, almost translucent undershirt that was slightly too small, especially when it was warm out and he planned on working up a sweat, as was the case today. Nor was he choosing the most challenging patterns to follow just because they were visually impressive, either: he needed to keep his skill set sharp, and he had several days' worth of training to make up for. He was used to being watched as he trained, whether by the Aida's guards, the soldiers of his revetha or any other passersby who found him entertaining. Velasin, like Markel, was just another observer, and if Cae was acutely conscious of his attention as he swung and blocked, lunged and pivoted, that was nobody's business but his own.

He may have been showing off.

And yet, for all that Cae was hyperaware of his husband's gaze, running the pattern still, mercifully, centred him. Pulse thrumming, muscles stretching, he let his frustrations bleed into action, using them to fuel each step, each stroke and stance, until all that was left was the clean joy of motion.

As he came to the end of one pattern, he caught sight of Velasin leaning indolently against a nearby post, arms folded as he tracked Cae's progress, and though he'd been at it long enough for his lungs to burn, he immediately launched into another set. *Just one more,* he told himself, and ignored whatever mix of ego and masochism caused him to pick Needle Braid, a lightning-quick pattern of sudden thrusts, sharp turns and tight blocks meant to simulate a fight in close quarters. Drawing on his reserves, Cae threw himself into a flawless execution, focus narrowed until nothing existed beyond the pattern, his sword an extension of his arm. The air blurred by, and when he finally completed the last, complex pivot and returned to first position, he felt almost giddy.

"Now *there's* a handsome sight," drawled a familiar voice.

Coming back to himself, Cae blinked and grinned at Liran, who'd just ridden in on his striking red-black mare, Jisi. "If I'd known you were coming, I'd have made an effort," Cae called out.

Velasin laughed at that, straightening and heading over with Markel. "If you'd tried any harder, your arms would've fallen off."

"You don't know that," said Cae, sheathing his sword as he ducked out of the training ring.

"I have my suspicions."

Liran dismounted, but kept hold of Jisi, politely waving away a nearby groom. He cocked his head at Markel, not having met him before, then looked inquiringly at Velasin.

"This is Markel, correct?"

"It is," said Velasin. "Markel, this is Ru Liran."

Markel gave him a small wave, which Liran returned with a grin, saying, "Excellent! Now that we're all introduced, I was wondering if the three of you would like to join me for an outing, as discussed. Although," he added, giving Cae an amused once-over, "you really ought to shower first, assuming you can peel yourself out of that poor excuse for a shirt and put on one that fits."

"I *like* this shirt," Cae muttered.

"Of course you do."

Cae glanced at Velasin. "Will you be all right waiting out here? I won't be too long."

"I'm sure I'll cope," said Velasin dryly, but softened it with a smile. "Go on, get changed."

Nodding, Cae headed over to the bench where he'd left his clean things—he'd planned ahead this time, to avoid another towel-wrapped trip through the Aida—and, after entrusting his sword to a passing guard for return to the armory, headed off to the showers. His neck prickled as he went; it wasn't that he distrusted either Velasin or Liran—or Markel, for that matter—but the prospect of his husband and his former lover conversing in his absence contained more possibilities than he was comfortable acknowledging.

With his sweat-stained things taken away to be laundered, he showered, dried off, rebraided his hair and dressed so quickly that he didn't process the reason for Liran's visit until he was halfway back to the Court of Swords. *He's found something,* he realised, and felt his spirits lift at the prospect of taking action.

He returned to find both Alik and Luya saddled and ready, their reins held in Velasin's hand.

"You're not coming too?" he asked Markel.

Markel shook his head and glanced at Velasin, who answered for him. "His side is still giving him pain, and Ru Zairin advised him against riding just yet. But," he said, and pitched his voice lower, "he's going to keep his ears open around the Aida while we're gone."

"That sounds extremely sensible," said Cae. He reached for Alik's reins and almost fumbled them at the brush of Velasin's fingers against his own. Liran made a small, polite noise that sounded suspiciously like stifled laughter, which Cae resolutely ignored in favour of mounting up. Velasin copied a moment later, as did Liran, and after waving farewell to Markel, the three of them headed out into the city.

"So," said Liran, once they were suitably distant from the Aida's gates. "I spent last evening sifting through my contacts, thinking who best to advise you about Khytoi artifex purchases, when I remembered someone I first ran into, oh, two years ago now, at an open collegium hosted by Ruya's Order. He's not exactly a merchant—more of a go-between for those who are looking to acquire particular items, often artifex, and those who are looking to sell them. His name's Ren Adan Akaii, and he's rather fascinating—his mother was originally Ralian, I believe," he said, glancing at Velasin, "but his father is a Khytoi merchant, so he deals a lot with their hunters and fur-sellers. If anyone in Qi-Katai will know who might've been looking to purchase a set of Khytoi hunting artifex, it's him."

"Thank you," said Cae wholeheartedly. "Will you take us there, or do you have other business?"

"I'll tag along, if permitted."

"Of course," said Cae. "Though it would be nice to know where we're headed."

"He keeps an office in the middle city, between the Pelt Market and the temple district." Turning to Velasin, Liran asked, "Have you been to the temple district yet? Architecturally, it's one of the oldest parts of Qi-Katai, and quite beautiful."

Velasin coughed. "I actually, ah . . . I haven't really seen the city at all."

"What? Not at all?" Liran exclaimed. "Cae, I'm scandalised—what have you been *doing* for this poor man?"

Somewhat chagrined, Cae replied, "Trying to keep him alive, mostly."

"Ah," said Liran. "Well. I suppose that is *some* excuse. And all the more reason to sort this mess out quickly, so Velasin can start to explore."

"Saints willing," Cae agreed. He thought again of Ren Vaia and winced. "Speaking of which, do you know of any magic that could be used to make a horse violent?"

Liran pulled a face. "Plenty, though a great deal depends on the type of violence. What's happened?"

As Cae relayed the most recent events, Liran's expression darkened. "Violence indeed," he murmured. "An abominable thing to do, but unfortunately quite easy, if you know the trick of it. Kicking is a reflex action: the brain sends signals to the nerves and muscles, and the body responds. That's as true of horses as it is of people. All a mage needs is a basic grasp of anatomy and sufficiently fine control to trigger the reflex on purpose—and a strong enough stomach to keep going, of course. Were it not illegal, you could do the same to a person just as easily, though the effect would obviously be different."

Cae shuddered. "Different, but no less damaging. You could make an archer release their shot, a swordsman stumble during a bout." He glanced at Velasin. "It's illegal here, to work magic on another without their consent, unless it's in self-defence or the pursuit of saving a life. Is it the same in Ralia?"

Velasin looked surprised. "No, actually. That is, if you were to *harm* someone with magic without due cause, you'd be held to account the same as if you'd hurt them in any other way, but if it was benign, there'd be no problem."

"Benign how?"

"Oh, you know—like changing the colour of someone's hair, making a friend slip over. Pranks, that sort of thing." His lip curled. "Of course, that only applies if you're someone who ought to be using magic in the first place—which is to say, a man of the right birth and background. Anyone else is likely to get in far more trouble, especially if they use it against their betters."

"Regardless," Cae said, "it ought to be harder, to have that sort of control over someone's body."

"Ideally, yes, but that's what's so fascinating about magecraft," Liran said, warming to his subject. "So many people think magic useless because it works on such a small scale—what good is it, if you can't wield lightning or summon dragons like the heroes in a story? But tiny levers can do big things, if you only know where to apply them. Body-magic is proof of that."

"I'd always wondered—" Velasin started, then stopped, ducking his head.

Liran cast him an amused glance. "Let me guess: You want to know how magery can reshape a person's most intimate parts, when it can't regrow a severed limb?"

Velasin grinned wryly. "Something like that, yes. Tithenai body-magic is whispered about in Ralia, but even Aline wasn't sure how it worked, not really."

"Allow me to enlighten you, then," said Liran. "Put simply, bodies aren't designed to rejuvenate, but we're all born to change. The shift from child to adult is perhaps the most dramatic example of this, and yet think of how many developments we undergo before then! A newborn babe doesn't have the same skull as an older child, for instance—they have softer plates of bone that help with being, excuse my bluntness, squeezed into the world. They don't even have kneecaps, did you know that? Little babies have no knees!" He laughed, delighted by the kneelessness of infants. "Which makes us wonder: How do our bodies know to change? What elements do we contain from birth that only emerge as we grow, to compel that greater development?

"I could bore you senseless with a long recitation of medical facts, physiological stages of development and so on, but the upshot is that, as we age out of childhood, our bodies—or certain of their internal parts, rather—produce an essence that guides our future physical changes. Or rather, a *mix* of essences, which is what you Ralians tend to find so upsetting. The same essence that turns a boy into a man is found in women, just as the essence that turns girls into women is found in men; it's just that, in most cases, one essence is much more prevalent than the other, you see? But even then, the ratios between them aren't remotely consistent, and the more mage-surgeons study it, the more variations they find.

"Which means that, when someone like me comes along, and especially when we know ourselves early enough to get in ahead of an uncontrolled adolescence, the right building blocks are already there. You just coax the body to produce one essence instead of another, then use that essence to reshape the parts you already have into what you want them to be, both inside and out. Which some kemi choose to tinker with too, in varying combinations—but the point is, it's a little lever that makes big changes. Slowly and over time, perhaps, but big changes nonetheless. And there you have it."

Cae, who'd heard Liran wax lyrical on the subject many times before, had been paying less attention to the speech itself than to Velasin's reaction. His husband had looked intrigued throughout, and now sat back in the saddle with a surprised little *huh!*

"It makes perfect sense, when you put it like that," said Velasin. "The way it's talked about in Ralia, you'd think it meant killing babies. But then," he added sourly, "too many Ralian men disdain anything they think of as *womanish,* up to and including actual women; I can only imagine how outraged they'd be if you told them that any part of their essence wasn't *purely* male."

Liran laughed. "Poor darlings! They'd be heartbroken."

At the mention of Ralian men, Cae's thoughts turned naturally to Killic, who with any luck was either already gone from Qi-Katai or very soon to be. He had a brief, unpleasant sense-memory of the smell of burning flesh, the way Killic's skin had crisped and seared beneath the soldering pen, and dispelled it by saying the first vaguely relevant thing that popped into his head.

"The theatres," he said, earning himself startled glances from his two companions.

"What about the theatres?" asked Liran, raising what Cae felt was an unnecessarily judgemental eyebrow.

"When this is over, I just thought . . . the theatres. I can take Velasin. If you'd like to go, of course," he amended, glancing at his husband.

"I would like that," said Velasin, daring a tiny smile. "Though you'll have to educate me on Tithenai productions—what sort of thing is in season here?"

Cae seized the change in topic like a drowning man lunging for a thrown rope, and with Liran's gracious (if clearly amused) help, he somehow managed to fumble his way through a discussion of Tithenai theatrical norms that lasted until just past the Pelt Market.

"It's down here," said Liran, returning them abruptly to the errand at hand. He'd steered them along a side street whose shopfronts were well-maintained while giving few clues as to what wares or services could be found inside. They halted at a small, open square between two buildings where a private guard oversaw a trough and hitching post; she bowed as they dismounted, and Liran tipped her as they left the horses under her watchful eye, after which he led them a little farther up the street.

Ren Adan Akaii worked in a slim red building with a glossy black door. Liran rapped smartly on the wood, and after a moment, the door opened to reveal a willowy Khytoi man dressed in immaculate greys and whites—or at least, Cae took him for Khytoi, given his petal-shaped eyes, smooth brown skin and distinctive, reddish-black hair. This latter feature was shaved high at the sides, so that what remained looked like a slicked-back crest; combined with his slim, sharp nose and irises that were so light a brown as to be almost gold, he resembled a bird of prey.

"Welcome to the office of Ren Adan Akaii," he said, in a curling Khytoi accent. "May I ask if you have an appointment?"

"We don't, I'm afraid," said Liran, dropping into what Cae recognised as his sugary, I'm-so-sorry-but-please-let-me-have-my-way register, "but Tierns Caethari and Velasin here would be *so* obliged if you'd give us a moment of Ren Adan's time. It's a matter of *deepest* urgency."

"Ah," said the man, eyes widening slightly as he took in Cae and Velasin. "Of course, Ren Adan is always willing to assist Clan Aeduria; however, he is currently attending to a business matter elsewhere in the city."

"When is he likely to return?" asked Liran. "We would be happy to wait."

"He should be back within the next half-hour, ren—?"

"Ciet Liran Faez," Liran said breezily, "but really, I much prefer to go by ru. And who do I have the pleasure of addressing?" He actually batted his lashes at this, forcing Cae to choke back a very inappropriate burst of laughter.

"Forgive me, ciet—ru, I mean," said the mortified man. "I am Ren Zhi Kai'ia, and you are all extremely welcome to wait for Ren Adan in the foyer." He stood aside to let them in, visibly flustered. "Please, come in."

"With *pleasure,*" purred Liran.

Cae really did snort at that.

The foyer was a well-appointed first-floor room, sufficiently furnished with couches, artwork and cushioning that Cae felt safe in assuming that the majority of Ren Adan's business was likely done here. A Ralian-style drinks cabinet in the corner only added to this impression, though given how the day had begun, it also reminded Cae that he deserved to get pleasantly drunk at some point in the near future.

"Can I offer you some refreshments while you wait?" asked Ren Zhi, clearly still embarrassed by his slip with Liran's title. "We have khai, white tea, Ralian brandy, Khytoi o'oa—"

"Tea would be *most* welcome," said Liran, and took a seat as Ren Zhi bowed again and hurried off towards what was, presumably, a small kitchen.

"I didn't take you for a cruel man," Velasin quipped, sitting down beside Cae on a low settee.

"Oh, don't fuss. I barely ruffled his feathers. And they are *beautiful* feathers," he added, craning his head for another glimpse of Ren Zhi—who was, Cae had to admit, well-favoured. "In any case, I got us through the door, didn't I?"

"Getting in was never in doubt."

Liran laughed. "Such confidence! Do keep this one, Cae, I like him."

"Your approval means the world to us both," Cae drawled, which was easier than saying *I like him, too.*

Ren Zhi returned with the tea, which was served in elegant glazed cups from a Khytoi-style teapot shaped like a dragon curled around a boulder; its curved tail was the handle, and the steaming liquid poured from its open mouth.

"That's a lovely piece," said Cae. "May I ask where it came from?"

Ren Zhi flushed. "It's my own, tiern. My clan-sister made it."

"Your clan-sister is talented indeed, then."

"How long have you worked for Ren Adan?" asked Liran, graciously accepting a cup of his own. "I would've remembered meeting you before now."

"Ren Adan was gracious enough to offer me employment as his secretary some three months ago," said Ren Zhi, pouring the final cup for Velasin. Cae noticed he'd made none for himself, and wondered if that was due to nervousness or habit. "Before that, I travelled with the Ei'iko Third Caravan."

"Ei'iko Third Caravan?" asked Liran. "Not Kai'ia?"

Ren Zhi stilled so minutely that, if Cae hadn't been looking right at him, he would've missed it. "My clan are not traders, ciet," he murmured. Liran opened his mouth to ask another question, but before he could do so, Ren Zhi bowed and said, "Please excuse me," retreating back to the safety of the kitchen.

Cae shot Liran an annoyed look. "You scared him off again!"

"An accident, truly!" Liran sighed and sipped his tea. "Still, it's unlikely he knows all his master's business. I'm content to wait, if you are."

"I have the patience of the very saints," Cae said loftily.

Liran waited until Cae had a mouthful of tea before stage-whispering to Velasin, "That's not remotely true, you know."

Velasin gave a discreet cough. "I'm aware of that, yes."

The nervousness Cae had felt earlier about leaving Liran and Velasin unattended together returned with force. *Ah,* he thought. *So* this *is what I was worried about.*

He was on the brink of mounting a protest to this assessment of his character when the front door opened, prompting Ren Zhi to come hurrying out from the kitchen.

"Zhi-u, can you get the door?" came a clipped, polished voice. "My hands are full."

"Of course," said Ren Zhi, rushing to comply. "But, Ren Adan, you have—visitors."

"There's nothing on the schedule," said Ren Adan. He came

suddenly into view, his arms heaped high with a bundle of furs, and blinked to find the three of them in his foyer.

"Tierns Caethari and Velasin Aeduria, and Ciet Liran Faez," said Ren Zhi quickly. "They wished to speak to you on a matter of some urgency."

Ren Adan took a moment to absorb this. He was younger than Cae had expected, his light brown skin set off by a fitted red lin over coal-grey nara and a creamy undershirt. The latter garment was narrow-sleeved and rolled to his elbows, displaying muscular forearms as he hefted the furs. He had a short, neat beard, intelligent eyes and a square jaw, and wore his unbraided hair tied back in a tail.

"Well," he said, smiling. "This is certainly unexpected, but if you gentlemen will give me a minute, I'll be happy to accommodate you."

"Of course," said Cae, and watched as both rens hurried upstairs to where, he assumed, Ren Adan kept his private office. He was half expecting them to take their time, but he'd barely finished his cup of tea when Ren Zhi returned and bowed to them again.

"Ren Adan will see you now," he said. "Please, go right upstairs. It's the first door, straight ahead of you."

"Our thanks," said Cae.

"You've been most helpful," Liran added, and winked at Ren Zhi in passing.

"You're incorrigible," Cae muttered as they climbed the stairs.

"I have no idea what you're talking about."

Velasin smothered a laugh.

The door at the top of the stairs was open, and in the doorway stood Ren Adan.

"Tierns!" he said, bowing. "And Ciet Liran, too—a pleasure to see you again! You honour me with your custom." He led them into his office as he spoke, taking care to shut the door behind him. "I'll confess, you've caught me during a busy time, but one must always be flexible about such things." He returned to his desk, which was both large and conspicuously neat, but didn't sit, his hands tucked neatly behind his back. "How may I be of assistance?"

"We were wondering," Cae said, "if you'd recently encountered or heard of anyone trying to purchase a Khytoi hunter's kit—an artifex crossbow and gloves, and something spelled to safeguard against falling from heights."

Ren Adan's brows lifted in surprise. "Not a commonly trafficked set of items within Qi-Katai," he said, casting an appraising look at Liran. "With no false modesty, I can see why you thought of me." He hesitated, then said, "Without wanting to pry into the tierns' business, may I first ask why you wish to know? I am happy to assist, of course; it's just that my work depends a lot on confidentiality, and while I trust that you would not ask for frivolous reasons, it would be . . . poor practice, shall we say, to simply disclose such information to anyone who asked. Even you." He inclined his head in apology.

Cae paused, weighing how much to conceal or reveal. "We have reason to believe these tools were used in an attack on Tieren Halithar, in the murder of a suspect in custody at the Amber Gate guardhouse and in escaping from the house of said murdered suspect."

"Truly!" Ren Adan exclaimed. He looked a little pale at this, and abruptly sat down. "That is . . . extremely disconcerting to hear." He swallowed, looking up at them. "Please forgive me, tierns—if I'd known what he intended, I would never have found it for him, I swear it—"

"Who?" asked Velasin, getting in ahead of Cae. "Who acquired the kit?"

"It was Varu Shan Dalu," Ren Adan said. "The head of the Amber Gate guardhouse."

29

It was almost anticlimactic, how easily Varu Shan Dalu was arrested.

When Cae and Velasin arrived back at the Aida, Liran having departed en route, they reached the stables just as Raeki was setting out to interview Varu Shan. Armed with Ren Adan's intelligence, Raeki changed his plans and quickly enlisted a small coterie of guards to accompany him. Cae wanted to go, too, but Raeki—and Tar Katvi, curse her—put their respective feet down about it, insisting he stay safe at the Aida. Cae complied with impatient ill grace, pacing through his apartments and flinging his knife at the wall, thoughts whirling with the many ways it could all go wrong.

And yet, nothing happened. Having paid a runner to alert them of the tar's return, Cae and Velasin knew the instant that Raeki and his guards were sighted on approach and hurried out to greet them. Side by side, they watched as a compliant but shackled Varu Shan was marched into the Court of Swords, his head held high despite his trembling. He was of average height and middle years, with short, thinning hair and a neat moustache that didn't quite match his bland, round-edged features. He wore no uniform, presumably as he'd been arrested at home, and his undershirt was pale enough to show fresh sweating beneath his arms, though whether that was the result of his walk to the Aida or anxiety was unclear. If forced to guess, Cae would've called it a mix of both.

As Kita and Mirae led Varu Shan down to the cells, Raeki saw the approaching tierns and scowled.

"We caught him preparing to flee," he said, "though he wouldn't tell us where, and as yet, he hasn't confessed to anything. But having spoken to some of his people at Amber Gate earlier today"—the scowl darkened significantly—"it's clear he's corrupt, and has been for years. I've had verbal accounts of bribery, intimidation, nepotism, negligence, both gross and petty misconducts, and once we've completed a proper search of his home and office, I've no doubt we'll find more evidence. Including his artifex gear," he added, after a beat. "We didn't find it lying around, but that's hardly surprising. He's likely hidden it somewhere."

"I'd like to question him now," said Cae.

"Me, too," said Velasin. "Or at least, I'd like to be present for it."

"No, you should do it," said Cae, surprising all three of them.

Raeki's eyebrows climbed into his hairline. "Are you certain, tiern?"

"If Velasin consents, then yes," said Cae. And then, to his husband, who was still processing this development, "I don't have your skill at reading people, responding to their cues."

"I'm hardly an expert—"

"You're better than I am."

"But that doesn't mean—"

"Velasin," said Cae, "will you do it or not?"

"Well, yes, but—"

"Just take the compliment, tiern," said Raeki, not ungently.

Velasin's mouth snapped shut. He nodded, jaw working silently, and with that they headed towards the cells, which were located under the barracks. To the best of Cae's knowledge, Velasin hadn't been down there before, but this was hardly an opportune moment to give him a guided tour, either. Instead, pitching his voice low enough that Raeki couldn't overhear, he murmured, "Are you sure you're all right with this?"

"I am," said Velasin. He looked at Cae sidelong and sighed, running a hand through his hair. "I'm sorry. I'm not . . . good, at accepting praise."

"I'll have to help you practice, then," said Cae. Unhelpfully, his brain reacted to this by conjuring up an image of Velasin, dishevelled and panting in his bed as Cae whispered filthy endearments into his ear. Cae slammed a mental door on that (very intriguing, absolutely to be considered later) prospect and returned his focus to the moment.

The air was cooler in the cells by virtue of their being underground, and stale by dint of their being largely unused, at least normally. The bandits captured at Vaiko were still in custody, and Cae made a point of stopping outside their cells to inspect the conditions. He'd never liked taking prisoners, but he had a greater dislike of seeing them mistreated, and was relieved to find no signs of sickness nor scanting of basic amenities.

"Gonna keep us here forever?" one barked at him, noting his scrutiny, but there was no bite to it. The man just sounded tired, and Cae experienced a pang of unwilling sympathy. Most who turned to banditry did so out of desperation, and while that didn't excuse their crimes, it had made it harder to fight them, knowing that, despite their efforts to kill him or his soldiers in the moment, most might yet be rehabilitated.

"Not forever," he said, and moved on, steeling himself for the confrontation with Varu Shan, whose malice was born of no such extenuating circumstances.

He'd been put in an interrogation room—not a torture chamber, though even in Tithena, there were those who saw the concepts as synonymous—furnished with a heavy wooden table and several equally sturdy chairs. The table was fitted with iron rings through which his shackles had been looped—the far more common cousin of Cae's anchor-cuffs, which were a delicate bit of custom work—but loosely enough for him to lean back in the chair. As the three of them entered, Kita and Mirae saluted, moving automatically to stand on either side of the door.

Velasin hesitated, then took a breath and sat down opposite Varu Shan, leaving Cae to stand to the side with Raeki.

"Do you know who I am?" he asked, voice even.

Varu Shan sneered. "You're the new tiern. The Ralian."

"I am," Velasin agreed. He folded his hands on the table, examining the disgraced guard. "I imagine you know why you're here."

"Feh. You're free to *imagine* all you want." It was a fine attempt at bravado, Cae thought, but there was a betraying tremor to his voice. "I've done nothing wrong!"

"Have you not?" said Velasin lightly. "Well then, Varu Shan—as you are innocent, tell me the thing you haven't done that we, in our foolishness, think you have, so that we can set about clearing your name."

Varu Shan froze. A calculating look flashed across his face, there and gone; but if Cae had seen it, then Velasin had certainly noticed, too. Slowly, leaning slightly forwards, he said, as though testing the waters, "Being varu, especially at a place like Amber Gate . . . it's the kind of thing that earns you enemies."

Velasin nodded, and when Varu Shan flashed a wary glance at Cae and Raeki, both did their best to project blank expressions. Emboldened by this, Varu Shan continued, "Jealous underlings wanting promotion, criminals whose business you've hurt or whose relatives got what they deserved—a varu could spend his whole life with clean hands, and still come away looking dirty through no fault of his own."

"You weren't running, then?" asked Velasin. "When Tar Raeki came to your house?"

"Running? Perish the thought! I was preparing for a visit home; my mother has fallen ill, you see; it's why I've been unavailable this past week." He adopted a pious tone. "If only I'd known what would befall Amber Gate, I'd have prayed harder to Mother Ayla."

The gambit was so barefacedly unoriginal, Cae had to exercise significant self-control to keep from scoffing, yelling or possibly just lunging forwards and shaking the man until he stopped lying. Instead, he clenched a fist behind his back, where Varu Shan couldn't see it, and gritted his teeth until his jaw ached.

"Of course," said Velasin, soothingly. "But you understand, don't you, why we have to investigate? The varu of Amber Gate must be seen to be above suspicion, and that means treating you the same as any other suspect—which, of course, you already know, as you were gracious enough to come quietly."

"I misjudged you, tiern," said Varu Shan, clearly thinking he'd won a sympathetic ear. He smiled at Velasin in a way that made Cae's skin crawl with the falseness of it. "Understand, I bear Ralia no ill-will—I didn't mean to get off on the wrong foot, it's just that, well. You know what it's like to be gossipped about as well as I do, I expect, and who amongst us hasn't fallen prey to rumour before?"

"I understand entirely," said Velasin. "So tell me, varu"—and here his silken tones turned hard, a dizzying change in register which turned Cae's thoughts once more in unhelpful directions—"assuming you *didn't* conspire to kill me, or Tieren Halithar, or have anything to do with the murder of Ren Baru Kasha, who would want us to think you did?"

Varu Shan went ashen. "W-what?" he stammered, staring from Velasin to Raeki to Cae and back again, as though waiting for a punchline. "Conspiracy? Murder? Tiern, that's not—I would *never*—I've skirted lines, yes, but nothing like t—"

"What lines, varu? What lines have you skirted?"

Varu Shan was sweating openly now, beads of perspiration dotting his forehead like cheap seed-pearls. "I—a man in my position, tiern—sometimes grateful citizens offer gifts, or divulge information which leads to arrests, but which cannot appear on official reports due to, to discretionary reasons; or else there are mistakes—honest mistakes! what officer has never erred?—but I swear by the saints, by Ruya, Zo and Ayla together, I have never conspired against Clan Aeduria, nor sought to see you harmed, nor the tieren neither!"

"But of course not," said Velasin, his silk-steel voice sending shivers up Cae's spine. "We already discussed your innocence. I didn't ask for your motives, varu; I asked *who would frame you.*"

Possibly the last few days had taken a greater toll on Cae than he'd allowed himself to realise, that he was reacting so . . . inappropriately, to Velasin's interrogation techniques. Or, more specifically, to his interrogation *voice:* he knew Velasin to be both witty and observant, but he also tended strongly towards self-deprecation and deflection, which were more upsetting than simple false modesty would've been. Knowing what he did of Velasin's history, not just with Killic, but within the vin Aaro family, Cae could see where his reticence came from, but that didn't make it easier to bear or fix. He'd been trying to coax him out of his shell since his first, disastrous day in Qi-Katai, and the more he learned of his depths, the angrier he was to think of such a man being slighted.

But seeing him as he was now—poised, controlled, *competent*—was thrilling in an altogether more familiar way. It was a skill Liran also possessed, and which Cae was self-aware enough to admit a preference for. He'd already been attracted to Velasin in its absence; to suddenly stumble on it here, now, was rather like being smacked soundly about the ears. Deep down, he knew, he was still processing everything, still conscious of the severity of the case at hand, of the crimes to which Varu Shan was linked, but he was also a healthy, newly married man with a very attractive husband, and promise of friendship or not, Cae was still only human.

"Who would frame you, Varu Shan?" Velasin repeated. "Or rather, who would frame you for this? Come now. You must, as you said, have some idea of your enemies."

"I don't know." Varu Shan spread his hands, shackles clanking ominously. "Tiern, when your tar brought me here, I thought—I assumed it was an accusation of negligence, over the death of Ren Baru. I did not think to be accused of the death itself!"

"Think harder, then," said Velasin, in a tone that made Cae shiver anew. "I'd love to believe you weren't involved, varu, if only for the sake of Amber Gate's reputation, but as you pointed out earlier, I am still new to Qi-Katai. What can I possibly know of her customs, her criminals and their habits, if you don't enlighten me?"

Varu Shan trembled, mouth working soundlessly for several moments, until an idea seemed to come to him. "Whoever implicated me!" he exclaimed, chains clanking once more. "Whoever told you it was me, that's who you ought to suspect!"

Dryly, Velasin said, "You'll forgive me, varu, if I require a little more convincing than that."

"Convincing!" Varu Shan exploded. In contrast to his earlier shock, this new surge of anger was turning him red in the face. "And how am I to convince you, pray, when I'm not even told of the accusations against me? How do I know that any of *you*—" He pointed waveringly at the room at large, until his finger was aimed directly at Velasin. "—haven't made this all up out of whole cloth, hm?"

"A very specific set of tools was used to accomplish both the attack on Tieren Halithar and the murder of Ren Baru; tools whose origins are distinctive, once you know what to look for. We have seen the ledger of purchase, Varu Shan: your name was on it."

"An imposter," Varu Shan declared, anxiously wetting his lips with his tongue. "An imposter using my identity, trying to set me up—"

"So name them," said Velasin. "I ask again, Varu Shan: If you are truly innocent, who would frame you for this?"

Varu Shan's hands trembled on the table. "I don't know," he said, agitated. "Tiern, I don't—I swear I don't know anything!"

"Then I suggest you think on it," Velasin said, and without another word, he turned his back on Varu Shan and walked straight out of the room. Cae shared a glance with Raeki and then hurried after him, leaving Kita and Mirae to see Varu Shan installed in a cell.

They caught up with Velasin at the top of the stairs, where he stood aloof in the late-afternoon sunlight, gilded as a saint.

"Well, tiern?" Raeki asked. "What do you make of him?"

Velasin sighed. "I don't think he did it; or rather, if he did, I don't think he knew the significance of what was asked of him. Either he was manipulated into buying the hunter's kit without knowing how it would be used, or someone truly used his name as an alias." He paused, scratching his jaw. "He's clearly a liar, but I don't believe he's that good an actor. When I told him why he'd been arrested, his shock was real. The man might be corrupt, but he's a pawn in this."

Raeki gave a frustrated nod. "That was my thought, too, but I also think he knows more than he's letting on."

"You think he's protecting someone?" Cae asked.

"That, or he's afraid of them, which would track with Ren Vaia's experience." Raeki made a fist, like he very much wanted to hit something, but was forced to let his hand drop in the absence of a target. "I'll see if Kita can get anything out of him—she's got a deft touch—but if not, I'll try him again myself tomorrow. Let him marinate overnight and see if it makes any difference."

With a sudden, sinking feeling, Cae realised there was nothing more to be done; or at least, not today. Against all reason and experience, some foolish part of him had hoped that Varu Shan's arrest would be the end of it—that he'd confess his crimes in some snarling rage, leaving them all with no doubt that the matter was solved. But instead, perhaps inevitably, they'd been left with yet more questions to which there were no easy answers.

"When you do," said Cae, resigning himself to it all, "try a different line of questioning. Ask him about what happened when Ren Baru was first brought in—where he was, what his orders were—and have it checked with the testimony of someone from Amber Gate who actually knows what they're doing, assuming such a person exists." He shook his head, seeking to dispel a sudden surge of bitterness. "Then ask about the lack of guards posted outside that night. That seems like the most promising link to me, how easily Amber Gate was breached."

"Of course, tiern," said Raeki. "Is there anything else?"

"No, Raeki. Thank you."

"Then I'll be about my business." He bowed and departed, leaving Cae alone with Velasin.

A light breeze stirred, ruffling the nearby grass that flanked the stone path leading to the cells. Cae looked at his husband, and witnessed the exact moment when the strength he'd shown in dealing with Varu Shan went out of him. It was a subtle thing, like sunlight shifting away from a window, and yet the change it left behind was not. Velasin slumped, rubbing wearily at his forehead, and smiled at Cae in a way that didn't reach his eyes.

"This has been a very long day."

"Yes," said Cae, inanely.

Velasin stared bleakly into the distance. "Will Vaia be buried yet, or is she still in the mortuary? Don't answer that," he added, as Cae opened his mouth to do so. "I don't think I want to know, just now."

Cae found himself wrestling with a complex well of emotions provoked by the exhausted line of Velasin's shoulder, the gentle arch of his neck. After several seconds, his mouth won part of the battle, and he said, "Velasin?"

"Mm?"

"This . . . friendship, that we've agreed to have. Does it include any casual intimacy?"

Velasin jerked his head up. "What?"

"Touch," said Cae, neck burning as his stomach churned. "It's been, as you said, an extremely long day, and I just . . . it feels wrong, to ignore the possibility of comfort."

"Comfort," said Velasin, who was not quite trembling in place like a spooked deer. "What—I don't know what—"

"Just touch," said Cae, and before he could lose his nerve, he stepped into Velasin's space and slowly, slowly, put his hands on his shoulders. Velasin looked up at him with wide, soft eyes, but there was no fear in him; just a spark of astonishment as his lips parted on a gentle *oh,* gaze flickering between Cae's eyes and mouth. Skin burning, Cae brushed his palms down Velasin's biceps and up again, letting his fingers curl over his shoulders. Tentatively, he squeezed, and like it was a dam breaking, Velasin made a small, involuntary noise and embraced him, arms wrapped warmly around Cae's back.

Cae drew a shuddering breath and closed his eyes, one hand cradling Velasin's head as the other supported his middle. He could feel Velasin's head pressed against his collarbone through the fabric of lin and undershirt; was aware, intimately and profoundly, of the way their bodies slotted together, chest to chest and hip to hip, as neat a fit as any he could've wished for. It struck him then that, though he'd held Velasin before, this was the first time where there'd been no extenuating horror forcing them together: no wounded Markel or bleeding leg; no threat of knives or murdered horse. The thought made him furious and sad in equal measure, a tender ferocity coiling behind his breastbone as he breathed in the scent of Velasin's hair.

He felt more than heard it when Velasin laughed, a burring vibration that passed between them.

"What's funny?" he asked, heart pounding all out of proportion to the question.

Velasin moved against him, and though it was impossible, Cae would've sworn he felt him smile. "Do you know how scandalous this would be in Ralia? Two men embracing in public, not pulling away . . . such a stupid thing. But here we are." He turned his head, so that he was facing into Cae's chest instead of away from it. "I keep forgetting it's *allowed,*" he murmured, raw in a way that hurt Cae's heart. "I've been so wretched since I got here, you have to hold my hand through every little thing, and yet it never occurs to me that you can, quite literally, hold my hand, or that I could hold yours."

"You can't learn a whole new culture overnight."

"Or unlearn an old one. No, I don't suppose I can. But it's nice to be reminded that the change is there." He laughed again and leaned back, looking up through his lashes in a way that was utterly unstudied, a product of their proximity and his lesser height only, and yet it took Cae's breath away. "You keep confusing me, that's all. I'm sorry for being slow."

"Confusing you how?"

"Not in a bad way, just—I have trouble, sometimes, sorting out what's specific to you, and what's simply the absence of Ralian logic."

Without quite meaning to, Cae tucked a stray curl of hair behind Velasin's ear, just as he'd desired to do that morning, and felt the shuddering breath this earned in every inch of his body. "Like what?"

"Like that," said Velasin, smiling crookedly. "Like the fact that you're willing to have me at all, despite my being spoiled."

Cae tensed. "You aren't spoiled. Velasin, you must know that, it isn't—"

"I don't mean because of Killic. Or not only Killic," he amended, ducking his gaze a little. "Just. It's foolish, like I said when we talked about money and householding, but some part of me keeps characterising my role as that of a Ralian bride, and brides, unlike husbands, are meant to come chaste to their marriage-bed."

"You aren't a bride," said Cae, trying very hard not to fixate on *marriage-bed*.

"Rationally, I know that. But there are all these little parts of me I never had to think of before that keep popping out at the oddest moments; ideas I would've sworn weren't mine at all before now, because they were invisible, you see? Like camouflage, but on the inside, too; a way of being within myself as well as appearing to others. But the camouflage doesn't fit here, and now I can see it, but that's not the same as being able to throw it out all at once."

"Velasin—"

"But my point is," said Velasin, fingers gripping the back of Cae's lin, "you have been—are being—extraordinarily kind to me, very often in ways I don't expect. Like now, for instance. And I don't, like I said, I don't know how much of that is *you*, just being yourself, and how much is simply your not being Ralian, but—"

He looked up, meeting Cae's eyes. "—but I'm starting to think it doesn't matter. Or, well," and here he glanced away again, a dark flush spreading across his cheeks, "obviously it *does* matter—I'm not about to confuse you with Raeki, or run off with the first handsome groom who tips me a wink—"

"I'm glad to hear it," Cae murmured, relieved beyond measure when Velasin chuckled.

"—but what I mean is, there's no point trying to subtract the Tithena from you, just like there's no point you trying to subtract the Ralia from me. We are as we've grown to be, and however we change in the future, that will always be where we've come from. So. I suppose what I'm trying to say is, if I had to be in this sort of mess with someone, I'm glad it's you."

"I'm glad it's you, too," said Cae.

They looked at each other, soft and intense in the fading light, and for a moment Cae could've sworn that Velasin was waiting to be kissed; his chin was angled just so, and his mouth was right there—

But friendship was what they'd agreed to. Friendship, and such physical intimacy as friends might share, in fellowship and comfort, which did not extend to Cae pushing him up against the nearest wall and doing things that he absolutely could not continue to think about while they were pressed so close together.

With a quiet huff, Velasin smoothed his hands over Cae's lin, unaware of the goosebumps he left in his wake, and stepped away. Cae's palms tingled at the loss of contact, and not for the first time, he wondered if he was going mad.

"I'm starving," Velasin said abruptly. "You?"

"I could eat," Cae admitted.

"Let's do that, then—but in our apartments, please, no public dining. I'm in no fit state for any company other than you and Markel."

All at once, Cae flashed back to a thousand years ago that morning, when he and Velasin had spoken to Yasa Kithadi. Velasin had said the same thing then, too—had finally said *our* instead of *your*—but the circumstances had been too fraught for it to fully register. It registered now, and Cae felt a dizzying rush of fondness that was laced with something suspiciously like hope.

"Of course," he said, and let Velasin lead them inside.

30

Cae dreamed of Velasin that night, and slept either very well indeed or extremely restlessly, depending on your point of view. Possibly he did both at once, if such a thing were possible: his dreams hadn't been quite that desperately graphic since he was fourteen, and the only difference was that now, unlike then, he didn't embarrass himself in his sleep. Even so, he woke sweaty and hard in his hipwrap, so jolted by the transition to wakefulness that it took him several heart-pounding seconds to realise that Velasin wasn't actually in the room with him.

I'm going to kiss him tomorrow, Cae thought stupidly, and as new arousal licked through him at the prospect, he hiked up his wrap and took himself in hand. He was close enough to the brink that he came within a handful of strokes, groaning softly as he flopped back on the pillow. He skimmed out of his hipwrap, used it to clean himself and tossed it in the hamper, grimacing a silent apology to the Aida's laundry staff. Orgasm had cleared his head, and for a few minutes he floated in a blissful white lassitude, untethered from the world and its responsibilities.

Inevitably, however, such a perfect state couldn't last. He sighed, ran a quick mental list of everything he might potentially be asked to do today, braced himself accordingly and got out of bed, only barely remembering to don a fresh hipwrap before venturing into the main room.

It was a good thing he'd bothered, as both Velasin and Markel were up already, having one of their silent conversations. It struck Cae forcefully that, despite his eagerness, he'd made little headway on learning their signs, and resolved to improve—right after he was bathed and dressed, of course.

"Good morning," he said, and was greeted with a cheery wave from Markel and a tired smile from Velasin.

"Good morning," Velasin replied. "Would you care for some khai? Ren Valiu sent some up."

"After I've washed, perhaps." He hesitated, then said, a little awkwardly, "Do you have any plans for the day?"

"Plans? Not as such, no, but I'm sure some new crisis will pop up and demand our attention sooner or later."

Cae snorted. "Well, once I've cleaned up, I'm going to get some training in, and afterwards, assuming the inevitable crisis is kind enough to postpone itself until afternoon, I was hoping you—both of you, that is—might teach me some more sign-speech."

"We would be very pleased to do so," said Velasin, after exchanging a look with Markel. "Does your training require an audience, or would you object if we headed into town? I still haven't taken my promissory documents to a bank, and I'd feel better for having some money to my name."

Cae hesitated. "Would you consent to take a guard with you? I've no doubt you can look after yourselves, but I'd rest easier for it."

"I suppose it's only sensible," Velasin sighed. "I'll see if Kita or Mirae is available; they're both decent company."

"Thank you," said Cae, relieved, and took himself off to the bathroom.

He showered rather than bathed, adjusting the height of the spout to stand beneath the flow, but didn't bother with his hair, knowing he'd wash it properly after training. The sound of the water was loud enough that he could only catch snatches of noise from the main room, which were easy enough to tune out. He was therefore surprised, once he'd dried, shaved and dressed, to find both Markel and Velasin in a noticeably more sombre mood than they'd been barely fifteen minutes earlier.

"What's happened?" he asked.

"Ru Telitha stopped by," said Velasin. "She had a book for Markel, as promised—" He cocked a thumb, indicating a slim red volume on the table that hadn't been there before. "—but she also invited us to a memorial service for Ren Vaia, to be held before the Little Aida at sunset." A muscle twitched in his jaw. "She had no kin, apparently; not even a sweetheart. Nobody to mourn her but the folk of the Aida. Her body's already been taken to Ayla's temple, but Yasa Kithadi apparently saved a lock of her hair. I don't know why," he added, finally looking at Cae, "but I assume there's some sort of ritual involved?"

"She'll burn it," Cae said softly. "Along with a feather, for her soul's migration, and a flower, for her body's return to earth."

"Oh," said Velasin. He laughed, short and sharp. "That's—that's better than what I was thinking."

"What were you thinking?"

"That I was given a braid of Quip's mane as a keepsake, and maybe the yasa wanted some of her servant's hair for a similar purpose, too. I'm sorry," he said, eyes downcast at Cae's wince. "That was uncharitable of me, to Tithena and your grandmother both. But the whole thing is just—"

"I know," said Cae, and dared to put a hand on Velasin's shoulder, squeezing gently. Velasin sighed and leaned into the touch, which felt as thrilling as if he'd somehow coaxed a wild hawk to his wrist. He let the contact linger a moment, then forced himself to pull away, conscious of the fact that Markel was watching them both like a naturalist in the field.

"If you don't want to go—" Cae said, but Velasin shook his head.

"No, I do. Or at least, I'd be ashamed of myself if I didn't." He ran a hand through his hair, which was unbound this morning, dark waves loose around his face. "That probably makes me sound awful, I'm sorry."

"Don't be," said Cae. "I know what you mean."

Velasin managed an almost-smile at that. "We'll see you here beforehand, then?"

"You will," Cae promised, and went to grab the clean things he'd change into once he was done with his training.

Heading down to the Court of Swords, he half expected to be accosted by someone, but no interruptions came. He fetched his sword, warmed up and ran through several combat patterns before, of all people, Tar Katvi showed up and asked if he wanted a sparring partner, which offer he accepted willingly. She was a capable swordsman, strong and precise in her forms, and what she lacked in imagination she more than made up for with the speed of her footwork, which quickened her reaction times considerably.

The bout was exactly what Cae needed, and when they stood back and bowed to each other over the hilts of their weapons, he was pleased to see that she, too, was flushed and smiling.

"My thanks for the match, tiern," she said. "It's good to get out from behind a desk and test yourself."

"I heartily agree, and my thanks to you, too." He hesitated, not wanting to ask and thereby return them both to the world and their roles within it, but duty was as ingrained in him as it was in her. "Is there any news on the investigation? I assume you've been keeping abreast of things with Tar Raeki."

"I have, tiern, but no, there's nothing meaningful to report. Or, well." Her lip curled. "We've plenty of proof of Varu Shan Dalu's corruption, now that we've searched his home—there'll have to be an independent investigation into Amber Gate, which'll be as much fun as a pissed-off barrel of cats, excusing my language—but we're still going through the ledgers from Ren Baru's office, and so far, there's nothing of use."

He sighed. "And Velasin's horse? Do we have any idea who might've killed it?"

Tar Katvi grimaced. "No, tiern. We've interviewed all the grooms, all the servants, but everyone was too distracted by that business with the stallion, and the gate guards haven't reported any unusual comings or goings." She let out an angry huff. "I hate to think there's someone working in the Aida who's been aiding and abetting all this, but it's starting to look that way. I'm loath to subject the entire staff to questioning about their loyalty—that sort of thing causes more rifts and fear than it does useable information, and we already know this person must be good at blending in—but if we don't find any new leads soon, we might be forced to try. Gods know, there's enough gossip and scaremongering among the staff already."

"Let's hope it doesn't come to that."

"Your lips to the saints' ears," said Tar Katvi, and bowed again before exiting the ring.

Cae watched her go, rolled his shoulders and set himself to moving through some of the simpler combat patterns as a cooldown exercise. As he did so, he thought back to last night's dinner, where Markel, with Velasin acting as translator, had relayed his observations of the Aida. Just as Velasin had said was the case in Farathel, people spoke freely around him to an extent that Cae found equal parts shocking and fascinating. Any other servant who lived so closely with an Aeduria would've been excluded from most casual gossip, but such was evidently not the case with Markel. He'd spent a great deal of time in the common mess and near the kitchens, and had picked up more in a day than most newcomers would in a month.

Markel—and through him, Cae—had learned that Riya's seneschal was widely disliked, as he'd never served at the Aida before joining her household, and yet considered himself a cut above the Aida's general staff by virtue of belonging to the tiera's personal retinue. By the same token, no fewer than three guards were evidently sweet on Laecia, who'd recently made a point of having extra beer from her own supplies sent to the barracks when the days were hot. It was reassuring to know that nobody appeared to take the attack on his father lightly—many viewed it as a personal affront, that anyone would so disrespect the tieren (and in his son's name, too!)—but, at the same time, worrying to hear that the tieren's intelligencer, Ru Daro, was slighted for his habit of putting too little stock (or so the servants said) in the knowledge of underlings.

It had been embarrassing for both Cae and Velasin to learn that Riya's tale of their supposed premarital correspondence had taken on a life of its own, to the extent that their marriage was now being characterised as a love match by some. Cae's ears had burned no less hotly than Velasin's cheeks to hear that a not insignificant number of the staff, though admittedly sceptical about Velasin's being Ralian, nonetheless thought he was good for Cae, if only because it meant he was settling down at last.

The more petty, gruesome gossip, inevitable in light of the past few days, was a joy to hear by comparison. Nobody suspected that Ren Vaia's death was the result of foul play, but an undercook and a junior groom had evidently come to blows over the question of whose unwanted advances might have driven her to try and flee the Aida, thus leading to her being in Silk's stall in the first place. The grooms in general were still shaken by the killing of Quip: more than just Ren Taiko had responded by increasing both their vigilance and their suspicion, and Ren Vaia's death had closed their ranks even further. This was on the brink of becoming a genuine point of contention with the stable hands, who felt they were being unfairly held to more rigid standards than previously, while certain guards and grooms were becoming antipathic to one another. Cae mentally cursed himself for not mentioning this to Tar Katvi as something to head off at the pass, and resolved to bring it up with Raeki before the day was out.

Mercifully few people, Markel reported, had concerned themselves with the matter of Killic, which spoke well to the discretion of Mirae and her guards. Inasmuch as he'd been noticed at all, he'd been thought of as a Ralian courier, perhaps bringing a message for Velasin, perhaps simply passing through, with no especial significance attached to him otherwise. Given how previous gossip had named Killic, along with Markel, as a potential lover for Velasin,

Cae had to assume this was due more to his name having been kept private than to any inherent lack of curiosity; that, and Riya's story about their romantic correspondence had shifted the narrative in more ways than one.

And then there was the marriage-gathering itself, due to be held tomorrow. The Aida was half in a state of excitement and half in a flurry of caution: nobody wanted there to be *an incident,* though as nobody could agree on what form such a disruption might take, certain imaginations were in danger of running away with themselves. Guard shifts had changed, serving rosters were being fought over and only by the good sense of Ren Valiu and certain other stalwarts of the Aida's senior staff was common sense prevailing.

Finishing his patterns, Cae returned his sword to the armory and went to wash up and change, taking more time than he had after the previous day's exertions. He was halfway back to the comparative safety of his apartments when Keletha, Riya and Laecia—an alarming trio to encounter at the best of times, which these were not—ran him to ground in a hallway.

"*There* you are," said Keletha, exasperated.

Cae blinked at her, attempting guilelessness. "Is there somewhere else I should've been?"

"Caethari," said Riya, "your marriage-gathering is tomorrow. Velasin is excused from organisational duties on the grounds of his not yet knowing how the Aida works—"

"And being Ralian," Laecia added helpfully.

"—and being Ralian, yes, but *you,* dear brother, have no such excuses, and cannot expect to remain exempt from everything."

"I thought that was all taken care of?" he said, turning pleading eyes on Keletha.

"Organisationally, yes," thei replied. "But you still need to know the order of events, and when to make your speech—"

"Oh gods, not a speech," moaned Cae, as they marched him off to Keletha's quarters.

"*Absolutely* a speech," said Laecia, revelling in his torment, "officially welcoming Velasin to Clan Aeduria, while also thanking your wonderful guests for their kind attendance."

"Can't I just wing it?"

"No," said Keletha firmly.

"I'll wing you," muttered Riya.

"Also," said Laecia, "have you even thought of a gift for Velasin? He's moved to your household, after all; you ought to give him something to signify your appreciation."

Hopefully, Cae said, "Did you have something in mind already?"

Riya cuffed him over the ear. "Be respectful! He's *your* husband, so *you* should choose the gift."

"Yes, yes," said Cae, wincing as he rubbed his head. "I was only joking."

"Your jokes were better before the bear."

The next few hours passed in a blur of dutiful activity. Cae penned as short a speech as Keletha would let him get away with, approved the order of events proposed by his sisters (while making sure to thank them lavishly for all their hard work; the praise made Riya roll her eyes, though Laecia primly accepted it as her due), and then ate lunch with the three of them. Afterwards, he had Keletha take him to the family vault to find something for Velasin. He'd known, of course, somewhere in the back of his mind, that he was meant to provide a gift; events had simply overtaken him, and he'd had far more and unpleasant things to dwell on the past few days than selecting an heirloom to pass on. Still, he was very much in favour of giving Velasin things—he steered his thoughts firmly away from the same territory into which his dreams had so eagerly veered; he was a grown man, not a green boy sniggering at his first dirty joke—and in the end, he picked what felt like an excellent present. Even Keletha approved, and promised to have it dusted, wrapped and ready in good time for the gathering.

With all that finally taken care of, he hunted down Raeki and passed on Markel's intelligence about the growing animosity between the grooms and guards, though without saying how he'd come by it. Raeki, who was starting to look distinctly greyer at the temples than he had before setting out to Ralia, thanked him and went back to glaring at a report on Ren Baru's recent business history.

He returned to find his rooms empty—Markel and Velasin, presumably, were still out in the city; he felt a small pang of worry at this, but quashed it with vicious pragmatism—and belatedly recalled the matter of Ren Vaia's memorial, which would require he wear something in the appropriate colours. One of the few cultural similarities between Tithena and Ralia was their mutual use of black as a colour for mourning and funerals; the main difference, as he understood it, was that Ralians had a vastly more complicated rulebook about degrees of mourning, how many black clothes to wear, for how long and under what conditions, whereas the Tithenai system was much simpler. Ren Vaia wasn't family, but she'd been in his family's service—or Yasa Kithadi's service, rather, which amounted to the same thing—and that ranked a black armband.

Knowing that neither Velasin nor Markel was likely to have such a thing in their possession, Cae fossicked around in the depths of his linen trunk until he came up with three, which he laid out on the table. As much to help pass the time as because he was thirsty, he rang for and received a bottle of chilled wine, pouring himself a modest cup to sip from as he lounged with his boots on the table.

It was in this attitude that Velasin and Markel found him on their return, idly flipping his knife in one hand as he held his wine in the other. Markel snorted through his nose and proceeded through to his room, a wrapped package cradled in his arms, while Velasin stared at him from the threshold.

"If I truly were a Ralian bride," he said, "and I came home to find my new husband with his feet up where we eat, tossing a knife and drinking in the middle of the afternoon, I would doubtless be pitied by all my friends."

"That's a considerable if," said Cae, though he did sheepishly return his feet to the floor.

"Quite," said Velasin dryly, but he smiled as he said it, taking a seat of his own. "How has your day been?"

"I was corralled into organising things for tomorrow."

"Sooner you than me," said Velasin, though with a certain studied lightness that said he, too, had been thinking about it. "Have there been any new developments otherwise?"

"None," said Cae, "though I don't know whether to be glad of that or fearful," and proceeded to relate what little there was to tell of his conversation with Tar Katvi.

Markel returned just as he was finishing, and after asking politely about their trip into town—they'd stayed wholly within the upper city and had, after Velasin's promissory documents were accepted at one of the merchant banks, done a little exploring in the Jade Market—Cae made good on his earlier promise and asked for a lesson in signing.

It was, he soon discovered, much easier to learn from two teachers than one, partly because Velasin could speak the words aloud as Markel shaped them fluidly with his hands, leaving Velasin's free to correct Cae's form, but mostly because they worked together so seamlessly. Since learning about the circumstances under which they'd first met, there'd been little opportunity for Cae to sit and digest the tale, but it came back to him now, evoking a sharp, fond pang beneath his breastbone. Markel was clever, wry and pragmatic, and to Cae's soldier-sense, he carried too the determined self-possession of a survivor; that almost indefinable capacity, not just to endure, but to recover. And then there was Velasin, so stubbornly kind that it was equal parts strength and vulnerability. He was also reckless, not quite because he didn't value himself, but because he valued others or other things more. Cae had barely known him a week, and it already drove him mad, if madness could be defined as wanting to take Velasin to bed and leave him too happy and satiated to endanger himself.

"Caethari?" said Velasin, in a tone that suggested he'd said it several times already.

Cae flushed, returning abruptly to the moment. "Sorry," he said, "I was whittling trees from firewood."

"We can stop, if you like—"

"No, no, please." He smiled, face hurting with how much he meant it. "I want to learn."

Velasin smiled back at him, and so the lesson continued until just before sunset, when Cae distributed the mourning bands and the three of them trooped solemnly down to the sika-studded lawn of the Little Aida. Half the Aida's staff were present, including all the grooms save Ren Taiko, who was doubtless still sitting his determined, lonely vigil in the stables. The crowd of guards and servants parted to let them through, until they were standing with Yasa Kithadi and Ru Telitha at the head of the crowd, where a small bronze brazier had been brought out and set on a tripod.

"Thank you for coming," the yasa murmured, and Cae was shocked by the nakedness of her grief: her voice was rough, her eyes red-rimmed, every trace of composure stripped away.

"Of course, grandmother," he said.

Yasa Kithadi opened her mouth, but paused as the crowd parted again, revealing Laecia, who bit her lip and came to stand awkwardly at Cae's side. She, too, was wearing an armband, which Cae noticed at the same time as their grandmother, whose eyes widened ever so slightly at the courtesy.

"Laecia," she said, surprised and touched. "You didn't have to."

Laecia shrugged. "It felt right," she said, and ducked her head.

Yasa Kithadi swallowed, then collected herself and began to speak.

"We are gathered here to mourn the death of Ren Vaia Skai, who lived and worked among us, and whose passing has come as a shock to us all." Her voice was clear and carrying, but laden with emotion. "I will not pretend to have known her as a friend, but she was nonetheless very dear to me. She joined my service at the age of fourteen, and was always a kind and cheerful girl." Her voice faltered. "The world has been robbed of her. I do not take it lightly. And now I ask that anyone who knew her, who might wish to speak, come forward and do so."

There followed a shuffling from the crowd as, one by one, a handful of the Aida's staff stepped forwards to speak their part. Most were grooms, including an older woman who spoke passionately on Ren Taiko's behalf as well as her own, tears streaming down her cheeks, but other servants joined in, too. And yet the service passed all too quickly—as fleeting an event, in the end, as Ren Vaia's life had been. It made Cae's stomach twist with rage and guilt, to know that she'd been murdered, and that her murderer as yet walked free. *We owed you better than this.*

With the speaking done, Yasa Kithadi stepped forwards once more, producing the lock of Ren Vaia's hair, a small white feather and a soft blue flower from the deep pocket of her nara. She laid them gently in the brazier, then nodded to Ru Telitha, who lit them with a match. The scent was odd, the unpleasant scents of singed hair and feather overlaid by a sweetness from the flower, the combination of which had Cae on the brink of sneezing. Thankfully, though, his senses adjusted, and as the thin streak of grey-white smoke drifted up to the sky, his grandmother sang the first part of the call and response that had been a part of Tithenai memorials for years uncounted:

"*Travel high, saints mark your passage; we remaining set you free.*"

And the crowd sang back:

"*The earth is paid, the sky is waiting; pass softly through the great between.*"

Velasin's hand closed gently around Cae's wrist; he startled at the contact, and then realised that it was Velasin's way of joining in, as neither he nor Markel knew the words.

"*Ayla made you, Zo watched you; now Ruya leads you into mystery.*"

"*Go well, go well; saints mark your passage; you who were known, be known again.*"

The smoke cleared; Velasin released his wrist; the crowd fell silent. Someone sobbed, then stifled themselves as the last of the light slipped past the Aida's walls.

"Goodbye, Vaia," the yasa whispered, and Cae heard the sentiment echoed through the watching crowd: *goodbye.*

A poignant moment, still with meaning. Then Yasa Kithadi sighed, and it was done: the crowd murmured as they dispersed, trickling back to homes and barracks, rest and duties, food and company, all the things Ren Vaia would never have again. Laecia smiled a sharp, sad smile and left without another word; Cae wanted to call her back, to thank her for being there, but couldn't find the words. He looked instead at his grandmother, who was staring into the brazier's embers, hands clenched by her sides.

Gently, Ru Telitha touched her mistress's elbow. "Yasa," she murmured, "come inside. Dinner will be waiting for you."

Yasa Kithadi shook herself. "Of course," she croaked. She frowned, visibly straightening, and then repeated, more smoothly this time, "Of course." She flashed a glance at Velasin and Markel, then rested her eyes on Cae. "Bring her justice, Caethari. Find who did this."

"I will," he said. "I promise."

"Good," she said, and let Ru Telitha lead her away, leaving the brazier to smoulder its last in the dusk.

Part Seven

VELASIN

31

The day of our marriage-gathering dawned as bright and clear as my spirits were not. I was powerfully anxious, plagued by a sort of restless confusion I didn't know how to articulate. To my Ralian mind, this marriage-gathering more closely resembled a wedding than the vows we'd taken before the justiciar. Though we were already husbands, I felt more keenly what I imagined was a traditional, pre-wedding nervousness; and yet there was another element to my feelings, too, some subtler thread I didn't dare tease out for fear of where it might lead me. I rose, washed my face, paced around my room and flung myself back into bed again, face buried in the pillow as I stifled a moan at the ridiculous predicament in which I'd found myself. *Only you, Velasin,* I told myself. *Only you would marry in terror, somehow convince your husband to be friends with you anyway and* then *figure out that you want to bed him.*

Because I *did* want to bed Caethari, I'd realised; I was just too scared to attempt it. I'd dreamed nebulously of Killic, which was hardly a good omen, and it made me jumpy to think that the aftershocks he'd left me with, those moments of irrational fear where my heart sped up and my body betrayed me, might suddenly return the instant I tried to act on my desires. It wasn't even that I thought Caethari would shame me for it, though I couldn't completely dispel the fear that his patience was bound to run out at some point. No: it was my pride that hurt, a stumbling-block entirely of my own creation. I wanted to be confident, desirable; I wanted to feel *myself* again, some version of me unblemished by either Killic's false love or his cruelties, and the fear that I might never be so was a vise around my heart.

Today would be a test, I decided. The Tithenai tradition of kissing two strangers and then one's spouse made for a perfect experiment, and if I froze up at any point, it would doubtless be attributed by the onlookers to little more than Ralian prudishness. Not, of course, that I *was* especially prudish by Ralian standards; or at least, I hadn't been before all this.

I sighed, and rose, and went about the business of getting dressed.

When Ren Lithas had brought me my new clothes, he'd drawn my attention to a matching set of nara, lin and undershirt that was more lavish than the rest, and though he'd not said as much in so many words, I gathered that it was this outfit I was meant to wear to the marriage-gathering. As the event itself was not set to start until midafternoon, however, I set the beautiful clothes aside and donned another, more practical outfit for the morning. Ordinarily, I would've showered first, but as I was going to have to bathe in a few hours anyway, I allowed myself to head straight out to breakfast.

Markel was already up, engrossed in reading the book he'd been gifted by Yasa Kithadi. It was an old Tithenai translation of a volume of Ralian fables whose original edition was no longer in print—exactly the sort of thing that Markel loved. Without wishing to slight the yasa, I suspected Ru Telitha's hand in the gesture, and wished, not for the first time in my life, that I had Markel's great ease with securing romantic prospects.

There was already a ceramic carafe of khai on the table, along with three cups and—I let out a small, delighted noise—a bowl of Ren Valiu's famous little suns.

"Now *there's* a treat," I said, and popped one into my mouth as I poured myself some khai. "Is Caethari up yet?"

"He woke early for training," Markel signed, "but he ought to be back soon." He grinned at me, then added, "I think he wanted to work off some nervous energy."

"Well, he's not the only one," I muttered, and consoled myself with another little sun.

Markel, annoyingly, had begun to have *opinions* about my marriage to Caethari. Specifically, he thought we were both ridiculous around each other, like two callow youths trying to navigate their first infatuation. Wretchedly, he wasn't entirely wrong. I'd explained the three kisses to him last night, so that he wouldn't be shocked when it happened, and he'd been reduced to paroxysms of silent laughter at the notion, though he wouldn't fully explain why. It was irksome in the extreme, but there was still a strange sort of comfort to be had in knowing that, however facetious he might be at times, Markel still liked Caethari, which was more than could be said of his feelings for most of my previous partners. He'd told me several times that I had appalling taste in men, but that under the circumstances—the circumstances being Ralia in general and Farathel's court culture in particular—he didn't blame me for taking what I could get, though he'd said this in a teasing way, not at all censorious.

I'd made a significant dent in the number of little suns by the time Caethari returned from his exertions, and his eyes lit up at the sight of them.

"Now *there's* a treat!" he exclaimed. Markel was so delighted by this accidental echo that he choked on his khai, grinning like he'd won a bet even as I thumped him on the back. Caethari, mercifully, didn't notice that there *was* something to notice beyond Markel's coughing, and having established that I had the matter in hand, he sat down to breakfast with us.

"Well, here we are," I said, aware that my tone was falsely bright but unable, quite, to make it otherwise. "What a day we have ahead of us!"

Caethari's face fell. "Velasin, if you don't wish for this to happen—"

"No! No, I'm sorry." I sighed, and my next sentence came out in Ralian. "That was churlish of me."

"What?" asked Caethari, whose Ralian vocabulary evidently lacked the word *churlish,* and so I repeated it for him in Tithenai. He grimaced, shaking his head. "You aren't being churlish. You were forced into this—"

"That's not it," I said, interrupting him. "I'm in an odd mood, that's all." And then, because he still looked morose, which no one should do in the presence of Ren Valiu's little suns, "It's just, this feels more like a wedding to me than the vows we took, and so I'm nervous. Moons help me, but I'm actually *nervous,* the way anyone might be before a wedding, except that we're already married, and that makes it even more foolish."

"It's not foolish," said Caethari, his expression clearing in a way that made my heart lift. "Truth be told, I'm nervous, too."

"You are?" I asked, and for all that Markel had quipped about his burning off nervous energy, my surprise was genuine.

"I am. Part of it is just that I don't like formal events—I always feel trapped, like I'm one wrong step away from being bailed up in a corner and lectured about economics—but this is . . . today is significant, for both of us. I want it to go well." He looked at me, dark eyes earnest in a way I could scarcely handle so early in the morning. "I want *you* to be well, Velasin, and I'm afraid—I'm more or less constantly afraid, if we're being honest—that I'm failing you in that."

My throat went dry. "You're not," I said. "That's—Caethari, that's absurd. You aren't failing me in the slightest. I'm, tonight . . . I'm not sure *eager* is quite the word, but is it wrong to say that I'm excited, despite everything?"

"You are?"

"I am," I said, and felt something shiver between us, some frisson of possibility that made my fingertips tingle. "I . . . I realised, last night, that part of me feels like I'm in a children's story, albeit an impossible one." I gestured shyly to Markel's book, and pretended not to notice his quiet glee at our conversation. "Marriage to a man—an open, true marriage—it's not a thing I ever thought would be possible; but in my secret heart, I think perhaps I yearned for it. To show that part of me to others, to be seen for who I am . . . and this is that, in a way. A real way. And whatever the context otherwise, it feels . . . I don't know. But it makes me *feel,* and that's what's making me snappish."

Caethari was smiling at me, so softly that it was almost unbearable; so I, provocative little brother that I still was, deep down, elected to break the moment by picking up a little sun and poking it rather forcefully at his mouth. His lips parted in surprise, and I felt the brush of my thumb against them—and then I laughed, as much to shield against the sensation as at the beautiful confusion of his face. He chewed and swallowed and then laughed, too, dark threads of damp hair loose around his ears where they'd pulled free from his braid, and I suddenly wondered: Would I ever brush it for him, braid it for him? It wasn't a service Ralian spouses customarily performed for one another, largely because Ralian men weren't expected to know anything about hair beyond the basics necessary for personal deportment, but the image of Caethari before me, sitting or kneeling as I ran my fingers through that dark, silky mass . . .

I coughed, laughed, helped myself to another little sun, and told myself very firmly that Markel did not, in fact, possess the ability to read minds.

We went without conversation for a time, sipping our khai and enjoying the morning air, until Markel abruptly snapped his book shut and signed that he was going to seek out Ru Telitha, to see if she could advise him about his role in the marriage-gathering. I bid him farewell—as did Caethari, who practiced his signs to do so—and suddenly found myself all alone with my husband, as unoccupied as either of us had been for days.

Refusing to find this awkward, I said, "Is there anything we're expected to do before the event itself, or do we just show up?"

"Well, it's generally considered appropriate to dress," said Caethari wryly, "but otherwise, no. That being said, I wouldn't be shocked if my sisters materialise at some point; if there hadn't been so much excitement to keep us all busy, they'd have been in and out the past few days like bees in a hive."

"Even Riya?" I asked. "I would've thought she was busy trying to negotiate her, ah, known paternity."

"Oh, she is," said Caethari, "but she's very capable of making time to pester me when it suits her."

"Such is the way of older siblings," I said knowledgeably, which led into an easy discussion of our respective siblings, swapping tales of Riya and Nathian, Revic and Laecia that soon had both of us laughing. It was the sort of conversation we ought to have had already, but aside from a vague notion that we were doing things backwards, I was pleased to have it come easily.

And yet, because I was still myself, I couldn't help but give voice to a lingering point of curiosity. "Forgive me if it's a delicate subject," I said, "but why did the Tierena Inavi leave? I know you told me you didn't fully understand it, but it's hard to believe that it came from nowhere."

Caethari stilled, and for an awful moment I thought I'd broken the rapport between us; but then he smiled, gentle and a little sad.

"She was unhappy," he said, simply. "I say I don't understand, and that's true at its core: I don't know when she first began to be discontented here, the details of what went wrong between her and my father, but looking back . . . I think he eroded her, wore her down the way water wears at a stone; not maliciously or with cruelty, but through simple lack of understanding. She changed more than him, I think; changed in ways that he didn't care to notice or examine in comparison to himself until it was too late. The thing I always think of was the magelights in the Garden Hall—she developed such a fascination with magic, and he was always so dismissive of it, as though her intelligence was of no consequence if it weren't turned to something he saw as useful."

"But you don't . . . you bear her no ill-will, for leaving you?"

He frowned. "That's a more complex question. At the time, I was angrier on Laecia's behalf than my own, her being the youngest, but looking back, I think it made me feel that I must've been older than I was; more adult, somehow, like Riya was, for my mother to think I no longer needed her with me. It was a year later when I fought the bear—wholly my own decision, of course, I don't blame her for *that*—but I suspect at least some of my bravado came from thinking myself a man grown already."

He rubbed his chin, staring thoughtfully at the near-empty bowl of little suns. "We've talked about it since, albeit in vague terms; it's not exactly an easy conversation to have. Perhaps I'd feel differently if she was open with me about it, but as things stand . . . no, I don't bear her any ill-will for leaving. For a while, I wanted to be angry that she chose herself over her children, but the older I get, the more sympathy I have with, with a fear of abnegation, if that makes sense? I can wish all I want that she might've stayed a few more years, but what would they have cost her? Perhaps nothing; perhaps something; perhaps everything. It's the not knowing that makes me angry now, the feeling that it's too late to ask, or that she might not tell me if I did. I want to be able to judge for myself, to see the truth of things, but I can't—" He made a frustrated noise, fingers flexing as if in physical search of a word. "—I can't expect that, even if I did so, it would make as much sense to me as it did to her."

All at once, I understood why I'd asked him about it, and felt something twist beneath my ribs.

"Caethari," I said, "I'm not her."

"What?"

"I'm not her," I said again, feeling on some level that we both needed to hear it. "I'm not her, and I won't be her, not in that way. I'm not unhappy here, and if I was, I would tell you; and if, on the basis of that unhappiness, I one day decided to leave this marriage"—my breath snagged oddly on the sentiment, as though I'd swallowed a tiny thorn—"I wouldn't leave you wondering."

He stared at me like I was an apparition. "Velasin—"

"I just mean," I rushed on, "that you don't have to keep being worried that you're failing me; that I'm going to up and vanish. I know I can be ridiculous and frustrating and sharp, especially when I'm in a mood, but even if I'm being an ass about something, you can rest assured that Markel will make me talk about it eventually. If I'm at all sane and well-adjusted, it's really down to him."

"I think that does you a disservice," said Caethari. "But . . . thank you. I hadn't—saints!" He shook his head, grinning crookedly in a way that made me want to press my thumb to the corner of his mouth—to the place I'd so impulsively kissed—and hold it there, as if to pin his smile in place. "You have a gift for seeing into people."

"I have a gift for being presumptuous in my declarations and questioning both," I countered.

He laughed. "You really are bad at accepting compliments, aren't you?"

"I admit it freely."

All at once, his earnestness lost its playful edge, becoming more serious. "Can I ask you something?"

"I'd be hypocritical to say no."

"That's not the same as a yes," Caethari pointed out.

"Ask away, then."

"Did you never consider coming to Tithena of your own volition?" I felt the breath go out of me. "It's only," he said, "your Tithenai is fluent, and as a younger son, there was no inheritance to hold you in Ralia. You must've known your preferences would find a greater acceptance here than there. So I wondered: Did you ever think of moving?"

I was silent for a long moment, reminding myself that I'd been the one to ask the first prying question, which Caethari had been good enough to answer honestly. I swallowed a mouthful of excuses and finally said, "I did truly consider it, once. But I was afraid."

"Of what?"

"Of everything." I laughed, ashamed and brittle. "What would my family think of me? Would they suffer in their friendships and alliances because of what I was seen to be? How would I make a living, if my father decided to cut me off? And what if I was wrong, about what I'd find here? I spoke the language, yes, but I didn't understand the culture. What if I came all this way, and it turned out that I'd misunderstood somehow, or the rules excluded Ralian spouses? But the worst fear—" And here I faltered, for this was the deepest truth of the matter, and though I felt Caethari was owed it, the words were still hard to utter. "—was, what if it *was* all possible, but nobody wanted *me*? To give up everything, only to learn that the fault was mine—that I wasn't—that I couldn't be wanted like that, not even in Tithena . . . I had rather stay in Ralia and never know, than leave and have that fear confirmed."

Caethari's eyes were impossibly soft. "Of all the things you have to fear in Tithena, Velasin, being unwanted is not among them."

Oh.

I ducked my head, heart pounding wildly. "That is . . . good to know," I said, and the words came out half-swallowed. I waited a moment, trying to master myself, but when I finally looked at Caethari, nothing could have prepared me for the expression he wore, an aching, tender hope that very nearly undid me. All by itself, it was almost enough to have me open my arms to him and see what happened next.

But I didn't. I didn't dare, not with the marriage-gathering still ahead of us. If I had one of my episodes now—if I gambled incorrectly, and set myself to reliving Killic—I didn't know how I'd get through the rest of the day without shaming us both. Drawing on every scrap of Farathel poise I'd ever possessed, I smiled at my husband and said, "You know, we still haven't had that game of kesh. Would you like to try it now?"

"I would," said Caethari, and rose to fetch the board.

32

The hours passed, both honey-sluggish and swift as deer, until we arrived at the brink of our marriage-gathering. Caethari bathed first, partly because he was riding high on his most recent kesh victory—we'd proven to be evenly matched, with two wins apiece and one stalemate—but mostly because his hair required more drying time than mine. I waited until I heard water running, then ducked into Markel's room and retrieved the gift I'd impulsively bought during yesterday's trip to the Jade Market, furtively returning it to my own quarters. I felt foolish about it now, as though I'd be saying more than I meant to if I handed it over, but it wasn't the kind of thing I'd have bought for myself, and so I resolved to gift it to Caethari before we joined the festivities.

Markel returned just as I was laying out my clothes, took one look at whatever face I was making and graced me with an expression that somehow conveyed concern, amusement and exasperation all at once.

"I know," I said, flushing. "I *know,* Markel. I'm doing my best."

"I know," he signed. "That's what makes it so funny."

I straightened up, running a palm over my outfit for the evening. The lin was made of heavy silk, dyed a beautiful forest green and embroidered with golden deer and white flowers. The undershirt was an astonishing pale gold colour, almost iridescent and made, as best I could tell, of a linen-silk blend, while the nara were a dark, tawny gold embroidered with green vines. So much work had gone into making these clothes, it surely wasn't possible that Ren Lithas had produced them on such short notice; not even with the aid of a whole shopful of assistants and apprentices. But then I recalled that the gold and green were Aeduria colours: more likely than not, Ren Lithas would've been instructed to start work on my marriage-gathering clothes long before anyone in Qi-Katai knew I was destined for Caethari instead of Laecia. The embroidery would've taken the most amount of time and could've been started beforehand; all they would've needed was my measurements.

Too late, I realised I'd been drifting again, and shot Markel an apologetic look. This time, his expression was one of concern alone.

Hands tentative, he asked, "Are you sure you're all right?"

I did him the courtesy of thinking before I answered. "Strangely enough, I think I am. A part of me thinks I shouldn't be, after Killic, but this . . . I think I'm looking forward to it. Does that seem odd?"

"Not at all," signed Markel, gracing me with a genuine smile. "I'd be more worried if you weren't looking forward to a party. Not counting those weeks of travel, I think this is the longest you've gone without attending a gathering of some kind since your father decided you were old enough to drink."

I laughed aloud at that; he was exaggerating, but not by much. "How's your side doing?"

"Better than it was. I stopped in with Ru Zairin earlier; thei did a healing cantrip and checked the stitches, which thei said are holding well, and gave me some painkillers to take at night, too, so it doesn't hurt when I move in my sleep."

"I'm so glad you recovered," I said, moving to squeeze his hand. Thus far, I'd managed not to dwell on the most terrifying *what if* of Ren Baru's actions, but the thought of having to do any of this without Markel . . . the concept rose up out of nowhere and threatened to choke me, and I knew he could read the unspoken fear in my face. "Please, don't go putting yourself in the way of any more blades on my account."

"You'd have done the same for me."

"Even so."

Markel's expression softened. "I'll do my best," he signed, then grinned. "It's hardly my favourite pastime."

"I'm very glad to hear it."

Just then, the bathroom door opened and Caethari called out, "Your turn!"

"Thank you!" I replied.

"Jewellery?" Markel asked, as I made to leave. "You really ought to wear something."

I grimaced. "We didn't bring much from Farathel, and most of that is silver. There might be a pair of gold earrings, though—can you have a look?"

"I'll do my best."

It would've been nice to luxuriate in the shower, but I was strung too tightly for it. I scrubbed and primped and overall took more care with myself than I had in days, including certain more intimate preparations whose inclusion, I told myself firmly, was merely routine, and no reflection on anything I might be thinking of doing. Once out, I towelled my hair so vigorously that my scalp tingled, then brushed it carefully, so that it would dry the way I wanted. In addition to the gift I'd bought Caethari, I'd also purchased some cosmetics and toiletries at the Jade Market; I was perfectly capable of applying skin-smoothing cream without supervision, but Markel was vastly more talented with makeup.

Wrapped in my towel, I slipped back to the bedroom and, for the first time in weeks, had Markel help me dress. It felt both right and comforting to have him act as my valet now, if only because the last time he'd been physically able to do so, I'd been too afraid to let him. It was soothing for the both of us: he helped me into my new good clothes, fastened the small gold earrings in my ears, rebrushed my hair and then had me sit on the end of the bed with my chin tipped up and my eyes closed as he carefully winged them with kohl. It was still a risqué thing in Farathel, for men to wear makeup, but at certain private gatherings and among friends, I'd allowed myself the indulgence and discovered a fondness for it, thanks in no small part to Markel's deft application.

When he was finished, he stepped back so I could see myself in the mirror. I inhaled, pleased and startled by the effect. I looked better than I had in days, and the simple drop earrings matched remarkably well with the golds in my Tithenai clothes.

"I've always said gold suits you more than silver," Markel signed, his expression smug.

"I like silver," I said, more out of habit than any present conviction. "You're right, though. It does suit me."

"Go out and show him, then." Markel glanced around the room, saw the gift still sitting on the bedspread and handed it to me. "And give him this, too."

"I will."

"Good. And now, if you'll excuse me, I need to go and get ready, too." He flashed a cocky grin. "Ru Telitha has agreed to accompany me, and I need to look presentable."

"I'll see you there," I said, and though I felt an odd pang to recall that Markel wouldn't be entering the party with me, it was reassurance enough to know that he'd still be in attendance.

I stood a moment, dithering, then forced myself to stop being ridiculous. Hands trembling slightly, I picked up the gift and headed out to the main room to wait for Caethari.

I didn't have to wait long: I'd barely sat down when he emerged from his own room, and I shot to my feet as the two of us stared at each other. I swallowed hard: his immaculate braid was wound through and bound with gold wire, while a single tear-shaped emerald set in gold dangled from his right ear. His clothes, like mine, were in Aeduria colours, but differently arranged: his undershirt was pale green, while his lin was made of stiff gold silk embroidered far more lavishly than my own, cut to emphasise the breadth of his chest and shoulders. It was longer than a typical lin, closer to the length of a Ralian tunic, and so was slit to the hip on each side, the better not to infringe on his freedom of movement. He was also wearing a belt, the butter-soft leather looped through dark green nara that were tucked into polished brown boots. He looked princely in a way that left me flustered, and so I was somewhat graceless as I stepped up and presented the small parcel to him.

"This is for you," I said, awkwardly. "A gift. A wedding gift of sorts, I suppose, though we're already married—you don't have to keep it if you'd rather not, but I thought—I wanted to get you something."

Caethari stared at me a moment, then took the parcel and unwrapped it. His eyes widened as he withdrew a jade-handled throwing knife in a sturdy leather sheath. The jade was clear green, the ring at the base cut and polished to a perfect loop, and when he removed it from the sheath, the leaf-shaped blade was bright steel, sharp along both edges. It was simple and beautiful, not something I'd expected to find at the Jade Market despite the namesake material, but after days of watching Caethari flip and twirl a knife whose balance was clearly *not* designed for throwing, I'd had to buy it for him.

"Velasin," he breathed. "This is exquisite." He met my gaze, searching my face for I knew not what. "Thank you."

I wanted to look away, make a joke, do anything to escape the sincerity of the moment, but what came out instead was, "I'm glad you like it."

"I'm going to wear it now," he said. I laughed, thinking he was joking, only to find that he was already attaching the sheath to his belt, positioning it so that the jade hilt showed like an ornament through the slit in his lin. "And yes," he said, getting in ahead of me, "I know I don't have to, just like you didn't have to buy it. But I want to."

"Thank you," I said, dumbly. I felt flushed, foolish, and suddenly far too cooped up in our apartments. "Shall we go? You'll need to lead me down, I might get lost if I go alone."

"Of course."

"Of course I'd get lost, or of course we'll go?"

"Why not both?" he said, and grinned as I tried and failed to come up with a witty reply.

The marriage-gathering was being held in the Gold Hall, which was, I'd been told, the main hall of the Aida and directly below the Garden Hall, though much grander in size and scale. I hadn't visited it before, and so took a moment to take in the splendour. It wasn't opulent by Farathel standards, but Farathel was a royal court, and I'd always thought its décor representative of a certain ugly vainglory. There were a few magelights here, in concession to the size of the space—these were placed mainly high up, in places where it would've been difficult to set and maintain candles—but neither these nor the bracketed torches were lit as yet, the afternoon sunlight still streaming in through tall glass windows.

The hall opened onto the Aida's main gardens, and it was through these double-doors that the guests would soon be arriving. Tables had been set up, including one on a dais that was meant for Clan Aeduria, with the centre of the floor left open for dancing, mingling and other such pleasant activities. There were flowers everywhere, spilling from vases, twining artfully around columns and braided into wreaths along the walls, a profusion of white and yellow blooms that filled the air with a sweet, pleasant scent. Liveried servants moved about adjusting place settings, and there was music, too—off in the corner, a trio of musicians were tuning their instruments, though they paused to bow when they realised I was watching them.

"This is beautiful," I murmured.

"I wish I could take the credit," Caethari replied, "but it's mostly Keletha, Riya and Laecia's doing."

"I'll be sure to thank them, then."

We made a circuit of the room, Caethari going out of his way to praise the arrangements to anyone he caught contributing to their upkeep. We were about to embark on a second lap when Tieren Halithar hailed us from across the hall. We both turned, and I did my best not to look visibly intimidated by my father-in-law.

"Everything running smoothly?" the tieren asked. Caethari confirmed that it was, and they went back and forth in that vein for a minute or two, as though each was reassuring the other that nothing had been omitted from plans to which, as best I could tell, neither of them had meaningfully contributed.

"We're not sure if the Ralian ambassador will make it," said the tieren, abruptly reclaiming my attention. "The last I heard, he was on his way from Qi-Xihan, so we felt it only proper to send an invite via the local embassy, but who knows if he'll arrive in time?" He snorted and clapped me hard on the shoulder. "Doubtless he's having a conniption over you wedding my son, but that's Ralians for you. Well, most Ralians, at least."

"Indeed," I said, hoping fervently that the Ralian ambassador, whoever he was, would be waylaid for the foreseeable future. It was possible that living in Tithena had altered his views on relations between members of the same sex, but that wasn't a theory I wanted to test in person.

The tieren moved to leave, then paused, his attention snagged by the throwing knife I'd gifted Caethari. Brows raised slightly, he said, "I know there's been some unhappy occurrences of late, but going armed to your own marriage-gathering seems a bit excessive."

"It was a gift from Velasin," Caethari replied, a clear note of pride in his voice.

Tieren Halithar's expression cleared instantly. "Ah, well. That's quite different, then," he said, and favoured me with an approving smile. "I'll leave the two of you be."

"What happens now?" I asked Caethari, as the musicians started to play a gentle, unfamiliar melody.

"We wait for the guests to arrive," he said, and for a mercy, we didn't have to wait long: Tithenai gatherings, unlike Farathel parties, were evidently punctual affairs, and within minutes, people began to trickle in through the doors to the garden, shepherded by the servants.

"Saints, here we go," Caethari muttered. I could feel him tense beside me, and on impulse I reached down and gave his hand a brief squeeze, withdrawing before he could do more than make a surprised, plaintive noise about it.

And then the guests were upon us, none of whom I knew—not of this first wave, at least—which meant that it fell to Caethari to introduce me, a task which, for whatever reason, he clearly found intimidating. Here were some of Qi-Katai's political leaders, officials whose posts derived from a mix of election, appointment and inheritance, but all of whom were responsible for various aspects of city governance. As such, they were technically subordinate to Tieren Halithar and thus to Clan Aeduria, but as I memorised names and ranks, shook hands and otherwise made small talk, I had the same intense sense of hierarchy, manoeuvring and dominion that had characterised my life in Farathel.

The familiarity of it almost made me laugh out loud, but I managed to restrain myself, savouring instead the delightful novelty of being introduced as a husband's husband to men who shared the title, or to women with wives, or to kemi of all inclinations, as well as those in what I couldn't help thinking of as more Ralian arrangements. There were guild leaders and merchants, too, whose political sway in the city was just as much as those of the officials I'd met; I realised it would likely take me years to understand all the tensions and histories to their relationships, exactly the sort of tangle I'd always loved to unravel, and I experienced an odd, delighted jolt to realise that years were exactly what I had.

As the silk merchant to whom we'd been speaking excused herself, Caethari's whole demeanour suddenly brightened. "Nairi!" he exclaimed, smiling at a tall, powerful woman with skin the gorgeous blue-black of deep twilight. She was dressed in red and white and accompanied by a trio of strangers whose mannerisms, even discounting their proximity to their rahan, would've marked them out as soldiers. "Come and meet my husband."

"So you're Velasin," she said, one perfect brow raised as she extended a hand. I shook it, noting both her calluses and the strength of her grip. "It's a pleasure to meet you. Don't call me rahan, it gives me hives from people who aren't in my revetha. Has he told you about Liran?"

"Nairi!" Caethari hissed, but I only laughed.

"I'm not sure what specific thing he ought to have mentioned, but I've met him, if that's what you're asking."

Nairi grinned. "It's a good start." She gestured to her fellow soldiers. "These are Dais Xani, Seluya and Kirit, who have promised to be on their very best behaviour."

"I promised nothing," said Dai Kirit, a lanky man with a wolfish grin. He tipped me a smile, then leaned in to embrace Caethari, the two of them slapping each other's backs. "Congratulations! If you had to wed a Ralian, at least you picked a handsome one."

"Please ignore Kirit, tiern," said Dai Xani, who wore a kem's green braid on the collar of thir lin. "He's an acquired taste, and you're under no obligation to acquire him for Cae's sake."

"This is slander!" said Dai Kirit, and promptly ducked as both Nairi and Seluya moved to cuff him about the head.

Their camaraderie worked wonders on Caethari's mood; his shoulders untensed, and for a precious few minutes, he was able to unbend from the formality of the evening to bicker with his friends, who seemed a pleasantly rowdy lot.

With the four of them distracted, Nairi lowered her voice and said to me, "Not to create a diplomatic incident, but if you ever break his heart, you and I will have an *encounter*."

I flushed all over, mouth gaping stupidly as I tried and failed to come up with a suitably witty reply that neither committed me to an impossible promise nor gave away my own feelings. Nairi watched me struggle, a slow smile spreading across her face, and I realised with a lurch that I'd already betrayed myself.

"*Ahh,*" she said, grinning. She didn't pat me on the shoulder, but she looked very much like she wanted to. "Well, I'm looking forward to our having a proper conversation at some point, but right now, there's too much wine in this blasted hall going tragically undrunk, which situation I am honour-bound to remedy. Excuse us, please." And with that, she somehow corralled all three of her dais, gave Caethari an affectionate punch in the shoulder and beelined towards the nearest drinks-bearing servant.

Caethari smiled to himself as they left, though there was something wistful in his expression, too.

"I like them," I said, and was unprepared for the way he beamed at me in response.

I was unprepared for most things about Caethari, it seemed, and had been since the first minute I'd set foot in Qi-Katai.

Markel and Ru Telitha arrived soon after, arm in arm. They made a fetching couple, and I refused to feel envious of the ease with which they leaned into each other, Ru Telitha to murmur in his ear or Markel to sign something back to her—evidently, she'd become more proficient in the language than I'd expected after their time in the infirmary, though I noted he still carried his slate and pen. We welcomed them both, and Markel winked at me as they moved to enter the throng of guests, which cheered me greatly.

Next came Riya, Laecia, Yasa Kithadi and Keletha, as imposing a familial quartet as I'd ever seen. The yasa was resplendent in a jewel-strewn, dove-grey halik—a more lavish, dress-like alternative to a lin that fell in panels from hip to ankle—over silk nara, with a slim coronet of braided wire set with diamonds atop her head. Keletha was more modestly dressed by contrast, as was thir preference, but for once thei wore the same colours as thir twin, and both wore their hair in a braided knot, coiled cleverly at their napes. Laecia wore a pale blue halik over dark blue nara, while Riya wore a red lin over red nara and a pristine white undershirt, her dark hair loose within a jeweled net.

Yasa Kithadi looked me over, lip twitching with what I hoped was approval. "You clean up nicely," she said.

"I aim to please," I replied.

The yasa laughed at this—and then, to my utter astonishment, she leaned in and embraced me.

"Look after him," she murmured, voice pitched for my ears alone. She hugged Caethari next, though whether she said anything to him, too, I couldn't tell; I was too preoccupied by a small internal crisis. It wasn't her words that had shocked me—it was, after all, a perfectly reasonable request to make of a grandchild's new spouse—but rather the abrupt realisation that this was all *real;* that I was *married to Caethari,* an Aeduria in truth. In much the same way that my nerves had fixed on the marriage-gathering as being more like a wedding than the vows we'd already sworn, apparently some inner Ralian instinct measured the validity of a marriage against the approval of dowagers, and all at once, I was suffused with feelings I scarcely knew how to manage.

As Riya and Laecia embraced me in turn, each calling me *brother,* I found myself on the verge of tears, though whether they were happy or sad or hysteric, I had no idea, as I was able to keep myself from shedding them. Yet something of my struggle must've been transparent to Keletha, who gripped my hands in lieu of a hug and said, simply, "We are glad to have you."

I must've managed some polite reply, but whatever it was vanished from my memory as soon as it left my tongue. My new kin moved on, and I experienced a sudden giddying confusion as everything I'd been told about the order of events flew out of my head like papers caught in a gust of wind.

"What happens next?" I hissed to Caethari.

"Once everyone has been welcomed, the guests mingle for a bit, and then—" He sighed. "—I have to give my speech. And after that, we're both fair game for kissing."

"Bring on the kissing," I muttered.

Caethari made a choked noise.

The next guests were local nobility, an even balance between those of an age with Caethari and me, and those who were friends and allies of Tieren Halithar.

"I wonder if Riya will ask any of the clans about paternity negotiations," Caethari mused. "I'd assumed she would've approached the local families already, but she might've been holding off until now."

"You'll have to ask her later," I said, and was immediately distracted from whatever reply I might've received by the arrival of Liran, who was waving at the pair of us. His locs were twisted up and back to form a fan-tail shape, and his halik was yellow, patterned with beaded flowers in red, blue and orange.

"You look a perfect matched set," he said, taking both our hands at once. "I'd paint you, if I had the time and tools."

"Another day," Caethari promised. "We need to get a portrait done at some point, anyway."

Liran's eyes, which were lined with kohl and dusted with gold across the lids, widened. "Velasin hasn't even seen my work yet!" He smacked Caethari's shoulder. "He might not like my style! Which would wound me terribly if so, but you still can't go promising to let me paint the both of you if he'd prefer a different artist! Honestly, Cae, stop being so dictatorial."

Caethari flushed at this, and didn't relax until Liran laughed to show he was teasing. "You simply are too easy to rile up, you know that? Oh! There's Nairi, I haven't seen her in an age. And Kirit! He's always fun, even if he is tragically uninterested in men." He squeezed our hands again, grinned and stepped back. "I'll see you both later. Remember to breathe, hmm?"

"Saints," Caethari muttered, casting a longing glance towards the wine. "This is exhausting. Why is this exhausting?"

"Because people are exhausting," I said, not without sympathy, and nudged him as yet more guests I didn't know approached us.

By the time we were done greeting this latest group of arrivals, my head was swimming with the number of new names and titles I'd absorbed in so short a period. As such, I nearly wilted with relief when Tieren Halithar approached and informed us that, bar the Ralian ambassador, who'd come late if he came at all, everyone who'd been expected to arrive was now present. This, finally, left us free to move throughout the gathering instead of standing in place like a pair of mechanical statues. We both made straight for the wine, sharing a relieved grin as we each took a glass, and within moments, Caethari had gone in search of Nairi and their fellow soldiers, while I did the same for Markel.

Much to my amusement, I found him smiling quietly as Ru Telitha, who was in on the joke, "translated" for a small group of Tithenai nobles, all of whom were intent on boasting to him about the wonders of Qi-Katai. We exchanged a look of private amusement and, seeing that both he and Ru Telitha were enjoying themselves, I slipped away before the nobles could be distracted by my presence. I caught sight of Liran, but he was having what looked to be a private, serious conversation with Riya, so I turned aside and, after exchanging some meaningless pleasantries with those I passed, made my way back to Caethari and his soldiers.

While it doubtless would've been more politic for me to ingratiate myself with the various nobles, guild leaders, merchants and politicians to whom I'd been introduced, I judged that there'd be plenty of time for that later. Nairi greeted me warmly, and I was soon included in the cheerful back-and-forth, with Kirit only too happy to explain their various in-jokes.

It made for such pleasant company that I soon lost track of time, and was therefore caught by surprise when the music stopped and Tieren Halithar called the hall to attention, thanking the attendees for coming and announcing that, in accordance with tradition, Caethari would now give a short speech welcoming me to Clan Aeduria.

I'd known it was coming, but I still flushed to be the centre of attention as, surrounded by applauding mostly-strangers, Caethari led me up to the dais, stood me beside him and began to speak.

33

The first part of Caethari's speech was much what I'd expected: a reiteration of the thanks his father had already extended to the guests, praise for the work gone into organising the gathering itself and an acknowledgement of the diplomatic underpinnings of our marriage, including the hope of improved relations between Ralia and Tithena in the future. I'd heard many such speeches over the years and allowed myself to relax into the rhythm of it, relieved to be spoken about more in the abstract than the specific—until, suddenly, Caethari's tone turned playful.

"Of course, we must acknowledge that my marrying Velasin was not the *original* plan." This won an amused murmur of laughter. "While I hope our union is equally honoured in Ralia as a diplomatic link, I will bear no grudge if it takes my husband's kinsfolk a little time to acclimate. But a little time only; for if they do not acclimate—or rather, do not try—I will be forced to pity them." He paused, then said, with a degree of genuine feeling that made me blush to the roots of my hair, "I would pity anyone who doesn't see Velasin's value. He is extraordinary."

He said this last softly, with a glance at me, as though we were speaking privately and not on display to a room full of people. My skin burned so hot, it was like I'd been stood in the midday sun, and in this flustered state, I was utterly unprepared for Keletha to step smoothly forwards, as thei'd evidently been waiting to do, and hand Caethari a small, cloth-wrapped parcel.

"Velasin," he said, and my name in his mouth was a benediction, "with this gift, though it cannot hope to approximate your worth, I welcome you to Clan Aeduria."

He held out the parcel flat on his palms. I unwrapped it, dry-mouthed, and became no less overwhelmed on seeing what it contained.

"Moons," I whispered, lifting the piece with trembling hands. It was a necklace of exquisite craftsmanship, quite easily the single most expensive thing I'd ever held. It was six layers of overlapping rings in a repeating pattern of gold, rose gold and platinum, with each layer one ring larger than the last. This meant that, rather than repeating identically along the vertical, the pattern shifted one spot over each time, creating a rippled effect like the iridescent sheen on scales. The outermost layer was fringed in a similarly alternating pattern of diamonds, pearls and flawless dark green jade, and only then did I see that there were matching earrings, too, still held on Caethari's palms, each consisting of three loops—one of each metal—from which dripped a single diamond, a single pearl and a single piece of jade.

Such a treasure would not have been an unfitting gift for a monarch—or, I suddenly realised, for the daughter of a yasa. Green, white, gold: the colours of Clan Aeduria. A single glance at Yasa Kithadi, who looked almost as shocked to see the jewels as I was to receive them, told me that these had originally belonged to the former Tierena Inavi. A treasure made to honour the clan she'd ended up leaving, and which her only son had now passed to me.

From the ripple of astonishment that went through the room, I wasn't the only one to understand the significance of the gift.

"It's beautiful," I said, which was a helpless understatement—and then, in a fit of madness, "May I wear it now?"

"Of course," said Caethari, voice rough with feeling. Carefully, so carefully, he swapped the earrings into my care and took the necklace, holding it spread between his hands. I was scarcely breathing as he came to stand beside me, alive to every brush of his skin against my hair, my cheek, as he raised the necklace over my head and drew it closed. I could feel his hitched breath against my nape as he fastened the clasp, and then he was in front of me, eyes fixed on mine as he removed the gold earrings Markel had affixed earlier and replaced them with the matching pair. The whole process couldn't have taken more than half a minute, and yet it felt infinitely longer, my throat swallowing and swallowing as his hands and fingertips brushed against my neck, ears, jaw.

"You should keep these safe," he murmured, pressing my original earrings into my hand.

I nodded, not trusting myself to speak, and almost jumped out of my skin when the whole room began to applaud, with one or two whistles thrown in for good measure. I laughed, half shocked and half embarrassed to have behaved so brazenly before an audience—and yet that was the point, wasn't it?

"And now," said Keletha, thir warm voice ringing through the room, "we shall see if the newlyweds can be tempted away from each other!"

A gale of laughter and yet more applause followed this remark, which I understood to be the traditional wording used to start the being-kissed-by-strangers portion of the evening. I felt light-headed and oversensitized, like I'd drunk too much wine in the sun on an empty stomach, and every glance at Caethari as we stepped down from the dais felt more heated than the last.

The music started up again, much livelier now, and before I knew it the crowd was lining up to dance in the generous space between the tables. I hung back, recognising the tune but uncertain whether the steps I'd learned in Ralia would translate here, but Caethari had no such compunctions, flashing me a grin as he stood up opposite Kirit.

I soon realised that the primary difference between Ralian dancing and Tithenai dancing was in the lack of gender segregation: the steps were largely the same, but where I was accustomed to seeing men on one side, ladies on the other, here the lines formed according to whichever person most wanted to dance which part, which I found delightful.

I watched Caethari dance two rounds, partnering alternately with Kirit and Nairi, before I ventured to join in myself. I ended up across from one of the young nobles, and though this dance had a few Tithenai variations I wasn't prepared for, I managed not to completely disgrace myself.

As I was returning to the fringes, Nairi caught me by the arm, grinned broadly, and called out to the room at large, "Witness, a temptation!" And then she leaned in and kissed me—not deeply, but a generous press of closed lips to mine, and I flushed to my newly ornamented ears as everyone cheered around us.

I cast around for Caethari and found him watching me from across the room. Heat coiled low in my gut at the look on his face, and something similar must've shown in my expression, too, for even at a distance, I could swear his eyes darkened. We were so preoccupied with each other, in fact, that I was equally as surprised as him when Xani popped up by his side, yelled "Witness, a temptation!" and stood on tiptoe to haul Caethari down for a smacking kiss. Everyone hooted once more, and then the dancing resumed as if nothing extraordinary had happened—but of course, by Tithenai standards, it hadn't.

I rejoined the festivities in a pleasant daze, helping myself to more wine along the way. As though I were a compass needle and he my north, I never lost my awareness of where in the room Caethari was, but anticipation was evidently a spice we both desired, for neither of us sought the other out. Dutiful, social spouse that I was, I used the time to ingratiate myself with nobles, politicians and merchants alike, employing the best of my Farathel charm and manners as I moved through the gathering, dancing here or talking there, learning the interplay of my new situation. I took note of which people were kind to Markel, and which dismissive; of who tried to rattle my Ralian sensibilities with facts or questions they thought would shock—including, to my deep annoyance, one tipsy ciet who leaned in far too close to tell me about Liran being metem—and who was welcoming.

As the music changed and I exited one conversation in search of another, I caught sight of Markel and Ru Telitha approaching Caethari. I grinned, thinking to join them, and so was taken by surprise when Ru Telitha called out, "Witness, a temptation!"

But it wasn't Ru Telitha who stepped into Caethari's space. It was Markel.

I lost my breath, staring in equal parts envy and wonder as my best friend placed a hand on Caethari's jaw and leaned up to kiss him—not a chaste kiss, such as Nairi had given me, or a comedic one, such as Xani's had been, but a proper kiss, sweet and compelling enough that Caethari closed his eyes and leaned into it. Markel lingered before drawing back, a sly smile on his face as the room once more erupted into cheers. Caethari looked stunned, and as I approached, I saw him sign to Markel, "Surprising!"

"It seemed fitting," Markel replied. And then, glancing at me as I came close, "Besides, I'd be lying if I said I'd never been curious."

"Markel!" I exclaimed, as Ru Telitha started giggling. And then, in signs, "You finally kiss a man, and it isn't me? I'm heartbroken."

"You're not my type," signed Markel, grinning as he winked.

I made an indignant noise in response to that, and though I'd meant it in good humour, Markel's expression instantly softened into concern.

"I'm sorry. Should I not have done it?"

"No, no! I'm not at all offended. And it was fitting, as you say." I smiled at him. "You just surprised me, that's all."

"I think I might've surprised myself, to be honest."

"Truly?"

"What can I say? He's got a nice mouth."

"Markel!" I exclaimed again, and then we were both laughing, my hand on his shoulder as he wheezed silently while I very near cackled.

"Please tell me I'm not being ridiculed," Caethari said, almost plaintively.

"You're not being ridiculed," I replied. "Quite the opposite, in fact."

"Oh!" he said, pleased. "Well. That's all right, then."

"I'm glad we meet with your approval."

"You do," said Caethari, and the note of warmth in his voice made me shiver pleasantly.

"I'll take that as my cue, then," said Liran, materialising beside me as if from nowhere. I swallowed, heart pounding, as he crooked a finger beneath my chin and called out, "Witness, a temptation!"

He leaned in, and I'm not ashamed to say I was quickly rendered breathless. His kiss was teasing, gentle but by no means tame, and when I dared to return it a little, I felt him smile against my mouth.

"He's all yours," he murmured as we broke apart.

The crowd cheered anew, and over the clapping and whistles I once more heard Keletha's voice ring out like a bell: "Temptation has been offered! Will we see it answered?"

"We will," said Caethari, stepping up to claim the space that Liran had smoothly vacated.

For a moment, we simply looked at each other. The breathlessness I'd felt before was nothing to what I experienced now. I could feel my pulse in my throat, my tongue; every inch of my skin was sensitized. Caethari's dark eyes were deep as wells; I saw his breath hitch, and I had one last moment in which to be achingly conscious of his beauty before he cupped my face with both hands, tilted my chin up and kissed me.

I made a noise in the back of my throat and grabbed his lin for purchase. It was a deep kiss, hungry and just the right side of bruising; I melted into it, kissing back as I clung to him. One hand skated up my cheek, his fingers threading through my hair in a way that shifted the angle between us. I felt him pull back and, forgetting our audience, chased his mouth with my own, pulling him to me with both hands. His thumb brushed along my jaw, hand fluttering down to rest half on the necklace he'd given me, half on the column of my throat.

Around us, the crowd burst into cheers, though I was scarcely conscious of them despite the noise. I sucked Caethari's lip between my teeth and felt him shudder, releasing him only as he pressed our foreheads together. We were both unsteady, moored only to each other; I wanted to kiss him again and again, and might've done, if I hadn't heard someone say, "Oh! The Ralian ambassador made it, after all!"

Sighing, I smiled at Caethari and inwardly braced to deal with my unknown countryman, whose reaction might be anything from baffled worry to outrage. I turned, scanning the crowd for Ralian clothes, and caught a flash of familiar patterns in my peripheral vision. I moved to track them—and froze, mouth open on words that wouldn't come, as I recognised Killic, now close enough to touch.

"*No,*" I gasped, "Killic, no—"

He shoved me aside so violently that I crashed into Markel, knocking him to the ground. I barely kept my footing, grabbing blindly to stay upright as Killic reached Caethari, reaching whip-fast into his pocket. Caethari saw him, eyes widening in horrified recognition, and stepped back just in time to avoid the terrible swing of Killic's small but wickedly sharp punch-knife. Someone screamed, space clearing as Killic swung and swung again, Caethari stepping away each time with reflexes honed through his combat patterns. Unarmed as he was, he couldn't mount a counterattack—

But he wasn't unarmed. The knife I'd given him hung at his belt, forgotten in the chaos. Guards were coming—I could hear the distant clatter of arms—but all it would take was a single blow, a single slice—

Caethari backed up beside me, arms raised to show he meant no harm—Killic's face was a snarl, contorted with animal rage—and in the moment where Killic's swing whistled past, I snatched the blade from Caethari's belt and lunged forwards. I had no real training in close combat, but I knew how to mercy-kill a hound, and it was this instinct that guided my hand to angle the blade upwards; to put all my weight behind it and brace as Killic's own momentum combined with my strike to drive it in to the hilt.

A terrible silence. Killic's face twisted, anger and pain becoming furious shock as he realised I'd been the one to stick him. My hand trembled; I could feel his blood on my fingers, and it was this sensation that provoked an even worse reflexive action: I yanked the blade out.

My hand spasmed open. The jade knife clattered against the floor. Blood gushed from Killic's unplugged wound as freely as if I'd tapped a spigot.

"Bastard," Killic whispered. "He swore you'd be unarmed."

And then, face visibly whitening, he dropped to his knees, swayed awkwardly and collapsed sideways, blood pooling where he lay.

I staggered back, hands shaking. Where was Caethari? I whirled and grabbed him by the shoulders, heedless of the blood on my hands. "Are you all right? Did he cut you?"

"Velasin." Voice raw, Caethari gripped my arms in turn. "Are *you* all right?"

"*Did he cut you?*"

"No, he didn't. I'm fine." He smoothed his shaking hands through my hair, and I realised both that I was hyperventilating, and that I'd switched instinctively to Ralian.

The arrival of the guards startled me; I would've jumped if not for Caethari's grip. Instead, I watched Tars Katvi and Raeki usher the shocked guests back—but as Raeki reached for the punch-knife, I wrenched away from Caethari, found my Tithenai and blurted, "Don't touch that!"

Raeki froze, turning to look at me in clear confusion. "Tiern?"

"The blade," I said, the words feeling thick and strange on my tongue. "I think the blade is poisoned." In the moment, I didn't know where this certainty came from; only that it felt true enough to be terrifying.

Raeki's expression darkened; Caethari swore, while the crowd began to murmur anew. I stared at Killic; at the terrible, sluggish seep of blood from his chest.

"Ru Zairin," I said, and this time it was Tar Katvi's attention I caught. "For Killic, someone should call Ru Zairin—"

"He's already dead, tiern."

The world swooped sideways like a sparrow evading a hawk's grasp. "What?"

"He's dead," Tar Katvi repeated, a terrible sympathy in her eyes. "You struck him cleanly, tiern. Right through the heart."

"No," I said, staring at Killic's—not his body, it couldn't be his *body*—I'd wished him ill, I'd wished him consequences, but not this, not death, not death at *my hand*—

Caethari's hand landed on my shoulder. I whirled at the touch, and suddenly my throat was tight almost to the point of tears.

"I'm sorry," I rasped. "I'm sorry, I didn't mean—I was scared for you, I thought—I didn't—"

Caethari swore and gathered me up, pressing a kiss to my forehead. I shut my eyes and leaned against him, feeling the reassuring thump of his heart where our bodies met.

"No apologies," Caethari murmured. "You did nothing wrong."

I pulled back and rested a hand on his cheek—an unimaginable intimacy just days ago, and yet touching him now felt nearly as vital as breathing. I ran my fingertips over his jaw, my free hand stroking worriedly along his arm, oblivious to the red I left in my wake. "He truly didn't cut you?"

"Not even a nick." He curled a loop of hair behind my ear. "What made you think the blade was poisoned?"

"He's done it before," I said, voice shaky. "Not—not to commit murder—not so far as I know, at least—but he told me once, before a duel, he sometimes edged his blade with a substance to make wounds more painful, harder to heal. I was horrified; he promised he rarely did it, and only to those who truly deserved the punishment, that men like us should make every possible effort to stay alive, even if it meant breaking the rules, but—" I swallowed, unable to look at Killic's body. "That punch-knife is so little. It's unlike him, not to look for an extra advantage. Would've been, I mean."

"You knew this man?" said a hard voice, sudden enough to startle me. It was Tieren Halithar, his face thunderous. "For he is most assuredly *not* the Ralian ambassador."

"Father," said Caethari, gulping. "I think we should speak in private."

34

With what remained of our marriage-gathering left in the more-than-capable hands of Keletha and Yasa Kithadi, and after announcing to the guests—boldly, I thought—that all would be taken care of soon, Tieren Halithar led us out of the hall and across to an empty office of some sort. He shut the door, then stood before us with his arms crossed.

"Explain," he said.

The question was directed at Caethari, but I forced myself to answer instead. Killic was—had been—my burden, and though I cringed to explain him to my father-in-law, the dead body I'd left on the floor of his hall said I owed him the truth of the matter.

"The—dead man is Lord Killic vin Lato," I said. The words came out calm, but I felt as though I were standing half a foot behind my own body, growing incrementally more distant with each word spoken. "He was once my lover, but he betrayed me. I left him. When my father called me home to discuss my betrothal, Killic followed. He—accosted me, in the gardens. Keletha saw us, but didn't know I'd been forced to it. He's why thei betrothed me to Cae instead of Laecia. I thought he'd fled back to Farathel, but he would've been ruined there. He came here instead. Dai Mirae found him at Vaiko; he'd been captured by the same bandits who attacked our party. But having him here . . ."

I faltered, unable to continue, and Caethari quickly took over. "He acted as though he'd never harmed Velasin," he said, the words coming fast and angry. "As though he still had a claim on him. Velasin knew he could've punished him under Tithenai law, but he didn't want their history known, nor did he want to risk a diplomatic incident with Ralia. So instead, we kept him here a day, and I branded him a rapist, in the Ralian fashion."

"*Branded* him?"

"On his hand, with a soldering pen." Caethari sounded exhausted. "Yesterday, Tar Raeki had him escorted to the gates of Qi-Katai. We thought him gone, but—" He gestured helplessly.

"Zo's sainted ballsack." The tieren ran a hand down his face. "So this was what—revenge? A lone man's twisted payback?"

"Yes," said Caethari.

"No," I said, belatedly thunderstruck. Father and son both stared at me, and I realised too late that only I had heard Killic's dying words, the significance of which hadn't registered until now. "When I—as he fell, he said, *He swore you'd be unarmed.* He got in by pretending to be the Ralian ambassador, but how did he get his hands on the invitation? How did he know to come at all?"

"Someone put him up to it," said Caethari. It wasn't quite a question, though I could tell he badly wished there was room for doubt.

"Specifically," said the tieren, "a man put him up to it."

"Or a kem," I said. "Killic doesn't understand the difference. Or wouldn't have, I mean."

A short pause followed, as none of us wanted to be the one to say what we were all thinking. It was Caethari who broke first, rubbing both hands across his face.

"This is the same person, isn't it. Who's been behind everything so far."

The tieren grunted. "It's a hell of a coincidence otherwise."

"At least now we know they're a man," I quipped, making a thin, transparently poor attempt at false cheer. "Or a kem, I suppose. That's more than we knew this morning."

"We know more than that, though," said Caethari, slowly. "Hardly anyone knew Killic was in Qi-Katai, let alone his connection to you, and only some of that group were men."

"Who?" the tieren demanded.

"The guards who returned from Vaiko with Dai Mirae, and the few who guarded him overnight. Tar Raeki, too, and potentially Ru Zairin, though I shudder to suspect either of them. It's possible some of the gossip got out, but that's still a good starting point."

"Our own guard is *not* a good starting point," the tieren growled. I flinched, thinking he was wroth with us, but he gave a weary shake of his head to indicate his anger was aimed elsewhere. "I've no more wish than you to distrust Tar Raeki, but under the circumstances, I'll put the investigation into Tar Katvi's hands."

"We should requestion Varu Shan Dalu, too," I ventured. "He can't have been the one to recruit Killic—he was locked up the whole time—but if they were both used by the same person, it might be a way to get him to talk."

The tieren's reply was forestalled by a knock on the door. "Enter!" he barked, his long braid swishing irritably, and in came Tars Katvi and Raeki. Both bowed, and when the tieren commanded, "Report!," it was Tar Katvi who spoke.

"The hall has been cleaned and the assailant's body taken to the mortuary," she said. "A cursory examination of his weapon suggests that Tieren Velasin's suspicions were correct: there is something on the blade, though Ru Zairin will have to analyze it to determine what, precisely, the substance is."

"*Fuck,*" I whispered, grabbing blindingly for Caethari's hand. He squeezed my fingers, and for a moment all I could hear was the pounding of blood in my ears. I hadn't wanted to be right, and having my panic confirmed was like watching the punch-knife whistle past my husband's vulnerable neck all over again. *He could've died. I could've lost him.*

"Have thim do it," the tieren said, sparing me a flash of concern. Tar Katvi bowed acknowledgement, and Tieren Halithar cut his gaze to Raeki, who smartly picked up the telling.

"The assailant—Lord Killic vin Lato—entered through the main gates of the Aida. He was, indeed, carrying the invitation Envoy Keletha sent to the Ralian ambassador, though how he came by it is yet to be determined. He was admitted the same as any other guest, albeit late, but as my guards had already been apprised of the ambassador's circumstances, no suspicion was aroused by this."

"Who sent word that the ambassador would be late?" I cut in, directing the question to Tieren Halithar. A terrible thought had occurred to me. "We've been working on the assumption that some anti-Ralian Tithenai faction is behind all this, as the early attacks were painted as such, but the invocation of the Wild Knife was always a distraction. What if we've got it backwards, and the real objection is Ralian—some faction within the court or such that doesn't want this alliance?" I swallowed, hating how plausible it suddenly felt. "My marrying Laecia would've been one thing, if there were factions opposed to mending the rift, but a union like this, between two men . . . far too many Ralians would view it as an insult. An outrage. Moons, we don't even know what King Markus thinks of it!" My chest tightened at the thought. "If His Majesty took this marriage as an insult, depending on the politics of how it was received at court, he wouldn't necessarily act against us in the open."

"But what of the timing?" Caethari countered. "Even mage-sent messages aren't instantaneous. News would have to pass from your father to Farathel, from Farathel to who knows where else in Ralia, and from there to Qi-Katai."

"You forget, it took me a fortnight to get here," I replied. "I was on the move before you ever knew I was meant for you; the same could be equally true of any Ralian action. But involving King Markus, that's pure speculation on my part. A factional objection is far more likely, especially if it was orchestrated by Ralians already present in Tithena. Consider: everything that's happened—everything since I first arrived in Qi-Katai—if you strip away the trappings, the unifying theme is trying to disrupt our marriage. To first scare me away by making me think you wanted me dead, and only then by striking at you directly."

I turned back to Tieren Halithar. "Sir, the . . . the circumstances

I related to you, of Killic being seen with me—even if it didn't explain why I'd been sent to Caethari instead of Laecia, it's the kind of scandal that soon grows wings. If the Ralian ambassador knew of it, or if his staff did, and if they were already looking to disrupt the alliance . . . Killic was turned loose at the gates of Qi-Katai, but what if he sought out the ambassador's residence, looking for aid? He could've spun any tale he chose about being branded unjustly, exiled unfairly, and he would've made the perfect tool: disposable, motivated and so clearly possessed of his own agenda that his actions could be written off as those of a lone agitator—a man seeking vengeance, as you said yourself."

"Ruya's grace," Caethari swore.

The tieren's face was a stormcloud. "These are not accusations to be levelled lightly," he said. "Ru Daro has heard nothing of this, but as you say, it would of necessity be subtle, and his inquiries have been directed elsewhere. A Ralian faction acting against the interests of its monarch is one thing; but if King Markus is himself involved, after all his talk of reparations—" He broke off, hands clenching in silent fury. He was silent for a moment, and when he spoke again, it was through gritted teeth. "Tar Katvi. Have my envoy and the yasa kept the guests in good humour?"

"Aye, tieren," she replied. "The tieras helped the envoy put it about that Lord Killic was a jilted lover, and if I may speak frankly, I'd say the crowd is loving the gossip. It's been a while since anything this exciting happened at a marriage-gathering."

To my great surprise, Tieren Halithar chuckled. "That business with Ciet Madani's secret common-born lover and her little twins; I remember. What a scandal!"

I looked at Caethari. "Forgive me, but I suspect I'm being Ralian again. What, precisely, was the scandal?"

Caethari grinned. "That he pledged to provide for his children and then did not, while also failing to mention either them or their mother in his betrothal contracts. His new bride was furious; she dissolved the marriage on the spot—she had clear cause to level fault and did so—and took both the lover and her children into her household. Last I heard, they were courting each other." He raised a brow at me. "I take it that's not how things would go in Ralia?"

"Very much not," I said, "but I like this version better."

"Well then!" said Tieren Halithar, clapping his hands. "Caethari, Velasin—let's get you cleaned up and back out there, hm?"

I made a face like a guppy out of water. "What?"

"Back to the marriage-gathering," he said. "You've hours still to go, and the tars can take care of things in the meantime. Oh, speaking of which"—he turned back to Tar Katvi—"have someone interview Varu Shan Dalu, will you? See if he might know anything about this Ralian link, or if he knows who might've involved Lord Killic."

"Of course, tieren."

Raeki looked slightly discomforted at this. "Respectfully, tieren, Varu Shan Dalu is part of my investigation. Shouldn't my people see to his questioning?"

"I want your people running extra perimeters and watching the gates," the tieren replied. "For all we know, Lord Killic was only one gambit; if anything else tries to disrupt this gathering, I want it stopped."

"Of course, tieren."

"But first," said Tieren Halithar, "I'd be obliged if one of you could procure some wash-water for my son-in-law."

"I'll do it," Raeki said.

As both tars bowed and exited, the tieren stepped forwards and clapped both Caethari and I on the shoulder. "One last question," he said, looking at his son. "Did you truly forget you were armed in there?"

"I didn't," Caethari admitted, with an ease that made the breath catch in my throat. "But I thought it would've made for a poor diplomatic showing if *I* was the one to strike at Killic. I'd thought to keep him at bay until the guards showed up—" He glanced at me, gaze softening in response to my distress. "—but I would've slain him in a heartbeat if I'd known his blade was fouled."

"Good," said the tieren brusquely. "I believe the yasa has your knife, by the way; a truly beautiful piece. Your husband has a good eye."

And with that, he left the room.

In the silence that followed, I looked blankly at Caethari. "Are we truly to go back out there?"

"If you'd rather not—"

I shook my head. "That's not it. I'm just . . . *surprised* doesn't seem to cover it, but I'm not sure what other word fits."

"If something akin to this had happened in Ralia, would the gathering be disbanded?"

"Moons, I don't know." I managed a scrap of laughter. "Probably not, if nobody too important was hurt and there was only the one assailant. Excitement makes for good gossip everywhere. It just . . . feels surreal, somehow."

I jumped as Raeki unceremoniously returned, bearing a washcloth and a bowl of water. I watched, nonplussed, as he set them carefully on the desk, bowed silently to the pair of us and bustled out again.

"What—?"

"Dear Velasin," Caethari said, both soft and sad. "You still have blood on your hands."

I froze in place, staring mutely at my palms, which were indeed tacky with Killic's blood—not much of it, but enough to be noticeable, and far more than I ever wanted to touch again. I was suddenly shaking, my breath too fast as I recalled the wet-crackle *skrnch* of the knife penetrating Killic's chest. It wasn't the same as I'd felt at Vaiko, killing the men who'd ridden at us; this was different, a bloodier intimacy than I'd ever cared to experience. For all that Killic had hurt me, he'd been my lover, too; and still I'd killed him. Not in cold blood, not quite, but up close and unhesitating in a manner of which I hadn't thought myself capable.

Something soft touched my hand, damp and warm. It jolted me out of my terrible thoughts, and there was Caethari, poised and ready with the washcloth.

"Let me?" he asked.

I nodded, reduced to mute sensation as he slowly, tenderly cleaned the blood from my hands. I was thrown back in time to the death of Ren Baru, when I'd performed the same service for him, and at that thought my breathing quickened for reasons other than fear. We were echoing each other, caught in some strange, impossible loop. I watched him as he washed me clean, and when he was done, I silently took the cloth from him and dabbed away the bloody marks my worried hands had left on his face and throat. It would've taken more laundering skills than I possessed to fully remove the staining from his pale green undershirt, but I did my best, only stopping when Caethari reached up and gently squeezed my wrist.

"That's enough," he said, voice rough. "They're only marks."

I shook my head, though I let him guide my hand away. "It's his blood. He shouldn't get to touch any part of you."

Caethari inhaled sharply, and all at once I was done with pretending. I dropped the cloth and grabbed his neck, pulling him in for a desperate kiss. I was hungry for comfort, for proof that we were both unharmed, and he met that hunger with need of his own, until we were grasping at each other, gasping at the power of both touching and being touched.

"We should stop," Caethari panted, kissing up my neck. "We need to stop, or I'm going to debauch you on some poor clerk's desk."

"Who says you get to do the debauching?" I squeezed the meat of his thigh and shuddered as he groaned in response. Neither of us, of course, was going to get undressed in a clerk's office barely one room away from a gathering full of friends and family, but the desire I felt—the raw wanting, all at once, to put my hands on as much of Caethari's skin as he would let me—was such that it almost felt like an option. *Like drinking salt water for lack of fresh,* some foolish part of me thought, and the comparison was odd enough that I broke off laughing, pressing my face against Caethari's lin.

"What's funny?" he asked, smoothing my hair away from my face.

"Nothing," I said, and smiled at him. "You're right. We do need to get back out there."

He sighed. "I detest being right."

I kissed his cheek by way of apology, straightened my lin—which had become somewhat rucked by the proceedings—and took his hand with more daring than confidence.

"Lead on, then," I said, and Caethari obliged me.

The corridor was empty, but the second we reentered the hall, we were greeted with raucous cheering from the guests. Not knowing what else to do, I sketched an awkward bow and was met with laughter—not the mocking sort, but the kind that invited me to join in.

"Let the gathering continue!" Tieren Halithar called, and as the crowd cheered again, the music switched to something wild and celebratory that had everyone scrambling to re-form the dancing lines.

As a space cleared around us, Markel rushed up to me, trailed by Ru Telitha, Liran, Nairi and her dais.

"Are you all right?" he signed, expression just this side of frantic. "They wouldn't let us out to see you, but that was Killic. Are you well?"

"I'm well," I replied—and then, aloud, in Tithenai, for the benefit of our other listeners, "I won't say it wasn't unpleasant, and I'll doubtless have to process it all later, but for now, I'm fine. I swear it."

Markel stared at me a moment, gauging the sincerity of my expression—after everything I'd concealed from him since we left Ralia, I couldn't begrudge him a whit of his suspicions—until, with a sigh of relief, he relaxed.

"I'm glad," he signed. "My only regret is not having killed him for you."

It was bizarrely touching, and very Markel. "I appreciate the sentiment," I signed back, and he gave a firm, pleased nod.

As Caethari began to offer verbal reassurances of a similar nature to the other concerned listeners, I turned aside and signed a quick summation of the conversation we'd had with Tieren Halithar, including my unpleasant suspicions regarding Ralian involvement. Markel's expression darkened at this, and by the time I was done, his shoulders were once more tense.

"It makes far more sense than I'd like it to," he signed, hands sharp with anger. "Fucking Farathel games! I should've known they'd follow us here."

"We don't know for sure it's Ralia; it's only a theory."

"A compelling theory, though, and one that fits." He straightened. "I'll keep my ears open, see if I can catch anything."

"I'd appreciate that," I said aloud, relieved.

He rolled his eyes at me. "You say that as if it were ever in question." And then, all at once, his expression turned sly. "Besides which, if I spend the evening roaming the Aida and then borrow a bed in the infirmary, nobody will think it odd. It's natural that I'd give the two of you privacy."

The heat which had not long vacated my cheeks rushed back in force. My reflexive instinct was to deny it, not for modesty's sake, but because I felt a sudden, queer sense of shame in my own desires, as though I'd made up my earlier fear of intimacy out of whole cloth. What did it say about me, that nothing I'd done this evening had triggered my worse recollections of Killic? Had I exaggerated the problem to myself somehow, or was I being arrogant in assuming it gone? And what might happen later, once the truth of his death and the fact that I'd caused it sank in? It ought to have been the perfect catharsis—and indeed, a small, vehement part of me insisted that it must be—but the rest of me was too accustomed to the unfairness, incohesion and general vagaries of personhood to believe it.

Belatedly, I realised I'd been staring instead of answering, and for long enough that Markel was now looking at me with genuine worry.

"I'm sorry," he signed quickly, when he realised he had my attention. "I shouldn't assume or make jokes about that. Of course I'll stay with you."

"No," I signed back, surprising both of us. "That's not it. I . . . I think I would like the privacy, if it doesn't inconvenience you. I just—" And here I paused, my hands hovering uselessly in midsign for several long seconds. "—I worry there's something wrong with me, for wanting this at all. For even feeling ready to attempt it. And it's not that I want to feel bad, but it doesn't seem right that any of this be easy, either."

"Velasin," signed Markel, a world of fond exasperation in both sign and expression, "there's nothing wrong with you. Let yourself want things. If Caethari is enough of an ass to mock or shame you for anything you might feel later tonight, then you can come find me, and I'll express my displeasure to him in whatever form you wish, but frankly, I don't think he's that man, and I don't think you do, either. If I even suspected him of it, I wouldn't offer to leave you alone with him in the first place. And I could be wrong! Moons know, I've certainly been wrong before. But I don't think I am now, and if you have a chance, a real chance, to make this the sort of marriage you deserve to have, then you should take it." He grinned. "For what it's worth, you have my blessing."

"It's worth everything," I said aloud in Ralian, and shocked us both by embracing him. He hesitated, which I understood—we'd spent a lifetime with our friendship hidden in public, constrained by Ralia's rigid sense of gender and class—and then hugged me back, quick and tight.

"Thank you," I whispered, and Markel made a tiny noise, a vocalisation I wouldn't have heard if we hadn't been pressed together.

We pulled apart, grinned stupidly at each other and then reverted to type when Markel whacked me on the shoulder. "I'm going dancing now," he signed. "You and your husband should try it."

"Flirt," I said fondly. Markel poked out his tongue and found his way back to Ru Telitha's side, convincing her to partner him by simple virtue of cocking his head towards the dancers, raising an eyebrow and smiling boyishly, to which she responded by laughing and linking their arms together, leading him away.

"Those signs of yours," said Nairi, suddenly enough that I jumped; for all that she'd been engaged in a verbal conversation not two feet away the entire time I'd been talking to Markel, I'd managed to tune her out. "They could be extremely useful in a military setting."

"We'd be happy to teach you," I said, after taking a breath to regain my composure. "Caethari is learning already."

"*Is* he now?" said Nairi, and for some reason her emphasis made my husband colour. "You'll have to keep me updated, Cae!"

"I'll consider it," he said.

And somehow, impossibly, the rest of the party went on from there, as parties are wont to do. We talked and danced, ate and drank—even laughed a great deal, which felt like a miracle if I stopped to think about it—and there was no further bloodshed; no sudden crisis or unpleasant scene to distract us from celebration. Yasa Kithadi sought me out to compliment me on the cleanness of my killing stroke, which was unsettling but not actively distressing; Riya praised my decisiveness in defending her brother, while Laecia seethed like a boiled-over pot at the *utter Ralian barbarity* (as she termed it) of putting poison on a punch-knife.

"It's insulting!" she said, gesturing wildly with her wine. "To Caethari *and* to whatever-his-name-was. Honestly! If you're going to poison someone, poison them; if you're going to stab them, stab them. Don't go mixing and matching like an urchin at a rag-cart!"

"I'm not quite sure you're drunk enough for this conversation," Riya said, deeply amused. "Would you like me to fetch you a brandy?"

Laecia scowled. "Brandy is *Ralian.*" She took a long swallow of wine and then scanned the crowd moodily. "I wonder if there's anyone here I could stand to fuck?"

Riya laughed. "That's the spirit!"

"I'm abandoning this conversation," Caethari said loudly. "Velasin, save me."

"Dance?" I asked, and he took my hand with gratitude.

35

By the time our marriage-gathering finally drew to a close, the sky was freckled with stars and I was exhausted in every way but one, the mere possibility of which lent me an unnatural energy. I was giddy, too, and not from wine—I'd drunk little after returning to the party, and though Ren Valiu had outdone herself in the kitchens, when the food was laid before us, I'd been too anxious to eat much of anything. Thankfully, there was no need to expend any effort in farewelling the guests: those who left early sought out both Caethari and I to pay their respects, but otherwise, the tradition was that the newlyweds should retire first.

When the moment came, we were cheered again as loudly as we'd been for each kiss. I looked for Markel in the crowd and caught a glimpse of him, one hand raised as he grinned at me. Then Caethari snugged an arm around my waist and led me out, and all other sensory input became abruptly secondary to the feel of him against me.

The halls of the Aida were largely empty, but whenever we passed a guard or servant, there was something of a smile to their expression, however they tried to stifle it: a knowing look that said they knew, or thought they knew, what we were on our way to do. I couldn't tell if it bothered me; I was too worked up. I wanted their inference to be true, but didn't want it to be known, except that I also did, and yet, and yet—

As we reached our apartments, the silence between us turned electric; even the mundane ritual of removing boots and socks at the door felt oddly charged. Dry-mouthed, I looked at Caethari, who looked at me, but before he could say anything, I blurted some nonsense about wanting to wash my face and made for the bathroom, shutting the door behind me.

The still air was cool and silent. I made my ablutions, certain of which expanded upon what I'd done while bathing earlier, then stared at myself in the mirror. I looked happy and hectic, utterly myself and yet somehow alien, though I couldn't have pinned down why. I closed my eyes and took a deep breath, steadying myself, wondering what I wanted; if I was right to want it; *if, if if.*

I thought of Caethari's mouth on mine, the burning heat of his callused hands, and opened the door again.

I found Caethari pacing, flipping the jade-handled knife—now cleaned of gore and returned to him by Keletha—from hand to hand, the blade a silver streak in the low light. He stopped when he saw me, his eyes intense, and set the knife down on the table as we drew close to each other.

"Cae," I said, and his hands were on my waist, thumbs stroking gently against my hips as he looked me over, looked and looked and looked. "Cae, is this—do you want—?"

"Do you?" he asked, and lifted a hand to cup my cheek. I leaned into the dear, rough warmth of it, then raised my own to lace our fingers together. Caethari drew a shocked, sharp breath. "Velasin, are you sure?"

"Vel," I said, and realised I was trembling. "Just Vel. And yes, I'm sure. As sure as I can be. I want—I *want*—"

He kissed me, and it felt like flying. I gasped into it, arms twining around his neck as our bodies pressed together. He gripped my hips, hands climbing the planes of my back to steady my shoulders, his mouth a sweet temptation that I chased and chased and chased. We broke apart for long enough to look at each other.

"Will Markel—?" he asked, and I shook my head.

"He's sleeping elsewhere," I replied. Caethari groaned and kissed me again.

By tidal increments, push-pull-push, we crossed to the threshold of his bedroom; a room in which, only days ago, I'd lain in fear of a horror that had never come and never would, because all men were not Killic, and Caethari, my Cae, was certainly not all men. He pressed me against the doorframe and I shuddered with want, arching between two solid points until he moved us farther in, eyes wide in the soft, warm light. A servant must have lit the candles, part of me thought distantly: a courtesy to their tierns.

His knuckles brushed my stomach as he freed the hem of my undershirt from my nara; brushed again as he slowly, slowly lifted my lin and pulled it over my head. I reached for his in turn, laughing as the greater length and heavier fabric proved more difficult to manoeuvre; but Cae laughed too, and the sound curled through me like music. He kissed me sweet and fierce, and when he drew my undershirt off, his touch was as reverent as his eyes were dark. He looked at me, and had I not already been shivering, his gaze alone would've seen me so. He brushed a thumb across the bud of a nipple, and I gasped aloud, then gasped again when he trailed his fingers along the body-warmed metal of the necklace. He stepped close, hands raised to undo the clasp for me, but I took his wrists and squeezed, shaking my head.

"Leave it on," I whispered.

"Vel," he said, sounding wrecked already. I smiled to hear my most intimate name on his lips, and divested him of his undershirt as neatly as he'd done for me, until I could drink my fill of his charms. I skimmed my hands along his torso, tracing the lines of the bear-claw scars until he twitched and gasped. We were close again, and when I looked up, his expression was bare in a way that had nothing to do with clothes. My heart twisted, a fierce, swooping joy; I held his face, thumbs smoothing across the arc of his cheeks, and drew his mouth to mine.

We moved together, bare hands sliding over skin, mapping the lines of each other. I lacked the will to be coy, and when I felt the hard heat of his cock press against my hip, I shifted to rut us against each other, clinging to his shoulders.

"Vel," he breathed again, and I felt his hands shake as he unbuttoned my nara, sliding both them and my smallclothes down until gravity left me naked before him, whimpering as he kneaded the curve of my arse. I did the same for him with what I felt was vastly less elegance, fingers slipping on the buttons, hands turned clumsy with eagerness, but the end result was worth it. I touched him slowly, savouring the shift from soft skin to scars, of which he had more than just those given by the bear, though none quite so dramatic. He made a low sound and bucked his hips in a way that said he was trying not to, and something about that undid me more than even his nakedness had. I took his length in hand, stroking up and down, just once, and felt my skin spark with sensation when he bent his head to place a sucking kiss on my throat, just above the necklace.

I released him, gasping, and let him steer us both to the bed. I was braced for him to throw me down, but instead he turned us, sitting and sliding backwards as he pulled me onto his lap.

"Oh fuck," I whispered, grinding against him. His hands were huge around my hips, and when he leaned in and kissed my chest, I tipped my head back and twined my fingers through his hair, pulling at the gold wire that bound his braid. I figured the trick of it by touch alone, casting the wire aside with a cry that was partly in triumph, partly for the scrape of his teeth against my nipple. His hair was dark and feather-soft; I carded it into a loose, black mane and sucked in breath to see him so dishevelled by my touch.

"Do you have oil?" I asked. He nodded and I ground against him, earning gasps from both of us. "Show me where."

"The drawer," he said, and I swayed over to reach it, anchored in place by his grip on my hips. My searching fingers found the vial, and as I resettled above him, I felt a power I'd seldom known in bed before: to be wanted in a way that held no fear, no shame, no caveats. I passed the vial into his hand and held his fingers around it, hypnotised by the plushness of his lips.

"What—" I began, but my voice skyed like a boy's. I laughed, embarrassment chased away by the crinkles around his eyes, and tried again: "What preference have you?"

His free hand skated along my flank, back and forth. "In general, or in this moment?"

"Both."

He leaned in, kissing my collarbone. "In general," he murmured, "I prefer, ah, giving to receiving, but in this moment—" He tipped his head to look at me, his eyes and voice both velvet-soft. "—whether you wish me rider or ridden, I am yours, Vel. Utterly yours."

I kissed him, heart pounding, and lost myself in the feel of him. His words unmoored a part of me, and only when I reclaimed it did I pull back and pant out, "Make me ready to ride you, then."

Cae groaned and oiled his fingers, reaching behind to slick me up. He circled me and pushed in, a slow-hot stretch as I groaned and pressed my head to his shoulder, mouthing at the line of his throat. My hips hitched, arching with him as he worked me open, and I set my teeth to the meat of his shoulder, a biting kiss that was sure to leave a mark. His fingers shifted, and suddenly I was whimpering, sucking on his bottom lip in a plea for *now, this, more.* He obliged me with a gasp of his own, one hand anchoring my head as he took control of the kiss; he moved as he did so, sliding his fingers free from me as he shifted us up the mattress, until his back was against the headboard.

"Vel," he whispered, gratifyingly awed, and for an answer I braced a palm on his unbitten shoulder, sought his slick length with my other hand and sank down onto him, slow-fast-slow, unable to keep from keening in pleasure that almost edged into pain, it was so intense. Moons, he was a lot to take, and there was a moment where I paused in place, breathing hard and shaking from the strain of holding myself just so as my body adjusted—and then it did, and I seated myself with a groan.

His hands slid reverent over my hips, and it felt like being devoured by worship, all of him within me and a look in his eyes that lit on my skin like lightning. The necklace glimmered at my throat, and the only sound besides our breath was the faint metal chime of my earrings as they swayed in place. I was full and bright and beautiful, and if any clouds would later scud across the risen moon of this moment, still it would remain unsullied, untouched.

"Cae," I whispered, and worked my hips, and started to ride him.

I'd always been a talented horseman, and though my former tutors would've doubtless burned to know this other use to which I'd put their lessons, still there was a transference of skill. My thighs were strong, my hips fluid; I rose and fell, braced and twisted, and every noise I wrung from Caethari wound us both tighter, higher. When he planted his feet and gripped my hips to thrust up in counterpoint, I cried out in near ecstasy; we both swore, my hands in his hair as we tried for a kiss that was lost in translation, desperate mouths brushing too shallowly to do more than tease.

Steadily, my hips lost their rhythm; I was near frantic, my skin so hot it felt like I was throwing off sparks. I whined in my throat, abruptly drained of energy; I wanted more than I could take, and something in how I pressed against Cae must've told him so, for he kissed my throat, slipped out of me—I gasped at the loss—and rolled us over, hitching my legs around his waist.

"Is this—?"

"Please, *please*—"

He braced a hand against my thigh and fucked back into me, holding me spread beneath him as I dug my heel into his back. He pressed in deep and kissed me breathless, and when I was near to seeing stars from that alone, he went to work with a strength that utterly undid me. I lost my Tithenai, slipping into Ralian as I clutched his neck, his shoulders, and then I had no words at all, my body a wire strung so tight, a wink would've set it thrumming.

Reaching between us, Cae ran his knuckles along my cock, and that was it: I bowed up beneath him and came as hard as I ever had, crying out as my vision went white. I felt him thrust twice more, and then he followed me over the brink, setting us both to shudder through the aftershocks. He caught his weight on his arms, kissing me at temple, cheek, jaw, and in an instant that lasted years, we separated, sticky-slick and satiated, shifting until my head was pillowed on his chest. We tangled our legs, and I tasted the salt that gleamed along his collarbone, heart rabbiting as we drifted in that bliss which is cousin to sleep, but sweeter far.

And then we did sleep, at least for a time, though I doubt that he meant to any more than I had. It was just that the day had been so long, like all the days before it, and now that we'd stumbled through the last of the barriers we'd managed to set between each other, the natural inclination was rest. But when I woke again, sticky and confused, it was to the gentle sensation of Caethari tending to me with a washcloth. The candles had burned low, and the room was suffused with a soft yellow light. I watched him, impossibly comforted by the slow sweep of his hands, and when he realised I was awake, he smiled at me, almost sheepish.

"I should have seen to you first," he said, "and instead I fell asleep like some inconsiderate lout."

"We both slept," I replied, though I was warmed by the sentiment. I lifted my head a little and winced to realise that both necklace and earrings had been digging into me. "Moons, I should've taken these off. If I've damaged them—"

"You haven't," said Cae, and leaned up my body to kiss me. I yielded, loving the way he crowded over me, and when he pulled back, he was smiling, his firm cock nudging against my hip.

I flushed, though I was just as hard. I was accustomed to feigning less desire than I felt, the better not to seem needy; I'd never been very good at it, which had delighted Killic in ways which, with the benefit of hindsight, should've left me wary—but now, I realised, there was no need for pretence. Or at least, I hoped there wasn't: the rules of assignations in Farathel might have been harsh, but even when they'd left me empty, I'd still understood them. But what was unfolding between Caethari and me . . . there were no rules for that, or if there were, I didn't know them. We were married, and after days of fear and misadventure on my part, we'd finally taken each other to bed, but what did that mean for what happened next?

"I can hear you thinking," Cae teased, lying down beside me. He toyed with one of my earrings, but his expression was soft. "Are you well?"

"I'm very well," I said. "I just don't know the rules for this."

"The rules?"

"For this," I repeated, gesturing between us. A flash of worry lit his gaze, and my stomach lurched so unpleasantly at the prospect of mangling things between us that I blurted out, "I want you." I swallowed hard. "I want you so much, but I'm not—I don't know how—am I meant to play coy? I've never been any good at it, but it's what I'm used to expecting."

"Vel," he said, so gently, "we're married."

"I know. But the way some husbands treat their wives, stringing them along for any little glimpse of affection, or how some wives let their husbands think them forever indifferent—"

"You're not my wife, Vel, nor am I yours. And," he added, before I could speak again, "this isn't Farathel."

I shut my eyes and leaned forwards, pressing my forehead to his. "I'm afraid," I whispered. "I hardly know of what, but I don't want to get this wrong."

"May I make a confession?"

"Please."

"I'm afraid, too." Our hands were moving as we spoke, sliding along bare skin, trailing sparks in their wake. "The thought of hurting you, of pushing you away—I can't bear it."

I made a breathy noise that was not quite laughter. "It seems we have a shared predicament, then."

"Mm," he agreed, and kissed my jaw. "Perhaps, then, we should agree to be honest with each other."

"Honest?"

"Mm."

"I may struggle with that," I admitted, the words coming out a gasp as his lips moved to my throat, "but I promise to try."

"I can ask for nothing more."

"Is this nothing, then?" I reached down and took him in hand once more, provoking groans from both of us.

"It's honesty." He caught my chin, looking into me. "I want you, Vel. And if you ever don't want me in whatever way, be it for an hour or a lifetime, you can tell me, and I'll listen. But if you want, as I do now—"

"I do," I breathed, "I want," and curled up to kiss him. And then, just as the kiss was deepening, I hissed frustration and pulled back. "Wait, wait."

"What is it?" He sat up straightaway, brow furrowed.

I laughed at his expression, waving a hand to show I meant nothing dire. "I really do need to take these off," I said, and rose enough to bare my nape to him. "Would you?"

He answered with an action, kissing my neck as he undid the clasp of his gift. I removed the earrings myself as he set the necklace down on the bedside table, passing them to him in turn. There was a moment where we looked at each other, and I almost froze with the sudden, absurd conviction that this was when it would all go wrong; that he'd turn away, or else that my darker memories would suddenly boil to the fore. But when I kissed him, nothing happened except that he kissed me back, and the incongruous relief was like having all my suppressed desires uncorked at once. I rolled us over, setting him beneath me, and felt my blood heat at how easily he went, though he was stronger than me; the way his eyes darkened in expectation.

"Honestly," I said, my lips to his ear, "I find I am not the least tired."

"Nor I," he rasped, and those were the last coherent sentences either of us spoke for quite some time.

Part Eight

CAETHARI

36

For Cae, waking to the warmth of a naked Velasin stretched peacefully beside him was a transformative experience, and not one of which he felt likely to tire. He'd thought his husband attractive from the moment he'd first laid eyes on him—what felt like months ago now, but was somehow, impossibly, only days—but in sleep, all Velasin's sharp-edged tension was smoothed away, replaced by the beautiful fan of his thick, dark lashes against his cheeks; the unruly curl of his hair. His skin was soft and, by Cae's martial standards, unscarred; which was to say, marked only lightly here or there, and not by deliberate violence.

The lone exception to this was the star-shaped mark on his thigh where the arrow had struck him at Vaiko, currently bared by the ruck of sheets around his slender waist. The scar tissue was taut and shiny, red around the edges and still scabbing in places; Ru Zairin's cantrips had accelerated the healing, but the body could only be rushed so much. Cae brushed his thumb lightly over it, heat pooling in his gut at the memory of Velasin riding him, Velasin under him, Velasin's hands and lips and voice—

"Shouldn't watch people sleep," Velasin mumbled, one eye slitted half-open and a sleepy smile on his lips. "'s rude."

"I'm a bad, rude man," Cae agreed, and leaned down to kiss him awake. Velasin made a sweet noise against his mouth and let himself be kissed, arms twining lazily around Cae's neck as he moved from his side to his back, legs falling open as he did so. Cae slid into that welcoming space with happy ease, and soon enough any languidness was replaced by gasping urgency as they rutted against each other. Cae took both of them in hand, groaning at the slip of Velasin's cock against his own, goaded by the urgency with which he rolled and arched beneath him. Though they'd more than satiated each other the previous evening, it wasn't long at all before they'd both made a mess of Velasin's stomach, Cae panting into his husband's neck as Velasin's fingers petted through his hair.

"I am debauched," Velasin murmured, kissing Cae's cheek. "How am I to go about my day after such an awakening?"

"A clear impossibility," Cae agreed, running his knuckles through their joint spill and feeling Velasin's muscles hitch beneath his touch. "Perhaps we should stay abed."

"Mmm," said Velasin, and then, "*Mmm, oh!*" as Cae sucked a mark on his throat.

That distracted them all over again, but as the morning light poured in through the window, not even Cae at his most enamoured could completely forget what responsibilities awaited them outside their apartments.

"We should rise," he said, regretfully.

"Only if you bathe with me," came the reply, which was such an agreeable prospect that Cae immediately swung out of bed, hoisted a startled, laughing Velasin into his arms and carried him through to the bathroom, where washing was very much not the first activity they engaged in.

By the time they eventually made it out to the main room, robe-clad and wet-haired, Cae was ravenous. He rang for breakfast, and was about to start braiding his hair for the day when Velasin said, somewhat shyly, "May I?"

It took Cae a moment to understand, but once he did, he flushed all over. Braiding someone else's hair was an act of great intimacy in Tithena, to the point where offering to do so for a non–family member was tantamount to a declaration of love. He knew that wasn't what Velasin meant by it—the same convention didn't apply in Ralia—but as he nodded and sat, handing comb and tie to his husband, he shivered to feel those long, dexterous fingers working through his hair. The last person he'd allowed to do his braiding was Riya, and that had been years ago, when he'd been learning some of the more complicated styles after their mother left and hadn't been able to figure them out alone.

"Did Liran ever do this for you?" Velasin asked, parting his hair into segments.

Cae's breath caught. "No," he said, swallowing a desire to explain the implications of both question and answer. So many times when they were together, he'd hoped that Liran might offer, but he never had—and that had stung, both then and for a long time afterwards. There were good reasons why Nairi had worried he was still hung up on Liran, who'd cared for him—still cared for him—but not in the way Cae had wanted him to. Wanted once, but no longer: he and Liran were better as friends, and as for what he wanted now—

"Should I grow my hair long, too?" asked Velasin, braiding steadily. "I've never grown it much past its present length—it's not done in Ralia, for men to have hair past their shoulders—but I've always wondered how it might look."

"If you wanted to grow it, I'd have no objections," said Cae, who was already imagining what it might be like to braid Velasin's hair in turn. He blinked, dispelling the fantasy. "Who taught you braiding, then, if you couldn't practice on yourself?"

Velasin laughed. "Grooms and horsemasters," he said. "For formal hunts and the like, a nobleman is expected to keep his mount looking presentable. Of course, there's many who prefer to delegate the task, but I've always found it soothing." He punctuated this by tying off Cae's braid and standing back. "There. All done!"

"And do I make a presentable mount?" Cae asked.

Velasin laughed. "I should hope so!"

Cae turned in his chair, took Velasin's hand and tugged him down for a kiss—or tried to, anyway. Velasin abruptly froze, and Cae let go the second he realised something was wrong.

"Vel?"

"I'm sorry," Velasin whispered. His voice had changed, and Cae was out of his seat in a moment, hands hovering protectively over his shoulders. "I'm sorry, I didn't mean—"

Too late, Cae recalled that Killic's predations had made Velasin shy of being grabbed and pulled like that, and he mentally cursed himself for forgetting.

"You've nothing to be sorry for. Can I touch you?"

Velasin nodded, and Cae embraced him, hyperaware of all the places where poorly tied robes meant their skin was touching. Velasin took a shuddering breath, leaned hard against him for a moment and then straightened, smiling crookedly.

"I'm all right now, I think," he said. "It was only a flash. I just wasn't expecting it."

"It's my fault, I'm sorry. I shouldn't have grabbed you like that."

"You ought to be able to take my hand."

"Still—"

"Hush," said Velasin, kissing the edge of his mouth. "If I'm not allowed to apologise, then neither are you."

Cae disagreed, but before he could say so, a servant knocked on the door and called out to announce the arrival of breakfast, which was a pleasant distraction for both of them. Moments later, they were once more seated, sipping khai and helping themselves to the fruits of Ren Valiu's very talented labour.

"So," said Velasin, recovered once more. "What delightful tasks does the day hold?"

Cae sighed. "Someone will need to approach the Ralian ambassador and his household about what happened last night—discreetly, of course, but it still needs to be done."

"Not a job for us, then?"

"Not at this stage, no. Gentle inquiries are more Keletha's territory, and in any case, even if we didn't suspect the ambassador, he'd still need to be told that a Ralian nobleman died last night." He suppressed a wince. "I know it's hardly your favourite topic of conversation, but—"

"I know, I know." Velasin rolled his shoulders and stared at the window, his profile framed by the curling steam from his khai. "I never had much to do with the rest of Killic's family, but the likelihood of Ralian pushback over his death is, I think, going to depend more on His Majesty than on Lord vin Lato, and that will depend in turn on how our marriage is being viewed by the court." He laughed, small and bitter. "Do you know, I hadn't even thought about how we'd be seen in Farathel until last night? I was too wrapped up in everything else. If I'd only stopped to consider—"

"Vel." Cae reached across the table and squeezed his wrist. Velasin gave a weary nod, a half-smile flitting across his face as he briefly twisted their fingers together.

"Regardless," he went on, after a moment, "given that Killic's . . . involvement with me is scandalous, his family may not wish to claim his body, the better to distance themselves from his disgrace. Even if they mourned him in private, they might be forced to act differently in public. But if either King Markus or some faction within his court feels more disdain for this alliance than disgust at Killic's preferences, then they might cast his death as an outrage." He made a face. "Of course, the fact that *I* was the one to kill him might see the whole thing written off as a sordid spat between *men like us:* no greater diplomacy necessary."

"Barbarians," Cae growled, stomach turning sour at the prospect. Then he winced, expression turning apologetic. "Sorry. I know they're your people."

"They are, for my sins. And I don't defend them. Or not that part of them, at least." He made a frustrated noise. "Ralia is what it is. I hope it can change, but who knows how long in coming such a thing might be?"

Cae nodded. "At any rate, Keletha will doubtless let us know if and when we need to do anything. As for the rest of it . . . Raeki will probably talk to Varu Shan Dalu again, see if he has any thoughts about Ralian involvement. I'll have him turn the bandits from Vaiko over to a magistrate, too; we can't just keep them locked up here indefinitely. And we should talk to Ru Zairin about the poison on Killic's blade; if we know what it is, we might be able to find out where he got it, which is a thinnish lead but better than nothing. Other than that, though"—and here he ventured a small, hopeful smile—"I believe we might have the morning to ourselves."

Velasin brightened considerably. "Could we go out, do you think?" he asked. "Markel and I saw a little of the Jade Market, but it's not as if we were given a guided tour."

"I would be very pleased to introduce you to any and all of Qi-Katai, should you wish it."

"I do," said Velasin, and Cae smiled helplessly at him.

Thus it was that, after breakfast was done and the plates cleared away, they dressed and made their way to the infirmary to consult with Ru Zairin. To Velasin's obvious delight, Markel was there already—as promised, he'd spent the night in his former sickbed, and grinned hugely when they walked in together—and so was included in the subsequent discussion of Ru Zairin's findings, such as they were.

"I wish I had more to report," said the ru, thir tone apologetic. "From what I can tell, it's ghostfruit sap. The good news is that he was definitely trying to kill you: the sap is harmless if it gets on your bare skin, but if ingested or introduced into the bloodstream, it can stop your heart or lungs within minutes if there's no antidote handy."

Cae blinked. "That's the *good* news?"

"Comparatively so, yes." Ru Zairin tipped thir chin at Velasin. "In the sense that your husband provably didn't overreact. If the deceased had cut you even once—if the guards had tried to subdue him, and he'd struck them in turn—then last night's outcome could've been catastrophic."

"Gods," said Cae, swallowing against the near miss. "And the bad news?"

"The bad news is that it's a very reliable verminicide, which means it's readily available throughout Qi-Katai. Apparently, what tastes vilely distinctive to us is irresistible to rodents."

"How is it sold?" asked Velasin, in the tone that meant he had an idea. "In vials, jars, pouches—what?"

"It varies from shop to shop. There's no single distributor. Licensed apothecaries should keep a record of all poison sales, but they're not the only ones to sell it."

Velasin nodded. "Has anyone searched the body?"

Ru Zairin blinked. "Not to the best of my knowledge, tiern."

"Then we should. Search it, I mean. If he kept whatever container the poison came in, that might narrow down where he bought it, and if we can do that, we might backtrace his steps."

"That sounds extremely sensible," said Ru Zairin. "I can take you to the mortuary now, if you wish?"

As Velasin nodded, Cae exchanged a meaningful look with Markel, who proceeded to step in front of Velasin and sign at him. His regular speed was still too fast for Cae to easily follow, but he thought the gist of it was: *You don't need to do this.*

"I'll be fine, Markel," Velasin said in Ralian, voice oddly gentle. "Seeing him dead won't hurt me more than knowing I killed him did."

Markel winced at this, but nodded and stepped aside, leaving Cae to fill the space at Velasin's elbow as Ru Zairin led them out of the infirmary.

"Don't you start, too," Velasin muttered.

"I wasn't going to," lied Cae.

The rest of their trip to the mortuary was silent, save for Ru Zairin's murmured greetings to those they passed in the Aida. Unusually but perhaps sensibly, they arrived to find the mortuary door minded by a duty-guard, who bowed to both Cae and Velasin as they entered. The room itself was cold, and Cae suppressed a shiver as Velasin moved slowly towards the one stone slab that was occupied.

Killic had been laid on his back, his hands crossed over the wound in his chest, though his Ralian finery was still stained with blood. His eyes were open, staring blankly at nothing, and Velasin's breathing hitched at the sight. He reached out a hand, fingers trembling, but snatched it back before he could touch the body. Then he slumped, and Cae was there in an instant, wrapping an arm around his shoulders to keep him upright.

"I'll do it," Markel signed, and Cae nodded thanks as Velasin leaned on him.

"I'm sorry," he whispered, eyes closed. "I thought—"

"Shh," said Cae, and watched as Markel rifled through the dead man's pockets. He was surprisingly adept at it, which made Cae wonder if it was something he'd done before; either way, he was hardly about to ask him *now,* but mentally filed the matter away for future investigation.

He hadn't really expected Markel to find anything, and so was genuinely surprised when he suddenly straightened, flourishing a small clay vial sealed with a cork stopper. He passed it straight to Ru Zairin, whose brows went up as thei examined it.

"Any clues?" asked Velasin, who'd evidently reopened his eyes.

"Hard to say," said Ru Zairin, turning the vial over in thir hands. "There's no apothecary mark, but that's not surprising. I'd venture to guess it wasn't sold in the upper city—clay vials are cheap—but I could be wrong." With a sigh, thei handed it to Cae, who gave it a cursory glance and then slipped it into his pocket. "Unless you want to go store to store asking if anyone recognises the make or recalls a Ralian customer, I'm afraid we've hit a dead end."

"It was worth a try," said Cae.

Beside him, Velasin straightened. "I'd rather like some fresh air," he said, and exited with a speed begrudged by no one. As Markel hurried after him, Cae made their farewells to Ru Zairin and did likewise, until they'd all three emerged into the sunlight. Markel was hovering by Velasin's side, hands raised as if he wanted to speak but wasn't quite sure what to say.

"I know," said Velasin, answering what hadn't been said. "You told me so. I'm a delicate hothouse flower, and I should've known better."

"Stop that," Markel signed instantly, followed by something too swift for Cae to follow.

"Death is never easy," said Cae. "Not seeing it, not dealing it, and certainly not both together."

Velasin laughed and rubbed his face. "And here we were having such a pleasant morning." His shoulders slumped. "I don't suppose that trip into town is still on the table?"

"Why wouldn't it be?"

Velasin opened his mouth. Shut it again. Blinked, and then, with a slow, brilliant beauty, smiled. "Why not indeed?"

37

In the end, it took them the better part of an hour to make it out of the Aida—Cae had to speak first with Keletha and Raeki, the latter of whom scowled at the idea of their venturing out for pleasure without actually vetoing the expedition—but it was worth the wait, to make Velasin happy. He was a natural horseman, and though Cae knew he still felt wounded by the terrible death of Quip, he visibly relaxed once mounted on Luya. They set off together, Markel waving cheekily; he'd been invited to join them, but had demurred, pleading his still-healing wound and a desire not to interrupt. Or at least, he'd said something to that effect: if Velasin's flush was anything to go by, the literal translation had involved more innuendo.

"Where to first?" asked Cae.

"You choose," said Velasin. "You're the one giving the tour, after all."

"I am," Cae said, and steered them towards his favourite part of the Jade Market, where the glassblowers kept their stalls. He felt curiously vulnerable doing so, as if Velasin might tease him, as certain pre-Liran lovers had done, for his love of delicate things, but he needn't have worried. Velasin shared his delight in the wares on display, insisting that they pass by again on their return trip to the Aida.

"I'd buy something now," he confessed, as Cae led him on towards the food stalls, "but then I'd spend the whole day worrying it might break before I got it home."

Home. His husband's casual use of the word sent a twist of feeling through Cae. It felt a momentous accomplishment, after days of Velasin referring to their shared apartments as Cae's alone; so much so that he half wanted to grab Luya's bridle and guide them back to pick up where they'd left off before breakfast.

But there'd be plenty of time for that later, and anticipation would make it all the sweeter—and of course, though the spirit was willing, even Cae was forced to admit that the flesh was no longer nineteen. As healthy and vigorous as they both were, taking a break between rounds was still a necessity.

And so Cae showed his husband the market, the pair of them talking easily all the while. They revisited a couple of places Velasin had already been with Markel—once to buy some particularly savoury grilled meat, which Cae agreed was delicious—but otherwise explored new grounds. Eventually, this meant dismounting, leaving Alik and Luya at a hitching post to visit the narrower, more eclectic back sections of the market on foot, Cae basking in Velasin's delight as though it were a second, private sun.

As they passed a booth selling used clothes and jewellery—all high-quality, though most of the fashions were out of date—Velasin stopped, a slight frown between his brows. He reached out to the nearest rack, absently fingering the fabric of a fur-trimmed cloak, but before the vendor could approach him, he turned back to Cae and said, "The outfit Killic was wearing. I've never seen it before."

The comment caught Cae off guard. "Should you have?"

"If this were Farathel, I'd say not. He always kept a good wardrobe." His frown deepened, mouth quirked in a way that Cae couldn't quite interpret. "But here . . . he lost his things at Vaiko, remember? The bandits saw to that. But his clothes last night were Ralian. So where did they come from?"

Before Cae could venture an answer, Velasin caught the vendor's eye and asked, "Do you sell any Ralian clothes, by chance?"

The vendor, a dignified older woman, wrinkled her nose. "Ralian? I'm afraid not, ren."

"Do you know of anyone who would?"

She considered a moment. "For a stage play, do you mean? Or actual everyday wear?"

"The latter."

"Hm. Then no, I'm afraid. At least, not in the upper city."

"My thanks," said Velasin.

"What are you thinking?" Cae asked, as his husband looped their arms together and started walking quickly back through the market.

"I'm thinking Killic's clothes had to come from somewhere, and it can't have been the Ralian ambassador's wardrobe—or not from him personally, at least. He wasn't in Qi-Katai soon enough—or, wait. Do we know that for certain?"

Cae pulled a face. "It's possible we were lied to, so he'd have plausible deniability. But as you've pointed out, we still don't know if he's the one involved in this, or if it's some other Ralian faction."

Velasin grunted, then swore as he realised he'd overshot a turning. Stopping hard, he spun on his heel and pulled Cae back in the right direction, muttering under his breath. Cae felt helplessly endeared by this, but shoved the thought aside to focus on the matter at hand, which suddenly seemed a much more promising lead than the bottle of ghostfruit sap.

"So," Velasin continued. "I admit, it's possible that whoever recruited Killic just so happened to have some Ralian clothes in his size on hand, especially if they're Ralian themselves, but for the sake of treating this like a lead, let's assume they didn't. There must be places in Qi-Katai where Ralian clothes are sold or, I don't know, a community who'd know where to get some at short notice. Either way, I'd wager there's fewer possibilities in that department than there are sellers of verminicide in the upper city alone. What do you think?"

"I think it's a good idea," said Cae. "Worth a shot, certainly. The problem is, I don't know where to look." He scratched his jaw. "We could always ask Liran again; it's not quite his area of expertise, but his circle of friends is broad."

"Or," said Velasin, slowly, "we could ask Ren Adan."

"Why Ren Adan? He deals with the Khytoi."

"Yes, but he's half Ralian, remember? He might well know of other Ralian migrants in Qi-Katai."

As they reached the hitching post where they'd left Alik and Luya, Cae swung himself into the saddle a heartbeat after Velasin, both of them nodding thanks to the attendant.

"I take it you want to go now?" said Cae, struggling to keep the amusement from his tone.

"Yes, unless you have any objections." Velasin paused, head tilted as they began to ride. "*Do* you have any objections?"

"None that spring to mind."

"Oh! Good, then."

Velasin fell silent as they exited the market, waiting until they were back on the main street to say, with an air of studied casualness, "I should warn you, once we've sorted all this out, I'll probably get a bit strange."

"Strange how?"

"Oh, the usual." Velasin flapped a hand. "Insecurity, mania, expecting you to read my mind, being generally impossible."

Carefully, Cae said, "I wouldn't quite call any of that usual."

"It is for me," said Velasin. "Believe it or not, this"—he gestured at himself, the city—"is how I look when I'm doing well under pressure. Admittedly, this has involved a deal more violence than I'm used to, but Farathel intrigues still require a certain amount of skulking about, solving clues and chasing leads, that sort of thing. But once they're done, I never know quite what to do with myself." He laughed, a little sad and a little fond. "Markel says I'm like a hound without a hunt—if I don't have a project, I go stir-crazy. So—"

"So we'll need to find you a project," said Cae. He thought for a moment, considering. "My holdings in the Avai riverveldt are certainly due for an inspection. You ought to see them regardless, but I'd value any opinions you might have concerning their usage, or how to better the lot of my tenants."

Velasin stared at him, mouth gaping slightly. "What?"

"My riverveldt holdings? I'm sure I've mentioned them, though admittedly not in much detail. Or if that's not to your liking, we could visit Qi-Xihan—I'd love to show you the capital." He frowned. "Come to think of it, we're probably meant to go there anyway. I have a feeling Keletha mentioned it at some point, and now I'll be clipped over the ear if I ask thim for details I presumably ought to know already."

"You," said Velasin, then stopped. Swallowed. "You're not bothered?"

"Well, I can't speak to how I'll react in the moment, and we're bound to squabble and get on each other's nerves at some point, but I don't see why you wanting a project would be an issue." When Velasin remained silent, Cae leaned over in the saddle and squeezed his shoulder until Velasin looked at him. "Vel. Did you truly think I'd mind?"

"I don't know. You keep confounding me," said Velasin, softly. "A Ralian gentleman is meant to be a man of leisure. Excelling at the masculine arts is one thing, and scholarship is always acceptable provided you don't become obsessive or support any unfashionable theories, but anything more substantial—it's too close to work, you see. To *labour*. And we're meant to be above that. To be *better* than that." His mouth curled with disgust, but before Cae could think of how to respond to any of this, Velasin murmured, half to himself, "I have lived a cramped life, it seems. So shy of having my greatest indiscretion discovered that I seldom dared indulge in simpler ones." He lifted his head and looked at Cae, his gaze both soft and piercing. "You must be patient with me, dear Cae, as I learn to inhabit myself."

Mouth dry, he replied, "For you, anything."

Velasin flushed and looked away, but not before Cae saw him smiling. Warmth flooded him, and for neither the first nor last time since they'd left the Aida, he reminded himself that there'd be time enough to return to bed later.

Having no pressing need to rush, they rode sedately through Qi-Katai, and when they began to speak again, it was about the city: its districts, its history, the sights and bustle around them. Cae relaxed into his role as guide, feeling a little thrill of pleasure whenever he was able to make Velasin laugh or smile with his commentary. He kept it up all the way from the upper city to the middle, relenting only when they both had to concentrate to remember the way to Ren Adan's business. For all his newness to Qi-Katai, Velasin proved to be an excellent sight-navigator, and after only one false turn, they soon found themselves on the right street, leading their mounts to the same guarded hitching post they'd used on their first visit.

They had just begun walking the rest of the way when Velasin did a slight double take at the sight of another passerby and called out, "Ren Zhi!"

The man in question stopped and turned, his surprised expression transforming into a smile of polite recognition.

"Well met, tierns," he said, bowing slightly. He was dressed in the same whites and greys that Cae remembered from their previous visit, though he also now bore a wicker basket over one arm, filled with a tantalising selection of hot food. "I was just fetching lunch," he said, gesturing with the basket, his Khytoi accent making the statement sound almost like a question. "Ren Adan has had a difficult morning."

"I'm sorry to hear that, as we were hoping to speak to him," said Cae. "Should we come back another time?"

Ren Zhi frowned, considering, then shook his head. "I think it should be fine," he said. "Or at least, if it is not, I believe he would want to tell you so himself. He is presently between appointments."

"Our thanks," said Velasin, and the three of them fell into step, Cae's stomach rumbling at the savoury scents wafting up from the uncovered basket. The grilled meat they'd bought at the Jade Market had been delicious, but not exactly abundant, and as they reached Ren Adan Akaii's red building with its shiny black door,

Cae made a mental note to take Velasin somewhere nice for lunch afterwards.

"Here we are—" Ren Zhi began, but broke off in surprise when the door opened onto a heated argument, loud enough to carry down the stairwell.

"—t my fault!" Ren Adan was yelling. "If it was as simple as holding his hand and walking him up to the gates, we wouldn't have needed him in the first place!"

"I gave you *one rule,*" a woman's voice shot back, so familiar that Cae froze. "One rule! However we do this, my family lives. It was *your* job to make that clear to him—"

"And how was I to do that, pray, without telling him he was expendable? You're the one who swore Caethari would defend himself, and instead—"

"If Baru had killed Velasin in the first place, we wouldn't be having this argument! Or if *you'd* managed it yourself, instead of running away!"

"Oh, fuck," Velasin whispered, grabbing frantically at Cae's hand at the sound of descending footsteps. "Cae—"

But Cae was rooted in place, staring helplessly as Laecia stomped into view. Her eyes went wide as she saw him, and for a fleeting instant her reaction mirrored his own, shock and hurt and just a trace of fear. But then her expression shuttered, lips settling into a tremulous smile as Ren Adan appeared behind her.

"Well, now," she said, as Ren Adan glared furiously at a paralyzed Ren Zhi. "This is awkward."

38

In the frozen instant that followed, Cae made a split-second decision to stand his ground. Velasin's instinct to run made sense, but while Cae didn't relish the prospect of having to physically subdue either his little sister or—saints help them—Ren Adan, he knew he could do so if necessary, and he wanted answers. Even so, the words stuck in his throat; the very notion was absurd, and despite the incontrovertible proof of what they'd just overheard, he didn't want to believe it.

"Laecia," he rasped out. "What have you done?"

His sister flinched. "What have *I* done?" she asked, voice brittle as she alighted the stairs. "What have I ever done, but try to be a good daughter, a good sister? And yet, no matter what I do, I'm always seen as lesser than you and Riya." She stopped two steps from the bottom, keeping herself on eye level with Cae. "Riya moved away to be with Kivali. You care more for your revetha than the running of Qi-Katai. And yet our father and grandmother can't agree between them as to which of you two should inherit what?" She thumped a fist against her chest, eyes sparking with grief. "But me? I was *never* considered!"

Cae blanched. "Laecia—"

"*Never once,*" she said, speaking over him, "until our father needed a diplomatic match with Ralia. Do you know how pathetically happy that made me, that I was the one he offered? Never mind that Riya was unavailable; he could've asked for a Ralian bride for you instead, but he didn't. He offered *me,* and I thought that meant he was reconsidering which of us would inherit, because how better to strengthen Qi-Katai than to marry its heir to the clan that holds the other side of the Taelic Pass?" She laughed bitterly. "And then *you* ended up with him anyway."

"And so you decided to kill me," said Velasin, softly. "To take away your brother's advantage before he could claim it." He cocked his head, staring past Laecia to Ren Adan. "I imagine it was you who recruited Ren Baru? A fellow merchant, one obsessed with the Wild Knife—it must've been so easy, to convince him you were acting as Caethari's agent. But how did—ah!" He laughed and shook his head, as if chiding himself for being slow. "The letters we found in Ren Baru's desk. Cae said they didn't read as if a Tithenai had written them, but you're Ralian-Khytoi. Did you use them to convince Ren Baru that Laecia already had a lover, or did you just want to show him how terrible Ralian marriages are?"

Ren Adan's smile was sharp as spite. "Oh, the letters themselves were quite real, tiern, though the copies I gave him were edited. My parents wrote the originals, and as you can see, my mother escaped her original match, or else I would not be here."

Cae inhaled sharply. A numb, bruising ache was building behind his ribs, and he felt it pulse as Laecia finally alighted, brushing past him into the foyer as though they were discussing nothing more serious than the weather. Ren Adan followed, but not before gripping Ren Zhi's shoulder, hard, and murmuring something in Khyto that made him wince, head ducking as he moved to shut the door.

Belatedly, Cae realised that Velasin's fingers were still curled tightly around his wrist. He glanced at his husband, trying to silently communicate that Vel should trust him. Velasin gripped him harder for a moment, hooded eyes unusually wide; then he let go and stepped back with a short, sharp nod.

Thank you, Cae mouthed, and received a fleeting, troubled smile in response. As buoyed by this as it was possible to be under the circumstances, he walked stiffly into the front room. Seeing Ren Adan already seated, he sat down opposite, fists balled on his thighs as Velasin perched beside him. Laecia, in a display of polite incongruity, opened the drinks cabinet.

"Brandy, anyone?"

"Thank you, no," said Cae. His sister flinched again, which somehow made him feel monstrous, then forced a shrug and went to sit beside Ren Adan. There was little comfort to be found in the fact that Ren Adan looked as angry at this turn of events as Cae felt; after all, the ren wasn't the one being betrayed.

"So," said Laecia, falsely bright. "I imagine you've got a lot of questions, and I don't object to answering them in principle, but the thing is, Cae, you've put me in rather a difficult position." Her voice shook; there was a pause as she mastered herself, and when she went on, her tone was earnest, troubled. "Please understand, I've never wanted to hurt you—I was furious that Killic poisoned his blade!"

"And yet you set him on me regardless?"

Laecia snorted. "That idiot? Please. You could've dispatched him in your sleep."

"You wanted a diplomatic mess," said Velasin, making Cae jump. "When Ren Baru's attack failed, you tried to scare me off by making me think the Wild Knife wanted to kill me; and when that didn't work, you set up Cae to kill a Ralian nobleman, hoping it would sour the alliance."

"Quite," said Laecia, glaring at him. Then her expression turned almost rueful. "I didn't take you for a killer, Velasin; apparently, I was wrong."

"That makes two of us," Velasin replied, smiling in a way that didn't reach his eyes. "I assume, then, that it was Ren Adan here who appeared in the tieren's chambers, killed Ren Baru and later tried to cut my throat in his house?"

"Yes," said Laecia, ignoring Ren Adan's hiss of protest. She flicked her gaze back to Cae, expression serious. "Our father was in no danger, Cae; for all he frustrates me, I only wanted him to take this all seriously!"

Cae stared at her. "And to distrust me, you mean."

Laecia flapped an agitated hand. "Yes and no. I needed Velasin to be scared, but I knew our father would never really believe you capable of murdering your intended; truly, Cae, I wasn't trying to turn him against you, not like that! I just needed him to think your *supporters* were dangerous." She huffed, annoyed, voice turning bitter again. "But then your clever Velasin had to ruin things by pointing out the difference it made, his being wed to you instead of me, and who would've known about it." She shot Velasin a resentful look. "If only you hadn't brought that up, Tar Raeki would've been slower to ask Ren Baru about it, which would've given us time to discreetly bribe Varu Shan into letting him escape—he is so very bribeable, you know—and there'd have been no need for Adan to take care of him at all!"

"So you slaughtered my horse," said Velasin, voice deceptively even. "As, what—punishment for speaking up?"

"It was only a *horse*," said Laecia, exasperated. "Yes, I was angry, but I really just wanted to scare you off. And you *should've* been scared, no matter that stupid story of Riya's about you swapping letters. So why weren't you? I haven't been able to figure it out at all."

"Guess," growled Cae.

Laecia glared at him. "Very well, be like that. The main point is, I never set out to harm *you*."

"And what of Ren Vaia?" Cae shot back. "She was barely more than a child! Laecia, please." *You came to her funeral,* he didn't say, though remembering was enough to make his heart hurt. He swallowed, already knowing the answer but hoping, somehow, impossibly, that it wasn't true. "Tell me you didn't."

"I did," said Laecia—calmly, but still he could see the betraying shake of her hands, the bob of her throat. "I regret that it was necessary, but she'd become a liability."

"A liability! Why was she even involved in the first place?"

"She was my go-between with Ren Baru. She thought she was

helping you and me, but for all her talk of loyalty, in the end, she cared more about horses. *Horses!*" His sister made a frustrated noise. "All that work, all her promises, and in the end, she betrayed me over an animal that didn't even suffer!"

"And what of Ren Vaia?" Velasin asked softly. "Did she suffer, Laecia?"

Laecia trembled, lifting her chin. "Yes," she admitted—and all at once, Cae was nauseated with memory: little Laecia, six years old and admitting that yes, she'd punched and pushed another child, *But only because she was mean to me! She deserved it!* His vision doubled, overlaying the past on the present: the same defiant-defensive tone, the same pushed-out chin and tightly crossed arms, and even before the present Laecia opened her mouth, he knew what she was going to say next.

"I'm sorry that she suffered," said his sister, "but she deserved it."

Cae felt his stomach turn over. *When did you become this? When did you grow so cruel, and why didn't I see it? When did you learn to hide?* He wanted to shout, to shake her by the shoulders and demand an explanation, but before he could do something stupid, Velasin spoke again.

"That's why she was out with the yasa's mare, the day I arrived at the Aida—you had her speak to Ren Baru?"

"The guard rosters changed last-minute. I had to let him know."

"And you had her lead out the mare in heat when Riya's seneschal rode in, to create a distraction while you—" He swallowed, pulling an ugly face. "—killed Quip."

Laecia clenched her jaw. "I did. But like I said, she loved horses too much. She sent you that apology note about it, and we could've been sunk if she'd run away—but then you let the whole Aida know you'd found it, and I could—" She swallowed, some darker emotion flashing briefly across her face. "—I had time, then, to stop her. To do what had to be done."

Sickened, Cae made to stand, but found himself held in place by Velasin's hand on his leg.

"All of that makes sense, after a fashion," said Velasin, staring intently at Laecia. "But how did you two get involved in the first place, and what does it have to do with Ralia?"

"Laecia," Ren Adan warned, but Laecia ignored him, enthusiasm warming her tone.

"We met months ago, at a collegium on magic. Unlike our father, Adan can see the value in artifex; the sort of good they could do for Qi-Katai. When the betrothal was first suggested, we were both excited by the possibilities of opening a more robust artifex trade with Ralia. We started to plan for it, even! Certain Ralian factions were very pleased by the idea, as were our Khytoi artifexers." Her expression fell, hands clenched into fists as she looked at Cae. "And then, just as we'd begun to make progress, word came that *you'd* be marrying Velasin, not me. We had to stall our plans, which was extremely inconvenient, and for a while, I thought I'd have to turn everything over to you. Again." Her voice went bleak. "Give up all my plans, my ambitions, and make them into a project for you—and I might've done, Cae, for Qi-Katai's sake. I truly did consider it. But you're not—you've got no *interest* in any of this, not magic or trade or artifex, and what if you didn't listen to me? Or what if you did, but you and our father took it all away from me? So I came up with a different plan."

She took a steadying breath and met Cae's gaze. "I decided to make my own alliance. Adan and I work well as partners, and he has his own links to Ralia—to the Ralian ambassador's staff, even, if you were wondering how we snared that invitation for Killic. It's not a stretch to think that your marriage would be controversial in Ralia, so why not start over from a clean slate—let your alliance falter, and then step in to salvage things with my own? And if the Ralians took too much offence, Adan is half Khytoi; we could always build our bridges there if need be."

"And of course," interrupted Velasin, "if our marriage ended up a diplomatic disaster, then that would be just one more reason for either your father or grandmother to bestow you an inheritance."

"They should've named me from the start!" snapped Laecia, and then, just as quickly, calmed herself, as though her anger had never been. She turned to him, a calculating look in her eyes. "So then, Velasin vin Aaro—as I've been kind enough to answer your questions, perhaps you can answer mine: After everything, how did you end up here? We couldn't decide if it was good luck or bad when Liran brought you here the first time—it made Adan visible to you, but it also made it so easy to point you towards Varu Shan. Not that he was ever involved with us, of course; he was just usefully corrupt. But I'm getting distracted—did you follow me here, or was it a hunch?"

"Neither," said Velasin, smiling thinly. "I just wondered where Killic's new Ralian clothes had come from, and I thought Ren Adan might know."

A stormcloud crossed Laecia's face. "Really."

"Really."

All at once, Ren Adan smacked the arm of the couch and said, furious, "Are you quite done helping them hang us, Laecia? Or are there any other secrets you'd care to offer up?"

"I'm not helping them," she said, gaze flicking back to Cae. "I'm explaining things so that my brother can make an informed decision."

"Oh?" asked Cae. "And what decision is that?"

Laecia folded her hands on her lap. She was trying hard to look calm, but Cae could see the cracks in her, the effort it was taking to maintain the façade, and a terrible part of him pitied her for it. "Caethari. I've told you the honest truth, and I expect it in return. Do you believe me when I say that I've never tried nor wanted to kill you?"

Cae bit back a sarcastic retort. Laecia's colour was up, her braided hair coiled in an elegant knot. She was his little sister, and his throat ached at the realisation that he didn't know her at all.

Except that, in some ways, he did. Or at least, he hoped he did.

"Yes," he said, softly. "I believe you."

Almost imperceptibly, Laecia relaxed. "Good," she said. "Because right now, you have two choices, and it matters that you understand how sincerely I mean them." She raised a delicate finger. "One, you and Velasin can elope. Leave Tithena, travel or live wherever else you wish with my blessing; the only conditions are that you don't come back, and that our conversation stays confidential."

Cae didn't laugh at this, though part of him very much wanted to. It felt like a bad joke. "Or?"

"Or," said Laecia, holding up a second finger, "I have the two of you locked away in Khytë."

Silence fell. Cae waited for a punchline that never came.

"Laecia," he said at last, "that's ridiculous."

Anger flashed in her eyes. "Is it now."

"It is. For one thing, even if you were foolish enough to think that I'd simply leave here without a fuss, I don't believe for a moment that Ren Adan does. Nobody in your position who aims to hold it leaves that sort of loose end lying around, not even for the sake of kinship, and especially not without any leverage—and you *have* no leverage, Laecia; only an expectation of my goodwill. And for another, as I don't intend to run off, you've no means of holding either of us."

"Caethari, please," she begged, "think rationally about this. Do you actually *want* to inherit? You've never been an administrator, and you hate political intrigues. If you run off to Father and tell him about this, you guarantee yourself a life spent doing what you hate, and for what? Our family might believe you, but tieren's privilege doesn't apply to cases involving the tierency. If a case was called before the judicate, you've no hard evidence with which to prove any of it; only your word against mine. You'd put our clan at the centre of a public scandal, and no outcome you could hope for would be greater than the damage done to all of us in the process. And as for my having no leverage—" She hesitated, visibly gathering herself, then said, "That brand you left on the late Killic's hand betrayed a great many things."

As Velasin tensed beside him, Cae's fingers curled into impotent fists. "You wouldn't," he said—reflexively, helplessly, knowing the plea was false even as he winced at the naivety of voicing it in the first place.

"Wouldn't what?" said Laecia, bitter once more. "Tell the Ralian ambassador that you took violent, extrajudicial action against a foreign nobleman under the guise of tieren's privilege, prompting him to seek public revenge? Embroil your marriage in a public, diplomatically loaded argument about rape and retribution?" She straightened, anger creeping into her face. "You're lecturing me about what I've done, but you've bent the rules to suit yourself, too! At least what I did, I did for the future of Qi-Katai—*you* only acted for yourself!"

That was just true enough to sting. "Laecia—" Cae said, then stopped. He had no desire to argue the semantics with her, though they swirled through his head regardless—that he'd acted in defence of Velasin, not for himself; that he'd harmed no innocents like Ren Vaia, only a guilty rapist. She'd blindsided him; her betrayal hurt, but what hurt more was the realisation that he didn't know his sister; that she'd turned so readily to calculated, cold-blooded violence.

"I'm so sorry," Cae said, voice rough. "I don't know when I failed you, that you became this and I didn't see it, but I'm sorry. I'm so sorry, Laecia."

He came to his feet, already running the mental arithmetic on how best to disable Ren Adan, who'd risen in turn to put himself between Cae and Laecia; the kindest way to bind his sister's hands and take them both back to the Aida.

"Stand down," he said to Ren Adan, whose forehead was already beaded with sweat. "I don't want to hurt you any more than necessary."

"*Wait,*" said Laecia, sudden and sharp and desperate enough that Cae heeded her. She rose unsteadily to her feet, hands twisted in genuine agitation as she pushed past Ren Adan. "Caethari, please—don't do this. I'm your *sister.* Forget what I just said about Killic and the

Ralians; I didn't mean it. I wouldn't—" She looked away, swallowed visibly as she fought for words, then continued, "Even if I could do that to you, I couldn't do it to Qi-Katai, to our *family.* You're right. I have no leverage; nothing with which to bargain but the love we bear each other." She took a tremulous step towards him, tears welling in her eyes. "Yes, I've done some terrible things—spoken terribly of them just now, to try and justify myself—but the truth, the real truth . . . Cae, I never wanted to do any of this, but what I want *doesn't matter.* Nothing I am has *ever* mattered."

Her voice cracked with hurt and rage. "I've a natural skill at magic, did you know that? Ruya's Order would've loved me. But our father has no use for it, and so it didn't matter. I work harder and do more on behalf of Qi-Katai than you and Riya; I know the names of everyone who works in the Aida. I know how to lead our clan into the *future,* Cae. I can make us prosper; make Qi-Katai thrive again. Can't you just forgive me? Can't you let me have this?" She fell to her knees on the carpet, looking pleadingly up at him. "We can make a different deal, the kind I should've made with you in the first place. You and Velasin can stay here, learn your marriage here, do everything you've planned to do. Just don't turn me in. Keep my secret; let Varu Shan Dalu take the fall. He's been corrupt for years, you must know that by now; he's hardly innocent. Please." She gripped his nara with one hand, swiping away her tears with the other. "*Please,* Cae. As you love me, don't turn me in."

For an awful, guilt-fuelled moment, Cae was tempted. He didn't want to hurt Laecia, and despite everything, he believed her when she said she'd never wanted to hurt their family. But Ren Vaia's life mattered; Ren Baru's life mattered; her lies and manipulations mattered.

Gently, he prised her fingers off him. "No, Laecia," he said, voice soft with regret. "I'm sorry, but no. I'll vouch for you to our father, that you never meant your family harm, but everything else you've done, you need to answer for." His gaze flicked to Ren Adan, who was still hovering uselessly behind Laecia. "Both of you. Now."

He stepped away from her, drew a breath and watched as his sister came unsteadily to her feet. "Like I said, I don't want to hurt you—"

"I didn't, either," said Laecia. A strange look had come into her eye, a thread of mania weaving through the sadness of her tone. "I really didn't, Cae. But you've left me no choice."

"Laecia, be reasonable—"

She laughed, the sound cracked. "You really do think so little of me, don't you?" She raised her hands, fingers twitching, and then—

Cae convulsed, a graunching spasm that made him cry out as he dropped to the floor. Straining to breathe through leaden lungs, he tried to move, but it was like being held down by weights. He didn't understand what had happened. Pain sang through him, lighting up every nerve and sinew; he lay as if paralysed, frozen below the neck. Eyes rolling helplessly, he could only watch as Velasin was felled in turn, collapsing across the couch like a fallen soldier.

"What—" he choked out, gasping as Laecia moved to stand over him. "What—?"

She smiled sadly down at him. "There's really not much difference between human nerves and the nerves in a horse—not when it comes to this, at least. All you need do is suppress or pinch or tweak them just so—" She gave an illustrative snap of her fingers, and Cae's right arm flailed violently for a moment, like a landed fish. "—and they do what you want them to."

His senses were garbled: vision spotting, ears filled with the terrible, incongruously loud sound of Velasin whimpering. "Illegal," he rasped out—stupidly, because she'd already crossed that line in myriad ways, and yet he was still shocked. Breaking the law was one thing, but the taboo against using magic on others without their consent was older than Qi-Katai. "Laecia, this—you're not—"

"Not a mage?" she asked, sharply. "No, I'm not temple certified. I might be now, if our father weren't so convinced of the uselessness of magic. But he is, and I'm not, and so I'm forced to improvise. Still, not even you can doubt that I've got a knack for it."

She crouched down, setting a palm to his cheek, and for a moment there was a flash of something like apology in her gaze. "I meant what I said, Cae. I've never wanted you dead. You can still walk away from this—you and Velasin both."

Unable to move the rest of his body, Cae did the only thing in his power and spat at her. White, foamy spackle landed on her cheek. Laecia froze, her face a mask of fury, and slowly rose to her feet.

"I'll give you a day," she said, voice shaking with anger as she wiped her face with a sleeve. "One day to change your mind, Caethari, and after that, whether by my will or yours, you'll both be gone from Qi-Katai forever."

Ren Adan's heavy boot arced towards his head, and the world became starbursting darkness.

39

Cae came to in groggy bursts of consciousness. His head swam; one eye was swollen shut where Ren Adan had kicked him, the injury radiating spikes of brighter pain against a backdrop of all-over hurt. He counted himself lucky that there was no odd, metallic taste in his mouth, which he knew from past experience to be a very bad sign indeed. He grunted, stomach churning with nausea, and cracked open his good eye, blurry vision clearing as he blinked. He was lying sideways on a stone floor, his wrists cinched tightly behind his back in a hog-tie linked to his bound ankles, holding his body in an unnatural arch. An unconscious Velasin lay nearby—not quite close enough to touch, had either of them been able to reach for the other, but not so far that Cae couldn't see the dark bruise forming on his temple. From his posture, he too was hog-tied, and Cae felt a swell of fury at the thought of Velasin being hurt yet again, after everything he'd already been through.

That they'd been left facing each other felt deliberate. It wasn't quite a kindness, but as it would've been crueler by far to keep them hidden from each other, Cae gritted his teeth and allowed himself to feel viciously grateful for it.

At least he could feel his limbs again. It was a relief to find that Laecia's magic had worn off, but whoever had bound him knew their knots: there was just enough give in the rope to keep his circulation from cutting off, and nothing more.

"You're awake, then."

Boots appeared in his vision: Ren Adan's, to go by the voice.

"I am," said Cae, who saw no point in denying it.

Ren Adan sighed. "I'd prefer to talk to you eye to eye, but you'll forgive me for not quite trusting you with a shorter rein."

"I'll forgive you nothing."

"Be like that, then." A brief pause; the boots backed up a step, and suddenly Ren Adan was hunkered down on his haunches, obscuring Cae's view of Velasin. "Your sister really does care for you, you know."

Cae choked on a bark of laughter, suppressing a wince at the various hurts the simple movement provoked. His neck was already starting to burn; much longer like this, and he'd stiffen up completely. "She's got a funny way of showing it."

"Perhaps," said Ren Adan, "but all things considered, neither of you would be alive right now if she didn't." He snorted, but when he spoke, his voice was strangely affectionate. "One day, she gives you. What the fuck does she think you'll decide in a day that you haven't already? But then, that's Laecia for you."

"I'll have to take your word on it."

"I suppose you will, at that." Ren Adan's expression darkened. "Did you know your father refused to let her study magic? A natural gift like hers, but even though he doesn't want her to inherit anything, he still wouldn't let her go to Ruya's Order."

Cae inhaled sharply. "I didn't know that."

Ren Adan sneered at him. "Of course you didn't. Why would the Wild Knife bother with something as trivial as a sister's dreams when there's Ralians to kill?"

Shamefully, Cae had no answer to that, and so made no defence of himself. Ren Adan peered at him for a long moment, lip curling when it became apparent that Cae wasn't going to speak.

"Here's the thing, tiern. What you said upstairs before, about how Laecia can't just expect the two of you to vanish and keep your mouths shut? We both know you were right, and deep down, so does she. Oh, she'd never admit it, but the cold truth is, you're a liability." He reached to his belt and withdrew a wicked-looking knife from a sheath, tapping the flat of the blade against his palm. "The way I see it, I'd be doing us both a favour if I killed you here and now. She knows you're a fighter; there's always a chance you could wriggle around, find something sharp to cut your bonds and free yourself, the better to attack me when I come to give you water. I'd tell her it was self-defence, and maybe she'd doubt me, maybe she'd rage and curse and find some way to punish me while she mourned—and she would mourn, tiern, I assure you—but in the end, you'd still be dead, and she'd know in her heart that it was for the best."

A terrible calm came over Cae then, both like and unlike what he felt in the midst of battle. "And what of Velasin?"

"Now, that's a little trickier." Ren Adan framed the knife between his hands, the thumb and forefinger of one hand pinching the blade while the hilt pressed into the opposite palm. "On the one hand, letting him live to run away makes him an excellent scapegoat, or at least a suspect. If both of you turn up dead, it's harder to explain, but just one of you, with the other missing? Well."

He let the knife hilt fall from his palm, dangling it briefly by the tip of the blade before swinging it into a proper grip, and Cae felt an incongruous burst of annoyance at both the unnecessary showmanship and the poor weapons-handling. "But on the other, if he's left alive and suspected of your death, then people will try and find him; to bring him back for questioning, or justice, or some other nonsense. The more sensible thing," he said, laying the cool flat of the blade on Cae's bruised cheek, "would be to let him be *seen* to run, and then kill him after."

"Don't," said Cae, the word lurching out before he could stop it. He gritted his teeth, aware that he was betraying a weakness by appealing to the sympathy of a man who had none, and yet he could do nothing but plead for Velasin's life. "Don't kill him. Please."

Ren Adan withdrew the blade and sighed once more. "Your sister's right. You're really not very good at this, are you?"

"I've never claimed to be."

A low moan sounded from behind Ren Adan, followed by a burst of dry coughing. Cae pulled against his bonds, trying and failing to crane his head.

"Vel? Vel, are you all right?"

"Head hurts," croaked Velasin, as Ren Adan pivoted to examine him. "Thirsty."

Cae watched, helpless, as Ren Adan did something to Velasin—touched him on the face or shoulder, he couldn't tell which; only that he extended an arm—before rocking back on his heels with a grunt.

"Very well," he said. "You shall have some water." He straightened and walked out of Cae's view. Cae listened to him go, noting it was barely five steps until the timbre of his footfalls changed, then counting a further eight up what he guessed to be a stone flight of steps before he heard the telltale creak of hinges.

His eyes met Velasin's across the floor, but before Cae could speak, his husband said, urgently, "Put your back to me."

"What?"

"Quickly, before he comes down again. Put your back to me!"

"I'm not sure I can," Cae grunted, but made an effort nonetheless. He rocked and wriggled, shoulders burning painfully as his wrists were yanked by each attempt to move his hips. He managed to rise up a little, but that was it: he couldn't fold his arms down or twist his feet sufficiently to roll over without dislocating something in the process. He swore and flopped back, giving a weary shake of his head. "Sorry."

"It's all right," whispered Velasin. "Just—whatever I say to him next, please believe I don't mean it."

"Of course. But what—"

The door creaked again and Cae fell silent, heart pounding in his ears as Ren Adan returned with a jug in one hand and a cup in another. Making sure to kneel where both captives could see him, he smirked, making an elaborate show of pouring water into the cup and then taking a sip himself, to show that it wasn't poisoned.

"You will not find my hospitality lacking," he said, and shuffled forwards on his knees, holding the cup to Velasin's mouth. Lifting his head with visible effort, Velasin drank awkwardly, water dribbling from his lips and running down his chin. He'd barely had a few swallows before Ren Adan pulled the cup away, chuckling as Velasin tried and failed to chase it.

"Please," croaked Velasin—in Ralian, not Tithenai. "Please, sir. I don't want to die here. I never wanted to be here at all."

"If you're hoping for a private chat," Ren Adan replied in the same language, "I'm told your husband speaks this language fluently."

"I know. I know he does," said Velasin, shooting a venomous look at Cae. It landed like a punch, so much so that it took Cae several agonising seconds to recall Velasin's warning, and by then, his husband was speaking again. "You've no idea what it's like. Those letters, the ones you left with Ren Baru—it was like reading about myself." A sob hitched his voice. "I loved Killic. Truly loved him. But when he followed me here, Caethari was so angry, so jealous—he branded him, made Killic believe I'd accused him of rape; he turned him against me! I never meant to kill him, but I knew he liked to poison his blades, and I was afraid—I've been so afraid—that he'd turn on me, next. It was self-defence." He swallowed, tears beading his lashes. "I never wished him dead."

Slowly, Ren Adan rose to his feet. He contemplated him for a moment, Velasin's head tilted to look up at him as best he could—and then, with no warning, Ren Adan kicked him hard in the stomach. Velasin made a gargling noise that choked into a pained cry; his body had tried to curl up around the injury, but the hog-tie meant he'd succeeded only in worsening his hurt. Cae thrashed angrily, but didn't cry out; Velasin was trying something, making a play to get both of them free, and he didn't want to disrupt it.

"Do you think," said Ren Adan, voice deceptively mild, "that I was born yesterday? If you truly were scared of the tiern and yearning for your Ralian lover, you would've bolted the instant he was named as the man behind the attack on you."

"Call me a liar all you want, it's true," panted Velasin. Ren Adan kicked him again, his execution almost lazy despite the clear strength in the blow, and Velasin made such an awful noise that Cae couldn't hold back a cry of his own, twisting against his bonds as his husband vomited all over the floor, whimpering as each racking spasm tortured his arms and legs.

"Please," coughed Velasin, more than a hint of sob in the word. "Even if I feared Caethari, what was the point in running? Until he showed up in Qi-Katai, I thought Killic was lost to me forever." He spat out bile on the floor, visibly trembling as he shut his eyes. "Our relationship was known in Ralia; he might've weathered the shame alone, but not if I went back, and after the way things ended with my father, I had nothing and nowhere else to turn to." He gave a terrible hacking laugh, and Cae was horrified to see a smear of blood on his lips as his eyes cracked open once more, peering wetly at Ren Adan. "Why would I run from a death threat when I already wanted to die?"

Velasin slumped, struggling to suck in air. Ren Adan drew his foot back for another kick, but when Velasin didn't react to the threat, he stilled. Cae couldn't see his face, but something about his posture said he was considering it; that maybe, just maybe, Velasin had sown a seed of doubt within him.

Cae didn't know what his husband's gambit was, but in that moment, he knew that he trusted him. "You lying snake," he rasped in Tithenai. "Is this what Ralian loyalty looks like?"

Velasin didn't answer, but addressed his next words to Ren Adan. "Please. I preferred him to death, but I don't want to die for his sake; not if there's a way for me to live. I'll disappear, you'll never have to see me again, just please—"

"Enough!"

Velasin obeyed, panting softly. The acrid stench of vomit was already strong in Cae's nostrils; it must've been ten times worse for Velasin, who was all but lying in his own mess.

"Save your pleading for Laecia," said Ren Adan, after several long seconds. "She's the one you need to convince, not me."

Velasin shut his eyes again and nodded tightly. "Thank you, sir."

As Ren Adan turned to leave again, Cae called out, "You can't just leave us like this!"

"Why not, tiern?" He sounded amused, but in the affected way of an angry man whose patience is being tested. "Your man there made his own mess; that means he gets to lie in it."

"*Him,* yes," said Cae, forcing a note of bitterness into his voice. He'd never been a great actor, and could only hope that any flaws in his performance were put down to the circumstances. "But why should I have to suffer? You might at least turn me over, so I don't have to smell it." He waited a beat, then added, "Or look at him."

Ren Adan laughed at that. "Sure thing, tiern. We'll even call it a courtesy." He moved over, bent down, gripped Cae's lin and none too gently manhandled him over, until he was facing the opposite wall. In place of Velasin, this new view contained several stacked crates, some iron-bound barrels and a basket of onions and root vegetables, confirming Cae's guess that they were in a cellar beneath the kitchen in Ren Adan's office.

"Enjoy the view," said Ren Adan, punctuating the remark with a slap to the back of Cae's head. Cae grunted as he absorbed the blow, then listened once more for his footsteps; for the moment when the creak of the door was followed by the unmistakeable sound of a key turning in a lock.

Cae waited several more seconds just to be on the safe side, then said, "Are you all right?"

"I've been better," Velasin admitted. "Cae, what I said—I'm sorry, I didn't mean a word of it, I was just trying—"

"—to get us out of here, I know. The same for me, too."

Velasin coughed wetly. "Thanks."

"Well, I got myself turned over, at least. What now?"

"Give me a minute."

Cae nodded, though he wasn't sure if Velasin could perceive the gesture, and shut his eyes, head throbbing. *Laecia did this,* he thought, and the knowledge was nothing but pain. He wanted to shove it away, deal with it later, but there was precious little else with which to occupy himself.

He felt ugly for having spat at her.

"Fuck," muttered Velasin. His voice sounded thinner than it had a moment ago, and Cae's pulse spiked with worry.

"What is it?"

"Hush," came the snapped response, though there was no heat in it. "I'm trying to concentrate."

Cae complied, forcing his thoughts elsewhere. He didn't know how long they'd been unconscious, but based on the fact that he was neither ravenous nor desperate for a piss, he doubted they'd been out for much more than the time it had taken Ren Adan—and Ren Zhi, presumably—to get them downstairs and safely tied up.

Ren Zhi. The name brought him up short: where did the Khytoi stand in all of this? For all that he'd brought them back to the offices, theirs had clearly been a chance encounter, and under the circumstances, Cae was hard-pressed to think of Ren Zhi as a knowing co-conspirator. It would've been easier when meeting them in the street, to steer them both elsewhere; to claim Ren Adan was too busy for guests, or else to stow them outside before going back to warn his master. And yet he hadn't helped them, either: whatever Ren Adan had said to him in their shared language had, if nothing else, left him frozen in the moment. Had he fought back or protested their capture, Cae would've expected to see him tied in the cellar, too; but then, that didn't necessarily mean he'd been swayed to his master's cause.

Thinking back to that first, more pleasant encounter with Ren Adan, Cae struggled to recall anything that Ren Zhi might've said about himself. Liran would know, because Liran had been interested enough to flirt with him, and because, for all his casual ease in such moments, he seldom forgot any details he learned in the process.

But Cae was not Liran, and all he could remember was the dragon teapot and something about it being made by a member of his clan. Nothing useful; nothing to help them now, when Ren Zhi might be their only potential ally in escaping—

"Ah!" cried Velasin suddenly, a wounded punch of noise that jerked Cae out of his thoughts. "Nearly—*ah*!"

All at once, the terrible pressure on Cae's wrists and shoulders vanished. He slumped in stunned relief, groaning as he stretched his arms and slowly, disbelievingly pulled them around to his chest. He lay on his back, blinking as the ropes slithered off him as though they'd never been tied at all, and only then did he realise he was unbound completely.

He sat up at once, scrambling to his hands and knees. "What did you do?"

"Magic," said Velasin, bloody-mouthed and smiling. There was blood trickling from his nose, too, and his skin was ashen in a way that Cae would swear it hadn't been before. "Told you—other day—I can undo knots." He made a wheezy noise that was, Cae realised, meant to stand in for laughter. "Just. Never done it from—distance. Always had to. Touch, before. And look. Need to look, to see or I'd have—done mine. First. But. Can't see behind me. So. Had to see. Yours."

Velasin's eyes rolled back in his head, snapping Cae from his stupor. "Vel!" he croaked, hurrying to his husband's side. Velasin was unresponsive, his breathing shallow. Swearing, Cae got behind him and set to work undoing his hog-tie the old-fashioned way, cursing as his blunt-nailed fingers snagged and stuck on firm, sticky knots. He cast around the room, annoyed but not surprised to find there was nothing sharp within reach, and tried to calm his fear.

"I'm no good at knots," he said, shakily. "No good at magic, either, though I wish now I'd learned. Vel?" No answer. "Saints, Vel, if you've damaged yourself with this I'll—" He swallowed, trying to think of something, anything. "—I'll make you eat Ralian food for a fortnight."

"Cruel," slurred Velasin. "Bad hus'bn."

Cae made a noise that was absolutely not a sob of relief. "A month, then. Two months." He picked furiously at a knot, and almost wept when it finally started to loosen. "I'll even tell Ren Valiu not to let you in the kitchens."

As the knot came free, Velasin groaned and flopped onto his back. Cae knelt beside him, untying the remaining rope with vicious satisfaction. When he was done, he leaned over Velasin's body and grabbed the cup and pitcher that Ren Adan had, presumably for his own amusement, left sitting just to the side of the vomit. Pulling Velasin into his lap, Cae cradled his head with one hand and held the water to his lips with the other, urging him to drink.

Shakily, Velasin raised his own hand and pressed it to Cae's, keeping it there as he took a sip. With aching slowness, he swilled it around his mouth then leaned to the side and spat, clearing out the foul taste. He did this three more times before finally drinking deep, but when Cae refilled the cup and offered him more, he shook his head.

"You have some, too."

"I'm not thirsty," Cae lied, but relented when Velasin tipped his head to glare feebly at him. The water was cool and clean, and he drank more than he'd meant to. Velasin looked smug at that, or as smug as it was possible for him to look with a bruise blooming on his cheek and dried blood crusted beneath his nose, and Cae retaliated by kissing his forehead, belatedly overwhelmed by all the fear he'd felt when Ren Adan had kicked him.

Setting the cup aside, he dipped his sleeve in the pitcher and gently cleaned the blood from Velasin's face. He'd never seen someone surpass their magical limits before, but he had a basic understanding of the consequences, and he shuddered to think of the drain on Velasin's body in addition to everything else. When he was done, he refilled the cup and returned it to Velasin, who took small sips with his eyes closed.

"Well," said Velasin, finally. "We're out of the ropes, at least. What now?"

"What now indeed," Cae murmured. "I'm fairly sure we're locked down here, so unless you've got a set of lockpicks hidden in your boot, we need to wait until someone comes in."

"I could try more magic—"

"Absolutely not." Cae stroked Velasin's hair, pausing for a moment with his hands on either side of his forehead. "As a last resort, maybe. But you've already passed your limits, and I'll have a hard time getting you out of here and back to the Aida if you're unconscious, never mind the damage to your body."

"Liar," Velasin murmured, lips twitching. "I already know you can carry me." But to Cae's relief, he didn't push the argument.

A beat of silence. Two. Then:

"Velasin. Can you get up at all?"

"Ask me in an hour."

"*Vel.*"

"No." He turned his head, staring at the far wall. "No, I don't believe I can."

Carefully, Cae asked, "Because of the magic, or because of the kicking?"

"A little of both, I suspect. But—" He winced, shifting to look up at Cae. "—mostly the magic. I've always used that charm on knots I could see and touch, and my area of effect is small to begin with—like I told you, I've no great talent. Working without touch, and at a greater distance . . . I won't say it's quite like trying to leverage a millstone with a teaspoon, but it's close enough." And then, more softly, "Your sister must be gifted indeed, to have done what she did to us."

Indulging himself, Cae dropped another kiss on Velasin's forehead and said, "Rest for now. There's no immediate rush."

Velasin let out a startled laugh. "We're locked in a cellar while your sister prepares to disappear the both of us."

"Well, yes. But I doubt she's here right now."

"What makes you say that?"

"Because she's not *here.* With us, I mean, in the cellar, assessing your apparent betrayal of me or making a decision about what to do next, and if she was *about* to come down, Ren Adan wouldn't have locked the door." He rolled his shoulders, trying to ease their tension. "That, and it'd be conspicuous if she just so happened to be out of the Aida the whole time we were missing—once people realise we're missing, that is." He winced, recalling Raeki's disapproval at their decision to go out unescorted. *Sorry, Raeki.* "Which won't be for a few hours yet at least."

"Huh," said Velasin. "That's . . . huh."

"What?"

His answer was forestalled by a muffled shout from somewhere overhead.

40

Cae jerked sharply, staring at the ceiling. Two seconds passed; then there came another shout and the scrabble of feet, followed by a terrible crash.

Another pause, longer than the first.

An awful thump.

Silence.

"That doesn't sound good," said Velasin.

"No," Cae agreed, pulse racing. "It doesn't."

"Get up," said Velasin, voice suddenly urgent. "If someone comes down here, you need to be ready to—"

"No."

"No?"

"No, I'm not leaving you helpless on the floor."

"Caethari—"

"Vel. No."

"Don't be such a self-sacrificing ass!"

"I'm not," said Cae, calmly. "Look: that stairwell is narrow and steep, and the door opens outwards. Ren Adan is armed, and he'll have the high ground. If I go up there I'll be at a clear disadvantage, not least because he could simply slam the door in my face. I'm confident I can take him in a fight, but I need him down here first."

Velasin digested this, then gave an indignant huff. "All right. But get me off your lap; you can hardly spring up if I'm pinning your legs."

"Fair," said Cae, and began to extricate himself. Once he had his feet under him, he grabbed Velasin under the arms and pulled him over to the wall, propping him in a sitting position. He'd barely had a chance to move the cup and pitcher back to their original spot before he heard the key turn in the lock, at which he swore and hurried to crouch at Velasin's side.

The door creaked open. Cae readied himself, fists flexing, waiting for the moment Ren Adan stepped fully clear of the recessed stairs. A blind charge was too risky: if Ren Adan noticed that Cae and Velasin weren't where he'd left them—and that was all too possible, depending on how much of the cellar was visible from the doorway—he might well have his knife in hand, and Cae would be of no use to either of them if he got himself carelessly stabbed.

The business end of a loaded crossbow appeared from behind the wall, held by a furious, sweating Ren Adan. A trickle of blood ran down his face; his eyes were wide and wild.

Cae froze in place.

"Fuck," whispered Velasin.

"How did you—?" Ren Adan began, then broke off. He was breathing heavily, his finger on the trigger. At such close range, the heavy bolts would be fatal. "Never mind. We're having a little change in plan." He raised the bow higher, aimed directly at Cae's head, and—

"You kill us, you kill yourself!" Velasin shouted.

Ren Adan aimed the bow at him, a manic grin on his face. "What happened to wanting him dead, hmm? You're a good liar, tiern, but not good enough."

"But Laecia's good enough, isn't she?" Velasin panted, bracing his palms against the floor. "And you let her go back to the Aida."

"What's that supposed to mean?"

"You said it yourself: there's no point in keeping us here overnight, and Laecia knows it. So why bother?" Velasin laughed jaggedly. "Because you're her patsy, ren. Because she's going to see everything pinned on you."

Ren Adan made an outraged noise and took a step closer, but

Velasin kept on talking, switching into Ralian as his words came faster. "Think about it. She only wanted Cae to live when she thought she could get away with this, but if it's a choice between him and her? Of course she'll choose herself! You became expendable the second we walked in here. Why else would she tell us everything? Either we'd be swayed, or it wouldn't matter."

The crossbow shook in Ren Adan's grip. "If that were true, she could've felled me along with you and had done with it."

"Really? You really think so? Taking out just the two of us the way she did, that must've cost her enormously. I'll bet she was tired afterwards, wasn't she? Adding in even one other person—that would've been too much. Besides, she needed you to control Ren Zhi; for the two of you to tie us up and haul us down here. She couldn't have done that all on her own."

"No," said Ren Adan—a refusal, not an agreement. "You know nothing of her!"

"I know she's a good enough liar to fool her whole family for years. I know she's smart and adaptable, and I know that, more than anything right now, she wants to *survive.*"

"She needs me," Ren Adan said, and Cae was startled to hear his voice crack. "Everything we've worked for, the future we're building—she *needs* me for that."

"Does she? Or does she just need someone *like* you?" Velasin cocked his head, grinning cruelly. "She already knows your contacts, and right now, what she *needs* is a culprit—not just for what you've already done, but for what she's going to do to us. And that's you, isn't it? You've always done her dirty work. You're the one who found Ren Baru, recruited him with your parents' letters and gave him the crossbow; you're the one who stole it back from his home when he didn't use it, and once he was arrested, it was you who used it to kill him; you who tried to kill me; you who accused Varu Shan in your stead. It was you who recruited Killic, you who clothed him, armed him and set him on Cae. And if you kill us, you'll have done that, too—and Laecia knew, didn't she, that you disagreed with keeping her brother alive? We heard you arguing about it. Didn't you say yourself that she'd forgive you our deaths, too?"

Velasin flopped a hand to indicate the cellar, the offices above. "Knowing that, why else would she leave you here with us, except that she wants you to kill us for her? That way, all she needs to do is point the guards in the right direction. And so many of the guards love her, don't they? All she'd need to do is whisper in the right ear, and you'd die resisting arrest, or in custody, and what more proof would the law need than our bodies in your cellar?"

Ren Adan stared at him, trembling all over. "And so what?" he rasped. "Say you're right. Why shouldn't I kill you both and leave Ren Zhi to take the blame?"

"Because you've already killed Ren Zhi," said Velasin, softly, "and because, no matter how far you run from this, Laecia will be forced to chase you, just as you'd have been forced to chase us."

A terrible silence followed. Ren Adan swayed, but didn't lower the crossbow. Chancing a glance at Velasin, Cae licked his lips and, for the first time, spoke.

"But if you let us live," he said, forcing himself to stay perfectly still as Ren Adan turned the bow on him, "we can speak for you. Just your word against hers, you know she'll hold the advantage. But with us as witnesses—"

"*Witnesses,*" Ren Adan spat. "Either way, I end up dead or jailed!"

"Not necessarily," Cae countered. "Not if I ask for clemency on your behalf. After all, my sister is the one with rank, who conspired against her kin. But you; you were just following orders. How could you have told her no, even if things got out of hand? And you're half Ralian; especially after Killic's death, there's the alliance to think of. I can make your life a diplomatic gift. After all, we both want more and better trade with Ralia, don't we? You won't get a better offer from Laecia; not now that she's looking to save her own skin."

Ren Adan wavered, looking between them. Silence stretched like a tendon overextended. Then:

"And I suppose," he said, readjusting his grip on the crossbow, "that you want me to let you out, too? For all of us to go up to the Aida together?"

Cae shot a worried glance at Velasin, who looked equally on edge. He was also frighteningly pale; whatever strength he'd summoned to speak his piece was fading rapidly, and he looked almost in danger of fainting.

"If you go alone," said Velasin, his Tithenai laboured, "Laecia could just arrest you—"

"*Liar!*" Ren Adan shouted—

And aimed at Velasin.

Cae was moving before Ren Adan even pulled the trigger, a hoarse cry ripping from his throat. As if in the terrible slowness of dreams, he heard the bolt fire, but couldn't turn to see its impact; could only lunge forwards, rage and fear a knot in his throat, coming almost within arm's reach of Ren Adan before the merchant dropped the bow and drew his knife, slashing blindly at Cae. The blade cut across his left bicep, scoring a line of hot, white pain, but however adept Ren Adan was at firing an artifex crossbow, he'd clearly never trained in hand-to-hand combat. Cae had: he took the strike with a grunt and used his right hand to intercept the downswing, grabbing Ren Adan around the wrist and squeezing hard, his thumb digging into the tendons. Ren Adan made a strangled noise and dropped the knife; Cae pivoted to the side, pulling Ren Adan's arm with him and yanking it up between his shoulder-blades, kicking viciously at the back of the merchant's knees.

As Ren Adan went down, his shoulder dislocated with an audible *pop;* he yowled in pain and doubled over, but not before Cae knocked the knife out of reach with his boot. His mind was screaming *Vel Vel Vel* but he didn't dare look until he had Ren Adan secured; couldn't risk being struck from behind. Shaking with adrenaline, he grabbed the nearest rope—the rope that had bound Velasin (*don't think of Vel don't look* don't look)—and roughly tied Ren Adan's hands behind his back with all the swift, merciless efficiency for which the Wild Knife was famed. He kicked Ren Adan on his side for good measure—he was bone-pale with the pain from his shoulder, panting for every breath—and only then did he rush to Velasin, heart in his throat at the sight of his husband slumped over.

"Oh gods, saints, please no, Vel, *no*!"

Cae crashed to his knees beside him, hands frantically searching for the wound, for blood. Vel's eyes were closed, and Cae choked back a sob to see he was still breathing, but his panic refused to abate. Where had the bolt struck? Ren Adan had fired too quickly, hadn't properly sighted the shot, but it was still an artifex bow, and he'd been standing so close—

"Stop patting me," Velasin mumbled.

Cae made a pained noise and cupped his face in his hands. "Where are you hit? I need to know, I need to stop the bleeding—"

"'m not hit."

"—pain can put you into shock, you might not feel it at first, but—"

"*Caethari.*" With enormous effort, Velasin lifted his head and looked weakly up at him with eyes whose lids were heavier than usual. "I'm not hit." And then, as Cae opened his mouth to protest this, "I fainted."

Cae looked at Velasin's too-pale face, and remembered the last thought he'd had before Ren Adan had fired.

Swallowing hard, he said, "You fainted?"

"Only a little."

"You *fainted.*"

"Yes."

"*Out of the way of a crossbow bolt?*"

"I am a man," croaked Velasin, with as much dignity as he could muster under the circumstances, "of many talents."

Cae made a noise that was equal parts sob and laughter. Bending over, he pressed their foreheads together.

"Don't scare me like that again," he whispered.

"I'll try my best, but I make no promises." And then, squinting, as Cae lifted back up again, "You're bleeding."

"Only a little." But he winced as he said it, relief at finding Velasin unharmed serving to make his own hurts more noticeable. "It's my left arm, and it's shallow enough. I'll be fine."

"You'd better be. Apart from anything else, I need you to help me up. And don't argue," Velasin said, before Cae could do just that. "I wasn't lying about your sister. We need to get back to the Aida and find out what's happening."

Cae blanched. Knowing Laecia had betrayed him was one thing, but to turn on her partner, too—

"You really think—?"

"I think it's her best option—or it was, when she left here—and if she's even half as clever as I think she is, she knows it."

"Fuck."

"Not now, dear, I'm busy."

Cae stared at his husband. Velasin blinked at him, guileless until a small smile twitched the corner of his mouth. Cae continued to stare; his heart felt at once three sizes too big for his ribs and yet so tender, a single wrong word would bruise it.

"You're ridiculous," he said, his own smile cracking across his face like pond ice thawed by sunlight. "You utterly ridiculous man, you can't even *stand*—"

"Lucky for me, then," Velasin said, looping an arm around Cae's neck, "that I've such a big, strong husband."

"Lucky indeed," Cae murmured. He'd meant to echo Velasin's teasing tone, but even to his own ears he sounded nothing but fond. Velasin's resulting flush stood out more clearly than usual against his ashen skin, and Cae felt fond about that, too; or possibly much more than fond, if he was being honest.

Shaking these thoughts aside, Cae slid his good arm around Velasin's shoulders and took his weight, knees braced as he began to straighten.

"See if you can get your feet under you," he grunted, and felt it when Velasin nodded in answer.

He stood slowly, ignoring the strain in his abused joints, and drew them both upright. Velasin swayed against him, but didn't fall when he tried to walk; just leaned on Cae and held tight to his lin for extra stability. Cae waited a moment, the better to ensure that Velasin wasn't about to faint again, and then carefully spun them both around, where they were instantly met with the pain-racked face of Ren Adan. He'd managed to lever himself back onto his knees, but otherwise hadn't moved.

Cae studied him, eyes narrowed. Ren Adan's dislocated shoulder hung at an unnatural angle, not helped by the way his hands were bound behind his back. Cae would've felt a little guilty about that, had the merchant not just tried to kill them both.

"What now?" rasped Ren Adan. He lifted his chin to bare his throat, or tried to; the effect was somewhat shakier. "Will you kill me, tiern?"

"No," said Cae, after sharing a look with Velasin. "You're coming with us, just like we said." They walked forwards together, and as Ren Adan stared uncomprehendingly at the pair of them, Cae bent down and picked up the trailing end of the rope he'd used to bind the merchant's wrists. "Walk up ahead of us," he said. "I'll tug on this if I have to, but your shoulder won't thank you for it."

Swearing in Khyto, Ren Adan staggered upright with considerable difficulty. Shooting a venomous glance at his captors, he started to move, hobbling awkwardly up the recessed stairs. Happily, these proved wide enough for Cae and Velasin to get up without too much difficulty, emerging into the kitchen.

Ren Adan stopped abruptly, staring at the side wall. Cae was about to chivvy him on when he saw the reason for the delay: amidst a spray of dropped utensils and pottery shards, Ren Zhi lay sprawled facedown on the stone, the pool of blood around his head lapping stickily at what he recognised, with an incongruous pang, as the smashed remains of the Khytoi dragon teapot.

"Walk around him," Cae said softly. Ren Adan cursed again—in Ralian, this time—but complied, head jerking as he stepped over Ren Zhi's outflung arm.

Moving through to the front room, Cae gently deposited Velasin on the couch, letting him rest a moment; he then urged Ren Adan over to the staircase, where he bound the trailing rope securely to the bannister. After a perfunctory frisk to check if Ren Adan had any concealed blades—he didn't—Cae nodded to himself and headed back to reexamine Ren Zhi.

"What are you doing?" Ren Adan asked, the snap of annoyance in his voice failing to mask his fear.

"Checking to see if you really did kill him."

Walking back into the kitchen, Cae crouched down by the Khytoi's supine body, examining the visible wound on the side of his head. Scalp wounds often bled dramatically, but the real danger came from the blood you didn't see, that bruised or pooled beneath the skull. Licking the tips of two fingers, Cae held them beneath Ren Zhi's nose and felt the faintest tickle of breath against them.

"He's still alive!" he called.

"Huzzah!" croaked Velasin, and promptly fell into an ugly coughing fit.

Frowning, Cae hastened back to Ren Adan. "The nearest healer," he said. "Where are they?"

Ren Adan just glared at him.

Resisting the urge to snap, Cae said, "Your shoulder is out of its socket, and fixing it will be harder the longer it stays like that. It's also in your best interests for Ren Zhi to live, so I ask again: Where is the nearest healer?"

Sullenly, Ren Adan said, "There's one at the end of this street," and gave the directions with the reluctance of an old man having his last tooth pulled.

Silently thanking the saints, Cae went back to Velasin and told him what he was doing, departing only when his husband nodded agreement. He left the building with Ren Adan's glare boring holes in his back and set off at a run, more aware that his bleeding arm and bruised, swollen eye were garnering him strange looks than he was of their respective hurts. So long as he had something to do, something that mattered, he was able to push through his own pain; the minute that ceased to be true, however, he knew he'd be in for a reckoning, not least because he was still alight with anxiety. What if Ren Adan broke free in his absence? What if he hurt Velasin? What if Velasin collapsed, and Cae was too late to help him? Ren Adan might easily have given him a false address; what if he wasted precious time wandering the streets, and something terrible happened in his absence?

He was equal parts shocked and relieved, therefore, to find that the healer's clinic was right where Ren Adan had said it would be. Given its location on an upmarket, mercantile street, the waiting room was unsurprisingly filled with well-off adults and a few small children, several of whom were audibly alarmed by his sudden, bloody appearance. He paused, not sure at first whether the healer was already in the room or elsewhere with a patient, until a middle-aged woman dressed all in red appeared from a doorway, her eyes widening at the sight of Cae.

"Ru, please forgive my appearance, but it's an emergency. I'm Tiern Caethari Aeduria, and there's a man been beaten near to death in a building nearby, as well as other injured parties."

Her sharp-eyed gaze raked the wound on his arm. "I can see that," she said. "What other injuries will I be treating?" *Besides your own* was the unspoken rider; her gaze flickered between his arm and eye with all the stern assessment of a teacher proctoring an exam.

"Magical overextension, the aftermath of a magical attack, a dislocated shoulder and a serious head wound."

A murmur ran through the room, and he realised that the gossip would be flowing fast the second he left the clinic. He was annoyed for all of an instant, and then imagined Velasin saying that it was ultimately to their advantage; that, if necessary, these people would be witness to the fact that he'd tried to aid both Ren Zhi and Ren Adan.

Velasin. Cae's heart twisted. *Please, let him be all right.*

Nodding, the ru called out instructions to her assistants, deputising this and organising that, until a stocky kem with wide, dark eyes and golden skin emerged into the waiting room, a healer's bag slung over one muscular shoulder.

"Right," said the ru. "Lead on, please!"

"This way," said Cae, and set off at a fast walk, refusing to give his fears the satisfaction of running. During the trip, he established the names of his helpers—Ru Irevis Tiek and Ren Cadi Ghon—and somehow managed to convey that Ren Adan was a criminal awaiting arrest and, as such, tied up, without coming off as deranged and untrustworthy. It helped that Ru Irevis had the unflappable air of a seasoned healer, which steadied the more wide-eyed Ren Cadi; even so, when they reached the door to Ren Adan's building, Cae's heart raced with panic, nightmare scenarios tumbling through his head.

To his intense relief, however, he found that Ren Adan was right where he'd left him, sweating and subdued, while Velasin had moved to slump by Ren Zhi's side. He looked up at the sound of their entry, smiling tiredly when he saw Cae.

"I thought I should sit with him," he said. "In case there was a problem."

Cae was saved from answering by Ru Irevis, who took one look at the situation and promptly deputised Ren Cadi to pop Ren Adan's shoulder back in, a task at which thei were evidently practiced. "You'll need to untie him, though," she added, beelining for Ren Zhi.

As Cae went to help Ren Cadi, Ru Irevis shot Velasin an assessing look.

"You'll be the magical overextension case, then?"

Velasin gave a sheepish nod. "Yes, ru."

"*Not* a habit you should get into," she said—and then, as she set about examining Ren Zhi, "Though these have been, I understand, extenuating circumstances."

"You could say that," Cae muttered, glaring at Ren Adan. He reached for the ropes, shooting the captive a pointed look. "Behave now, or I'll dislocate the other one, too."

"Of course," snarked Ren Adan, though his defiance was somewhat undermined by the pained groan he let out as his arms were freed. This promptly morphed to a groan of annoyance as Cae, who wasn't feeling especially trustworthy, retied the rope around Ren Adan's good wrist, yoking him once more to the bannister.

Standing back to give Ren Cadi space, Cae watched as thei took his wrist in one hand and ran a calculated assessment up the rest of the arm with the other, all while a whey-faced Ren Adan stood trembling, mouse-meek and silent. Ren Cadi grunted to thimself—and then, without any outward warning, performed a deft manoeuvre, twisting Ren Adan's wrist while pulling on his forearm. As his shoulder clicked back into place, he bellowed as though he'd been kicked in the jewels, then stood, panting and wide-eyed, as Ren Cadi grinned at him.

"You're welcome," thei said, and walked off to help Ru Irevis, who was running her hands over Ren Zhi's skull, assessing his injury with a healer's cantrip.

With nothing more to do, Cae thumped down on the couch before his legs could buckle. He was, all at once, exhausted; far more so than could be accounted for by his external injuries alone. But then, he supposed, using magic on people without their consent was forbidden for a reason; whatever Laecia had done to subdue them, his body was still suffering the after-effects, which in turn was making his other hurts increasingly difficult to ignore.

As his arm began to throb anew, Cae felt a sudden awful pang for Laecia; what might she have become, if she'd only been allowed to study magic? Nobody had forced her to the path she'd chosen—she was a grown adult, responsible for her actions—and yet his gut twisted bitterly, to know their father's prejudice had impacted her so badly; and worse, that he hadn't known it.

"It's not your fault," said Velasin, softly. His hooded gaze was fixed on Cae. "She hid herself from you."

Grief knifed through him, sharp and sure. "If I'd been a better brother, she'd have trusted me."

"You can't know that for certain."

"Maybe not," Cae whispered, and hung his head.

Part Nine

41

Sitting on the couch in Ren Adan's foyer, mouth sour with the aftertaste of a restorative draught, I submitted meekly to Ru Irevis's examination. Having already pronounced my bruised stomach to be of no immediate concern—"Unless, of course, you start passing bloody stools or water, or bringing up blood"—her main concern was my magical overextension. Merely feeding me her draught, it seemed, was insufficient: she also insisted on checking my eyes, ears, nose and throat, as well as repeatedly taking my pulse to make sure it kept steady.

"I blame you for this," I said to Caethari, now seated beside me with a freshly bandaged arm to match his purpling eye. "You didn't *need* to tell her I tried a contactless charm over distance—"

"Yes, he did," said Ru Irevis, sternly. "For a nonpracticing mage in your current physical condition, it was dangerous indeed—and yes, I know it was necessary, and no, that doesn't change my assessment," she added, before I could get a defensive word in edgewise. "Working magic is the same as working a muscle: you have to build up your strength, know your limits and only test them under safe conditions. Human magic draws primarily on the ambient energy of the world—but *you*, young man, are very much a *part* of the world, and whenever your reach exceeds your grasp, it's your body that power is drawn from. To do that, after you'd already suffered both magical and physical abuse at the hands of another—you're lucky you didn't rupture an organ!"

"I'll bear that in mind," I said weakly.

Ru Irevis glared at me, as if searching for any sign of sass; then she softened, patted my cheek and stood, as though I were a wayward nephew come to his aunt for courting advice.

"I'm glad to hear it," she said. "I recommend at least two days' rest, but I imagine that might have to wait."

"I'm afraid so," said Caethari, who'd been given his own, much less pungent restorative draught and was now visibly impatient to leave. He took a breath, glancing to where a studious Ren Cadi was monitoring the still-unconscious Ren Zhi, and then said, "I hate to impose on you further, ru, but under the circumstances—"

"I quite understand," said Ru Irevis, cutting him off. "Leave your wounded friend with me; I'll see he's taken care of and that this building is watched until you're able to send your people to secure it."

Caethari stood, bowing low to her. "My thanks. I'll be sure to see you recompensed for the trouble."

"Oh, it's no trouble," said Ru Irevis. "If nothing else, you've given my apprentices a good day's practicum. But," she added, a touch of humour in her eyes, "reimbursement is still, of course, appreciated."

With that, she stepped away, leaving my husband to help me up. I was dizzy as I came to my feet, but the feeling subsided after a moment and, to our mutual relief, I found I was able to walk unaided.

Ren Adan waited by the stairs with all the grace of a kicked dog, his wrists bound tightly before him. He was still clearly pained by his shoulder, which ought by rights to have been in a sling, but as untrustworthy as he'd proven to be, that particular medical courtesy would have to wait.

"What a sight we'll make," he said sourly as Cae untied the rope from the bannister, "parading through the streets like this. Like a dog on its hind legs. Would you like to collar me, too?"

"Collar, no," said Caethari, "but I'd be tempted by a muzzle."

In an unprecedented display of wisdom, Ren Adan didn't reply to that.

Still, he wasn't wrong: the sight of two visibly battered men leading a captive third attracted stares once we reached the street, while the poor attendant at the hitching post looked somewhere between stricken and outraged.

"This man is in the custody of Tierns Caethari and Velasin Aeduria," said Cae, in weary explanation.

"Which is us," I added, helpfully. And then, when the attendant still seemed uncertain, "We'll be sending guards soon, to secure his offices. Please feel free to report to them if you've any doubts."

"Of course, tiern. I mean—no, tiern. Yes. Sorry." She sketched an awkward bow and backed away, watching nervously as we unhitched Alik and Luya.

Whatever Ru Irevis's restorative draught had done to shore up my stamina, my torso still ached abominably. For the first time since childhood, I flubbed my first attempt at mounting up, kicking poor Luya in the quarters as I failed to swing a leg over the saddle. Ren Adan laughed, and was instantly punished with a swift jerk on his bound wrists by Cae, who of course had mounted seamlessly despite being in charge of our captive. Setting my jaw, I gripped the pommel, set one foot in the stirrup and boosted up, landing in the saddle with all the spraddled dignity of a jellyfish dropped on a rock. I wheezed quietly for a moment, patting Luya's neck before slowly, painfully straightening.

"Are you all right?" Cae asked, as though that wasn't an entirely absurd question.

I laughed, unable to help myself. "As amusing as it might be to see our friend here try and keep up with a canter, let's stick to a fast walk, shall we?"

And so we did, with Caethari leading and Ren Adan hurrying alongside. With the end of his rope bound to Caethari's saddle, he had no hope of tugging himself free and less slack than he would've liked, and so was forced to content himself with cursing at the pair of us.

By now, it was early afternoon and the streets of Qi-Katai were busy with onlookers. I'd have felt less conspicuous towing a corpse. More than once, we were hailed by city guards who came to see what we were doing with Ren Adan; each time, Caethari stopped and gravely explained both our rank and business, often resulting in flustered apologies from his interlocutors.

Though necessary, I found each forced delay maddening, not least because of my hurts. It rendered me quite waspish, and after the fourth such interruption, I snarked, "Perhaps we should write our business on a banner and hold it aloft, to save time."

Cae glanced at me—just a glance!—and all my anger vanished. "I'd worry more if they didn't stop us," he said. "It would mean the guards of this city were content to see a captive man and not ask questions."

"In that case," I said, "I'll make a note of all the guards I see who don't stop us, so you can yell at them later."

Cae smiled and said, "Please do," and suddenly I didn't hurt quite so much, after all.

By the time we reached the Aida, we'd been stopped a total of six times, while I had a mental list of a further five guard-pairs who'd seen us pass but let us be, the most recent of which, I was somehow unsurprised to note, had been around Amber Gate.

As the Aida's duty-guards let us through, Caethari halted and drew their attention to Ren Adan.

"This man is behind the recent attacks on myself and my husband," he said. "His accomplice is in the Aida. Until they've been brought to justice, nobody else is allowed in or out save by my express command or that of the tieren. Shut the gates. Do you understand me?"

Though startled, they saluted without hesitation. "Yes, tiern!"

We rode on to the stables, the massive gates creaking closed behind us. I'd allowed myself to be grouchily preoccupied on the ride up, but now my wits began to sharpen, recalling the threat of Laecia. It was possible, certainly, that she'd no intention of betraying her co-conspirator, but my Farathel instincts said otherwise, and either way, once she saw the three of us here, she'd be forced to confess or act. It felt trite to recall the old hunters' saying about a cornered animal being the most dangerous, and yet it applied—or very soon would, at least.

As we finally drew to a halt, Ren Taiko came hurrying out to meet us, his tired eyes widening at the sight of Ren Adan and our injuries both.

"Tierns!" he gasped. "Are you well? Should I send for Ru Zairin?"

"We're as well as can be, and will see the good ru in time," said Caethari. He paused to dismount, and I followed suit with a very undignified groan, leaning heavily against Luya's flank as my legs attempted mutiny. My husband looked at me, concerned, but I waved him off with a flap of my hand, silently willing my treacherous muscles to uncramp. As I did so, Cae reiterated the message he'd given the guards at the gate: that nobody was to be allowed out except by his word or his father's.

"But if someone does want to leave and won't be dissuaded," he said, "don't try to stop them yourself. The guards at the gate will do that; just come and send word to us."

"Of course, tiern," said Ren Taiko, and mercifully asked no more.

By this time, our captive's early muttering had long since tailed off, and a glance at his face told me why: Ren Adan was exhausted, near as ashen and sweatier by far than he'd been when Caethari first dislocated his shoulder. With his rope untied from Alik's saddle, he stumbled along before us as we made for the Aida proper, and I suppressed a pang of sympathy for his pitiable state.

We'd barely made it inside before Markel came hurtling around a corner and stopped dead at the sight of us, a look of panicked relief on his face as he took in our injuries.

"We're fine," I signed to him, before he could ask. "It's Laecia, Markel. She's the one behind all this. We're trying not to spook her, but she's a powerful mage, and she's dangerous."

Markel went utterly still. He nodded once, then looked between Cae and me. "How can I help?"

He signed it slowly enough that Caethari must've understood, for he answered, "Find Ru Telitha. Have her tell my father, my sisters and grandmother, along with Tars Raeki and Katvi—and Keletha, if thei're here—to come to the Tieren's Small Hall." This, I vaguely understood, was less a hall than it was a chamber of office: the place where Tieren Halithar conducted most of his business. Very possibly, he was there already.

"Of course," signed Markel, and promptly hurried away.

"You're not worried about his safety?" Cae murmured as we kept walking. "If Laecia tries to take him hostage—"

I smiled grimly. "If she does, it's because she knows he's more valuable to her alive, which is more than can be said for just about anyone else we could send. And in any case, believe me: Markel knows how to look after himself."

"I wonder—"

"Looking for me, brother?"

We stopped in our tracks, my heart racing as Laecia appeared before us. Even knowing how easily she might've learned of our approach, I hadn't expected her to come to us, and my gut lurched with the wrongness of it. Aside from a slight flush, she looked even more composed than she had earlier: she'd changed her clothes, so that she was dressed in various flattering shades of blue, and her freshly coiled braids were immaculate.

"We are," said Caethari, voice even.

For a fleeting moment, Laecia's gaze landed on Ren Adan, and I saw him tense, though in expectation of what I couldn't have said. But she looked away without granting him further acknowledgement, and his fists clenched at the slight. She lifted her chin, as bold as she'd been in his offices, and for a horrible moment I thought she was going to disable us again, or else use some new magic to aid in her escape.

Instead, she asked us mildly, "Well. I suppose we should have this out like civilised people, shouldn't we? Where are we headed?"

"The Tieren's Small Hall," said Caethari, after an almost imperceptible pause.

Laecia smiled at him, and it didn't reach her eyes. "I'll lead on, then."

42

The most awkward silence following the most awkward remark at the most awkward Farathel gathering I'd ever had the misfortune of attending couldn't hold a candle to the awkwardness that followed. Acting as though nothing at all was amiss and without so much as a word to her captive co-conspirator, Laecia led us silently to the Tieren's Small Hall, a squarish room whose high windows let in stripes of light, and whose raised stone dais was dominated by an imposing wooden desk, its surface set with the bureaucratic tools of the tieren's office. Portraits of past tierens, tierenas and tierenai hung from the walls like a built-in jury, presiding over the rows of seats that faced both desk and dais.

"I imagine you've sent for the others," Laecia remarked.

It wasn't a question, but Caethari nodded anyway, and I felt a spike of rage on his behalf, that his own sister had first betrayed him and was now behaving as though it were of no consequence.

"In that case," she said, "I see no need to stand on ceremony." She eyed the identical rows of chairs that stretched almost to the back wall, divided down the centre by a single aisle, before finally seating herself on the right, three rows back from the front and two across.

It felt wrong to sit, as though by doing so we'd somehow be taking the bait of the trap that was Laecia, but pragmatism and physical tiredness won out over suspicion, and after a moment, led by Cae, we sat side by side in the first row on the left, with Cae playing out enough slack in Ren Adan's rope that he could take the corresponding front-row seat on the right. There were no entrances to the rear of the room, and yet it felt imprudent to take our eyes off Laecia, which meant we all sat twisted around—even Ren Adan, whose expression now was one of affronted confusion.

"You know," said Laecia, sounding amused, "you could watch me more easily from the back."

"And leave nothing and no one between you and the door?" Caethari replied. "I'd rather not."

Laecia snorted. "Oh, please. We both know I could have you writhing on the ground in a heartbeat if I wanted."

"Then why don't you?" I asked.

"Good manners?" she suggested, making a show of examining her nails.

"Or magical exhaustion, more like," I said. Her head jerked up at that, and I had the brief satisfaction of feeling that I'd won a point. "Truly, what you did to us was extraordinary—to wring that much power from a charm? It was a charm, wasn't it? Or have you mastered silent cantrips?" When she didn't reply, I went on, "It's impressive either way, of course, but impressive acts come at a price."

"A price with which I'd be more familiar than you, I'm sure," she shot back.

I smiled and said nothing, and mercifully, neither did she—not until some minutes later, when Riya came hurrying in.

"What's going on?" she demanded, her expression and tone shifting comically as she noticed Ren Adan's bonds. "What—?"

"Don't strain yourself, sister," Laecia drawled. "Just take a seat. You'll find out soon enough."

Riya baulked at this, only to be told by a weary Caethari, "She's not wrong, Ri. Just sit."

Riya complied with ill grace, foot tapping impatiently until the next arrival. Raeki took one look at our visible injuries and scowled, but otherwise made no comment, silently assuming a watchful stance on one side of the doors while Tar Katvi, with whom he'd entered, mirrored him on the other. Keletha came next, which surprised me—I'd assumed thei'd be out of the Aida—and promptly sat down by Riya. Next came Yasa Kithadi, attended by both Markel and Ru Telitha, as regal as a queen. She did not sit, but moved to stand at the base of the dais, Ru Telitha staying by her side as Markel hurried to mine.

Which left only Tieren Halithar.

Minutes ticked by in an agony of silence that no one was either willing or able to break. With Raeki and Tar Katvi guarding the doors, there was technically no need to keep watching Laecia, and yet I felt compelled to do so. Perhaps I was imagining it, but it seemed to me that her father's tardiness angered her: she sat straighter the longer he took to arrive, hands perfectly still in her lap, but though her face was set in an expression of disinterest, it was the feigned unconcern of a house cat sprawled by a hole in the skirting-board.

When the tieren finally arrived, the atmosphere of the room changed so sharply, it felt like the shift in air before a storm, an impression aided by the rumbling *thud* of the double-doors shutting behind him. Dressed immaculately in matching shades of grey, his silver braid swinging behind him, the tieren assessed the room with a cool, sharp gaze and moved to stand beside Yasa Kithadi, directly before his desk but below the dais.

"Caethari, Velasin," he said. "You've asked for us, and now we're here. I'd like an explanation."

Slowly, Cae stood, and I stood with him. As though they'd coordinated the movement, both yasa and tieren stepped aside, making room for us in the shadow of the dais, the rope in Cae's hand stretched taut where it led to Ren Adan. I kept my eyes fixed on Laecia, but her attention never wavered: of everyone in the room, it was Tieren Halithar she watched, and him alone.

"There's no pretty words for this," Caethari said, "and so I'll speak plainly. This morning, Vel and I were attacked and imprisoned by Laecia and her co-conspirator, Ren Adan—" He gave a brief, demonstrative jerk of the rope, which coincided with a startled murmur from those listening. "—who've been behind the many recent breaches of the Aida's peace, including the murder of Ren Vaia Skai."

Yasa Kithadi let out a cry at that. She looked at Laecia in furious, grieving disbelief and took a half step forwards, but Ru Telitha gripped her wrist and murmured something I didn't catch, and the yasa, glaring balefully, subsided.

"You accuse your sister?" the tieren asked, shocked. "On what basis?"

"On the basis of my own eyes and testament," said Caethari grimly, "and the evidence of Ren Adan."

And with that, he began to lay out the whole sorry business, beginning with Laecia's bitterness about being denied magical tuition—the tieren blanched at that, but didn't interject—her association with Ren Adan, and their joint aspirations for the governance of Qi-Katai. From there, the bungled conspiracy was laid out like a hand of cards: the recruitment of Ren Baru, his foolish (but for me, fortuitous) choice of knife over crossbow; Ren Vaia's role as their intermediary; the provocative "attack" on Tieren Halithar; the slaughter of Quip and the murder of Ren Baru; Ren Adan's failure to either end my life or retrieve the missing crossbow bolt; the murder of Ren Vaia; the recruitment of Killic and, voice growing hoarse by then, the events of the past few hours, including Laecia's use of magic, Ren Adan's use of the crossbow and the near-death of Ren Zhi.

With our tale done, Caethari hauled Ren Adan to the fore, where he first grudgingly and then defiantly confirmed both his and Laecia's part in things before Tieren Halithar's questioning. The tieren remained stone-faced throughout, but his clenching hands and a tic in his jaw said that he was far from unmoved.

"You have no regrets, then?" he asked Ren Adan.

Ren Adan laughed hoarsely. "I'm a merchant, tieren; as is the way of traders, I have gambled on reward over risk and, as is sometimes the case, I have lost. Why should I regret it? All great ventures come with the risk of casualties. I had the aid and sanction of an Aeduria, and I do not believe our plans would've been to the detriment of Qi-Katai—quite the opposite, in fact." Though swaying on his feet, he lifted his head and met the tieren's gaze. "That you have a prejudicial view of magic is your own failing, one for which your daughter has suffered. Yet even so, we never sought to usurp your rule; instead, we aimed to ensure its legacy. Hold such crimes against me as you will; I have said my piece."

With that, he sketched a mocking bow, or as much of one as his bound hands and injured shoulder permitted, and stretched out his rope to resume his seat. Then:

"Laecia," said the tieren, in a voice like the first, betraying rumble of an avalanche. "What have you to say in your defence?"

All eyes turned as Laecia rose from her seat and traversed the aisle, coming to stand before her father. Head held proudly, she ignored Yasa Kithadi's venomous stare and said, "In my defence, I never aimed to break anything of value that I didn't intend to fix. I didn't try to kill you or Cae. I only sought to secure an inheritance which, for *stupid* reasons—" Her voice cracked on the word, though she was quick to recover. "—has always hung in the balance between my siblings. Never me. No matter what I did, how hard I worked, it was *never me*!"

"You idiot girl," the yasa cried, stepping forwards at last, "of *course* it was you! Do you think your father and I are fools? Did you think us oblivious to Caethari's preferences, to your skills and ambitions? We both favoured *you*!"

The words hit Laecia like a slap. Incredulity washed across her face, chased first by shock and then by anguish. "What?"

"Laecia," said the tieren, voice heavy with grief, "why else would I refuse to let you study with Ruya's Order? Temple-sworn mages cannot serve as city officials or administrators; you *know* that. If I never wanted you as an heir, of course I'd have let you go."

"*Then why not say so?*" Laecia screamed, a terrible sob in her voice. Her composure had utterly melted away; she looked so young, and I didn't want to pity her, but in that moment, she reminded me so strongly of Revic near the end that the feeling snuck up of its own accord. "Why not ever *say* so? Why let me flounder in the belief that I was never enough; that nothing I could do would ever matter?"

"Because you always rose to the challenge," said Yasa Kithadi. "Everything you did, it proved your willingness to work, to embrace the thankless but necessary tasks of rule and do well by them."

"And because you weren't floundering," the tieren added, softly. "Not that we could see."

Laecia laughed, ugly and jagged. "How could I have let you see, when I wanted to show only strength?" And then, with a suddenness that was downright eerie, her whole demeanour shifted: all her grief went sharp and flat, like a cleaver turned blade-down. "No," she hissed. "I don't believe you. I don't believe either of you!"

Of all the things she'd said, it was this that struck Tieren Halithar most deeply; he let out a noise, so soft as to be almost inaudible, as something vital went out of his eyes, some lingering spark of hope. Laecia stepped away from him, staring wildly around the room; I'd no doubt she'd come in with a plan, but she'd been left unmoored by this last, unlooked-for revelation, and was now caught between doubt and action. She turned in place, looking at everyone present as if in search of an answer, until her attention finally snagged on Ren Adan, whose expression I found unreadable.

And then she began to laugh.

"I never needed you," she said, between horrible bursts of laughter. "*I never needed you!*"

Ren Adan shrank from her. "Laecia—"

"*No,*" she snarled, whirling back to her father. "What I *needed* was a sign, any sign, that you valued me. But you never did, did you?" She scrubbed a hand across her eyes, smiling awfully. "That's why our mother left, you know that? You stopped caring, or stopped acting like it, and after a while, that's really the same thing."

The tieren went rigid. "I valued your mother as highly as I've ever valued anyone."

"And what good was that, when she couldn't tell?" Laecia shot back. "You valued what she did for you, not who she was. You started seeing only the tierena and stopped seeing Inavi, so Inavi *left.* She left you, just like I tried to leave. But you wouldn't let me go!" She laughed again, the sound like breaking glass. "You might've spared me from this, if you'd only known how to be kind."

"Your choices were your own. Whatever my faults might be, I cannot—"

"*Might* be? What they *might be*?" She stepped into his face, then paused, her wildness transmuting into something else. Her features stilled, and when she spoke again, her voice was almost calm. "You'd have let me doubt my whole life, wouldn't you? Both of you," she added, sparing a flat, uncanny glance for Yasa Kithadi. "I'm still angry at you, grandmother, but—" She shrugged, not quite smiling. "—I never thought you liked me in the first place, so it doesn't sting as much. But you?" She turned back to her father, and just for an instant, I saw mania in her eyes. "You should've known better. But you wouldn't learn." Her expression raised the hairs on my neck. "You won't learn," Laecia whispered, and before I could move—before anyone could intervene—she raised her hand and *twisted.*

Tieren Halithar's jugular stood out like a cord along his throat. He made a single, strangled noise and collapsed against the dais.

His face and eyes were red—not from exertion, I realised with horror, but because his blood vessels were bursting. He opened his mouth—to scream, to beg—but only blood came out. As Riya shrieked and ran to help, Caethari grabbed for him, kneeling to try and keep him upright, but all the tieren could do was clutch at his arm, blood dribbling from his mouth, before he spasmed and went suddenly, awfully slack.

He was dead.

43

No!" sobbed Riya. "No, no, *no*—"

She fell to her knees beside her father, gripping his lin and shaking, but the light had already gone from his eyes.

Horrified, Caethari stared up at his murderous sister. "Laecia," he whispered. "What have you done?"

Laecia didn't answer. Like Riya, she was staring at the fallen body of Tieren Halithar; unlike Riya, she showed no sadness, only a sort of brittle disbelief.

"I broke his heart," said Laecia, more to herself than to anyone else. And then, more loudly, almost triumphant, "I broke his *fucking* heart!"

Yasa Kithadi was ashen with shock, swaying where she stood. Ru Telitha grabbed her on one side, and suddenly Keletha was there, too, supporting thir sister's elbow as Tar Katvi, face frozen in fury, approached with her sword drawn.

"Tiera Laecia Siva Aeduria, you are hereby detained for the murder of Tieren Halithar. Should you resist, I am authorised to act—"

"Then act," said Laecia.

Tar Katvi dropped, spasming in a way that recalled the nerve-trick to which we'd already been subjected. Laecia lifted her head and smiled terribly at the room at large, all of us rooted in place, all powerless against her abuse of magic. With Katvi still under her control, Laecia stooped and claimed the tar's sword; Raeki rushed forwards, but within seconds he, too, was on the ground, watching through bulging eyes as Laecia slashed through Katvi's throat. Ru Telitha cried out at that, a horrified shriek as Katvi's blood gushed onto the floor.

"Stay down, Raeki," Laecia warned, pointing the dripping sword at him. "Or you'll be next."

Turning, she walked over to Ren Adan, who'd watched the violence unfold with the same incomprehension as the rest of us. Gesturing with her stolen blade, she said, "Hold up your hands."

Mutely, he obeyed, flinching as Laecia sliced through his bonds with a blank, eerie calm.

"Come," she said, as if to a dog.

Ren Adan came slowly to his feet, eyeing the sword with trepidation. "Laecia," he tried gamely, "I don't think—"

"Correct. You don't think. I do."

"Laecia," he said, "you need to stop. This can't work. You just killed your fath—"

The sword flashed once, and Ren Adan dropped with a red gash where his throat had been.

"Oh gods," I whispered. Something had broken in Laecia, and as she turned and stared at us, there was nothing behind her eyes at all.

When that empty gaze fixed on me, my heart stopped.

"Velasin," she said. "Come here."

Behind me, I heard Caethari scrabble, struggling with his father's dead-weight. I felt his hand grab at my leg. "Vel, no—"

"It's all right," I said, though it wasn't at all. I walked to Laecia. As casually as if she'd performed the same manoeuvre a thousand times, she gripped the back of my neck with one hand and set her blade to my throat with the other.

"Get up, Cae. You're letting me out." The wet blade kissed my jugular, and oh, its edge was sharp, so sharp. "He's my *leverage.*"

"All right." Caethari rose on unsteady legs, his hands held up in a show of peace. "All right. Whatever you want."

"Oh, it's too late for *that,*" said Laecia. "You go first. Walk out there. Clear a path. Tell them I'm inviolate or your husband dies, you understand?"

"I do," said Cae, and did as she commanded.

Out into the hall we went, my pulse hammering. It felt surreal, impossible that I'd just watched the woman who now held my life in her hands murder three people, and yet I could feel the blood of Tar Katvi and Ren Adan as a sticky line against my skin; could almost hear the drip of it from the sword-blade onto my clothes. Laecia was shorter than me, but not by much; just enough that she had to angle the sword up to keep it in position, which left me walking with my chin raised high, so that most of what I saw was ceilings, walls and empty air. As if in a dream, I heard the terrified shouts of servants; Caethari's desperate commands to keep them calm.

And then, of all the ironies, I remembered the night I'd pressed a blade to my throat of my own volition, and had to choke back a gale of terrified laughter.

Apparently, I didn't do a good enough job of it.

"What's so funny?" Laecia snapped. "And don't say *nothing*."

I giggled, an absurd, fatalistic part of me suddenly desperate to say just that. Struggling to master myself and not quite succeeding, I said, "All this time, you never knew why I trusted your brother; why your Wild Knife ploy didn't work." The word *knife* set me off again; I was absolutely terrified, and still I could barely stop laughing. "And this, what we're doing right now, it reminded me of why."

"Oh?" said Laecia. "And how's that?"

I grinned so hard it hurt. "Because I tried to kill myself, my first night here. I put a knife to my neck, but your brother stopped me. Saved me. How could I think he wanted me dead, after something like that? And yet here we are, and you'll likely kill me anyway."

"Huh," said Laecia, and I swear I heard her tilt her head, considering. She laughed a little, too, a tiny *hah* that I felt on my neck. "You're right, Velasin. That *is* funny."

Sunlight broke over us, lancing into my eyes as we entered the courtyard. Unable to see my footing, I stumbled, forcing the blade to score a line across my neck. I barely felt the sting of it, but the anguish in Cae's voice as he cried out to me was almost more than I could stand.

"It's just a scratch," I made myself say. "I'm fine."

"Quiet," Laecia hissed.

Reflexively, I raised my hands to show my obedience, as Caethari had done—and then, through my panicked stupor, I recalled that I had two voices.

With that realisation, my scattered wits came scrambling back like off-duty soldiers summoned by a war-horn. I had no wish to die today, and in a sudden burst of thought, I dared to hope that I might not have to.

Dipping my head as much as I dared to make sure Caethari could see me, I signed at him, small and slow, using the alphabet to spell out words for which he didn't yet know the signs. His eyes went wide, and I'd just completed my message when Laecia, belatedly noticing, forced my head up again.

"None of that!" she snarled. "Put your hands down!"

I obeyed, heart racing, and could only hope Caethari had understood me; that he trusted what I was trying to do.

We reached the stables, the scent of hay and horse strong in my nostrils. I couldn't see Ren Taiko, but I heard his dismayed exclamations as Caethari stopped him from intervening with Laecia.

"What was that?" snapped Laecia—suddenly, from my perspective. "No whispering, Caethari!"

"I was just telling him to go," said Cae. "He doesn't need to be here for this. I'll fetch your horse myself."

"Do it, then."

I shut my eyes, listening to the familiar sounds of a horse being saddled, trying to ignore the fading burn of the cut on my neck, the tackiness of the secondhand blood, the stench of my own fear-sweat. Minutes passed with all the comfort of ants crawling over naked flesh, and still I startled to hear the clip-clop of approaching hooves. There was a whuffle as the horse stopped at my shoulder, and for a handful of glorious moments, the blade was gone from my neck as Laecia mounted up. Yet I didn't dare move: the threat of her magic was too strong, and within seconds, the blade was back, this time angled down, so that I could see again. It came as a shock when she grabbed my hair, fisting it tightly enough that I yelped.

Evidently, Laecia was a skilled enough rider to steer with her knees: she clicked to the horse and it walked on, leaving me to stumble along beside her in an uncomfortable echo of Ren Adan's trip to the Aida.

With Caethari still leading, we passed the Court of Swords and headed for the main gates, which were still shut tight. Caethari yelled to the guards to open them and stand back, and as I gauged the distance between us and the Aida, us and the gates, I realised I had no time left in which to act. I could only hope Caethari had understood my signs; could only hope I was right in thinking he'd passed that message to Ren Taiko; could only hope Ren Taiko in turn had delivered it; that the delivery had been acted upon. Because if it hadn't—

I raised a hand, grabbed Laecia's lin and, with Ru Irevis's earlier warnings clear as a bell in my thoughts, I summoned fire.

Not just a spark, as I usually would—as I'd feared to do with Killic in my father's garden, what felt a thousand years ago—but *fire.*

Laecia's clothes went up like tinder. She shrieked in pain and shock and—as I'd hoped—let go of me in instinctive favour of trying to put out the flames. Her horse screamed beneath her, bucking in fear, and though my body went cold all over, teetering once more on the brink of magical overextension, still I forced myself to *run:* to get out of Laecia's range. Every instinct screamed at me to head for Cae, but that would've put me once more between her and the gate, where I had no desire to be. I made instead for the stables, stumbling on fawn-wobbly legs as my body throbbed and Laecia screamed and I hoped against hope against hope that Caethari had listened, and Taiko, and Markel—

Laecia's screams abruptly cut off in a horrible, choking gargle. I turned, sight briefly greying out, in time to see an arrow protruding from her throat, the wooden shaft already catching alight as she burned like a taper. I tipped my gaze up to the Aida's walls, following the line of the shot, and saw a cluster of familiar figures standing on a balcony. There stood Raeki, Keletha, Riya; there Ru Telitha and Yasa Kithadi; and dearest of all, his skilled hands holding the bow, there was Markel, sighting down the length of another arrow.

He let it fly. The second shot took Laecia through the forehead, and as her terrified horse screamed and reared again, hooves pawing at the air, her burning body toppled over backwards and hit the ground with a dull, ugly thump.

Gasping, I fell to my knees. My vision swam. I wanted to throw up, but also felt like I might lose a lung if I did. I had a dim sense of Caethari running towards me, shouting my name, but he sounded as though he was calling from underwater. He reached for me, and for a strangely perfect second, all I could see was the arc of his braid as it swung through the air, the light glinting off it like gold leaf over obsidian.

Then the world went dark.

44

I woke somewhere soft and possibly familiar, though it was hard to tell at first. There was a strange pressure on my right hand, my vision was fuzzy and I couldn't remember where I was or how I'd come to be there. I frowned at this, perturbed, and tried to focus on a nearby blur, which I suspected of being responsible for the odd feeling in my hand. I tried to clear my throat, but what came out was a rasping noise—at which point, the blur jerked and rose, becoming a lighter shape with dark around the edges.

I blinked several times, attempting to clear away the fog, until the blur resolved itself into Caethari's face. One eye was still bruised, but less than it had been in a way that spoke to magical healing, though both were red-rimmed and heavy with bags. I smiled at him, dopily pleased by his presence, then frowned again when he started to weep. He was clutching my hand, I realised—the pressure I'd felt—and now he raised it to his lips, kissing my knuckles over and over.

"Saints, Vel," he whispered, voice utterly wrecked, and yet his eyes were bright as new coins behind his tears. "You've got to stop scaring me like that."

"Like what?" I croaked, and then it all came back to me, the memories hitting like a slaughterhouse hammer. "Oh."

"*Oh,* he says." Caethari rubbed his eyes, smile tremulous but achingly real, then broke the moment by reaching for a pitcher and cup on a nearby table. "Here, you need to drink. Ru Zairin was very emphatic about getting your fluids up once you were awake again."

I complied with relish; my throat was sore, but I hadn't realised how parched I was until I started drinking and couldn't seem to stop. I just about emptied the pitcher, Caethari refilling my cup each time and holding it to my lips, so careful that he never spilled a drop. It was only when I'd finished that I realised the enormity of what he'd lost, and the circumstances under which he'd lost it, and felt my chest ache in sympathy.

Testing my left hand, which felt like lead but was nonetheless mercifully operable, I lifted it and reached clumsily for his cheek, warmed all the way through when he leaned into the touch.

"I'm so sorry, Cae. Your father—"

"Please, don't." Caethari shut his eyes, and I realised then that his tears were for more than just my survival. "Not yet. I can't—right now, I just need to know that you're well. That someone I love made it out of this undamaged."

My heart about stopped in my chest. "I'm someone you love?"

Caethari laughed weakly. "I ought to hedge, I suppose, but yes. I'm too tired to lie. My sisters—" He broke off, raw pain in his eyes, before continuing, "—my *sister* will tell you, I've always been prone to falling fast, and you, Vel . . . I've been falling for you since the day you got here." He inhaled sharply, looking away. "And I'm—I'm sorry if that's too much, too soon, but I can't—under the circumstances, I can't bring myself t—"

I reeled him in by the nape of the neck and kissed him. Not a deep kiss, as I lacked the energy, nor even open-mouthed, as I surely tasted terrible, but a lingering press, into which I put all the dizzying things Cae made me feel.

"I can't say it yet," I whispered, when we finally broke apart. "I'm not—it doesn't come easy to me, but I think—I feel—if you give me time—"

"Take all the time you need," Cae rasped, and pressed a kiss to my forehead. His lips were dry and cool, and if I felt a tear or two slip into my hairline, I didn't remark upon it.

"How long was I out?" I asked, when he sat back again. We were in the infirmary, I realised. Only one bed other than mine was occupied, but it still felt odd that nobody else was in attendance.

"A little over a day," he said. "After . . . after, ever since, we've been taking turns to sit with you. I didn't want to leave, but there's been—there's been so much to do, and I—"

"Oh, sweetheart," I said, the endearment slipping out of its own volition. Cae made a wounded noise and pressed his head to the edge of the mattress, crying into the linen. I stroked his hair, still bound in yesterday's messy braid yet streaked with new threads of silver, and wished his heart could be healed as easily as his flesh.

Finally, Caethari lifted his head and managed what was almost a smile. "I need to tell the others you're awake," he said. "Markel especially, but Ru Zairin and Ru Irevis will want to see you, too."

I blinked. "Ru Irevis is here?"

He nodded. "Yesterday, after . . . after, we sent Raeki and some of his people down to secure Ren Adan's offices, and the healers were still there with Ren Zhi. He was brought up here on a stretcher, and Ru Irevis didn't want to leave without knowing he'd recovered. Also, she said something about giving her apprentices another practicum day, and I wasn't about to argue with her." We both smiled at that.

I peered anew at the other occupied bed, just able to discern a bandaged head peeping out from beneath the blankets. "That's him, then? How's he doing?"

"He's stable, apparently. He still hasn't woken, but he's no longer unconscious: Ru Irevis put him in a healing sleep last night, and if all goes well, he's due to wake some time tomorrow."

"That's a relief."

Caethari nodded. Reluctantly, he said, "I really do need to tell them you're conscious, now."

"I'll be right here," I replied, and counted it a victory when he nodded.

Within minutes, Markel came hurtling in, beaming hugely. He flung himself at me, hugging me around the neck, and though I was slightly winded, I appreciated his fervour, reaching up to hug him back.

"No more magic!" he signed emphatically. "That visiting ru was very specific: no more magic for at least five weeks, or you'll damage yourself irreparably."

"I've no desire to attempt it ever again," I assured him. And then, because Cae wasn't there to be hurt by it, "You saved my life, you know. I saw your second shot. She wasn't an easy target, but you made it clean. Thank you."

Markel's expression turned grave. "It gave me no pleasure. Anyone else, I would've shot to wound, but that magic of hers—I was terrified that she'd lash out again, do one of those tricks she used on the tars or the tieren. And if she'd lived and woken still feeling murderous but with her strength restored, what then?"

"What then indeed," I whispered, and swallowed a horrible pang of guilt. Eventually, Caethari and I would have to talk about my role in Laecia's death: how I'd summoned fire, and how I'd earlier signed to him *I'll distract, Markel shoot* and left him to act on that message without knowing whether *shoot* would mean death or wounding. In the moment, I'd thought only that Laecia was untouchable within melee range: that a bow alone could take her out, and only—if I wanted to live; or rather, if the shooter did—if the blade was gone from my throat and she was unable, somehow, to retaliate against me while I fled. That it had worked at all was miraculous, but beyond my survival, the victory was hollow. Caethari had still lost both his father and sister, and for all her evils, I didn't doubt that he'd loved her.

I was distracted from these maudlin thoughts by the arrival, first of Rus Zairin and Irevis, for whom Markel immediately made way, and then of Caethari, who dragged his chair to the foot of my bed and sat with a hand curled possessively over my ankle as I was thoroughly poked and prodded.

I allowed myself to voice a small worry. "Is it a bad sign that I'm not desperate to relieve myself?"

"Not at all," said Ru Zairin, to my considerable relief, not least because I didn't quite feel capable of standing. "Oddly, it's a side effect of the magical overextension, though it ought to clear up once you get some nutrients into your system."

After that, I complained as much as I dared, which wasn't very, and received an extremely stern reprimand from Ru Irevis on the precice nature of my foolishness, which she softened by saying she was glad to see me recovering. After consulting together, both healers agreed that I ought to stay abed for the next three days at least—"By which I mean *resting,* tierns," said Ru Zairin, looking pointedly at a blushing Caethari—and to exert myself only gently for a week after, making sure to stop and rest the moment I started to tire. I promised to do my best and was treated to a matched pair of withering looks, after which Ru Zairin also said that I'd likely need to eat and drink more than usual in the coming days, and to consider an increased appetite a positive sign.

At the mention of food, my stomach rumbled. "I could eat," I admitted, and Markel was promptly sent to the kitchen for a tray of food, with Ru Zairin writing out a list of suggestions for Ren Valiu which, in thir opinion, were most likely to speed my recovery.

With that done, Ru Zairin excused thimself once more, while Ru Irevis gave Ren Zhi a quick once-over before departing. Caethari waited until the sound of her footsteps had faded, then moved his chair back to its original position and took my hand once more.

"Vel," he said, "I'll understand if you don't feel up to it, but Riya—Riya wanted to speak to you, too. To both of us, really, but I don't know what it's about."

"Of course," I said. I had no fear of Riya, and she'd lost every bit as much as Caethari had, with her wife too far away to be of immediate comfort. "We can see her now, if you like."

Caethari smiled in relief. To my surprise, he rose, walked to the infirmary door and poked his head into the hallway, returning a moment later with his sister.

Riya's eyes were bloodshot from weeping, her usual elegance

frayed with grief. She sat in the chair that had been Cae's, her brother standing beside us both, and was silent for a long, pained moment.

"I'm so sorry," she said at last, her voice hoarse with emotion. "I don't—I hardly know how to process this. What Laecia did to you—"

"You don't need to apologise for her," I said, as gently as I could. "You're no more to blame than Caethari."

Riya looked like she wanted to argue, but bit her lip and nodded. After a moment, she went on, "I'm—I'm the heir, now. I won't lie and say I never thought I would be, but this is sooner—" She broke off, twisting in her seat to look at her brother. "Do you want it?" she asked suddenly. "The title, that is."

Caethari flinched. "No," he said, firmly. "Come to that, I don't want our grandmother's inheritance either, but that's a bridge we hopefully won't have to cross for a good many years."

"From your lips to the saints' ears," Riya murmured. She shook her head at some thought or other to which I wasn't privy, then said, "Well. There'll still have to be a confirmation ceremony, after the—after the funerals, but to all intents and purposes, I'm the tierena now, and a tierena needs an heir. Which is, after all, a part of why I came home in the first place." She took a deep breath, then said, "At your marriage-gathering, I ended up speaking to Liran. And I realised, I've always liked him, he's smart and kind, and he's unconventional enough not to baulk at negotiated paternity. So I asked him if he was interested in siring mine and Kivali's child. And he said yes. But only on the condition that the two of you had no objections." She looked uncertainly at Cae. "So. Do you?"

Caethari's mouth hung open; I doubt he could've looked more stunned if his sister had produced a fish and smacked him about the face with it. "Liran's child," he said at last. "By your body, or Kivali's?"

"We haven't formally decided yet," she admitted. "Why, does it matter?"

Caethari blinked—and then, impossibly, he laughed. "No," he

said. "Not in the slightest. Ri, I'm so happy for you! Liran, siring my future nibling!"

"I've no objections either," I added quickly, before their enthusiasm could dim. "It sounds like an excellent idea."

Riya promptly burst into tears; I was briefly alarmed, but then she started laughing, too, and I realised it was happy crying—or as happy as crying could be, right now. Impulsively, I took her hand and squeezed; Caethari bent down to hug her, and soon I was wiping away tears of my own, the prospect of such joy amidst grief a balm to my deeper hurts.

"Thank you," Riya said, once she'd wiped her eyes. "I'll go and tell him, then." Her smile dimmed a little. "I can't promise that I'll fill him in on the rest of what's happened beyond the main details, but—"

"He's always welcome to visit," said Cae. "Now more than ever. We'd both be happy to see him."

Riya nodded, relieved, and when she rose to her feet once more, she carried with her a little of her customary poise. "I'll tell him so," she said, and with a parting smile, she exited the infirmary.

"You truly don't mind?" asked Caethari, his tone more curious than anything.

"Why should I?"

"No reason at all," he said, and leaned in to kiss my cheek.

We'd just progressed to a different type of kissing when Markel returned with a tray overflowing with food. Grinning at the pair of us, he handed the tray to Caethari, snagged himself an extra chair and sat down at the bedside. "Ren Valiu insisted on sending enough for three," he signed, "and I don't know about your husband, but I'm starving!"

I conveyed this to Cae, who looked quite overwhelmed by such a simple courtesy, and within moments, the three of us were eating together, jidha and little suns jostling alongside savoury greens and pork dumplings, with three cups of khai into the bargain.

As we ate together, a strange sensation startled to bubble beneath my chest: a sort of fizzing lightness like champagne bubbles. Here were the two people I cared about most in all the world, grinning at each other and me as we shared a meal: a tiny pocket of joy in the midst of a turbulent world. The feeling reached out of me like tendrils, encompassing the prospect of Riya, Kivali and Liran's child; the friendship offered by Nairi and her soldiers; the growing bond between Markel and Ru Telitha. It almost felt familiar, but it wasn't until Caethari dropped a little sun on Markel's plate and urged him to try it, lighting up at the rapturous expression that crossed his face when he did so, that I realised what it was.

It felt like family.

45

Three days later, I lay in bed with my husband's head curled against me, running my fingers through his hair. The morning light warmed both of us, though not as much as we warmed each other, and for all that we hadn't spoken of it, I suspected we'd both been mentally counting down the days of Ru Zairin's injunction to *only rest* in bed until now.

It was, after all, one of a very few pleasant things we'd had to look forward to.

"I don't want to get up," Caethari murmured. The arm he'd slung over my hips tightened incrementally. "I don't want to go out there."

"I know," I said, gently. *Out there* meant organising funerals for his father and sister, sharing in Riya's terrible grief as they struggled to contact their absent mother; *out there* meant skirting Yasa Kithadi's as-yet-polite but nonetheless painful requests to talk about his becoming her official heir to the yaserate. Nor were all the burdens his: for me, *out there* meant meeting with the Ralian ambassador, who was frantic to hear my account of all that had happened with Killic; *out there* meant facing the diplomatic repercussions of Laecia's death at mine and Markel's hands and, eventually, an audience with the Asa Ivadi Ruqai in Qi-Xihan. "I don't want to go out, either."

Out there contained a great many things that neither of us, in that particular moment, felt equipped to deal with—but *in here,* in bed, we had only each other.

Caethari had said he loved me.

I didn't know what to do with that, except be dizzied by it. Under the circumstances, it felt wrong, grotesque, that I should have such a miraculous thing as knowledge of a husband's love to warm me, when the husband in question was mired in loss. I wanted to say it back to him, if only so that he, too, would have something bright to cling to, but could no more twist my tongue to utter what I wasn't yet sure of than I could force my fumbling heart to rush its verdict—and in any case, I felt in the very core of me that Cae would know if I feigned reciprocation. He deserved the truth, whatever that was, not false comfort given in duty, but though I wasn't yet sure that what I felt was love, he was dear to me, and wonderful.

And handsome, too, a part of me whispered. *And naked, and in your bed.*

"You don't mind it?" Caethari asked suddenly.

"Don't mind what? Staying in?"

"I mean my hair," he said, oddly self-conscious. "I didn't think I'd go grey so soon."

I laughed. "Not grey," I corrected. "Silver."

"Grey, silver—what does it matter? It makes me look old."

"You're not old," I said, looping a silver-threaded lock behind his ear. "Besides, I think it suits you."

He lifted his head slightly, a touch of heat in his gaze. "You do?"

"I do," I said, as an answering warmth began to pool in my stomach. We had so much yet to discuss between us; so much that was fraught and complex. I didn't know how long it might take to rid myself of Killic's ghost, but though I yet carried the shadow of his actions and the weight of mine, on that morning, in that moment, I was light.

"How much do you like it?"

I smiled at him. "Come here and I'll show you."

"With pleasure," he said, and did so.

Acknowledgments

Depending on how you measure it, the first draft of this book was either written in five months or five years: a period during which, among other things, I moved from Scotland to Australia to America while struggling with my health—both mentally and physically—more than I ever have at any other time in my life; and that was before the pandemic. That I managed to get the book written at all is a species of miracle, but one that wouldn't be possible without the constant support of my husband, Toby, who carried me through when I was all but falling apart.

Deepest thanks to Liz Bourke, the first and most enthusiastic reader of this story, and to Sarah Loch, B R Sanders, and Chris Brathwaite, who joined her in cheering me on. I couldn't have done it without you.

An enormous debt of gratitude is also owed to my wonderful agent, Hannah Bowman, who reached out to me when my confidence was shot and helped me to get back up again, and to my editor, Claire Eddy, who understood this book on a fundamental level, and whose kind, insightful work has helped to make it stronger.

Thanks to the Bunker, for friendship and sanity amidst the chaos of publishing; thanks to more writer friends than I have space to name, for simply being yourselves. And special thanks, as ever, to my family, for their ceaseless encouragement of my writing: to my mother, who has always believed in me, and in loving memory of both my mother-in-law, Janie, who passed away on January 2, 2021, and my father, Charles, who passed away on June 14, 2021. I miss you both.

Turn the page for a sneak peek at
the next Tithenai Chronicle

Available Winter 2023 from Tor Books

PRELUDE: ASRIN

Six months I'd been in Eliness; six sunfucking months of going unnoticed, working hard and drinking just enough to dull the sting of it, and all for nothing. Six months without so much as winking at another man, let alone screwing one, and Lord Sun knows there were men enough to be tempting. My office stood in sight of the docks, which teemed with strapping, broad-shouldered roughs, hauling cargo or doing whatever sailors do in port that isn't drinking or fucking, and there I sat, as celibate as an Attovari monk and twice as miserable. No men, nor any sociable vices that might lead to a lapse in judgement; I even drank alone, or on rare occasions with Yarrick, whom I wouldn't have fucked in a fit but who was, at least, reasonable company.

Six virtuous, miserable months, and still the Shade came for me anyway.

I'd just left work on a grim and drizzling evening when he materialised from the fog and blocked my path, sudden enough that I shrieked.

"Asrien bo Erat," he intoned. His voice was deep and mocking, and he omitted my title because he could, patrician features exuding superiority the way other men exude sweat. The rain turned the grey in his hair to silver, glinting in the low light. A hatefully handsome comeuppance.

"Lord Cato," I grit out, embarrassed and angry and fearful. "What a surprise."

"An unpleasant one, no doubt." Smiling thinly, he gestured ahead. "We will speak in private."

He set off for my lodgings unerringly and at speed, leaving me with my far shorter stride to struggle along in his wake. A less confident man would've kept his eye on me, worried I might flee; the Shade, however, had no such insecurities. Spymasters seldom do.

"As you know where I live," I said acidly, "I wonder you didn't wait for me there instead."

"I had business elsewhere. Your office was on my way."

He didn't deny that he could've broken in, had he wanted to. There was no point.

The drizzle had soaked me through by the time we reached my dingy rooms. The landlady, normally stationed in the central parlour, was nowhere to be seen as I unlocked my door and entered. The Shade watched, perversely amused as I shrugged out of my wet coat—his own was sturdy black wool, elegantly cut and far better suited to the time of year than my flimsy former finery. I claimed the only chair with a child's defiance, staring up at him with what little fire I could muster, but regretted it the instant he stepped forwards and loomed over me, his long features hard as iron.

"You speak Tithenai, do you not?"

I stared, waiting for him to continue. He didn't, and after several infuriating seconds, I realised he wanted me to answer.

"I do," I bit out. "You know I do. It's half my sunfucking job."

He twitched at the profanity, but otherwise remained impassive.

"Good," he said. "You will require the use of it."

A long pause followed.

"Yes?" I prompted eventually. "And?"

"In your . . . former circles," said Cato, the euphemism dripping with distaste, "did you ever encounter Velasin vin Aaro?"

The *vin* said he was gentry, but the Shade's apparent disdain for his title could've meant any number of things. I racked my brains and came up empty. "No. Or if I did, I never knew his name. Who is he? What's this all about?"

Again I waited. Again he said nothing. The Shade's pale lip curled in a grimace, and all at once I realised that, whatever he was here to say, it disgusted him—and that could mean only one thing.

"Oh, I see." I leaned back in the chair, letting my legs sprawl open, grinning like I'd caught his eye at the kind of bar that wasn't supposed to exist in Ralia. "This is litai business, isn't it?"

Cato snarled, and I had half a second to bask in having unsettled him before he backhanded me for it. My head snapped to the right, and I laughed because I'd learned early that it was better to laugh at blows than cry from them. My ears rang as my top lip throbbed, and when I touched it, my fingertips came away bloody. I blinked through the resultant dizziness and stared at the hand he was flexing, open and shut, open and shut, like he wanted to wipe it clean but not where I could see him. As if admitting he found me repulsive would've meant showing weakness.

I snorted. As if I couldn't tell anyway.

"Velasin vin Aaro," said the Shade, continuing with pseudo-calm, "is the third son of Lord Varus vin Aaro, to whom His Majesty recently granted such lands and powers as formerly belonged to the traitor Lord Ennan vin Mica."

Now there was a name I recognised, as would most anyone in Ralia. I nodded grudging comprehension, still thumbing my split lip, and Cato continued.

"At the encouragement of King Markus, Lord Varus arranged a marriage between Velasin and a Tithenai noblewoman out of Qi-Katai, to help mend the rift vin Mica's banditry caused. But." And here he stopped, a look on his face like he'd bitten into a particularly sour quince. "Owing to some . . . indecorous behaviour on Velasin's part, the Tithenai envoy was made aware of his . . . unconventional preferences. And being Tithenai, their solution was to—offer him a groom, instead. Which offer he accepted, and which has now been formalised, *without* His Majesty's consultation."

It took a moment for the words to sink in, and when they did, a stupid grin spread across my face. My cut lip split wider and I didn't care, the sting of it nothing compared to the Shade's distaste.

"Oh, that's priceless!" I cackled. "A diplomatic litai marriage, and your lot have to eat it!"

A triumphal sneer crossed Cato's face, and too late I remembered why he was telling me this in the first place.

"We will not, as you say, be *eating it* for long." He leaned in close, and I shrank back without meaning to. "Because *you,* Asrien, will end it."

"Me?" I spluttered. "I'm no assassin—" But even as the words left my mouth, I knew that wasn't what he meant.

"Would that death were an option," the Shade said bitterly. "In this case, however, as Ralia's official, traditional stance on such unions is widely known, and as better relations with Tithena are genuinely desired"—*despite their perversity,* he didn't add, though his tone and scowl clearly implied it—"we have determined that even a seemingly accidental death would be laid at our feet, and however unpleasant the current situation is, we do not wish for a new diplomatic crisis. As such, we are taking a different route." His expression sharpened to a terrible smile. "You, Asrien, will go to Tithena. You will insinuate yourself into the confidence of Lord Velasin vin Aaro by whatever means necessary, and you will seduce him away from his . . . from Tiern Caethari Aeduria. Or, should that prove the more difficult option, seduce the tiern away from him. As a Ralian will be seen to be acting shamefully in either case, we do not especially care which of them you cozen."

He paused, his black eyes raking me with a coldly speculative look. "Although," he murmured, "looking as you do, you could easily pass for a Palamite." He smirked. "Or would it be more than passing? Your mother has always denied it, but—"

"I don't speak Palamish," I snapped, knowing my cheeks were flushed bright red and hating it even more than usual. Some Ralians might be light-haired or light-eyed or both, especially in the south, but even paired with plain brown eyes, my too-blond hair and too-pale skin spoke more of Palam or Attovar than Ralia, and nobody had ever let my mother or me forget it.

Least of all my father. Or, it seemed now, Lord Cato.

"A pity," said the Shade, savouring my discomfort like a good brandy. Then he shrugged. "Regardless, all that matters is that the marriage of Velasin and Caethari ends—and is seen to end—because of their inclinations, and not our intervention."

Feeling slightly hysterical, I asked, "And what if I end up married to one of them instead?"

"Don't be disgusting," Cato snapped. But then, after a moment, he muttered, "If that's what it takes, however . . . it would still be embarrassing, but the diplomatic union would be ended, and we'd have no need to formally acknowledge whatever broke it. But—" And here he paused, disdainful gaze flicking over me once more. "—I highly doubt it will come to that. Your value, such as it is, lies wholly in your usefulness as an instrument to your betters; beyond that, you bring nothing to anyone."

The worst thing was, he didn't say it to twist the knife, but as a bored statement of fact. It hurt in a way that made me harden, baring my teeth at him.

"Once I'm in Tithena, what's to stop me from doing as I please?"

"Two things," said the Shade, with deadly softness. "One, your beloved mother is still in a position to be ruined by your antics, should they be made public, and two—" He reached into his coat and withdrew a wicked knife, fitting the point beneath my chin and lifting, so that my head tipped up. "—there would be no diplomatic consequences to killing *you*."

The pressure on the knifepoint increased. I felt a sting, gulping as a thin trickle of blood ran down my bared throat. The Shade tracked its descent with idle curiosity, until it reached my collar and began to dampen the fabric there. Then he looked up again, holding my gaze for longer than was comfortable; long enough that my starved libido gave a jolt, like maybe he was about to lean across the blade and—

Sunfucking stars, I'd been in Eliness too long.

"You'd have to find me to kill me," I said, attempting bravado.

"One lone man who won't return to Ralia—that's a waste of the crown's resources, surely."

"You're right," said the Shade, and gently scraped the blade's edge against my throat, as if in parody of giving me a shave, though all this achieved was smearing the trickle of blood around. His mouth smiled, but his eyes were cold as week-old embers. "*You* would be hard to find. Your mother, however—"

"*Don't,*" I gasped, all bravery gone. "You can't, she's done nothing wrong, she's loyal to King Markus—"

"Accidents do happen," Lord Cato said softly, "and in any case, one might argue that producing a son like you is treason enough."

My chest felt suddenly inverted, fleshless ribs behind my naked heart. I valued few things in this world—stars knew, I cared little enough for myself, most days—but my mother . . .

"What if I fail?" I asked, and it came out a whisper.

"That will depend entirely upon the manner of your failure. Should your *native powers of seduction*"—the words dripped with loathing—"prove insufficient, there is an alternative." Lord Cato bared his teeth in what was almost, but not quite, a smile. "You see, there is *one* instance in which the death of Velasin vin Aaro would be deemed acceptable. As it stands, his former . . . *entanglement,* Killic vin Lato, pursued Velasin to Qi-Katai. On being rebuffed, he reacted violently, and Velasin killed him." Ugly relish coloured his tone. "As such, if Velasin were to be killed in turn by another jilted lover . . . well. You could almost call it poetic. And who could blame the crown for that?"

Brusque in victory, the Shade withdrew the knife, wiped the tip on my stinging cheek and resheathed it discreetly.

"Should you behave yourself," he went on, as mildly if we'd been discussing the weather over tea, "and provided you succeed in your mission in whatever capacity, you are free to remain in Tithena. We might even see our way to extending you a small stipend by way of recompense—though not, of course, if you engage in a public union with either Velasin or Caethari; or any other man, for that matter." His lip curled. "And, of course, your debts here will be erased."

"And my mother?"

"Your mother will come to no harm, provided you do as you're told."

I digested this, numbness spreading through me. There was no way out, and never had been. If Lord Cato had been some garden-variety blackmailer, I'd have feigned agreement, slipped out the second his back was turned and run home to get Mother on the next ship out of Ralia, and damned to the consequences. But I couldn't outrun a Shade. They were the crown's eyes and ears and hands, spies and secret-stealers and hidden knives, named for the spectral guardian of the underworld, and among their hidden ranks, Lord Cato, it was whispered, stood closer to the king than anyone but his own shadow.

Gulping, I asked, "How soon do I leave for Qi-Katai?"

"You don't," came the reply. "You're headed for Qi-Xihan."

I blinked at him, confused. "But you said—"

"Qi-Xihan is more swiftly reached from here," said the Shade, "but even if it wasn't, they'll be headed there soon enough. Besides which, you'll have more excuse to approach them in the capital, and your presence will seem . . . less coincidental, shall we say, if you arrive there first."

"What of my work here?" I asked—desperately, as I hardly liked it at the best of times. "What will you say to—"

"Asrien," said Lord Cato, and here he sounded almost amused. "I am a Shade in the king's employ. Do trust that I know what I'm doing."

I looked away and forced myself to swallow. "Yes, my lord."

"Good boy," he said, and smiled.

Part One

VELASIN

1

We'd been at Caethari's holdings in the Avai riverveldt just long enough for me to fall in love with them when the summons came. A courier rode in on a fine bay mare and handed the message to Cae in person, bowing from the saddle in one breath and departing in the next, her job done. A sense of foreboding tickled my neck as my husband broke the elaborate wax seal on the missive and unrolled its fine paper, frowning at the contents. I'd been happy enough for long enough—which is to say, for nearly three weeks—that I'd grown suspicious of my own felicity, and when Cae's mouth twisted in annoyance, some cynical part of me rejoiced in perverse vindication. *See?* it seemed to say. *We knew this couldn't last.*

"We're wanted in Qi-Xihan," said Cae. He swallowed, glancing at me. "Her Majesty Asa Ivadi Ruqai desires an audience."

Whatever crisis I'd been expecting, this wasn't it. I blinked at him. "What?"

"The asa wants to see us," Cae repeated. He shot me a look that was equal parts confused and frustrated. "She doesn't say why; only that we're to appear at our earliest convenience, which is a polite way of saying *as soon as is humanly possible,* and that this is her personal request."

I grimaced, thoughts whirling. "There must be trouble with Ralia over our marriage," I said. "Either King Markus objects, or one of his factions does, and we need to give an accounting of it all." I faltered. "That, or—the other thing."

My husband winced and looked away, leaving me to silently curse myself. *The other thing,* I'd said, as though the deaths of Caethari's father and sister, the former at the latter's hands, was a sordid afterthought. The only reason he wasn't dressed all in black was in deference to the newness of our marriage: Tithenai custom held that to observe full mourning before a new couple's second and final marriage-gathering was bad luck. As such, Cae wore a dark lin edged with black and had wound black ribbons into his braid, but was otherwise dressed normally. My lin, too, was trimmed with black, and as my hair was yet too short for a proper Tithenai braid, I wore my matching ribbons bound around my wrists. Cae had tried to say it wasn't necessary—I'd scarcely known his father, while his sister's last act had been to take me hostage—but I'd ignored him and done it anyway. Honouring his grief seemed the very least I could do, under the circumstances.

I placed a hesitant hand on Cae's shoulder, relieved when he leaned into the touch.

"You needn't talk around it so," he said, raising his opposite hand to squeeze my fingers, this gentleness in contrast to the bitter scrape of his voice. "Call it what it is: Laecia's treachery."

"I'll call it whatever hurts you least."

"There is no *least hurt,* with a thing like this." And then, with a sigh, "I'm sorry, Vel. I shouldn't snap. It's just . . . I thought we'd have more time here."

"Me, too," I admitted, and took a moment to ache at the thought of leaving. When we'd first set out from Qi-Katai, I'd been apprehensive, worried that whatever rural charms Avai might offer would prove an insufficient sap to my fractious brain and urban predilections. What would it mean for my marriage if I couldn't find some means of self-occupation that neither endangered the pair of us nor drove Cae to distraction? The prospect of helping administer his holdings here was a potential lifeline, and one I was all too afraid would fray apart in my hands.

But the moment we'd ridden down the broad, paved drive to the main estate—the same drive in which we presently stood—I'd felt myself bewitched. It was calm in Avai, the sort of calm that sinks across your shoulders like a soft, cool fur and eases whatever tension you've been carrying. The scent of the Eshi River was everywhere—not acrid and foul, like so many city rivers come to be, marred by human refuse and the leavings of industry, but bright and clean. Birdsong cut through the elegant, curving branches of trees I'd never seen before, while neat fields and orchards in late-autumn hues of brown and russet patchworked the valleys between gentle, rolling hills. I'd found nature beautiful before, of course—I'm not made of stone—but Avai felt different.

Perhaps it was simply that my life, since leaving Farathel, had been one overwrought commotion after the next, such that the pretty quietude of this patch of Tithena was a balm I hadn't known I'd needed. Perhaps my tastes were maturing as I aged—and moons, but this recent span of weeks had certainly aged me!

Or perhaps I only felt what I did because of Caethari. For all that our marriage and acquaintance both were scarcely a month old, I had come to care for him as I'd cared for few others in my life. In the aftermath of his sister's betrayal, he'd confessed his love for me, and though I didn't yet trust that the depth of my feelings matched his own, the knowledge that he didn't expect direct reciprocation—that he was content for me to be as I was, at least for now—meant more than I could say. Avai mattered to him: was that why it mattered to me? I rubbed my beribboned wrists together, unsettled by the prospect.

"Wait," said Cae, suddenly. "There's a second page."

"A second page?"

"Or, not a page—there's something stuck, here—" He held up the letter and flipped it over, blunt nails scrabbling ineffectually at the edges. I watched him struggle for a moment, suppressing a smile at the peek of tongue protruding from his mouth, then took the paper from him. At first glance, it seemed a single, ordinary piece of stationery, albeit an expensive one; but at the top, where the broken wax seal had started to flake, a careful eye could just make out the leading edge of a second sheet stuck perfectly to the first. It was a technique I'd seen before, though not recently—for a brief time in Farathel, it had been all the rage to send secret, doubled missives like this—and so I knew the trick to prying it loose.

"Markel!" I called across the lawn, to where my dearest friend and ostensible servant was lazing contentedly on the grass, pretending to take no notice of us. "Can I borrow your letter-knife?"

"I've got a knife," Cae muttered not-quite-sulkily, indicating the leather-sheathed blade with its ring handle of polished jade that I'd given him as a marriage gift.

"I know," I said, and kissed his cheek to show I'd meant no slight. "But this calls for delicate work, and your blade isn't thin enough."

"Hmph."

Markel ambled over, one brow raised at the pair of us and a crooked grin on his face. He passed me the letter-knife handle-first, a flash of recognition in his eyes as he watched me slip it between the two pressed pages.

"Haven't seen this in a while," he signed—more slowly than was usual between us, partly in deference to the fact that Cae was still learning sign-speech, but also because he was using a new, syllable-based sign alphabet designed to spell out Tithenai words more easily, the better to enable more fluent communication with Cae. It was all Markel's development, something he'd shyly admitted to having worked on for a while, but which he'd altered to work with Tithenai more than Ralian, and in the fortnight since he'd introduced it to us, it had done wonders to improve Cae's confidence with signing.

I nodded absently, refocussing on the paper. The hidden sheet was thinner than I'd first assumed, like the finest rice paper, the edges sealed so neatly with adhesive that it was hard work not to tear it. Still, I managed in the end, and with a little *hah!* of triumph, I peeled away the second page and handed it to Cae.

He held it up to the sky, letting the wintry light illuminate the contents. Unlike the primary letter, this one was neither written in the neat, precise hand of a professional scribe nor inked in the customary black or blue. Instead, the writing was small and curlicue, difficult to make out, and written with an ink (if the term applied) that bleached instead of stained. The message was pale and indistinct even with the aid of direct sunlight: held normally, you could scarcely see it at all.

"It's in the asa's own hand," Cae said, startled. "She writes, 'I bid you travel discreetly. Observe the state of Tithena and report your findings to me.'"

"She wants us to *spy* for her?" I exclaimed.

"You needn't sound quite so delighted," Cae said dryly, "but yes." Carefully, he rerolled both pieces of paper. "Asa Ivadi is well-known to be fond of issuing private games and challenges to her subjects, like sending a hidden message to some noble or minister asking for their private observations. If they don't find it, she'll know them to be incurious and unobservant; if they do, their compliance tells her what they think is valuable information and how good they are—or not—at acquiring it."

"I like her already."

Cae snorted. "You would," he said. "This is much more your thing than mine."

That stung, though I was sure he hadn't meant it to. "We can always pretend we didn't find it, if you prefer."

"What? Of course not!" Cae looked at me, a worried furrow between his brows. I'd aimed to keep both my tone and expression neutral, but I mustn't have succeeded; that, or he was getting eerily good at reading me, for he promptly leaned in and kissed the corner of my mouth, so lightly that I shivered. "I'm sorry, Vel. That wasn't meant as a dig."

"I know," I said, flustered. I wasn't used to being so sweetly perceived, and it threw me off-balance. "It's me who ought to apologise, spoiling your good humour—"

"You haven't spoiled anything, saints!"

"I only meant—"

"I know what you meant, I just—"

Markel cut us off with a throaty noise of amusement, grinning from ear to ear. I flushed and ducked my head, smiling into the collar of my mourning lin. It was still a new and wonderful thing, to be bedding a man approved of by my oldest friend; almost as new and wonderful as the fact that, in Tithena, we could openly claim each other. In Ralia, the lifelong necessity of keeping my inclinations secret had sickened me like a slow cancer; here, we were two men married, and while ours had been a political match forged in unpleasant circumstances, I'd sooner have lopped off a hand than repudiated Cae.

"You're very married today," signed Markel. Before I could reply to that, he nodded his stubbled head to indicate the asa's letters. "Does this mean we're headed to Qi-Xihan?"

"It does," I said, "and immediately. Though if you'd rather stay here or return to Qi-Katai, I'd understand."

Markel favoured me with a withering look. "I'll go and see about packing," he signed, and strode off towards the main house with a sarcastic wave over his shoulder.

"Well," said Cae, after a moment. "That would seem to be settled, wouldn't it?"

"Quite decisively, yes."

He laughed and stepped closer, sliding an arm around my waist. "Look on the bright side. I'll get to show you the capital." He leaned in, kissing up my throat to my ear. "And the palace accommodations are *very* luxurious."

I made an involuntary sound and turned to face him, looping my arms around his neck with the closest approximation to coy ease I was capable of mustering. "Are they now," I said, and for an answer he kissed me properly, both hands on my hips as he drew us together. I melted into it, heart hammering with a mixture of new anticipation and old fear: I wasn't yet used to being intimate in public without risk of either discovery or censure, and so it yet felt illicitly thrilling to kiss my husband outdoors. Though Cae was, as

I'd quickly learned, a consummate kisser; even in private, he left me dizzied and wanting.

All too soon, he broke away again, raising a hand to smooth his thumb across my cheek. I flushed as he brushed the stubble—I'd been lax with my grooming the past few days, not bothering to shave—and was on the brink of apology when he murmured, "It suits you, you know."

"What does?"

"This." He repeated the gesture, rubbing back and forth across the unshaven grain. "It makes you look rakish."

I scoffed to hide how flustered I was. "You're the rakish one, with your fine salt locks." I stroked the new silver at his temple, smiling around the lump in my throat that rose whenever I thought on how he'd acquired it. "Especially with your ribbons, the effect is quite piratical."

"Piratical?"

"Dashing, then."

"I can work with dashing," he said, and kissed me again—a light press of lips, but I deepened it greedily, pulling him close once more.

We had talked, my new husband and I, albeit somewhat awkwardly, about our mutual expectations around bedplay. Knowing his feelings to be deeper than my own, Cae had made it clear that he didn't want to pressure me; that he was, in fact, actively afraid of doing so. For this reason, he'd said, I should be the one to instigate things, at least for now, and in the moment, I'd been so overwhelmed by the consideration that I'd proceeded to do so eagerly. But volition is a tricky thing, and in the weeks since, my contrarian nature had reared its head: having struggled my whole romantic life in Ralia to play at seeming disaffected, to show less than I felt, now that I had express permission to do as I wished, I found myself holding back. What if Cae became bored with me? What if my need and greediness lost me his regard? *Or what if,* my insecurities whispered, *he's already tiring of you, and this is his way of slowing things down?*

About the Author

Foz Meadows is a queer Australian author, essayist, reviewer, and poet. They have won two Best Fan Writer awards (a Hugo Award in 2019 and a Ditmar Award in 2017) for yelling on the internet, and have also received the Norma K. Hemming Award in 2018 for their queer Shakespearean novella, *Coral Bones*. Their essays, reviews, poetry, and short fiction have appeared in various venues, including *Uncanny, Apex Magazine, Goblin Fruit, HuffPost,* and *Strange Horizons*. Meadows currently lives in California with their family. *A Strange and Stubborn Endurance* is their fifth novel.

@fozmeadows